Jill Mansell worked for many years at the Burden Neurological Hospital, Bristol, and now writes full-time. Her novels include TWO'S COMPANY, NADIA KNOWS BEST and STAYING AT DAISY'S, all of which have been *Sunday Times* bestsellers.

*Also by Jill Mansell*

# Kiss

## and

# Sheer Mischief

Jill Mansell

**headline**

KISS first published in 1993
by Bantam Books, a division of Transworld Publishers Ltd

SHEER MISCHIEF first published in 1994
by Bantam Books, a division of Transworld Publishers Ltd

First published in this omnibus edition in 2004
by HEADLINE BOOK PUBLISHING

A HEADLINE paperback

10 9 8 7 6 5 4 3 2

ISBN 0 7553 2256 8

Typeset in Times by Avon DataSet Ltd,
Bidford on Avon, Warwickshire

Printed and bound in Great Britain by
Mackays of Chatham plc, Chatham, Kent

Papers and cover board used by Headline are natural,
recyclable products made from wood grown in sustainable
forests. The manufacturing processes conform to the
environmental regulations of the country of origin.

HEADLINE BOOK PUBLISHING
A division of Hodder Headline
338 Euston Road
London NW1 3BH

www.headline.co.uk
www.hodderheadline.com

# Kiss

For Cino and Lydia
With all my love

# Chapter 1

'I just want to know,' Katerina said slowly, 'whether your intentions towards my mother are honourable.'

And despite the fact that it was snowing hard, she stood her ground in the doorway, refusing to allow Ralph inside.

'What a little darling you are.' He grinned and ruffled her hair, because he knew how much it annoyed her. 'And whatever did your disgraceful mother ever do to deserve such a daughter? If you were a few years older, Kat, I swear I'd whisk you off to Gretna Green myself.'

'Ah, but would I be silly enough to go? Besides, we aren't talking about my marital prospects,' she continued, her expression stern. 'I asked you a question and I'm still waiting for an answer.'

'Of course. Are my intentions honourable?' Frowning, he paused for a second to consider his reply. Snowflakes, melting in his hair, were sliding down his neck. It was very cold. 'No, sorry,' he said finally. 'Absolutely not.'

Katerina shrugged. 'That's all right, then,' she replied cheerfully, stepping to one side and waving him through. 'Mum can't stand honourable men. She's in the kitchen, by the way, dyeing her hair.'

'Go away,' grumbled Izzy, her voice muffled, her head plunged upside down in the sink. 'You're early.'

'No, I'm not.' Ralph pinched her bottom, denim-clad

and excitingly stuck out. 'You're late. What colour is it going to be, anyway?' Peering more closely at the mass of curling, dripping hair, he saw that the rinsed-off water in the washing-up bowl was an ominous shade of indigo.

The final jug of hot water cascaded down, splashing into the sink and on to the floor. When Izzy had wrung out her hair and wrapped an enormous pink towel turban-style around her head she resumed vertical posture and planted a wet kiss on Ralph's cheek before he could dodge out of the way.

'Glossy Blackberry. It'll be irresistible, darling.'

She was already irresistible, he thought as he followed her through to the cluttered living room – untidy, but irresistible. And although they were supposed to be going to a party in Hampstead he was beginning to have second thoughts about it now, despite the fact that an extremely useful film producer was rumoured to be attending. It would take Izzy at least an hour to get herself done up and it was arctic outside. The prospect of a quiet night in – just the two of them in front of the fire – was becoming increasingly inviting.

'Going out?' he asked hopefully, addressing Katerina. Stretched out across the entire length of the cushion-strewn sofa with her bare legs dangling over the arm, she was engrossed in a book.

She didn't even bother to look up. 'No.'

Why couldn't Katerina be like normal teenagers, he thought with a trace of exasperation, and go out on a Friday night? The mother-daughter package might have its small advantages – and the fact that Katerina was able to *organise* Izzy was an undoubted plus – but her total disinterest in the social whirl, at times, could be a distinct pain.

He seriously doubted whether Katerina even knew the meaning of the word enjoyment in its generally accepted sense. At seventeen, she didn't have a boyfriend, didn't like discos or parties and deplored teenage magazines. She never gossiped. Her idea of a really good time, it seemed, was to hog the sofa and devour a few chapters of *Gray's Anatomy*. God knows, she was a *nice* enough girl, well mannered and charming, funny when she wanted to be and undoubtedly beautiful. Why she wasn't out every night making the most of it he simply couldn't imagine.

But the fact remained that she wasn't, and since she didn't appear to be showing any sign of moving from the sofa either, Ralph reconciled himself to the idea that they may as well go to the party after all.

'I'll be five minutes,' lied Izzy, heading towards her bedroom with the pink towel trailing damply behind her like a matador's cape.

'Mum, your hair's blue.' Katerina, who failed to understand why anyone should even *want* to change the colour of their hair, let alone practise it on a monthly basis, gazed after her mother with a mixture of exasperation and tolerance.

'No, it isn't,' replied Izzy loftily over her shoulder. 'It's Glossy Blackberry. It'll be irresistible. When it's finished.'

There really weren't many greater luxuries in life than this, Izzy decided. Chronic lack of money, the frustration of being wildly talented and as yet undiscovered, the sheer *bother* of having to wonder how much longer their revolting landlord was going to allow them to stay in their less-than-luxurious flat . . . these problems simply faded into insignificance when one was lying in a warm bed with a gorgeous man, caressing deliciously warm flesh and knowing that one didn't have to get up for hours. It was positively blissful.

'Skin contact,' she announced, pleased with herself for having recognised its importance.

'Hmmm?'

'The three most pleasurable experiences known to man.' She smiled, sliding closer still and plastering the entire length of her body against his side. 'Sex, sneezing and skin contact. No, make that sex, skin contact and sneezing. Touching skin is the second greatest pleasure. And it's certainly more fun than a cold.'

A foot brushed against her shin, moving experimentally up and down. 'Only if the other person remembers to shave her legs.'

Izzy raked her fingernails down his chest in protest. 'I did remember! I did them the other night.'

'While you were dyeing your hair?' said Mike. 'Just think, you could have dyed your legs and shaved your head by mistake. What a thought.'

'How can you be so sarcastic at ten o'clock on a Sunday morning?' demanded Izzy grumpily. Realizing that she was hungry, she wondered whether Kat would be amenable to the idea of cooking a gigantic breakfast.

'It comes naturally.'

'It isn't fair.'

'Life isn't fair.' Mike hauled himself into a sitting position, since natural sleep was clearly going to be denied

4

him. 'The fact that I only see you two nights a week isn't fair. Izzy, if we're going to have a proper relationship we should organise ourselves more effectively.'

That was the trouble with Mike, thought Izzy, smiling beneath the bedclothes. It was also part of his charm; only Mike could expect her to 'organise herself more effectively'. As far as she was concerned, their relationship was perfect. Each week she spent two nights with Mike, two with Ralph and two nights working. Wednesdays were for rest and relaxation. And if that wasn't perfect planning, she didn't know what was.

'You're busy, I'm busy . . .' she murmured vaguely, cuddling up to him once more. 'Besides, you'd get bored. I lead a pretty mundane life, after all. You'd soon go off me if you had to sit and watch me scrubbing the kitchen floor and hoovering the hallway.'

Nothing Izzy ever did was mundane, thought Mike. He also seriously doubted that she even knew what a Hoover looked like, but sensed nevertheless that arguing the point would be futile. 'OK,' he said, gathering her into his arms and breathing in the faint, unmistakably Izzyish scent of her body. 'I give in. I'll expand my business empire and you can hoover to your heart's content. Just so long as *you* don't get bored and find yourself another man.'

'With a daughter like mine to give the game away?' said Izzy smiling up at him. 'Some chance.'

# Chapter 2

'I don't understand,' said Gina hesitantly, her mind blotting out the words she knew she must have heard incorrectly. 'You aren't making sense. Let me get you a drink . . . there's roast lamb for dinner and it won't be ready for another thirty minutes.'

Moving jerkily towards the drinks cabinet in the corner of the sitting room, she became hideously aware of the fact that she no longer knew what to do with her hands. They seemed huge and ungainly, flapping at her sides as she walked. It was with relief that she picked up the bottle of Gordon's and poured Andrew his drink – half an inch of gin, three inches of tonic, just as he always liked it when he returned home from work.

But now she was faced with the new problem of where to look. Andrew, she knew, was watching her and although he couldn't possibly have meant what he'd just said, she found herself incapable of meeting his gaze. Her co-ordination had gone. She didn't know whether to stand up or to sit down. And how could something so *silly* be happening to her body when it was only a simple misunderstanding anyway? In less than a minute, no doubt, they would be laughing at her ridiculous mistake and her hands and eyes would behave normally once more.

But Andrew wasn't laughing. He shook his head when

she finally held the drink towards him, gesturing instead to a nearby armchair.

'Sit down. You'd better have that drink. God, I'm sorry, Gina – you must think I'm a real bastard, but I truly didn't expect anything like this to happen. I didn't want to hurt you . . .'

Gina tensed, unable to do anything but wait. Any minute now he'd break into a grin and say, 'I'm joking, of course,' and she would be able to relax and get on with the dinner. The parsnips needed to go into the roasting tin and the onion sauce, simmering on the stove, could probably do with a stir.

'I would have thought you'd be throwing things by now,' Andrew went on, hating himself for what he was doing but needing to provoke some kind of reaction. When Gina finally looked up at him he saw fear and confusion in her eyes.

'Are you joking?' she whispered at last, and the flicker of hope in her voice was almost too much to bear. Steeling himself against it, taking a deep breath, Andrew prepared to repeat the words which he had hoped to have to say only once.

'Gina, this isn't a joke,' he said, more brusquely than he had intended. 'I'm moving out of the house and I want a divorce. I've met someone else – I've been seeing her for almost six months now – and my staying here isn't being fair to either of you. I've rented a flat in the Barbican and I'll be going there tonight. I'm sorry,' he repeated helplessly. 'I really *didn't* want to hurt you, but sometimes these things just happen . . .'

'But you're my husband,' whispered Gina. Her knees

were beginning to tremble uncontrollably – he'd always said how much he liked her knees – and she was finding it hard to swallow. Placing the tumbler of gin and tonic carefully on the table beside her before she spilled it, she rose to her feet, then abruptly sank back down. 'We're married,' she said incredulously. 'We're *happily* married! Everyone's always saying how happy we are.'

Sympathy mingled with exasperation. Why couldn't she hurl something at him, for God's sake? Why wasn't she screaming, shouting, swearing and generally raising hell? It would, he thought grimly, make telling her the rest of it easier.

'I was happy,' he told her, willing her to react. 'But now I've fallen in love with someone else.'

'You said you didn't want to hurt me!' Gina's knuckles whitened as she pressed clenched fists into her lap. With a huge effort, she burst out, 'I could forgive you for having an affair. We don't have to be divorced . . . if you don't want to hurt me you can tell her it's all over and we'll carry on as if it never happened. It's only a fling,' she concluded breathlessly, choking on the words as hot tears – at last – began to fall. 'It doesn't mean anything, really it doesn't. Lots of men go through this kind of thing . . . it doesn't mean we have to get a divorce . . .'

'I want to marry her,' said Andrew tonelessly.

Gina stared at him, uncomprehending. Wasn't she giving him every opportunity? Wasn't she being as understanding as any woman could possibly be? 'But why?'

He reached for the tumbler of gin and tonic and drained it in one go. 'Because,' he replied slowly, 'she's pregnant.'

* * *

Brandishing her mascara wand and treating her lashes to a second coat, Izzy belted out the second verse of 'New York, New York!'. 'Kat, do you want a lift to the library, because I'm leaving in five minutes.'

The next moment Katerina appeared behind her, in the mirror. Izzy, overcome with love for her precious, clever daughter, spun round and gave her a hug.

'What would I do without you, hmm?'

'Get yourself into a muddle,' replied Katerina, ever practical. 'Now, are either of them likely to phone tonight?'

'Ralph might. He wants me to have dinner with him tomorrow . . . tell him I'll meet him at Vampires at eight-thirty. Mike shouldn't be phoning but if he does, just say that—'

'You're going for an audition,' supplied her daughter. 'Don't worry, I won't forget.'

'You're an angel.' Izzy hugged her again, then stepped back and regarded her with mock-solemn dark eyes. 'Am I really a disgrace?'

Katerina, at seventeen, knew nothing if not her own mind. Izzy had her faults — and her chronic untidiness could be particularly irritating at times — but as a mother she was one of the best. And who could ever describe such a warm, generous, optimistic and loving person as a disgrace?

'You've been seeing Mike for over a year,' she replied calmly. 'And how long has Ralph been around, nearly two years? You're faithful to them. You haven't promised to marry either of them. Everybody's happy . . . what can possibly be so wrong with that? When I grow up,' she added airily, 'I fully intend to go for multiple, part-time lovers myself.'

'And long may they drool,' said Izzy, who never failed to be amazed by the extent of her daughter's irrefutable logic. She glanced at her watch. 'Help, I really am going to be late. Do you want that lift or not?'

Katerina shook her head. 'Too cold outside. I can pop in on my way to school tomorrow morning. I've got an essay to be getting on with tonight, anyway.'

'OK.' In the chilly hallway, Izzy wrapped herself up in her brown leather flying jacket and flung a white woollen scarf around her neck. Grabbing her keys and helmet, she gave her daughter a final kiss. 'I'll be back by one-thirty, fans willing!'

'You'll be back a lot sooner than that,' said Katerina drily, holding up the carrier bag which Izzy had forgotten, 'if you don't take your clothes.'

Izzy hummed beneath her breath. Her teeth were chattering too violently to risk singing the words aloud; she'd end up with a shredded tongue. Her beloved motor bike, a sleek, black Suzuki 250, was a joy to ride during the summer months, and it was certainly economical to run, but travelling to and from work in sub-zero temperatures was – she couldn't think of a better way of describing it – a real bitch.

Still, at least the roads weren't too icy tonight. Maniacs notwithstanding, she'd be at the club in less than twenty minutes. And who knew, tonight might just be the night to change her life . . .

★ ★ ★

Having cleared away the debris of their early evening meal, changed out of her school uniform into black sweatshirt and leggings and emptied a packet of Liquorice Allsorts into a pudding bowl for easy access, Katerina settled herself in front of the fire and wondered what it must be like for people who hated solitude.

Katerina adored it, as much as she adored their small but cosy flat, situated over an ironmonger's shop in a quiet road just off Clapham High Street. It was only rented, of course, but Izzy had thrown herself into redecorating with her usual enthusiasm and flair for the dramatic the moment they'd moved in eighteen months earlier. And although she might not have been able to afford the luxury of wallpaper she had more than made up for it with richly shaded paints, striking borders and her own dazzling sense of style. Many hours of multi-coloured stencilling and artful picture-hanging later, the effect had been as spectacular as Katerina had known it would be and within the space of four days the flat had become a home.

It was one of Izzy's more unexpected talents and if Katerina had been less loyal, she might have wished that her mother would consider a career in interior design, or even good old painting and decorating. Admittedly, it wasn't likely to bring her fame and fortune beyond her wildest dreams, but it was decent, gainful employment and was even rumoured to bring with it a reasonably regular wage . . .

Katerina simply couldn't imagine what it might have been like, growing up with a mother who didn't sing. As far back as she was able to remember, Izzy had always been there, careering from one financial crisis to the next and at the same time eternally optimistic that the inevitable big break was just around the corner. When she was very small Katerina had perched on beer crates in dingy, smoke-filled pubs and working men's clubs, sipping Coke and listening to her mother sing while all around her the audience got on with the serious business of getting Saturday-night drunk. Sometimes there would be appreciative applause, which was what Izzy lived for. At other times, a fight would break out among the customers and Izzy's songs would be forgotten in the ensuing excitement. Periodically, the hecklers would turn out, either joining in with bawdy alternative lyrics or targeting Izzy directly and laughing inanely at their own imagined wit. Katerina's eyes would fill with tears whenever this happened and the longing to land a seven-year-old punch on the noses of the perpetrators would be so great that she had to grip the sides of the crate upon which she sat in order to prevent herself from doing so. In her eyes, her mother was Joan of Arc, a heroine hounded by ignorant peasants. Afterwards, Izzy would laugh and say it didn't matter because she'd earned £3.40, she would press the 40p into her daughter's small hand and give her a hug. It didn't matter, she would explain cheerfully, because everybody needed to start somewhere; that was a fact of life. And anyone who could survive an evening in a working men's club on the outskirts of Blackpool was going to find Las Vegas a doddle in comparison.

At school the next day, Katerina's teacher had found her poring over an atlas in search of that elusive town. In answer to the question, 'What's it like in Las Vegas?' Miss

Brent had replied with a disapproving sniff, 'It's a town where everybody gambles,' and Katerina had been reassured. Lambs gambolled in fields. In her imagination, Las Vegas became one big, emerald-green field, with all its inhabitants skipping and bouncing and smiling at each other. 'My mum's going to take me to Las Vegas,' she confided happily. 'When we get there, I'm going to gamble every day.'

Las Vegas, needless to say, hadn't happened. Izzy's big break had stubbornly failed to materialise and life had continued its haphazard, impecunious course, although at least working men's clubs were now a thing of the past. Platform One, where Izzy had worked for the past eighteen months, might not be Ronnie Scott's, but it was situated in Soho and the clientele, on the whole, were appreciative. Here, in London, as Izzy always maintained, there was always that *chance* of a chance . . . one never knew who might walk through the door one night, hear her singing and realise that *she* was the one they needed to take the leading role in the show they were currently producing . . .

This didn't happen, of course, but Izzy had never tired of the fantasy. Singing was her passion, what she was best at. She was doing what she *had* to do and Katerina didn't begrudge her a single impoverished moment of it. Who, after all, could possibly begrudge a mother who would cheerfully splurge on a primrose-yellow mohair sweater for her daughter and survive on peanut-butter sandwiches for the next week in order to redress the precarious financial balance? And if her impulsive generosity never failed to alarm Mike, who was one of those people who got twitchy if their electricity bills weren't paid by return of post, Katerina adored her mother's blissful disregard for such mundane matters as financial security. If the bomb was dropped tomorrow she'd much rather have a deliciously soft, mohair sweater to keep her warm, than wander the rubble-strewn streets wondering how all this was going to affect her pension plan.

She was a third of the way through the Liquorice Allsorts and already on to the second page of her essay when the phone rang. It was two minutes past eight. Smiling to herself – for despite all his apparent sophistication Ralph could never bring himself to miss *Coronation Street* – Katerina picked up the receiver.

'I suppose your mother's out,' said the brusque voice of Lester Markham.

Katerina replied sweetly, 'I'm afraid she is. How are you, Mr Markham? And how is—'

'Never mind that,' he interrupted harshly. 'I'll be a damn sight better when I receive the last two months' rent your mother owes me. Tell her I'll be round at nine o'clock tomorrow morning for payment. In full.'

Katerina popped another Liquorice Allsort – a black-and-brown triple-decker, her particular favourite – into her mouth and gave the matter some thought. Lester Markham looked a lot like Jim Royle from *The Royle Family*, only maybe a bit grubbier. He didn't have as much of a sense of humour either.

'I thought we only owed one month,' she said carefully.

'Plus another month in advance,' snapped Lester Markham, 'which she used up in December and

14

conveniently appears to have forgotten about.'

Oops, thought Katerina. So that was how Izzy had acquired the money for their splendid Christmas Eve dinner at Chez Nico.

'Of course,' she replied in conciliatory tones. 'I'll tell her as soon as she gets home, Mr Markham. Don't worry about a thing.'

'I'm not worried,' he said in grim tones. 'You're the one who should be worried. Just tell your mother that if I *don't* receive that money – and I mean *all* the money – tomorrow morning, you'll both be out of that flat by the end of the week.' He sniffed, then added quite unnecessarily, 'And I'm not joking, either.'

# Chapter 3

Gina didn't know why she was doing this – she wasn't even sure any more where she was – but she did know that she couldn't go home. Anything was better than returning to that empty house and having to relive the nightmare of Andrew's departure.

Her fingers tightened convulsively, gripping the steering wheel of the Golf so hard that she wondered whether she'd ever be able to prise them free. And she was definitely lost now, but since she didn't have anywhere to go, it hardly seemed to matter.

Having packed a couple of suitcases with guilt-ridden haste, Andrew had left their Kensington home at ten minutes past six and Gina, not knowing what else to do, had switched off the oven and run herself a hot bath. Then, unable to face the thought of taking off her clothes – she felt vulnerable enough as it was – she had pulled out the bath plug, watched the foaming, lilac-scented water spiral away, and reached instead for her coat and car keys.

Driving around the Barbican for forty minutes had been both stupid and unproductive. Gina knew that, but knowing too that somewhere amid the multi-layered nests of purpose-built apartments was her husband, she had convinced herself that if only she could locate him, he would come back to her. She had even found herself peering up at lighted windows, willing him to appear at one of them. Looking down into the street he might recognise her car. Then, overwhelmed by remorse he would rush down, fling his arms around her and beg forgiveness . . .

But, of course, it hadn't happened, because there were simply too many apartments and because by this time his silver-grey BMW would be locked away in one of those expensive, security-conscious car-parks. Furthermore, her husband would undoubtedly have far more interesting things to do than gaze out of a window. He had a mistress, a pregnant mistress, who was probably with him at this minute, exulting in her victory and listening with quiet amusement as he relayed to her the events of the afternoon.

How To Discard An Unwanted Wife, thought Gina bleakly, a lump rising in her throat once more as she accelerated, pulling out to avoid a haphazardly parked car. Andrew and his mistress were probably talking about it right now, reassuring each other that since they were in love, nothing else mattered. What was a used wife among friends, after all? They were probably in bed, too, making passionate love and laughing at the same time because Andrew had been so clever and it had all been so wonderfully *easy* . . .

Blinded by tears, she didn't see the junction looming ahead until much too late. The next moment a sickening thud and the grating shriek of metal against metal shuddered through the car. Screaming, Gina slammed on the brakes and slewed to a halt as another dull thud echoed violently through her eardrums. Trembling so violently that she could barely get the seat belt undone, she fought rising nausea and wrenched open the car door. Fear and panic propelled her – somehow – towards the figure of a motor cyclist lying immobile in a pool of ice-blue light reflected from a nearby cocktail bar. My God, she thought, whimpering with terror, I've killed him . . . he's dead . . . oh please, God, don't let this be happening . . .

Izzy wasn't dead. Dazed, distantly amazed by the extent of the pain tearing through her legs – and by the astonishing fact that she wasn't kicking up more of a fuss about it – she lay in her crumpled position at the roadside and listened to the sound of an hysterical female yelling, 'I've killed him . . . someone help . . . I've killed him.'

Opening an experimental eye, Izzy found herself at grating level. Now *everything* was starting to hurt and to add insult to injury the icy wetness of the road was beginning to permeate her clothes. But at least she could see her bike which was oddly reassuring, even if the front wheel was badly buckled and the handlebars appeared to have twisted in all the wrong directions.

Then she saw the legs of the female who was making all the noise. Thin, pale-stockinged legs in high-heeled, mud-splashed shoes loomed before her.

'He's not dead!' screamed the voice that went with them, and Izzy began to lose patience. Attempting to raise her head in order to see the injured man for herself – how many people had been involved in this accident, for heaven's sake? – she couldn't understand why she wasn't able to do so. Embarrassed by her own weakness, she glared at the skinny, stupid legs in front of her. 'Make up your mind,' she said irritably. 'And will you *please* stop screaming? He's still going to need a bloody ambulance, whether he's dead or not.'

'She isn't quite herself, but you mustn't let it worry you,' explained the young male doctor reassuringly. He neglected to mention that Izzy – to the delight of the night nurses – had just informed him that he had a gorgeous body. 'It's the after-effects of shock combined with the sedatives we needed to give her,' he continued, his eyes kind. 'She didn't sustain any concussion.'

It was three-thirty in the morning and the rest of the ward was in darkness as the doctor showed Katerina into the side ward beyond the sister's office. Dry-mouthed with trepidation, Katerina stood at the end of the bed and gazed down at her mother, propped up against a mountain of pillows and apparently asleep. With her dark hair spilling over her shoulders and her make-up smudged around her closed eyes she looked so small and pale that Katerina found it hard to believe that all she had sustained were cuts, bruises and a broken leg.

Then, as if sensing that she had company, Izzy opened her eyes.

'Darling!' she exclaimed, holding out her arms. 'Come here and give your poor battered mother an enormous hug.'

'How are you feeling?' Katerina said, kissing Izzy's cheek and sending up a silent prayer of thanks for whoever had invented crash helmets.

'Well, absolutely delightful as a matter of fact, but that's because of the pills they've been shovelling down me. Tomorrow, no doubt, everything will hurt like hell. Did they tell you about the madwoman ploughing straight into me? Apparently I went flying through the air like a trapeze artist, then . . . splat!'

'At least you're alive,' said Katerina, tears pricking her eyelids as she gave Izzy another hug.

'And you're positively indecent,' replied Izzy sternly, doing up the unfastened top buttons of her daughter's white cotton shirt. 'Make yourself respectable, child, before that young Adonis behind you starts getting ideas.'

'Mum!' She stifled a smile, not daring to turn around.

'Don't laugh. I know what these doctors are like. Do you hear me, young man?' she went on, waving an admonishing finger in his general direction. 'This is my daughter, seventeen years old and as pure as she is beautiful, so I want you to control yourself.'

'Don't worry about me, Mrs Van Asch.' The doctor, busy filling in charts at the foot of the bed, sounded amused. 'I'm a married man.'

'They're the worst kind,' said Izzy darkly, her eyes narrowing even as Katerina attempted to cover her mouth. 'And you should be ashamed of yourself for cheating on your wife. Why, she's probably at home right now, thinking you're busy at work, while all this time you're here instead, you wicked man, drooling like a pervert over my innocent teenage—'

'*Mother!*' It came out as an agonised whisper. Long accustomed as she was to Izzy's outrageous talent for extracting blushes from people who'd never blushed before in their lives, this was too much. This was truly mortifying.

'It really is quite all right,' the doctor smilingly assured Kat, as the door to the side ward slid open once more. 'Ah, you appear to have another visitor. Just five minutes, I think, then Mrs Van Asch really must get some rest.'

Having flown into a panic after receiving the call from the hospital, not believing for a moment that Izzy had sustained only 'minor injuries', Katerina had phoned Ralph and luckily found him at home. It was Ralph who had brought her to the hospital, Ralph who'd been waiting in the dimly lit corridor outside the ward, and Ralph, blond and handsome, who now entered the room and moved towards Izzy's side with love and concern in his eyes.

'Sweetheart, we were so worried about you . . .'

'I'm fine,' said Izzy happily, lifting her face for a kiss. Then she pointed at the metal cage covering her legs and gave him a woeful look. 'Well, I'm fine but my leg isn't. We aren't going to be able to have sex for *weeks*. Oh Mike,' she concluded piteously, 'isn't it just the most depressing thing you ever heard?'

# Chapter 4

In medical parlance it was known, enigmatically, as 'complications' and they took a desperate turn for the worse the following day. Having hastily explained to Ralph that Izzy was under the influence of mind-bending drugs, Katerina had only partially – minimally, even – succeeded in convincing him that it had all been a ridiculous slip of the tongue. And when Mike had telephoned the flat the next morning to speak to Izzy, and Katerina had told him about the accident, she reasoned that she could hardly have done anything else. The man was in love with her mother, after all. He had to *know* that she was in hospital.

Consequently, and quite naturally, Mike had rushed in to visit Izzy, and to deposit armfuls of exotic hothouse flowers around her bed. It was sheer bad timing, combined with Ralph's lurking suspicions, which brought about the unfortunate *tête-à-tête-à-tête* that had subsequently ensued.

Although not a coward, Katerina was glad she hadn't been there. The way Izzy told it afterwards, it had all been too farcical for words.

'. . . so there was Mike, sitting on the side of my bed unravelling miles of Cellophane and dumping all these incredible flowers into hideous tin vases, when all of a sudden Ralph wrenched open the door and *erupted* into the room, just like the Wicked Witch of the North.' Izzy shuddered as she recounted the scene. 'Then he just stood there in the doorway and said, "Don't tell me, this is Mike." And of course Mike said, "Yes, I'm Mike. Who are you?" and Ralph – my God, darling, never go out with an actor – made himself look as tall as possible and said . . . no, *proclaimed* . . . "I am Izzy's other lover." '

She knew she shouldn't be enthralled, but Katerina couldn't help herself.

'Go on,' she urged, silently willing Izzy to have pulled it off. If anyone was capable of handling such an odds-against situation it was her mother.

Izzy shrugged, reading her mind. 'I'm sorry, darling, but what could I do? The nurses told me afterwards that Ralph had been lurking in the corridor for hours; obviously he'd been waiting for Mike to turn up. And you know how proud and dramatic he is. He simply delivered his lines – "It's over, Izzy. You'll never see me again" – and swept out.'

Katerina had liked both Ralph and Mike, although Ralph had definitely been more fun. He had also, she felt, been more of a match for Izzy, whereas Mike was quieter, more serious and more inherently thoughtful.

'And Mike?' she asked hopefully, aware that she was clutching at straws. He might be thoughtful, but he wasn't completely stupid.

'And Mike,' echoed Izzy in thoughtful tones. 'Well, it was all rather sad, actually. He gave me one of his looks – the same kind of look he uses when I eat chicken legs with my fingers – and said, "I'm sorry, Izzy, but I thought I could trust you. It seems I can't." Then he took all of the flowers out of the vases, wrapped them back up in their bloody Cellophane packets and left.'

'Oh, Mum,' said Katerina brokenly. It was all so sad and so unnecessary. It had also – at least partly – been her fault.

Izzy patted her arm. 'What will be will be,' she said philosophically. 'I know it's a bummer but I suppose I can't really blame them. Besides,' she added with a shrug and a smile, 'there'll be other flowers.'

Her mother was being so determinedly brave that Katerina knew she had to be upset. Between them, Ralph and Mike had made Izzy's life happy and complete. Now, through no fault of her own, she had lost them both and the unfairness of it all hit Katerina like a hammer blow.

'It isn't fair,' she repeated aloud. Izzy didn't even know yet about their imminent eviction from the flat and the implications, job-wise, of a broken leg had clearly not yet dawned on her. 'And maybe it isn't their fault. But I know who *is* to blame . . .'

It was surprisingly easy to find the house, tucked away though it was at the end of Kingsley Grove, a cul-de-sac a couple of hundred yards away from Holland Park. Although tucked wasn't really the word to describe it: an imposing three-storey Victorian residence with pale stone walls beneath ornate russet roofs and its larger-than-average, frost-laden garden, it dominated the other houses in the road. The garden, although overcrowded, was well tended and fresh paintwork surrounded glistening, flawlessly polished windows hung with draped and swagged curtains. Katerina, pausing at the front gates, pursed her lips and wondered whether all this soulless perfection was maintained with the help of outside staff or if Death-on-legs, as Izzy had casually referred to the driver of the Golf GTi which had mown her down, did it all herself.

She was relieved, however, to see the offending car in the driveway. The fact that it was there – gleaming, white and polished to within an inch of its life – indicated that its owner was indeed at home, which meant that Katerina hadn't caught two tubes and had her bum pinched at Westminster for nothing.

Despite the morning sunlight, it was desperately cold outside. Stamping her feet in an attempt to restore feeling in her toes and pulling her crimson coat more tightly around her, Katerina pushed open the gate and made her way up to the front door.

She wasn't by nature a vindictive person and her intention in coming here wasn't to deliberately hurt or to upset the woman. She simply couldn't bear to think of her shrugging off the incident, dismissing it from her mind and carrying on with her life as if nothing of any importance had ever happened. She needed to make sure the woman realised – truly *understood* – the extent of her careless actions, and that while her own life might proceed unhindered she had certainly succeeded in casting a blight over another human being's existence.

When the front door finally opened she was genuinely taken aback. If she *had* wanted to upset this woman she would have felt cheated, because obviously nothing could possibly make her more upset than she already was. The expression on her face was pitiful, her grey eyes red-rimmed and swollen from crying. Her pale skin looked as fragile as tissue paper about to disintegrate.

Katerina hadn't imagined for a moment that the accident would have affected her this drastically – the woman was positively *distraught* – and for a moment she was overcome by guilt. How embarrassing. And how on earth could she justify her sudden appearance on the doorstep without causing the poor, guilt-ridden woman even further distress?

'Yes?' said Gina wearily, barely seeming to notice Katerina. Her gaze was fixed upon a trailing tendril of creeper which had come adrift from its moorings above the porch.

'I'm sorry,' said Katerina, her voice gentle, 'but I felt I should come and see you. My name's Katerina. I'm Isabel Van Asch's daughter.'

Gina very nearly said, 'Who?' but managed to stop herself just in time. The name was obviously supposed to mean something, though she couldn't imagine why the girl should be looking so sympathetic.

Then . . . Van Asch. Of course. This was the daughter of the woman she had driven into the other night, the motor cyclist she had thought was a man. Normally she wouldn't have been able to think of anything else, but the past few days hadn't been exactly normal. Gina knew she should feel ashamed of herself, but somehow she couldn't summon the energy to worry about other people . . . Andrew had wrecked her whole life and the turmoil of simultaneously loving and hating him was tearing her apart . . .

'Of course,' she said, running agitated fingers through her lank, blonde hair. 'You'd better come in.'

'Th-thanks,' said Katerina, through chattering teeth. She was glad now that she had skipped school and come here; at least she could put the poor woman's mind at rest, before she made herself really ill. Guilt was a terrible thing, she thought with a fresh surge of compassion. How idiotic of her not to have realised that Gina Lawrence would be blaming herself and in all probability feeling every bit as bad as Izzy.

'Would you like some coffee?' said Gina, glancing up at the clock as she led the way into the immaculate sitting room. Walls of palest green were hung with tasteful prints and the peach velvet three-piece suite exactly matched the curtains. Katerina prayed that her best trainers weren't treading mud into the flawless carpet.

'No thanks.' She shook her head, deciding to come straight to the point. 'Look, you really mustn't blame yourself for what happened, Mrs Lawrence. I know it must have been a terrible shock for you, but it *was* an accident ... it could have happened to anyone. If I'd realised you were taking it so badly I would have come round sooner. But what's done is done and thank God it wasn't any worse. Mum's quite comfortable now and the doctors say she'll be out of hospital within the next week, which is brilliant news. So you see, you really mustn't take it too much to heart,' she concluded reassuringly. 'It was just one of those things . . .'

Eleven-fifteen, thought Gina, gazing blankly at the girl with the sherry-brown eyes, pink-with-cold nose and dreadful black trainers. Andrew would be in his office now, working at his desk and scribbling down notes with the Schaeffer pen she had given him last Christmas. She wondered whether he was wearing one of the ties she had bought for him and whether the framed photograph of her which had stood on his desk for the last ten years was still there. Or had it been hidden away, replaced by a picture of Marcy Carpenter, the woman with whom he had replaced her?

The thought was so terrible that tears welled up in her aching eyes once more and she brushed them away hastily, although the girl had already seen them.

'Oh God, I'm so sorry . . .' wept Gina, sinking into a chair. 'Forgive me, but I just can't help—'

'Of *course* we forgive you,' Katerina broke in, leaping to her feet and rushing over to her. The woman definitely needed professional help, but psychiatry was a branch of medicine in which she'd become particularly interested recently, and it wasn't every day you came face to face with a real life case of reactive depression. Besides, Gina Lawrence was beginning to make *her* feel guilty.

Putting her arms comfortingly around the woman's heaving shoulders, she said, 'Maybe I'll have that cup of coffee, after all. You stay here and I'll make us both some.'

When she returned several minutes later carrying a tray bearing cups and matching saucers and a plate of chocolate biscuits, the storm of tears had subsided.

'I must say you have a lovely home,' said Katerina, placing the tray on a slender-legged coffee table which scarcely looked capable of supporting it. But she sensed that Gina Lawrence wouldn't approve of tea trays being plonked on the floor. 'I've never seen such a big kitchen before. And everything's so . . . tidy!'

'I haven't been able to stop cleaning things,' sniffed

Gina, shaking her head as the girl offered her a biscuit. 'Ever since Monday night I just haven't been able to stop myself *doing* things. I can't sit still . . . I can't sleep . . . it's so *stupid* . . . I've been getting up in the middle of the night and before I even realise what I'm doing I've scrubbed the kitchen floor. Last night I spent five hours cleaning and polishing all the windows and they didn't even need cleaning but I just had to be *busy* . . .'

'I understand how you must feel,' said Katerina firmly, 'but you have to force yourself to come to terms with what happened before you make yourself ill. We don't blame you for Mum's accident, so you mustn't blame yourself.'

For a long moment, Gina stared at Katerina as if she was quite mad. Not having taken in before what she was saying, only now did she realise that their entire conversation had been conducted at cross purposes. And that the girl seriously thought she was going through this living-bloody-hell purely on account of a stupid, unavoidable accident.

'I'm afraid you've made a mistake,' said Gina, realizing that she was teetering on the edge of hysterical – and horribly inappropriate – laughter. Thankfully it didn't erupt. 'I'm not like this because of . . . your mother. I mean, I'm sorry, of course, but it *is* only a broken leg . . .' She floundered, knowing that she wasn't making herself plain and searching for the right words. Not having told anyone of Andrew's departure, she was dimly able to appreciate the irony of having to say it aloud for the first time to a total stranger. 'You see, on Monday . . . my husband left me. For another woman.'

Later, much later, Katerina would send up a prayer of thanks for the fact that she wasn't a practising psychiatrist. The urge to hit the woman was so strong that she actually had to clasp her hands together.

As it was, she simply stared into the woman's tear-streaked face and said, very slowly, 'You selfish bitch.'

It was almost a relief to have someone to rail against. Gina, tears momentarily forgotten, threw her a withering look.

'You can't be more than sixteen. How could you possibly understand?' she demanded. 'My husband has left me and my life is ruined. I can't think straight, I can hardly *see* straight and here you are, expecting me to feel sorry for your mother simply because she has a broken leg? The insurance company will take care of that,' she went on derisively. 'But my life is over and who's going to take care of *me?*'

Katerina had had enough. She wasn't a bloody psychiatrist, anyway. How this woman had the bare-faced cheek to dismiss Izzy – who was funny and brave and so optimistic that it could bring tears to your eyes – in order to wallow in self-pity, simply because she was too much of a wimp to stand on her own two feet, was beyond her.

'Now you just listen to me,' she said evenly, because screaming abuse – tempting though it was – wouldn't achieve her objective. Death-on-legs would only scream right back and she wanted what she had to say to be listened to, to really sink in. 'You were the one who caused that accident. Thanks to you, my mother has lost her job, her home and two long-term boyfriends. She has nothing left and by the end of the week we'll both be homeless, so

don't you *dare* ask me who's going to take care of you –
you should be *ashamed* of yourself!'

Then, because she hadn't meant to let herself get quite
so carried away, she stood up abruptly, rattling the coffee
cups as she did so. 'I'm sorry, I suppose I've been very
rude. I'd better go.'

'Yes,' said Gina icily. 'I think you better had.'

# Chapter 5

Being in hospital wasn't so bad, Izzy decided. James Milton Ward, for orthopaedic cases, was really rather pleasant because patients with broken bones weren't actually sick, and now that she had been moved out into the main ward she didn't even have time to be lonely. The ward was a mixed one, morale was high, the food was surprisingly good and the fractured femur in Bed Twelve was absolutely gorgeous, even if he was a dentist in real life.

She had also been taught to play a mean game of poker, which was far more entertaining than battling with a weave-it-yourself laundry basket or with the increasingly grey and frazzled piece of knitting that the occupational therapist had urged her to 'have a go at'.

But for the moment, peace reigned. Those in traction were either dozing or reading, and everyone else had disappeared into the television room at the far end of the ward; they were desperate to watch some vital half-hour of a soap of which Izzy had never heard, but which they evidently lived for. Izzy, taking advantage of the brief hiatus, was engrossed in painting her fingernails a particularly entrancing shade of fuchsia. She couldn't reach her toes; they would have to wait until Katerina arrived later.

Her attention was caught moments later by the

appearance in the double doorway of a visitor, chiefly because of the sound of her high heels tapping rhythmically against the polished wooden floor. Glancing up, Izzy saw a tall, slender woman with blonde hair fastened in a chignon and an extremely sophisticated ivory-and-black Chanel-style suit. Pausing uncertainly in the centre of the ward, she surveyed the beds lining each side of the ward and adjusted the bag slung over her padded shoulder with a nervous gesture.

'They're all in the TV room,' said Izzy, pointing towards it with her nail-polish brush. 'Shit!' she exclaimed, as a glossy blob of fuchsia landed in her lap, wrecking for ever her second-best white T-shirt. Then she grinned, because the visitor had assumed a determinedly unshockable expression and was approaching the foot of her bed.

'Sorry. These things are sent to try us. Who is it you're looking for?' Privately, she had already made her decision. This had to be either the dentist's wife or Wing Commander Burton's daughter. Nobody else on the ward could afford even to know someone who wore those kind of clothes.

'Actually,' said the woman, her gaze flickering to the name card fastened above Izzy's bed, 'I think I'm looking for you.'

Not having known what to expect, Gina was nevertheless taken aback by the sight of Isabel Van Asch. When *she had been* lying in the road, her face obscured by the visor of her motor-cycle helmet, she had at first mistaken her for a man. Then, following that decidedly unnerving visit from her daughter, Gina had mentally envisaged her to be a large, somewhat butch female in her mid-forties, with short hair and an aggressive manner.

But this person sitting before her now was small and undeniably feminine. With her expressive dark eyes, smiling mouth and riotous bluey-black hair framing a heart-shaped face, she wasn't at all what Gina had had in mind while she had been plucking up the courage to come here. She looked younger than Gina herself, she was wearing a white T-shirt and bright pink, lycra cycling shorts and she didn't look the least bit intimidating.

Gina, however, who had learned over the past difficult few days not to take anything or anyone at face value, was intimidated anyway. Doing herself up to the nines and finding first the right hospital and then the right ward had sapped her strength completely. On the verge of losing her nerve, she sat down on Izzy's empty visitor's chair with a thump.

'But I don't know you,' said Izzy, looking puzzled. Her dark eyebrows disappeared beneath her haphazard fringe. Her fingers, their nails still wet with pink polish, were splayed in the air before her. Then, with a trace of suspicion, she said, 'You aren't a social worker, are you?'

'I am not,' replied Gina, as shocked as if she had been suspected of prostitution. Did she look like a social worker, for heaven's sake?

But now that the moment had arrived, she was unable to find the words to introduce herself. And surely, she thought with a surge of resentment, that terrifying teenage daughter would have described her to her mother. Isabel Van Asch must know who she was; she was just extracting maximum pleasure from an awkward moment.

'Oh well,' said Izzy, remarkably unperturbed. 'It's nice

to have a visitor, anyway, even if it is an anonymous one.' Reaching with difficulty for a half-empty box of chocolates in her locker drawer, she offered them to Gina. 'Would you like a rum truffle?'

'I'm Gina Lawrence,' Gina blurted out, because someone had to say it and the woman clearly wasn't about to oblige.

The expressive eyebrows remained perplexed. Izzy shook her head and Gina caught a waft of expensive scent. Thorntons truffles and Diorella, she thought darkly; so much for the homeless, impoverished, six-feet-below-the-breadline sob story spun to her by the daughter.

'I was driving the car that collided with your motor bike,' she said, enunciating the words with care. Although the accident had undoubtedly been her fault, her solicitor had cautioned her most sternly against admitting anything at all.

'Oh, right!' exclaimed Izzy, through a mouthful of truffle. Then, to Gina's amazement, she stuck out her hand. 'Gosh, no wonder you were so twitchy when you came in. And how nice of you to come and see me. I'm sorry, I really should have recognised you, but I was in a bit of a state that night. Apart from your legs, I didn't take much in at all. God, sorry – I didn't realise my nails were still wet . . . look, are you quite sure you won't have a chocolate?'

Bemused, Gina shook her head. 'Your . . . daughter,' she said falteringly, 'came to see me yesterday morning.'

'She did?' Now it was Izzy's turn to look stunned. 'Why on earth should she have done that? She didn't even mention it last night.'

'Mrs Van Asch,' began Gina. 'She—'

'Miss. I'm not married. But please call me Izzy,' said Izzy, chucking the box of truffles back on to her locker. 'But how strange. What did she want, anyway?'

'My husband left me,' said Gina hurriedly. There, another hurdle cleared. If she said it fast enough, it didn't make her cry. 'And your daughter told me that I was a selfish bitch. She said that as a result of the accident you'd lost two ... er ... boyfriends. I don't really *know* why I'm here, but I suppose I thought I ought to come to see you and apologise. And something else I don't understand,' she added with a burst of honest to goodness curiosity, 'is how you can lose two boyfriends at the same time. What happened?'

'So, she made you feel guilty,' mused Izzy, a wry smile lifting the corners of her mouth. 'My God, that girl has a positive talent for digging at consciences. She does exactly the same to me when I haven't hung my clothes up for a week. Still,' she added sternly, 'she shouldn't have called you a selfish bitch. That's going too far. Don't worry, I'll have a word with her about that. And you really mustn't worry,' she added, leaning forward impulsively and resting her hand upon Gina's. 'She can be a bit self-righteous at times but she doesn't really mean it. You know what teenagers are like.'

Gina shook her head, sadly. 'No, I don't.'

'Well!' Izzy rolled her eyes. 'Let me tell you that they can be the living end! Kat's an absolute angel but sometimes I almost wish I could disown her – like now. She might have twelve GCSEs, but she can still make an idiot of herself when she wants to. I really am sorry she upset you, Mrs Lawrence. And when I see her tonight I promise you I'll give her a good slapping.'

'Oh, but you mustn't—' Gina broke off, realizing a couple of milliseconds too late that the other woman was joking. Colour rose in her pale cheeks. 'Please,' she amended hastily. 'My name's Gina.'

She hadn't fooled Izzy, however, and they both knew it.

'Tell me about the boyfriends,' said Gina, changing the subject, and Izzy pulled a face.

'It has its funny side, I suppose, although I was too out of it at the time to appreciate the humour, and when I did realise what I'd done I was pretty pissed off. Maybe it'll be funny in a few weeks' time.' She shrugged, pausing to admire her painted nails, then briefly outlined the details of the mix-up, culminating in the prompt departure of both Mike and Ralph from her life.

The unorthodox arrangement – not to mention Izzy's pragmatic attitude towards it – was something quite outside Gina's experience. She'd never met anyone like her in her life.

'Aren't you devastated?' she said finally.

Izzy looked thoughtful. 'I suppose so, but wailing and weeping isn't going to do me much good, is it? Besides, Kat says it would only give me wrinkles.'

'Mmm.' Gina, who had spent the majority of the past few days weeping and wailing, experienced a twinge of guilt. At this rate, she supposed she was lucky not to look a hundred and fifty years old. 'Your daughter also told me that you were about to be thrown out of your flat. What will you do when that happens?'

'Well,' said Izzy in a confidential whisper, as a nurse strode briskly past, 'since I'm between men, as they say, I thought I might as well seduce my landlord. See if I can't persuade him to change his mercenary old mind . . .'

'Are you joking?' asked Katerina, two days later. She didn't know whether to laugh and the expression on her mother's face was making her feel decidedly uneasy.

'Of course not,' Izzy replied with enthusiasm. 'Would I joke about something as serious as our imminent vagrancy? It's perfect, darling. The answer to a desperate mother's prayer.'

'But she's an old witch!'

'She is not.' Seeing the mutinous glitter in Katerina's eyes, Izzy knew she had to be firm. 'She's just going through a rough time at the moment. I thought it was amazingly kind of her to make the offer – and it isn't as if we have much of an alternative, anyway,' she reminded her daughter briskly. 'I was going to ask Rachel and Jake if we could stay with them for a while, but they really don't have the room, whereas Gina's rattling around on her own in that big house of hers and she needs some company at the moment . . .'

'What about money?' Katerina demanded. The idea of having to keep that woman company was positively chilling; she'd rather share a hot bath with Freddie Kruger.

'Rent free for the first month,' Izzy replied with an air of triumph. 'And then the same as we've been paying Markham. Now isn't that a great deal?' she exclaimed. 'Be honest, where would you prefer to live, Clapham or

Kensington? Or was a plastic bench on Tottenham Court Road tube station what you'd really set your heart on?'

Since there wasn't really any satisfactory answer to that, Kat said nothing.

'There you are then,' concluded Izzy, glad that it was sorted.

'I still don't like her.'

'We're renting a couple of rooms in her house, we don't have to *marry* her.' She flashed a flawless smile at the dentist as he zipped past in his wheelchair with his smashed-and-plastered leg stuck out at right angles before him. 'And since we don't have any choice, we may as well make the most of it. Sweetheart, who knows? It might even be fun!'

# Chapter 6

Gina didn't know what she'd got herself into. She was suffering from a severe attack of doubt which erupted from time to time into near panic. Never one to act upon impulse, she couldn't understand why she should have done so now, when her entire life was in the process of being turned on its head anyway and the last thing she needed was more trauma. And although she had tried to shift the blame on to Andrew, she was uncomfortably aware that from now on she wasn't going to be able to do that. As from last week, she had become unwillingly responsible for her own life and already she was making a diabolical mess of it.

Visiting Isabel Van Asch in the hospital had succeeded in taking her mind off Andrew for an hour, which was miraculous in itself. She had gone in order to salve her vaguely pricking conscience, and had come away impressed. She'd never met anyone like Isabel – Izzy – before and the novelty of the woman had been a revelation. Imagining what it must be like to live so carelessly, to be so *unworried*, had occupied her thoughts for the rest of the afternoon. But since she wasn't Izzy, and because she was quite incapable of casting off her own worries, as darkness had fallen so she had sunk back into depression. Women like Izzy simply didn't understand what it was like, not being able to stop thinking about disaster, Gina had realised miserably, whereas she was constantly haunted by reminders of Andrew.

And then at eight-thirty that evening, quite unexpectedly, Andrew had arrived at the house and she didn't need to imagine him any more because he was there in the flesh, achingly familiar and even more achingly businesslike.

'We have to discuss the financial aspects of all this,' he told Gina, refusing with a shake of his head her offer of a drink and opening his briefcase with a brisk flick of his thumb. He wasn't quite meeting her eyes and a fresh spasm of grief caught in her chest. Handle this with a shrug and a smile, Izzy Van Asch, she thought savagely. It was no good, it couldn't be done. When it was the husband you loved in front of you it wasn't humanly possible.

'We don't have to,' she had wailed. 'You could come back. I *forgive* you . . .'

Even as the words were spilling out she had been despising herself for her weakness. And they hadn't worked anyway. Andrew had given her a pitying look and launched into a speech he had prepared earlier, the upshot being that Gina was going to have to realise that money didn't grow on trees. The house was hers, inherited from her parents, and he naturally had no intention of staking any kind of claim upon it, but the credit cards were no longer going to be fair game, always there to allow herself such little treats as new furniture, holidays in the sun and the latest designer outfits.

'I've spoken to my solicitor,' Andrew had explained, more gently now. 'And I'll be as fair as possible, but I have to warn you, Gina, I won't be able to give you much at all. That flat of mine is costing an arm and a leg just to rent. And my solicitor says that, basically, there's no reason why you shouldn't be able to get yourself a job—'

'A job!' shrieked Gina, horrified. 'But I don't work. My job is looking after my husband! Why should I have to suffer when I haven't done anything wrong?'

Andrew shrugged. 'The law is the law. You don't *need* me to support you. You have this house . . . Marvin suggested that you might like to take in lodgers.'

The prospect was more than terrifying, it was unthinkable. When Andrew had – with undisguised relief – left the house thirty minutes later, Gina had made every effort not to think about it. By midnight she had come to the unhappy conclusion that pretending it wasn't happening wasn't going to make it go away. Andrew's third suggestion, that she might sell the house, move into a small flat and live off the interest on the money saved, was out of the question. She had spent her entire life here and the future was going to be scary enough without having to uproot herself from the only home she had ever known.

A job . . . the mere thought of it sent a shiver of apprehension through her. Apart from two terrible years spent ricocheting from one office to another in search of a job that was even semi-bearable, she had never worked. Andrew had burst into her life and she had abandoned the tedium of nine to five, office politics and fifteen-minute tea breaks without so much as a backward glance. The relief had been immeasurable; looking after a husband

and a home was all she'd ever wanted to do, for ever and ever, amen . . .

The very idea of allowing strangers into her house – lodgers, tenants, paying guests, call them what you will – was equally alarming. Pausing finally to consider this unpalatable option, Gina actually poured herself a vodka and tonic. Who hadn't heard the horror stories, after all, of dubious, fraudulent, sinister and sometimes downright sex-crazed characters lulling their landladies into a false sense of security and then either making off with the entire contents of the house or finishing them off with machetes? Gina, only too easily able to envisage her remains bundled into the chest freezer alongside the sole *bonne femme*, took a hefty gulp of her drink. Then she realised that she *was* going to pieces. The tonic was flat.

'I still don't understand,' said Katerina in challenging tones, 'why you're doing this. Why *did* you go back to see my mother and ask her – us – to come and live with you?'

It was a shame, Gina thought, that the daughter hadn't inherited her mother's happy-go-lucky nature. She thanked God that her house was a large one.

'I didn't ask her to come and live with me,' she replied coolly. 'I offered her a place to stay, and she accepted.'

Katerina dumped the assortment of cases and bags on to the narrow bed and gave the rest of the room a cursory glance. Magnolia walls, beige-and-white curtains, beige carpet; not awfully inspiring but exceptionally clean.

'But why?'

Gina decided to play her at her own game. 'If you must know, it was sheer desperation. If you really have to know,' she continued, her tone even, 'I need the money.'

'Of course,' murmured Katerina, not even bothering to sound scathing. Moving across to the window, she looked out over leafless treetops at the roofs of the elegant houses lining the street, and at the gleaming, top-of-the-range cars parked outside them. Gina's claim to 'need the money' was so ridiculous it was almost laughable, but she wasn't in a position to laugh. And Izzy had insisted that she behave herself.

'Well thanks, anyway.'

'That's all right,' said Gina awkwardly. 'I hope you'll both be happy here.'

'We've always been happy,' Katerina replied simply. 'Wherever we've lived.'

Then, glancing out of the window once more, she spotted an ancient white van hiccuping down the road. 'Great, here comes Jake with the rest of our things. I'd better go down and guide him into the drive.'

'Into the drive,' echoed Gina, paling at the sight of the disreputable vehicle being driven by a man whose hair was longer than her own. Marjorie Hurlingham was cutting back her forsythia next door. She prayed that Jake and the van wouldn't stay long.

'I can't get over it, this is fabulous!' declared Izzy later that afternoon. Seeing her new home for the first time, and observing with some relief that relations between her daughter and their new landlady weren't as bad as she had feared, a smile spread over her face. Katerina had obviously decided to behave, the house was wonderful and there was real central heating that actually worked . . .

* * *

It was eight-thirty in the evening. Izzy, her plastered leg flung comfortably across Jake's lap, was still regaling everyone with tales of her stay in hospital. Rachel, Jake's wife, had opened another bottle of wine and was singing happily along to the music playing on the stereo – which appeared to be the only electrical appliance Izzy possessed. Katerina, lying on her side on the floor, was eating raisins and looking through an old photograph album, pausing from time to time to show off the more embarrassing snaps of Izzy during her flower-power days.

Gina perched unhappily on the edge of a chair. She felt rather like a hostess no longer in control of her own party. Not having had time to think about Andrew – and the ritual of brooding over her past life with him had become comforting, even necessary – she was also feeling somewhat dispossessed. And Izzy, Katerina and their friends were so utterly relaxed in each other's company, laughing and teasing and giving the impression of being entirely at home in Izzy's bedroom, that she felt even more of an outsider than ever. This was her *own* home, she reminded herself, yet already her immaculate guest room was unrecognizable.

Despite his long hair and gold earring, Jake had seemed remarkably normal; nevertheless, Gina was glad when he and Rachel finally made a move. He might be a lecturer in history at one of London's largest polytechnics, but she couldn't help wondering what the neighbours would be saying about his terrible van. And now that they were leaving, she could do likewise and retire to the sanctuary of her own room. To sit in peace and think about what

Andrew might be doing, thinking and saying at this moment . . .

'Don't go,' Izzy urged, rolling on to her side and stretching out for the half-empty bottle of wine. 'Sod it, can't reach. Kat, do the honours will you, darling? Fill Gina's glass to the brim. Gina, don't look so nervous! Come on now, relax.'

Relaxing didn't come easily to Gina, particularly when she was instructed to do so. Her legs were knotted together and she didn't know what to do with her hands. Glancing at her watch, she said, 'I really should be—'

'No, you shouldn't,' said Katerina unexpectedly. Handing Gina her drink, she added, 'You're looking a lot better than you were when I last saw you, but you're still twitchy. Why don't you tell Mum what's been happening with your ex-husband? She's awfully good at cheering people up.'

Katerina still hadn't forgiven Gina for her selfishness the previous week, but she was also slightly ashamed of her own behaviour that day. This was her way of making amends.

'Of course I am, I'm brilliant,' said Izzy, her dark eyes shining. 'Tell me all about it, every detail. It's so unfair, isn't it, that men should be such pigs. Why on earth do we still fall in love with them?'

'. . . he was my whole world,' Gina whispered fifteen minutes later. Her wineglass, unaccountably, was empty. Her feet were tucked up beneath her. 'When we were first married I thought we'd have a family, but Andrew told me that we didn't need children to be happy because we had each other. After that, every time I mentioned it he just said he didn't want children ... they were too expensive or too time-consuming or he needed to be able to concentrate on his career ... and if I got upset he'd buy me a nice necklace or take me away on holiday ... I wanted a baby *so much*, but he always managed to convince me he was right. And now,' she concluded hopelessly, 'he's got some woman pregnant and he's changed his mind. So I'm left on my own without a husband or a family and it's too late for me to do anything about it. I'm too old to have children now ... I haven't got anything ... it's all been *wasted* ...'

Izzy, who had been listening intently, now looked perplexed. 'I'm sorry,' she said, eyebrows furrowed, 'but I'm not with you. He's been a bit of a shit, I'll grant you that, but why exactly has your marriage been a waste?'

'Because now I don't have a husband or a child,' sniffed Gina with a trace of irritation. 'If he'd told me ten years ago that he was going to leave me eventually, I could have cut my losses and married someone else who *did* want a family.'

Izzy's frown deepened. 'But you're only thirty-six.'

'Exactly! How long is it going to be before I even *feel* like looking for another man? How long is it going to be before I find someone I want to marry? It's just not fair,' Gina sniffed, tears glittering in her eyes. 'By then it'll be too late, I'll be too old.'

'This is crazy,' Izzy burst out, jack-knifing into a sitting position and spilling half her wine into her lap. 'If you want a baby that badly, you can have one. Nobody's going to stop you!'

Gina wondered for a moment what it must be like to be Izzy, to live so carelessly and with such total disregard for the conventions which had dominated her own life.

But it was too great a leap, even after three unaccustomed glasses of wine.

'*You* don't understand,' she said defensively, hanging her head. 'I couldn't do that. It isn't the kind of thing I could cope with on my own.'

'But you don't know that,' argued Izzy, struggling to curb her natural impatience. 'You just *think* you wouldn't be able to cope . . . I'll bet you any money you like that once it all started happening you'd sail through it. Well,' she amended with a grin, 'I would if I had any money to bet with.'

'It's no good, I'm not that kind of person,' Gina replied, defiant now but still close to tears. It *wasn't* any good; she had hoped that some of Izzy's optimism might rub off on her, but all she felt was intimidated. Their personalities, their attitudes to life were just too different. Rising somewhat unsteadily to her feet, she said, 'I'm going to bed.'

Izzy, equally frustrated by Gina's inability to realise that what she had been trying to say made absolute sense, glanced at her watch. 'It's only ten o'clock. Stay and have another drink, *please* . . .'

'I'm going to my room,' put in Katerina helpfully. 'I've got two essays to finish.'

'No, no,' said Gina, wondering what she had let herself in for. Her guest room looked and felt different – it even smelled different, thanks to Izzy's scented candles – and now she was beginning to feel like a hostage here. It had all been a terrible, impetuous mistake, which only served to underline the vastness of the gulf between them. She simply wasn't cut out to be impulsive and she was damned if she'd ever do it again. 'I'm tired,' she concluded, not daring to even glance up at the cuckoos who had invaded her own private nest at her own stupid instigation.

'OK,' said Izzy, conceding defeat. Then she brightened, because it was only a temporary defeat. 'There's no hurry, after all. We'll talk about it again tomorrow.'

# Chapter 7

'So, how's it going at home?' asked Simon as Katerina cleared a pile of text books from the chair next to his and collapsed into it with a sigh. It was lunchtime and the sixth-form common room, buzzing with gossip, sounded more like a cocktail party in full swing. Handing her his half-empty can of Coke, he admired afresh Katerina's clever, slender fingers and her ability to look so amazingly good, even after three rigorous hours in the physics exam. Having quietly idolised Katerina Van Asch throughout their years together at King's Park Comprehensive, actually getting to know her and eventually becoming her best friend meant more to him than anything else in the world. If it hadn't been for Kat, he would have left school a year and a half ago; she was the one who had persuaded him to stay on and study for A levels and for that he would be everlastingly grateful. He had a sneaking suspicion that abandoning further education in favour of bumming around the country as a bass guitarist in a rock band might not, after all, have been as much fun as he had first imagined.

He was, nevertheless, fascinated by Katerina's bizarre lifestyle, wonderfully Bohemian in his eyes and as far removed as possible from his own sedate upbringing. Living in a semi-detached in Wimbledon with a bank manager father, housewife mother and two pain-in-the-neck younger sisters wasn't exactly wild.

Katerina, whose mother didn't nag her to keep her feet off the furniture as his own mother was forever doing, flung her long legs across the arm of the chair and tore open a packet of crisps.

'How's it going at home?' she repeated thoughtfully. 'Well, not great. Dreary Gina can't seem to talk about anything but her husband, Mum's hell-bent on cheering her up and I keep out of the way as much as I can. The really bad news is that our four weeks of living rent free are up and Mum's leg is still in plaster. When I left her this morning she was poring over *The Stage*, but how can she possibly get work in her state?'

'Elizabeth Taylor did *The Little Foxes* in a wheelchair . . .' began Simon excitedly, but Katerina quelled him with a look that would have stripped the eyebrows of a lesser man.

'That was Elizabeth Taylor, this is the real world.'

'So, what are you going to *do*?' he persisted, enthralled by her casual acceptance of the situation.

She paused, considering his question for a moment, then shrugged and said, 'Find myself a job, I suppose. Something in the evenings that pays well and doesn't interfere too much with my homework. Failing that, I could always find my mother a new and dazzlingly wealthy man.'

She grinned suddenly and lobbed her empty crisp packet into the bin. 'Now that *would* be a smart idea. I could be the devoted stepdaughter. I'd make a great stepdaughter, don't you think? And the more money he had, the more devoted I'd be . . .'

Worried, Simon said, 'You're joking.'

'Of course I'm joking.' With a howl of despair, she pretended to hurl the Coke can at his head. 'Who needs men, for heaven's sake? Now stop agony-aunting and tell me everything you know about the medulla oblongata. It's human biology this afternoon, and I've got an essay to finish.'

Simon broke into a grin. 'I thought you didn't need men.'

'I don't,' Katerina replied crisply. 'I just need information. Besides, you aren't a man. You're a boy.'

Damn, thought Sam Sheridan, finally hanging up the phone at Heathrow and realizing that he and his suitcases had a couple of hours to kill before they could make their collective way to Kingsley Grove. Andrew was out of the office, there was no reply from the house and jet lag was already threatening to set in, which possibly served him right but didn't necessarily make it any easier to bear. If he had slept on the plane instead of falling into conversation with a rather intense but decidedly attractive female solicitor, he wouldn't be feeling quite so tired now.

But Gina was a creature of habit, he reassured himself, glancing at the watch he'd adjusted as the plane had neared the end of its transatlantic journey. Almost four o'clock, and it was a sure bet that she would be back home soon in order to prepare dinner. If he caught a cab he could be there by five, in time to stop her doing so. Then, when he'd grabbed himself a couple of hours' sleep he could take them both out to dinner to celebrate his return. It would be great to see Andrew again, after nearly six months away. And as for Gina ... well, teasing and shocking dear, uptight, ever-shockable Gina had always been one of his very favourite pastimes ...

Damn, thought Izzy, hopping helplessly into the sitting room and glaring at the now silent phone. Didn't people realise how much longer it took a broken-legged person to even reach the room the phone was in, much less get a chance to actually pick up the receiver? And was there anything in the world more frustrating than not getting that chance to find out who had been on the other end of the line?

Chucking a cushion at the offending machine – and missing it by three feet – she allowed her imagination to run wild for a few seconds. A single telephone call, after all, was potentially capable of changing entire lives.

Why, it might have been Andrew Lloyd Webber, begging her to accept the lead in his latest and greatest musical. It could have been Doug Steadman, her agent, phoning to tell her that an American producer wanted her – and only her – to replace Shirley MacLaine in a Broadway show. It might have been – it just *might* have been ... a salesman ringing to make her a fabulous offer on double glazing ...

'Damn,' repeated Izzy, aloud this time. Wheeling around, she headed into the hall, picking up her jacket and bag *en route*. Now that she was downstairs she might as well exercise her good leg and take a trip out to the shops before they closed. Having rashly promised to cook dinner for Kat and Gina tonight, it might be an idea to buy something edible. She had a feeling Gina might be expecting something a bit more substantial than tinned tomatoes on toast.

Through the side window of the cab Sam observed with fleeting interest the dark-haired girl in the short yellow skirt who was swinging her way along the pavement on crutches. Her legs, one encased in plaster and the other shapely and black-stockinged, were what had immediately captured his attention. But now, as the cab reached the end of Kingsley Grove and slowed to a halt, he glimpsed the girl's face in the orange light of the street lamp and was further impressed. For a brief second, as she paused to search in her jacket pocket for her keys, their eyes met. Dark eyes, wide mouth, crazy corkscrewing hair and an indefinable air about her . . . of vitality and humour and . . . daring . . . caused something, somewhere inside him, to click. Jet lag miraculously forgotten, Sam smiled at her without even realizing he was doing so, but it was too late. The girl had turned away.

Then, even as he watched, she moved – peg-leggedly but very definitely – towards Andrew's and Gina's house.

Better and better, he thought, hauling his cases out of the cab and pressing notes into the driver's hand. Within seconds, he had caught up with her on the front doorstep. 'Hi,' said Sam, flashing her a brilliant smile, one that this time she couldn't possibly miss. 'Well, I don't know who you are, but your timing's perfect. I thought Gina would be home by now.' He gestured towards the darkened windows. 'But she obviously isn't. And I'm afraid I've lost my front-door key.'

The girl, returning his gaze but not his smile, said

nothing. Realizing his mistake – he must be more jet lagged than he appreciated – Sam said, 'I'm sorry, how rude of me. I haven't even introduced myself. I'm—'

'I know exactly who you are,' Izzy interjected rapidly, at the same time wondering at the colossal nerve of the man. Glancing briefly down at the suitcases littering the doorstep she said, 'Gina didn't say anything about this to me. Have you spoken to her? Is she *expecting* you?'

Taken aback by the unpromising abruptness of her manner, Sam shrugged and said, 'Well . . . no, not exactly. As I said before, she was out when I phoned. But she won't mind, if that's what you're worried about. After fifteen years she's perfectly used to my—'

'I'm sure she is,' Izzy retorted, interrupting him for the second time and deciding it was high time somebody told Andrew Lawrence precisely what they thought of him and his diabolical behaviour. Not having seen any photographs, she had envisaged a slightly older, altogether less casual man, the type who favoured pin-stripe suits rather than scuffed-leather flying jackets and ancient Levi's, but even in the semi-darkness she could see that he undoubtedly possessed more than his fair share of good looks and charm. Only men with that particular, lazy, *uncultivated* degree of charm could do as he had done and expect to get away with it. And only a man with a total lack of humility, she thought darkly, could expect to roll back home and be forgiven, just like that.

'Oh yes, I'm sure she is,' repeated Izzy, leaning against the cold stone wall of the porch and with great deliberation dropping the front-door key back into her pocket. 'But that doesn't mean she has to keep on putting up with it. She may be too scared of offending you to tell you what a neat job you've done of wrecking her life, but I'm not. Look,' she snapped, realizing that Gina's husband didn't have the slightest intention of showing remorse, 'hasn't it occurred to you for even a single second that Gina might *not* welcome you with open arms when you turn up on her doorstep?'

'To be frank,' said Sam, wondering what the hell was going on, 'no.'

'Well, it bloody wouldn't, would it? You really are *incredible . . .*'

'I really am very tired.' He was beginning to lose patience now. 'Look, why don't you just tell me exactly what it is I'm supposed to have done wrong. Then, when you've got that off your chest, maybe you could introduce yourself. No, strike that. Tell me first who *you* are and let me decide whether or not I should even bother to listen to you. And where the hell are Gina and Andrew anyway? If they aren't coming back here tonight I'll save you the trouble and find myself an hotel.'

'Oh shit.' Izzy stared at him, appalled, then sagged slowly back against the rough stone wall behind her. Would there ever come a time in her life, she wondered, when she wouldn't go around saying *exactly* the wrong thing to *exactly* the wrong person, in the very worst way possible?

'Look, I'm going,' said Sam irritably. Turning to leave, he added, 'If it isn't too much trouble, maybe you could tell them I called.'

Grabbing his arm so quickly that she almost lost her balance and toppled over, Izzy said, 'Please, I'm sorry. I've made a hideous mistake. You must come in.'

By this time Sam was almost certain he was the one who'd made the hideous mistake. That initial, almost instantaneous attraction had taken a smart step backwards. This woman wasn't just rude, he thought, glancing down at her cold fingers around his wrist, she was downright weird.

'*Please*,' begged Izzy, reading his mind and fitting the key hastily into the lock. 'I'm really not mad, but until I explain everything you can't possibly understand. Look, let me take your jacket. What would you like to drink?'

'Sit,' commanded Sam firmly, steering her into the sitting room, switching on lights as he went and flinging his jacket over the back of Gina's immaculate sofa. Pouring hefty measures of Scotch into two tumblers, he handed one to the obediently seated madwoman and settled himself in the armchair opposite.

'Now, maybe we should start again. Properly, this time, and without resorting to a slanging match. How very pleasant to meet you, Miss . . .'

'Van Asch,' murmured Izzy, thankful that he had taken charge, and that he didn't appear to have taken her insults too much to heart. 'Izzy.'

'Yes.' He nodded, a smile hovering on his lips. 'You look like an Izzy. And my name is Sam Sheridan.'

'Hallo, Sam Sheridan.'

'And who exactly did you think I was?'

'Gina's husband,' she confessed, her brown eyes huge as she searched his face for a reaction. Then, hurriedly, she added, 'As soon as you said it, I knew you didn't know. They've split up. Andrew moved out a few weeks ago and Gina's absolutely distraught.'

'What happened?' said Sam, no longer smiling. He could imagine the effect Andrew's departure must be having upon Gina. Her entire life had revolved around him.

'He met someone else,' Izzy explained. 'And she's pregnant. They're living together in the Barbican.' Then she paused, eyebrows furrowing, and said, 'Are you a friend or a relative?'

Sam sipped his drink. 'Friend. Old friend.'

'Of Andrew's?'

'Yes.' He shrugged. 'Of both of them really. I was the best man at their wedding. When I moved over to the States six years ago they gave me a key to the house. Whenever I come back I stay here. Jesus,' he shook his head in disbelief, 'Gina must be going through hell.'

'Andrew should have warned you,' said Izzy. While he was otherwise occupied she seized the opportunity to observe this startlingly attractive 'friend of the family' about whom she had hitherto heard nothing at all. The tan, for a start, coupled with those mesmerizing grey-green eyes, would alone have been enough to seriously impress. But Sam Sheridan didn't stop there; his hair, streaky and sun-bleached, was just long enough to be interesting while the eyebrows were contrastingly dark and wonderfully expressive. His mouth was perfect. And as for the rest of the body . . . Having found herself in something of a sexual limbo recently, it made a nice change to be able to sit and admire such spectacular good looks. They might have got off to an unpromising start, she thought cheerfully, but who knew what might happen if Sam Sheridan were to move into what Kat had taken to calling 'The Nunnery'?

'I've been in Hawaii for the past month,' he said. 'Maybe he tried to contact me, and couldn't.' Then he glanced once more at Izzy and said, 'But I still don't know who *you* are.'

This was more like it, decided Izzy, running the fingers of her free hand through her rumpled curls in a casual manner. She grinned, suddenly.

'I live here. We're Gina's new lodgers.'

'We?'

'My daughter, Katerina. But we're almost completely housetrained,' she added, catching his look of alarm. 'And there's no need to panic, I'm sure this house is big enough to cope with one more.'

She was older than he'd first thought, a woman rather than a girl. Sam, guessing her to be around thirty, nevertheless found it extraordinarily difficult to imagine her as a mother. She didn't *look* like one. Furthermore, much as he liked children – in measured doses – he wasn't at all sure he wanted to share a house with some screaming toddler who doubtless would be up at unearthly hours of the morning just when he most needed to be asleep.

'I don't know,' he said, glancing at his watch. 'Now that the situation's changed I really think it might be better if I book into an hotel.'

At that moment they heard the front door open and close and Gina's high heels clicking across the hall.

'You talk to her,' said Izzy, martialling her crutches and manoeuvring herself to her feet. 'I'm sure she'd want you to stay. If you want me,' she added with a provocative smile over her shoulder, 'I'll be in the kitchen. You aren't a vegetarian, are you?'

'No.' She *was* weird, decided Sam. Beautiful, but definitely weird. 'Why?'

'I'm making a Stroganoff,' explained Izzy patiently. 'And since it's your fault that it's going to be late, the very least you can do is shoulder the blame and stay for dinner.'

# Chapter 8

'Oh Sam, how could he have done it to me?' sniffed Gina over an hour later, dabbing at her mascara-smudged eyes with a sodden handkerchief, but knowing that the worst of the tears were over. Embarrassed at having broken down in front of him, but at the same time immensely comforted by his presence, she realised afresh what a good friend he had been to them both over the years. She'd always enjoyed his visits but this time his arrival was just what she needed. Sam, who could cheer anyone up more effectively than anybody else she knew, was on her side. And that knowledge strengthened her more than she'd imagined possible.

'Men,' said Sam, getting to his feet, 'are notorious for not knowing what's best for them. Sweetheart, I'm just going to see how Izzy's getting on. That Stroganoff smells great and I'm starving.'

'Don't get your hopes up,' said Gina waspishly. 'Izzy's cooking isn't her strong point. The most ambitious meal she's conjured up so far is fish-finger sandwiches.'

'You aren't Izzy,' said Sam, entering the steam-filled kitchen and beginning to feel somewhat surreal. A tall girl with swinging, shoulder-length, sherry-brown hair was standing at the table, carefully tipping sautéd potatoes from a frying pan into a shallow blue dish. She looked up, unsurprised by the intrusion.

'I'm Kat. Mum's upstairs trying to have a bath. Dinner will be ready in five minutes.' She paused, then added kindly, 'You look confused.'

'I am confused,' said Sam, running a hand through his hair, then shaking his head. 'I was expecting you to be about five years old. At the very most.'

She smiled, covered the dish of sautéd potatoes and put them into the oven. 'I'm mature for my age. How's Gina?'

'Damp, but she'll live. Did you make all this?' Deeply appreciative of good home cooking, he leaned forward to take a closer look at the Stroganoff into which she was now stirring double cream.

'It isn't difficult,' said Katerina. Then she added wryly, 'Unless you're my mother.'

'Well, I'm impressed. I'd planned on taking Gina out to dinner this evening, but I'm glad now that I didn't. What are you, a professional chef?'

'She's a professional schoolgirl,' said Izzy, who had been watching them from the doorway. Pink-cheeked from her bath and now wearing a white tracksuit, her glossy dark hair cascaded past her shoulders. Apart from the fact that the tracksuit top was unzipped to display a distinctly adult amount of cleavage, she looked absurdly young. 'So, what's the verdict?' she continued, her tone light but her eyes bright with challenge. 'Are you going to stay or is the thought of sharing a house with three neurotic females too much to cope with?'

'Objection,' put in Katerina calmly. 'Two neurotic females and an extremely staid schoolgirl.'

'All this,' murmured Sam, running his fingers through his hair once more, 'and jet lag too.'

Sam Sheridan hadn't got where he was by ignoring or underestimating women. Having grown up quietly observing his brother Marcus – a useful four years older than himself – plough through school and university, causing havoc with his flashing smile and superlative seduction techniques and provoking equally dramatic showdowns whenever he tired of his girlfriends and unceremoniously dumped them, Sam had gradually come to realise that his brother didn't even like the opposite sex all that much. Girls were for sleeping with. They were what one talked about rather than to. They were, as far as Marcus was concerned, nothing more than appendages. And, like cigarettes, when he'd finished with them he stubbed them out. Sam, on the other hand, had never found girls a bother, and as he grew older he found his brother's attitude towards them even harder to understand. He genuinely enjoyed their company and found them every bit as interesting to talk to as males. Then, of course, there was also the added attraction of sexual chemistry . . .

But Sam miraculously never encountered the problems which had so complicated Marcus's own life. For although there were many girls who were friends as opposed to actual girlfriends, such was his easygoing charm and immense popularity during those growing-up years that the amount of kudos attached to being one of Sam's girls-who-were-friends had almost outranked the other kind, simply because girlfriends were par for the course, whereas friendship without sex indicated that you had a personality really worth getting to know.

And since Sam had always made a point of remaining on good terms with his ex-girlfriends, he engendered virtually no bitterness. He enjoyed instead a riotously happy three years at university, ending up with a better-than-expected 2:1 in economics and a vast circle of friends of both sexes, none of whom could for the life of them envisage Sam Sheridan holding down a job in any kind of financial institution where his degree might be of any practical use at all.

But Sam, despite his easygoing nature, had – unbeknown to his peers – already hit on the answer to his needs, which were access to a good standard of living coupled with the indescribable pleasure of non-stop socializing. The weekend parties he had thrown in the crumbling Victorian house he had rented with three other students had been legendary. Naturally a night person, Sam revelled in them; they made weekdays bearable and the thrill of never knowing who might turn up at the next party – the Swiss penfriend of somebody's sister or the actress aunt of somebody else's flatmate – never ceased to send the adrenalin pumping through his veins. In three years he'd never held an unsuccessful party. In three years he'd become renowned for throwing *great* parties where people met, argued, debated, laughed and fell in love with each other. Some had even gone completely over the top and subsequently married each other.

But it was the art of creating the perfect atmosphere in which any or all of these events could be achieved that had really captured Sam's imagination. People enjoyed themselves and he was the one who had made it happen.

And he couldn't help wondering whether there was possibly a nicer way of spending the rest of his so far happy and ridiculously charmed life.

It had not, however, been easy. Persuading the banks to lend him money had required far more intellectual agility than finals; some of his financial arrangements had been frankly dubious and, when he had taken over the lease on the first less-than-desirable premises in Manchester, weekly juggling acts had ensued between the demands of the finance companies and his own staff. Then, as news of the latest night-club began to spread, sustaining the necessary balance between a desirable clientele and money-waving non-desirables occasionally taxed even Sam's determined mind. But, above all else, he knew that his very own club must maintain an impeccable image from the outset. It wasn't necessary for his clientele to be mind-bogglingly wealthy; it was simply imperative that they be the *right* kind of people, people who would contribute to the very particular ambience he needed in order to ensure that The Steps became and *remained* the ultimately desirable place to go and to be seen having fun in.

And – although not without a serious struggle at first – it did. Sam's reputation grew and within two years he had bought the premises. Eighteen months after that, he had sold it at a staggering profit, moved to London, and found to his relief that if the streets weren't paved with gold, they nevertheless held more than enough people desperate for his particular brand of night-club to make The Chelsea Steps more successful than even he had imagined possible.

His circle of friends had widened. The number of women in love with him – secretly or otherwise – increased. Men, aware of Sam Sheridan's reputation, prepared to dislike him and, having met him, promptly failed to do so. Sam was genial, charming, easygoing, able to talk about any subject under the sun with enthusiasm, and he never pursued other men's wives or girlfriends.

This in particular reassured the men immensely. It cheered the single girls even more. And the irresistible challenge he presented to the women who were attached – and with whom Sam steadfastly refused to become involved – was indescribably exhilarating and only made them want him even more.

The formula had been a winning one and Sam had wisely stuck to it. When, six years ago now, he had announced his plans to set up a new club in New York, his friends had been horrified. Everyone had warned him of the financial riskiness of such a venture, but he had done it anyway, handing over the reins of The Chelsea Steps to his under-manager, Toby Madison, and allowing himself a year in which to either make or break his long-cherished American dream.

And, being Sam, he had succeeded where everyone had feared he would fail. The New York Steps, founded at precisely the right time and in exactly the right location, had worked from the start. Sam's international circle of friends expanded still further and his success, seemingly effortlessly achieved, followed suit. No one knew quite how Sam Sheridan did it, but it worked. And Sam himself, treating the whole thing as a huge private joke, lived life to the full, never seemed to sleep and made sure he extracted as much fun as possible from his extended American holiday.

But although New York was magical, over-the-top and indeed his kind of town, it wasn't home. For the past couple of years his trips back to England had become not long enough, had gradually increased in importance. When he had begun to dream – seriously dream – about English rain and girls without shoulder pads, Marmite on toast and people who'd never been psychoanalyzed in their life, he knew that the time had come to return home.

Meanwhile, back in Gina's dining room, Izzy's steadily increasing interest in Sam was being monitored by Gina with anxiety bordering on dismay. Dinner wasn't even over yet and already they had achieved an easy, mutual rapport.

Sipping her wine, she gazed across the candlelit table at Izzy, who was so obviously enjoying herself. And she made it look so effortless too, thought Gina with resentment. Why, she was positively *glowing*. It would have taken years for her to get to know someone well enough to ask them the kind of questions Izzy was asking after just a couple of hours.

'But how can you possibly have spent six years in New York and not got married?' Izzy was demanding now, pushing up her sleeves and resting her brown arms on the table. Idly, she picked a slice of courgette from the vegetable dish and paused to admire it before popping it into her mouth. 'Everyone gets married in New York.'

'Maybe I'm gay.' Sam's dark eyebrows arched with amusement.

'But you aren't.'

'Mum,' said Kat warningly. 'You don't know that. Stop being embarrassing.'

'Of course he isn't gay,' said Izzy with an impatient gesture. 'So, come on, Sam, tell us everything. Did you leave New York because of a woman? Was it true love? Was it sordid? Was she too rich or too poor? Was she—'

About to say married, she stopped herself just in time, out of deference to Gina's feelings. Sam, second-guessing her and stepping effortlessly into the breach, said, 'She was certainly persistent. Every fisherman's dream, in fact. The one who wouldn't go away.'

'Pushy,' observed Izzy, helping herself to another slice of courgette. Then she grinned. 'I couldn't be like it myself.'

'My mother,' sighed Katerina. 'The original pre-shrunk violet.'

'I don't want this to sound funny,' Gina began, lacing her fingers together and looking decidedly ill at ease.

'In that case,' replied Izzy, deadpan, 'I won't laugh.'

Having known Sam for as long as she had, Gina was only too well aware of his reputation where women were concerned. In his apparently irresistible presence they simply forgot how to say no. And now she could see it about to start happening all over again, right here in her very own home.

But inveigling Izzy into the kitchen in order to talk to her alone had been the easy part. Finding the right words for what she knew she had to say wasn't easy at all.

'Look, this might not sound very fair,' she began, then

paused and took a deep breath. Her fingers, of their own accord, were reducing a paper serviette to shreds.

'It's certainly frustrating,' observed Izzy good-humouredly, 'waiting to hear what "this" is all about.'

'Sam's a very attractive man,' Gina blurted out, and Izzy's eyebrows shot up.

'My God, I don't believe it,' she laughed. 'You're secretly crazy about him and you want me to put in a few words on your behalf. Well, say no more . . . I shall be the soul of discretion and before you know it you'll be—'

'No!'

Izzy was still smiling. Gina was so easily shocked. 'Well,' she said, 'if it isn't that, what *is* it?'

'I've seen the way you've been looking at him and the way he looks at you.' In her distress, the words fell out in a rush. 'And I couldn't bear it if you and Sam were to—'

'Were to *what?*'

'Have an affair,' said Gina unhappily. 'In my house. My husband's left me for another woman, I've never been so miserable in my life and I absolutely couldn't cope with it.' She paused once more, then went on in a low voice. 'I'm sorry, I can't help it. I did warn you that what I had to say wasn't fair.'

Izzy tried and failed to conceal her dismay. Fixing her gaze upon the little pots of chocolate mousse lined up on the kitchen table and realizing that she was no longer hungry, she said, 'You want Kat and myself to leave.'

'I didn't mean that.' Gina, more embarrassed than ever, shook her head. 'And no, of course I don't want you to leave. I just don't want you and Sam to . . . start something. I don't want to feel like a gooseberry in my own home.'

'And if I promise to leave him alone you'll be happy?' This time Izzy had to hide her smile. Did Gina think she was a complete nymphomaniac?

'I've forgotten how to be happy,' said Gina, immeasurably relieved. Since Izzy's amusement hadn't escaped her she shrugged and managed a small smile of her own. 'Let's just say I'll be bearable.'

# Chapter 9

'What a cheek,' Katerina protested the following morning. Polishing off the last of the chocolate mousse, she scraped the dish with vigour. 'That's emotional blackmail.'

'Financial blackmail,' corrected Izzy, who had unearthed a tube of glitter and was sprinkling it liberally over her hair and shoulders. 'She knows we can't afford to move out.'

Katerina gave her an old-fashioned look. 'He is rather gorgeous, though. Has this blighted your plans? Are you going to sink into a Victorian decline?'

'Not at all. It's rather exciting.'

'Hmm.' Katerina wasn't convinced. 'Doesn't sound very exciting to me.'

'You're too young to understand,' Izzy informed her cheerfully. 'Men like Sam aren't used to not getting what they want. I shall dazzle and intrigue him, and the longer he has to wait the more tantalized he shall be. It's going to be the most enormous fun.'

'How would you know?' Katerina gave her spoon a final, appreciative lick. 'You've never played hard to get before.'

Izzy looked serene. 'Don't worry, it always works. I read it in a Mills and Boon.'

Sam could easily have slept right through the day but he

knew from experience that the only way to beat jet lag was to ignore it. Besides, he had a lot to do.

'Oh, are you going out?' said Gina fearfully when he arrived downstairs at midday wearing a crumpled white shirt and Levi's, and with his hair still wet from the shower. With his deep Hawaiian tan and sun-bleached hair he looked even more startlingly exotic than usual and Gina wondered unhappily how on earth she could seriously expect Izzy to remain immune to his charms.

Edgy because she knew that sooner or later he would be seeing Andrew, she averted her gaze and busied herself with the coffee maker. 'Black or white? If you're hungry I could make you a bacon sandwich . . .'

'I don't want you to wait on me,' said Sam, who knew exactly what was bothering her. Removing the packet of ground coffee from her grasp, he pushed her gently towards a chair, realizing as he did so just how much weight she had lost. 'And if anyone needs a bacon sandwich, you do.'

'I haven't got much of an appetite at the moment,' muttered Gina. Then, defensively, she added, 'Don't worry, I'm not anorexic.'

Sam nodded. 'OK. It's allowed, I suppose, under the circumstances.'

Gina, however, wasn't going to be side-tracked. Abruptly, she said, 'You still haven't told me where you're going. Have you spoken to Andrew yet?'

'No.' Sam, who intended phoning him that afternoon, was able to reply honestly. 'I'm going to the club. And I have to sort out some transport – I'll rent something for now – then I thought I'd take a look at some properties.

Who knows,' he added teasingly, 'I may end up living next door. Isn't that the most terrifying thought ever?'

'It's not a terrifying thought,' said Gina, realizing that he was attempting to cheer her up. Giving him a quick, awkward kiss on the cheek, she said, 'And you don't have to rush out and buy the first thing you see. It's lovely having you here.'

Her utter inability to lie was one of her most endearing traits. Ruffling her smooth, blonde hair, Sam said, 'Thank you, sweetheart.' Then he grinned and added, 'But a word of advice. If you were thinking of going into politics . . . don't.'

Old friendships died hard and Sam had no intention of criticizing Andrew's actions. These things happened, long-standing marriages bit the dust every day and Sam wasn't about to apportion blame. In the long run it could well turn out to be the best thing that could have happened to both Gina and Andrew.

As long as Andrew, he reflected drily as he drove towards the Barbican in his extremely clean, newly rented car, hadn't made the biggest, most Godawful mistake of his life.

The tapas bar was crowded with after-work commuters having a drink before bracing themselves for the journey home. Although there were a couple of free tables outside – it was a mild, sunny afternoon that had seen the seasonal re-emergence of the Ray-Bans – Andrew evidently preferred the gloom of the bar's interior. As he paid for a bottle of Rioja and a bowl of tapas, Sam observed that he, too, had lost weight; his charcoal-grey suit was too big for him and the collar of his shirt was loose. It was six months since he'd last seen him and he looked five years older.

'So, are you happy?'

Andrew filled their glasses and grimaced. 'I've done it, haven't I? Too late to change my mind now.'

Sam said nothing, waiting for him to continue. Listening to other people was what he was good at.

'You'll meet her,' Andrew continued, glancing at his watch. 'She's joining us at six-thirty. God . . . I don't know . . . I thought I was in love with her, but it isn't easy. If opposites really do attract, she and Gina should get on like a house on fire. Do you know, she hasn't cooked a single meal since we've been in that flat?'

'Does she work?' asked Sam mildly, trying not to smile.

'Handed in her notice the day I left Gina. She doesn't do any housework . . . she doesn't do *anything*.' Andrew spilled his wine in his agitation. 'Hell, we'd have a nice view if we could only see out of the windows. So we go out instead; I spend a fortune I can't afford in Italian restaurants because she's developed a craving for spaghetti *alle vongole*, and we spend every evening telling each other how lucky we are to have found each other. Then we go back to the flat and screw ourselves stupid. After that,' he concluded lamely, 'Marcy falls asleep and I iron a shirt for the following day.'

'Is *she* happy, do you think?' said Sam, by this time seriously struggling to keep a straight face.

'Is the Pope Catholic?' Andrew riposted. 'Of course she's happy – she doesn't do a single thing she doesn't want to do, she has everything she's ever wanted . . .'

'So, what are you going to do?'

Andrew spread his hands in despair. 'Haven't I done enough? She's having my child – because she couldn't even be bothered to remember to take the bloody Pill – and I've left my wife. There's nothing I *can* do now, except live with it.' He shook his head, then drained his glass, pushing the bowl of tapas away untouched. 'Lust isn't love, Sam. Take a tip from an expert and don't ever let it fool you into thinking it is.'

Marcy arrived late, swaying into the darkened bar at ten to seven. Sam's first thought was that Andrew hadn't been kidding when he had told him Gina and Marcy were complete opposites. Not yet enormously pregnant, she was nevertheless decidedly plump; her legs, in pale grey tights, reminded him of those stone-carved cherubs that cavorted around fountains and her pink lambswool dress strained across an impressive bust. Although she had an undeniably pretty face – pink cheeks, big grey eyes and a small, rosebud mouth – her shoulder-length auburn hair looked distinctly uncombed and the only make-up she appeared to be wearing was the remains of yesterday's mascara smudged beneath her eyes.

She wasn't what he'd been expecting at all, and for once in his life Sam found himself caught completely off-balance by the enormity of the gulf between expectation and reality. Marcy's laid-back, extremely elocuted voice, her languorous gestures and the almost monotonous slowness with which she proceeded to plough through four bowls of fresh tapas, all combined to give the impression that her batteries were on the verge of giving out. Not that she said anything wrong; she seemed perfectly friendly and even smiled whenever necessary. It was just that Sam couldn't for the life of him imagine her being capable of summoning the energy to actually laugh.

'So, you're staying with Gina for the time being,' she observed, when she'd soaked up the last of the salad dressing with a chunk of crusty bread. 'How does she seem to you? Poor Gina, we're so concerned about her. Is she coping well?'

Sam envisaged Gina's reaction, should she ever find out that she had Marcy's sympathy. Spontaneous combustion, he decided, at the very least.

'As a matter of fact,' he replied easily, 'she's coping extremely well.'

'It must be awful for her,' Marcy continued, pushing her hair away from her face and taking a sip of Perrier. 'I hope you can understand our situation. We didn't mean this to happen, it just . . . did. The last thing I ever wanted was to hurt someone else, but when two people fall in love they can't help themselves, Sam.' She paused, then smiled across at Andrew. 'They really can't.'

'Oh Kat, you *must* come to the club,' pleaded Izzy. 'Sam's invited us. It'll be wonderful.'

'Simon and I have a lot of work to do,' Katerina replied calmly. Unwinding a long, navy-blue cotton scarf from around her neck, she dumped a pile of books on the kitchen table and motioned Simon to sit down.

Simon, enthralled by the invitation and as overwhelmed as ever by Izzy, said, 'Well, maybe we could just . . .'

'No, we could not . . .' Katerina quelled him with a look. 'A night at The Chelsea Steps isn't going to enhance my life half as much as a physics A level will. And there's no need to look at me like that, Simon – I'm just being practical.'

There were times, thought Simon darkly, when Kat was a damn sight too practical. Glancing across at Izzy for support, he was further cast down when all she did was shrug and say flatly, 'She is not my daughter. I took the wrong baby home from the hospital, I know I did. Somewhere out in the big wide world my real daughter is out having *fun*.' Then, making up for it slightly, she blew a kiss which encompassed them both. 'Darlings, I hope you have an exhilarating evening. Meanwhile, we old fogies will totter off and try to enjoy ourselves. Now, where did I put my bus pass . . . ?'

# Chapter 10

By ten-thirty The Chelsea Steps was almost completely full. Sam, having concluded his brief business meeting with Toby Madison and reassured himself that all had been running smoothly in his absence, was reacquainting himself with old friends. Izzy, in her element, was engrossed in flamboyant conversation with a racing driver whose right arm was in plaster. Gina, finding herself briefly alone at the bar, wondered if she'd ever felt more uncomfortable in her life.

It wasn't fair, she thought miserably. Everyone else appeared to be able to switch with perfect ease into night-club mode; was she the only one genuinely incapable of doing the same? As Andrew's wife she had been an adequate conversationalist, if not a sparkling one, yet here . . . now . . . she couldn't even begin to imagine how it was done. This kind of socializing was what single people did – it was what single people like Sam and Izzy evidently excelled at – but she had been married too long even to remember what being single was like. She couldn't do it. All she wanted now was to be able to go home, crawl into bed and pretend that the events of the last few weeks had never happened.

Moments later, Sam materialised at her side.

'That bad, hmm?'

'It . . . it's a lovely club,' stammered Gina, not wanting

him to think her a complete wimp. Gesturing around her at the midnight-blue-and-bronze décor, she said, 'And it's obviously going well. Everyone's enjoying themselves . . . having fun . . . I'm always reading about it in the papers . . .'

'You don't have to feel guilty just because you aren't enjoying yourself,' he told gently. 'I'm sorry, I shouldn't have persuaded you to come.'

'I don't think I'm a terribly clubby person,' said Gina, her expression despondent. 'Izzy's having a marvellous time and she makes it all seem so easy.'

'She's had plenty of practice,' replied Sam drily, his gaze fixing upon Izzy. Shedding glitter at a rate of knots, she and the racing driver were now making their precarious way towards the bar in search of yet another bottle of champagne. As strong as his initial attraction had been towards her, Sam wasn't blind to her faults and keeping Gina company was the least she could have done, under the circumstances. Taking Gina's arm, he said, 'Come on, let's go home.'

She looked alarmed. 'We can't leave Izzy.'

'Why not?' said Sam evenly. 'She left you.'

The thought of Sam and Izzy having an affair had filled Gina with horror, but the prospect of friction between them was even more unnerving. Leaping to Izzy's defence, she said, 'Only for a couple of minutes, truly.'

He grinned. 'Don't panic, I'm not suggesting you kick her out into the streets. I'm just saying that she can be a bit thoughtless now and again. Loyal,' he conceded, the memory of her verbal attack on him last night still fresh in his mind, 'but still thoughtless, nevertheless.'

'But we *can't* abandon her,' Gina protested miserably. 'And you don't want to leave either. Why don't I just get a cab? I'll be fine, really I will.'

'Oh shut up,' said Sam, his tone affectionate. 'Come on, we'll tell Izzy we're going. She's a big girl, I'm sure she can find her own way home.'

Only Katerina Van Asch, thought Simon with rising frustration, could spend three solid hours discussing – in dizzying detail – the human reproductive process and not even spare a thought for the effect it might be having on her partner-in-revision.

'So,' she was saying now, as she stretched across the velvety carpet for the saucer of Liquorice Allsorts, 'let's just run through it again. I'm still not quite happy about testosterone levels.'

Simon wasn't happy about his own testosterone levels, which were skyrocketing; he was sure it couldn't be good for his health. Hauling himself into a sitting position he cast her a reproachful look.

'What?' said Katerina, twisting on to her side and meeting his gaze. Even in her frayed orange sweatshirt, khaki combats and holey green socks she looked irresistible. 'Simon, whatever's the matter with you tonight? You really aren't concentrating at all.'

Plucking up as much courage as he possessed, Simon pushed back his straight blond hair and said, 'Do you think it would be sensible to take an important maths exam without ever having worked out a single mathematical equation?'

He really was in an odd mood tonight, decided

Katerina. Humoring him, she replied obediently, 'No, of course it wouldn't.'

'Or . . . a chemistry exam, when you've never conducted an actual chemical experiment yourself?'

'No.'

'Yet you expect to pass biology purely on the strength of what you've learned from books,' he persisted, flushing slightly. 'Doesn't that seem . . . illogical?'

Having considered his argument for a few seconds, Katerina broke into a broad smile. 'You mean I should murder you, then dissect your body with Gina's best carving knife and eyebrow tweezers? Simon, it's a generous offer, but—'

The next moment his arms were around her, his mouth fastening upon hers and his frantically racing heart pounding against her chest. Astonished, Katerina almost laughed out loud but sensed it wouldn't be the diplomatic thing to do. She might be lacking in experience but even she knew that kissing and laughter didn't mix. 'I love you, Kat,' mumbled Simon, scarcely able to believe that his dreams were at last coming true. 'You must know how much I love you, it's been driving me crazy . . .'

'And you think we'd stand a chance of improving our grades if we got a little practical experience on the subject,' she said, pulling gently away from him. If this was what sexual passion was all about, well . . . on the whole she preferred Liquorice Allsorts. 'Simon, it's lovely of you to offer, but I really can't. It wouldn't be . . . right, somehow.'

'Oh damn,' Simon muttered unhappily. Realizing that he'd well and truly blown his chances – maybe his only chance – with Katerina, he slumped back on one elbow and gazed morosely at the pile of books lying open in front of the fireplace. 'I suppose you won't want to see me again, now.'

'Don't be daft,' she replied, smiling and passing him his half-empty can of lager. 'You're my best friend, aren't you?'

His expression still truculent, he said, 'I'd rather be your boyfriend.'

'No, you wouldn't.' She squeezed his hand. 'I'm a seventeen-year-old virgin and probably frigid to boot. There's nothing I can do about it; maybe subconsciously I'm rebelling against my upbringing. But it isn't your fault, OK?' she persisted, more forcefully this time. 'It's mine.'

'One day,' said Simon with resignation, 'some man will come along and sweep you off your feet and you won't know what's hit you.'

'He won't know what's hit him,' Katerina replied briskly. 'But it'll probably be my physics textbook. I've told you, Simon, I'm really not cut out for all that love-and-sex business. It just isn't *me*.'

There was nothing like a bit of good, old-fashioned sexual attraction to put a spring in one's step, thought Izzy, gazing down at her decidedly unspringy left leg the following morning. But although the sexual attraction was still there – on her part, at least – last night's plan appeared to have misfired in somewhat spectacular fashion. By chatting to Nicky Holmes-Pierce, cavalier racing driver and ex-husband of one of her oldest friends, she had hoped to prove to Sam that she wasn't overkeen on him and at the same time pique his interest. Instead, however, he had simply left the club with Gina and so far this morning had seemed totally unpiqued. And she'd put make-up on, too.

Now, with the sun streaming through the kitchen windows, he was ignoring her totally, poring instead over a pile of estate agents' details spread across the kitchen table. With Gina out shopping and Katerina at school, their previous easy camaraderie appeared to be in genuine danger of evaporating completely. Izzy was in danger of losing all faith in Mills and Boon.

'I could help you look for a flat, if you like,' she offered, swinging her good leg against her stool and making an effort to redress the balance.

Without even glancing up at her, Sam said, 'I'd have thought you'd be too busy, looking for some kind of job.'

Charming, thought Izzy. Aloud, she said idly, 'Why, is Gina worried about her rent?'

'She hasn't said anything,' Sam replied in even tones. 'She's too well mannered. Maybe that's why I thought I should mention it.'

Flicking her hair away from her face, she said crossly, 'I did *have* a job, right up until the moment when this terribly well mannered madwoman hurtled into my life. The accident wasn't my fault, you know.'

'I know.' Sam smiled slightly, because she looked so indignant. But he wasn't to be deflected. 'And I'm sure you wouldn't take advantage of her generosity,' he continued, more gently now. 'But I'm very fond of Gina and she's had a rough time of it recently. She needs as much support as she can get.'

'I'm not an underwired bra,' Izzy retorted, her dark eyes flashing.

You aren't wearing one either, thought Sam, admiring the faint outline of her breasts beneath the khaki army surplus shirt. Picking up the list of addresses, he rose to his feet. 'OK, don't sulk. Do you want to come with me or not?'

'Are you going to be beastly to me?' Izzy regarded him with suspicion.

'Only if it's what you really want.'

The tension had melted. She grinned, suddenly. 'I'd prefer outrageous flattery, if you could manage it.'

'Outrageous flattery,' mused Sam, his expression deadpan as he held the door open and waved her through. 'In that case I shall tell you that I heard you singing in the bathroom this morning, and I have to confess that I was impressed. Most impressed. You have an exceptional voice, Miss Van Asch, in fact a truly spectacular—'

'Bullshit.' Izzy burst out laughing. 'That was Liza Minnelli on the radio.'

# Chapter 11

Within two hours of setting out on a whistle-stop tour of select properties in highly desirable areas of London, during which time he glanced at and summarily rejected apartments which Izzy would have given her eye-teeth to live in, Sam found what he'd been looking for. Situated on the top floor of a chic but unflashy low-rise apartment block in Holland Park, it was light, extremely spacious and commanded spectacular views over the park itself.

'Yes, this one,' he said simply, returning from his inspection of the bedrooms and standing in the centre of the vast sitting room. Pushing his hands into the back pockets of his Levi's, he gazed out of the floor-length windows at the park and nodded once more for emphasis. Then, turning to the dumbstruck estate agent, he said, 'I'll take it.'

Watching Sam choose a home had been an edifying experience. Izzy, thrilled by the ease with which he'd done it, said admiringly, 'I've known men take longer to decide on a new shirt.'

'Ah, but I know what I want,' said Sam, his eyes glittering with amusement. 'And I know what I like. So why waste time?'

With an involuntary shiver Izzy wondered whether – beneath that super-cool exterior – he wanted her. The thought was extraordinarily enthralling. Damn, she thought, she would have given anything right now to be out of this plaster cast . . .

Since it was lunchtime, they retired to a nearby winebar to celebrate. Sam raised his eyebrows when Izzy ordered a bottle of very expensive wine.

'Don't panic,' she said mockingly, unearthing her purse from her bag and waving it at him. 'We have the technology, we have the means to repay them. And it isn't as if I could even begin to do a runner.'

Aware that she was making the gesture to prove a point, Sam waved acceptance and sat back in his chair. 'OK, if you're sure.'

'I'm sure,' said Izzy, greedily perusing the menu. 'You aren't the only one around here who knows what he wants . . . and what I want is lobster salad. Come on now, choose something wonderful. It's on me.'

Sam raised an eyebrow. 'Have you been stealing credit cards?'

'Mr Sheridan, what a nasty, suspicious mind you have.' She gave him an admonishing look, then winked. 'Only little gold ones.'

'So, tell me,' she said five minutes later, 'how's Andrew? Did you meet the bimbo? Is it really the greatest love affair of all time?'

'How did you know I'd seen him?' countered Sam with genuine surprise.

Izzy shrugged. 'It stands to reason, doesn't it? He's your friend and you have a habit of not wasting time. You were bound to see him.'

'I suppose so.' He smiled, conceding the point. He

liked women who were on the ball. 'Well, it isn't going brilliantly. If Marcy wasn't pregnant he'd be back with Gina like a shot.'

Izzy, idly stirring her wine with a finger, said, 'Then it's lucky for Gina that Marcy is pregnant. Otherwise she just might be stupid enough to take him.'

'And you and Katerina would have to find somewhere else to live,' observed Sam drily.

Izzy bristled. 'That's a cheap shot. I don't happen to have a very high opinion of men like Andrew Lawrence; he's a shit of the first order.'

'Did your husband leave you for another woman?'

'Me?' She looked surprised, then shrugged dismissively. 'Kat's father did offer to marry me, if that's who you are thinking about, but I turned him down – very politely – and got out while the going was good.'

'Why?' asked Sam, interested.

'Because sooner or later I would have ended up like Gina.' Pausing, taking a sip of her drink, she added, 'And because he was already married when I met him.'

'Hmm.'

'I didn't know that, then. I was eighteen and gullible, and by the time I found out he had a wife it was too late; I was already pregnant. End of sordid story,' declared Izzy, as the waiter approached with their food. 'And don't look at me like that, because it wasn't tragic and it didn't ruin my life. I have a better daughter than any mother has a right to expect and the experience taught me everything I needed to know about men. I only told you about it so you'd understand why I feel as strongly as I do about Gina and Andrew. And you still haven't said anything about Marcy,' she complained, steering him neatly back to the subject in hand. Picking up a lobster claw and tilting her head to one side, she said, 'You met her, didn't you? So, what is she, a complete dog?'

'Oh, it's a hard life,' said Katerina mockingly as she washed up after dinner that evening. Izzy, who had propped herself against the draining board in order to dry the dishes, was regaling her with details of her day.

'It's such a beautiful flat,' she said with enthusiasm. 'They were *all* beautiful flats . . . and just think, darling, one day when we're rich beyond our wildest dreams, we'll live in a penthouse apartment every bit as fabulous as Sam's. Won't that be great?'

'Do excuse my mother, she's an incurable fantasist.' Katerina grinned at Sam, who had just walked into the kitchen. Then, her attention returning to Izzy, her expression changed to one of alarm.

'Mum, your gold chain – you aren't wearing it!'

Izzy's hand went automatically to the V of her open shirt. Then she shrugged. 'I must have left it upstairs.'

'But you never take it off,' began Katerina. 'You *always*—'

'It's upstairs,' Izzy repeated firmly, before she could say any more. 'Now give me that dish before you wash the pattern off it. When I'm rich beyond my wildest dreams I'm going to get myself a new daughter,' she continued smoothly, addressing Sam and silently defying him to comment on the fact that her cheeks were ablaze with colour. 'One who doesn't nag her poor old mother to death.'

* * *

When Sam returned to the living room he found Gina curled up on the sofa working out sums on the back of an electricity bill. Despite the fact that he had written her out a sizeable cheque that morning, her narrow blonde eyebrows were still furrowed with concern.

'Everything OK?' he said, touching her shoulder and making her jump.

'As well as can be expected.' Gina managed a wan smile. 'I hate to sound like a helpless housewife, but I simply hadn't realised how much it costs just to live.'

Experiencing a fresh surge of irritation as he recalled Izzy Van Asch's own cavalier attitudes towards such mundanities as household budgeting, he said brusquely, 'Particularly when you have freeloading lodgers to support. Sweetheart, you're too easygoing . . . if Izzy doesn't cough up soon, you'll have to ask her to leave.'

Gina looked up, surprised. Then, with a vigorous shake of her head, she said, 'Oh, I didn't get a chance to tell you. She's paid me two months' rent.'

It was now Sam's turn to look surprised. 'Good,' he replied, somewhat mollified. 'And about bloody time too.' She must have sold the necklace while he was signing forms in the estate agent's offices, he decided. At least it proved she had a conscience of sorts.

Pleased with himself . . . and, to be fair, with Izzy . . . he said, 'My little chat with her this morning must have sunk in after all.'

'I don't know, maybe it did.' Gina had turned her attention back to her sums. Then, absently, she added, 'But Izzy gave me the money yesterday.'

* * *

Having the plaster cast removed from her leg the following Friday was sheer bliss. Another advantage, Izzy discovered upon returning home several hours later, was that she could move silently once more, without her arrival everywhere being heralded by the noisy, give-away clunking of crutches.

'I'm back!' she announced delightedly, flinging open the door of Katerina's room.

Katerina, who was lying on top of her bed, jumped a mile and hastily shoved the book she'd been reading under the pillows. 'Mother! You're supposed to knock.'

'I wanted to surprise you,' said Izzy serenely. Advancing towards the bed, she added with a lascivious grin, 'And it rather looks as if I have. What's that you're hiding?'

'Homework,' Katerina protested, turning pink and wondering why she had to have the nosiest mother in the entire world.

But it was hopeless; no longer hampered by her plaster cast, Izzy was upon her in a flash, tickling her ribs unmercifully with one hand and tearing the book out from its hiding place with the other. Then, retreating triumphantly to the safety of the doorway, she held it aloft.

'*The Joy of Sex!* Honestly darling, what a waste of money. I could have told you how nice it is, for nothing.'

'Give it back,' wailed Katerina, mortified. When Izzy was in this kind of mood there was no stopping her, and no knowing what she'd do to extract maximum pleasure from Kat's embarrassment.

'But sweetheart, I thought you weren't interested in

boys,' continued Izzy gleefully. 'And even if you were, these pictures would be enough to put *anyone* off them for life. Will you look at that chap's haircut? And as for his beard . . . yuk!'

Katerina wasn't interested in boys, but Simon's unexpected and clumsy seduction attempt the previous week had had a more profound effect on her than she'd first realised. Just for a fraction of a second, she was able to admit to herself later, she had been tempted to go through with it just to see what 'it' was like, and only getting the giggles had saved her.

But had she really been saved? Sex might be a mystery to her, but everyone else seemed to enjoy it and if it were really that marvellous, then maybe she was missing out. Having given the matter a great deal of serious thought, Katerina had decided not to initiate a return match with Simon – great friend though he was, she felt instinctively that there should be more *emotional* involvement between lovers – but to pay at least a little attention to the more technical aspects of the procedure. It was only sensible, after all, to be prepared. Then, when the right person did come along, at least she wouldn't run the risk of making a complete idiot of herself by getting it hopelessly wrong. That, she thought with a shudder, would be even more humiliating than coming last in a chemistry exam.

But now, faced with her mother's helpless laughter and realizing that only the truth would do, she said firmly, 'It's research, that's all. Don't make a big thing of it, Mum.'

'A big thing . . .' murmured Izzy, catching sight of one of the more detailed illustrations in the book and wiping tears from her eyes with the back of her hand. 'Oh Kat, don't look at me like that . . . it's just so *funny* . . .'

'I could always break your other leg,' Katerina offered, moving towards her. 'Look Mum, why don't you calm down and just give me back the—'

She lunged forwards, but it was too late. Darting back through the doorway and out on to the landing, Izzy hurled the book down the stairs.

At precisely that moment, they both heard the front door open.

Katerina held her breath. Izzy, still shaking with laughter, sidled barefoot along the landing and peered over the carved wooden banister rail at Sam, who was standing at the bottom of the staircase with the book in his hand.

'Please mister,' said Izzy, adopting an expression of wide-eyed innocence, 'can we have our book back please?'

Observing the fact that the long-awaited removal of the plaster cast had taken place, Sam glanced at the cover of the book, then – without a flicker – returned his gaze to Izzy.

'Have I interrupted something,' he said drily, 'or is this an invitation?'

Stifling a giggle, Izzy said solemnly, 'Revision. Now that I've got my leg back, I thought I'd better refresh my memory. It's been so long, I may have forgotten how it goes.'

# Chapter 12

Bored to the back teeth with inactivity, Izzy celebrated her return to the two-legged world by going out and getting herself re-employed.

Job prospects on the singing front being as dire as ever, it took two hours of cajoling and an extremely short skirt to persuade Bernie Cooper to take her back on at Platform One, the none-too-ritzy club in Soho at which she had been working up until her accident.

But in the mean time, she had been replaced by an enormously well-endowed blues singer called Arlette and Bernie was only able to offer her one evening a week, which meant she was forced to take a pub job as well.

The work at Brennan's Bar – in nearby Covent Garden – was hard, the atmosphere frantic and the pay ridiculously low, but at least it left her with most days free so she was able to attend auditions.

Gina's nights, meanwhile, were becoming increasingly prolonged and unbearable. The days she could just about cope with, because then at least the shops were open, but the evenings alone – when both Izzy and Sam had disappeared to their respective places of work and Katerina had retired to her room to study – were miserable and endless. Worse still, and because she was such a light sleeper, she invariably was woken at around three in the morning by the sound of Izzy and Sam returning home, laughing and joking together as they shared a late-night snack and watched a video before finally retiring to their beds an hour or two later.

One night, having told herself firmly that of course they weren't discussing her, Gina slid out of bed and pulled on a thin dressing gown. They sounded as if they were having so much fun downstairs . . . and she was so *lonely* . . .

But the laughter had subsided by the time she'd crept across the hall and when she paused by the sitting-room door she was able to hear their lowered voices quite clearly.

'. . . it's so crazy,' Izzy was saying with characteristic impatience. 'I've tried to make her realise that she's wasting her life, but she simply refuses to do anything about it. It's almost as if she enjoys being unhappy.'

Gina shivered, clutching the wall for support.

'Of course she doesn't,' she heard Sam reply in more reasonable terms. 'She just isn't able to help herself at the moment. I know it's frustrating—'

'Damn right it's frustrating,' said Izzy hotly. 'She spends more money on clothes than all the Royals put together, then panics because she can't pay the gas bill.'

'According to your daughter, that's exactly what you do.'

'But I don't panic, I enjoy it!' Izzy retaliated. 'What's really frustrating is the fact that Gina does it and she's *still* miserable.'

'She needs something to occupy her mind,' said Sam, above the clinking of glasses. 'Some kind of job, although when I mentioned it to her the other day you'd have thought I'd suggested prostitution.'

'She could take over my job.' Izzy was laughing now. 'And I'll take control of her cheque book. Poor old Gina, I do feel sorry for her, but there are times when I wish I could just shake some sense into that head of hers. For God's sake, how many weeks is it since she even *smiled?*'

'She's unhappy,' chided Sam. 'Haven't you ever been unhappy?'

The next moment, Izzy shrieked. 'Damn right I have! In fact, I'm unhappy at this very moment. Sam, how *could* you?' she protested, her voice rising in anguish. 'That last slice of pizza was mine!'

'Right, we're going to get you sorted out,' Izzy announced a couple of days later, steering Gina out on to the patio for what, hopefully, would be a productive woman-to-woman talk and waving a bottle of Chardonnay for emphasis.

'It's only eleven-thirty,' Gina protested, gazing in horror at the wine.

'Ah, but the clocks go forward tonight.' Izzy winked, then continued with great firmness. 'Besides, it's necessary. I want you to be totally honest and I want you to *relax*. If this fails,' she added cheerfully, 'we resort to Pentothal.'

'I know what you're going to tell me,' said Gina with a trace of defiance. This was like being fifteen all over again.

'I'm not going to tell you anything,' Izzy replied, pouring the wine, then kicking off her shoes and making herself comfortable on the wooden bench. 'For one thing, I'm hardly in a position to lecture. For another, your problems aren't – strictly speaking – any of my business.'

'Then why have you dragged me out here?' Gina demanded.

'Drink your wine before it evaporates,' replied Izzy sternly, knowing from experience that Gina was capable of nursing the same glass for hours. 'The thing is, I'd like to help, so I wondered if there was anything I *could* do?'

Feeling awkward and thinking that if she hadn't overheard Izzy's conversation with Sam she would have been touched by her concern, Gina shrugged and said, 'I don't think so.'

It was like pulling teeth. Waiting until Gina had taken a decent slug of wine, Izzy tried again. 'Look, I really do want to help. What would you like most in the world?'

Startled by the abruptness of the question, Gina's eyes filled with tears. 'I'd like the last two months to have never happened.'

'But they have,' said Izzy relentlessly. 'So, taking that into consideration, what *else* would you like most in the world?'

This wasn't fair. Gina, fumbling for a handkerchief, mumbled, 'I don't know.'

'Well, would it be nice to feel a bit more confident and start getting out and making some new friends?'

'Don't tell me.' Gina's mouth narrowed. 'I should get myself a job.'

'I'm not telling you to do anything,' Izzy reminded her, although it was a struggle not to. Then, struck by an idea, she said, 'Shall I tell you what *I'd* do, if I were you?'

Anything was better than enduring this inquisition. Gina nodded.

'I'd want to make sure my husband had really left me for good,' said Izzy, sitting back and improvising rapidly. 'I'd want to see him with his new girlfriend, so that at least I could stop *wondering* about her. It wouldn't be easy, but it would be worth it, because then I'd know it was over and I could get on with the rest of my life. And yes, I would get myself a job of some kind, even though I'd be scared to death because I hadn't been out to work for so many years that I'd think I'd make an idiot of myself . . . oh, please –' She broke off, realizing that Gina was crying harder than ever. 'I'm sorry, I've gone too far. Look, I'll stop. I won't say another word, but please don't cry any more.'

'No, no,' wailed Gina, her handkerchief by this time soaked through. 'You're absolutely right,' she sniffed. 'That's exactly what I *do* want to do!'

'We should have phoned,' Gina said fearfully as Izzy reversed the Golf into a parking space beneath Andrew's apartment building. Her courage was failing her now that they were actually here.

'No way,' said Izzy briskly, switching off the ignition and cutting Cliff Richard off in mid-flow. 'This time, you're going to have the upper hand. Here you are, dressed up to the nines.' She gestured with approval at Gina's svelte silk dress, the silver jewellery and the perfectly made-up face. 'And there *they* will be, all unsuspecting and unprepared. It's going to be the most brilliant fun,' she concluded with determination, praying that she wasn't making a hideous mistake.

* * *

Marcy, when she opened the door, was certainly unsuspecting. Her own auburn hair was tangled, her unflattering baggy sweater and tracksuit bottoms looked as if they'd been slept in and her face was pale.

'Yes?' she said, hanging on to the door handle and regarding the two women with disinterest. Behind her, a television blared.

Whatever Gina had imagined during those endless tortured nights, it wasn't this.

'We've come to see Andrew,' said Izzy helpfully, when it became apparent that Gina was too stunned to say anything at all.

'Oh, he isn't in.' The woman, who had a sleepy, cultured voice, sounded relieved, as if his absence solved the problem.

'Are you expecting him back' – Izzy allowed herself a tiny pause – 'shortly?'

'He's just popped out to the supermarket.' Unexpectedly, Marcy smiled. 'He shouldn't be long.'

In all the years she had been married to him, Andrew hadn't so much as registered the existence of such objects. Astounded by the thought that he was at this moment actually in one, and almost laughing out loud at the absurdity of the idea, Gina recovered her nerve.

'In that case,' she said, so smoothly that even Izzy gazed at her in admiration, 'perhaps we could come in and wait. I'm Gina Lawrence, Andrew's wife. And this is my friend, Izzy Van Asch.'

The flat was an absolute tip. Small and low-ceilinged to begin with, the suffocating central heating and incredible amount of clutter strewn around the room rendered it positively claustrophobic. Gina was cheered still further by the terrible sight. Marcy's lack of response to her introduction had been disappointing – she had geared herself up for high drama and received only a mildly surprised 'Oh, well then, of course you must come in,' in return – but other than that she could have hugged Izzy for bringing her here. This was all so much less terrifying than she had imagined, and meeting Marcy had filled her with such sudden, wild optimism, that she knew she couldn't fail. Baby or no baby, Andrew was bound to come back to her sooner or later. This plump, slow-moving, slovenly creature was no threat to her marriage after all . . .

'Tea,' announced Marcy, returning from the kitchen with two unmatched mugs, a soup spoon with which to fish out the teabags and a king-size bag of prawn-cocktail-flavoured crisps. 'Well, I must say this is all very civilised.' With a sigh of relief, she collapsed into a chair. Then, her grey eyes swivelling between her two guests, she gestured vaguely at the mugs of tea and smiled once more. 'I'm so glad you felt able to visit us. Problems with exes and in-laws are so unnecessary, I've always thought . . . please Gina, do help yourself to the crisps . . .'

Andrew's reaction, when he arrived back at the flat fifteen minutes later, was far more gratifying. Grinding to a halt in the doorway, bulging carrier bags dangling from both hands, he stared at his estranged wife and said, 'Jesus.'

Izzy opened her mouth, ready to leap into the breach once more, but Gina was too fast for her.

'Andrew,' she acknowledged gracefully, crossing one slim leg over the other and smoothing the silk dress over her knees with a composed, almost regal gesture. 'How pleasant to see *you* again, after all this time. I'm afraid we've called unannounced, but I didn't feel such an important matter could be properly discussed over the telephone. I hope you don't mind us coming here to your . . .' The word 'love-nest' hung unspoken in the air between them. Izzy held her breath. '. . . home,' continued Gina, the merest hint of a smile lifting the corners of her mouth. 'But we really do need to discuss the details of our divorce.'

'That was terrific!' exclaimed Izzy as they made their way back to the car. Bursting with pride, she said, '*You* were terrific. Really, I'm so impressed. And did you see the look on his face when you started talking about the divorce . . . !'

'Yes,' said Gina, so wrapped up in her own thoughts that she could barely concentrate on what Izzy was saying.

'And how about that female he's landed himself with. What a ditz. I thought he'd at least have gone for something with a bit of go about her . . . but you were so *brilliant* . . .' Lost in admiration, she shook her dark head, then broke into a grin. 'Don't you feel a million times better now that you've faced them?'

'Better than I've felt for months,' agreed Gina happily. Stopping at the edge of the pavement and glancing up at Andrew's rented apartment, she realised that now, at last, she was feeling alive again. Unable to stop herself, she reached out and clutched Izzy's arm. 'Better than I've ever felt in my life! Oh Izzy, I thought I'd lost him . . . it didn't even occur to me that I could get him back. And it's all thanks to you for making me come here . . .'

Izzy ground to a halt. Her heart plummeted. Somehow, somewhere along the line, she and Gina appeared to have got their wires very crossed indeed. 'But you don't want him back!' she countered strongly. 'He's a liar and a cheat and you're better off without him. You came here to prove all that to yourself . . . to lay the ghost . . .'

'But now I've found out that I don't need to,' replied Gina, her eyes alight with joy. 'And I can stop worrying, because it's all going to be all right. He doesn't love her, don't you see? He *will* come back.'

'Oh God,' said Izzy with a groan. But Gina didn't even notice; she was miles away.

'He will come back,' she repeated with dreamy conviction. 'To me.'

# Chapter 13

'It's all my fault,' Izzy admitted gloomily as Sam gave her a lift to work that evening on his way to The Chelsea Steps. Peering into her hand mirror and putting the finishing touches to her lipstick, she said, 'I've made an absolute pig's ear of the whole thing. And all I was doing,' she added with an impatient gesture, 'was trying to help.'

'I wondered why she was so much more cheerful,' remarked Sam drily. Then, swinging the car into the outside lane to avoid a braking cab, he said, 'But is that really so terrible?'

They had reached Trafalgar Square. Reminded by the sight of Nelson's Column that she had a Cadbury's Flake in her bag and immeasurably cheered by the thought, Izzy rummaged until she found it, then offered half to Sam. Even more happily, he shook his head, which meant a whole Flake to herself. 'Gina's like an addict with a fix after six weeks of cold turkey,' she informed him, between mouthfuls. 'It's completely disastrous! Just think what she'll be like when it wears off.'

Amused by her agony-auntish attitude, as well as by her ability to eat chocolate and apply mascara at the same time, he said, 'Don't you ever make mistakes?'

'Oh zillions.' Make-up completed, Izzy dropped the mascara back into her capacious bag and polished off the last of the Flake, licking her fingers with panache. 'But

102

that only makes me more of an expert at seeing where everyone else is going wrong. And the one thing I'd never do,' she added as a careless afterthought, 'would be to lust after a man who didn't lust back. Now that *is* asking to be kicked in the teeth. That's just *stupid*.'

Brennan's Bar was still relatively empty when Ralph walked in. Izzy's stomach did a quick backward somersault and for a millisecond she considered diving down behind the bar. Since she was in the process of giving a fat businessman his change, however, it wasn't entirely practical.

Ralph, on the other hand, didn't even flinch when he saw her. 'Hallo, Izzy,' he said evenly. A faint smile lifted the corners of his mouth. 'Well, well. Of all the bars in all the world you had to be working in this one.'

He might be an actor, but the casual line didn't fool her for a moment. With a grin, she said, 'You knew I was here.'

'Word gets around.' Leaning against the bar, tanned and narrow-eyed, looking only slightly over the top in a beige trenchcoat worn open over a T-shirt and white jeans, Ralph surveyed her with practised thoroughness. Then he lit a Gauloise and Izzy realised that he was doing his Alain Delon bit, which meant that beneath the cool façade he must be nervous. 'So, how are you?'

At least he wasn't using a French accent. Stepping back and showing him her legs – and glad now that she'd worn her short, charcoal-grey lycra dress – she said simply, 'Mended.'

He nodded. 'And how's Kat?'

Ralph and Katerina had always got on so well together. An unlikely father figure, he had nevertheless formed a close and genuinely affectionate relationship with Kat, and their good-natured verbal sparring had been capable of keeping them happily occupied for hours. Experiencing a rush of belated gratitude, Izzy seized a bottle of Lanson and said, 'Come on, my treat. It really is lovely to see you again.'

Happily, the bar remained quiet and she was able to catch up on all the gossip concerning their old friends.

'And what about you?' she asked finally. Knowing Ralph as she did; she was perfectly well aware that he was holding out on her.

He half-smiled, trying not to look too pleased with himself. 'Oh, not too bad. This and that, you know.'

'How can I know unless you tell me?' she persisted, beginning to enjoy herself. Sam was still off-limits, after all, and if Ralph had finally decided to forgive her . . . well, she reasoned, he did have the most gorgeous eyes, and he could always make her laugh. Besides, when Sam had caught her with Kat's sex manual, there had been more than a modicum of truth in her riposte that she was badly out of practice . . .

'Well, as a matter of fact my agent rang me this afternoon,' he admitted, breaking into a grin at last. 'To tell me that I've landed the lead in a new TV drama series.'

Izzy's shriek of delight startled even the seen-it-all-before stockbrokers sitting at a nearby table. 'Ralph, that's fantastic! My God, you must be so thrilled . . . tell me everything, every *detail* . . . quick, have another glass of champagne . . . you should be out celebrating!' Leaning across the polished bar, she took his face in her hands and gave him a kiss. To her further delight, he didn't show the least sign of resisting.

'Maybe I wanted to celebrate with someone who'd really understand.' Then, his eyes narrowing once more, he said, 'Are you still seeing that other guy?'

'Of course not!'

'Anyone else?'

Not yet, thought Izzy, crossing her fingers beneath the bar. 'Whoever in the world would want anything to do with a hopeless case like me?' she said lightly. Then, since he continued to glare at her, she smiled and shook her head. 'No. Nobody else.'

Ralph relaxed at last. 'In that case, what time can you get away?'

'Ah, there you are,' said Sam, crossing to the bar and observing with amused interest the way Izzy jumped at the sound of his voice. Even more intriguing was the sudden rush of colour suffusing her cheeks, since as long as he'd known her she'd never blushed.

'Sam . . . what on earth are you doing here?' she demanded, far too quickly.

'Such gratitude!' He tut-tutted with mock reproval, then winked and pulled her purse from his jacket pocket. 'I found it on the floor of the car. It must have fallen out of that disgraceful bag of yours while you were doing your make-up. Oh, and I phoned Kat in case you were panicking about it,' he continued easily, apparently quite unaware of Ralph's glowering presence beside him. 'She said that if we were thinking of stopping off at the Chinese on our way home, could she please have lemon chicken with egg fried rice and double pineapple fritters.'

'What did I say?' protested Sam, as they made their way back to the house several hours later.

Izzy, with six boxes of Chinese food balanced precariously on her lap, threw him a suspicious sideways glance, but his immaculate profile was giving nothing away.

'You know exactly what you said,' she told him, still undecided whether to laugh or empty the carton of prawn crackers over his head.

'OK.' He nodded, keeping his own amusement to himself. 'But what did I say that was so wrong? That guy stormed out so fast I didn't even get a chance to admire the medallions around his neck.'

'He doesn't wear medallions.' Despite herself, Izzy smiled into the darkness. It had been she, two years ago, who had had to break the news to Ralph that real men didn't wear necklaces. 'And before you say anything else,' she continued in severe tones, 'you're talking about the man I loved.'

But Sam was already acquainted with the saga of Izzy's recent entanglements. 'Don't you mean one of the men you loved?' he remarked, deadpan.

'It isn't funny,' she said, with a touch of irritation. 'And you deliberately said those things to give him the wrong impression. You might find it amusing, but I spent my entire evening's wages on that bottle of champagne.'

'And now I've spoiled your hopes of a romantic reconciliation,' he mused cheerfully. 'Really, Isabel. I thought you didn't lust after men who didn't lust after you. If he can't even cope with tonight's little misunderstanding, he can't be that smitten.'

Enraged, she shouted, 'You've wrecked my non-existent love life and it has nothing whatsoever to do with you! How would you like it if I stuck my oar in, just as you were about to make *your* move with some bimbo at The Steps?'

How indeed? Having known Izzy Van Asch for some weeks, Sam's feelings towards her were still decidedly mixed. That initial jolting attraction had knocked him sideways, but there was so much more to Izzy than simply the physical appeal of big brown eyes, riotous hair, a curvy body and stupendous – now that they were both visible – legs. She exuded fun, laughed more than anyone he'd ever known and her optimism was irrepressible.

Yet at the same time, she could be thoughtless, illogical and infuriatingly cavalier in her attitudes and lifestyle. Wildly generous one day, she would be shamelessly cadging a fiver from her daughter the next, and although she was undoubtedly capable of hard work when it suited her, she was also better at whiling away an afternoon in sybaritic indolence than almost any other woman he knew. She was so exasperating, loving, sometimes downright astounding – and he was never entirely sure whether the things she said and did were deliberately calculated to shock – that Sam couldn't decide what he wanted to do more; shake a bit of much-needed sense into her dizzy head or tumble her into bed.

And there, he reflected ruefully, lay the other half of his dilemma. Attracting women was not something he'd ever had to think about before. It just happened, and gently rebuffing the ones who didn't attract him in return had been the only mildly tricky part. But surely, no other woman on this planet had ever sent out signals as conflicting as those signalled by Izzy. Time and time again, just as he'd thought he had her sussed, she would move smartly into reverse and he would be left wondering . . . once again . . . whether he even knew her at all.

Until now he'd been both amused and intrigued by her behaviour. Tonight, however, something had changed. And maybe tonight, Sam mused as he drew up outside the house and switched off the car's engine, he should do something about it.

'You still haven't answered my question.' Izzy spoke with an air of truculence. She hadn't forgiven him yet.

'Ah yes, the bimbo.' Sam nodded, giving the question some thought. Then, taking the cumbersome pile of boxes from her lap, he gave her a brief smile. 'I suppose it would rather depend,' he said finally, 'on what she was like.'

It wasn't the most romantic of situations, thought Izzy, but at least it was finally happening . . .

She had been dumping the dirty dishes into the sink when Sam had moved up behind her, resting his hands on the edge of the draining board on either side of her so that she was effectively pinned in. There was no physical contact, but she could feel his warm breath stirring her hair and smell the faint scent of his aftershave.

Hoping that he, in turn, couldn't see the tiny hairs prickling at the nape of her neck, Izzy turned on the hot tap and squirted far too much Fairy Liquid into the bowl.

She hadn't planned on actually doing the washing-up, but it looked good, and such a show of domesticity was bound to impress. Sam was always making pointed remarks about her appalling lack of it.

'Come on now, be honest,' he murmured, as she watched the foam cascade over the edges of the bowl like champagne. 'Ralph really wasn't your type anyway.'

'He was my type for two years,' Izzy replied with outward calm. Her hands, however, were shaking so she seized Gina's beloved rubber gloves, pulling them on in a hurry and plunging them into the washing-up. Then, nodding towards the tea towel, she said, 'And if you really want to be useful, you can dry.'

Taking half a step backwards, Sam admired the deep V of tanned flesh revealed by her dress, which was virtually backless. Resisting the urge to run a finger down her spine, he said mildly, 'You're changing the subject.'

'I don't know what the subject is.' She took a deep, steadying breath and sloshed fresh water over a haphazardly scrubbed bowl. 'I just know that Gina does her nut if the dishes aren't put away.'

'Izzy,' he said gently. 'You may be many things, but you aren't stupid.'

Unable to think of a suitable reply to this statement, she played safe and said nothing. A moment later, Sam's mouth brushed the nape of her neck and Izzy, who had been bracing herself for something like this, was quite unable to prevent the shudder of longing which ricocheted up from her stomach. When his warm hands came to rest at her waist and his lips travelled to her bare shoulder, she almost gave in.

But this was Gina's house and she had made her a promise. Besides, Sam was due to move out in less than a fortnight . . . and a little waiting had never harmed anyone. Least of all, she reminded herself firmly, a man like Sam Sheridan, who had probably never been kept waiting before in his life.

But his tongue was idling along the line of her collar bone now, a manoeuvre to which Izzy had always been particularly susceptible, and that wasn't fair at all. Squirming with suppressed desire, she had to employ every last ounce of will-power in order not to turn around. Instead, concentrating fiercely on the washing-up, she managed – somehow – to clean another plate. Then, when she finally judged herself able to speak in something approaching normal tones, she said with deliberate flippancy, 'Did they slip something extra into your sesame king prawns, Sam, or do you just have a bit of a thing for Marigold gloves?'

With a shrug, he dropped a light kiss on the top of her head and stepped back. 'I'm just curious.'

'About me?' said Izzy, torn between relief that he had stopped and irritation that he couldn't have tried a little harder. There was such a thing as giving up too easily, after all. 'You thought I'd be a pushover,' she continued, her eyes bright with challenge. 'Is that it?'

'Not at all.' Moving across to the dresser, he uncapped a bottle of Scotch and poured hefty measures into two glasses. 'I was simply curious, as I said. I don't want to shock you,' he added with a glimmer of a smile, 'but when two people find each other attractive, when they're both unattached and over the age of consent . . . well, sometimes they . . .'

'I know about all that,' replied Izzy swiftly. Not wanting to annoy him, she smiled back. 'Kat told me all about the birds and the bees when she was twelve. But . . .'

'But?' Sam echoed with a trace of irony.

Uncomfortably aware that she hadn't really thought this through, Izzy wiped a tendril of hair from her forehead with the back of a foamy hand and said as cheerfully as she could, 'Well, it might spoil things. We get on well, now. We're friends, aren't we?'

Sam nodded, not believing her for a moment but intrigued nevertheless to hear what she was going to come up with.

'So, it might spoil our friendship,' she continued hurriedly, 'and that would be awful.'

'It might not, and then it wouldn't be awful at all.'

This time she drew a deep breath. 'It still isn't a good idea.'

'OK.' He held up his hands. 'If that's what you really feel. And there's no need to get into a flap about it, anyway. It was just a thought.'

'Well, it was nice of you to think of me,' said Izzy lamely, miffed by his refusal to make any kind of serious attempt to seduce her. If this was the extent of his persistence, she wasn't surprised he'd never been married.

'That's OK,' said Sam, by this time openly amused. 'My mistake. I should have realised that you weren't that sort of girl.'

'No hard feelings?'

He gave her a rueful smile. 'Hardly any at all now, thanks.'

'Good.' She was pushing her luck, she knew, but victory over someone as desirable as Sam was infinitely sweet. And next time . . . in about two weeks' time to be precise . . . she would achieve an even greater one. Chucking the washing-up cloth into the sink and crossing the dimly lit kitchen, she stood on tiptoe and planted a careful, sisterly kiss on his cheek. 'Good friends are more important than lovers,' she murmured. 'Every time.'

'Depends how good they are,' said Sam, keeping himself firmly under control. The bitch, he thought. Now he knew she was playing games.

'Good night, Sam,' said Izzy serenely.

'Good night, John-boy.'

# Chapter 14

Galvanised into action by the realization that she could get Andrew back, Gina had embarked upon a whirlwind plan of campaign in order to do so and stubbornly refused to listen to Izzy's protests that this wasn't what she'd meant at all. The terrible apathy which had dogged her for the past months was stripped away like Clark Kent's office suit, to be replaced by a positive tidal wave of enthusiasm. Having lost almost a stone in weight – which didn't particularly suit her – she regained her appetite and began eating again, had her hair rebobbed and her legs eye-smartingly waxed. Oblivious to the bank manager's unamused letters she launched into a fresh orgy of spending, but this time it was carried out joyfully and with real purpose because nothing was too good for Andrew and whoever would dream of wearing underwear which didn't match their clothes and clothes which didn't match their Kurt Geiger shoes anyway?

And since nothing seemed impossible any more, gaining new-found independence in the form of a job no longer struck terror into Gina's soul. Her determination to prove herself different in every way from that slothful, unkempt creature with whom Andrew had so stupidly – and *temporarily* – gone to live was a far more effective incentive than Izzy's airy exhortations to 'get out and do something' had ever been.

'Where are you going?' Izzy demanded with suspicion a couple of days later when Gina presented herself downstairs made up and scented and wearing a new, navy-blue Chanel-style suit which looked suspiciously like the genuine article and which would no doubt reduce the bank manager to new depths of depression. At this rate, Izzy could almost feel sorry for him.

Gina, who had been practising a new, slightly deeper and hopefully more authoritative voice in the privacy of her bedroom, said, 'I've got a job interview.' But Izzy only looked more alarmed.

'Are you going down with something infectious?'

'No, I am not.' Disappointed, Gina reverted to her normal tones. 'And you're supposed to be encouraging me.'

'I tried doing that,' Izzy reminded her. 'And it went horribly wrong.' Then she pulled herself together. 'But I'm glad you're looking for work; it'll do you the world of good. What kind of job is it?'

It was indeed going to do her a world of good, thought Gina, scarcely able to control her smile. She had run through the plan a hundred times, yet the thought of it still sent the adrenalin racing through her body. The interview, set for eleven o'clock, was bound to be over by midday. Then, having secured the job she would arrive at Andrew's office just before twelve-thirty and insist . . . *insist* that he join her for lunch in order to celebrate. From there on the details grew a little hazy; all she knew was that Andrew would be seeing her at her new and absolute best, she would be seeing him without that awful Marcy in tow and it would be the happiest afternoon of her life . . .

'Are you *sure* you're OK?' Izzy waved a hand in front of her face, bringing her back to earth.

'Of course I am. It's a sales job,' said Gina with renewed pride, 'at Therese Verdun, just off Bond Street.'

Therese Verdun was one of the most exclusive dress shops in London.

Of course, thought Izzy wryly, silly me for asking.

'Yes?' snapped Andrew, when his secretary buzzed through to his office at midday.

'Er, Mr Lawrence, your wife is here to see you,' said Pam, struggling to contain her excitement. Having stayed up late the previous night to watch *Fatal Attraction*, she had high hopes for this real-life confrontation. Gina didn't look as if she was carrying a gun, but you never knew. And Andrew Lawrence had been in such a lousy mood for the last couple of weeks that whatever he had coming to him now, Pam condoned absolutely.

'Send her in,' commanded the tinny voice over the intercom. Gina smiled at Pam. Pam, deciding that maybe she wouldn't take her lunch hour just yet after all, smiled back. Andrew, ensconced in his office, didn't smile at all.

'Darling!' said Gina, when the door was safely shut behind her. Swooping down on him like a thin, elegant bird and enveloping him in a cloud of freshly applied Shalimar, she kissed his cheek. 'Isn't this a surprise? I should have phoned, but I was so excited I simply had to come and tell you . . . I've just found myself the most marvellous job and I wanted you to be the first to know!'

'That's—' began Andrew, caught totally off-guard by

her arrival, but Gina had rehearsed her lines too often to allow him to interrupt.

'And it's all thanks to you, because if you hadn't left I would never have even thought of going out to work!' she gabbled joyfully. 'So I insist, absolutely, upon taking you for lunch.'

'Ah, well . . .'

'No excuses,' she continued with mock severity. 'I checked with Pam to make sure you didn't have any other appointments, and besides . . . what on earth is the point of having a civilised divorce if one can't treat one's husband to a superb lunch at Emile's once in a while?'

It was all going disastrously wrong, she thought numbly an hour later. Here she was, doing and saying everything according to plan, here they were in Andrew's favourite – and ruinously expensive – restaurant, and here was Andrew refusing to co-operate with all the quiet stubbornness of a small boy who doesn't want to return to boarding school.

'Another bottle of wine?' she asked in desperation, but he simply shook his head and glanced yet again at his watch. Gazing helplessly around at the other tables, Gina saw only couples enjoying themselves. She was running out of bright conversation at a rate of knots now. Her new job had become more and more grand . . . she was practically running the entire company . . . and Andrew still wasn't as impressed as he was supposed to be. He also took little apparent interest in her wildly exaggerated stories of what sharing a house with Izzy and Sam was like. Unless he pulled himself together and started making an effort very soon, thought Gina as the first signs of real panic began to gnaw at her stomach, she didn't know what she might do.

'I hope Marcy isn't cooking you a huge dinner,' she said, although he hadn't really eaten much at all.

Andrew shook his head. If he looked at his watch one more time, thought Gina, she would tear it off his wrist and hurl it across the room.

'And the baby?' she continued, too brightly. 'Is everything going smoothly there? I expect Marcy's up to her ears in ante-natal classes at the moment . . .'

'Gina, don't,' he said abruptly. 'Look, thanks for the lunch and I'm really very pleased for you about the job, but I have got to get back to the office. There's no need for you to drive me back, I can take a cab.'

The fantasy hadn't materialised; the charade was over. Unable to bear it, Gina's eyes filled with tears and she rose jerkily to her feet, knocking the fork from her plate and splattering the front of her skirt with Madeira sauce. 'Andrew, please, you can't just leave like this. You don't understand—'

'I do understand.' He didn't know whom to feel most sorry for, Gina or himself. He was merely unhappy, whereas she was chronically insecure. 'You've landed yourself a wonderful job, you're making a new life for yourself and I'm *glad* about that.'

The tears were in full flood now, streaking her make-up and attracting the attention of other diners. 'But I don't *have* a new life,' she sobbed, scrubbing hopelessly at the burgundy stain on her skirt with a snowy napkin. 'And I don't have a wonderful job, either. I don't have any kind of job because they turned me down. They told me I needed experience,' she wailed accusingly, 'and I didn't have any because all I'd ever been was a wife!'

Somehow he managed to get her out of the restaurant. A handful of tenners he could ill-afford to lose only just covered the bill. By the time they reached the car, Gina was shivering violently and barely able to stand. The fact that she was oblivious to the stares of passers-by convinced him that her grief was genuine.

'I can't drive, d-don't make me d-drive,' she begged, through chattering teeth. 'The last time I was like this I nearly k-k-killed someone.'

'All right, don't worry,' he said rapidly, praying he wasn't over the limit. 'I'll take you home.'

'I'm so ashamed.'

'Blimey,' said a man unloading a van. 'What's she got, syphilis?'

'Get in the car,' ordered Andrew, torn between irritation and sympathy. Once again the crushing weight of responsibility was bearing down on him. While he accepted that he was to blame for this entire sorry mess, he couldn't help wondering why he should be the one with the wife who couldn't handle it while other men seemed to escape scot-free.

'Blimey.' Katerina, spending the afternoon studying at home, unknowingly echoed the van driver when she answered the front door and saw Gina's swollen, ravaged face.

'I'm sorry.' Andrew waved apologetically in the direction of the doorbell. 'Gina couldn't find her key.'

Katerina regarded him with interest. Gina in tears was nothing new – although she did look quite spectacularly dreadful – but as far as Katerina was aware she had left the house this morning in unusually high spirits, looking forward to her interview. From the look of her now, she could only assume that Gina hadn't been offered the job. 'That's OK,' she replied easily, wondering if this man was the owner of the dress shop. 'But I'm intrigued. Who are you?'

It was a bizarre situation; for the moment Gina was quite forgotten. Having already deduced who Katerina was, Andrew could only return her unflinching gaze. She was wearing a faded honey-coloured sweatshirt and knee-length white leggings and her glossy brown hair hung straight to her shoulders. Her eyes were huge and light brown, her teeth very white. In her right hand she held a pen; in her left a marmalade sandwich.

'Andrew Lawrence,' he said and waited for her expression to change to one of disdain. Izzy's dislike of him had been only too evident during their brief meeting the previous week.

Katerina, however, broke into a smile and gave him a look of such complicity that he knew at once she was on his side. The relief was overwhelming.

'Right, of course you are.' She stepped aside, enabling him to lead Gina towards the sitting room. Andrew found himself unable to tear his eyes from her rear view; those slim hips and long legs were almost hypnotizing in their simple elegance. She couldn't possibly be more than eighteen.

'Well, I'd better leave you to it.' In the sitting room,

text books littered the carpet. Within seconds Katerina had retrieved them and was standing in the doorway. When she had watched Andrew deposit his wife in one of the peach upholstered armchairs she said calmly, 'Do you know who *I* am?'

He straightened, adjusting his tie and dropping Gina's car keys on to the coffee table. He might not have contributed much towards the conversation in the restaurant, but he had at least listened. 'You're the clever one,' he told her, his voice even, 'who does the washing-up.'

'Right.' This time Katerina laughed. 'Of course I am. And how clever of *you* to have guessed.'

Having planned to drop off Gina and leave immediately, he found himself phoning the office instead and telling them he wouldn't be back that afternoon, which would fuel office gossip no end. And after thirty minutes of half-heartedly attempting to console his inconsolable wife, he was rewarded by the sound of footsteps descending the staircase. Snatching Gina's teacup from her hands and murmuring something about a refill, he shot out of the room and slap into Katerina.

She was wearing a denim jacket and carried a vast canvas bag stuffed with books.

'How's it going?'

Andrew pulled a face. 'Same as ever. Look, it's about time I was leaving, but I'd like to talk to you ... about Gina. Can I offer you a lift to wherever you're going?'

She gave him another of those solemn mesmerizing looks. 'I'm afraid not.'

'Oh.'

'It isn't that I don't appreciate the offer,' she explained, breaking into a slow smile. He looked so dismayed, it was almost heartbreaking. She leaned closer and said in a stage whisper, 'But you don't have transport.'

'Damn.' At the same time, Andrew experienced a surge of relief, because the rejection wasn't personal. Putting the memory of the lunch he couldn't afford behind him, he said, 'I'll phone for a cab.'

Katerina's smile widened as she hauled her heavy bag over her shoulder. 'Why don't we just walk to the tube station? Then we can talk on the way.'

I'm in the Victoria and Albert Museum and something very strange is happening to me, thought Katerina carefully, an hour later. She didn't know how or why it was happening; it just was. And there was nothing, absolutely nothing on earth she could do to either stop or control it.

She didn't even know what they were doing in the museum, for heaven's sake; there had simply been too much to say and not enough time in which to say it, until Andrew had suggested they stop *en route* for a coffee and *en route* had somehow become the dear old V & A. Now, as they sat side by side in the ground-floor restaurant, surrounded on all sides by noisy, overweight Americans and tiny, chattering Japanese tourists, Katerina was aware only of the momentousness of a situation she didn't even fully comprehend. On the outside she was still herself, twirling a strand of hair between two fingers as she discussed – in purely practical terms – Gina's lack of confidence and what they could possibly do about it.

But on the inside she wasn't herself at all. While her mouth was doing the talking, her stomach had tied itself up in a gigantic knot and the inside of her wrist, where Andrew had accidentally brushed against her, was still tingling, really *tingling*, as a result of that momentary physical contact.

As long as she continued to talk, however – and discussing his marital problems in a detached, adult manner was astonishingly easy – she was able to study Andrew Lawrence in detail. And while he wasn't as startlingly good-looking as some men ... Sam, for example ... there was something about his shadowed grey eyes, thin cheeks and floppy, light brown hair that was somehow infinitely more attractive. He looked careworn, exuding an air of fighting against the odds to make the best of what he had to put up with, and when he actually smiled his features were transformed; his whole face lit up and the years melted away.

'I shouldn't really be telling you all this,' he said eventually, stirring milky coffee which had long since gone cold. 'It isn't your problem, after all.'

'But it's so awful!' exclaimed Katerina, her eyes on the verge of filling with uncharacteristic tears. 'And so unfair ... God, we have no idea! Mum did say that—'

'Yes?' Andrew prompted gently. 'What did Mum say?'

Incapable of lying to him, fixing him with those huge brown eyes, she murmured, 'Well, she mentioned in passing that Marcy was a bit of a ditz.'

He acknowledged the words with a thoughtful nod, then smiled because at least he was here, with Katerina Van Asch. Life, it seemed, had its compensations. He just wondered how he was going to cope with the particular compensation facing him at this minute. The urge to touch her once more . . . accidentally, of course . . . was almost overwhelming.

'It's all my fault; I've been a complete idiot,' he admitted. 'I was married, I thought I'd fallen in love with another woman . . . and by the time I realised I hadn't, it was too late.'

'You shouldn't blame yourself,' said Katerina indignantly. 'Getting pregnant was her own stupid fault. Plenty of other men would have just dumped her.'

The restaurant was rapidly emptying; it was almost six o'clock and cleaners were pushing mops around. Aware of their baleful stares, and of the fact that time was running out, Andrew was unable to stop himself. Taking Katerina's hand and giving it a brief squeeze, he smiled. 'Thank you. I wish I'd met you six months ago.' Even better, he thought, he wished he were twenty years younger and still single.

But Katerina, knowing only that Andrew Lawrence had already changed her life and throwing seventeen years of caution to the wind, reached for the hand he had withdrawn and held it between her own. She was trembling slightly, her stomach had long since disappeared and she had never been happier in her life.

'It doesn't matter,' she heard herself saying, as if from a great distance. 'You've met me now.'

# Chapter 15

Determined not to be too obvious or too eager, but at the same time nerve-wrackingly aware that single men like Sam were in constant danger of being snapped up by less patient women than herself, Izzy maintained a decorous distance when he eventually moved out of the house and into his new apartment and, in a state of intense and delicious anticipation, managed to hold out for almost an entire week.

Waking up the following Saturday afternoon, however, and realizing that now was the perfect time to see Sam and put her brilliant plan into long-awaited action, the anticipation became at once almost unbearable. It was sunny. It was warm. She was – boasting apart – looking great. And best of all, Izzy discovered when she eventually got up and moseyed into her daughter's empty bedroom, Katerina had decided against wearing her new pink denim skirt. If that wasn't fate, she thought happily as she slung it over one arm and headed towards the bathroom, she didn't know what was.

Gina was downstairs, disconsolately watching an old black-and-white film on the television.

'Going somewhere nice?' she asked, when Izzy appeared in a pale pink denim skirt worn with a minuscule white vest and clinched at the waist with a twisted charcoal-and-pink fringed scarf. Navy-blue eyeshadow and more mascara than usual conspired to make her eyes look enormous and she was even wearing pink lipstick. Stupid question, thought Gina miserably. Of course she was going somewhere nice.

Recognizing the note of desperation in her voice and realizing that Gina was likely to ask if she could come along too, Izzy replied briskly, 'Audition,' then smiled to herself, deciding that in a way, that was exactly what it was. And a mutual one at that.

'Oh.' Losing interest, Gina returned her attention to the film which was bound to make her cry. 'Kat asked me to tell you that she's gone over to Simon's house, by the way. She won't be back until late.'

Snap, thought Izzy cheerfully, scooping Katerina's alligator earrings out of the bowl on the mantelpiece and fastening them into her ears. Aloud, she said, 'Hooray for A levels,' because Katerina hated it when she borrowed her earrings. Then, tipping her head to one side as she examined her reflection in the mirror, she added, 'Although if you ask me, there's more to these disappearing acts of hers than meets the eye.'

'What on earth do you mean?' Gina, who had watched a nightmarish programme about teenage junkies the night before, thought immediately of drugs. God, that was all she needed . . .

'Kat and Simon,' explained Izzy patiently. 'They can't possibly spend this much time together simply revising. Haven't you noticed how different she's been these past few weeks? Physics and chemistry haven't done *that* to her,' she concluded with satisfaction, fluffing up her hair and adjusting the straps of her top to reveal a fraction more cleavage. 'I know, I can hardly believe it myself, but it seems that my brilliant, backward daughter has finally discovered what little boys are made of. Bless her little heart, she's in *lurve*!'

'There are crocodiles in your ears,' observed Sam, who had been in the shower when the doorbell rang. The fact that he was wearing only an olive-green towel slung around his hips made Izzy unaccountably nervous, which was ridiculous. If she got her way later on this evening, she reminded herself, he would be wearing rather less than a bath towel, after all.

'There are hares on your chest,' she countered; a feeble joke even by her own terrible standards.

He winked. 'Ah, but I didn't borrow them from Katerina without asking her first.'

'How do you know I didn't ask her?'

'If you had,' he said with a grin, 'she would have said no.'

Izzy almost bit her lower lip but all that would achieve was unattractive lipstick-stained teeth, so she settled instead for an expression of penitence. 'Are you going to call the police?'

'Not if you've brought champagne,' he said, glancing at the bulky carrier bag clasped to her chest.

'Single men are famous for keeping their fridges stocked with champagne,' she replied, making her way through to the kitchen. 'And very little else. I've brought something much more useful. Food.'

'You mean you're going to cook something?' Sam looked alarmed. 'To eat?'

'Don't panic, I went to the Italian delicatessen,' she said soothingly. 'All we have to do is unwrap it.'

He couldn't quite put his finger on it, but there was definitely something different about Izzy. Over a leisurely late lunch of smoked salmon, marinated mushrooms, salads, French bread and Camembert, the effortless conversation continued as ever ... business at The Chelsea Steps, Katerina's budding love life, Gina's third unsuccessful interview ... but there was something else, too. Two small glasses of champagne hadn't had this much of an effect on her; Izzy was definitely hiding something.

'Never mind Katerina and Simon,' he said at last, eyeing her with suspicion. 'What's been happening with you? Are you in love?'

Izzy popped a black grape into her mouth and smiled. 'Me? Whoever would I be in love with?'

'I don't know. Somebody wildly unsuitable, no doubt.' Recalling the medallion man he had met at the pub the other week, Sam experienced a twinge of irritation. He was surprised to find how much he minded. 'You have terrible taste in men, you know.'

She shook her head vigorously. 'I don't.'

'Yes, you do.'

How sweet, thought Izzy, in raptures. And how ironic. Twirling a tendril of hair between her fingers, she fixed Sam with an innocent gaze. 'Are we having our first quarrel?'

'Possibly.' God, she was infuriating. 'Why, is that the reason you came over here?'

'Not at all. It's just that I'm right and you're wrong and I love it when that happens.'

As far as Sam was aware, it never *had* happened. Izzy had a positive talent for mistakes, she got *everything* wrong. 'So, who is he?' he said, attempting to sound as if it didn't matter to him anyway.

Izzy, enjoying herself enormously, began to dismantle the last bunch of grapes. 'Well, I don't know whether I'm actually in love, but there's definitely a bit of lust involved. He's wildly attractive.'

'Oh, top-priority stuff,' Sam retaliated. 'Don't tell me, he wears white, patent-leather shoes, too.'

'There's no need to make fun of me,' she said, deadpan. 'Looks *are* important. Would you go out with a dog?'

Realizing that he was in danger of losing this particular argument, he said, 'So, is it fairly serious between you and this . . . man?'

The bait had been well and truly taken, Izzy appreciated happily. Her mission accomplished – for now, at least – she drained her glass and pushed back her chair. With a careless shrug, she said, 'Who knows what will happen? It may turn out like that. Whichever, it'll certainly be fun finding out.'

As she reached for her bag, Sam said, 'Are you working tonight?'

Izzy pulled a face. 'Yes. And you?'

He nodded.

'Right. Well, I'm off.' Tossing her bag over her shoulder, she gave him a dazzling smile. 'Have a nice night then, Sam. And enjoy yourself. I'm certainly going to!'

\* \* \*

It was just after midnight when Sam caught a glimpse of Izzy through the crowd at the edge of the dance floor. She had her back to him and he was unable to see who she was with, and for a few seconds he hesitated at the bar, unsure whether he actually wanted to meet this new man of hers. Having felt uncharacteristically edgy all evening he didn't altogether trust himself not to say something he shouldn't.

But Izzy, at that moment turning and spotting him, smiled and waved and made her way over. Looking dazzling in an iridescent petrol-blue dress he hadn't seen before and with her hair piled up in a glossy, disorganised topknot, she gave him a quick kiss.

'Sam, I love this place! I've just bumped into Robbie Williams . . . !'

'As long as you didn't sing to him,' replied Sam evenly. If it meant furthering her career, Izzy wouldn't think twice about pulling such a stunt. Glancing over her shoulder, he said, 'So where's Mr Universe?'

'Who?'

'The white-shoed wonder. You didn't bring him along, or has he collapsed under the weight of his jewellery?'

Izzy smiled and leaned against the bar. 'Ah, maybe he's here. Maybe I'm just playing it cool like they tell you to in all the magazines.'

'You mean he isn't here,' said Sam with some relief. 'Come on, I'll buy you a drink.'

'I don't want a drink.' She shook her head at the approaching barman, paused for a second, then said slowly, 'I want to dance. With you.'

It was like dancing with a cyberman. 'I'm sorry,' said

Sam in her ear. 'I can't do this. I just don't dance with my customers.'

'I can see why,' Izzy replied, disappointed by the temporary setback. She was doing her best, the slow, sensual music was – God knows – doing *its* best, but Sam remained as unrelaxed as it was possible for a cyberman to be. 'And I'm not even a real customer,' she chided, 'so I shouldn't count.'

'I know, I know. But people are watching.' Sam wondered if Izzy had any idea how uncomfortable she was making him feel. Furthermore, how was it possible that she was able to dance with such apparent decorum – their bodies were barely touching, for heaven's sake – while at the same time managing to give him the distinct impression that this was more of a seduction than a dance?

'Your reputation will be in tatters,' she murmured, moving fractionally closer so that he could breathe in her scent. 'You know what women assume about men who can't dance.'

'I can dance,' replied Sam through gritted teeth. 'I just can't do it here.'

'Oh.' Izzy smiled. 'So, where exactly *can* you do it?'

'What?'

'Go on, prove it.'

Something was definitely going on. There was a deceptive innocence about her eyes, yet at the same time she looked as if she was bursting with the most marvellous secret. As the music ended, Sam reached for her hand and led her off the dance floor, resolutely ignoring the looks of intrigue he was receiving from regular customers.

When they reached his office on the first floor he

steered Izzy inside and closed the door firmly behind him.

'Right. What's this all about?'

'Alfieee,' sang Izzy under her breath. But, encouraged by the fact that he still hadn't let go of her arm, she said, 'I just want to know if you really can dance.'

'Very funny.'

'Gosh, Sam.' She fluttered long eyelashes. 'You're awfully attractive when you're angry.'

'Izzy, the club is packed, Ewan McGregor will be arriving shortly and the Press are milling around outside like meerkats on heat. I have better things to *do* than stand here and—'

'Why don't you shut up,' said Izzy fondly, 'and give me a kiss?'

# Chapter 16

Two minutes later she took an unsteady step backwards and slowly exhaled.

'Gosh, Izzy. You're awfully attractive when you're ruffled,' mimicked Sam.

She shook her head, putting up a hand to smooth her hair. 'I didn't expect you to . . . well, do that.'

'You asked.' He shrugged, a faint smile tugging at his lips. 'You got.'

'Oh I got, all right.' Izzy wondered whether a repeat performance might be on the cards. 'I'm just surprised.'

'Because you wanted to shock me and you didn't? Really, Izzy, I'm not that naïve . . . and you aren't that subtle, if you don't mind me saying so, although I still don't understand why you should have changed your mind about me. A couple of weeks ago,' he reminded her pointedly, 'you didn't think I was such a great idea.'

Having planned on being the seducer, Izzy was now caught on the hop. She certainly hadn't expected Sam to be this masterful, so totally in control. 'A couple of weeks ago,' she murmured, colouring slightly at the lie she was about to tell, 'you were still living in Gina's house. I didn't think it would be kind to her, if anything should . . . happen . . . between us. She's feeling lonely enough as it is.'

'Really,' drawled Sam. 'How incredibly thoughtful of you.'

Izzy shrugged and maintained a modest silence.

'And there I was,' he continued softly, 'thinking it might have had something to do with the fact that Gina had actually asked you not to get involved with me while we were both living under her roof.'

She burst out laughing. 'You cheat! What have you been doing, crossing off the days on the calendar and laying bets with yourself on how long it would be before I hurled myself shamelessly into your arms like the brazen hussy I am?'

'Laying bets with my entire staff, actually.' He managed to keep a straight face, but Izzy's ability to laugh at herself was one of the things he found most irresistible about her. Far too many women, desperate to make a good impression, lost their sense of humour completely whenever they themselves were the butt of the joke.

Izzy, however, was still smiling, quite unabashed. 'And did you win?'

As he drew her towards him once more, breathing in the scent of Diorella and feeling her body quiver helplessly beneath his touch, Sam recognised that her state of arousal was equal to his own. 'I think,' he murmured in her ear, 'I'm just about to find out.'

The shrill of the phone on his desk moments later provided a rude interruption. Izzy, who was practically sitting on it at the time, jumped a mile.

'That'll be Wendy, ringing from the front desk to let me know that Ewan McGregor's arrived,' said Sam with some reluctance.

Izzy pulled a face. 'Tell him he's just lost himself a fan.'

But when Sam picked up the receiver and began to listen, she knew at once that something was wrong. 'Tell her I'm not here,' he said tersely, and Izzy's heart sank. Then, eventually, he snapped, 'OK, OK, I'm coming down,' and slammed down the phone.

'Shit,' said Sam with feeling.

'Seconded,' she murmured, bracing herself for the worst. 'Who is it?'

Glancing at his watch, then back at Izzy's disappointed face, he heaved a sigh and said, 'Her name's Vivienne Bresnick; I met her just over a year ago in New York and we had one of those on-off relationships . . . it was doomed to failure from the start, but Vivienne is one of those women who are hard to shake off. She wouldn't give up. She wasn't the reason I left New York,' he said evenly, 'but she was certainly an added incentive.'

'So, you aren't madly in love with her?' Izzy brightened at the thought that all was not lost.

'I am not,' he replied, his tone firm and a glimmer of amusement lifting the corners of his mouth. 'But she's turned up here in the middle of the night and she isn't likely to leave quietly on the next flight back to the States.' Running an affectionate finger along the curve of her cheek, he added with a regretful smile, 'I'm sorry about this.'

Talk about *coitus interruptus*, thought Izzy. Apart from anything else, she had shaved her legs for nothing. 'Not half as sorry,' she said ruefully, 'as I am.'

Having laid a private bet with herself that Vivienne

Bresnick would be tall, tanned and dangerously blonde, Izzy would have recognised her immediately, even if she hadn't been surrounded by suitcases – matching Louis Vuitton suitcases at that.

'Sam!' exclaimed Vivienne, tossing back her practically waist-length hair and flying into his arms the moment he reached the bottom of the staircase. 'I know I should have phoned, but I wanted to be a surprise!'

'There but for the grace of Vivienne go I,' muttered Izzy under her breath as she slipped, unnoticed, along the dimly lit oak-panelled hallway and out of the club. Maybe she'd stop off at the Chinese on the way home and pick up pork su mai and prawns with pineapple as a treat for Katerina.

But when she let herself into the house forty minutes later, her daughter wasn't there.

How was it possible to be this happy? wondered Katerina, still unable to believe that such a state – and such an all-engulfing state of *rightness* – could truly exist. As they turned into the road which would lead them back to Kingsley Grove, however, some of the pleasure began to dissipate. She leaned closer into the curve of Andrew's arm around her waist, praying that the evening could stretch on into infinity . . .

'I wish there could be more,' said Andrew, seemingly able to read her thoughts.

In reply, Katerina squeezed his arm. 'I don't care, this is enough. At least we have each other.'

'But I *want* more.' Gazing moodily at the rooftops of the opulent Georgian terrace silhouetted against an orange-tinted sky, he considered the irony of so many houses and nowhere to go – nowhere to spend an entire night with Kat.

Now, drawing her slowly into the shadows and leaning back against a high stone wall, he kissed her and said, 'It's not fair on you.' Then, as she opened her mouth to protest, he covered it with his fingers. 'It isn't fair on either of us, but particularly you. This isn't how a beautiful seventeen-year-old girl should be spending her evenings.'

'You don't know what my evenings used to be like. All I ever did was study. You wouldn't believe how *important* I thought it was! I just didn't realise there were other things in life that could be more important . . .'

'And you don't realise how important you are to me,' murmured Andrew, 'but this still isn't what you deserve. I'm too old for you, I'm going through a divorce and I'm trapped in a hopeless relationship with a woman who—'

'But that isn't your fault,' Katerina interrupted, before he could mention the baby. She hated to even think of it; in her fantasies Marcy broke down in tears, confessed that Andrew was not, after all, the father, and promptly emigrated to New Zealand.

'What difference does it make?' Andrew frowned into the darkness. 'I'm screwed, financially. All I want to do is whisk you away to an hotel and at the moment I can't even afford to do that.'

Katerina was privately relieved. Despite everything she felt for Andrew, her conscience still troubled her; as long as they weren't sleeping together, she was able to tell herself that she wasn't doing anything *too* terribly wrong. And although she knew she was being silly, she was

also afraid of taking that final step. Being with Andrew . . .
kissing him, spending hours in his arms and acknowledging their mutual desire . . . was one thing, but actually
*doing* it was quite another, and an altogether more
alarming prospect. She wouldn't know what to do. She
could get it all embarrassingly wrong and Andrew might
lose interest in her. The idea was too terrifying even to
contemplate.

'It doesn't matter,' she repeated, smoothing Andrew's
hair away from his forehead and watching his frown lines
magically disappear. If only she could solve their other
problems as easily.

'I love you,' said Andrew, and she shivered. How could
those small words make her *shiver* like this?

'I know,' she said simply, moving back into his arms
and resolutely refusing to think of Gina, Marcy . . . the
unborn child . . . 'I love you, too.'

'But I *love* you,' repeated Vivienne, frustrated beyond belief
by Sam's uncompromising attitude. Flinging herself down
on to the sofa and tossing back her hair, she deliberately
didn't bother to adjust the rising hem of her skirt. She
was wearing a pale grey jersey top which emphasised the
unEnglishness of her tan; only faint shadows beneath her
spectacular eyes betrayed the fact that she had gone far
too long without sleep. 'And there's no need to look at
your watch, either,' she said in despairing tones. 'Jeez,
Sam, you sure know how to make a girl feel welcome.'

It was five o'clock in the morning and he had been
wondering whether Izzy was asleep. If Vivienne hadn't
turned up with her usual miraculous sense of timing . . .

'You should have let me know you were coming over.' Not wanting to sit down, he was pacing the sitting room, drinking black coffee and watching the sun rise over the park.

'You would only have gotten crazy.' Vivienne pouted, wriggling still further down in her seat, and Sam realised how quickly he had readjusted to the English accent; her lazily elongated vowels sounded incredibly put-on. In addition, she had always adored a bit of drama.

'I would have told you that it was a wasted journey.' A full-scale row wasn't what he needed right now; he had a business meeting at nine o'clock and a couple of hours' sleep beforehand would have helped.

'Oh, Sam!' Kicking off her shoes, she drew her feet up beneath her. 'So, what are you going to do, kick me out on to the streets?'

That was really likely. The reason Vivienne found it so hard to believe he was no longer interested in her wasn't a million miles removed from her bank balance. The only daughter of Gerald Bresnick, a genuine Texan oil baron, she could in all probability – if she really wanted to – rent every suite in the Savoy and have change left over for the doorman.

'I'm going to bed,' said Sam quietly. He didn't have time for arguments. 'You can sleep in the spare room, if you're staying.'

'That takes me back,' mused Vivienne, her tone playful. 'You're beginning to sound like my ex-husband.'

Sam, moving towards the door, didn't reply.

'And there I was,' she continued softly, 'thinking that you might be my next husband.'

He turned back to face her. 'Vivienne, it's over. You really shouldn't have come here.'

'Maybe I shouldn't.' She shrugged, apparently unperturbed, then gave him a slow, languorous smile. 'But, on the other hand, maybe I should. My mom always taught me that if a man was worth chasing, he was worth chasing all around the world, so flying over from the States wasn't even that far to come. Besides,' she added with a careless gesture, 'what the hell did I have to lose?'

For the second time, Sam kept his mouth very firmly shut. A mental image of Izzy flashed through his mind . . . notoriously impatient, unreliable, why-stop-at-one-man-when-you-can-have-two Izzy Van Asch, with whom he would so much rather have spent the night. Vivienne might not have had anything to lose, he thought drily, but if her intention had been to come over here and put paid to any romantic attachments he might be in danger of forming, she had certainly won the first round, hands down.

# Chapter 17

It was so hard, struggling to appear cheerful when all you wanted to do was crawl into bed and let the rest of the world carry on without you. And it was harder still, Gina decided sourly, when she had to put up with Izzy indulging in one of her favourite pastimes – getting ready to go out.

Now, as Izzy burst into the sitting room for the third time in fifteen minutes and did an extravagant twirl to show off her red velvet dress – with the red shoes, this time – Gina gave up trying.

'Well?' said Izzy, glossy-mouthed and seeking approval. 'Which looks better, red or black? And are the stockings too much . . .?'

The stockings had red hearts stencilled up the back of them. Izzy, who was booked to sing at a charity ball in Henley, looked like a saloon girl. She also looked, thought Gina, exactly like . . . Izzy.

Irritation, which had been welling up, now spilled over 'Since you ask,' she retorted, 'they're perfectly hideous. But I'm sure you'll wear them anyway.'

Izzy halted in mid-twirl. 'What?'

'You wanted my opinion, I gave it to you.' It was surprisingly satisfying, watching the expression on Izzy's face change and the wide smile fall away. Why did she always have to be so bloody cheerful anyway? 'Although I don't know why you bother, because you never take a blind bit of notice of anything I say,' Gina continued, inwardly amazed at her own daring but at the same time almost exhilarated by it. 'You simply carry on regardless, thinking everything's great and not even stopping to wonder what other people might think of *you*.'

Accustomed as she was to dealing with the occasional heckler when she was working, Izzy was so stunned by this full-frontal attack on her personality that for a moment she couldn't even speak.

'I see,' she said finally, wondering whether Gina might be in the throes of some kind of nervous breakdown. Apart from hogging the bathroom for an hour earlier she couldn't imagine what might have annoyed her enough to trigger such an outburst. 'And what exactly *do* other people think of me?'

'I don't know,' said Gina, her expression truculent. The adrenalin-rush was ebbing away; she had wanted to hurt Izzy and she'd succeeded. Now she felt slightly ashamed of herself.

'No, go on. Tell me.' Izzy's eyes were beginning to glitter. 'I'm interested.'

'You're nearly forty,' Gina said defensively. 'You shouldn't be wearing stuff like that.'

'And?'

Gina shifted uncomfortably in her chair. 'OK. If you must know, I find it embarrassing when my friends ask me what you do for a living and I have to tell them you're a barmaid.'

There, she'd said it. And it was true; apart from anything else, Izzy was too *old* to be a barmaid.

'I see,' said Izzy again. Shock was giving way to anger

now; how *dare* Gina look down her nose at the way she earned enough to pay their rent? Tilting her head to one side, she enquired softly, 'And are you embarrassed when they ask you what you do for a living?'

Bitch, thought Gina, turning red. Pushing back her hair with shaking fingers and beginning to feel out-manoeuvred, she said, 'At least I'm not reduced to working in a bar.'

'Of course you aren't. You're lucky,' Izzy retaliated. Then, out of sheer pride, she added, 'And that isn't my *career*, anyway. I'm a singer.'

'I know you're a singer. Everybody knows you're a *singer*,' blurted out Gina, without even thinking this time. 'You tell the whole bloody world about it and if you really want to know, that's what makes it all so laughable . . . As far as I can gather you've spent your entire life thinking that one day you'll be discovered and turned into some kind of *star* and you don't even realise that there are hundreds of thousands of other people out there who can sing just as well as you. Being able to sing is . . . nothing!'

All her frustration was spilling out now. The frustration of being unloved and always alone while the rest of the world had fun. The frustration of finally falling asleep at one o'clock in the morning, only to be woken again at two by Izzy's key in the front door and the sound of her footsteps on the stairs. The frustration of answering the phone for the past two and a half months and endlessly having to say, 'It's for you . . .'

'Well, thanks,' said Izzy finally. 'So, tell me, how does it feel to be perfect?'

\* \* \*

Wearing her stencilled stockings with defiance, Izzy sang her heart out during her hour-long set at the Davenham Ball, although whether anyone truly appreciated it was another matter. Spirits were sky high and the general noise level incredible. She could have sung hymns and they would have carried on shrieking and dancing regardless.

It was also blisteringly hot and, by the time she left the stage to patchy applause, both her stockings and her pinned-up hair were beginning to droop.

But it wasn't until she saw Sam, waiting for her at the side of the stage, that she realised how thoroughly miserable she really was.

'Oh, hell, I never cry,' she mumbled against his chest, reluctant to move away because then he would see the mascara stains on his clean white shirt. 'I can't think what you're doing here, but I'm awfully glad to see you . . . it's been the most horrible night . . .'

Bread rolls, as is apparently their wont at such functions, were hurtling through the air. Sliding his arm around her waist, Sam guided Izzy through the maze of bottle-strewn tables and gyrating dancers and led her outside.

'I truly never cry,' she repeated in a subdued voice when they at last sat down on a stone bench. Blowing her nose in the handkerchief he'd passed to her, she shook her head and shivered. 'But honestly you wouldn't believe the go Gina had at me this evening . . . and now we'll have to move out and it's such rotten timing, what with Kat's A levels coming up . . .'

'Gina rang me. She told me what happened and asked me to come and find you.'

'What for?' Izzy sniffed. 'Did she think up another dozen or so reasons why I should be ashamed of myself?'

'She's sorry,' he told her firmly. 'She wants you to know that she didn't mean any of it, but she was afraid that if she came here herself you'd refuse to listen to her.'

'She was right.'

'And she was also afraid,' he went on, 'that you wouldn't go back to the house tonight.'

'You mean she was worried in case I crept in, packed my things and made off with her precious Royal Doulton dinner service,' Izzy retaliated, lifting her chin in defiance. 'According to Gina, I'm the laughing stock of London and the Home Counties, and about as socially acceptable as a bed bug.'

'Look, she really is sorry,' said Sam, relieved to see that the tears had stopped. 'And if you were to give her a hard time, nobody would blame you. But it isn't you she's really getting at . . . it's herself.'

'Really?' It was gratifying to know that Gina was consumed with guilt, but Izzy wasn't going to give up that easily. 'She certainly had me fooled.'

'And you aren't the kind of person to hold a grudge,' Sam continued, his voice low and encouraging. 'It isn't your style.'

'Nobody's ever spoken to me like that before,' she countered, 'so how would anyone know what my style is? She *hurt* me, Sam.'

'I know, I know, but she envies you.'

Izzy pulled a face. 'And there I was, just beginning to believe you. Now you've really blown it.'

'You're happy, she's not,' he said simply.

'I'm not happy. I'm a barmaid.'

He gave her a hug. 'You're a singer.'

'But an unsuccessful one, without any future.' Drawing away from him, she shook her head and looked miserable. 'That was what *really* hurt, Sam. Gina was right about that.'

For the first time, Katerina was seriously tempted to tell her mother about Andrew. The way everyone took care of Gina, sheltering her from real life and making endless allowances for her, made her sick. Sharing her wonderful secret with Izzy would make it all that much more bearable.

And although she hadn't planned on falling in love with Andrew Lawrence, in a peculiarly satisfying way it evened the score, which would surely cheer Izzy up . . .

Some sixth sense, however, prevented her from saying the words. Perching on the edge of Izzy's bed, Katerina handed her a mug of coffee instead and said, 'Look, you mustn't even *think* about my exams. She's a complete bitch and I don't care where we live or how soon we move.'

Considering that it was eight-thirty in the morning, Izzy was astonishingly alert. Rumpling her daughter's glossy hair, she grinned. 'We aren't going to move. Gina's apologised and it's all behind us now.'

Katerina pulled a face. 'I can't imagine Gina apologising for anything. What was it like?'

'Oh, very *Little Women*. She cried a bit, grovelled a bit, lied a bit . . . and I was terribly understanding; wounded and subdued, but prepared to forgive her because I'm such a wonderful human being.'

'Yuk. Sounds horrible.'

'It wasn't horrible.' Izzy assumed a saintly expression. 'It was quite spiritually uplifting, as a matter of fact. From now on, I'm sure we're all going to get along wonderfully.'

'Why?' Katerina shot her a suspicious look.

'Because forgiveness is a virtue, my darling.' Then Izzy winked and drained her coffee cup with a flourish. 'And because to make up for being such an old bitch, the old bitch has waived this month's rent!'

# Chapter 18

Doug Steadman was on the phone when Izzy pushed open the door and waded through the piles of junk in his office. Other theatrical agents, she reminded herself with amusement, had plush suites, glittering windows and rows of filing cabinets lined up, military style, against the walls. They had computers, air-conditioning and alarmingly efficient staff capable of working both.

Only Doug, however, could operate out of such Dickensian chaos and manage – somehow – to make a living out of it.

He gave her an abstracted wave, straining the seams of his shirt as he did so, and said, 'Yeah, fine, I'll tell him when he next calls.' The moment he replaced the receiver, it rang again. Izzy, who was familiar with this pattern of events, removed a couple of bulging box files from the only other chair in the office and sat down.

Ten minutes later, Doug finally left the receiver off the hook, took a noisy slurp of Diet Coke from the can teetering on the edge of his desk and mopped his face with a massive handkerchief. Then he grinned and said, 'Hi.'

'I should have worn my dark glasses,' Izzy chided. 'Then you'd have thought I was Cher and unplugged the phone straight away.'

'I would have told you to come back this afternoon.'

He roared with laughter at the idea. 'Her appointment isn't until three-thirty.'

'Dream on, Doug.'

He shrugged, still enjoying his own joke. 'We all have our little fantasies . . . anyway, how did it go last night? Some twenty-first birthday bash in Wimbledon, wasn't it?'

His memory was about as efficient as his filing system. Much as she adored her agent, Izzy often wondered whether her once-in-a-lifetime big break might not have come and gone without her even hearing about it because Doug, overworked and under pressure, had allowed it to slip his mind.

'Davenham Hall,' she reminded him, slipping out of her jacket and pushing up the sleeves of her white shirt. The sun was beating through the dusty windows but if she risked opening them a single draught of air might send five million pieces of paper swirling and Doug's fragile filing system would be destroyed for ever. 'In Henley,' she added as she settled back into her chair. A germ of an idea had begun to unfold and in order to press her point further she gave him a look of gentle reproach.

'Whatever,' said Doug with an airy, unrepentant gesture. Then, glancing sideways at the disconnected phone, he remembered that time was money. Mopping his face once more, he said, 'So, what brings you here, my darling? Not that it isn't always a treat to see you, but . . .'

'A year or so ago you got me a fortnight at an hotel in Berkshire,' said Izzy, leaning forward and propping her elbows on his desk. 'Allerton Towers, I think it was called. And I shared the bill with another client of yours, a blond chap in his twenties who sang and played a guitar. He isn't with you now – he told me he was going back to teaching. Doug, can you remember his name?'

He frowned, thought hard for several seconds, then shook his head. 'Can't say I do, sweetie. Can you give me any more clues?'

Izzy hadn't seriously expected him to remember. Doug's memory banks were notoriously selective; when he no longer needed to remember something, he didn't. But by trekking into his Soho office she had hoped to bully him into ploughing through a few box files in search of an answer.

'No,' she said helplessly, 'but I really need to contact him. His name's Billy or Bobby . . . something like that . . . and he was living in Willesden at the time. You must have some kind of Cardex,' she went on. 'If you could give me a list of all your ex-clients I'm sure I'd recognise his name as soon as I saw it.'

She needed to find that name – it was why she had come here, after all – but the fact that Doug was shifting uncomfortably in his seat – if he possessed such a list he clearly had no idea where to lay his hands on it – seemed at this moment to be almost propitious.

'You don't have a list,' she declared flatly.

'I do, I do,' Doug protested. 'Somewhere . . .'

'You need a personal organiser.'

He frowned. 'You mean a Filofax? Izzy, spare me that!'

'I mean the walking-talking-filing-hardworking-*organising* kind of personal organiser,' announced Izzy triumphantly. 'And I know just the person for the job.'

By this time Doug was looking plainly horrified. '*You?*'

'Don't be silly,' she replied with tolerant amusement. 'I said organised, didn't I?'

The last thing in the world Gina wanted to do was work for Douglas Steadman, but after the events of the last couple of days she didn't have the courage to say no. She had behaved abominably and this was her penance, she told herself as she adjusted the shoulders of her neat navy-blue suit and checked the line of the skirt in her wardrobe mirror. Besides, it might not be too awful; all she had to do, according to Izzy, was pull a filing system into some sort of order, answer the telephone and set up appointments. She would be a clerk-cum-receptionist and at least it meant that while she was sitting at her desk she would be meeting new people and taking the first steps towards building a new life for herself . . .

Izzy was lying full-length across the sofa when Gina returned home less than two hours later. Stuffing the envelope upon which she had been scribbling into her shirt pocket, she sat up and said bleakly, 'You've walked out.'

'That place is a pigsty,' Gina retaliated, standing her ground and daring her to deny it. 'Why didn't you tell me?'

'You wouldn't have taken the job. And now you're giving up, simply because it isn't *Homes and Gardens* enough for you.' Then, with a trace of irritation, she added, 'And what on earth are you planning to do with that?'

Having dumped her bag on a chair, Gina was now painstakingly removing the price sticker from a large aerosol spray of anti-perspirant for men.

'Who says I'm giving up?' she countered, dropping the aerosol back into her bag and moving towards the door. 'I came home to change into something more suitable. That place needs a damn good clean.'

'With deodorant?' said Izzy faintly, and for the first time in weeks Gina broke into a real smile.

'That's for Douglas Steadman,' she replied, her tone brisk. 'You told me he was a nice man, and he is. But Izzy, somebody has to *do* something about him. He *smells*.'

Doug Steadman might not have known what had hit him – or his poor office – in the days that followed, but for Gina they were some of the most satisfying of her life. Much to her own amazement she was really enjoying herself and the sheer pleasure of transforming unkempt, dusty chaos into pristine order brought a glow to her cheeks that had been absent for months. She was achieving something, doing something worthwhile . . . and the fact that the task was such an enormous one only made tackling it that much more fun.

With the files stacked in tea chests and Doug – together with his precious phone – relegated to the broad corridor outside the office, Gina scrubbed and scraped at every last disgusting corner, threw out the ancient tattered rugs on the floor, polished the floorboards, cleaned the windows until they glittered and washed down the nicotine-stained walls. Then, just as he breathed a sigh of relief – it was over; he could move back in – she reappeared with three enormous cans of vinyl emulsion and proceeded to paint everything white.

Apart from the ceiling, which she had decided should be primrose yellow.

'My God,' Izzy gasped, when she saw it for the first time a week later. 'Where's the plaque?'

'What plaque?' said Gina, looking worried. If she'd thrown away some irreplaceable award . . .

'The one Princess Anne's going to unveil!' Izzy stuck her arm through Doug's – so much nicer to be near, nowadays – and gazed around the office, whistling approval. Shamed into action by Gina's untiring efforts, Doug had allowed himself to be trundled down to John Lewis and had miraculously forked out for yellow vertical blinds, brass spotlights and a charcoal-grey desk whose price had left him gasping but which Gina assured him was perfect. Even the theatrical posters were now neatly framed, Izzy noted, instead of being taped up, yellowing and curly-edged, on the walls.

And the office wasn't the only thing to have changed, she thought, pleased with herself for having engineered the situation so brilliantly. The transformation of Gina, if anything, was even more startling; whoever could have imagined that she would enjoy getting so dirty, and that she could *smile* like that . . .?

'It's nice, isn't it?' Gina was saying now, her eyes alight with pride and her hair still paint-streaked. 'It looks like a real office. Of course the filing system still needs to be organised, but if I start on it right away I should be able to get it sorted out by Friday.'

The files were still dumped in their tea chests, but the cabinets, dust free and gleaming, stood empty and at the ready. Having listened to Doug and got the gist of what would be necessary, she had already decided how the system should be run. And at least they were agreed on one thing: no computer. Indexes and cross-referencing she could handle, but programs and floppy discs were way out of both their leagues.

'It's great, really great,' said Izzy, gazing longingly at the tea chests. 'And as soon as this lot's organised you'll be able to tell me the name of that chap who played the guitar at Allerton Towers.'

Gina looked surprised. 'Allerton Towers? Andrew and I went there quite regularly last year . . . we had friends in Berkshire.' She frowned for a moment, concentrating hard, then her face cleared. 'You aren't by any chance talking about Benny Dunaway, are you?'

# Chapter 19

It was egg-and-chicken time, Izzy decided a couple of days later. Gina was out at work, Kat was at school and she had the sun-drenched patio all to herself. In three hours' time she would be seeing Benny – still living in Willesden and now working as a maths teacher at a local comprehensive – and he would be able to tell her which came first, but overcome with shame at her own ignorance she was desperate to have something . . . anything . . . to show him, to prove that she was serious.

And all she had so far, she thought, were untidy, scribbled-on scraps of paper which looked more than anything else like a harassed housewife's shopping lists.

Gloomily surveying them now, she realised that if he were to mark her out of ten she'd be lucky to get one and a half. These were the motley sum of her ideas so far and they looked – even to her own eyes, let alone those of a mathematician – pathetic.

Deciding that she could at least make them *look* more impressive – Presentation is Important, as her old English teacher had been so fond of chanting, particularly when Izzy's work had been under scrutiny – she shuffled the scraps of paper together and jumped to her feet. Katerina, to whom perfect presentation came naturally, possessed A4 refill pads, rulers, felt-tipped pens and highlighters galore . . .

* * *

Not wanting to disrupt any work in progress, Izzy first helped herself to a selection of coloured pens, a ruler and a startlingly pink highlighter, then sifted carefully through the A4 pads in search of a decent-sized batch of unused paper. Most of the papers were filled with incomprehensible essays, neatly executed diagrams and equations. My clever daughter, she thought with renewed pride, turning over another page and catching a loose sheet of folded, unlined paper as it slid out into her lap.

Idly unfolding it, Izzy began to read.

Ten minutes later, having read the contents of the page three more times and given them a great deal of thought, she rose slowly to her feet, folded the single sheet of paper into quarters and slipped it into the pocket of her jeans.

'Izzy, it's great to see you!' Benny Dunaway, standing in the doorway of his Victorian terraced house, opened his arms wide and gave her a big kiss. Izzy, briefly ashamed of the fact that she hadn't even been able to remember the name of this genuinely nice man, hugged him in return and allowed him to lead her inside.

'That'll give the neighbours something to gossip about,' he told her cheerfully. 'Now that I'm a staid schoolmaster I don't get much opportunity to kiss gorgeous women . . . apart from my wife, of course,' he added with an unrepentant grin. 'Now, come into the kitchen and tell me what you've been up to. What would you like, tea, coffee or a beer? No, sit in this chair, that one's got a wonky leg . . .'

It was all very well for those who didn't mind taking

the risks, he explained over coffee, but when the baby had come along – ten months ago, at eight and a half pounds and with a shock of white-blonde hair that made her look like a dandelion puff – he had been forced to face up to his responsibilities. Teaching might not be as much fun as singing, but he was good at it, it paid the mortgage and the family wouldn't starve. Every now and again he was able to take his guitar down to the local pub and let off a little gentle steam, and in his spare time he still indulged in the odd bit of song-writing . . .

'And this, of course, is where you come in,' he said, refilling her coffee cup before settling back down in his chair and lighting a cigarette. 'So, come on, tell me exactly what kind of help it is you need.'

'You must think I have a terrible nerve,' said Izzy, 'contacting you out of the blue. I'm still singing but I'm not . . . getting anywhere. And I'm not rich,' she added with a brief smile. 'Benny, if I'm ever going to achieve anything, I have to learn how to *write* songs, and I haven't the least idea how to go about it. Is it something anyone can do? Which comes first, the melody or the lyrics? And is it possible to teach a complete nincompoop,' she concluded shamefacedly, 'who's totally . . . musically . . . illiterate?'

Benny threw back his head and roared with laughter. 'You aren't serious . . . you really can't read music?'

'Can't read it, can't write it, can't play any musical instruments,' confessed Izzy. 'I know, I'm nothing but a fraud with a great memory. And if there's any way you think you *can* teach me, I'd better warn you now that I wouldn't even be able to pay you because I'm so broke.' She paused, then gave him a hopeful, beguiling smile.

'But I could promise you years of free babysitting . . .'

Great teacher that he was, Benny enjoyed nothing more than a real, honest-to-goodness challenge. Izzy had a great voice and more enthusiasm than an entire classful of fifth formers . . . just sitting opposite him now she positively radiated energy and eagerness to learn.

'I can do songs in my head,' she continued anxiously, terribly afraid that he was on the verge of turning her down. 'I make them up all the time, but I just can't write them down . . . I even sang into a cassette recorder once, but it sounded so silly afterwards . . . I'm sure I *could* do it properly, though, if only I could get the songs *out* . . .'

'In that case, maybe we'd better give it a go. How could I ever forgive myself, after all,' he added drily as Izzy let out a shriek of delight, 'if I missed out on the opportunity of teaching the songwriter of the century?'

'Just call me McCartney.' Izzy, tossing back her tangled curls, gave him her breeziest smile.

'My pleasure,' said Benny, imitating the gesture and running his fingers through his thinning, short blond hair. 'Just call me Mr Twenty Per Cent of the Profits. What *is* twenty per cent of eighty-seven million pounds?'

'You're the maths teacher, I'm the genius songwriter,' Izzy scolded. '*You* work it out.'

If Vivienne Bresnick wasn't embarrassed to open the front door wearing only a small towel, Izzy wasn't going to let it put her off her stride either.

'Hi,' she said, removing her sunglasses and envying the girl her tan. 'Lucky I'm not the man who's come to read the meter.'

'Lucky for who?' countered Vivienne, appraising Izzy in turn. 'You might have been gorgeous.' Then she paused and burst out laughing. 'No offence intended. What I meant was, you might have been a gorgeous man, whereas in fact you're Izzy Van Asch. Am I right?'

'Brilliant.' Izzy was impressed, both by the accuracy of the guess and the fact that the girl appeared to have a sense of humour, which was something she hadn't expected. 'I know who you are too.'

'Great, so now we don't need to bother with all those boring introductions. Nice to meet you, anyway,' said Vivienne, stepping back and waving Izzy into the apartment. 'Sam isn't here, he had to go to some meeting, but he should be back soon. Can I get you a drink while you're waiting?'

'Just coffee, thanks.' Izzy's admiration increased further when she saw the state of the sitting room. Evidence of female occupation – in the form of stray shoes, a discarded négligé, scattered glossy magazines and a variety of earrings and cosmetics littering the mantelpiece beneath the mirror – abounded. The girl was untidy, and defiantly so. It must, she thought with the kind of comradely cheerfulness which could only come from a fellow sufferer, be driving Sam wild.

'I know, I know.' Vivienne, observing the look on her face, gave an unrepentant smile. 'The place is kind of a mess. I don't understand how it happens . . .'

'It's the same with me,' Izzy told her reassuringly. 'My daughter says I have a primaeval need to mark out my territory.' Then, in case Vivienne thought it was some kind of sly dig, said, 'So, how did you know I was me?'

The kettle was taking its time. Picking up the ivory satin négligé and pulling it on, Vivienne allowed the towel to slide to the floor and stepped away from it. Then, tilting her head to one side and considering Izzy for a thoughtful second, she replied, 'Sam told me. An upfront lady with crazy hair, he said . . . or words to that effect. You have a neat daughter, no money and a pretty good singing voice, right?'

'Right,' said Izzy with a grin. It seemed a fair enough resumé, after all. 'Except that I'd have preferred "great" for the voice. And my daughter,' she added as an afterthought, 'isn't just neat. She's brilliant.'

'I can't sing for toffee,' said Vivienne comfortably. 'Go on, it's your turn now. What did Sam say about me?'

'Rich. Blonde. And rich.' Izzy burst out laughing. Was this really her rival in love? 'I can't think what's wrong with him . . . I'd marry you tomorrow!'

Having finally remembered to make the coffee, Vivienne handed her one of the cups and dropped gracefully on to the sofa. 'Something he didn't tell me . . . excuse me if this is a rude question . . . were you and he having a fling when I turned up? Did I put a kind of spoke in the old wheel?'

'No,' Izzy replied truthfully, to the first part of the question.

Vivienne nodded. 'Well, good. That makes things less complicated, I guess.' Then she shrugged and grinned. 'It's just that something else Sam didn't mention was how pretty you are.'

A compliment for a compliment, thought Izzy. She sipped her coffee and said slowly, 'Well, I saw you on the night you turned up at The Steps. And I can't tell you how much I admired your . . . luggage.'

You couldn't help warming to the kind of girl, Izzy decided fifteen minutes later, who, when she heard Sam's key turning in the front door, appeared to notice for the first time the damp towel crumpled in a heap in the centre of the carpet and who, instead of picking it up, kicked it vaguely in the direction of the coffee table. Much to her own surprise she found herself liking Vivienne more and more. She was also mightily intrigued to see the two of them together. Whatever Sam might have said that night at The Steps, Izzy found it hard to believe that he could be sharing his apartment with Vivienne and not sleeping with her.

'Look, darling . . . Izzy's here,' announced Vivienne delightedly, and Izzy had to force herself not to fluff up her hair because the last time she'd seen him she'd been looking diabolical and she didn't want him to think she was turning into a frump. Quite suddenly, next to Vivienne, she felt small, dark and decidedly insignificant. How, after all, could jeans and a floppy black sweatshirt compare with ivory satin, miles of deeply tanned leg and a staggering amount of cleavage?

Sam's expression, however, gave absolutely nothing away. The habitual lazy grin, when it appeared a second later, was unchanged. Izzy wondered if he was ever really taken by surprise.

'We've been getting along just fine,' Vivienne continued, her Texan drawl deepening as she stretched like a cat and patted the seat next to her. Then, with a wink in Izzy's direction, she added, 'Talking all about you.'

'No, we weren't,' put in Izzy hastily. Beaming at Sam, who hadn't taken up Vivienne's unspoken offer – he was leaning against the window-sill instead – she said, 'As a matter of fact we were talking about someone far more interesting. Me.'

'Far more interesting, of course,' he agreed, attempting to keep a straight face.

'Of course,' she echoed, unperturbed. This was, after all, why she had come here. 'I was just telling Vivienne, I'm going to write songs. This brilliant friend of mine is going to help me . . . before you know it we'll be out-Garfunkeling Simon and Garfunkel . . .'

'The last time Izzy got this excited about something,' Sam informed Vivienne drily, 'it was peanut-butter ice-cream.'

'This time I'm serious,' she insisted with pride.

'But you said you can't read music.'

'Ah, but Benny can. I have all the ideas,' Izzy explained, tapping her forehead, 'and he has the know-how. It was what Gina said the other night that made me realise. I had to *do* something . . . and now it's going to happen!'

'And you never thought of doing this before?' enquired Vivienne looking genuinely puzzled.

'I didn't think it was physically possible,' Izzy confessed. 'What with me not being able to play any kind of musical instrument, I suppose I just thought it was one of those things which can't happen, like waking up in the morning and suddenly being able to speak Russian, or looking in the mirror and realizing that your eyes have turned green.'

Vivienne burst out laughing. 'Honey, all you had to do was ask. I would have lent you my tinted contacts.'

# Chapter 20

It was certainly an odd situation to find oneself in, Izzy mused as she got herself ready for work that evening. Until this afternoon, Vivienne Bresnick had been nothing more than an untimely intrusion. Now, having met her, she found herself liking the girl immeasurably and almost wishing her and Sam well. They were such a striking couple . . . in many ways so perfectly matched . . . that it was impossible to imagine them not being happy together.

As far as Izzy herself was concerned, she didn't know whether it was sad or funny. And even more frustrating was the fact that she *still* didn't know whether or not Sam and Vivienne were once again sleeping together.

Putting the finishing touches to her mascara, then stepping back and idly wondering how she'd look with long, white-blonde hair and Bahama-blue eyes, Izzy said aloud for the second time in twenty minutes, 'She really is a nice person, you know.'

Gina, who was kneeling on the sitting-room floor sifting through a carton of tattered files, glanced up at Izzy's reflection in the mirror.

'Of course she is,' she replied evenly. 'She's Sam's girlfriend, isn't she? Whyever would he want to waste his time with some brainless bimbo?'

Izzy shrugged. 'Men have no taste; it's a common failing.' She considered holding up Andrew as a case in point, then decided against it. Since starting work at the agency, Gina had seemed so much happier. If the old wounds were beginning to heal, she wasn't going to be the one to reopen them.

'Not Sam,' replied Gina flatly, leaning back on her heels and flexing her aching shoulders. Really, she sometimes wondered whether Doug even knew the meaning of the words 'alphabetical order'. Given this box, a chimpanzee could have produced more organised chaos. 'But aren't you glad that *you* didn't get involved with him?' she continued in cheerful tones. 'You can see now that it would never have worked . . . you aren't Sam's type at all.'

Katerina was working in her room, attempting to con-certina a week's homework into one evening and trying to banish all thoughts of Andrew from her mind while she concentrated instead on the less exciting prospect of her forthcoming exams. Love and essays didn't go together – she knew it, but she didn't care – and, although she was shamefully behind with her revision, she couldn't even summon up the energy to panic.

It was almost one o'clock in the morning when she heard Izzy letting herself into the house. Clipping her felt-tipped pen to the top of her writing pad, Katerina wriggled into a sitting position and hoped her mother would arrive bearing prawn crackers.

'Hi, sweetie.' Pushing open the door to her daughter's bedroom, Izzy wondered whether it was possible physic-ally to burst with pride. How could a seventeen-year-old girl – the miraculous product of her own disorganised and undeserving body – be so beautiful, so brilliant . . . and so good?

Katerina, surrounded by books, grinned back at her. Izzy was indeed carrying a haversack-sized bag from the Chinese takeaway. 'How was work?'

'The pits, but what's new?' Collapsing on the bed and heaving an extravagant sigh, Izzy helped herself to a handful of Liquorice Allsorts. She enjoyed their night-time chats, when it seemed that the rest of the world was asleep. 'But I don't care. I know you think I'm doing my usual pie-in-the-sky thing, but I really do have a gut feeling about this song-writing business. And just think, if that took off . . .'

If seventeen years of being her mother's daughter had taught Katerina anything, it was never even to attempt to quash her eternal optimism. They had survived everything, and that in itself was an achievement of which to be proud. Leaning forwards, she gave Izzy an affectionate kiss. 'If anybody can do it, you can.'

'With Benny to help me,' Izzy admitted. 'Sam thinks I'm quite mad; he said it would be like instructing a blind man to paint a masterpiece.'

Katerina nodded; the observation was somewhat apt. 'But even if you can't write music,' she protested, 'you can do the lyrics. Look at Tom Rice . . . he's made an absolute fortune!'

Izzy laughed. 'Tim Rice, darling. But yes, lyrics are important.' Here was the perfect opening, she thought with some relief. 'As a matter of fact, I—'

'Mum, if that pub's so terrible, why don't you leave?' Katerina interrupted. She had been giving the matter some thought recently, and the solution was so obvious she couldn't understand why Izzy hadn't thought of it herself. 'Why don't you ask Sam if you can work at The Steps? The tips would be better, the pay couldn't possibly be any worse and at least it isn't a dive. It's the very opposite of a dive,' she added persuasively, recalling an item in last week's *Daily Mail*. 'And if it's good enough for royalty . . .'

Izzy shifted uncomfortably on the edge of the bed. Picking idly at the remains of the Liquorice Allsorts, she said, 'I've already asked him. He said he didn't have any vacancies.'

On behalf of her mother, Katerina was outraged. 'The pig! So what does that mean, translated into English?'

'He doesn't want me there.' It had bothered Izzy, which was why she hadn't mentioned it at the time, but she wasn't going to let Kat pry into the possible whys and wherefores. In her more optimistic moments she had managed to convince herself that company policy decreed no mixing of business with pleasure. And if it wasn't that, it meant he simply knew her too well, which didn't exactly boost a girl's confidence.

Besides, she had more important matters to discuss with her daughter. 'Kat,' she began. 'I've got something to—'

'The big shit!' Katerina exploded, her brown eyes flashing with indignation. 'Who *does* he think he is?'

'It doesn't matter,' said Izzy, more sharply than she had intended. 'Kat, working in a night-club – even The Steps – isn't my ultimate fantasy. Now stop interrupting, because I'm trying to tell you something.'

'Sorry,' said Katerina, immediately contrite. Folding her arms and leaning back against her plumped pillows, she assumed a listening expression.

'And this is important,' Izzy told her seriously, 'because you know I would never deliberately pry into your personal . . . things.'

If Katerina had been a thermometer, her mercury level would at that moment have plummeted. Quite simply, she froze.

'This morning,' her mother continued, apparently oblivious to the effect her words were having, 'I needed some writing paper and I knew you'd have some, up here.'

'Yes,' replied Katerina in guarded tones. So this was it. Unable – for obvious reasons – to send her letters through the post, Andrew had taken to handing them to her as they parted, so that when she returned to the house she could read them, over and over again, in the privacy of her own room, and know that his feelings for her were genuine.

And whereas every other mother in the world would react with shock and revulsion to the discovery of such letters, she realised with rising panic her own mother was about to behave with typically Izzyish non-conformity. She was going to be *understanding*, and indulge in one of those embarrassing woman-to-woman discussions of hers which no daughter should ever be asked to endure. Besides, she thought as resentment mingled with panic, those letters were addressed to her, and she had taken the utmost care to hide them among the pages of her physics homework, where no sane mother would ever think to look. They were *private*.

'I found this,' Izzy continued, reaching into her bag and pulling out a folded sheet of paper.

'Mum, it's none of your business,' said Katerina, prepared to fight.

'I know, of course I know that,' her mother replied, her tone unrepentant. 'But now that I've read it, it is.'

She was unfolding the letter now. Realizing that she was planning to read it aloud, Katerina experienced a rush of fear. First the humiliation, then the interrogation, she thought wildly. And there was absolutely no way of telling what else Izzy might do. She wouldn't put anything past her.

'This isn't fair,' she pleaded, unable to even contemplate the horrific possibilities. If Izzy were to tell Gina . . . 'It's private, and I don't want to discuss it, so why don't you just give me that' – jack-knifing forwards, she attempted to snatch the letter back, but Izzy whisked it out of reach – 'and forget you ever saw it.'

'Young love!' exclaimed Izzy, her dark eyes alight with amusement. 'Really, darling, I'm not so ancient that I can't remember how it feels . . . but this is nothing to be ashamed of.' Tapping the page with her forefinger, she continued triumphantly, 'It's brilliant! Better still, it *works*.'

'Works,' Katerina echoed, falling back against her pillows. That was it; she gave up. Closing her eyes for a second, then slowly reopening them, she said wearily, 'Mother, what on earth are you talking about?'

Izzy said, reading aloud:

'Never, never
Understood how
The rest of the world
Felt, until now.
Was I ever, ever
Alive before now?
You showed me how
It could be.
Lucky me, lucky world,
I'm a woman, not a girl.
You taught me how
To love. And now,
As long as I have you,
You'll always, always
Have me.'

Izzy stopped reading. Katerina, so geared up for the confrontation that she almost shouted, 'But that isn't what we were talking about,' had to exert actual physical control in order not to.

Her secret was safe, after all. She had been reprieved and as the realization sank in, she knew that it had indeed been a lucky escape because never in a million years would Izzy have taken the news of her involvement with Andrew as lightly as she had – for those few bizarre moments – imagined. Not even Izzy, thought Katerina wryly, was that liberal.

'It's a poem,' she said, sagging still further into her cocoon of pillows, but disguising her relief with truculence. 'And it's totally crappy. You shouldn't have read it.'

'It isn't totally crappy,' Izzy contradicted her. 'Admittedly, I don't think Wordsworth need lose too much sleep over it . . .' She paused, then squeezed her daughter's cold hand. 'But that's what I was trying to tell you, darling. When I read it, it *wasn't* a poem . . . it was a song! I heard the music . . . I knew exactly how it would sound . . . powerful and haunting, happy and sad at the same time . . . it's the kind of song people remember for the rest of their *lives*.'

Despite herself, Katerina smiled. 'Mother,' she said tolerantly, 'you're mad.'

'No, I'm not,' Izzy insisted. 'I'm right!'

'Quite mad.'

Izzy waved the sheet of paper. 'But will you let me give it a go? Can I at least *try*?'

In a few days, thought Katerina, her mother would have forgotten all about it. Her enthusiasms, wildly embraced, seldom lasted. This one would be lucky if it survived the week.

'Of course you can use it,' she conceded, 'if you really want to.'

'You're an angel,' declared Izzy, enveloping her in a hug. 'And just think,' she added with an air of triumph, 'this could really be the start of something big . . . fame, fortune and toyboys coming out of our ears . . .'

'I'm too old for toyboys,' protested Katerina.

'They're for me, silly.' Izzy gave her a pitying look, then broke into a grin. 'You don't need them – you've already found the love of *your* life. And speaking of love,' she continued, lowering her voice to a conspiratorial whisper, 'what did he say when he read the poem? What did Simon think of it?'

Reminding herself that at least she wasn't telling a lie, Katerina returned her mother's gaze with equanimity. 'Nothing,' she replied, her voice calm. 'I didn't give it to him.'

# Chapter 21

The doctor had been quite definite, although Marcy still didn't understand how it possibly could be true. Now, back at the flat, she gazed at her naked reflection in the mirror, running a trembling, experimental hand over the rounded swell of her stomach. However could she *not* be pregnant, looking like this?

But . . . a phantom pregnancy, he had told her. A non-existent baby. God, nature was weird, thought Marcy, not knowing whether to laugh or to cry at the bizarre trick that her own body had played on her. And not only a bizarre trick; a particularly cruel one as well. Having longed for a baby so desperately that at times it seemed as if she were incapable of even *thinking* about anything else, the realization that she was finally pregnant had been one of the most wonderful discoveries of her life. She had felt complete . . . replete . . . and so happy it was positively sinful.

She had guessed, of course, that Andrew's own initial reaction had been less enthusiastic. The professed delight had been tempered with unease, maybe even a trace of alarm, but that was only to be expected under the circumstances. Consequently, she had put no immediate pressure upon him, merely revelling in her own private joy, allowing him to come to terms with the idea in his own time and only mentioning in passing that maybe this was the excuse he had been waiting for – the perfect opportunity – to leave his unhappy marriage.

And gradually, as she had known would happen, he *had* come to terms with the idea. The pull of impending fatherhood was strong; Andrew had realised that this, after all, was what was important, what was *needed* in order to complete their lives, and her own happiness had in turn become absolute. It was all so perfect . . .

And it had all been a lie, because there was no baby. Even the cravings for salt-and-vinegar crisps and spaghetti *alle vongole* had been nothing more than an inexplicable illusion.

Pulling on her dressing gown, covering her traitorous body, Marcy turned away from the mirror and experienced the first pangs of fear. It wasn't her fault. She hadn't done it on purpose. But would Andrew believe that?

Telling him that she was on the Pill had been only the first lie. The second, that the home pregnancy testing kit had proved positive, wasn't going to be so easy to explain away.

Yet she truly hadn't meant to deceive him. It had just seemed so unnecessary under the circumstances, and upon discovering that such silly little kits cost almost ten pounds she had reeled away from the chemist's counter in shock and spent the money instead on the latest Jackie Collins novel and a tub of Häagen Dazs chocolate ice-cream.

Now she fervently wished she hadn't, but the chilling question remained: what was Andrew going to say when he found out?

She didn't have long to wait. Unusually – and because, unknown to Marcy, Katerina had been unable to meet him straight from the office as she usually did – he was home by five-thirty. And this time she was painfully aware of his look of irritation when he glanced around and saw that, yet again, she hadn't tidied the small flat.

'Darling,' she said, going up to him and giving him a kiss. It would have landed on his mouth if he hadn't turned his head at the last moment, leaving her only his pale, aftershaved cheek. 'You're early.'

'Would it have made any difference?' he countered, gesturing towards the coffee table littered with magazines and teacups. He was early, hungry and tired, and still Marcy was incapable of making any effort. That, combined with the fact of not being able to be soothed by Katerina, fuelled his annoyance. In her panicky state, it also made Marcy only more hyper-aware of the precarious state of her own situation.

'I'll make us something to eat,' she said, at the same time wondering what on earth she might possibly conjure up. All she knew for sure was that there was enough maple-and-walnut-flavoured Angel Delight to feed an entire school, an awful lot of crisps and maybe some malt loaf that was only slightly mouldy. 'Sweetheart, you look worn out. Why don't you sit down and relax?'

'I have to go out again, later.' Andrew's gaze was fixed on the television screen as he spoke. Katerina had said she might be able to meet him at nine. 'A party of Dutch clients are staying overnight; they've invited me to join them at some restaurant in Belgravia.'

'In that case, you'd better not eat now,' said Marcy,

overcome with relief. It also meant she would be able to watch her favourite soap in peace.

Andrew nodded, his mind elsewhere. Then, as if remembering his duty, he said, 'So, what have you been doing today?'

The icy grip of fear churned in Marcy's stomach. Instinctively, she rested her hand upon the fraudulent bump. 'I went to see my doctor.'

Now she had Andrew's attention. He sat forward, his grey eyes searching her face. 'What did he say? Is anything wrong?'

She loved him. He had left his wife for her. And it wasn't her fault that nature should have chosen to play such a vile trick on her.

Crossing her fingers beneath the folds of her dressing gown, Marcy smiled and shook her head. Like Scarlett, she would think about it tomorrow. 'Nothing's wrong,' she said, her tone gently reassuring. 'I'm fine, darling. We're both *fine*.'

Recognizing the back view of the person ahead of him, Sam braked and slowed his car to a crawl, admiring as he did so the allure of such very good legs and such a perfect bottom. What this particular person was doing being carted along the pavement by a sandy-blond Great Dane he couldn't imagine, but they certainly made a striking pair . . .

'Hi,' he said, when he had pulled alongside her. The dog, tail wagging, immediately bounded up to the open window and sniffed with interest.

With a pointed glance at the heavy chain around its

neck, Sam shook the proffered paw and said solemnly, 'You must be Izzy's latest boyfriend.'

'Very witty,' said Izzy with a half-smile. 'Where were you when we needed you, anyway? Jericho didn't want to take the tube, which means we've had to walk *all* the way from Hampstead.'

Jericho, whose dark brown eyes were even larger than Izzy's, barked in happy agreement and attempted to lick Sam's face.

'And now you're almost home,' he remarked, pushing the dog away while he still had some aftershave left. 'Of course, I *would* offer you a lift, but . . .'

'You forgot to bring the juggernaut,' supplied Izzy, holding up her free hand. 'It's OK, we're getting used to it. The cab drivers we tried to flag down felt the same way.'

He laughed at the expression on her face. 'So, what's this all about? You've given up song-writing in favour of professional dog-walking? I don't know how to break this to you, sweetheart, but you're going to have to walk twice around the world before this new venture makes you rich.'

'He's ours,' Izzy replied proudly. 'Our new male lodger.' Then she broke into an irrepressible grin. 'But this time we've got ourselves one who's housetrained.'

Sam, whose new washing-machine had broken down, and who had driven round to Kingsley Grove in order to use theirs, had been quietly surprised by the news that Gina had acquired a dog. It wasn't until he saw the expression on her face when Jericho loped into the kitchen that he realised that Izzy had done it again.

'Aaagh!' said Gina, backing away into the corner next to the fridge.

'Woof,' replied Jericho, regarding her with polite interest.

Despite himself, Sam wished he had a camera.

'Whose dog is that?' Gina squeaked, pointing at the intruder with a shaking finger. Whereupon Jericho, ever hopeful of a biscuit, stepped forward and attempted to investigate the outstretched hand before it was snatched away. Disappointed, he snuffled around Gina's slim ankles instead.

'Isn't he gorgeous?' sighed Izzy, blithely unaware of the havoc she was causing. Then, thrusting the end of the chain in Gina's cowering direction, she announced, 'He's yours.'

'No, he isn't!'

'Of course he is; he's a present. A thank-you present,' she added happily, 'because if it hadn't been for you, I never would have realised that I had to be a song-writer if I was ever going to get anywhere. You've changed my life, Gina,' she concluded, her eyes alight with gratitude. 'And I'd been wondering for *days* what to get you . . .'

A husband, thought Gina numbly. And a peaceful, dog-free, Van Asch-less home.

'. . . then I saw this advert in the paper this afternoon and it all fell into place, so I rushed over to Hampstead and snapped him up!'

'He looks as if he wants to snap me up,' Gina said, her voice faint, but Izzy was already down on her knees, fondling the enormous dog's ears with affection and freeing him from his chain.

'He's just hungry, bless him. We both are. Oh look, he's shaking paws again . . . isn't he adorable? And just think,' she added triumphantly, 'of all the advantages of having a dog!'

'Burglars,' said Sam. Izzy was an utter disgrace, but her heart was unarguably in the right place. A dog lover himself, he was incapable of remaining as impartial as he should have been. As long as he had known Gina he had known how much she mistrusted dogs.

'Men!' exclaimed Izzy, so thrilled with her own reasoning that she was unable to keep the discovery to herself. 'You see, that's what's so brilliant! I was reading an article in the same paper about husband-hunting . . . about ways of meeting new men,' she amended rapidly. 'And taking your dog for a walk in the park was top of the list. It's sociable without being obvious, you start off by saying, "Hallo, how are you this morning?" and before you know where you are, the dentist with the golden retriever is inviting you out to dinner. It's a cinch!'

Sam had to admire her style. Helping himself to a can of lager from the fridge, he sat down to enjoy the ensuing argument.

'It's great exercise, as well,' Izzy added as an afterthought, since Gina didn't appear to be as thrilled with her present as she should have been. 'And of course Sam's absolutely right; he'll see off any burglars, not to mention carol singers, in a flash . . .'

'I'm scared of dogs.' Gina spoke through gritted teeth; at this very moment in time Jericho was eyeing her keenly, salivating and presumably anticipating the prospect of her ankles. If Izzy had to give her a dog, why couldn't it at least have been something small and manageable?

'But that's ridiculous,' Izzy declared passionately, still on one knee and with her arms open wide. 'Nobody on earth could possibly be afraid of Jericho! The only reason his previous owners had to let him go was because *he* was scared of their poodle. He needs love and understanding,' she went on, sensing weakness, 'to build up his confidence. And lots and lots of wonderful walks in the park . . .'

It said much for Izzy's powers of persuasion that within the space of two hours she had managed to dispatch Gina and Jericho, albeit with some reluctance, to the nearby park, with instructions to take a turn around the pond and enjoy the last of the sun.

Sam, however, was doubly impressed by Izzy's subsequent dash to the phone and her heartfelt pleas with not one but three dog-owning male friends. If they would just do her the biggest favour in the world, take their animals for a quick zip around the pond on the east side of Kensington Gardens and say something friendly in passing to the nervous blonde with the Great Dane, she would be for ever in their debt . . .

The real miracle, of course, was that they agreed to do so. But if Izzy possessed anything in abundance, Sam reminded himself, it was charm. Besides, she also had some extremely weird friends.

'Your washing's done,' she observed, as the machine finally subsided into exhausted silence forty minutes later.

'And you're trying to change the subject.' Clean shirts were only half the reason for his visit. Stranger even than Izzy's friends had been the urge . . . almost a physical *need*

. . . to see her again. He might still be saddled with his own unwanted house guest, but Sam hadn't forgotten that evening in his office, whereas as far as Izzy was concerned it might never have happened. They were back to square one, he thought, and her apparent amnesia for the event was becoming, as far as *he* was concerned, bloody irritating.

'I'm worried about that red shirt,' said Izzy, who hadn't forgotten at all. Before, biding her time and enjoying the interplay between them had been fun. Now, however, the situation had changed. Knowing and liking Vivienne had put a real dampener on things, and she had decided to keep her distance until the situation resolved itself. It wouldn't do any harm, she had told herself, and in the mean time she could concentrate her attention on her work.

Now, slightly flustered, she repeated, 'Your red shirt. It might have run.'

Sam simply looked at her and said nothing.

'Oh, shit,' said Izzy, with feeling. For something to do, she yanked open the door of the washing-machine and began pulling out damp clothes. 'Look, whether you wanted it to happen or not, the fact remains that Vivienne is living with you in your flat.'

'Staying,' he corrected her. 'Not living.'

'Whatever,' she sighed. It was easier to talk when she didn't have to look at him. Serious eye contact, under the circumstances, was decidedly unsettling. 'For once in my life I'm trying to do the honourable thing, so it really isn't fair of you to give me a hard time.'

'It isn't very fair on me, either,' Sam pointed out.

Drumming his fingers against his now empty lager can, he wondered just how much this had to do with the new man she'd told him about, the 'very attractive' man after whom she had lusted so vigorously. He frowned. 'Are you still seeing that guy?'

Izzy, who had forgotten all about her own private joke, assumed he was referring to Benny Dunaway. Still with her back to Sam, she said, 'Of course I am.'

'Of course,' he echoed with a trace of irony. Determined as she was not to come between Vivienne and himself, the question of her own monogamy never even occurred to her. In her eyes, it simply wasn't an issue.

A volley of barks interrupted his train of thought at that moment, which under the circumstances, Sam decided, was just as well. As long as Vivienne remained in his flat and Izzy continued to see her partner-in-lust, there was precious little to either say or do.

The next moment, Jericho clawed open the kitchen door and, recognizing Izzy crouched before the washing-machine, hurled himself at her in a frenzy of delight. Sam's red shirt went flying and landed in the bowl of water which had been set out for Jericho earlier.

'Well?' said Sam. Gina's face was flushed and she was out of breath.

'Well, what?'

'Did he behave himself?' said Izzy brightly, and Gina swung round, looking more startled than ever.

'Who?'

Izzy rolled her eyes in despair. 'Jericho! Are we keeping him or must he go back to face a life of miserable tyranny at the paws of a poodle named Pete?'

'Oh . . . he was very well behaved,' Gina replied, not altogether truthfully. With a quick glance in his direction – he was at this moment burying his nose up the sleeve of the hapless red shirt – she took a gulp of air and attempted to steady her breathing. 'I don't think it would be very fair, sending him back,' she continued with a brief, tentative smile. 'Not now that he's got to know us.'

'Of course it wouldn't.' Izzy smiled back, making a playful grab for the dog's ears. 'Ah, look at him . . . he's tired. But how about you, did *you* enjoy the walk?'

Gina sat down suddenly on one of the kitchen chairs, her eyes brighter than ever. 'As a matter of fact, I did. And I didn't believe you when you said it,' she added, torn between a mixture of embarrassment and pride, 'but you were certainly right about meeting other people walking their dogs. It just seems to . . . well, *happen*.'

'Heavens, how exciting!' Izzy sent up a silent prayer of thanks. She'd been pretty sure of Tom and Luke, but Alastair had said he might not be able to spare the time. 'So, how many men actually spoke to you?'

'Well,' said Gina, blushing prettily. 'As a matter of fact, five.'

# Chapter 22

It wasn't easy, transmitting her definite ideas as to how 'Never, Never' should sound to someone who then had to battle with the logistics of such a scheme and make it workable. Frustration hadn't been the word for it; at times Izzy found herself with her fingers ravelled up in her hair and her voice hoarse with the effort of attempting to imitate the precise tone of a tenor saxophone, while Benny frowned and enquired for the tenth time whether she was absolutely *sure* it should precede the vocals by half a beat. Didn't she think it would be better to synchronise the notes and allow the piano to form the echo effect . . .

But slowly, with much concentration, a few tense moments and many hours of hard work, the miracle began to happen. The song was coming together in a recognisable form and if Izzy had broken a few of the very oldest rules in the book, Benny had demonstrated one of the talents possessed by every great teacher and allowed her to do so. Some of the mistakes had been horrendous. Astonishingly, others had worked, and it was the very unexpectedness of those departures from tradition which helped to create an indefinable sense of magic.

And Izzy, like a child finally mastering the art of riding a bike, didn't want to stop. Having adapted 'Never, Never' from Katerina's poem, she was now bursting with ideas of her own. Lyrics tumbled effortlessly on to the pages of her writing pad and as soon as she saw them she found herself able to hear the accompanying music. Benny had to struggle to keep up, roughing out her ideas before they slipped away. Biting his tongue whenever she made such remarks as, 'This bit's a duet for voice and clarinet,' he allowed Izzy's untutored imagination free rein. And there was indeed a lesson to be learned by musicians everywhere, he discovered later in the evenings when she had left to go to work and he went back over the annotated scores he had scribbled down according to her jumbled instructions. Some of her ideas were downright impossible, while others, though technically feasible, he knew would never work in practice. But some, he had to concede, were astonishingly good. Izzy hadn't been joking when she'd told him she knew she could do it. And a shiver snaked its way down Benny's spine as he realised for the first time that with expert help, the right backing and a lot of luck, she could maybe . . . just maybe . . . be great.

'Boy, am I glad I phoned you,' confided Vivienne, stirring her drink and offering Izzy a cigarette. 'It gets *sooo* boring here, what with Sam doing the rounds and me not knowing a soul. I'm sure the only reason he encourages me to come to The Steps is because he's hoping I'll meet some other guy and leave him in peace.'

'Do you think you will?' Izzy tried not to look too optimistic.

Vivienne laughed. 'Are you kidding? Izzy, we have what the columnists call "a tempestuous relationship" . . . it'll take a lot more than this little fall-out to send me running home to Daddy. I haven't given up on Sam yet, not by a long chalk.'

Oh sheeit, thought Izzy, because a Texan drawl is alarmingly infectious.

'But that isn't to say I can't have a little fun in the mean time,' Vivienne added, her eyes dancing. 'And who knows, once Sam sees me having fun with other people, he might get his act together.'

'I could do with meeting some new people myself,' Izzy mused, recalling the depressing conversation she'd had earlier that day with Benny. 'You wouldn't happen to know any rich record producers, I suppose?'

Vivienne stubbed out her barely smoked cigarette and pulled a face. 'I'm such a selfish bitch – I haven't even asked how you're getting on with this song-writing kick. How's it *going*?'

'Brilliantly,' said Izzy, then she shook her head. 'But writing the songs is the easy part. The next move is taking them into a recording studio and getting a demo tape made up.'

'Hey, that's great . . . so, when does it happen? Could I come and watch?'

Izzy smiled. 'It happens when we can afford to rent out a recording studio. Remember what Sam told you about me: crazy hair, great voice, no cash? Well, hiring a halfway decent studio for even a single day costs twelve hundred pounds, which is more than either Benny or I can raise . . .'

'Oh.' Vivienne looked bewildered; this was something outside her own experience. Then her face brightened. 'Borrow it,' she said promptly. 'From Sam! He'd lend you the money in a flash, and then as soon as you get rich you can pay him back.'

It was a solution which had occurred to Izzy. For a second she reconsidered the idea, then shook her head once more. 'I really can't.'

Vivienne looked perplexed. 'Why not?'

Wriggling uncomfortably in her seat, Izzy said, 'It's hard to explain, but I just know I've got to try and do this on my own. As far as Sam's concerned, I'm a walking disaster, financially. A spendthrift. And, of course, he's absolutely right,' she admitted with a brief smile, 'but I can't help it, it's just the way I am. If I asked him to lend me the money, I'd feel ... uncomfortable.' It wasn't the word she'd been looking for, but it would do. Being in Sam's debt, she felt, would only confirm his opinion of her. And a girl had her pride, after all.

'You mean he'd lecture you?' asked Vivienne, still trying to understand. 'He'd keep asking you when he was going to get his money back? Jeeze, what a bastard! I never thought he was like that.'

'Oh, no,' Izzy said hastily. 'He isn't. He wouldn't say a word about it.' With a gesture of despair, she concluded, 'That's *exactly* what would make it so unbearable.'

'No, please don't,' said Vivienne a moment later, as Izzy reached for her purse and made a move to stand up. 'My treat. I dragged you down here, after all.'

Izzy burst out laughing. 'Don't tell me, I've spun my poor-little-match-girl-story and now you're having a guilt attack. Listen, the nice thing about spendthrifts is they can always afford to buy a round of drinks, so instead of looking at me like that, why don't you tell me what you'd like? Another tequila sunrise?'

But Vivienne, clasping her arm and pulling her back down into her seat, shook her head. 'Hey, Sam brought me here tonight, so the least he can do is keep us fed and watered. And the only reason I suggested him just now was because I thought you two were such great friends. What I'd really like,' she went on, catching the attention of the bar manager and mouthing her request, 'would be to lend you the money you need, myself.'

Izzy's mouth dropped open. Having just declared herself a bad risk it hadn't occurred to her for a moment that Vivienne would make such an offer. 'My God,' she said eventually. 'Do you really mean it?'

'Why wouldn't I mean it?' countered Vivienne cheerfully, as the bar manager materialised with a bottle of Moët and two glasses. 'It's not such a big deal. You can pay me back whenever you like.' She smiled and thanked the bar manager, then winked at Izzy. 'And Sam need never know.'

'This is fantastic,' said Izzy, overwhelmed with gratitude. 'I don't know how to thank you.'

'Hell, what are friends for?' Vivienne laughed and began to pour the champagne into their glasses. Izzy hastily covered hers with her hand.

'I wouldn't want Sam to accuse me of freeloading. I'll stick to orange juice. Really.'

'We're celebrating,' insisted Vivienne, removing her hand and sloshing Moët into the glass. 'Don't let Sam intimidate you, honey. It isn't your style.'

'Oh well, in that case,' said Izzy happily, 'cheers.'

Ten days later, she stood gazing out at the view from the

window of Doug Steadman's office and listened to the sound of her own voice echoing through the room. Behind her, Gina and Doug, Benny and Vivienne were sitting in silence, hearing the finished results of a single nineteen-hour day in the recording studio recommended to them by a friend of Benny's. The demo tape held four tracks and now they were nearing the end. Izzy's voice soared, echoing the haunting, plaintive notes of the tenor saxophone, then dropped to barely a whisper as the final bars of 'Never, Never' approached. A heartbeat of silence, then the rising crescendo heralded by a gently gathering drum roll . . . She had striven for the effect of Juliet's last impassioned words to the absent Romeo . . . the final, powerful line which this time rose high above the sax . . . and it was over.

Awaiting her audience's reaction was worse than any stand-up audition. Unable to turn around, she reached out instead and encountered Jericho's smooth head. His whiskers tickled her wrist. Her fingers were tingling and she felt dizzy . . .

The moment's silence, however, was broken by an ear-splitting whistle of approval rendered as only a true Texan knows how. Vivienne cried jubilantly, 'Izzy, you're a star!' and when Izzy finally turned to face them, it was Gina who led the round of applause. Jericho, realizing that his enforced silence was over, released a volley of joyful howls and sent a coffee cup flying from the desk with his tail. Benny was grinning broadly. Gina, still applauding, said, 'That was fantastic,' over and over again.

But Izzy was waiting for Doug, who had so far said nothing. She had taken the financial gamble and done her very best, but as her agent and as a professional she needed, above all, his approval. Regarding him with mounting nervousness she tried to say, 'Well?' but the word stuck in her throat and all that came out was a laryngitic croak.

But Doug, hauling himself out of his chair and mopping his face with a blue-and-white spotted handkerchief, had no intention of saying anything. Instead, crossing the small office, he came to a halt in front of Izzy and waited a full second before breaking into a smile. Then, reaching up and taking her head in his hands, he gave her a resounding kiss first on one cheek then the other.

Izzy's eyes promptly filled with tears.

'Do you really like them?' she whispered, as he stepped back and held her at arm's length.

'Do I like them?' Doug shook his head, experiencing a rush of almost paternal affection for the confident, wayward girl whom he had known for so many years. Her optimism and energy were boundless; she had never been afraid of anyone or anything in her life. Now, seeing her uncertainty and desperate need for approval, he only loved her all the more.

'You know me' he told her, with a reproving look. 'I *like* Roger Whittaker and Val Doonican. Your songs might not be my personal cup of tea, but even I can tell that they're good. Very good.' He paused, then admitted gruffly, 'I didn't expect them to be, but they are.'

Izzy's cheeks were wet and her mascara was dissolving fast. She sniffed and smiled. 'Don't you like them even a little bit?'

'Stop crying,' Doug ordered. 'Of course I do. When have I ever disliked anything that's going to make me rich?'

# Chapter 23

With her light brown hair swept up in a glossy topknot, her neat little black dress and unaccustomed high heels, Andrew realised that Katerina had worked to make herself look older, and was touched by her efforts. She could easily pass for twenty-one now, which – under the circumstances – was less eyebrow-raising than seventeen. Not that the discrepancy in their ages bothered either of them any longer, but sly glances and unsubtle smirks weren't exactly calming.

Katerina, however, was less inhibited. Arching her own eyebrows in amazement when she heard Andrew give the pretty hotel receptionist their names, she promptly burst out laughing. Even the receptionist had to smile.

'What's the matter?' He looked round, puzzled.

'Mr and Mrs Lawrence,' giggled Katerina. 'You can't put that! We don't have to pretend to be *married*, do we?'

It was so sweet of him to want to observe the proprieties, she thought with a rush of affection. Then, seeing the expression on his face, she tucked her arm through his and gave it a squeeze. 'And there's no need to be embarrassed. People will only guess, anyway, when they see us talking non-stop through dinner. Real married couples don't do that – it's written into their contracts.'

Andrew gave the receptionist an abashed smile and handed Katerina his pen. She signed her name with a flourish. 'There! Who needs to travel incognito, anyway?'

I do, thought Andrew wryly. At least he would be settling the account in cash, even though he could barely afford it. Then again, he wasn't going to run the risk of letting Marcy discover a giveaway Visa slip in his suit pocket . . .

'Shall I ask the porter to take your luggage up to your room?' said the receptionist, grinning at Katerina and wishing that even half her guests could be as honest.

'That's OK.' Katerina winked. 'I wouldn't want him to hurt himself. It really is an incredibly heavy toothbrush, after all.'

She couldn't help wondering whether her hunger pangs were psychological. Did she really want to eat or was she simply playing for time, putting off the moment when there would be just the three of them alone together: Andrew, herself and that great big double bed?

But no, although the devil-may-care bravado might be a front, she was happy to discover as the first course arrived at their table that the hunger was genuine.

'So, where does your mother think you are tonight?' said Andrew, as she demolished the last langoustine with her fingers. Having no appetite himself, he had left his own plate virtually untouched; watching Katerina enjoy her food was pleasure enough.

'Staying with the love of my life.' She grinned with her mouth full. 'Simon, of course, although it's not terribly likely that she'll remember; apparently Mum played her demo tape to Doug this afternoon and he was impressed. By the time I got home from school there was an extremely noisy party going on, so I told them I couldn't possibly study for my exams with that kind of distraction, and that I was going over to Simon's house. They won't miss me,' she concluded airily. 'As I was leaving, Sam's girlfriend was teaching Gina to Charleston and Mum was doing her Bette Midler impression, using a courgette as a microphone. Benny and Jericho were playing the piano . . . rather badly, I must say . . . and Doug was pleading with them to do "Paddy McGinty's Goat" . . .'

It all seemed highly unlikely; Andrew simply couldn't envisage such goings-on in sedate Kingsley Grove. The Neighbourhood Watch must be bristling with disapproval.

'We don't have a piano,' he said finally.

Katerina licked her buttery fingers. '*You* didn't,' she corrected him. '*We* do.'

He couldn't imagine Gina dancing the Charleston, either, despite Katerina's repeated assurances that – slowly but surely – she was loosening up. 'Coming along nicely', was how she described it, and although they had initially struck sparks off each other, their relationship had evidently mellowed in recent weeks. Katerina approved of the fact that Gina had finally 'got off her bum' and started working, while Gina, in turn, appreciated Katerina's culinary abilities, as well as her aptitude for washing-up. Even more strangely, Katerina was quite open to discussion where Gina – his estranged wife – was concerned, whereas any mention of Marcy was met with instantaneous freezing out.

'When do your exams start?' he asked, more out of a desire to change the subject than anything else. As long as he had known Kat, she had been gearing herself up for

A levels, but now she rarely even mentioned them.

The waiter arrived at that moment with their main course, delectably pink lamb cutlets for him and *tournedos Rossini* for Katerina. She shrugged and smiled. 'Nine o'clock tomorrow morning.'

'You're joking!'

'Don't panic.' She seized his hand, just as she had done on that first day in the Victoria and Albert Museum. 'The only reason I didn't tell you was because I didn't want it to spoil our night. When you said you'd booked us into this hotel I was so *happy*. Nothing else matters, only us.'

For a split second, Andrew wondered whether knowing in advance would have been enough to make him cancel the night. Although he loved Katerina desperately, he was still achingly aware of the differences separating them, and he knew how important her exams were to her.

But no, he had to admit that he wouldn't have done so. Their precious time together was even more important to him. And this night of all nights was to be the culmination of such long-awaited yearning . . .

'We'll have to leave here by seven-thirty,' he warned her. The rush-hour traffic from rural Berkshire into central London was diabolical.

'In that case,' said Katerina, her eyes shining and her hand trembling slightly as she raised her glass to his, 'we'd better have a very early night.'

But had there ever been a more nerve-wracking exam than the one she was about to face? In the bedroom, Andrew waited for her. Katerina, gazing at her reflection in the bathroom mirror, reminded herself that as long as a couple truly loved one another, nothing else mattered. She didn't understand why she should be feeling this way. If making love was so natural and . . . wonderful, why did she feel as if she were about to be sick?

She was being stupid, she thought briskly, reaching for her toothbrush and running the cold tap full pelt. What a wimp; seventeen years old and behaving like a child. Since there was absolutely no need to be scared, she wouldn't be. *Nothing* was going to be allowed to spoil the most momentous night of her life . . .

Much later, when Andrew had fallen asleep, Katerina rolled on to her side and gazed at the luminous blue figures of the digital clock beside the bed. One-thirty in the morning, she had done it and it had been OK. Nothing like in the movies, she thought with a wry smile, but then what was? OK was OK, it was at least better than she had been expecting, and it really hadn't lasted long at all, which was an added bonus. She hadn't stuck her big toe in Andrew's ear, giggled at the wrong moment or got herself hopelessly entangled in one of those terrifying positions described in that book of which Izzy had made so much fun.

She hadn't made an idiot of herself, and for that she could only be grateful. Ecstasy might – and hopefully *would* – feature at a later date, but in the mean time it was something she could quite happily live without. At least she hadn't lost her pride.

'Darling,' murmured Andrew, his arm sliding around her slender waist. As he pulled Katerina towards him, he realised that he was becoming aroused once more. 'Are you too tired . . .?'

He was kissing her neck. Wriggling away, terrified he'd forget, she reached under the pillows and drew the small, flat box out from its hiding place.

'This is the last one,' she said, feeling ridiculously like her old schoolteacher doling out coloured felt pens.

'Wrong.' Andrew, who had set the alarm clock for six-thirty, smiled into the darkness. 'There are always three in a packet.'

'Wrong,' replied Katerina, secretly relieved. 'I filled one up with water earlier, and swung it about a bit. Just to make sure they really worked.'

Simon was hovering at the school gates when Andrew's car screeched to a halt at five past nine and Katerina, still wearing last night's little black dress, leapt barefoot out of the passenger door.

'Jesus, Kat! Are you out of your mind?' His voice betrayed his agitation and anger. How she could take such stupid risks was beyond him.

Unable to look at the driver of the car, he averted his eyes as Katerina leaned through the open window and gave Andrew a hasty goodbye kiss.

'No need to panic,' she said briskly, detaching his clammy hand from her arm as Andrew's car disappeared and Simon attempted to drag her through the gates. 'I'm here now, with seven minutes to spare. We've even got time for a quick coffee if we—'

'What!' Simon shouted, his blond hair practically standing on end. She broke into a grin.

'Just my little joke.'

'You're the joke.' He glared at her. 'I can't believe what's happened to you, Kat. Having an affair with a married man isn't clever, it isn't an *intelligent* thing to do . . . and you don't even seem to realise the kind of *risks* you're taking . . .'

Attempting to chivvy him out of his bad mood – which was something she'd never encountered before – Katerina smiled. 'I may not be intelligent, but even I've heard of safe sex,' she riposted. 'Condoms rule, OK?'

But Simon's eyebrows remained ferociously furrowed. 'I'm not talking about those kind of risks.'

'And you don't have the experience to lecture me on any other kind,' declared Katerina flatly as they climbed the steps leading to the main entrance of the school. 'So don't lecture *me*.'

Shaking his head, he said, 'You're making a fool of yourself.'

In reply, she gave him an icy stare. 'And you're becoming incredibly boring.'

Ahead of them at the end of the corridor was the examination room. Standing in the doorway, their physics teacher gestured frantically to them to hurry up and take their seats.

'I'm trying to be your friend,' said Simon in a low voice.

Katerina, feeling slightly ashamed of herself, squeezed his hand. 'I know you are,' she whispered back. 'You're just going about it the wrong way. Oh Simon, I haven't revised for a week. I'm scared. Give me a kiss for luck?'

'No,' he said grimly, recalling the incident at the school gates. 'You've had one of those already.'

# Chapter 24

'There was no need for you to come all the way down here,' Gina protested, when Izzy arrived in the office. Breathless with the effort of hanging on to Jericho's lead as he belted across roads without looking, Izzy collapsed in a heap on to the window-seat and drained a can of Perrier in one go.

'I'm excited,' she said, wiping her mouth and kicking off her sandals. Jericho promptly grabbed one and buried himself beneath Gina's desk. 'Go on, tell me again what they said on the phone.'

'The people at MBT have listened to your tape,' repeated Gina patiently. 'They found it interesting. One of their A&R men will be coming to listen to you tonight at Platform One. His name is Joel McGill and he'll introduce himself after the show.'

Izzy liked the sound of Joel McGill. It was a good name, a good omen, and she had been singing it in her head all the way from Kensington to Soho. She had also been able to picture him in her mind quite clearly; he would be tall and dark with gypsyish eyes, a gorgeous smile and positively *no girlfriend*. And he, in turn, would be dazzled, absolutely *smitten*, by Izzy Van Asch . . .

'Gina,' she said, breaking out of her reverie, 'would you be an angel and lend me a hundred pounds?'

Gina looked startled. 'You're going to bribe him?'

'A new dress,' Izzy begged. 'Oh please, I need some-thing special.'

'But Izzy, you possess an entire wardrobe of special somethings at home. There must be something among your collection you could wear.' Gina, who hadn't allowed herself a single new item of clothing for over a month, shuffled papers and looked disapproving. 'Can't Vivienne lend you the money?'

'I tried her first,' confessed Izzy with disarming honesty. 'She was out.'

Less than two minutes after Izzy, Jericho and Gina's one hundred pounds had collectively departed, the door swung open again. Gina sat up straight and gave the visitor her best receptionist's smile.

'Hi,' said the visitor, smiling back at her in such a way that she almost looked over her shoulder to see if someone more interesting was lurking behind her. 'You're new. And so is this office.' With only a slightly over-the-top double take, he paused to survey the pristine surroundings before returning his gaze to Gina. 'I came to see Doug. Am I in the wrong building?'

She felt the colour rising in her cheeks. Unfortunately, it had a distressing habit of collecting in blotches around her neck, too. Goodness, he was handsome.

'Right building,' she said, almost as breathless as Izzy had been earlier, 'but I'm afraid Doug's out at the moment. Perhaps I can help you?'

'I'm sure you can.' Dropping into the chair opposite her, he pushed his fingers through his hair and gave Gina the benefit of his attention once more, with such perfect thoroughness that her knees, beneath the desk, became boneless.

'I'm Gina Lawrence,' she said, in order to break the silence which didn't appear to bother her visitor in the least. 'I'm . . . I'm Doug's new assistant.'

He nodded, still smiling, then gestured around the office. 'And you did all this?'

This time it was Gina's turn to nod. Her neck, she realised, had gone completely numb.

'Then you are a miracle worker. I can't believe the difference you've made to the old place.'

Gina couldn't believe the difference he was making to *her*. Since Andrew's departure she had been physically incapable of reacting even faintly normally to the attentions of any man. Not that there had been a great deal of opportunity, but the odd friendly word or appreciative glance had left her icily unmoved. She was immune to the opposite sex.

But here, now, long-dormant hormones were unaccountably slithering back to life at a rate of knots . . .

'I'm sorry, how rude of me,' said the visitor, delving in his jacket pocket and pulling out a large, folded envelope. 'You're busy and I'm wasting your time. My name's Ralph Henson and I came here to return a contract. I've read it and signed in the appropriate places. All Doug has to do now is bury it . . . except that there doesn't appear to be anywhere left for him to bury anything.'

Gina, glad of something to do and relieved to discover that her legs still worked, turned back from the D to J filing cabinet with a bulky, charcoal-grey file. 'It all goes in here, from now on.'

Ralph grinned. 'Amazing. More than a miracle.'

'Gosh, ITV,' said Gina, gazing at the contract.

Nervy but attractive, thought Ralph, admiring the excellent cut of her sleek blonde bob as she bent her head to return the file to its rightful place in the cabinet. Better still, his name obviously didn't mean anything to her.

'I know,' he said with a modest shrug. 'The producer warned me that once the series goes out, my life will never be the same again. I don't really know whether to celebrate or panic.'

'But that's amazing.' Gina's eyes shone. 'You must celebrate.'

'OK.' Ralph, rising to his feet, rested his hands lightly on the edge of the desk. 'But only if you'll celebrate with me. Tonight.'

Gina could smell his aftershave. She knew she must have misheard him.

'What?'

'Dinner at Bouboulina's. Eight o'clock,' he said steadily. Touching her left hand with his index finger, he added, 'You aren't married; I checked first.'

'But . . . but I don't know you,' she stammered. Nothing like this had ever happened to her in her life before. One minute she was harmlessly fantasizing, the next it was becoming scarily true. 'And you don't know me.'

Ralph, who had thought he'd known Izzy Van Asch, simply shrugged. 'Sometimes that's the best way. All you have to do is say yes.'

'No,' said Gina, panic-stricken.

'Are you scared of me?'

'No!'

'Then say yes.'

She closed her eyes for a second. What would Izzy do now? Was going out to dinner with an attractive man such a huge ordeal, after all? And which would she most regret later: accepting the invitation or refusing it?

'OK,' said Gina, before she had the chance to start panicking all over again. 'OK, yes.'

'That's better.' Ralph, who had overheard Izzy cajoling Gina into lending her some money and had watched Izzy leave the building ten minutes earlier – she was being towed along the pavement by some massive dog and looking extremely pleased with herself – couldn't wait to see her face when he turned up at her house this evening. Pulling a battered Filofax from his other pocket, he picked up a pen. 'Just give me your address and I'll pick you up at eight sharp.'

For once, Andrew didn't even notice the state of the bedroom. Pushing aside a towelling robe and a box of tissues, he sat down on the edge of the bed and stared at the wall. Behind him, Marcy wiped her eyes and reached for his hand.

'Oh darling, I'm sorry.' The words came out jerkily, between sobs. To her relief the tears flowed on cue. 'It happened yesterday afternoon. I wasn't feeling terribly well all morning, then after lunch I started to get these terrible cramping p-pains. It all happened so . . . quickly.' Encouraged by the fact that Andrew was holding her hand, she allowed her eyes to fill up once more. 'By the time the doctor got here, it was all over. The b-baby was gone.'

Andrew took her in his arms and held her while she sobbed quietly against his chest. 'You should be in hospital,' he said, stunned by the news. 'You should have *phoned* me, for God's sake.'

'The doctor examined me, made sure I was OK,' whispered Marcy bravely. 'And I didn't want to disturb you . . . I knew how important your conference was. There wasn't anything you could do, and I wanted to be on my own to have time to come to terms with . . . what had happened.'

'You should have phoned,' repeated Andrew, stroking her hair and wondering how it was possible to feel this numb. Guilt warred with relief that she hadn't tried to contact him, but for the loss of the baby he was unable to summon up any emotion at all. A child wasn't something he'd ever wanted in the first place, and even knowing that Marcy was pregnant, he'd found it curiously difficult to envisage the end result.

Except that now, there would be no end result. Which meant that his fate – Marcy, marriage and fatherhood – was no longer sealed. Katerina . . .

'Poor darling,' he said absently, his mind racing on ahead. 'Can I get you anything? What would you like?'

Sex would have been nice. Marcy wondered how soon she could decently resume that side of their relationship. The prospect of weeks of enforced celibacy wasn't exactly cheering.

'I'm OK,' she said, her voice husky from crying. 'How did your conference go, anyway?'

'Hmm?' Andrew was still lost in thought. He had arranged to meet Kat later this evening; clearly he

Jill Mansell

wouldn't be able to do so now. He could scarcely abandon Marcy, but dare he run the risk of phoning her at Gina's house to let her know of the change of circumstances?

'The conference,' Marcy repeated, nestling into the curve of his arms and thankful that he hadn't asked any further difficult questions. 'Was it a success?'

An image of Katerina, sitting up in bed sipping her morning coffee and smiling at him, flashed through Andrew's mind. Naked, happy and utterly desirable, she was everything he'd ever dreamed of.

'Oh yes,' he said, wondering whether the telephone cord would stretch as far as the bathroom. 'It went very well. Very well indeed.'

# Chapter 25

Izzy hadn't decided whether to be amused or annoyed with Ralph for playing such a filthy trick. On the one hand, it was flattering to know that he still cared, yet on the other it was poor Gina who was being used, and who was going to be hurt, and Izzy herself who, in turn, would have to suffer the inevitable consequences.

The decision was made for her in a flash when she answered the door at a quarter to eight. Ralph, in all-too-familiar acting mode, did the faintest of double takes and said in astonished tones, 'I don't believe it! Izzy . . . ?'

'Oh, cut the crap, Ralph.' Grabbing his arm, she hauled him briskly inside. When they reached the sitting room she closed the door and leaned against it, taking in the sharp, charcoal-grey suit, pale pink shirt and . . . ugh . . . grey shoes. When he lifted his arm to push back a lock of hair she even glimpsed a flash of gold bracelet. Thank goodness Sam wasn't here.

'Now look,' she began, her voice low and her expression deadly serious. 'Gina will be down here any minute, and because she doesn't know what a bastard you are, she has spent four hours getting ready to go out with you. She hasn't so much as looked at another man since her husband left her. This is her first date in probably fifteen years. So I'm just warning you, if you hurt her, you're in big trouble.'

'But—' said Ralph, looking injured and inwardly cursing the failure of his plan. He had been relying on the element of surprise; it simply hadn't occurred to him that Gina would tell Izzy the name of the man who had invited her out to dinner.

'But nothing.' Izzy was listening to the sound of Gina's footsteps on the stairs. 'Just remember that if you hurt her, I shall personally kill you.'

'Did I hear the doorbell?' said Gina. Her nerves had miraculously vanished and she was feeling quite giddy with excitement. At that moment the phone rang.

'Ralph and I were just introducing ourselves,' Izzy explained. 'Don't worry, I'll answer it. You two go off and have a lovely time. And make sure he takes you somewhere expensive,' she added, giving Ralph the benefit of her most innocent smile. 'He looks as if he can afford to show a girl a good time . . .'

'Don't take any notice of Izzy,' she heard Gina saying as she left the room. 'She's only joking.'

Izzy picked up the phone in the kitchen and said, 'Hallo?'

Andrew hesitated. It wasn't Gina, but was it definitely Kat?

'Hallo,' repeated Izzy in neutral tones, still planning in her mind a suitably apt murder.

On the other end of the line, Andrew anxiously waited for her to say something else so that he might glean a clue as to the identity of the voice, and Izzy, who could hear him breathing, rapidly answered his prayer. In a voice rigid with disdain, she said, 'Piss off, pervert,' and hung up.

Definitely not Kat, thought Andrew.

* * *

If Joel McGill was as tall, dark and handsome as she had imagined, thought Izzy, then he must be hiding beneath one of the tables. For no man fitting that description – in even its loosest terms – was visible to the naked eye.

She was not, however, going to let that put her off. Since nobody in the audience was wearing a jacket emblazoned with the famous yellow-and-white MBT logo, nor even a discreet badge proclaiming, 'I am an A&R man,' she had simply sung her heart out and ensured that even the least interested and most unlikely looking customer had been singled out during the course of the set for special attention and a dazzling smile.

Now, for the penultimate song of the evening, she stepped down from the stage and moved towards the nearest tables, where a group of businessmen had been applauding with particular enthusiasm. Behind her, Terry the pianist struck up the bluesy opening chords of 'My Baby Just Cares For Me', and the audience, recognizing the song, broke into renewed applause. The regulars among them knew that this was one of her particular favourites. For her finale, Izzy would return to the stage and belt out 'Cabaret' and every spine in the house would tingle because the power and passion in her voice made it impossible not to.

The evening had gone well, the audience were appreciative and Izzy was enjoying herself as she swayed among the tables. When the song was almost over she began to make her way back towards the stage, smiling as she did so at one of the quieter-looking middle-aged businessmen. She was mid-verse when she let out a scream. 'OUCH!'

The quiet, middle-aged businessman's hand, which had shot up the back of her skirt and pinched her thigh, was gone again in a flash. Izzy swung around, stared at him, saw his leery smile. She continued singing, as if the hesitation had been deliberate, and coolly ignored the nudges of his companions.

'Last song, now,' she murmured into the microphone, and nodded to Terry to indicate that she was staying where she was. The audience applauded once more as Terry moved smoothly into 'Cabaret', and Izzy, giving the quiet businessman an encouraging smile, prayed harder than she'd ever prayed before in her life that he wasn't the man from MBT.

As she sang her way through the opening verse, she moved closer to him, swaying her hips like Liza Minelli and reaching out until her fingers were only inches from his shoulder. He was grinning up at her now, his yellowed teeth revealed and his face glistening with sweat.

It was like ripping off an Elastoplast, all over in a flash. Izzy, dancing away, was up on the stage almost before he realised what had happened.

'. . . *Life is a grey toupee, old son, come to the grey toupee* . .' she sang joyously, waving the trophy above her own head like a big hairy handkerchief, and the audience, many of whom had witnessed the businessman's initial crude assault, rocked with laughter. The ensuing cheers almost brought the house down. Izzy bowed and tossed the toupee back to its apoplectic owner, whose friends were laughing more loudly than anyone else.

'Since I doubt very much whether I still work here,' Izzy announced cradling the microphone in both hands,

'I shall just say that I hope you enjoyed the show. You've been a wonderful audience. Thank you, and good night.'

Joel McGill was still crying with laughter when he entered the tiny cubbyhole which Izzy called her dressing room. She had to sit him down on the only chair, hand him a box of Kleenex and pour him a drink before he could even speak.

'I thought it was part of the act,' he managed to say eventually, though his shoulders still shook. 'Then I realised it wasn't . . .'

'That's nothing,' replied Izzy. 'Think how I felt, not knowing whether he was you . . . or you were him . . .' She thought for a second, then shrugged. 'If you know what I mean.'

'I know what you mean,' he agreed, wiping his eyes with a handful of peach-shaded tissues. 'That was fantastic. I think I love you.'

That had been one half of the fantasy, thought Izzy with a wry smile, but the rest of it appeared to have gone somewhat awry. Joel McGill wasn't supposed to be five feet two, with orange hair the texture of a Brillo pad, tiny round spectacles and the very smallest nose she'd ever seen. Neither had it occurred to her, while she was scouring the audience, to seek out a man wearing a powder-blue Argyll patterned pullover, an orange shirt and the kind of tartan trousers more commonly found on a golf course.

'You don't look like an A&R manager,' she said finally.

'No?' Still smiling, Joel McGill blew his nose with vigour. 'What do I look like?'

Izzy knew what she thought. Instead, tactfully, she said, 'Jack Nicklaus?'

He gave her a look that told her she'd disappointed him. 'Really?'

'OK. A train-spotter,' she confessed with reluctance, and he burst out laughing once more.

'I don't know why you had to make me say it,' Izzy grumbled. 'It isn't exactly enhancing my career prospects, after all.'

'Listen,' he said, leaning forward and stuffing the tissues into the back pocket of his terrible trousers. 'I'm one of the best A&R managers in the business. This means, happily, that I don't need to try and look like one. What's important to me is spotting new talent, assessing its potential and signing it up. Now, I spent a great deal of time yesterday listening to your demo tape, and tonight I've seen you . . . in action, so to speak.'

'Mmm?' said Izzy with extreme caution. Her pulse was racing and her fingernails were digging into her palms.

'And since I liked, very much, what I both heard and saw, why don't you stop grumbling and let me be the one to worry about your career prospects?'

'You mean . . . ?'

'I'm offering you a contract on behalf of MBT Records,' said Joel McGill, with an oddly engaging grin. 'Although there must be, I'm afraid, one proviso.'

Anything, thought Izzy passionately, anything at all. If it were stipulated in the contract, she'd even wear baggy tartan trousers.

Almost speechless with joy and gratitude, the most she could manage to get out was, 'What . . . ?'

'The trick with the toupee,' he informed her, struggling unsuccessfully to keep a straight face. 'Whatever you do, don't try it out on the president of MBT. Not unless you really want to die young.'

Guiltily aware that she should be studying for tomorrow's exam, which was chemistry, Katerina had baked herself a chocolate-fudge cake instead and eaten it while mindlessly watching an hour-long episode of a serial she had never seen before, and which she would certainly never watch again. At least both Gina and Izzy had been out, which meant that neither of them realised she had spent the earlier part of her evening sitting alone in a winebar in Kensington High Street, sipping Coke and waiting for Andrew to turn up. When, after an endless ninety minutes he still hadn't arrived, she had returned home and tried hard not to allow her imagination to run riot. He could be in hospital, he could be dead, Marcy could be in hospital . . . the possibilities had been both endless and agonizing . . .

When the phone shrilled at eleven-fifteen, Katerina and Jericho both jumped. Cake crumbs showered on to the carpet as she raced to answer it.

'Hallo?' she whispered, and this time it was so unmistakably her voice that Andrew didn't need to hesitate.

'Darling, it's me. I'm so sorry, I've been trying to get hold of you, but I'm in the bathroom and Marcy's next door.'

'You're OK?' Her hands were shaking uncontrollably. She slid down the wall, ducking to avoid Jericho's chocolatey kisses, and rested on her heels. 'What's happened?'

'Marcy had a miscarriage yesterday.'

'What!'

'She lost the baby,' Andrew repeated, his tone even. It would be indecent to sound too overjoyed, yet at the same time it was the answer to their unspoken prayers . . .

'Oh, poor Marcy,' breathed Katerina, her palms now clammy with perspiration. At the same time relief flooded through her, because Andrew was all right. 'Is she . . . very upset?'

'Yes,' he said briefly. 'That's why I couldn't leave her. Darling, you understand, don't you. I wanted to see you tonight, but—'

'Sssh.' Unbidden, the image of Andrew and herself in bed flashed through her mind. While she had been losing her virginity, Marcy had lost the baby. Overcome with shame, she said, 'Don't say that. Of course you have to stay with her. Look, I have to go now. Someone's coming home.'

'But—'

Quietly replacing the receiver, cutting him off in midprotest, Katerina realised that she felt sick. She was the Other Woman, and quite suddenly she was no longer sure whether she was equipped to deal with it. Simon had been right; it wasn't clever and it wasn't a game. It was becoming suddenly, frighteningly real.

From her vantage point, she held the phone in her lap and watched Gina – the other Other Woman, if she only knew it – wave a fond goodbye to Ralph.

'Gosh, you startled me.' Gina's eyes were bright. She looked so *happy*.

'Sorry,' said Katerina, rising to her feet and feeling old.

'I was on the phone. So, how did your date with the actor go? I thought you might have invited him in for coffee.'

She had been looking forward to seeing Ralph and out-acting him. Now she was glad she didn't have to.

'I did ask, but he has to be up at five o'clock tomorrow morning.' Gina, blushing slightly, looked happier than ever. Katerina, summoning up a smile, thought, You coward, Ralph.

'But did you have a nice evening?' she prompted. 'Do you think you'll see him again?'

'We had a wonderful evening,' Gina replied proudly. 'And yes, I'm seeing him again. Tomorrow night, as a matter of fact.'

'Tomorrow!' Katerina tried not to look too astonished. 'Good heavens, he must be keen.'

'I know,' said Gina, so dazed with joy that when she tried to hang up her jacket she missed the coat stand altogether. 'It's incredible. We just seem to have so much in common . . .'

# Chapter 26

Seduction Rule Number One, thought Vivienne cheerfully as she knocked on Sam's bedroom door: catch your subject naked and unaware.

After a long silence, Sam said, 'Go away,' which wasn't the most promising of starts, but Vivienne had decided that enough was enough. The way they had been carrying on for the past few weeks was plain silly. Smiling to herself, she knocked once more.

'I said . . . go away.'

Rule Number Two, Vivienne reminded herself: offer your subject unimaginable delights.

'I'm making breakfast,' she explained. 'Bacon and mushroom sandwiches . . . but if you'd rather go back to sleep . . .'

There was another long silence. Finally, he grumbled, 'I'm awake now. OK.'

'Such gratitude,' Vivienne replied lightly. 'It'll be ready in ten minutes.'

Moments later, she heard the shower begin to run, as she had known it would. Grinning to herself, she returned to the kitchen and turned the heat under the grill down very low indeed.

The noise of the shower meant that Sam didn't hear the bathroom door click open. Vivienne, revelling in the voyeuristic pleasure of watching him through the frosted glass, slipped out of her robe and moved quietly towards the shower cubicle.

'What the—' spluttered Sam, as flesh encountered flesh.

'Sssh, no need to panic,' Vivienne murmured, behind him. 'I'm a trained lifeguard. You won't drown.'

It was no good; she had caught him out. Before he even had time to protest, he knew he was lost. Vivienne, running her hands over his body with soapy, slippery ease, pressed herself against him. Within seconds Sam was aroused.

'This is crazy,' he sighed, willing himself to ignore the erotic effect of her warm, wet flesh and teasing fingers, and failing absolutely.

'But hygienic,' Vivienne murmured, her breasts sliding tantalizingly against his back, her tongue circling one shoulder-blade. Unable to contain her amusement, she said, 'This must be what you British call Good, Clean Fun.'

Turning finally to face her, acknowledging defeat with good grace, Sam took her in his arms and kissed her. Moments later, with a crooked smile, he said, 'We British call it risking life and limb.'

'Oh well,' Vivienne replied huskily, switching off the shower, 'if you want to be staid and boring, I suppose we'll just have to retreat to the safety of a bed.'

Afterwards, Sam rolled on to his side. 'Well?' he demanded. 'Was that staid and boring?'

Vivienne, so happy she thought she would burst, smiled back at him. 'As you British might say,' she informed him solemnly, 'it was very pleasant indeed . . . jolly well done . . . ahbsolutely mahvellous . . . top notch . . . altogether rahther splendid . . .'

'Good,' he interrupted in brisk tones. 'So, now can I have that bacon sandwich?'

'Oh, Izzy!' cried Vivienne, beside herself with delight. 'This is fantastic . . . Jeez, you really *are* on your way, now!'

Izzy grinned as the chauffeur, who swore his name was George, held open the door of the gleaming, ludicrously elongated limousine. 'The first of my lifetime ambitions,' she explained, running her hands lovingly over the ivory-leather upholstery. 'Even if it is only mine for six hours.'

'What's your second lifetime ambition?' Vivienne demanded, pouncing on the cocktail cabinet.

Izzy winked at the chauffeur. 'Wild sex in the back of a limo.'

'God, count me out. George, you aren't listening to this, are you?'

'No, madam,' replied George, maintaining a straight face.

'So, where are we going?' continued Vivienne, pouring enormous drinks and handing one to Izzy as the huge car purred into life.

'Are you kidding?' Izzy looked pained. 'In this thing, *everywhere.*'

By the time they arrived at The Chelsea Steps it was almost one-thirty and a huge crowd of paparazzi were milling around on the pavement outside. Within seconds, they were swarming around the rented limousine.

'My God,' said Izzy, awestruck. 'I got famous quicker than I thought.'

The photographers' expressions soon changed, however, when George opened the rear door.

'Shit, you aren't Tash Janssen,' exclaimed one with evident disgust.

'Never said I was,' Izzy replied loftily. 'Nincompoop.'

He shrugged and sighed. 'So, who are you? Anybody?'

Ignoring him, Izzy turned her attention to the chauffeur. 'Don't let anyone touch the car, George. We won't be longer than a couple of hours. And no gossiping to nincompoops in the mean time, if you value your job.'

'Very well, madam.' He tipped his cap to her.

The photographer regarded Izzy with suspicion. 'Hey, *are* you somebody?'

In reply, she gave him a pitying half-smile. 'Why don't you ask Tash Janssen if I'm "somebody", OK? He'll be here in five minutes. Maybe he'll tell you.'

The club was absolutely heaving with bodies. Izzy, peering through the crowd, said, 'There's Sam. What do you want to do, be polite and say hallo, or ignore him?'

Vivienne coughed delicately. Her green eyes sparkled. 'Ah well . . . as a matter of fact, you aren't the only one with a bit of good news to celebrate.'

'You mean . . .' Izzy stared at her. 'You and Sam?'

'Oh hey, we aren't getting married or anything,' Vivienne giggled. 'No need to look that stunned.'

'But you . . .'

'Got laid,' supplied Vivienne with characteristic bluntness. She heaved a blissful sigh. 'And it was as great as

215

ever. I mean, really. Sam Sheridan is seriously fantastic in the sack.'

I bet he is, Izzy thought ruefully, but she was able to smile and be pleased for her friend. What she'd never had she couldn't miss, she reminded herself, and even if she didn't happen to believe that particular bit of propaganda, at times like this it came in useful.

'I'm glad,' she said honestly, as Sam made his way towards them. 'But don't forget, I want to keep this recording contract a secret for the time being. He still thinks I'm a dumb female and I want to wait until there's something to really show him . . .'

'Izz, I won't breathe a word,' protested Vivienne. 'I *adore* our secret. Why, just this afternoon he was running you down something rotten and I stuck by you all the way.'

Incredulous, Izzy demanded, 'What was he *saying* about me?'

'Oh . . . something about this guy Tash Janssen coming to the club tonight,' said Vivienne vaguely. 'Sam said that if you saw him you'd turn instant groupie.'

'And what did you say?' Izzy's dark eyebrows had disappeared beneath her hair.

Vivienne winked. 'Why, honeychile,' she drawled teasingly. 'I said no way some rich rock star would get it for nothing. You'd charge!'

So annoyed with Sam that she didn't even trust herself to speak to him, Izzy left them to it and went for a wander. And although she tried hard not to think about her lost opportunity with Sam, not to mention the new and ludicrous pairing of Gina and Ralph, she couldn't help

216

noticing that the rest of the world appeared to be going around in twos.

I don't need a man, she reminded herself crossly. I have a recording contract instead.

But it had been an awfully long time; the days of Ralph and Mike and the happily synchronised subterfuge which had made her life so complete were long gone, and now even Katerina had fallen in love . . .

She had to step aside to avoid a couple with their arms locked adoringly around each other's waists. As she did so, she glanced across and saw Vivienne laughing with Sam, over at the bar. Never mind Gina, thought Izzy with a forlorn attempt at humour quite at odds with her previous high spirits; at this rate it wouldn't be long before *she* was the one carting Jericho around the park in search of men.

As soon as she returned from the loo, where excitement was high and lipsticks and Schwarzenegger-strength hairsprays were being wielded with abandon in anticipation of Tash Janssen's rumoured arrival, Izzy observed the hive of activity around the entrance and realised that he had indeed turned up. Famous though The Chelsea Steps might be for its laid-back, no-fuss policy, and although there were no actual stampedes or hysterical screams of delight, the appearance of one of the world's most outrageous and successful rock stars couldn't help but evoke more than a frisson of interest.

Despite herself, Izzy smiled as freshly lipsticked, miniskirted blondes streamed out of the loo and gravitated towards the dance floor. The DJ, who evidently had a sense of humour, promptly played a record to which it was almost impossible to dance. The blondes, first hesitating then retreating in temporary defeat to the sidelines, pretended they hadn't wanted to dance anyway and shot him looks of icy disdain.

'Hmm,' murmured Vivienne, reappearing at Izzy's side and gazing unashamedly in Tash Janssen's direction. 'I have to admit, he is *disturbingly* gorgeous. If I weren't in love with Sam I might even be tempted to have a go at him myself.'

Izzy watched the Janssen entourage – all male, for now at least – settle themselves around The Chelsea Steps' most coveted table. The singer, with his spiky dark hair, heavily lidded, even darker eyes and thin, tanned face, was casually dressed in a red shirt and black jeans. There was an air about him of deceptive languor, as he picked up his drink and murmured a few words to one of his black-suited minders. When he drained his glass in one go, another appeared before him within seconds.

'Definitely dangerous,' pronounced Vivienne, sounding excited. 'Will you look at that mouth . . .'

Despite herself, Izzy was intrigued; how could a man who wasn't, in truth, *that* good-looking, possess such an extraordinary degree of attraction for so many women? And had that attraction preceded the fame or become unleashed as a result of it? Whatever must it be like to exude such an aura . . . to be recognised by literally millions of people the world over . . . to simply *be* Tash Janssen?

'You aren't drooling,' Vivienne observed, giving her a sharp sideways glance.

Izzy, who had been miles away, murmured absently, 'I'm thinking.'

'Never think,' Vivienne declared, because it was one of her father's favourite sayings. 'Just act.'

Izzy grinned. 'Don't tempt me.'

'Will whatever it is annoy Sam?' Vivienne was looking interested now.

'Oh yes.'

'Will he be angry with me?'

'Nooo . . .'

'In that case,' said Vivienne, smiling with relief and clinking her glass against Izzy's, 'what the hell are you doing, hanging around talking to me? Go for it.'

'I don't believe it,' murmured Sam, twenty minutes later, as the larger of Tash Janssen's minders made his way in a direct line across the dance floor and approached Izzy, now sitting demurely on her own at a small table in the very furthest corner of the club.

'Maybe he's asking her to dance,' suggested Vivienne, doing her best not to laugh. The minder was addressing Izzy now, indicating that she should follow him.

'What *is* she playing at?' Sam had never quite overcome his fear that one evening Izzy – who knew no shame – would burst into song in front of one of his more celebrated guests . . .

Vivienne, reading his thoughts, squeezed his arm. 'No, you cannot go over there,' she admonished in stern tones. 'He invited her, didn't he? She hasn't exactly forced herself upon him . . .'

With some unwillingness, Sam conceded that this was

true. But he still wasn't happy. 'She planned this, some-how,' he said darkly, his eyes narrowing as he watched Tash Janssen rise to his feet and shake Izzy's politely proffered hand. 'I don't know how she did it . . .'

'Oh my,' said Vivienne good-humouredly. 'All this fuss over Izzy. Sweetheart, are you sure you aren't just the teeniest bit jealous?'

'Of course I'm not jealous,' Sam replied evenly. Pausing, he took a sip of his drink. 'I just don't want her to start *singing* . . .'

# Chapter 27

At close quarters, Tash Janssen was even more devastating to look at. Izzy, sitting next to him with her hands clasped modestly in her lap, wondered how many times he had enjoyed wild sex in the back of a limo, then hastily abandoned such thoughts in case he was able to read her mind.

'Well,' he announced finally, when he had finished subjecting her to a slow up-and-down scrutiny. 'I have to say that I've had plenty of notes passed to me in my time, but none quite like yours.'

'No?' said Izzy with the utmost politeness. The note, which she had handed over to her favourite barman, now lay on the table in front of them, but Tash Janssen quoted the first sentence without even glancing at it.

*'I'm not offering you my body, I don't have blonde hair and I am old enough to be your mother. But I would like to make you the very serious offer of a song which may interest you a great deal.'*

'Yes,' Izzy replied simply.

'You aren't old enough to be my mother,' he observed with a crooked smile.

'My only fib,' she conceded, the corners of her own mouth beginning to curl.

'And you're telling me that this song is great?'

'Oh, the greatest.'

'Another . . . fib?'

He was amusing himself. Izzy knew perfectly well that he wasn't taking her seriously. Yet at the same time she sensed that even if he didn't actually believe her, she had captured his interest, temporarily at least.

'This song,' she said mildly, 'is the best.'

Tash Janssen laughed and glanced briefly at his watch. 'Look, are you sure you wouldn't like to change your mind about sleeping with me?'

'It would take *five* minutes . . .' Izzy protested, realizing that the softly-softly approach wasn't working and that she was in danger of losing him.

His eyebrows shot up. 'Excuse me, but that just is not *true . . .*'

'To listen to my song, stupid.'

He raised his hands in relief. 'I thought we were discussing my sexual prowess. OK, OK, why don't you send me a tape, care of my record company? I promise to listen to it.'

'No,' said Izzy, opening her bag, lifting out her copy of the demo tape and flicking it away from him when he reached out to take it from her. 'I have a car waiting outside. Come and listen to it now.'

'I . . . do . . . not . . . *believe* . . . it,' said Sam, through gritted teeth.

Vivienne, beside herself with joy, replied consolingly, 'Now, now. She is an adult, after all.'

'That woman is the second most amoral adult I know.' Sam, glaring at the departing figures, observed that Tash Janssen's hand was resting lightly upon Izzy's shoulder.

'And she's just walked out – practically arm in arm, for God's sake – with the first.'

'Maybe,' suggested Vivienne, ever helpful, 'they've gone to feed his meter.'

Izzy, adoring the expression on the face of the photographer who had earlier doubted her, grinned at Tash Janssen, said, 'Your car or mine?' and took three steps towards her own rented limousine before he could open his mouth. With a shrug, she continued smoothly, 'OK, mine. Thank you, George . . . would it be rude to ask you to wait outside the car for a few minutes? Mr Janssen and I have some private business to discuss.'

'Full of surprises,' remarked Tash, when they were safely inside, protected from prying eyes and lenses by blacked-out windows. Leaning closer to Izzy, he murmured conspiratorially, 'Have you ever done it in the back seat of one of these things?'

'Since before you were born,' replied Izzy with a sigh. Pushing him upright, she went on. 'Look, nobody can hear us now, so you can drop the big rock-star act. Just behave like a normal human being for five minutes and listen to my song.'

He laughed. 'Have you ever thought of becoming a schoolteacher?'

'Sssh.' Izzy fitted the cassette into the tape deck and adjusted the balance for quadraphonic sound.

'Your hands are shaking,' he observed.

'That's because I'm nervous.'

He looked interested. 'You practically kidnapped me. Why should *you* be afraid?'

Turning to face him, her dark eyes huge, she said slowly, 'This is important to me. I'm afraid that you won't take the trouble to listen properly, because you're treating this whole thing as a joke, whereas I'm serious.'

After a moment, he took her hand in his, kissed it, then replaced it with care on the seat beside him. 'Sorry,' he said, 'I'll listen properly. I can be serious, too.'

The opening bars of 'Never, Never' flooded the car and he listened. Izzy watched him listen – with his eyes closed and his long legs stretched out in front of him – and scarcely dared to breathe for the entire four minutes.

When the song ended and he didn't move, she thought for a second that he was asleep. Then, slowly, he opened one eye. 'Play it again.'

'Please,' murmured Izzy, rewinding the tape.

He smiled before closing his eyes once more. 'Please.'

Fifteen minutes later, when 'Never, Never' had finished playing for the fourth time, he sat up and ejected the tape, turning it over in his fingers and looking thoughtful. Since he still hadn't said anything about it, Izzy was by this time almost paralysed with anticipation.

'Well?' she said eventually, and with great difficulty because her tongue was by this time stuck to the roof of her mouth.

'I'm impressed,' he replied, sounding faintly amused. 'But then you knew I'd be impressed, otherwise you wouldn't have gone to all this trouble to drag me out here. What I don't understand is why *you* don't want to sing it.'

'I didn't drag you out here,' she reminded him evenly. 'And I do want to sing it. Very much indeed.'

'Then why offer it to me?'

Izzy took a deep breath, inhaling the scent of leather upholstery, cigars and cologne. 'Because I want us to sing it together.'

He looked stunned. 'A duet?'

'That is, I believe, the technical term for it,' she agreed with a brief smile.

'I don't do duets.'

'Maybe you should. The public likes them. Look at Tom Jones and Cerys Matthews.'

'And?' prompted Tash.

'Bryan Adams and Mel C.'

Tash shot her a wry look. 'Not to mention Kermit and Miss Piggy.'

'George Michael and Aretha Franklin!' Izzy swiftly intercepted him before he could start making fun of her again. 'Oh please . . . the fans *love* that kind of thing.'

'Is that right? And how many fans do *you* have?'

'Approximately seventeen,' said Izzy, deciding that it might be prudent to exclude Toupee-Man from the list. She paused, then added, 'And a dog.'

'I see,' said Tash thoughtfully. 'Is the dog small or large?'

She risked a smile, because he still hadn't actually said no . . . and because he was still here in the car . . . and because she was beginning to think that maybe, just maybe, he might be seriously considering her suggestion. 'Why?' she countered, her expression innocent. 'Is size really important?'

'You tell me,' he countered, lying back and tapping the cassette idly against his denim-clad thigh. Then, turning abruptly to face her and regarding her with shrewd, dark eyes, he said, 'No, tell me how long you've been planning this.'

For a second, Izzy wondered whether he would be more impressed if she said weeks, or months. Maybe if he thought she had written the song specifically with him in mind . . . that it had never even occurred to her that anyone else *could* sing it . . .

But they weren't really the kind of eyes you could lie to, she realised, and the events of the evening were beginning to catch up with her. She simply didn't have the energy left to start improvising now.

'About an hour ago,' she admitted with a small shrug. 'When you arrived at the club.'

Tash was struggling to keep a straight face. 'So, it was a spur-of-the-moment decision, an impulsive gesture. How very flattering.'

'But does that make it a bad idea?' Izzy demanded with a trace of irritation because he was laughing at her now. 'Is your rock star's ego too great to cope with the fact that I didn't write the song *for* you?'

'A little diplomacy never goes amiss,' he replied, deadpan, 'but I daresay I'll recover, in time. Is this really your name?'

He was holding the cassette up to the dim light, his eyes narrowing as he scrutinised the label for the first time. Izzy, caught offguard by the abrupt switch in his train of thought, said crossly, 'Of course it's my bloody name.'

'Hmm.' He paused, apparently lost in thought. The next moment, without even glancing at her, he had reached for her hand once more and raised it to his lips.

The gesture was innocent enough. Its effect, however, was wildly erotic. Izzy, tingling all over, murmured faintly, 'Hmm what?'

'Tash and Van Asch,' he said, breaking into a smile. 'I don't know about you, but it sounds pretty good to me . . .'

# Chapter 28

Sam, who didn't enjoy musicals and who had been given a pair of much-coveted tickets to see the latest Andrew Lloyd Webber show, newly opened in the West End, dropped round to Kingsley Grove the following afternoon and offered them to Gina.

Gina adored musicals and was delighted. 'Stay for dinner,' she urged, returning her attention to the mixing bowl of pastry she was in the midst of kneading and inclining her head towards the plate of steak fillets on top of the fridge. *'Boeuf en croûte*, and I'm making far too much, so you really must join us.'

Sam hesitated. 'I only really called by to give you the tickets,' he said, not even allowing himself to wonder where Izzy might be, or whether she had even returned home last night. 'Vivienne's expecting me back at the flat . . .'

'Phone her,' said Gina happily. 'Tell her to come round, too. The more the merrier!'

A moment later he heard a footfall upstairs, and the sound of a bedroom door opening. 'Is that Izzy?'

Gina, now energetically rolling out the pastry, puffed a strand of hair away from her forehead and shook her head. 'I heard her come in at around six this morning, but by the time I got home from work she'd disappeared again. That was Kat you just heard.'

Sam tried hard not to think of Izzy and Tash Janssen in bed together. Instead, turning his attention back to Gina and realizing how much better she had been looking over the past few weeks, he said, 'You're cheerful.'

Gina stopped rolling and smiled at him. 'I am, aren't I?'

At least he could be pleased about that. It was about time Gina had some luck. He tilted his head slightly. 'So?'

'Oh, Sam,' she breathed, wiping her cheek with her forearm and streaking it with flour. 'I've met someone, someone really nice . . . and I know it's far too soon to even think about the future, but he's so *special . . .*'

'I'm glad,' said Sam, getting up from his chair and kissing her unfloured cheek. With mock severity, he added, 'And you're not so bad yourself, Mrs Lawrence, so don't let him think he has some kind of monopoly on special-ness.'

Gina shook her head. 'At the moment I still can't believe how lucky I am. And you'll meet him, if you stay for dinner. He's due here at six-thirty.'

'In that case,' said Sam, reaching for the phone, 'how can I refuse? I'll tell Vivienne to pick up some wine on the way over.'

When he had replaced the receiver, he said, 'Now, what can I do to help?'

The doorbell rang. Gina, whose arms were floury up to the elbows, smiled. 'Answer that.'

Since neither Sam nor Gina were aware of Ralph's alarming tendency towards over-punctuality, which Katerina had always maintained was a by-product of the fact that the acting profession was so notoriously insecure, it didn't occur to either of them that the doorbell ringing at five forty-five could have any connection whatsoever with his expected arrival at six-thirty.

Sam, opening the door and recognizing him at once, was only momentarily surprised. 'Oh. Hi,' he said easily, glimpsing a gold bracelet and suppressing a grin. 'Izzy's not here, I'm afraid. Was she expecting you?'

'Er . . .' Ralph's composure had temporarily deserted him. Behind Sam, he could see Gina hovering in the hallway.

'She may be back soon,' Sam continued, cheerfully unaware of the havoc he was creating. 'Why don't you come in and wait?'

'Er . . . er . . .'

'What's going on?' said Gina, her voice unnaturally high. She felt as if someone had switched channels in mid-programme. All the colour had drained from her face.

Sam, who had a good memory for names, stepped aside so that she had an unimpaired view of their visitor. 'It's Ralph, sweetheart. Have you two met before? I was just saying that if he's arranged to meet Izzy here he must have a drink with us while he's waiting.'

Gina stared, first at Ralph, then at Sam. Slowly, wondering whether she might be going mad, she said, 'What are you . . . talking . . . about? Is this a joke?'

Improvisation had never been Ralph's strong point. 'Oh, shit,' he said with feeling.

'What?' demanded Sam, glancing in turn at Gina and realizing that she was on the verge of keeling over.

It was her stricken expression that finally gave it away.

His heart sinking, he echoed beneath his breath, 'Oh, shit.'

Izzy, returning home at seven, found Sam waiting for her in the kitchen, alone. Buoyed up by her day at the head offices of MBT in Mayfair, where she had been introduced by Joel McGill to the company's president, its manager and financial directors and the producer with whom she would be working, she was in tearing spirits. And this evening she was having dinner with Tash.

'Hallo, darling!' she exclaimed as Jericho, scrambling to his feet, hurtled towards her. Then, grinning at Sam and realizing that it was no good, she couldn't keep her wonderful secret from him any longer, she said, 'Hallo, Sam. Guess where I've been?'

Then, as he looked up at her, she saw the cold fury in his eyes. 'You mean apart from that creep's bed?' he spat with contempt. 'I really don't know, Izzy. You could have been anywhere, stirring up any amount of trouble and disrupting any number of innocent lives.'

Izzy, stunned by the unexpectedness of the verbal assault, gazed blankly at him for a second. She'd never seen Sam so angry before. Then she twigged: he meant Tash. Sam had warned her not to approach him and she had ignored the commandment. Rock stars, it seemed, weren't the only ones with big egos . . .

'Not that it's *any* of your business,' she replied crossly, because she had come home bearing glad tidings and now he was spoiling it all, 'but I didn't sleep with Tash Janssen. I have no *intention* of sleeping with him—'

'Of course you don't,' Sam jibed, fuelling the words

with sarcasm. 'Come on, let me guess. You spent last night admiring his art collection!'

'We spent last night talking about music,' Izzy retaliated, a faint smile lifting the corners of her mouth. Heavens, she hadn't dreamed that Sam would react this strongly. He must still care about her, after all . . .

'So, you two were "talking about music",' he continued, his tone dangerously even.

'We had a cup of tea as well,' volunteered Izzy, beginning to enjoy herself now. 'And I ate six chocolate biscuits.'

'Where was Gina?'

'What?'

'Last night,' prompted Sam, moving inexorably in for the kill. 'While you were out. Where was she?'

'You mean *our* Gina?' Izzy, confused by yet another abrupt switch in the conversation, said, 'She wasn't there! She went out to dinner with . . . someone else.'

'And who exactly did she go out to dinner with?'

'Oh, hell!' Izzy, understanding finally what he was saying, closed her eyes in dismay. 'Bloody hell. *Bloody* Ralph . . .'

'Bloody who?' he demanded, suppressing the urge to shake her until her teeth dropped out. Izzy's ability to swan through life absolving herself from all blame was positively breathtaking. 'How the fuck could you stand by and let it happen? You *condoned* it . . .'

'I did not!' Her fingers gripped the edge of the dresser. She was quivering with rage now. 'I told him not to hurt her.'

'And if you'd told her in the first place, she wouldn't be

232

hurt now. But you chose not to, didn't you? Because it amused you to play along with the charade . . . because it made a good story to tell your friends.' He gestured towards her with disdain. 'You probably told Janssen about it, last night.'

Unable to contain her fury any longer, Izzy picked up the nearest object to hand and hurled it at him. The Victorian china ginger pot, missing him by several feet, crashed in spectacular fashion against the far wall and shattered into a million pieces.

Sam, who hadn't even flinched, sneered derisively. 'Oh, well done. Gina *will* be pleased.'

'I'll replace it,' shouted Izzy.

'Of course you will,' he replied, his tone icy. 'Just as soon as you've managed to persuade her to lend you the money.'

'Stop it,' said Gina quietly, from the doorway. 'Both of you.'

Izzy's eyes promptly filled with tears. 'I'm sorry.'

'It doesn't matter.' Gina, stunned by her reaction – Izzy *never* cried – shook her head. 'Andrew bought it for me last Christmas. I never liked it.'

'I meant . . . Ralph,' sniffed Izzy. 'I wasn't trying to deceive you, although I know I did . . . but you just seemed so happy . . .'

'I know,' said Gina soothingly. 'It wasn't your fault. I was a bit shocked when I realised who he was, but it's hardly the end of the world, is it?'

Sam, outraged by the fact that she was siding with Izzy against him and making such light of the matter, said, 'But you told me how much you liked him. You said—'

'Maybe I did,' Gina intercepted, without looking at him. 'But how upset do you honestly expect me to be? I was married to Andrew for fifteen years. For heaven's sake, I only met Ralph a few days ago.'

Izzy, rummaging blindly in her bag for a tissue and still desperate to make some kind of amends, encountered her purse. The first thing she'd done after leaving MBT's offices had been to rush to the bank and cash a good proportion of her advance cheque. Now, stung by Sam's earlier jibe, she pulled out a fat wad of notes.

'Here's the money I borrowed the other day,' she said rapidly, stuffing them into Gina's startled hands. 'And here's something to replace the pot.' Then, because she didn't have enough cash in her purse to be able to make the ultimate grand gesture and hurl it in Sam's horrible face, she withdrew her cheque book instead and scribbled out a cheque for £1300. Pushing it across the kitchen table towards him, she said, 'That's for Vivienne. Don't worry, it won't bounce.'

As he rose to leave, Sam cast a single, derisive glance in her direction. 'She was right, then,' he said evenly. 'You *do* charge.'

'I don't know why he should have turned on you like that,' said Gina later, while Izzy prepared to go out. 'It's not like Sam at all.'

'Don't apologise on his behalf.' Izzy, concentrating on her mascara, dismissed him with a shrug. 'He's a moody pig and I couldn't care less what he thinks of me. Look, are you quite sure you'll be OK here on your own this evening? Because you can always come along with me.'

Gina laughed. 'I'm sure Tash Janssen would enjoy that. What's the problem – do you think you might need a chaperone?'

'According to Sam,' replied Izzy, glossing her lips and pulling a fearsome face, 'I'll need six.'

When Katerina poked her head around the sitting-room door five minutes later, Izzy was saying, '. . . really am sorry about Ralph, you know.'

'Of course I know,' Gina replied in reassuring tones. 'It was only Sam getting hold of the wrong end of the stick. I know you'd never do anything deliberately to hurt me.'

Katerina, who had been about to announce that she was going over to Simon's house, felt her heart skip a couple of beats. How would Gina feel if she knew that in less than an hour she would be meeting Andrew? Could there be any more deliberately hurtful gesture? Was she really the world's worst bitch, or simply a helpless victim of circumstance?

Abruptly, avoiding Gina's eyes, she said, 'I'm off now.'

'Don't be late home.' Turning, Izzy smiled at her. 'And cheer up, sweetheart. Just think, one more paper tomorrow morning, then that'll be it. Oh, and tell Simon I'm taking the two of you out to dinner tomorrow night, to celebrate. We'll go somewhere splendid!'

Katerina hesitated, then said unhappily, 'I don't know whether Simon . . .'

'I'm taking you *both* out,' repeated Izzy, in firm tones. 'Because you damn well deserve it. And this way I can thank Simon for all the help and hospitality he's given you over the past few weeks. Ask him if there's anywhere in particular he'd like to go, will you, so that I can book the table in advance.'

# Chapter 29

Izzy, twisting round in the passenger seat of the dark grey Bentley and watching the electronically controlled gates swing shut behind her, felt a sudden affinity with Little Red Riding Hood. Ahead, just visible through the trees which lined the curving driveway, Stanford Manor loomed multi-turreted and magnificent. Izzy swallowed and tried hard not to look too impressed. Jericho poked his head between the front seats and whimpered. When the car slowed to a halt at the top of the drive, Izzy wrapped his lead around her wrist three times in case Tash kept guard dogs.

There were none in sight, however, when he came out to greet her. Jericho, shamelessly fickle, leapt at once towards him and investigated him with evident delight.

'Your greatest fan, I take it,' Tash observed, patting him. Izzy, realizing how desperately Jericho was moulting, prayed that the car's upholstery wasn't too covered with hairs.

'My chaperone,' she corrected him, shivering suddenly despite the fact that it was still warm. When Tash transferred his attention back to her, she felt her legs begin to tremble of their own accord.

Last night, persuading him to listen to her music and take her seriously had been all-important, and she hadn't allowed herself to even consider how seriously attractive he really was. Now, however, it hit her like a brick. He was stunning. It was official. Several million females, she thought with a brief half-smile, couldn't be wrong.

The driver who had picked her up and brought her to Stanford Manor had, by this time, disappeared. Following Tash and Jericho into the vast, high-ceilinged entrance hall, Izzy admired Tash's tall, athletically proportioned body. This evening, dressed in a pale pink shirt, faded denims and no shoes, and smelling cleanly of Calvin Klein aftershave, he seemed altogether more normal than he had done last night. It was bizarre to think that he owned this great house, not to mention two other *pieds-à-terre* in Paris and New York. It was mind-boggling to think how much money that gravelly, sexy voice had earned him . . .

'How old are you?' she asked, gazing up at the stained-glass windows and at the minstrel's gallery running along three sides of the hall.

Tash cast a sideways glance in her direction. 'Old enough to be your son, according to you.'

'Seriously, I'm interested.'

'Thirty-three.'

Three years younger than me, thought Izzy. 'And you've been married how many times?'

Looking amused, he replied, 'Only twice. Although I do have a tendency to find myself engaged. Every time I buy a pretty girl a ring it turns out she expects me to marry her.'

If anything about Tash Janssen was more famous than his voice, it was his predilection for blondes. Startlingly beautiful, *always* tall, these blondes were famous in turn for their less-than-dazzling intellect. One or two had even been suspected of not yet having come to terms with the complexities of joined-up writing. Izzy couldn't help wondering why someone like Tash, evidently no intellectual slouch himself, should confine himself to bimbos when he could have anyone he chose. 'Maybe you should stick to signed photographs in future,' she suggested absently.

He smiled. 'Maybe. How about you?'

'Heavens, how kind.' Izzy feigned surprise. 'I'd like a motor bike.'

'I'll make a note of it in my diary. Through here.' Opening a carved oak door, he waved her through to the dining room. 'I meant how old are you and how many times have you been married?'

'Thirty-six,' said Izzy. 'And never. I'm not the marrying kind.'

' "Never, Never",' Tash observed drily, pulling a dining chair out for her and ensuring that she was comfortable before seating himself opposite. The table, which would easily have accommodated a rugby team, was covered with a dark blue linen cloth and laid for two people with heavy silver cutlery, glittering crystal goblets and a bottle of Chablis in an ice bucket. Lighted candles, spilling snaky trails of beeswax down their sides, cast an apricot glow over the proceedings.

Izzy placed her forefinger momentarily over the flame of the nearest candle then held it up, blackened, and said, 'Isn't this what happens when you get married?'

He grinned and poured the wine. 'Financially, you mean? Of course it is, if you're me.'

The divorce settlements obtained by his ex-wives were

legendary, yet he didn't seem perturbed.

'Don't you mind?' said Izzy, genuinely interested.

Tash shrugged and replied lazily, 'What the hell, it's only money. And it seems to keep the girls happy.'

'I want to be rich,' said Izzy, with longing.

Deadpan, he replied, 'That's easily achieved. All you need to do is marry and divorce me.'

At that moment another door opened and their dinner was served to them by a brisk, plain, middle-aged woman with the air of a schoolmistress. Izzy, half-expecting to be reminded to eat up all her vegetables, smiled at the woman as the dishes were laid out and received a blank stare in return.

'Mrs Bishop makes it a strict rule to disapprove of my female friends,' Tash explained, when they were alone once more.

'I didn't expect you to live like this.' Izzy shook her head, bemused by the formality of it all. Having imagined wall-to-wall groupies, non-stop music, cans of lager and pinball machines, all this silence and *House & Garden* perfection was unnerving. 'Do you have fun here? Are you *happy*?'

Tash's dark eyebrows arched in surprise. 'You mean has becoming a multi-millionaire ruined my life? Sweetheart, I grew up on a council estate in Neasden with three brothers and two sisters. This is how I can afford to live now. Would *you* be unhappy?'

Izzy, however, still wasn't convinced. Despite the excellence of the food she had lost her appetite. 'I might be,' she replied, pushing her plate to one side. 'Of course, that's something you never find out until it's happened, but I've always been poor and I'm curious. I have fun spending money on things I know I can't afford, like going out for a wonderful meal when I really should be saving the money to pay the gas bill.' She paused, then added helplessly, 'But what do *you* do, when you want to have fun?'

'I can't believe you asked that question,' drawled Tash, his dark eyes glittering with amusement. All pretence at dinner abandoned now, he rose slowly to his feet and held his hand out towards her. 'Come on.'

'What?' Izzy gulped, her stomach leaping helplessly as his fingers curled around hers. 'Where . . . ?'

'You wanted to know what I do when I want to have fun,' he reminded her. 'Come with me and I'll show you.'

The recording studio, situated in what had once been a wine cellar, was a revelation – as far as Izzy was concerned – in every respect. Making the demo tape at the prestigious Glass Studios on the Chelsea Embankment had been exciting, but then she had been the performer, singing when she was instructed to sing and generally doing as she was told, while the producer and sound engineers worked their inscrutable magic in the control room next door.

Now, sitting at the amazingly intricate thirty-two track console and actually being allowed to experiment with the wondrous effects of the midi-synthesiser, a whole new world was opening up to her. Who needed to be able to write music when any notes played on the keyboard were instantly displayed on a computer screen and stored on disc? Who needed to be able to play the drums when at the touch of a button the same keyboard could transform any note into that produced by a snare, a kick-drum, a crash cymbal or a hi-hat? Who *needed* to struggle to emulate the exact degree of reverberation required at the end of a verse, when they had a machine like this, capable of doing it for them?

Even more stunning, however, had been the change in Tash. Gone was the lazy, laid-back demeanour, the air of boredom which she had first observed at The Chelsea Steps. The moment he had pulled up a chair and begun to demonstrate the different functions of the myriad machines before her, he had come properly alive. Making music – this was what gave him pleasure. This was Tash Janssen's idea of fun and for all his earlier double entendres Izzy realised that now if she were to pull off her jeans and top and dance naked around the studio, he would take no notice at all.

'Flick that switch,' he instructed her, so engrossed in the columns of figures on the computer screen that he didn't even realise his fingers were resting on Izzy's knee. Izzy tried hard not to notice, either. Whereas it had been easy to rebuff his good-natured advances yesterday, this abrupt switch to indifference – and the fact that he was no longer *trying* to seduce her – was ridiculously erotic. Pressing the switch he had indicated, she glanced around the room in order to take her mind off his proximity. Each wall was lined with cork tiles of different thicknesses in order to deaden the acoustics and the stone-flagged floor was covered with matting. More inviting was the slightly battered, green velvet sofa positioned against the wall behind them. Apart from the faint whirring of the tape she had set in motion, the room was in total silence.

'Now press play,' said Tash, when the tape had skittered to a halt.

Izzy, entranced by his seriousness, obeyed. Moments later, as the first bars of 'Never, Never' filled the studio, she sat upright and said, 'Oh . . . !'

When the tape ended she gazed at Tash with new respect. 'You did all that from memory.'

He smiled briefly. 'Since you wouldn't let me keep the tape, I didn't have much choice. It isn't exactly the same, but I wanted to experiment with the vocals . . . I'm pretty out of practice as far as this kind of singing's concerned.'

'I knew you could do it,' sighed Izzy. Unaccustomed though he might be to producing anything less than hard-driving, full-tilt rock, that husky voice was wonderfully suited to the slower, gentler pace of 'Never, Never'. Despite herself, she felt a lump form in her throat. She *had* known he could do it, but she hadn't imagined he would do it this well. Now, for the first time, she realised just how much of an effect last night's impulsive intro-duction could have on her life . . .

Two hours later, dropping the headphones she'd been wearing on to the desk and rumpling her hair back into some sort of shape, Izzy collapsed on to the sofa. Adrenalin was still bubbling through her veins and it didn't appear to have anywhere to go. Trying not to gaze at Tash's rear view – at the way his jeans clung to his narrow hips as he leaned across the mixing console to close down the computer – she said, 'So, this is what you do when you want to have fun.'

'Mmm.' He had his back to her, but she thought he

was smiling. 'Better than sex, don't you think?'

'That depends on who you're doing it with.'

He was definitely smiling now. 'I thought you didn't want to sleep with me.'

'I didn't want to sleep with the famous Tash Janssen,' she replied carefully. 'But you're different.'

Izzy held her breath as he turned and came to stand before her, then slowly reached out and drew her to her feet. Even more slowly, he traced the curve of her cheek with a forefinger. Hopelessly excited, incapable of concealing her own longing, she was pink-cheeked and trembling.

'We have a business partnership,' he reminded her. 'I don't think it would be a wise move. I really don't think we should risk spoiling that.'

Oh bugger, thought Izzy, not knowing whether to argue the point or give in gracefully. The humiliation of it all! And how Sam would laugh if he ever found out that she had been rejected by none other than Tash Janssen, the most unscrupulous seducer since Valentino.

'Right,' she said bravely, attempting to sound business-like and uncrushed. 'Of course. Look, it's past Jericho's bedtime. I'd better be making a move . . .'

But she didn't move anywhere, because at that moment Tash bent his head and kissed her, slowly, luxuriously and with stunning finesse. It was about the most unbusiness-like kiss she had ever encountered, and her senses reeled. Izzy was now thoroughly confused.

'Just checking,' murmured Tash, glancing over her shoulder and meeting Jericho's calm, unflinching gaze.

'What?'

'That dog of yours. He is one lousy chaperone.'

She looked surprised. 'Of course he is. Would I have brought him along otherwise?'

'I don't know.' Pausing, he slid his hand beneath her hair and idly stroked the sensitive nape of her neck. 'I don't know what you might do.'

Izzy thought she might be in danger of exploding with frustration. Trying not to squirm, she said faintly, 'Look, you said we were business partners. This isn't very fair . . .'

'You said you didn't want to sleep with me,' he reminded her for the second time. Then he smiled. 'Maybe I was lying, too.'

'I wasn't lying,' Izzy protested, wanting him to understand. 'I just changed my mind.'

Suppressing laughter, Tash pulled her towards him once more. 'Well, don't do it again. At least, not for the next couple of hours . . .'

# Chapter 30

Tash was a light sleeper. Through half-closed eyes he watched for some time while Izzy crept about the bedroom struggling to locate her clothes in the dark. Finally, he said, 'What on earth are you trying to do?'

'Find my shoes.' Izzy, who had barely slept at all, didn't turn to look at him. She had been lying awake, bitterly regretting her actions, even before he had flung out a bare arm and murmured, 'Anna,' in his sleep. She'd already known she'd made a mistake, but that was the moment when she realised she could no longer stay. She'd behaved just as Sam had predicted and now she was suffering the inevitable consequences. She was nothing but a tart. And where the bloody hell *were* her shoes, anyway?

'You don't have to leave.' Tash sounded amused but made no move towards her. 'Breakfast will be served from eight-thirty onwards. Why don't you just come back to bed and—?'

'No, thanks.' Izzy abruptly intercepted him, sensing that he was humouring her. Just as he must have humoured so many other women in the past, she thought with a surge of shame. 'I'm going home.'

This time he yawned and made a non-committal gesture. 'If that's what you want, OK. Don't say I didn't offer.'

'Don't worry,' she replied evenly, dredging up every last vestige of pride. 'I won't say anything at all.'

Tash smiled to himself as the two figures came into view ahead of him, imprisoned in the twin beams of his headlights. Izzy Van Asch was one hell of a stubborn lady. A barefoot stubborn lady, at that. He was impressed they'd managed to get this far in the twenty minutes or so since they'd left the house.

Slowing to a crawl alongside them, he lowered his window and held out one of her shoes. 'OK, Cinderella, you've made your point. Were you really thinking of walking all the way back to Kensington?'

Since Kensington was over twenty miles away, Izzy certainly was not. As soon as she reached the nearest village – she could have sworn they'd passed one on the way here last night – she was going to find a public callbox and phone for a cab. But the village had mysteriously distanced itself from Tash's isolated home, the soles of her feet were burning with pain and she was *hungry* . . .

'Come on, get in,' said Tash, admiring her spirit. 'Look, poor old Jericho wants a lift, even if you don't.'

Jericho, with characteristic shamelessness, was pressing his nose against the window. Izzy couldn't help smiling at the expression on his face. When Tash opened the car's rear door the dog scrambled on to the back seat with all the grace of an eager groupie.

'I don't turn out at five-thirty in the morning for just anyone, you know,' he remarked as Izzy slid into the passenger seat.

'I'm not just anyone.'

'Of course you aren't. You're a damn sight more bloody-minded than most people I know.'

They had breakfast at an hotel in Windsor, sitting out on the terrace and watching a string of polo ponies setting out on their dawn gallop across the dew-drenched lawns of Windsor Great Park. Jericho, wolfing down sausages and basking in the pale, early morning sunlight, was in heaven. So were the hotel staff, when they realised they had Tash Janssen on the premises.

'I felt cheap,' Izzy explained, feeling immeasurably better after five bacon sandwiches and several cups of strong black coffee.

'Maybe I did, too.' Behind his dark glasses, Tash gave her a mocking grin. 'Hasn't it occurred to you that whenever some woman wonders what it must be like to go to bed with a rock star, I'm the one on the receiving end? They don't want *me*, they just want to screw a celebrity and it's up to me to put in a good performance, otherwise they'll rush out and tell all their friends how hopeless I was.'

Izzy, who hadn't thought of it that way, pinched a grilled mushroom from his plate and said, 'You weren't hopeless, you were very good.'

'Of course I was good!' He raised his eyebrows in mock despair. 'That's because it wouldn't be healthy for my ego if you were to go belting off to the papers screaming, "We were going to record a song together but he was so terrible in bed I couldn't bear to go through with it. I'm going to sing with Des O'Connor instead." '

'Des O'Connor,' breathed Izzy reverently. 'I hadn't thought of him. How *stupid* of me . . .'

Katerina's heart sank when she rounded the corner and saw Andrew waiting for her in his car. It wasn't what she needed right now, but at the same time she wasn't particularly surprised to find him here. Last night had been awful and he hadn't taken it at all well. Katerina wondered whether he'd had as little sleep as she had. The big difference, of course, was that he wasn't due to take a final physics exam in less than half an hour.

'Kat, we have to talk.' Andrew certainly didn't look as if he'd slept. His thin face was almost grey with anxiety and the inside of the car was thick with cigarette smoke. Since a group of Katerina's classmates were meandering past, however, she wasn't about to get involved in a shouting match on the pavement. Pulling the passenger door shut behind her, she said wearily, 'I'm not going to change my mind, Andrew. We can't carry on seeing each other. It's *wrong* and I've been a selfish bitch—'

'But I love you,' he said urgently, trying to take her hand. 'And you love me, so how can it possibly be wrong? Nothing else *matters*.'

'Gina matters.' Katerina closed her eyes. When she opened them again a second later she saw Simon heading towards them, pretending not to look inside the car. 'Marcy does, too. She's just suffered a miscarriage. You should be looking after her.'

She was holding herself rigidly away from him. Andrew, longing to take her into his arms, knew she didn't really mean what she was saying.

'I want to look after you,' he told her, willing her to stop this stupid game. 'Kat, I've never loved anyone as much as I love you.'

Simon, rounding the final corner, swallowed hard when he saw who was waving to him by the school gates. Shit, now what was he supposed to do?

'Simon!' Izzy called out to him, as if he could have failed to notice her. Whoever could miss Izzy Van Asch? he thought, colouring with pleasure at the sight of her even as his mind raced ahead to the immediate problem of preventing her from seeing Kat and Andrew together.

'I had to come and wish Kat good luck for this morning and she hasn't arrived yet,' she explained, her dark eyes alight with amusement. 'I can't believe it – for the very first time in my life I'm early and she's late.'

Simon, crossing his fingers behind his back, said, 'She'll be here any minute now.'

'And how about you? Are you nervous?'

'Uh . . . yes.' That was an understatement. He promptly turned one shade pinker as Izzy gave him a kiss on the cheek.

'Well, don't be. You'll both do brilliantly, I know it. And then there's tonight to look forward to,' she added cheerfully. 'Where have you decided you want to go?'

Simon, who didn't have a clue what she was talking about, hesitated for a second. 'Well, Cambridge is my first choice. Although Mum isn't so keen on the idea of me leaving home.'

Izzy burst out laughing. 'I'm talking about restaurants, not universities. Honestly, that daughter of mine! Didn't she even tell you I'm taking the two of you out to dinner tonight?'

Distracted by the realization that the sleek bronze car parked at the kerbside was the very latest Mercedes, and that the big, ungainly dog peering out of the open window was Jericho, Simon said, 'Um . . . she must have forgotten to mention it.'

'It's Tash Janssen's car.' Izzy, who had followed his gaze, smiled at the expression on his face. Clearly, Kat had kept equally quiet about Tash.

He gulped. 'Really?'

'Really. So, how about this meal tonight, then? Where would *you* like to go?'

Katerina's mother really was amazing, thought Simon. Awestruck, he craned his neck sideways in an effort to catch a casual glimpse of the driver. The tinted windows didn't help, but he was just about able to make out the silhouette of his hero, wearing sunglasses and drumming his fingers idly against the steering wheel.

'I've always wanted to go to Planet Hollywood,' said Simon hopefully, wondering if by some miracle Tash Janssen might be there, too.

Planet Hollywood? Good grief. Awash with disappointment, Izzy said, 'Not Le Gavroche?'

'Anywhere. Anywhere.'

Delighted, she pushed back her hair. 'Le Gavroche it is, then. As long as we can get a table at such short notice. Simon, where *is* Kat?'

Just around the corner, arguing with her lover. Simon, panicking all over again at the thought of the proximity between mother and daughter, muttered hastily, 'Don't worry, she won't be late. Do you really *know* Tash Janssen?'

Izzy paused, wondering where Kat might be. It wasn't likely, but there was always the faint possibility that she might have overslept. 'We're recording a song together,' she replied absently. 'Do you think we should be looking for her?'

'No!' Simon shuddered. 'She's never late. She'll *be* here. Le Gavroche . . . isn't that a bit expensive? Do they serve English food?'

'They serve the *best* food,' declared Izzy, with an expansive gesture. The next moment her gaze slid past Simon and her eyes lit up. 'There she is! Darling . . .'

Katerina wasn't in the mood for hugs and kisses and Walton-type endearments. Behind her, she could hear the tyres of Andrew's car squealing as he made his ill-tempered getaway. Ahead of her stood Izzy, still wearing last night's clothes, looking hopelessly unmotherly in skin-tight jeans and a lacy off-the-shoulder top. Simon, obviously entranced, towered over her and several fellow pupils were lingering on the pavement close to a sporty, metallic-bronze car which Kat just *knew* had to be connected in some way with Izzy.

'Mum, I've got an exam.'

'Of course you have! Sweetheart, I've just been talking to Simon. We're all set for dinner at Le Gavroche, but we couldn't resist coming to wish you luck. Down, Jericho! Kat, you must say hallo to Tash Janssen. Tash, this is my brilliant daughter.'

Izzy, flushed with pride, pulled open the driver's door of the Mercedes and the girls lingering on the pavement gaped. Katerina, desperately on edge after her difficult encounter with Andrew, could scarcely bear to meet the eyes of Tash Janssen. She wished she could murder her mother.

'Say hallo,' prompted Izzy, puzzled by her daughter's lack of enthusiasm. 'We drove all the way over here to see you . . .'

'I didn't ask you to,' Katerina retaliated crossly, realizing she was on the verge of tears. This was all too much, too embarrassing for words. The other girls were giggling like five year olds, pushing each other closer to get a better look at this stupid rock star, and she was the one who would have to put up with their inane questions later. Trust Izzy, she thought bitterly, to turn her A level exams into a bloody circus.

Simon, glancing at his watch, said, 'It's nine o'clock, Kat.'

'We have to go,' she explained brusquely, beginning to edge away.

Disappointed, Izzy gave her a hug. 'Well, good luck, darling. You'll do brilliantly, I know you will.'

Katerina tried not to flinch as her mother kissed her; it was too reminiscent of the way Andrew had tried to put his arms around her just now in the car. 'Don't, Mum,' she said in pained tones. 'Everybody's watching.'

'So what?' declared Izzy, trying to coax a smile out of her and failing absolutely. 'Who cares?'

'I care,' snapped Katerina. Then, more cruelly than she had intended, she added, 'We don't *all* long to be the centre of attention, you know. Not *all* the bloody time.'

# Chapter 31

It was no good. By mid-morning, it was glaringly obvious that his inability to concentrate was affecting his work. Even Pam, his secretary, had been moved to enquire whether anything was wrong.

Everything's wrong, Andrew had wanted to shout at her, hating the way her eyebrows rose in polite disbelief as, emphasizing every mistake, she proceeded to read his dictation back to him.

'Maybe you're going down with summer 'flu,' she suggested, not believing for a second that he was really ill. Something was up, and her fertile imagination was at work figuring out what it might be. Three times this week she'd fielded phone calls from Marcy Carpenter, telling her Andrew was in a meeting when in reality he'd slipped out of the office for yet another prolonged 'lunch appointment'. Pam, who spent her own meagre lunch breaks devouring egg-and-cress sandwiches and Mills and Boon romances borrowed from the local library, couldn't help hoping that Andrew and Gina would get back together. Gina had always remembered her birthday, complimented her on her cardigans and been interested enough to ask her how she was, whereas Marcy Carpenter was nothing but a selfish, idle trollop.

'I do have a bit of a headache,' lied Andrew. His headache was persuading Katerina to see reason, making her understand that guilt and a ridiculous sense of obligation towards Gina weren't valid reasons to end their love affair.

Ever practical, Pam said, 'I've got some aspirins in my handbag.'

Gina had always carried aspirins around in her bag. For a fleeting moment Andrew wished she'd swallow a whole tub of them, then she wouldn't be able to stand in the way – however unwittingly – of his own happiness. It was ludicrous, he thought with rising frustration, that Katerina should feel compelled to make such a noble gesture simply to save the feelings of the wife from whom he was separated. Who, after all, could say whether Gina would even *care* . . . ?

'Thanks,' he replied absently, rising to his feet and almost knocking a stack of files to the floor as he did so. 'But I think I'll take a breath of fresh air instead. I'll be back by two if anyone needs to speak to me.'

He was out of the office within seconds. Although it was only eleven forty-five, Pam pulled her packed lunch out of her capacious handbag and settled down to enjoy a few extra chapters of *A Marriage Made in Heaven* by Desirée Bell. She deserved that much at least, she told herself as she bit forcefully into an apple. If Andrew Lawrence couldn't even wish her a happy birthday he needn't expect *her* to slave away over his rotten, incompetent dictation.

Andrew knew vaguely where Gina was working because Katerina had once told him, but he had to use the *Yellow Pages* in order to get the full address. Fired up with enthusiasm – it was so blindingly obvious, he couldn't think why the idea hadn't occurred to him earlier – he drove straight over to Doug Steadman's office and took the stairs two at a time, only pausing for breath when he reached the door at the top of the landing, upon which a small, highly polished plaque announced D. STEADMAN, THEATRICAL AGENT.

'Andrew!' Gina looked up, startled. Automatically, her left hand smoothed her straight, blonde hair, as it always did when she was caught unawares. The fact that she was no longer wearing her wedding ring was, he felt, an encouraging sign.

'I had to see you,' he explained, his eyes bright with purpose, and Gina felt her heart begin to pound. Could it all be over between Andrew and Marcy? Had he come here to ask her to forgive him? Did he really want to come back to her?

'Y-yes?' she stammered, twisting a pencil between her fingers and wishing she'd worn a dress that wasn't four years old. She hadn't had time to blow dry her hair with her customary attention to detail this morning, either. And why, oh why, had she allowed Izzy to bulldoze her into leaving off her wedding ring?

'We have to talk, Gina. About something very important.'

At least Doug was out of the office. An audience would be more than she could cope with, thought Gina faintly, although it certainly hadn't seemed to bother Debra Winger in *An Officer and a Gentleman*.

'OK,' she murmured, reaching out with trembling fingers and taking the phone off the hook. She'd just have to pray that no one came into the office and interrupted them. 'What do we have to talk about?'

Having intended coming straight out with it, Andrew now understood that in order to avoid confusion he must first fill Gina in on one or two other pertinent details.

'Look, the situation with Marcy and me . . . well, it isn't working out. I thought I was in love with her, but I realise now that I was wrong. If I'm honest, it started going wrong almost straight away.'

My God, thought Gina, struggling to contain herself. This is really happening! I can't believe it . . .

'The baby,' she murmured, feeling so light-headed she had to grip the edge of her desk.

Andrew looked momentarily surprised. He'd forgotten she didn't know about that. 'Oh, she lost it.' He dismissed the subject with an airy gesture. 'Miscarriage, a couple of weeks ago. I shouldn't say it, of course, but in some respects it was a bit of a relief, what with the way things were going between us. As soon as she finds herself somewhere to live, Marcy will be moving out of the flat. It was just one of those things, really. I suppose we all make mistakes.'

Oh God, thought Gina. Oh God, he wants me back . . .

'So, that's that out of the way.' Andrew took a deep, steadying breath. 'I had to explain, otherwise you'd have thought I was behaving badly. The thing is, you see, I've met someone else now. And this time it *is* for real. The only problem at the moment is the fact that she thinks you might be upset if you found out about it.'

Gina attempted to smooth her hair, but her arm was so heavy she couldn't lift it. Her entire body felt like lead.

Her heartbeat had slowed to an ominous, funereal pace.

'What?'

'Of course, *I* knew you wouldn't mind,' continued Andrew, adopting a hearty manner. It was quite the best way, he'd decided; if he was forceful enough he could make Gina realise it was the only sensible attitude to take. 'We're practically divorced, after all, but she was still worried.' Leaning forward, he added confidentially, 'I think she's afraid you might never speak to her again, or some such ridiculous thing.'

Gina sat there, paralysed. It was like thinking you'd won an Olympic medal, then being told you were being disqualified through no fault of your own. And in the few mind-numbing seconds following the realization that Andrew was talking about another woman, she had struggled to envisage the stranger – a chic, dark-haired divorcée, possibly – with whom he had fallen in love.

But now . . . now he was making it plain to her that the woman was someone she actually *knew*, and not only was that so much worse than any imaginary stranger, but she couldn't for the life of her even begin to guess who it might be.

Until Andrew, in his eagerness to sort the matter out, said, 'And she'll be moving into my flat, so you don't have to worry about any awkwardness at home.'

It was becoming progressively harder for Gina to breathe. Betrayal hit her like a hammer blow. She couldn't believe it.

'You. You and . . . Izzy . . .' she said faintly.

'*Izzy?*' Andrew, staring at her in amazement, almost laughed. How could anybody get something *so* wrong?

'Do me a favour, old thing! It's not Izzy I'm talking about. It's Kat.'

Izzy, having spent the day with Tash at his record company's headquarters, had discovered how the other half of the music industry really lived. MBT, the label to which she herself had been signed, was a young and thrusting company with a great reputation for fostering promising new talent. By contrast, Stellar Records was quite simply *the* biggest label in the business and it had the headquarters to prove it. Stellar House, situated in Highgate, was as big as a museum and twice as impressive. Open-mouthed, Izzy had followed Tash along endless, record-lined corridors and been introduced to people-who-mattered along the way. Within an hour of their arrival his manager was summoned and faxes started to fly. Meetings were set up between Tash's 'people' and hers. Contracts were drafted over a stupendous lunch. And Izzy was warned in no uncertain terms – on at least five separate occasions – that under no circumstances whatsoever must she either do, say or even think anything which might have a detrimental effect upon Tash Janssen's career. At all costs, his reputation must stay intact.

At this, Tash had cast her a sideways glance and awaited the explosion, but Izzy had thought it so funny she'd simply laughed. 'You mean like letting slip his deepest, darkest, most *shameful* secrets?' she had countered, with a subtle wink in his manager's direction. Harvey Purnell had coughed, straightened his bow tie and replied stiffly, 'I mean precisely that, Miss Van Asch.'

'OK, don't panic,' she replied with a grin. 'I won't

breathe a word about the fact that he knits all his own sweaters. Not to *anyone*.'

'I've heard of bringing your work home with you,' Vivienne grumbled as Sam set the word processor down, 'but this is ridiculous.'

He never seemed to *be* at home these days, she amended fretfully. And now it looked as if even those few precious hours when he was were going to be taken up with yet more boring paperwork.

Sam, however, replied drily, 'Don't sulk. It's for Katerina.'

'Oh yes?'

'She's just finished taking her A levels and I wanted to give her something which would be useful when she starts her medical training. Since we're in the process of replacing our computer system at The Steps, I thought she may as well have this.'

Vivienne softened. Sam was extremely fond of Katerina, who worked hard and appeared to possess so many of the attributes which Izzy – as far as *he* was concerned – sadly lacked. Privately, Vivienne had never before encountered a seventeen-year-old girl who dreamt about logarithms and who seemed to have no interest whatsoever in boys. As far as she was concerned, attractive girls like Katerina weren't meant to devote their teenage lives to serious study. It surely wasn't *natural* . . .

# Chapter 32

When they arrived at Kingsley Grove at six-thirty that evening, however, only Gina was there.

'It's a present for Kat,' explained Vivienne with enthusiasm as Sam carried the word processor through to the dining room and placed it carefully on the highly polished table. If he could get it up and running before she returned home, so much the better.

'Katerina doesn't live here any more.'

'What?' Sam straightened and turned to face Gina, who had spoken the words in a tone that was almost nonchalant. 'She was here yesterday.'

'She doesn't live here any more,' repeated Gina with a shrug.

Sam was frowning. Vivienne, hearing the click of the front gate, peered through the dining-room window and said, 'Well it doesn't matter, because she's here now. Quick, Sam – plug it in and make it do something intelligent!'

'Don't plug it in.' As Katerina's key turned in the door, Gina's gaze flickered momentarily towards the fireplace. Hurling her wedding ring into it earlier had given her enormous pleasure. Emptying the contents of Katerina's carefully annotated A level files on top of it and watching the whole lot go up in flames had been even better.

\* \* \*

'So tell me,' she enquired evenly as Katerina entered the room, 'how long have you been screwing my husband?'

Katerina froze. Simon, who was one step behind her, almost fell over.

Shit, I don't believe this, thought Sam.

'Tell me,' Gina repeated with mechanical slowness, 'how long you've been . . . sleeping with him.'

Oh God. Katerina, clinging to the door handle for support, met the steely grey gaze and experienced a surge of nausea. She hadn't wanted this to happen. She hadn't wanted to hurt Gina. She didn't want *anyone* to be hurt . . .

But it had happened and there was no escape. Gina knew. The game was up. She wished she didn't feel so sick.

'Not long,' she replied in a voice that was barely audible. 'A few weeks, that's all. Gina, I'm so sorry—'

'You aren't sorry. You're a lying bitch,' hissed Gina, her grey eyes narrow with hatred. 'A lying, hypocritical, back-stabbing *bitch*.'

Katerina looked as if she was about to pass out. Since Simon was clearly not planning on being any use at all, Vivienne rushed forward and caught her, putting her arm around Katerina's thin waist and guiding her into the nearest chair. Shocked by Gina's venomous outburst, astounded and inwardly enthralled by the revelation, Vivienne was having to make a lightning reappraisal of Izzy's daughter. 'It's OK, it's OK,' she murmured sympathetically. The poor kid was evidently no match for Gina at full throttle, for the moment at least. She needed someone on her side.

'I still can't believe I'm hearing this,' said Sam. Since he knew Katerina rather better than Vivienne, he was even more stunned. Instinctively, however, he moved towards Gina, who had just been through the worst six months of her life and who was now being delivered yet another body blow. Andrew and *Katerina*, for heaven's sake.

Simon, who had been looking forward to Le Gavroche all day, and who had been forced by his mother into wearing his father's best tweed jacket for the occasion, jumped a mile as the front door swung open and shut once more. The next moment he broke into a sweat; Izzy had brought Tash Janssen back with her. Oh God, oh God . . .

'Goodness!' Izzy exclaimed, surveying the frozen tableau before her. '*Hasn't* it gone quiet all of a sudden!' Grinning at Vivienne and pointedly ignoring Sam, she went on cheerfully, 'You must have been talking about me.'

'Mum . . .' It came out as an agonised croak. The expression on Izzy's face changed and in a flash she was at Katerina's side.

'Sweetheart, your exam! Was it awful? It couldn't have been *that* awful, you've worked so hard for it . . .'

'Your daughter isn't upset about her exams,' Gina cut in icily. 'She's upset because I've found out about her sordid affair with my husband.'

Katerina was clinging to Izzy. Sam placed his hand on Gina's arm. From his position in the doorway, Tash let out a low whistle. This was interesting.

'Don't be ridiculous.' Izzy frowned, her gaze shifting

enquiringly from Gina to Vivienne. Was Gina having some kind of breakdown? And if so, why was everyone simply allowing it to happen? How could they stand there and let her hurl accusations at poor Kat when they were so patently untrue?

But everyone *was* letting it happen. And Vivienne, her customary smile now absent, was nodding at her as if silently to confirm that what Gina had said was correct. With mounting unease, Izzy said, 'Come on! Is this some kind of joke? Kat doesn't even *know* Andrew.'

'Oh, she knows him all right.' Gina, shaking slightly, wished someone would pour her a drink. 'She knows him in every sense of the word. Apparently, they're *in love* with each other, and just as soon as he manages to dump Marcy, Katerina's going to be moving in with him. It's all terribly romantic . . .'

Izzy gripped Katerina's hands. Slowly, evenly, she demanded, 'Is this true?'

'No.' Katerina shook her head, pleading with her to understand. Her voice broke as she went on, 'Well, not all of it. I'm not seeing him any more. It's over, now.'

'But you *have* had an affair with him?' Izzy had to make sure she'd got it absolutely right. 'With Andrew Lawrence?'

The picture of misery, Katerina nodded. 'Yes.'

Sam was prepared for almost anything, except what happened next. The slap resounded through the air and Katerina's head jerked backwards, the imprint of Izzy's hand white on her cheek. Even Gina looked appalled.

'How could you have *done* it?' Izzy shrieked, oblivious now to their audience. Her dark eyes were ablaze, her whole body rigid with fury. 'You stupid, callous, cheating little bitch!'

Before she could slap her again, Sam intervened. Izzy, it seemed, had sailed through the last seventeen years without ever having had to deal with the problems traditionally associated with motherhood. Now, however, shocked and appalled by her daughter's lapse – and by the evidence that she was not, after all, perfect – she was unable to control herself.

'OK, OK,' he said, drawing her away as Katerina burst into tears and Vivienne attempted to comfort her. It occurred to him that Izzy's reaction was a touch hypocritical, anyway. She wasn't exactly the greatest example in the world for any daughter to follow.

'It is *not* OK!' yelled Izzy, struggling without success to get free and close to tears herself. 'It's disgusting! We live in this house,' she went on, turning to face Katerina once more and almost choking on the words, 'and you've abused that privilege in the worst way possible. You're nothing but a shameless slut. Oh God . . . I'm so *ashamed* of you . . .'

In the throes of her misery, Katerina had nevertheless assumed that the one person in the world who would understand her situation, and who would automatically defend her, was her mother. As she had supported Izzy through years of unconventional living, subterfuge and chaos, so she had expected comfort and understanding in return. But that hadn't happened. Izzy had let her down. Even more unbelievably, for the first time in her entire life, she had slapped her.

'I'm not a slut,' she shouted back, her long hair

swinging as she jumped to her feet. 'You're the one who sleeps with drug-crazed rock stars, for God's sake. If anyone's a slut, it's you!'

Tash, both amused and faintly bemused by the goings-on, had seconds earlier been thinking he could use a joint right now. At this, he raised one eyebrow and smiled, earning himself a look of undiluted disgust from Sam.

'How dare you lecture me on *my* morals?' Katerina's fists were clenched with fury at her sides as she continued her tirade. 'You've never even behaved like a proper mother! Real mothers listen to their children and look after them. They have real homes. Sometimes they even have husbands. Why couldn't I have a mother like that?' she wailed, dimly aware that she had gone too far, but unable to take it back now. 'Why did I have to get *you*?'

The appalled silence which greeted this final, terrible insult was broken by the drainlike rumbling of Simon's empty stomach. Utterly mortified, he hung his head and mumbled, 'Sorry.' Tash, standing beside him, was once again unable to disguise his amusement.

'You aren't the one who needs to apologise.' Izzy, still shell-shocked, turned to Simon. 'Oh, you poor boy . . . how could Katerina have done this to you? It must be so terrible for you, finding out like this . . .'

Oh God, oh God. Abruptly, Simon found himself embroiled in the very centre of the deception. Crimson-cheeked, he tried to look cheated-on, but Katerina soon put paid to that.

'Let's get everything straight, shall we? Simon is not – and never has been – my boyfriend.' Then, because it didn't matter any more, she added with an air of careless triumph, 'Although he has, of course, been a great alibi.'

Within the space of two seconds flat, poor cuckolded Simon became in-on-it-all-along Simon, partner in deception and now public enemy number two. The expressions on the faces of Izzy and Gina said it all.

Sam, who had known Andrew Lawrence longer than anybody else in the room, wondered what the hell Andrew had thought he was doing. Separated from his wife, currently in the process of dumping his pregnant girlfriend and now involved in an affair with a hopelessly inexperienced teenager. It was sheer madness . . .

Meanwhile, however, somebody had to do something before Izzy and Kat came to real blows. Taking his car keys from his pocket, he said, 'Vivienne, take Kat back to the flat.'

'Andrew's flat?' Gina intercepted in cutting tones. 'Won't it be a little crowded?'

'Stop it.' Sam quelled her with a look, then turned to address Tash. 'Maybe you should leave us to sort this out.'

Two things intrigued Tash. Firstly, Sam Sheridan clearly wasn't too impressed by the fact that he had arrived here with Izzy, making him wonder whether there might not have been something undercover going on between the two of them until very recently. The set-up in this house, he reflected daily, was downright *complicated*.

As for the other item of interest . . .

'I was just leaving,' he drawled, unable to resist the opportunity to say what had apparently not yet occurred to anyone else. Stepping towards Izzy, he kissed her briefly on the mouth. 'Give me a call tomorrow and let me know what you decide.'

Distracted and confused, she said, 'Decide about what?'

'The deal.' Carefully, he pushed a strand of dark hair away from her cheek. 'You signed a contract with Stellar this afternoon, but I'll understand if you don't want to go ahead with it now.'

Izzy was still puzzled. What on earth did that have to do with Andrew Lawrence?

'Your daughter,' explained Tash with a brief, sardonic look in Simon's direction. 'And those touching lyrics of hers. I think we can safely assume, in the light of all this, that she wasn't dreaming of old Roy of the Rovers here when she wrote "Never, Never".'

# Chapter 33

'You can stay here with us,' Sam told Katerina the following morning. Having slipped out of the flat at eight-thirty and returned half an hour later with a copy of *Loot*, her black coffee had grown cold beside her as she proceeded to study and circle the small ads. Pale, gripped with determination and refusing to even discuss yesterday's calamitous showdown, she now chewed the top of her felt-tipped pen and shook her head.

'Of course I can't stay. You're the good guys and I'm the social leper. Don't worry, I'll find something in no time.'

'A rat-infested hovel,' Vivienne put in, helping herself to a slice of the toast which Sam had made for Katerina, and which hadn't even been touched. 'Honey, you can't do that. How will you *live*?'

Hollow-eyed from lack of sleep, Katerina shrugged. 'I'll get a job.'

Sam had already offered her money and been politely but firmly turned down. She was every bit as stubborn as her mother, he thought with a trace of despair; the only difference was that Izzy would have pocketed the loan without even blinking.

'Let me phone Izzy,' urged Vivienne, through a mouthful of toast. 'Look, she was upset last night – she'll be over that now. Oh please, let me call her.'

'No.' Bleakly, Katerina recalled the terrible things they had said to each other . . . the slap on the cheek . . . Izzy's reaction when she realised that 'Never, Never' had been written not for Simon, but for Andrew . . . 'I don't want to see her. I *won't* speak to her.'

Vivienne gazed at the girl before her, dressed in an olive-green T-shirt and white shorts and with her long brown legs tucked beneath her on the chair. Until yesterday, she had envied Izzy her easy, uncomplicated relationship with her daughter. Now she couldn't even begin to imagine what her friend might be going through. 'Sweetheart, your mom loves you. She's *worried* about you.'

'Bullshit.' Katerina didn't look up. Dangerously close to tears once more, she said, 'Do you think I haven't worried about *her*? I've supported my mother all my life. This is the very first time I've *ever* needed her to support me . . . and she didn't. She's let me down and I don't think I'll ever forgive her for that. She hates me for what I've done and I hate her back. From now on, she can do what she likes with her stupid men and her stupid music. I don't care any more what kind of a mess she makes of it all.'

'Forget Izzy for the moment,' countered Sam, deciding to risk another outburst. Personally, he thought Andrew deserved castration at the very least. 'What about you and Andrew?'

This time Katerina did look up. He saw the sadness in her eyes, and the determined line of her mouth. 'That's what makes it so ironic,' she replied bitterly. 'I really had finished with him . . . put it all behind me. But now that all this has happened, I may as well carry on seeing him after all.'

'Kat, get back into the car. You aren't even going to *look* at this one.'

It was three-thirty in the afternoon and Sam was beginning to lose patience. Katerina's search for a bedsitter had led them from one unbelievably dreary address to another and the accommodation on offer had been so sordid he could hardly bear it. Still in a belligerent mood, she had initially been reluctant to allow him to accompany her, but he was bloody glad he had, otherwise the chances were she'd have been raped or murdered by now. Even in daylight the buildings were sinister. And now here they were in the depths of the East End outside 14 Finnegan Street, whose windows were cracked and opaque with grime and whose crumbling front wall was holding up a row of bleary-eyed, bottle-wielding tramps.

'It's cheap,' Katerina replied briefly, ignoring him. 'I can afford it.'

Sam couldn't let her go in alone. Locking the car, he put his hand on her shoulder as they approached the front door. 'Look, you really can't live in a place like this, temporarily or otherwise. I don't understand why you won't let me lend you enough money to rent somewhere decent.'

'Oh, please.' Katerina threw him a look of resignation. 'We've been through this before. I happen to know how you feel about lending money to a Van Asch.'

She knocked at the door and read the graffiti sprayed over it. 'Whoever wrote that can't spell.'

'You aren't Izzy,' persisted Sam. 'This isn't the same thing at all.'

'Of course it's the same thing.' She half-smiled. 'I wouldn't be able to pay you back for years.'

'But that doesn't matter!' Exasperated, he reached for her hand. 'Come on, we're leaving. There's no one here.'

As the door began to creak open, an overpowering smell of mould and cats' pee billowed out to meet them.

'Just a quick look,' said Katerina, who had no intention of borrowing so much as a bus fare from Sam Sheridan. 'Come on. Who knows, it might have hidden depths.'

It didn't have hidden depths. The depths were all there on display, from the damp-blackened walls to the hideously matted rug only half-covering bare floorboards. The furniture, such as it was, was unbelievably decrepit, the curtains were too small for the filthy window and the only light was provided by a naked bulb dangling from the ceiling.

When the scrawny landlady offered Katerina the room and she in turn accepted, Sam couldn't even speak. She was doing it deliberately, he now realised, and there was nothing on earth he could do to stop her.

'Well?' he drawled, when they were out of the house. 'Happy now?'

Beneath the calm veneer, Katerina was feeling slightly sick. Nothing seemed real any more. It was as if her body was making the decisions without consulting her brain. Finding work and somewhere to live were just things she had to do.

'Does it matter?' she countered with an offhand gesture. 'At least everyone else will be happy.'

'Oh yes, delirious.' Revving the car's engine and startling the tramps out of their collective stupor, Sam screeched away from the kerb. 'They'll all be thrilled, I'm sure, when they find out where you're going to be living.'

Katerina was gazing abstractedly out of the window. 'It's none of their business, anyway,' she murmured. 'And it's been very kind of you, driving me around like this, but my problems aren't actually anything to do with you, either.'

She was determined to punish herself. More than ever now, Sam longed to confront Andrew and make him realise the extent of the damage he had caused. A mid-life crisis was one thing, he thought irritably, but this was wrecking people's lives.

In response to his phone call, Izzy had arrived at Sam's flat at seven o'clock. Judging by her outfit – a new, black-sequinned dress and ludicrously high heels – she wasn't exactly prostrate with concern for her only daughter.

'She's moved into a bedsitter in Stepney and got herself a job in BurgerBest,' he said shortly. 'She also tells me she isn't going to medical school.'

'So?' countered Izzy, still boiling with resentment towards him and hating the way he was now trying to make *her* feel like a wayward schoolgirl. 'What am I supposed to do about it? Kidnap her and lock her up in a cupboard?'

'How nice to see you taking your parental responsibilities so seriously.' Sarcasm fuelled his own annoyance. Izzy's *laissez-faire* attitude might have worked in the past, but it was the last thing Katerina needed right now.

As if she realised this, Izzy's expression changed. Sinking down on to the arm of the settee, she stopped glaring at him and heaved an enormous sigh. 'OK, OK, of course I'm not happy about it, but there really isn't a great deal I can do to stop her. She's almost eighteen years old and she's been carrying on an affair with a man old enough to be her father, for heaven's sake. Maybe a few weeks in a bedsitter will give her time to think it through.'

'Izzy, this particular bedsitter had to be seen to be believed. It's a health hazard.' Handing her a piece of paper, he said, 'Look, here's the address.'

'No.' She shook her head, refusing to take it. 'I won't do that. I'm not going to approve of what Kat's done.'

'You're making a mistake,' Sam said warningly. 'She needs you.'

Izzy's eyes glittered, her temper flaring once more. 'And you're her long-lost father figure, I suppose,' she retaliated, stung by the criticism. 'Maybe when you've brought up a child of your own, *on* your own, I might listen to your brilliant advice. But until then, I'll do what I – as a parent – think is best. OK?'

He had injured her pride. Too late, Sam realised that if he had urged her to disown Katerina, there was every possibility Izzy would have done the opposite.

'At least keep the address,' he said with resignation. 'And if you should happen to bump into her, try and make her see that she can't give up her place at medical school.'

Izzy cast him a derisive look. Comments like that only

went to prove how little he really knew Katerina. 'She might have said it, but she didn't mean it,' she replied in almost pitying tones. 'Medicine means more to her than anything. It's all she's ever wanted to do.'

'Cut!' yelled the director, and with a gurgle of relief Izzy collapsed into Tash's arms.

'Ever felt overdressed?' he drawled, helping her out of the full-length, dark green velvet coat which clung to her damp body.

'Ever thought of hiring a hit man,' Izzy countered, 'to take care of whichever sadist dreamt up this idea?'

The set, upon which part of the video for 'Never, Never' was being shot, depicted winter in Moscow. In reality, the first week of August was proving to be the hottest of the summer so far and the temperature had rocketed to 90°F in the shade. Izzy simply couldn't understand how forty seconds' worth of video could possibly take seven and a half hours to produce.

'You're looking at your watch again,' Tash observed drily. 'What's the problem? Supposed to be meeting your lover?'

It was a month since Izzy had even seen Sam, yet for some peculiar reason Tash continued to suggest that the two of them were indulging in some clandestine affair. At times he only appeared to be half-joking. Frustrated by the fact that – for once – she was innocent of such a crime yet at the same time touched by this evidence of Tash's own unexpected insecurity, she reached up and kissed the corner of his mouth.

'I told you this morning,' she said patiently, aware of

the fact that the make-up girl and lighting cameraman were eavesdropping behind them. 'There's a house in Wimbledon I'm going to look at. The estate agent's meeting me there at six.'

'What d'you want a house for?' Tash frowned. Over the past weeks, they had spent most of their time together. Nothing had been said . . . no formal arrangements had been made . . . but it had just so happened that a number of Izzy's clothes had gradually taken over one of his wardrobes. The almond-scented shampoo she always used was propped up on his bathroom shelf next to her toothbrush, and several spare pairs of shoes littered his bedroom floor. 'What's wrong with my house?'

'Nothing, except that it *is* your house.' Izzy grinned. It was possibly the most romantic thing he'd said to her, so far. 'I want one of my own.'

'Why?'

'Because I've never had one before. Not a decent one,' she corrected, unscrewing a bottle of lukewarm mineral water and pausing with it halfway to her mouth. 'Besides, it's been over a month now since Kat left. It's time to get that little matter sorted out, and since she can hardly move back to Kingsley Grove I thought I'd get us somewhere neutral.'

Initially attracted to Izzy by her determination and natural independence, Tash reflected now that such qualities had their drawbacks. He wasn't used to being turned down in any shape or form, yet this was what she was doing to him.

'She might not want to live with you,' he retaliated, holding the dark green velvet coat towards her as the director signalled that they were ready to go once more.

'Of course she will,' said Izzy, who didn't doubt it for a minute. There had been an argument, during which they had both said and done things they didn't mean, but now was the time for it to be put behind them and for Katerina to come home. 'She isn't the kind to hold a grudge. By this time tomorrow the whole silly business will be forgotten. And don't look at me like that,' she added, as the snow machines started up and a flurry of polystyrene pips hurled themselves like wasps against her face. 'She's my *daughter*, for heaven's sake. I've known her for years!'

# Chapter 34

Katerina felt like a zombie, not like herself at all. Everything was so hideous she no longer stopped to think about it, to consider the awfulness of this new life of hers, because if she did she knew she wouldn't be able to bear it.

But bear it she must, because this was her new life and it was what she deserved. Every day she worked gruelling shifts in BurgerBest, enduring the leers of the customers and the eternal smell of fried onions which clung to her skin and never seemed to wash away completely. Her feet ached, her head spun with the banality of it all and the money was poor. She didn't have the energy, when she returned home each night, to do more than bathe, listen numbly to the transistor radio which was her only luxury and fall into bed.

And all because of Andrew Lawrence; that was the strangest part. Everything happened for a reason, Katerina would remind herself, and Andrew had been hers.

He still loved her, of course, and came round to see her whenever he could, but Marcy was deliberately making things as awkward as possible for him and had made no attempt at all to find herself another flat. Katerina, who hadn't been lying when she'd told Sam she no longer loved Andrew, was half-grateful to Marcy for staying put, relieving her as it did from the necessity of making any further mistakes – which was what she now knew moving in with Andrew would be.

It was all such a muddle, though. Some evenings she found herself looking forward to his visits simply because of the comfort it gave her to know that someone still cared. Luckily, the old dragon of a landlady didn't permit overnight stays so she was spared the difficulty of refusing to allow him to spend the nights with her. But while sex no longer appealed, hugs and sympathy were very much needed. Particularly when she reminded herself that her future no longer lay in medicine, but in chargrilled triple-decker cow-burgers . . .

Katerina had thirty seconds' warning of Izzy's imminent arrival, thanks to Mrs Talmage's passion for curtain-twitching.

'Blimey, there's an 'elluva car pulled up outside,' her landlady reported, peering through the grimy glass while Katerina counted out the week's rent. 'Like somefing outta Dallas . . . 'ere love, come and 'ave a look at this! Some woman wiv a bloody great dog's gettin' out.'

Katerina's hard-earned money disappeared in a flash inside Mrs Talmage's apron pocket. Katerina, glancing through the window, said, 'That's my mother.'

'Never! Wiv a car like that?'

Wearily, Katerina envisaged her rent doubling. Her landlady's pale little eyes were alert with interest, her brain undoubtedly working overtime.

'It isn't her car,' she replied in abrupt tones. 'She's just showing off, as usual. Mrs Talmage, could you tell her I'm not here?'

The pale eyes widened, registering astonishment. 'What, you don't want to see your own mother? Get away wiv you, girl. She's come to visit, and the least you can do is offer her a cup of tea. Tell her you're not 'ere, indeed. I don't know . . .'

'Darling!' cried Izzy, just as Katerina had known she would. 'Come here and give me a great big hug!'

It was absolutely typical of her mother, thought Katerina, to erupt into the room in a swathe of scarves and perfume, wearing way too much make-up and pretending that nothing at all had happened. Added emotional blackmail had been provided, of course, in the form of Jericho, who barked delightedly and leapt up at her in a frenzy of adoration.

But happy as she was to see Jericho again, she had no intention of allowing Izzy to bulldoze her into daughterly submission. When Izzy enveloped her in an embrace she submitted politely but said nothing, concentrating instead on remembering how bitterly her mother had attacked her when she'd needed her most.

'Well, well,' Izzy said, kissing Katerina's cold cheek and gazing around the bedsitting room, with its badly painted walls and dreadful furniture. 'We've lived in some God-awful places in our time, sweetheart, but this has to be the pit to beat all pits. And was that your landlady who answered the door just now? I thought her piggy little eyes were going to drop out of her head when she saw me.'

'Probably because you're wearing false eyelashes,' Katerina observed, easing herself out of her mother's grasp. 'Would you like a cup of tea?'

'What am I, some old great aunt?' Izzy had already spotted the ancient two-ring stove, upon which stood a battered tin kettle. More than anything else, the pitiful sight of those two objects fuelled her determination to get her precious daughter out of this terrible place. 'Sweetheart, you're looking thin . . . you need a splendid meal inside you. Grab some shoes and come with me to Langan's.'

Katerina, who hadn't been eating much at all recently, was almost tempted. Then she shook her head.

'No, thanks.'

'But I've booked a table for eight-thirty,' protested Izzy, her composure beginning to slip. Outwardly cheerful and calm, no one could have guessed at the turmoil she'd been going through. This evening's rapprochement was something she'd been carefully planning for days.

'You can still go.' Katerina, struggling to remain calm herself, wasn't going to fall for emotional blackmail. More brutally than she had intended, she added, 'I'm sure you and Tash will enjoy yourselves there.'

'Oh Kat, don't.' Izzy looked stricken. Fiddling with the emerald-green silk scarf around her neck, she backed away and sat down abruptly on the edge of the unmade single bed. 'Sweetheart, we can't carry on like this. I've missed you so much. We have to talk about it.'

'We've already talked about it,' replied Katerina coldly. 'I know exactly what you think of me, and that's your prerogative. I just don't have to listen to you saying it if I don't want to.'

This wasn't going according to plan at all. Izzy, almost in tears now, wrenched off the stupid false eyelashes so painstakingly applied by the make-up girl earlier. 'Listen,' she pleaded in desperation, 'I understand about Andrew. I won't say a word against him. But Kat, you can't carry on living in this terrible place . . . I came here to tell you I've rented a house in Wimbledon, just for the two of us. We can go back to how we always were before . . .' In a hopeless attempt at humour, because it might win Katerina over, she forced herself to smile and added, 'Only richer, of course.'

Katerina had never seen her mother beg before. For a second she wavered. But it was no good; the damage had been done and it was too late to try and pretend it hadn't.

'We can't go back,' she replied bleakly, ignoring the look of desolation in her mother's eyes. 'Everything's different now. We have our own lives – and you've got the two things you always wanted: success and money.'

Izzy swallowed. Was that really how Kat thought of her?

'What about medical school?' she asked finally, to change the subject. 'Will you be able to cope, living here and commuting to Westminster every day? You won't be able to study and work in the evenings as well.'

Past caring by this time, Katerina went to the door and held it open in the hope that Izzy would take the hint and leave. 'That isn't going to be a problem,' she said, her tone blunt, but at the same time almost casual. 'Because I'm not going to medical school.'

'But—'

'And that isn't a threat, it's the simple truth. They wouldn't accept me now, anyway. You see, I've failed my exams.'

* * *

When Andrew arrived an hour and a half later, Katerina was in bed.

'You've been crying,' he said, putting his arms around her and feeling – as Izzy had done – how thin she had become. 'Angel, you mustn't cry. Everything's going to be all right. Marcy's moving out of the flat on Monday . . . in less than four days we'll be able to be together for the rest of our lives.'

Katerina, the brief outpouring of bitter tears behind her now, gritted her teeth and crawled back beneath the bedclothes. Today, it seemed, was her day for being offered somewhere to live by people she no longer wanted to live with.

But she wasn't up to another argument tonight. What she most needed now after the fraught meeting with Izzy earlier was physical comfort and a bit of tender loving care. And here was Andrew, in his crumpled grey suit, sitting on the edge of her bed and wondering what on earth he could do to cheer her up.

Gazing around the cheerless little room in search of inspiration, he said anxiously, 'How about a nice Chinese takeaway? I could pick up some chicken and pineapple with fried rice . . .?'

It must also be her day, she thought drily, for being offered food she didn't even want to eat.

'I don't want Chinese.' Slowly, almost absent-mindedly, she slid her hand beneath his jacket, running her fingers along the side seam of his shirt. At once, his breathing quickened and the expression in his eyes became hopeful. He understood that the past few weeks hadn't been easy for her, but constantly being rebuffed whenever he made any kind of physical advance hadn't exactly been the greatest ego boost in the world for him, either. They hadn't made love for over six weeks and the strain of wanting Katerina as badly as he did – while in turn having to live with Marcy, who wanted *him* – was beginning to tell.

'No?' Proceeding with caution, in case he was reading too much into the tentative gesture, he held his hand up to her forehead with mock concern. 'You don't want a Chinese takeaway? Shall I phone for the ambulance now?'

Katerina smiled. 'Not just yet.'

'How about an Indian, then? Lamb Passanda? Chicken Tikka and Naan bread?'

With a pang, Katerina remembered that Lamb Passanda was one of Simon's favourite Indian meals. Poor Simon, she hadn't treated him very well either.

But she needed the comfort of Andrew's presence, for now at least. And although she might be taking advantage of him, it wasn't as if she was asking him to do something unspeakably awful. For heaven's sake, it would make him *happy* . . .

'I don't want an Indian takeaway,' said Katerina, loosening his tie and wondering whether she would ever be truly happy again. 'I want you to stay here tonight, with me. I want sex. I want you . . .'

# Chapter 35

Since their last meeting hadn't exactly been a raging success, Sam acknowledged Izzy with a cool nod and carried on talking to the Australian actor who was currently wowing audiences in a West End show, and who had turned up at The Chelsea Steps with a particularly fetching little blonde.

Not to be put off, however, Izzy simply stood at his shoulder and waited for the small talk to run out, glancing with disinterest at the underdressed blonde and ignoring the attentions of her companion.

'Did you want to see me?' said Sam eventually, turning and looking mildly surprised. For good measure, he scanned the crowd around them and added, 'Not with your boyfriend tonight?'

'No. And yes, I would like to see you.' Izzy, not in the mood for games, was brief and to the point. 'What time will you be finishing?'

'Four o'clock.' He frowned, sensing that something was amiss. 'Maybe three-thirty. Why, is anything wrong?'

'Yes, there is,' she replied flatly, turning to leave. 'Very wrong indeed.'

The club was still busy when Sam handed over to Toby Madison and left them all to it. Although it was only three-fifteen, Izzy was waiting outside at the wheel of a double-parked Mercedes, drinking Coke from a can and fraying a small tear in the knee of her faded jeans.

Concerned by her obvious low spirits, Sam winked and gave her fingers a brief squeeze as he slid into the passenger seat. 'OK. Your place or mine?'

This earned him the first smile of the evening – just a small one.

'I thought maybe somewhere more neutral,' said Izzy, switching on the ignition. 'Like Bert's.'

Bert had died fifteen years ago, but his son Quentin, who now owned and ran the Chiswick transport café, hadn't let the side down. He still turned out the best and biggest fry-ups in London and nobody ever suggested that the café should be renamed.

If anything was capable of cheering her up, Izzy had decided, it was the steamy, friendly, no-hassle atmosphere of Bert's – which was *always* busy, no matter what time of day or night – and a plate loaded with fried mushrooms, bacon and tomatoes.

Now that the food was in front of her, however, she couldn't for the life of her imagine being able to eat it.

'Look, you were right and I was wrong,' she said eventually, watching Sam stir sugar into his tea. 'That should cheer *you* up, surely.'

'You mean Kat?' He had guessed what this must be about. Izzy was hardly likely to come to him if she was having problems with Tash Janssen.

'I feel so awful,' she blurted out, her dark eyes almost feverishly bright. 'I've never had to try to be a good mother before . . . I've never *needed* to try . . . and now that all this has happened I've been working so hard to do the right thing, but it just gets worse. I stayed away because I thought she needed the time to sort herself out, and it almost killed me to do it. But tonight I went to see her . . . I thought we could put everything behind us . . . and she just wasn't interested. Oh Sam, I think she really does hate me. And now I don't know what else to do.'

'She doesn't hate you,' he said firmly. 'Of course she doesn't. She'll come round sooner or later, she obviously just needs a little more time.'

Much as the Australian actor at The Chelsea Steps had admired Izzy's figure earlier, so a couple of lorry drivers at an adjacent table were eyeing her now with evident appreciation. They looked frankly startled when she began to cry.

'I went to see a h-house in Wimbledon this afternoon,' she explained, between sobs. Wordlessly, Sam handed her a paper napkin as the tears began to plop on to her plate. 'It was a beautiful house, a hundred times better than anything we've ever rented before – apart from Gina's place, of course. I wanted it for the two of us, but Kat refused to even consider it. She won't move. She says she's failed her A levels, so medical school's out of the window. I don't know whether she's trying to punish herself or me and I can't bear to think what she's doing to her life . . .'

'Sssh,' murmured Sam, as her voice wavered. 'You're blaming yourself and you shouldn't.'

'Of course I should,' she wailed, pushing her plate to one side and wiping her cheeks with the napkin. 'It's all my fault.'

The other diners were by this time enthralled. Ignoring

them, Sam got up and made his way around the table, sitting down next to Izzy and putting his arms around her. Accustomed to her noisy, exuberant ways and eternally optimistic attitude towards life, he hadn't imagined her capable of such vulnerability and it touched him more deeply than he could have believed.

For Izzy, the comfort of being listened to by Sam – and of being held by him – was infinitely reassuring. Her desperate concern for Kat was hardly something she could share with Gina, and Tash simply wasn't that interested.

'Will you talk to her?' she begged, clinging to him and breathing in the familiar, delicious scent of his aftershave. 'She doesn't hate you. She might listen . . . take some notice of what you say . . .'

'I'll do my best,' Sam assured her, in turn recalling the last time he had been this close to Izzy. That night at The Chelsea Steps when Vivienne had turned up without warning. Who knew how things might have turned out if Vivienne's journey had been delayed for even a few hours? 'No guarantees, but I'll try. And if you really aren't going to eat any of this food, I think we'd better leave. Who knows what Nigel Dempster would make of this if he were to walk in now.'

Sam drove. Even the shared car journey through the empty streets reminded him of their trips home from The Chelsea Steps, with Izzy balancing boxes of Chinese food on her knees, telling him the terrible jokes she'd heard that night and mimicking with wicked accuracy the more bizarre customers she'd served in the bar.

This time, however, she wasn't laughing.

'It's all such a waste,' she said hopelessly when – to

take her mind off Kat – he asked her how the music thing was going. ' "Never, Never" is being released in eight days' time. I heard it being previewed on the radio yesterday and the DJ tipped it to go to Number One. This morning we recorded an interview for Capital. This afternoon we finished shooting the video and tomorrow we have three more interviews lined up with the music press and the *Mail on Sunday*. It's everything I've ever dreamed of,' she concluded with a dismissive gesture which took in the soft leather upholstery of the Mercedes, 'and this is my car, which is a dream come true in itself, but it doesn't even *mean* anything any more, because Kat isn't here to enjoy it with me. I wanted her to be so *proud* of me . . . and she isn't, so it's all wasted . . .'

They had reached Kingsley Grove. Dawn was breaking, streaking the sky violet, and a milk float clattered along the street as Sam drew to a halt and switched off the ignition.

'I know it isn't easy, but maybe a bit more time is all she needs.' Once again he had to prise Izzy's fingers from the ripped knee of her jeans. The amount of fraying had increased spectacularly. 'I'll go and see her. Talk to her. But she isn't necessarily going to take any notice of what I say.'

Izzy's lower lip trembled and he fought the urge to kiss her.

'She likes you,' she said wistfully. 'And I know she respects your opinions.'

Squeezing her hand, he smiled. 'In that case, I shall make them known to her. And in the mean time, you just have to be patient. Look, when are you moving into your new home? Do you need a hand with any of that?'

Sam was so kind, so thoughtful. Izzy, closing her eyes for an instant as exhaustion swept over her, reflected not for the first time how lucky Vivienne was to have him.

'Thanks, but it's OK.' She shook her head. 'I didn't sign the lease. That house was supposed to be for Kat and me. Now that I know she isn't interested, there's no point in my taking it.'

'Hmm. Well, at least Gina will be pleased.'

Izzy was watching the milk float as it rattled back past them at a sedate ten miles an hour. She wondered whether the milkman, who was whistling and looking cheerful, had a normal happy family and a normal happy life.

'I don't know whether she'll be pleased or not,' she replied slowly. 'But I'm still moving out of Kingsley Grove. Tash has been asking me to go and live with him.'

Sam's heart sank. He'd had no idea the relationship between them had progressed that far. And the man's reputation for bedding and discarding women wasn't exactly encouraging.

'Would that be a wise move?' he said, the tone of his voice indicating his own views on the matter.

Izzy, however, simply shrugged and flicked back her hair with a gesture of defiance. Unconsciously echoing Katerina's explanation for staying with Andrew, she fixed her dark eyes on Sam and replied, 'Does it really matter? It may not last for ever, but who cares? My daughter doesn't want to live with me, so I might as well settle for someone who does.'

# Chapter 36

There were mistakes and mistakes, Izzy thought idly a week later. And considering the almost universal disapproval which had greeted her decision to move into Stanford Manor with Tash, the signs so far were that, all in all, it had been a pretty good mistake to make.

'You hardly know each other,' Gina had said, a trifle waspishly, when Izzy had announced her intentions. But Gina, she knew, was more concerned with the fact that she would be left on her own at Kingsley Grove, with only Jericho for company.

'It's bloody stupid,' Sam had remarked dismissively, but that was only because he didn't like Tash and was probably jealous of the fact that Izzy would be living in a house worth almost four million.

Even Doug Steadman had been doubtful. 'If you ask me, pet, you're making a mistake,' he had told her, his forehead creasing with concern. 'Not that your personal life is any of my business, but isn't he going to think you're . . . well, easy?'

At least Vivienne didn't tell her she was making a fool of herself. Vivienne thought it was an absolute scream, a wildly exciting adventure, and Izzy had turned to her with gratitude, ignoring the boring scaremongers and concentrating instead on the fun aspect of the situation. She was going to be wealthy in her own right, successful, famous

. . . and the live-in mistress of one of the most glamorous and desirable men in the world. Who cared if other people thought she was easy? Tash had already had her body; now he would have the pleasure of her cooking, too.

And so far, it *had* been exciting. The prophets of doom might be muttering away to each other behind their hands, but she was enjoying herself, and the novelty of it all had at least partially distracted her from the problem of her estranged daughter.

Yes, there were definite advantages to being a rich man's mistress, Izzy decided, pushing the thought of Kat firmly from her mind and gazing out over the swimming-pool which glittered turquoise in the August sunlight. Having demolished a plateful of smoked-salmon sandwiches – peeling the salmon out of the centres and leaving the bread – she was in the mood for a swim. She was in the mood for Tash, but he was buried in his recording studio, working on ideas for the next album and showing no sign at all of needing a break.

Neither, evidently, did he welcome company during the serious business of song-writing. Izzy, reflecting that it was just as well she hadn't expected an initial honeymoon period to their living together, was finding herself with plenty of time on her hands to explore her new home and make the most of its splendid facilities. But although she was having fun, she was finding it less easy to relax than she'd expected. Topless sunbathing was out of the question because of the silent, unnerving presence of the security guards who roamed the grounds, and who treated her in the kind of distant, off-hand manner which indicated they thought of her as simply one more in a long line of female guests whose name was hardly worth remembering. And despite her best efforts to be friendly, the formidable Mrs Bishop was even less communicative than she had been on the night of her first visit. Attempts at conversation fell on the very stoniest of ground. Any compliments regarding the food were met with an impassive stare. Izzy had even idly contemplated her reaction if she were to lodge a complaint about the cooking, except that there was never anything to complain about. Everything at Stanford Manor was run with pristine efficiency, because that was what Tash wanted and demanded from his staff. And she hadn't managed to catch any of them at it yet, but *someone* was actually screwing the top back on the toothpaste tube in her bathroom . . .

Tash finally emerged outside four hours later, by which time Izzy had swum and dozed off, and – having forgotten to renew the Ambre Solaire – acquired a distinctly pink tinge to her tan.

Adjusting his sunglasses, he surveyed her in sleep, her dark hair spilling around her in glossy abandon, splendid breasts swelling out of her peacock-blue bikini, one hand trailing in the plate of desecrated sandwiches.

Izzy, adorable Izzy, both intrigued and amused him, and an added bonus was the fact that she was about as unlike his usual girlfriends as it was possible to be. Shrewd, sharp-witted and determined to succeed in her chosen career, she was nevertheless touchingly naïve at times. He was particularly entertained by her innocent ideas regarding the music business, and her plans to enjoy the money success would bring into her life.

Fishing an ice cube from the drink in his hand he dropped it into the hollow of her navel and grinned as, with a yelp, she ricocheted into a sitting position.

'Wake up. Mrs Bishop wants to know why you saw fit to massacre her sandwiches. She says unless you eat up every last crumb, she's leaving.'

'Oh God . . . oh, *you!*' Realizing belatedly that he was joking, Izzy sank back against the sunlounger and aimed the ice cube at his crotch. 'That would be too much to hope for,' she grumbled, glancing over her shoulder in case the old dragon was hovering, lurch-like, behind her. Then she examined her ominously rosy chest with dismay. 'And this isn't funny either. Hell, what am I going to look like tomorrow? We've got that photo session and I'm going to have a burnt nose . . . ouch, that *hurts!*'

She squirmed as he ran his fingernails along her collarbone, then smiled because at least he was in good spirits. While Tash would never describe himself as temperamental, she had already discovered his tendency towards moodiness whenever work refused to go well. Life wasn't all roses. Capable of the utmost charm when he chose, several wasted hours in his precious recording studio could change his mood to one of picky, tricky irritation and short temper. Izzy, who couldn't see the point of such irritability – since it didn't solve anything – steadfastly refused to be intimidated and either laughed or ignored him when it happened. But it was undoubtedly nicer, she reflected drily, when it didn't.

'Someone might be watching,' she protested, trying to

wriggle away as Tash began to slide the straps of her bikini away from her sunburnt shoulders.

'So?' He hauled her back before she landed on the plate of sandwiches. 'Would that really be so terrible? Sweetheart, it's half the fun.'

No doubt his past girlfriends had gone along with such suggestions, but Izzy wasn't about to set herself up as a floorshow for the security staff. Rising to her feet, she hooked a finger through one of the belt loops on his jeans and led him uncomplainingly inside. When they reached the bedroom, she slowly unbuttoned his white shirt and murmured, 'This is more fun.'

Afterwards, as he lit a joint and slowly exhaled, Tash said, 'I forgot to tell you. Someone phoned earlier, wanting to speak to you.'

Izzy didn't approve of drugs of any kind, but since he only laughed and called her a prude whenever she tried to tell him of the damage they could do, she no longer bothered. At least it was only marijuana, she consoled herself. It could have been much worse.

'And?' she said, stretching lazily and revelling in the luxury of not having to get up and go to work in either a crowded pub or a smoky, un-air-conditioned club. 'Who was it? Do I have to call them back?'

Tash shook his head. 'Nope. He said he was flying out to the States this afternoon, so I took a message. It was your friend Sam Sheridan.' Aware of the fact that Sam disapproved of his relationship with Izzy, he spoke in faintly mocking tones. 'He just wanted you to know that he'd had a word with Katerina, but that it wasn't a great success.'

'What!' In a flurry of bedclothes, Izzy jerked into a sitting position. 'Why couldn't you tell me earlier? Why on earth didn't you come and find me when he phoned?'

Tash's eyes darkened. He fixed his gaze on the glowing tip of the joint between his fingers. 'I was busy. I didn't know where you were. Look, what's the big deal? The man's a jerk and what he had to say was hardly of earth-shattering importance, anyway.'

Shooting him a look of disdain, Izzy grabbed the phone by the bed and punched out Sam's number. Seconds later, abruptly disconnecting the call, she said, 'Bloody answering machine. Thanks a lot, Tash. My daughter might mean nothing to you, but she *is* important to me.'

And don't we all know it, he thought with resignation, taking a final, long drag before stubbing out the cigarette. Izzy's obsession with Katerina was beyond his comprehension. Rebellion was part of growing up. When he was seventeen years old he'd left home and gone to live in a squat in Bayswater, sharing the icy, unfurnished basement flat with an acid-head and a fifteen-stone transvestite. It hadn't done him any harm, for Christ's sake.

But the marijuana was taking effect and he really couldn't be bothered to get into a fight.

'Angel, calm down,' he said placatingly. 'OK, OK, I'm sorry if I upset you. But I *was* pretty busy when the phone rang . . . and I would have come and found you if Sam had had something more positive to report, of course I would.'

Izzy digested this in silence. Maybe she had reacted too strongly. Tash wasn't being deliberately obstructive, he simply hadn't thought it that important.

'All right,' she said finally, only too well aware herself of the fact that the last thing they needed right now was a major row. The publicity machine was revving up to full throttle; practically every day for the next fortnight they were scheduled for interviews with journalists eager to get the low-down on Tash's latest relationship. 'All right, I'm sorry too. I just can't help worrying about Kat, that's all.'

'No big deal,' he said easily, relieved to have averted the crisis. Sliding out of bed, he strode naked across the room to the vast chest of drawers and took out a slim, matt black jewellery box. 'Here, I was saving this for the day "Never, Never" went to Number One.' With a crooked smile, he dropped it in her lap. Izzy needn't know that the emerald-and-sapphire earrings from Bulgari had been bought for Anna. Splitting up with her three days before her birthday had had its small advantages, after all; he'd never bothered returning them to the shop. 'But maybe you should open it now. Just a little something to cheer you up.'

Kat might not want her but at least Tash did. Overwhelmed by the size and beauty of the stones, and by his thoughtfulness in choosing the kind of earrings he knew she would love, Izzy rose to her knees and slid her arms around his neck. Too moved to speak, she leaned closer and kissed his handsome mouth.

'I'm too old for this,' murmured Tash.

'I'm sure you can cope,' Izzy replied, her lips curving against his as she smiled. 'What the hell, anyway? I'll risk it if you will . . .'

# Chapter 37

Later, much later, Gina would come to appreciate the significant part two fingernail-sized slivers of pink tissue paper had played in her life. At the time, however, it didn't even occur to her; she was having far too much trouble keeping a straight face.

The rain was still hammering down outside. It had been the dazzling spectacle of forked lightning against an indigo sky which had drawn her to the window less than two minutes earlier. Doug, hunched in his chair with his ear welded to the phone, glanced up and said hopefully, 'Coffee?' but Gina didn't hear him. In the street below, emerging from a cab and pausing briefly to examine his reflection in the rain-streaked side-mirror was Ralph, whom she hadn't set eyes upon since that humiliating afternoon at Kingsley Grove. All the air seemed suddenly to have been sucked from her lungs. He was one of Doug's most successful clients and she had known she should be geared up to seeing him again, but now that it was happening she was still unprepared. No matter how many times she told herself he didn't mean anything to her, it never quite rang true. Ralph was too charming and attractive ever to be ignored. He was the epitome of *cool* . . .

'With three sugars?' wheedled Doug, who wasn't cool at all. Thanks to Gina's gifts of deodorant and aftershave

298

the aura of BO had dissipated and he no longer smelled anything but sweet, but whenever he was caught in the throes of clinching a deal nothing on earth could prevent those damp patches forming on the underarms of his shirts. Poker, as Izzy had once gravely informed him, was never going to be his forte.

But making coffee would at least give Gina something to do so that she wouldn't have to sit there like a lemon while Ralph made polite conversation and inwardly smirked at her gullibility. Moving away from the window and flicking the switch on the kettle, she began spooning instant coffee into two cups and listened to the rhythmic beat of Ralph's footsteps as he confidently ascended the stairs.

The beige Burberry trenchcoat was rain-spotted but otherwise immaculate, as were – of course – the matching scarf and umbrella. The collar-length blond hair had grown blonder still with the recent addition of expensive and artfully styled streaks. The tan was deeper and smoother than ever. Intimidated by such perfection – as she had known she would be – Gina bent her head to the task of spooning far more sugar than usual into Doug's cup. Since she habitually under-sugared in a vain attempt to reduce his paunch, he would think it was his birthday.

'Doug, how are you?' Ralph, who had in fact taken particular care with his appearance because he was anxious to impress Gina – OK, so he had used her initially to get back at Izzy, but he had rapidly grown to *like* her – stepped forward and shook his agent's pudgy hand with enthusiasm. 'God, what weather! I just called by to let you know that we've finished filming the TV serial. The producers are really pleased with me, and the director has suggested I put myself up for a play he's involved with, so things are on the up. Hallo, Gina,' he added, as if seeing her for the first time. 'You're looking well. Very well. Working for this old slave-driver obviously suits you.'

He was . . . *golden*, thought Gina, forcing a brief smile and attempting to appear unconcerned by his presence.

'Less of the old,' complained Doug, glancing between the two of them and realizing that something was going on. Not always famed for his diplomacy, he nevertheless sensed that a trip to the newsagents around the corner might be in order. 'Hell, I've run out of cigarettes. Gina, make this young man a coffee and keep him entertained until I get back, will you? I'll be five minutes.'

'Fine,' said Ralph.

Help, thought Gina, oh help.

But for once in her life, help was on its way. As the door slammed behind Doug, Ralph settled easily into the client's chair and unwound the cashmere scarf around his neck, and the miracle Gina had been praying for finally happened.

'I wanted to see you again.' He assumed a confidential air, pushing his streaked hair away from his forehead and tilting his head slightly to one side as he studied her. 'You really have bloomed, Gina . . . look, I'm sorry about that misunderstanding we had, but I'm sure we could put it behind us now.'

Gina couldn't speak. If she tried to open her mouth she knew the giggles would erupt. If it had been anyone else, the fact that they had cut themselves while shaving wouldn't even *be* particularly funny, but it was perfect Ralph, the picture of *GQ* sophistication.

With a gulp she gazed, transfixed, at the two torn shreds of pink toilet paper dangling from his throat. Dotted with dried blood, they were an inch and a half apart, which only made them look that much more like a vampire's bite. Exactly on cue, a fresh downpour of rain rattled the windows and forked lightning illuminated the office, causing the lights to flicker in true *Hammer Horror* fashion. As the ensuing roll of thunder shook the building, Gina pressed her lips together and clenched her fists until the nails dug into her palms. The spell had been well and truly broken; no longer perfect, it was now Ralph's turn to look foolish and she was going to make sure she enjoyed every single, wonderful moment . . .

'What's so funny?' he demanded with a trace of suspicion, and she shook her head.

'Nothing . . . nothing. Thunderstorms make me a bit nervous, that's all. Um . . . I can't remember whether you take sugar.'

From the expression on his face she might have been enquiring whether he injected heroin. Ralph took fanatical care of his body.

'Thanks.' Taking the cup, he flashed her a winning smile. Imagining for a moment that his incisors seemed slightly elongated, Gina quelled a further explosion of giggles, and sat back down in her own chair with a bump.

'Am *I* making you nervous?' He spoke gently this time, shaking his head with mock disbelief. The ludicrous shreds of pink toilet paper fluttered in sympathy. 'Sweetheart, there's really no need. Why don't we put the past behind us and try again? I'm free this evening if you'd like to come out with me for dinner.'

'I . . . I'm busy tonight.' With an effort she managed to get the words out. 'Sorry.'

He shook his head once more. Flutter, flutter. 'Oh sweetheart. Don't tell me you're still cross with me.'

'Not . . . cross.' In serious danger of wetting herself, Gina pressed her knees together. 'Just b-busy.'

Ralph shrugged and leaned forward to take a sip of coffee. It was the shrug that finally did it. Absolutely transfixed, Gina watched as one of the dislodged shreds of tissue landed in his cup.

'. . . priceless! So, what did he do? What happened next?'

Gina, who hadn't laughed so much since she was a child, wiped her eyes with a mascara-stained handkerchief. She had an aching stitch in her side. Every time she thought the hysteria was dying down, she only had to envisage the expression on Ralph's face as he'd peered at the alien object floating in his coffee, and it erupted once more.

'He . . . he . . . recognised it!' she gulped, clutching Doug's sturdy arm for support. 'And then of course he realised how stupid he must have looked, and his face went all p-p-purple like an aubergine. I couldn't help it after that, I just burst out laughing and he went even *purpler* . . . then he leapt up, shouted, "You bloody little bitch," and stormed out. I'm afraid your door hinges might never be the same again . . .'

Doug grinned; poor old Ralph. In puncturing his ego, Gina had dealt him the cruellest of blows. He would undoubtedly now find himself a new agent, but Doug didn't even care. How could anyone – particularly someone as imperfect as himself – possibly resist such a wonderful tale? And to see Gina enjoying her much-deserved triumph was a positive delight.

'I suppose I am a bitch,' she continued, her tone unrepentant. 'If it had been anyone else – you, for example – I would have told them straight away, just as you'd tell someone if the label on their sweater was sticking out. But Ralph is so *vain* . . .'

And she was off again, rocking in her chair and clutching her side. Suddenly emboldened by their shared secret and the mood of almost festive celebration, Doug glanced at his watch and said, 'It's five-thirty. Are you really busy this evening, or d'you fancy slipping round to Russell's winebar for a drink?'

Her second dinner invitation in less than an hour. This time Gina didn't even hesitate. 'I think I'd better,' she said with a grin. 'For my own safety. Can you imagine what people will think if they see me giggling to myself all the way home on the tube?'

Over a shared bottle of Beaujolais and succulent ham-and-asparagus quiche in a corner of the dark, crowded winebar, they continued to laugh and shamelessly mock Ralph for his pretentious ways and over-co-ordinated wardrobe.

'But you must have liked him to begin with, otherwise you wouldn't have gone out with him,' ventured Doug finally.

Gina toyed with her glass. 'I suppose so. Well, I was flattered because he seemed so charming and attentive, but he was never really my type. It had just been so long since any man had paid me that amount of interest that I kind of . . . fell for it.'

It was beyond Doug's comprehension why anyone of Gina's calibre should be starved of male attention. As far as he was concerned she was eminently desirable and if he hadn't long ago come to terms with the fact that such women were way out of his league, he would have made his own interest obvious months ago.

'In that case,' he said, eyes twinkling, 'it sounds to me as if you had a narrow escape. Or should I call it a close shave?'

'Oh no,' gasped Gina, almost choking on her wine. 'Don't make me laugh again . . .'

'Really, my dear,' he protested, all innocence. 'Can I help it if I have a razor-sharp wit?'

'Doug . . . !'

'OK, OK. I've stopped. So, tell me, what kind of man *would* be your type?'

Gina thought for a moment. 'Someone as unlike Ralph as possible.'

Doug felt his heart inadvertently quicken. Fingering the frayed cuff of his badly ironed shirt, he experienced a faint – a very faint – surge of hope. Of all the men in all the world, he thought, surely none could possibly be more unlike Ralph Henson than he was.

# Chapter 38

In Izzy's experience, throwing a party had always involved working out how much money she couldn't afford to spend, roughly doubling it, then staggering back from the off-licence with enough crates of lager and boxes of wine to ensure that no one could possibly go thirsty. Huge vats of chilli con carne or spaghetti mopped up the alcohol and her rickety but reliable cassette player provided the music. If whichever flat she was living in at the time could comfortably hold thirty guests, she invited fifty and jammed them in willy-nilly because that way they could more speedily get to know each other and have fun. The party continued until the last guest fell asleep and whoever stayed the night helped with the clearing-up the following morning.

Well, that was how it had always been in the old days, thought Izzy drily. Throwing a party at Stanford Manor, however, wasn't going to be like that at all.

But not having to worry about the cost certainly had its advantages. As she adjusted her upwardly mobile, bottle-green lycra skirt, smoothed the strapless green-and-gold sequinned bodice into place and ruffled her hair for the last time in front of the mirror, she could hear the band tuning up downstairs in the main hall, their music punctuated by the stentorian tones of Mrs Bishop as she bullied the outside caterers and made absolutely certain they understood who was boss. The food, it went without saying, would be spectacular, the flow of vintage champagne never-ending and none of the two hundred or so guests need worry about being press-ganged into helping with the washing-up.

By ten o'clock the party was in full swing. 'Never, Never', having entered the top ten the previous week, was expected to go to Number One tomorrow and everyone was celebrating in advance. But it wasn't until the huge front doors swung open and Simon, with Katerina at his side, entered the hall, that Izzy truly began to celebrate.

She was about to rush towards them when Vivienne yanked her unceremoniously back. 'You're supposed to be playing it cool, remember,' she admonished. 'What did Sam tell you? She wants to be treated like an adult. Whatever you do, don't *gush*.'

'I won't.' Izzy, dizzy with delight, determined to be as ungushing as possible. Telephoning Simon and inviting him and Katerina to the party had been a master-stroke. In reasonable tones, she had explained that, although she and Katerina weren't on the best of terms at the present time, there was no earthly reason why they couldn't be civil to each other on a purely social level. Knowing how star-struck Simon was, he had been a foregone conclusion, and she had banked on his powers of persuasion – together with Katerina's deep-seated curiosity – to get her here tonight.

And it had worked, she thought joyfully, making her way towards them. It had really worked . . .

'You made it. I'm so pleased you're both here.' Gosh, it was hard not to gush.

'Simon wanted to come.' Katerina wore a guarded expression, as if she were expecting a more extravagant welcome.

'Well, it's exciting,' said Simon defensively, the colour already rising in his cheeks. Stepping forward, he dropped an awkward kiss on Izzy's cheek. 'And I think it's brilliant, your single doing so well.'

Izzy wondered whether Katerina was wearing jeans and an old, black T-shirt to make a point. Now that she was finally making real money, she ached to shower her daughter with lavish gifts. Instead, taking care to hide her true feelings, she smiled up at Simon and said, 'Thank you. I think it's brilliant, too.'

'Our A level results came through yesterday,' said Katerina abruptly. 'I didn't fail them.'

'Oh darling . . .'

'But the grades are too low for medical school, so I might as well have done.'

'Oh.' Swallowing her disappointment, forcing herself not to react as Kat appeared to want her to, Izzy managed another, slightly wan smile.

'Well, never mind. Look, the band's about to start up again and our eardrums could suffer. Why don't you two head through that archway, get yourself something to eat and drink, and take a look around?'

Simon was already looking. Ogling. This threatened to be the most exciting night of his life and he had already spotted several famous faces, not to mention real bimbos, enthrallingly underdressed.

'There's the drummer with Blur,' he said, his voice hushed with reverence. 'And that girl in the bikini – isn't she Fiona whatsername?'

'For heaven's sake, don't gawp,' said Katerina, determinedly unimpressed. Pushing him in the direction of the bar, she added in a fierce whisper, 'And don't you *dare* ask anyone for their autograph . . .'

'Well done,' said Vivienne approvingly, when Izzy returned to her side. Raising her exceedingly strong vodka and tonic in a semi-salute, she surveyed the departing couple with amusement.

'Poor old Kat, what a muddle. She and Simon actually make a good couple, if only she'd realise it. And if only,' she added as an afterthought, 'poor old Simon could control his unfortunate blushes.'

'Speaking of good couples,' said Izzy, her tone casual, 'why isn't Sam here with you? Does he still disapprove of my being with Tash that much?'

They were making their way out to the floodlit pool. Vivienne, impressively encased in shell-pink satin, undulated like an eel in heels. With a shrug, she replied, 'Who knows? Sam keeps his thoughts pretty much to himself these days. He doesn't ask me what I'm up to any more, and when I tell him, he doesn't even seem to listen. I'm bored to tears and all he says is why don't I get some kind of job. Can you imagine what *that* kind of advice does to someone like *me*?'

Izzy frowned. 'So, what are you going to do?'

'What would any normal human being do? It's practically an invitation to misbehave!' Vivienne tossed back her golden hair and grinned in passing at Tash's drummer, who had quite wickedly dissipated blue eyes. 'Hell, why else would I damn near give myself a hernia trussing myself up in this dress? I'm going to dazzle and delight, honeychile, like it's going out of fashion. This beautiful body is fed up with being ignored . . .' Her voice trailed away for a second, then added, '. . . and I think I may just have spotted the man not to ignore it. Izzy, who *is* that guy over there? The one in the dark blue shirt . . .'

'Oh, Vivienne, what about Sam?' Izzy was beginning to get worried. She clearly meant business.

'Since when did a little jealousy go amiss? And stop changing the subject. Tell me at once who he is, and how much money he earns. This is *definitely* the man for me.'

Izzy didn't think he was, but Vivienne was unstoppable. Refusing even to listen to Izzy's reminder of how very amiss her own love life had gone as a result of the mutual jealousy between Ralph and Mike, she made a beeline for the object of her desire and wasted no time at all introducing herself.

Since Tash was far too busy being chatted up by a rapacious, heavily bleached blonde either to notice or to care what Izzy might be up to, she danced with Benny Dunaway and marvelled – not for the first time – that such an accomplished musician could dance quite so badly. At this rate, her poor feet were in danger of doubling in size.

'Oops, sorry.' Benny, unused to champagne cocktails, looked hopelessly unrepentant. 'Now you know why my wife refuses to dance with me.'

'I don't mind,' said Izzy valiantly, giving him a hug to

prove it. 'If it weren't for you, none of this would have happened. Are you enjoying yourself?'

'Are you kidding? This is how the other half lives.' He flung his arm wide to indicate the splendour of the occasion. 'And from now on, it's how *you're* going to live. You've cracked it, my darling, and I couldn't be more pleased for you.'

She was touched. 'Really?'

'Well, it hasn't exactly done my street-cred any harm.' Benny trod on her toes once more and grinned. 'Did I forget to mention it earlier? The entire fifth year have issued demands for signed photographs. No hurry, tomorrow morning will be soon enough.'

'Nice to know I'm popular with some teenagers,' sighed Izzy, watching out of the corner of her eye as Katerina – sitting temporarily alone in one of the carved stone window-seats – rebuffed the attentions of a pony-tailed youth wielding a chicken leg in one hand and a bottle of Sol in the other.

'Not you,' said Benny cheerfully. 'It's Tash they're interested in, stupid.'

Having been abandoned by Simon, who was deep in conversation with Tash Janssen's bass guitarist, Katerina covertly watched her mother dance first with Benny, then with an horrendously dressed male who had to be Joel McGill. She was clearly enjoying herself in her new home, she thought, somewhat piqued by the fact that Izzy had paid her virtually no attention at all this evening. Everybody seemed to know everybody else. Extraordinary amounts of alcohol were disappearing down throats and several of the guests were on their way to getting stoned. It was certainly a good job Sam hadn't turned up, she thought, glancing in the direction of the pool and observing Vivienne wrapped around a complete stranger in the shadows.

Deciding to explore the rest of the undeniably spectacular house, Kat rested her orange juice on the window-ledge and set off in the opposite direction, away from the crowds and noise, before the jerk with the ponytail could come back and start pestering her again.

'Are you always this, er . . . forward?' asked Terry Pleydell-Pearce, his expression somewhat bemused. 'Not that I'm complaining, you understand, but I wouldn't want you to think I was somebody wealthy or influential, or anything like that.'

'Do I look like the kind of girl who would only be interested in money?' Vivienne protested, genuinely dismayed by the implied slur on her character. She'd practically fallen in love the moment she'd set eyes on this charming, funny, self-deprecating man. The very idea that the attraction might not be mutual filled her with something close to panic.

'Well, yes,' he said, in reply to her question, 'as a matter of fact, you do.'

'OK.' Determined to sweep his objections aside, she changed tack. 'We'll be honest with each other, shall we? I don't make a habit of telling people this, but it really wouldn't matter *how* poor you are, because I have money of my own. Oodles of the stuff. *More* than oodles . . .'

'Stop it. You're scaring me.'

'I'm supposed to be reassuring you!' It came out as a wail. Then he grinned and she realised he had been teasing her. 'Oh, that's not fair.'

'But it *is* scary. When a wealthy, gorgeous Texan blonde shows this much interest in an impoverished, forty-one-year-old widower, it's . . . well, nerve wracking.'

He'd called her gorgeous. Enormously encouraged, Vivienne said gently, 'How awful, your wife dying. Do you have any children?'

'A boy and a girl. Theo and Lydia.'

'And is that why you're so poor? You had to give up your job to raise your kids?' She could have wept; it was all so sad and so noble. This wonderful man, with his kind, careworn eyes and rumpled dark hair had abandoned a career in order to give his young family the love and emotional security they so badly needed . . .

'Good God, no.' Terry burst out laughing. 'Lydia's married with two children and Theo's working as a junior houseman at St Thomas's. When I said I was impoverished, I was speaking relatively. I work as a GP.'

'A medic? So you *can't* be poor,' she countered, her eyes alight with triumph. 'My gynaecologist back home has his own Lear jet.'

'Believe me.' Terry Pleydell-Pearce's expression remained deadpan. 'It isn't like that in this country, particularly if you work for the NHS. Of course, some days I can afford to eat. Others, I simply take a walk through Regent's Park and steal bread from the ducks . . .'

Vivienne's eyes narrowed. 'Forty-one,' she declared accusingly.

'I beg your pardon?'

'You said you were forty-one years old. And your married daughter has *two children?*'

The expression of guilt on his face was an absolute picture. At that moment, Vivienne fell irrevocably in love.

'When a wealthy, gorgeous, Texan mathematical genius shows this much interest in an impoverished forty-one-year-old widower, it's nerve-wracking,' he reminded her. 'But if the impoverished widower happens to be forty-six, it's positively traumatic.'

Moving closer, aching to kiss him, she touched his cheek, 'It needn't be traumatic.'

'And you're taller than me.'

It was the mildest of protests. Slipping out of her heels, she brushed his dry mouth with a trembling forefinger. 'Not any more.'

'I've never met anyone like you before in my life.'

This time, Vivienne smiled. 'I should hope not.'

'So, what happens now?' said Terry Pleydell-Pearce, his voice no longer quite steady.

She raised a delicate eyebrow. 'You're the doctor, doctor. You tell me.'

# Chapter 39

'Oh,' said Katerina, coming awake suddenly and realizing that she was being watched.

Tash looked amused. 'It's a talent of mine.'

'What is?'

'Staring at people when they're asleep. Subconsciously, they become aware of it and wake up. Is the party that boring?'

As she struggled into a sitting position he came and sat down on the opposite end of the sofa. Caught off-guard, she replied, 'Of course not. I'm sure it's a very good party. I was just tired, that's all.'

For a fraction of a second, Tash considered offering her a couple of the pills in his shirt pocket, then decided against it. The girl was straight, too straight, and he didn't want to run the risk of being busted, particularly with the next single due for release bearing an anti-drugs message.

'So, what do you think of my games room?' he said instead, gesturing around the huge, candle-lit room to include the pinball machines, snooker and table-tennis tables and giant video screen.

'Impressive.' There was an edge of sarcasm in her voice. 'Look, you don't have to make polite conversation with me. Shouldn't you get back to your guests?'

Tash's dark eyes glittered with amusement. 'It's my

party. I can do whatever I like. Are you always this stroppy?'

'I don't know why you're talking to me,' replied Katerina evenly. 'Unless it's because my mother asked you to. Is *that* why you're here, to give me another lecture?'

He shrugged. 'What you choose to do with your life is nothing to do with me. Now there's line for a song . . .'

Of course he wasn't interested, she realised. If she had agreed to move into the house in Wimbledon, Izzy would be living there with her instead of here with Tash.

For some reason, the thought cheered her. Reaching over, she removed the drink from his hand and took a mouthful to lubricate her sleep-dried tongue. To her surprise it was unadulterated tonic water.

Tash, who had been admiring her slender body, said, 'Do you play snooker?'

For the first time, Katerina smiled. 'Is Steve Davis boring?'

'OK.' Clasping her hand, he hauled her to her feet. 'Rest time over. Game well and truly on.'

'I can play. I didn't say I was any good.'

'No problem.' Tash winked as he began setting up the table. 'I'm a great teacher.'

Vivienne was nowhere to be found. Izzy, who had gone out to the pool in search of her, found herself buttonholed instead by a dippy-looking girl with fuchsia-pink cheeks, matching eyeshadow and the kind of candyfloss hair more commonly found on Barbie dolls. She was wearing an electric-blue rubber dress which emphasized the puppy fat around her midriff, and purple stilettos. Izzy held her breath in order to avoid the reek of Poison.

'You're Izzy Van Asch,' said the girl with a giggle. Holding out her hand, then realizing that a cigarette still burned between her fingers, she said, 'Oops, my mistake. I'm Mirabelle. Hi.'

You certainly are, thought Izzy, glancing around the pool and wondering where Tash had got to. This girl was seriously out of it.

'I saw the video the other night. Great song. Wild,' continued Mirabelle. 'Tash is great, too, isn't he? I know he's a bastard, but I just love him to death. Wild.'

'Hmm.' Izzy couldn't see Kat anywhere, either. 'Have you known him for long?'

Mirabelle smiled, revealing very small white teeth. 'Oh yeah. Nearly seven months now. I'm Donny's girlfriend.'

That figured. Donny, the band's keyboards player, might be musically talented, but he possessed about as many brain cells as the average Webb's lettuce. Izzy, growing increasingly desperate to escape, scanned the poolside once more in search of someone – anyone – she might use as an excuse to escape. Even Mrs Bishop . . .

'Yeah, and I was Anna's best friend,' continued Mirabelle, swaying slightly as she took another drag of her cigarette. 'You know, Tash's girlfriend before you.'

'I know,' replied Izzy carefully. Was this conversation perhaps leading somewhere after all?

'You're ever so much older than her.'

'I know that, too. Look, is there some kind of problem? Do you have something you want to say to me?'

'Well yes, I guess I do.' Mirabelle twirled a strand of candyfloss white hair around her fingers, hiccuped twice and gazed at her, wide-eyed. 'Hey, like, I just wanted you to know, it's cool. No problem at all. As long as you're with Tash, I'll be your best friend too.'

Tash should have called it the fun-and-games room. The first time he had brushed past her on his way around the table, Katerina had given him the benefit of the doubt. Three reds, a pink and a green later, she realised he had other benefits in mind.

'You should splay your fingers more to make a firm bridge,' he said, moving up behind her and reaching forward to correct the angle of her left arm. In doing so, his body came to rest against hers; Katerina felt the gentle pressure of his lean thighs and allowed herself a grim smile.

'That's much better,' he said, when she'd potted the ball. 'You see, all you need is a little guidance.'

All Tash needed, she thought, was a little bromide. But she wasn't about to object yet; it was going to be fun seeing just how far he thought he could go.

She didn't have to wait long to find out. Tash, who had earlier been indulging in some of the excellent coke brought along by Mirabelle, was finding Izzy's daughter increasingly desirable. She had the most gorgeous figure – and the longest legs – he'd seen in years. And as for that glistening, almost waist-length hair . . .

The next moment his arm had snaked around her waist and he was pulling her round to face him. Serious, conker-brown eyes regarded him with heartbreaking intensity.

'My mother could walk in at any minute,' said Katerina in a low voice.

'She'll have to bulldoze the wall down first.' Tash grinned. 'I've locked the door.'

His hands were sliding upwards. The next thing she knew, he had lifted her up on to the snooker table and insinuated his body between her thighs.

'She'd still be hurt if she knew what was going on.'

Tash, who had never understood the female obsession with monogamy, simply shrugged.

'I think we both know how to keep a secret, don't we?'

'But doesn't it worry you,' Katerina persisted, 'that you might be hurting her?'

His dark eyebrows arched in amusement. 'At this precise moment? No.'

'Oh, well . . .' she said slowly, 'in that case, I won't let it worry me that I'm about to hurt you.'

'Aaargh,' grunted Tash, as her right knee shot up, scoring a direct hit. Clutching his groin, he staggered backwards.

Katerina, jumping down from the table and eyeing him with disdain, said, 'Oh, for God's sake, did you seriously think you were *that* irresistible?'

'Shit . . .' groaned Tash, as the pain intensified.

Katerina, who had by this time reached the door and unlocked it, gave him a mock-pitying look. 'Yes, I'd say that just about sums you up,' she declared triumphantly. 'Tash Janssen, despicable little shit. My God, you and my mother deserve each other.'

Izzy was talking to Simon in a corner of the sitting room. Her eyes lit up when she saw Katerina coming towards them. 'Darling, we were beginning to think you'd gone home! Where on earth have you been?'

'Making polite conversation,' replied Katerina briskly. 'It's what you're supposed to do at parties, isn't it? And it's been great fun, but now we are going home.' She patted Simon's back pocket, locating his car keys. 'Ready?'

'Do we have to?' He looked dismayed. The party would go on for hours yet. It seemed almost sacrilegious to leave so soon.

But Katerina was determined. 'Yes, we do.'

'You've enjoyed yourself, though,' Izzy put in eagerly. Despite Kat's abrupt tone, she looked cheerful, almost elated. 'Who were you talking to, someone nice?'

Katerina only just managed to keep a straight face. 'Tash.'

'Oh, I'm so pleased!' Izzy knew she mustn't gush, but it was such encouraging news. She'd always known that Kat and Tash would get on well, once they got to know each other properly. 'Sweetheart, it makes such a difference, knowing that you really like him.'

Katerina savoured the moment. Out of the corner of her eye she glimpsed Tash, now evidently recovered, sliding his arm around the plump brown shoulders of a girl in a blue rubber dress. For a fraction of a second she debated telling Izzy exactly what had gone on in the candle-lit games room, less than fifteen minutes earlier. But then, why should she? Izzy deserved to find out the hard way and it damn well would serve her right for siding against her own daughter when she should have been supporting her.

Katerina, who had endured so much misery in the

past weeks, now revelled in the sensation of her own power.

'Did I say I liked him?' she enquired with exaggerated politeness. 'And is my opinion of Tash Janssen really relevant anyway? I tell you what, Mum. You don't lecture me on my choice in men and I won't lecture you on yours. OK?'

# Chapter 40

By four-thirty Izzy was seriously beginning to wilt. Although most of the guests had left, those that remained showed no signs of giving in. Music blared from amplifiers around the pool, people were still dancing and joints were being passed around between unsteady fingers. A well-known actress, currently starring as a nun in a top-rated TV series, was swaying in time with the music and slowly removing her dress to raucous acclaim. Behind her, Tash lay on a white sunlounger, and smiled his deceptively sleepy smile as a slender redhead began to massage his shoulders.

Izzy wished it could all be over. Tired and sober, her head was pounding and her eyes ached. Joel and Benny had long since disappeared, there was no one left she particularly wanted to talk to, and she was having a hard time shaking off the whisky-sodden attentions of a red-faced man who insisted that in real life he was a concert organiser.

'You name it, I've organised 'em,' he declared expansively, reaching for his drink. 'Yeah, all the greats . . . all the biggest venues . . . an' it could be you next, up there on that great big stage. Cute li'l thing like you could have a real future an' I'd be there to look after you, sweetheart . . .'

No longer listening to his drunken ramblings, Izzy

wondered where Vivienne was and hoped her friend had at least enjoyed the party more than she had. Everyone was yelling and applauding the actress as she discarded her camisole top and began to undo her bra. All they needed now was for a member of the paparazzi to leap out of the bushes with a camera.

Idly she watched as Mirabelle, not to be outdone, staggered to her feet and made her way over to Donny.

'Dance with me, baby,' she wheedled, crouching beside him in her high heels. 'Come on, just one little dance with me?'

Donny wasn't interested. 'Nah, dance on your own.'

'But that's no fun,' wailed Mirabelle, clutching his arm as he attempted to open a can of Newcastle Brown. 'Donn*eee*, that's no fun at all. I want to dance with *you*.'

Shaking off her hand, he grabbed the hem of her dress and twanged it. Then he started to laugh. 'Whiney bitch, always moaning. Haven't you seen that film, *Flashdance?*'

'Yes, but . . .'

Reaching for another rubbery handful of the electric-blue dress, he said loudly, 'Well, this is Splashdance,' and twanged again. The next moment, with a shriek, Mirabelle had toppled into the pool.

'Can she swim?' asked Izzy some moments later, when all that had surfaced were bubbles.

Everyone else seemed to find it highly amusing. Amid much laughter, Tash drawled, 'She'll be safe, she's wearing a big enough condom.'

Izzy wasn't so sure. Mirabelle still hadn't risen to the surface and she was far too stoned to be fooling around.

Shaking Donny's shoulder, she repeated urgently, '*Can* she swim?'

But Donny scarcely seemed to be aware of his surroundings. With a vague gesture, he said, 'Hey man, how should I know? How d'you get the lid off this sodding can, anyway?'

The night was warm but cold sweat prickled beneath Izzy's arms as she was gripped by a premonition of doom. All around her, people were still laughing. Nobody was going to make a move to help. The horrible party was turning into a nightmare . . .

Izzy wasn't a strong swimmer but she knew there was no time to waste. Kicking off her shoes, she held her breath and dived in.

The heavily chlorinated water stung her eyes and when she touched the bottom of the pool a jab of pain shot through the sole of her foot, but by some miracle she found Mirabelle almost at once.

Sequins grazed her inner arms as she struggled to grab hold of the inert body, slippery in its rubber casing. Feeling as if her lungs were about to explode, Izzy slid her arms securely around the girl's ribcage and hauled with all her strength. Bizarrely, the water around them was turning cloudy pink like something out of a *Jaws* movie. Kicking her feet, blinking as Mirabelle's candyfloss hair plastered itself against her face, Izzy strained towards the surface of the pool. Strangely, in the dim distance, she could hear people cheering . . .

Only the concert organiser deigned to help. Between the two of them they eventually managed to haul Mirabelle – like a large, ungainly seal – out of the pool.

Gasping for breath, wiping her streaming eyes, Izzy searched for and eventually found a weak pulse, but the girl's chest was ominously still.

'Get an ambulance,' she croaked, tilting the slack head back and pinching Mirabelle's nose. Kneeling over her, she bent her own head and breathed into the cold, rubbery mouth.

'Hey, this is more like it,' yelled an indistinguishable male voice. 'Better than a porno film. Watch out, Tash, you've got competition there.'

Shovelling Mirabelle on to her front, Izzy pressed down on her lungs in a desperate attempt to clear them. This was worse than any nightmare. And although she couldn't see where it was coming from, there seemed to be blood everywhere, mingling with the water from the pool and staining the beige concrete upon which Mirabelle lay.

But finally, just as she was about to give up all hope, Mirabelle's chest heaved and water gushed out of her mouth. With a moan – as the water was followed by vomit – she flailed her arms and struggled to raise her head. Izzy rolled her on to her side so she wouldn't choke and sent up a prayer of thanks as the girl's ribcage rose and fell in something approaching a regular pattern.

'I say,' observed the actress in conversational tones, swaying as she bent to take a closer look. 'That's an awfully good trick.'

Izzy spoke through gritted teeth. 'Did they say how long it would take before the ambulance got here?'

Behind her, Tash said, 'She's OK. Just let her sleep it off. Ambulances screaming up the drive would only give the neighbours something else to complain about, and drowning drug addicts aren't exactly the kind of publicity we need.'

Coughing and spluttering, Mirabelle wiped her mouth with the back of her hand and moaned, 'Where's Donny? I'm c-cold.'

'Get some blankets and call an ambulance,' snapped Izzy, fixing the concert organiser with a steely glare. '*Now*.' Then, still kneeling with Mirabelle's head in her lap, she turned to face Tash and his guests.

'You selfish, stupid . . . bastards – all of you. Is anything more important to you than getting stoned? You're lucky she isn't *dead*, and all you care about is bad publicity. Any one of you could have fallen into that pool . . . and not *one* of you is capable of doing a damn thing to help.'

'Christ, this is all we need,' said Tash lazily. Glancing up at the redhead still massaging his shoulders, he winked and added, 'Don't you just hate moralizing do-gooders? Aren't they *the* most boring people to have at a party?'

Trembling with rage, repulsed by the knowledge that this was her lover speaking – and that she didn't know him at all – Izzy said icily, 'You are the most despicable man I've ever met in my life. You are *pathetic* . . .'

Tash's dark eyes glittered with amusement. 'Ah, but at least I'm not boring.'

At that moment a tall figure stepped out of the shadows and moved swiftly towards Izzy. For a fraction of a second she thought she was hallucinating.

But Sam, who had been listening to the heated exchange for the last thirty seconds – long enough to figure out what was going on – didn't waste any more time. Scooping Mirabelle up into his arms, he said briefly,

'Come on, we'll take her to the hospital in my car.'

'*Oh, when the saints go marching out,*' sang Tash, as they passed him. Izzy, who was limping behind Sam, paused. Beyond words, she turned and slapped his thin face as hard as she could. It wasn't enough, but it was better than nothing at all. If she'd had a gun she would have used it, without so much as a second thought.

It wasn't until she emerged from the casualty cubicle and found Sam waiting outside that she finally managed a weak smile.

'I've just seen myself in a mirror. No wonder they thought I was the patient.'

Sam's expression softened. With her white, mascara-streaked face, dripping wet hair and blood-streaked legs, Izzy had presented a far more convincing picture of an accident victim than half the patients in the waiting room, and she didn't look that much better now. With a glance at her bandaged foot, he held out his arm in order to support her back to the car. 'Does it hurt?'

She pulled a face. 'A bit. There was broken glass in the bottom of the pool and I managed to land on it. Oh Sam, should we be leaving? What about Mirabelle?'

He led her firmly through the double doors. 'They've admitted her for observation just to be on the safe side, but they're pretty certain she'll be OK. And there's no need to look at me like that,' he added with a grin. 'I'm in charge. You're absolutely wiped out and I'm taking you home.'

'Home,' murmured Izzy, her expression doubtful.

They had reached the car. Opening the passenger door

and helping her inside, Sam said briskly, 'My home.'

When they reached the flat, he deposited her on the sofa, threw a large towelling dressing gown down beside her and headed towards the kitchen.

'Change into that while I make the coffee.'

Exhausted though she was, Izzy nevertheless summoned up the energy to make her lie sound convincing. 'I thought Vivienne would be here. She left the party ages ago, saying she was going to have an early night.'

Pausing in the doorway, Sam merely looked amused. 'But not in her bed, it seems. Never mind, Izzy. Nice try.'

By the time he returned with the coffee and a packet of chocolate digestives, however, the shock had begun to set in. Izzy, enveloped in the white towelling robe, was shivering so much the sofa practically vibrated beneath her. She looked so uncharacteristically frail and unhappy that Sam's heart went out to her.

'I suppose you've been looking forward to this,' she said, clasping the mug he offered her between both hands in order not to spill the contents.

'To what?'

'Saying, "I told you so." '

'I *was* looking forward to it,' he said truthfully, 'but it doesn't seem all that relevant now. I'm more concerned with how you're feeling.'

Izzy shrugged, her dark eyes enormous but mercifully dry. 'Lucky, I suppose, to be out of it in one piece. Angry, gullible . . . oh, Sam, how could I have been so *stupid*? When I first met Tash I really thought he was a nice person.'

'That's because he wanted you to think he was.'

She sniffed. 'God, I'm a lousy judge of character. Imagine the damage I could do if I was ever called for jury service.'

Easing his long legs up on to the coffee table and tearing open the packet of biscuits, Sam said evenly, 'Anyone can make a mistake.'

'You never do.'

'I let Vivienne move in with me.'

The signs of Vivienne's occupation were strewn around them. Having absently helped herself to a biscuit she didn't want, the chocolate now melted between her fingers as Izzy gazed at a pair of black-and-gold stilettos occupying a chair, and at the CDs littered like playing cards on the floor beside the stereo. The system had been left switched on, with a half-empty wineglass balanced precariously on top of it. In a small way, it was comforting to know how much Vivienne's untidiness irritated Sam. Maybe he was right, after all.

'But she isn't . . . scary, like Tash. She doesn't get out of her brains on drugs. He doesn't care about anyone or anything . . . he's practically psychopathic. You can't compare them, Sam. Vivienne's only unhappy because you aren't paying her enough attention.'

She was speaking more calmly now, and her teeth had stopped chattering. Lifting a semi-damp tendril of hair from her neck and breathing in the chlorine, Sam shrugged.

'That just proves my point. If I hadn't made the mistake of letting her stay here in the first place, she wouldn't be unhappy now. If Vivienne and I were genuinely happy together, I'd *be* paying attention.'

'It doesn't bother you that she didn't come home tonight?' Izzy still found it hard to believe. In her own mind, they were such a *good* couple.

'I'm relieved.' He paused, then added drily, 'It's easier this way. She can make her own decision, and her pride will still be intact. As you may have noticed, Vivienne has more than her share of pride.'

Izzy was finding it hard not to notice his warm fingers at the base of her neck, idly smoothing back her hair. She shivered uncontrollably and gazed down at the chocolatey mess in her hand.

'What you need is a hot bath and plenty of sleep,' he continued gently and for the first time her eyes filled with tears. What she *most* needed was a real hug, and someone to tell her she wasn't an all-time prize idiot.

To her utter dismay she heard herself saying in a small, pathetic voice, 'You're such a nice person. You used to like me, didn't you, Sam? I wish you hadn't stopped liking me. I . . . I wish you didn't hate me now.'

She didn't get her hug. Taking a deep breath and giving her shoulder a brief, meant-to-be reassuring squeeze, he said, 'Don't be silly, of course I don't hate you,' and rose to his feet.

'I'm sorry,' mumbled Izzy, wiping her eyes and feeling more idiotic than ever.

Sam, continuing to exert almost superhuman self-control, dismissed the apology with a brisk gesture. She was vulnerable, exhausted and deeply upset about Tash. Now was hardly the time to tell Izzy how he really felt about her.

'You've had a traumatic night,' he said with a taut half-smile. 'I'll run you that bath, and then you're going to bed.'

In a hopeless attempt to redeem herself, Izzy said weakly, 'Will you do me a big favour?'

This, thought Sam, was precisely what he was struggling so hard not to do. 'What?'

'Can I have Badedas in it?'

# Chapter 41

It wasn't as if they were doing anything *lewd*, but it was still kind of embarrassing being caught on the sofa with the new love of your life, particularly when the person doing the catching was your new love's grown-up son.

'Well, well,' he declared in arch tones, dumping a tartan overnight case on the living-room floor and surveying the cosy scene. Vivienne, whose bare feet had been resting in Terry's lap, leapt guiltily into a sitting position and tried to make her cleavage less prominent.

'Theo, for heaven's sake.' Terry was looking equally discomfited. 'I thought you were working this weekend.'

'Somebody wanted to swap shifts,' replied Theo easily, 'so I thought I'd drop in on my old man, make sure he was OK.' He winked at Vivienne. 'I thought he might be lonely . . . in need of a bit of company . . .'

Theo Pleydell-Pearce, sandy-haired and built like an American football player, had his father's blue eyes and endearing freckles. Deciding to brazen it out – since Terry was clearly too embarrassed to say much at all – Vivienne grinned at him and replied, 'I had exactly the same idea.'

'So, you aren't a patient.' The blue eyes sparkled with amusement. 'For a moment I thought I might be inter-rupting a reverse housecall.'

'Theo, this is Vivienne Bresnick. We met at a party last night . . .' Floundering for an explanation, Terry pushed his fingers agitatedly through his hair. 'We came back here for coffee ... we've been talking all night ...'

'What your father is trying to say,' Vivienne intercepted kindly, 'is that our relationship has not been consummated. Yet.'

Since morning surgery started at nine, Theo drove Vivienne back to Kensington. Above the roar of the ancient MG's engine, as they careered along narrow country lanes with the hood down and the cassette player blaring out Bruce Springsteen, he yelled, 'So, tell me, what exactly *is* going on here?'

'Excuse me?'

'Between you and Dad. It would be simpler if you just told me the truth. Was it a drunken one-off or do you really intend seeing him again?'

Leaning across, she switched off the music. Theo obligingly reduced his speed so that she could speak without shouting.

'Your father is one of the nicest men I've ever met,' said Vivienne carefully. 'And more than anything else in the world, I'd like to continue seeing him.'

He nodded. 'OK. I'm sorry if I've offended you, but you must understand why I needed to ask. Since my mother died, he's had his share of women interested in him, but you aren't exactly ...'

'I know, I know.' Vivienne had spent the entire night listening to this argument. 'I'm not a country lady in twin set and brogues, with a Labrador at my heels and a shooting-stick up my bum. I've never baked a "scone" – whatever the hell that might be – in my life. But the moment I set eyes on your dad, something . . . clicked. I really like him,' she concluded with a simple gesture. 'And I think he likes me.'

With a sideways glance, Theo took in the clinging, shell-pink satin dress, the expanse of tanned thigh, the astonishing bosom and cascading blonde hair. 'I'm not surprised.'

Vivienne smiled. 'I have a great personality, as well.'

'So I'm beginning to realise,' he admitted wryly. 'What I really can't wait to see are the faces of all those tweedy county ladies, when they find out what kind of competition they're up against.'

Sam, in white cotton trousers and a grey sweatshirt, was stretched out on the sofa surrounded by paperwork when she let herself into the apartment. Vivienne, who hadn't expected him to be up at this time of the morning, hesitated in the doorway before kicking off her shoes and dropping her bag into a chair. Despite the exhilaration of the last twelve hours, she was now gripped by a spasm of self-doubt. Sam was *so* stunningly handsome, so physically perfect, how could she even think of leaving him? Yet she had adored him and it hadn't been enough. Nothing she could do would ever make Sam adore her in return. She had done everything in her power, but the necessary spark simply wasn't there.

He glanced up from his paperwork. 'Good party?'

'It had its moments.' Vivienne pushed her fingers through her tangled, wind-blown hair. Then, with a trace of exasperation, she said, 'Well? Aren't you even going to ask me what I've been doing?'

It was a last-ditch attempt to force some kind of reaction, some shred of jealousy, but all Sam did was glance across at her opened bag and look faintly amused. After pausing to pencil in an alteration, he replied, 'Since your bra is hanging out of your handbag, I think I can probably guess.'

So much for jealousy and belated protestations of love. The pale pink bra was new and expensive but a size too small, and Vivienne had merely removed it in the early hours of the morning in order to be comfortable. She hadn't been unfaithful to Sam, yet he had calmly assumed the opposite and *still* didn't even have the decency to care . . .

'How did you ever get to be so *unfeeling*?' Her voice rose to a wail and at last Sam reacted.

'Ssshh,' he said sharply. 'Izzy's asleep in the spare room. Don't make so much noise.'

Despite everything, Vivienne was instantly diverted. '*Izzy's* here? Why?'

'While you were elsewhere, flinging off your bra and enjoying one of your . . . moments, Izzy realised what a bastard Tash Janssen really is.' Sam, who hadn't been to bed, abbreviated the facts. 'She's left him.'

'And she came here?'

'I brought her back here.'

Vivienne, bewildered, shook her head. 'You mean she phoned you up?'

'I thought you might have wanted a lift home,' said Sam evenly. 'So I drove out there when I'd finished at the club. But you weren't around, and Izzy was.'

At that moment her gaze travelled past him and

fixed upon the green-and-gold sequinned bodice draped damply over the back of a chair. It was recognizably the top Izzy had been wearing earlier.

Still confused, she frowned and said with a trace of suspicion, 'Are you and Izzy having an affair?'

'No.' Sam, looking not in the least put out by the suggestion, shook his head. 'We are not.'

'Hmm.' Overcome suddenly by fatigue, Vivienne turned and headed for the bedroom. 'So that makes none of us. No wonder we're all so bloody fed up.'

'How do I always manage to make such an incredible mess of everything?' said Izzy despairingly, over lunch at Langan's. It was three days since the party, two days since she'd moved back to Kingsley Grove, and the question had been preying on her mind ever since.

'I don't know.' Gina attempted a witticism. 'I suppose some people are just naturally untidy.'

'Ha, ha.' Izzy pulled a face. 'No, I'm being serious. Look what's happened to me over the past few months. A spectacularly failed love affair and an alienated daughter. OK, Kat speaks to me – but only just. We used to have such *fun* together . . .'

'A few months ago,' said Gina spearing a bite-sized piece of chicken breast in tarragon sauce, 'you'd never even seen the inside of a recording studio and you worked in a sleazy club for peanuts. Today you're buying me lunch, having driven me here in your very own Mercedes, and you have a single at Number Two in the charts. All you've ever wanted to be is a success and now you *are* one.'

'Ever heard of sleeping your way to the top?' Izzy retaliated, taking a slurp of wine. 'Everyone treats me as Tash Janssen's sidekick, that's all. Without him, I'd still be a nobody. And I'm hardly a successful mother, for heaven's sake.'

It was a tricky subject. Gina still froze every time Katerina's name was even mentioned. With a shrug, she glanced sideways at the diners at the next table and saw that they were still watching. It was heady stuff, being ogled by two such attractive men, even if most of the attention was going Izzy's way.

'Your daughter's choice of partners is hardly your fault,' she replied stiffly.

'But it's still my concern! Everything's been spoiled and I simply don't know where I've gone wrong. I've never been so miserable in my life. And you,' she continued in accusing tones, 'have never looked better. God knows, I'm glad you couldn't make it to that terrible party, but what's been *happening* with you? Is Ralph back on the scene . . . ?'

Indirectly, Gina supposed, Ralph had been responsible for her new-found sense of well-being. For some reason she had been unable to fathom, she simply had felt better since sending him away with a flea in his ear that stormy afternoon when he had erupted, brimming with self-confidence, into the office. In deflating his ego, she had boosted her own immeasurably, and the relationship between Doug and herself had subsequently improved in leaps and bounds. Almost overnight he had become less of an employer, more of a real friend . . .

For a moment she was almost tempted to tell Izzy that

Doug was taking her to the theatre this evening, but she held her tongue. Izzy would either leap to conclusions and imagine some grand romance or gaze at her with fascinated disbelief, which would spoil everything. It wasn't as if she was going out on some kind of date, after all. She simply enjoyed being with Doug and was able to relax in his undemanding company.

'Ralph is definitely not back on the scene,' she said briskly, finishing her lunch and feeling decidedly in control. 'Credit me with some sense, *please*.'

'I'm the one with no sense.' Izzy gazed gloomily at her own barely touched food. 'I'm an abysmal failure.'

'Excuse me.' The bolder of the two men at the table next to theirs leaned back in his chair and attracted her attention. 'Aren't you Izzy Van Asch?'

Being recognised wasn't turning out to be quite as much fun as she'd imagined, either. It always seemed to happen at the wrong moments. But she forced a gracious smile. 'Yes, I am.'

'We thought so.' He smirked at his friend, then said, 'What's it like then, screwing Tash Janssen?'

Gina cringed and held her breath, waiting to see what would happen next.

Finally, Izzy smiled.

'Terrible,' she replied sweetly. 'His willy's even smaller than yours.'

Disasters, as a rule, came in threes. As far as Doug was concerned, however, they were threatening to run into double figures. The harder he tried, the more things seemed to go wrong.

'I'm sorry,' he said again, pulling out his handkerchief in order to mop his forehead and managing to spill whisky down the front of his jacket as he did so. 'This is the worst play I've ever seen. You can't possibly want to go back inside. Shall we skip the second act and find somewhere to eat instead?'

If this had been a proper date, Gina might have been equally embarrassed by the almost farcical events of the evening. But since it wasn't, she couldn't understand why Doug should be so distraught. It was hardly his fault, after all, that his car should have broken down in Park Lane and needed pushing to the side of the road, just as it wasn't his fault that the new play he had brought her to see was one of the unfunniest comedies ever staged. Since it wasn't a real date it didn't even matter that she had ended up with rain-soaked hair, oil stains on her coat and two broken fingernails. All that mattered was that despite all these setbacks, she was still *enjoying* herself . . .

'We can't leave now!' She looked shocked. 'Mavis is expecting us to go backstage afterwards and congratulate her. The play may not be up to much, but she's acting her heart out on that stage and it's her first big break. The least we can do is tell her how great *she* is.'

Doug didn't understand how she could be so cheerful. Gazing down at his damp jacket, he was further mortified to realise that his new shirt, fresh out of its box, was displaying tell-tale box-shaped creases. He couldn't remember the last time he'd put so much effort into getting ready to go out. Now he was unhappily aware that he still possessed about as much sartorial elegance as a hippo in a mac.

Worse was to come. It seemed impossible to imagine that someone so uptight could fall asleep, but to his utter shame Doug found himself jerking awake halfway through the second act. The noise that had awoken him was his own snoring. Gina, beside him, was in fits of suppressed giggles.

'I'm a lost cause,' he said mournfully, when they had done their duty and visited a stiff-upper-lipped Mavis in her tiny dressing room. Leaving via the stage door, which led out into a narrow side-street, they found that the rain was bucketing down harder than ever, and there wasn't a cab in sight.

'Of course you aren't.' Gina squeezed his arm as they set off up the road. 'You gave the audience their best laugh of the evening for a start. And the really nice thing about awful plays is they do wonders for your appetite ... look, why don't we try this little Italian place on the left, then we don't have to worry about finding a taxi.'

Doug winced as the slender-hipped waiter whisked past, missing him by millimetres as he disappeared into the kitchen. Moments later the swing doors burst open once more as another waiter shimmied past bearing plates of steaming pasta. Anthony Hopkins, he thought darkly – because someone had once said he looked a bit like him, and because that great actor had always secretly been his hero – would never be dumped at the worst table in the house.

Gina, apparently unperturbed, was engrossed in the menu. 'I'm going to have the *moules marinière*.'

'You'll get food poisoning.' He looked more lugubrious than ever. 'That should round off the evening nicely.'

The meal, in fact, was exquisite. By the time they had finished their strega coffees Doug found himself in imminent danger of actually cheering up, but fate hadn't finished with him yet.

The manager, with a discreet cough, appeared by their table. 'I'm sorry, sir,' he said, not sounding sorry at all, 'but have you some other means of payment? This credit card is out of date.'

'It really doesn't matter,' Gina insisted for the fourth time as they climbed into their taxi. 'You can pay me back tomorrow if it makes you happier, but there's no need to keep apologizing. It could have happened to anyone.'

It wouldn't have happened to Anthony Hopkins, thought Doug with silent despair. Bloody expiry dates, bloody sanctimonious restaurant managers, bloody broken-down cars, bloody, *bloody* rain . . .

# Chapter 42

The weather continued to deteriorate. On the third Friday in October, London and the south-east of England cowered in the grip of one of the worst hurricanes of the decade. With Izzy away in Scotland pre-recording a television Hogmanay 'special' and her own television out of action as a result of the power lines going down, Gina decided the only sensible course of action was to have an early night. By the light of a flickering candle she made her way slowly up the stairs, prayed that the tiles wouldn't be ripped from the roof by the blistering storm, and wondered if she'd ever be able to get to sleep.

She was just dozing off an hour and a half later when the phone rang downstairs, jerking her back to wakefulness and instant apprehension. Whoever would be calling at twelve-thirty at night with anything but bad news?

The parquet floor was cold beneath her bare feet. Gina's heart was still hammering as she picked up the receiver. Guardedly, she said, 'Hallo.'

At first she couldn't make out who was on the other end. It was a terrible line, awash with crackles and electronic hisses. Eventually, straining to listen through them, she heard what sounded like uneven sobbing and gulps for breath. Not Izzy, surely not Izzy...

'Hallo, who is it?' she said, more loudly this time. The

all-enveloping darkness was eerie and the wind still howled outside.

'Mum,' came a small voice, amid more sobbing. 'Mum, is that you?'

Gina had neither seen nor spoken to Katerina since that nightmare day when she'd learned of her affair with Andrew. Now her grip tightened on the receiver and apprehension gave way to annoyance.

'Your mother isn't here,' she replied coldly. 'She's in Scotland.'

'Wh-what? Where?'

'Edinburgh. She's due back on Monday evening.'

A static-riddled silence ensued. Then, with almost animal anguish, Katerina wailed, 'But I want my mum!'

She sounded in a terrible state. Gina, whose initial instinct had been to slam down the phone, relented slightly and took a deep breath.

'Look, she's left me the number of the hotel, but there's a power cut here and it'll take me a while to find it. Why don't you phone directory enquiries and ask them; she's staying at the Swallow Royal in Edinburgh.'

'I want . . . my . . . mum,' repeated Katerina, her voice choking on the words. 'I . . . want . . .'

'What's the matter? Are you ill?'

'I want my mum.'

She sounded almost demented with grief. Feeling increasingly ill at ease, Gina said, 'Directory Enquiries. The Swallow Royal in Edinburgh. They'll be able to give you the number. But look, Katerina, if you're ill . . .'

The phone went dead. Katerina had hung up on her. With a sigh, Gina replaced the receiver and began to feel her way towards the staircase. Katerina's problems were no concern of hers.

But it was no good. After a second of deliberation she turned back, fumbling in the inky darkness for the notepad next to the phone, upon which Izzy had scrawled the hotel's number. By the time she managed to locate the matches and relight her candle she would be able to speak to Izzy herself, discover what was going on and put her own mind at rest. Then she'd be able to get back to sleep.

Forty minutes later, her teeth chattering with fear as much as cold, Gina edged the car out of the drive and set off up the road at a crawl, wincing as the storm buffeted the sides of the little Golf and sent twigs and leaves hurtling against the windscreen.

The telephone lines to Scotland were down. While she had been ringing Sam's flat and getting no reply, her own phone had gone dead. The hurricane was wreaking havoc everywhere. And although she had tried to tell herself that Katerina deserved everything she got, the sheer anguish in the girl's voice had shaken Gina to the core. Listening to her on the phone, she'd sounded more like seven years old than seventeen, and desperately in need of help. She was suffering, and alone. And Gina knew only too well how *that* felt. Driving across the storm-swept city, she wondered if she'd ever been more scared in her life. The streets were mercifully empty of pedestrians and cars, but the air was thick with swirling leaves and rubbish. When a triangular roadworks sign smashed into the passenger door Gina screamed aloud but kept going. She couldn't give up now. It couldn't be more than a mile to Katerina's bedsitter. Not more than another ten terrifying minutes . . .

She hammered on the front door for what seemed like an eternity, struggling to remain upright against the howling gale and make herself heard above it. Finally, just as she was about to give up, the door opened. Katerina's face, pinched and white, appeared in the narrow gap behind the security chain.

'Oh my God,' she wailed. 'What do *you* want?'

It wasn't quite the welcome Gina had been expecting. Hopelessly on edge after her nightmare journey, she snapped back, 'Charming. Are you going to let me in?'

Katerina's eyes filled with fresh tears. 'Why?'

'Because it's almost two o'clock in the morning and I've driven here to make sure you're all right.' Gina spoke through gritted teeth – so much for genuine concern. 'But if all you're going to be is fucking ungrateful, maybe I'd better just leave.'

Katerina wiped her wet cheeks with the back of her hand and digested these words in silence. She'd never heard Gina swear before.

'OK,' she muttered, because it didn't really matter any more; she no longer cared what happened to her. 'Come in.'

The electricity supply had by this time been restored although Gina almost wished it hadn't. The grim little bedsitting room was an absolute tip and Katerina – normally so fastidious – looked dreadful. Now, gazing defensively around at the mess and twisting her fingers, she said, 'Oh, I'm sorry, isn't this good enough for you? If you'd only let me know you were coming I'd have polished the silver and put on a party frock.'

She looked as if she'd been crying non-stop for a week. Her long hair, normally as clean and shiny as a conker, hung in rats' tails and the dark blue sweater and jeans she wore seemed three sizes too big. The unmade bed in the corner of the room was littered with dozens of sheets of foolscap paper.

'Go on,' taunted Katerina, observing the look of distaste on Gina's face. 'Tell me I've let myself go and it's no more than I deserve.'

There was no heating in the room. With a shiver, Gina replied evenly, 'Well, you've certainly let yourself go.'

'Oh, get *out* of here!' With a howl of grief, Katerina's face crumpled and she turned away. This was too much to bear. 'Just leave me alone . . . I didn't ask you to come here . . . I want my mum . . .'

That final heartfelt cry was too much for Gina to bear. It was what had brought her here in the first place, a poignant echo of the grief she had felt when her own mother had died so many years ago. Without even thinking, she crossed the room and took Katerina's thin, shaking body in her arms.

'Kat, stop it. You can't carry on like this. I'm here because I'm worried about you . . . we care about you . . . and you're going to make yourself ill if you don't let us help.'

Katerina went rigid. For a fraction of a second Gina thought she was going to hit her. Then, falteringly, and with tears still streaming down her face and neck, she turned and clung to her, burying her head against Gina's shoulder.

'I'm sorry, I'm so sorry, I don't know what's the matter with me,' she sobbed hopelessly. 'I thought I was having a nervous breakdown, but people aren't supposed to know when it's happening to them. I've felt horrible for weeks but the last few days have been like a nightmare ... everything's got worse and worse and I can't do anything any more except cry...'

'Sshh,' murmured Gina in soothing tones. Despite her lack of experience with young children, she was finding it easy to treat Katerina as a distraught seven year old. 'Come on, sit down and tell me all about it. Tell me everything, then we can sort it out.'

Katerina, sniffing, still clung to her. 'Do you really not hate me?'

'I'm here, aren't I? Of course I don't.'

'But I've been such a bitch. *I* hate me.'

Gina, tempted to suggest that a bath might improve matters, gave her a hug instead. 'And now you're punishing yourself. Hasn't it even occurred to you that it was just as much Andrew's fault as yours? More even. He was the one who should have known better, after all.'

Something had evidently gone wrong between them. Surprising herself, Gina experienced relief on Katerina's behalf rather than her own. Andrew was weak, whereas Kat had simply been gullible, and she deserved better.

'I hate him,' said Katerina bleakly. 'And now I'm going to tell you something that really *will* make you hate me.'

'What?'

'I think I'm pregnant.'

The seven year old in her arms had vanished. Izzy's daughter was, after all, a near-adult with adult problems.

Gina, her heart sinking, said, 'Have you told him?'

Katerina nodded.

'And?'

'He said, "Oh fucking hell, not again." '

The hurricane had blown itself out by early morning. With the boot of the Golf loaded up with carrier bags of Katerina's belongings, Gina drove her back through the debris-strewn streets to Kingsley Grove, then ran her a very hot bath, threw the dark blue sweater and disreputable jeans straight into the washing-machine and started cooking breakfast.

'I can't believe I'm here.' Katerina, reappearing downstairs forty minutes later in one of Izzy's dazzling silk dressing gowns, gulped down a cup of strong coffee and attacked her bacon and eggs with enthusiasm. 'I can't believe I'm actually enjoying this food . . .'

She may have been lacking personal experience in such matters, but Gina had heard enough tales of woe from pregnant friends in her time to seriously doubt whether Katerina could be similarly afflicted. Coffee and fried food at eight o'clock in the morning was an absolute no-no under such circumstances.

'The phone lines are back in action,' she said, inwardly wincing as Katerina smothered her eggs in tomato ketchup and black pepper. 'I've just checked with the operator. You can phone Izzy as soon as you've finished eating.'

Katerina hesitated, then gave her a tentative smile. 'Mum's busy. I don't want to send her into a panic. Besides, I'm feeling better now.'

'Good.'

'You really think I'm not pregnant?'

Katerina had wound herself up into such a state over the past few weeks that Gina thought it hardly surprising her period hadn't arrived. Having initially said this in order to calm her down, however, she now erred on the side of caution.

'As soon as the chemist opens, I'll go down and pick up one of those tester packs, then we'll know for sure,' she said carefully. It was strange, but nice, to be discussing such a personal matter with Katerina. 'Although you did say you'd taken precautions.'

'Oh yes.' For the first time, and because it was such a relief to have finally confided in someone, Katerina nodded and broke into a grin. 'And it's a known fact,' she added, crossing her fingers and praying that Gina was right, 'that good Mates don't let you down . . .'

# Chapter 43

When Izzy arrived back at Kingsley Grove three days later she thought at first she must be hallucinating. As astonishment gave way to delight, however, she carefully didn't ask too many questions and accepted her daughter's return as a much-longed-for miracle.

To her great joy as well, it was as if the past traumatic months hadn't existed. Katerina, bright-eyed and good-tempered, was her old cheerful self. She had also retained her old forthright way with words.

'Who did that to your hair?' she asked in reproving tones and Izzy – who had been marched along to a Mayfair salon by one of MBT's chief stylists – hung her magenta head in shame.

'I know, they said it had to be this colour to show up under the TV lights.'

Katerina was in the process of making a cheese soufflé. Having finished whisking the egg whites, she paused and wiped her hands on a damp cloth. 'The colour's fine. I like beetroot. I meant you let them cut it.'

'It's not cut,' said Izzy defensively, 'it's layered.'

But Katerina was eyeing the end result with disapproval. Izzy and her wild mass of ringlets were part of each other while MBT, it seemed, was attempting to transform her into something altogether more sophisticated. 'I've always cut your hair,' she said. 'I know it

349

better than anyone else. Tell your trendy record company that in future we'll be taking care of that side of things. I'll cut and you dye, just like we've always done before.'

Best of all, though, was discovering that Katerina had made the decision to retake her A levels. When she wasn't cooking – as if that in some way made amends for her past misbehaviour – she spent hours poring over her text books and painstakingly rewriting the notes which Gina had destroyed.

'I still don't know how you did it,' said Izzy gratefully, when she and Gina were alone the following evening. 'I'm almost afraid to ask.'

Jericho, almost certain that Izzy had dropped a Smartie down the back of the sofa, was burrowing frantically among the cushions. Gina hauled him off. 'She just came to her senses in her own time,' she replied, her voice calm. Since there was no sense in rocking the boat she had felt it unnecessary to even mention Katerina's false alarm. Two pregnancy tests had been negative, which was all that mattered, and a trip to her doctor had assured them that as soon as she relaxed and started eating properly once more, her periods would return.

Izzy regarded her with the merest trace of suspicion. 'There must have been more to it than that,' she persisted, but Gina simply shrugged and fondled Jericho's ears.

'We had a man in common. A stupid, weak man, maybe . . . but at least we both knew what the other had been going through. Once she realised that, the rest was easy.'

'Well, hooray for stupid men,' said Izzy, emptying the last of the Smarties into her hand and pretending to ignore the piteous expression in Jericho's eyes. 'But I still don't think you've told me everything.'

Gina grinned. 'Kat and I are members of an exclusive club. Now maybe if *you* were to have an affair with Andrew . . .'

With a yelp of gratitude, Jericho wolfed down an orange Smartie, his favourite colour. Izzy pulled a face. 'Pass.'

'. . . and just so long as you wouldn't be expectin' me to treat you like some great la-di-da duchess, waitin' on you hand and foot and finger at all hours of the day and night . . . I mean, you seem like a nice enough young thing at this moment in time, but let me tell you, some people have a funny old side to their characters when it comes down to it and I wouldn't be puttin' up with any of that kind of nonsense for even so much as one minute . . .'

Izzy, absolutely fascinated, held her breath and said nothing for fear of breaking the spell. Lucille Devlin from Dublin was quite simply the most amazing woman she'd ever met in her life. And she spoke in the longest sentences.

'. . . but if you're agreeable to my terms and you think we might suit each other,' continued Lucille, who didn't appear to need to draw any breath of her own, 'then I'd be happy to keep your house up together for you, seein' as it would give me a break from that no-good miserable old pig of a husband of mine . . . I sing a bit myself, you know, they used to say I had the finest voice in all Ireland, but of course it turned out to be a curse as much as a blessin', for wasn't it how I went and met the old bugger in the first place, me at nineteen years of age singin' in Daley's bar and him proppin' the bloody thing up . . .'

* * *

Izzy, lying in the bath, couldn't understand why she wasn't the happiest woman in the world.

She had Katerina back, as good as new and working like a Trojan to ensure that this time her A level results would be dazzling.

She had the house of her dreams, a splendid four-storey Georgian property in Bloomsbury which she had rented from one of the MBT executives while he and his family spent a year in Los Angeles.

She had her debut solo album in mid-production with the first track from it, entitled 'Kiss', coming out as a single next week.

She had public appearances lined up beyond Christmas, a carrier bag overflowing with fan mail in the corner of her bedroom, the offer of a European tour sponsored by a soft drinks manufacturer . . .

And she had buxom Lucille Devlin, with her tomato-soup-coloured hair, Technicolour clothes and endless capacity for conversation, who was a full-scale entertainment in herself. How could anyone in the company of Lucille possibly fail to be amused? wondered Izzy, drumming her toes moodily against the tap end of the bath. Lucille could cheer up Russia.

But for some reason it wasn't working for *her*. The success she had craved for so long, and which should have been making her so happy, wasn't doing the trick. Public recognition – even in the form of Lucille hoovering like a maniac and singing, '*I want you to kiss me, To know that you've missed me,*' over and again in her rich Irish contralto – simply wasn't enough to eradicate the leaden sensation in her stomach and the feeling that somehow there should be *more*.

Three hours later, too restless to stay at home and vaguely searching for that elusive 'more', Izzy entered the comforting familiarity of The Chelsea Steps. She was almost certain that Sam, who had recently been over in the States again, was now back. It was silly, she knew, but the longing to see him again had been almost overwhelming. And now that she was here, even her heart was beating a little faster in anticipation . . .

Sam, however, noticed the commotion before realizing that Izzy was the cause of it. Cursing beneath his breath and moving swiftly across the packed dance floor to the smaller bar at the far side of the club, he knew instinctively that the problem involved the two arrogant and mega-rich Argentinians whom he'd had his doubts about from the moment they'd arrived. The Chelsea Steps, famous above all else for the fact that there was never any trouble within its doors, needed this kind of guests like a hole in the head. Sam's blood ran cold as another yell of male outrage reached his ears and he imagined what a hole in a mega-rich Argentinian's head would do for business. All he could do was pray that neither of them was carrying a gun.

When he reached the source of the trouble, arriving just in time to see Izzy land a stinging slap on the younger Argentinian's tanned cheek and deliver a torrent of abuse to the pair of them, Sam cheerfully could have killed her himself. Cutting through the crowd which had gathered around to watch Izzy in action, he grabbed her by the arm and hauled her unceremoniously to one side.

'Calm down,' he said sharply, because Izzy forever seemed to be getting herself embroiled in some fracas or other and it couldn't always be the other person's fault.

'That oily bastard!' Izzy had no intention of calming down. Her dark eyes flashed as she glared at the thin, equally furious Argentinian, now gabbling frantically in his own language. 'He shoved his revolting hand down the front of my dress.'

'What dress?' countered Sam, glancing down at the skimpy apricot-pink creation which clung to every curve and ended at mid-thigh. It seemed to him that the more money Izzy spent on clothes, the less of them there became.

'Oh, so that gives him the right to *grope* me?' she demanded furiously, colour mounting in her cheeks as she realised that he was landing the blame on her. 'Come *on*, Sam! Whose side are you on?'

Sam was so tired he could hardly think straight. The reason he'd had to fly over to New York was because his supposedly dependable manager there had been busted for possession of cocaine. Now, back in London and suffering more badly than usual from jet lag, he had this to contend with. Izzy might not realise it at the moment but she was in danger of jeopardizing the good reputation of The Chelsea Steps.

'I'm on the side of keeping your voice down and letting the other guests enjoy their evening,' he replied evenly, steering her towards a small table and pressing her rigid body into one of the chairs.

'But he *assaulted* me . . .'

'And you are in my club, not a wrestling arena. For heaven's sake, Izzy, if you wanted to make a complaint all you had to do was come and tell me about it, then I could have dealt with the matter quietly.'

Sam could be such a disappointment sometimes. Izzy, who had been so looking forward to seeing him, felt her eyes fill with angry tears. 'You mean I should have *quietly* let them gang rape me—'

'Don't be ridiculous,' he snapped back. 'I'm just saying that it always seems to happen to you, doesn't it? And what do you honestly expect, coming out on your own dressed like some kind of high-class hooker? Anyone's going to think you're looking for attention . . . God knows, all you've ever *wanted* is attention . . . and now that you're becoming well known you're going to have to learn to handle it in the proper manner.'

'Stop it!' shrieked Izzy, unable to bear the unfairness of it all a moment longer. Now, her heart really racing, she wrenched her hand from Sam's patronizing grasp and rose jerkily to her feet. 'I'd rather be groped by greasy perverts than lectured to by a bastard who cares more about his precious club than his friends. And some friend *you* turned out to be,' she added through gritted teeth. 'When I think of all the nice things I told Vivienne about you . . .'

Vivienne. Another problem Sam didn't need right now. Vivienne had been behaving decidedly oddly during the past few weeks. 'You shouldn't have bothered,' he said in abrupt tones as Izzy turned to leave.

'You're telling me,' she hissed with as much sarcasm as

she could muster. 'But don't worry, it was all lies. And she didn't believe me anyway.'

# Chapter 44

'I'm miserable,' announced Vivienne when Izzy answered the phone the following morning. 'Come shopping with me.'

'What's Sam been telling you?' Izzy demanded suspiciously, and a noise like a snort greeted her ears.

'Sam who?'

They set out to do some serious damage in and around Bond Street, Vivienne the acknowledged expert and Izzy an enthusiastic newcomer to the art of real spending. South Molton Street was a particularly good starting-point; after twenty minutes in Browns, Izzy realised that she had blown more money on a pink suede skirt and a white cashmere sweater than she used to earn in an entire month. Vivienne, who had been weaned on designer labels and who never wasted any time glancing at price tags, kissed her gold card and became the proud new owner of a coffee-coloured silk dress and matching jacket, three pairs of trousers and a spectacular black-and-bronze sequinned top by a young Japanese designer with an awful lot of 'Ys' in his name.

'Better?' said Izzy two hours later when they stopped at a crowded bistro for a cappuccino and several slices of Amaretto-soaked chocolate-fudge cake. Glancing down at the slippery pile of carrier bags propped against the table legs, she estimated that they must have spent enough money to cover the cost of a holiday in Barbados.

Vivienne lit a cigarette. 'It helps, I suppose. It always helps.' Then she leaned closer. 'But I still haven't told you yet why I was miserable in the first place.'

'That's easy.' Izzy pulled a fearsome face, startling several nearby customers. 'You live with an unspeakable bastard. It'd be enough to make anyone miserable.'

'I love him so much.'

'Oh, Vee.' Izzy's expression softened. 'Do you still? I really thought you were getting over him.'

Vivienne, who had been idly scooping the froth off her cappuccino with a teaspoon, frowned. 'Not Sam, dumbo. I'm talking about Terry.'

'What!' Izzy, jack-knifing forwards, didn't even notice that she'd landed her left breast in the chocolate-fudge cake. 'Who? You haven't told me anything about this!'

Vivienne hadn't told anyone, so afraid had she been of breaking the spell. But now she simply couldn't help it.

'The man I met at Tash's party,' she explained, stubbing out her cigarette and immediately lighting another, even though Terry passionately disapproved of smoking. 'Oh Izzy, he's wonderful. I love him to pieces . . . he's everything I've ever wanted in a man.'

Reluctant though she was to spoil the fairy-tale, Izzy said cautiously, 'You said that about Sam.'

'Yes, but Sam's never loved me back.' Vivienne shook her head, then half-smiled. 'And Terry does.'

'In that case, I don't understand why you aren't deliriously happy. You love this guy, he loves you . . . so the two of you are crazy about each other . . . and you're miserable!' Izzy was seriously confused. Then she said, 'Uh oh, don't tell me – the dreaded M-word.'

'No, he's not married. He's a widower, with two grown-up children. I've met them, I get on well with them, they like me. Hell, even his bloody cat likes me . . .'

By this time almost bursting with frustration, Izzy screeched, 'Then *what*?'

'He won't take me seriously.' For a moment Vivienne looked as if she was about to burst into tears. 'Oh Izzy, it's ridiculous. He says I'm too young, too beautiful and far, far too rich to be interested in someone like him. I've tried telling him until I'm blue in the face that none of those things matter, but he simply refuses to believe me. And what can I do?' She spread her hands in despair, her cigarette almost setting fire to the trousers of a passing waiter. 'I can't make myself *older*.'

Despite Vivienne's tragic expression, Izzy had to smile. She was envisaging the world's first face-lift-in-reverse.

'Maybe if you stopped wearing make-up?' she suggested hopefully.

'I tried that last week. All I did was look ill.'

'And what did he do?'

'Took my blood pressure.'

'My God! Is he a pervert?'

This time, even Vivienne laughed. 'No, a doctor.'

Izzy, relieved to see that she was at last beginning to cheer up, was absolutely fascinated. 'So, what's he like to sleep with?' she said avidly. 'I've always thought the medical profession must be spectacular in bed because they know exactly where everything is . . .'

To her amazement, Vivienne actually blushed. 'He is

spectacular,' she admitted, lowering her voice in order to frustrate the middle-aged couple at the next table who had been frantically eavesdropping for the last ten minutes. 'Although we've only done it twice, so far. He wouldn't for ages, because he said he was afraid of getting too deeply involved, so in the end I had to seduce him.'

This was all too romantic for words. Izzy, breathless with anticipation, said, 'And?'

Vivienne's green eyes sparkled. The blush and the Texan drawl both deepened. 'OK, you guessed right. He knows *exactly* where everything is.'

They were interrupted several minutes later by the arrival of a waiter bearing a bottle of rather good Beaujolais.

'With the compliments of the couple at the next table,' he murmured with a discreet nod in the direction of their neighbours.

'Good heavens.' Izzy swivelled in her chair to take a proper look, and saw that they were about to leave. 'How very kind, but I don't know what we've done to deserve it.'

'You're Izzy Van Asch,' said the woman shyly. 'Our son Giles is absolutely crazy about you. All he ever does is sing "Never, Never", and fill his scrapbook with photos of you from the papers.'

'Gosh.' Absurdly flattered by the compliment and not yet accustomed to the attentions of total strangers, Izzy went even pinker than Vivienne had done earlier. 'I'm so pleased he likes me. How old is your son?'

'Seven.'

When she had scribbled a greeting and a rather ornate

autograph on the back of the menu, the middle-aged man took it, hesitated for a second, then slid a business card on to the table next to the wine. 'Actually,' he said with a diffident smile, 'I hope you won't think us impertinent, but the wine is for your friend as much as you. We'd so much like to know whether everything turns out all right,' he explained, meeting Vivienne's astonished gaze, 'between you and this nice doctor of yours.'

Izzy thought it all terribly funny. 'I know,' she said with a mischievous grin. 'Wouldn't we all!'

'Well, you can't disappoint that nice couple,' she admonished when they were alone once more. Pouring the wine, she added, 'And it isn't really that surprising, the good doctor's reluctance to take you seriously. You are still living with another man, after all.'

'Sam isn't a man, he's a machine.' Vivienne flicked back her blonde hair with new determination. 'And you're right, of course. The time has come to act. I tried my best, but I guess I simply wasn't his kind of woman. He always complained that my only hobby was shopping; I think he needs someone with interests of her own, either a brilliant career or an obsession with mountaineering . . .' She paused, took a sip of Beaujolais, then said a trifle shamefacedly, '. . . something that keeps her too busy to chase after him like a lost puppy. All I ever did was chase Sam, but what he really needs is an independent woman. Somebody he admires enough to chase for himself.'

# Chapter 45

After the merry-go-round comings and goings of the past few weeks, Gina found it almost a relief to have the house to herself once more. Arriving home from work to peace and quiet – apart from Jericho's initial volley of welcoming barks – definitely had its advantages.

An even greater luxury was the fact that the bathroom was always empty and the water hot. This evening, having invited Doug round for supper at eight-thirty, she decided to shower first and cook later; that way she wouldn't miss the first showing of Izzy's new video, 'Kiss', on *Top of the Pops* at seven-thirty.

Gina had a terrible singing voice, but since she was alone in the house it didn't matter. '*I want you to kiss me, To know that you've missed me, Like I've missed you and your smile . . .*' she warbled tunelessly, closing her eyes and letting the needles of blissfully hot water bombard her face. Shampoo, cascading down her body, had completely blocked her ears which improved the sound of her singing no end.

It was minutes later before she realised that downstairs the doorbell was ringing and Jericho was going absolutely frantic in his attempt to answer it and discover who was there.

Definitely not Doug, thought Gina, leaping out of the shower and hurriedly half-drying herself before tying her

362

old towelling dressing-gown securely around her waist and running downstairs.

'Who is it?' She had to raise her voice to make herself heard above the noise of Jericho's barking.

'Me.'

Gina froze. For several seconds she was unable to move. Finally, reaching down and grabbing Jericho's collar, she dragged him – whining in outraged protest – into the sitting room and locked him inside.

Returning, opening the front door, she gazed expressionlessly at her visitor. 'What do you want?'

'To see you.' Andrew glanced uneasily over her shoulder, in the direction of the sitting room. 'What on earth was that? Sounds like a pack of werewolves.'

'He'll calm down in a minute. Why do you want to see me?'

Clearly unnerved by his close encounter with Jericho, and shivering as a blast of icy November wind ricocheted around the stone porch, he said, 'Gina, can I come in?'

She led the way into the kitchen, wondering why on earth he had really come here and at the same time marvelling at her own self-control. This was her ex-husband – no, he was still her husband, the divorce hadn't been finalised yet – and she had loved him for over fifteen years. Now, however, it was like coming face to face with a virtual stranger about whom she had heard unpleasant things, and the very idea that they had once been man and wife seemed almost ludicrous.

She guessed that he had come straight from the office; his grey suit was crumpled, his light brown hair uncombed. Realizing that her own hair was still tangled and wet from the shower, Gina marvelled at the fact that her hands remained comfortably in her dressing-gown pockets, and that she felt not the slightest urge to even attempt to make herself look more presentable. If Andrew had been the milkman she would have done so, but he wasn't. He was only her husband . . .

'Well?' she said evenly, sitting down on one of the kitchen chairs.

Andrew took a deep, steadying breath. It wasn't the most promising of welcomes, but he was here now, and he had been rehearsing for this moment all week. He was aware of the fact that he'd behaved badly, but that had all been part of some mystical mid-life crisis, something a lot of men went through, and like all crises it had passed. He now knew that this was where he belonged. And Gina was his wife; she would forgive him . . .

'Darling, I realise how much I must have hurt you. I've behaved like a fool, but it's all behind me now. It's you I love, only you I've ever really loved.' Damn, he hadn't meant it to come out sounding like something from a Noël Coward play. The words, so carefully planned, seemed ridiculous now even to his own ears. Panicking slightly, Andrew took a step towards her. 'No, don't say anything. I'm trying to tell you that all I did was make a terrible mistake and I'm sorry. I don't understand it myself. Marcy and Katerina didn't mean anything to me, not like you! Oh darling, I want us to forget the past year. I want to love you and make you happy again, as happy as you were before . . .'

Gina gazed up at him, dumbfounded. The next moment before she had a chance to realise what was happening,

Andrew had dropped to his knees beside her chair and pulled her into his arms, enveloping her in an embrace so ferocious she could scarcely breathe.

It would have been laughable if she hadn't been too stunned – or too winded – to laugh. Having done his best to destroy not only her own happiness but that of Kat and Marcy as well – and those were only the ones she *knew* about – Andrew seriously seemed to think she still loved him enough to forgive and forget, and welcome him back to married life as if nothing had ever happened.

Meanwhile, he was still here, wrapping himself around her like Sellotape and frantically kissing her exposed shoulder.

Still inwardly marvelling at her ability to remain calm, Gina stole a quick glance at her watch – it was now twenty-five past seven – and murmured, 'You don't know how many times I dreamed of this moment. I prayed so hard that one day you'd come back to me . . . and now at last it's happened. I can hardly believe it.'

'Oh darling.' Andrew, hugging her tighter still, covered her face with triumphant kisses. 'I knew you'd understand. I love you so much.'

Drawing slowly, reluctantly away, trailing her slender fingers down his forearms and giving his hands a gentle squeeze, Gina whispered, 'Do you want to make love to me? Now?'

Andrew quivered with lust. He hadn't had sex for weeks. Wrenching off his tie and scattering shirt buttons across the kitchen floor, he gasped aloud as Gina's fingers moved to his belt buckle and began to unfasten it.

'Oh my God . . . yes, yes . . .'

She had him just where she wanted him. Gina had never felt more powerful in her life. Tilting her head in order to hide her smile, she reached behind her with her free hand and found the short, sharp, serrated knife with which she had planned to slice the tomatoes for the lasagne.

Andrew, opening his eyes with a start as cold metal made unexpected contact with warm flesh, gasped again. When he saw what Gina was holding he moaned aloud in horror.

'That's interesting,' she said in almost conversational tones. 'Your whole body's gone rigid with fear. Well, *nearly* your whole body.' Her smile broadened. 'Of course a certain small part of it remains as disappointing as it ever was. Some things don't change.'

'G-Gina. For G-God's sake . . .'

She could hear his teeth chattering. Idly turning the knife this way and that so that the blade glittered in the light, she glanced at her watch once more. Very nearly seven-thirty.

'It's a good job I'm not a raving lunatic, Andrew,' she told him pleasantly. 'Because a raving lunatic abandoned wife wouldn't hesitate for a second. She'd cut off this troublesome little appendage quicker than you could say . . . well, knife. And many people might applaud her for doing so.' She paused, then shook her head and tossed the knife into the sink out of harm's way. Leaning back in her chair, she said in cheerful tones, 'Luckily for you, I'm not a lunatic. And I wouldn't want to go to prison . . . just imagine the field-day my respectable neighbours would have when they read about it in the papers. So you can put it away now' – with a brief nod in the direction of the petrified acorn, she drew her dressing gown more securely around her and pulled the belt tight – 'and leave. I'm sure you can find your own way out.'

When he had gone, Gina poured herself a large gin and tonic and made her way through to the sitting room to be sullenly greeted by Jericho, who was very put out at having been excluded from all the fun.

'Cheer up, sweetheart,' she consoled him, rubbing his ears and for once allowing him up on to the sofa beside her. 'It was a pretty delicate situation, after all. And you might not have exercised as much self-control as I did.'

With a noisy woof of forgiveness, Jericho attempted to climb on to her lap. Gina waved the remote control at the television in the corner. 'Now shut up and pay attention, Jericho. *Top of the Pops* is about to start, and your favourite singer's on tonight. No, *not* Cilla Black . . .'

Unable to face slicing up those dear little cherry tomatoes, she had abandoned the idea of home-made lasagne and sent Doug out instead to pick up a takeaway from the new Mexican restaurant in Kensington High Street. Not until they had finished eating did she relate what had happened earlier.

'Well, I think it's marvellous,' declared Doug, when she had told him everything. As his face creased into a smile of genuine admiration he wondered how he could ever have thought of her as 'that skinny, nervy, *bossy* broad'. Over the months, Gina had metamorphosed into a calm, elegant woman who knew her own mind and no longer needed to live her life through the kind of men who treated her like dirt and didn't even deserve her. Doug had never been married; he had never even been in love, but he was aware now of skating perilously close to the edge. He knew, too, that he would never treat Gina like dirt.

The chief fly in the ointment, of course, was the fact that he seemed unlikely to ever get the chance to treat her badly or otherwise, since she had shown no signs at all of even recognizing that he *was* a man, in that particular sense of the word.

'I definitely scared him,' she agreed now, with some satisfaction. 'Oh Doug, you should have seen the expression on his face . . . I wish Kat and Izzy could have seen that expression . . . I still can't believe I really did it!'

'You can do anything you want to do.' He was so proud of her. First Ralph, now Andrew. And her elation was contagious; raising his glass of Mexican beer he saluted her, wondering if he dared pluck up the courage to give her a brief, congratulatory kiss. It was what *he* wanted to do more than anything else in the world.

Gina nodded, still smiling to herself. 'You're right. Know what you want and just go for it. That's Izzy's motto and it's worked wonders for her. From now on, I'm going to make sure it works for me.'

It was more than good advice, he thought as she lifted her own glass and clinked it rakishly against his. It was fate. He was here and Andrew wasn't. They were friends, celebrating together, and Gina – in a crimson cashmere sweater and cream linen trousers – had never looked more desirable. He'd even, thankfully, decided against wearing the new burnt-orange shirt which would have clashed so horribly with her red top. It was fate, it *had* to be.

Quickly, seizing the fateful moment and deliberately not giving himself time to back down, he leaned across and aimed for her cheek. Miscalculating slightly, his mouth landed on her chin, just down and to the left of her lower lip. That wasn't right; that was plain silly. Still clutching his beer he shifted position and felt his arm accidentally brush against the cashmere swell of her breast . . . oh God, her actual breast . . . before managing more by luck than judgement to locate her mouth . . .

Gina, astonished for the second time that evening and breathing in the somewhat overpowering scent of the aftershave she had given her boss for his birthday, tried hard not to flinch. Doug was simply pleased for her and proud of the way in which she had dealt with Andrew, she told herself, quelling the urge to dodge out of the way. Besides, it didn't do to flinch at a kiss from a friend, no matter how clumsy and damp it might be.

Having patiently waited for it to end, however, and finding herself still waiting several seconds later, she placed a firm but gentle restraining hand against his shoulder and disentangled herself from his grasp. It was impossible to be annoyed with Doug; he was too inoffensive . . . too *kind* . . . but enough was enough.

'Your drink,' she said kindly, as yet more dampness – icy dampness, this time – invaded her lap. 'Doug, I think you're spilling it.'

So much for fate, thought Doug, passion deflating as he saw how unmoved she was. Was it ever even *remotely* like this for Anthony Hopkins?

'I'm sorry,' he mumbled, his face burning with shame.

The moment of madness had passed; he supposed he should be grateful that at least he had escaped with his private parts intact. 'I'm sorry, it was just—'

'It's nothing at all,' Gina intercepted briskly, realizing that he was about to start apologizing all over again. With a bright smile, she jumped to her feet. 'Really. These trousers are brilliant. Just chuck them in the washing-machine and they come out as good as new, every time.'

# Chapter 46

Izzy, practically dead on her feet following eleven gruelling hours in a south London recording studio, took a while to get the gist of what her housekeeper was actually telling her when she returned home at seven in the evening. Lucille, sensing her confusion, poured her an enormous gin and tonic and splashed a couple of inches of Bushmills into a glass in order to keep Izzy company while she drank it.

'He telephoned an hour ago,' she repeated patiently, 'and I told him you were out, but that you'd be back for sure by eight. Well y'see, he sounded such a charming gentleman and I could tell he was disappointed not to be speakin' to you so I happened to mention that you hadn't any plans for the rest of the evening, what with havin' to catch that early flight of yours to Rome tomorrow mornin', and then it occurred to me that maybe the good fellow might want to pop round and see you before you leave.' Pausing momentarily for breath and an invigorating gulp of the Irish whiskey to which only a heathen would add ice, Lucille licked her lips in appreciation. 'Well, he said that would suit him just fine so I told him to turn up at any time after eight-thirty so as to give you a little while to get yourself ready beforehand. Izzy, I'm tellin' you, that man has a beautiful smilin' voice . . . he all but broke my heart, just talkin' to him . . . oh, and I told him not to eat first because he might as well share something here with you.'

The last of the Bushmills disappeared down her throat with a flourish. Izzy watched it go. Then she watched, helplessly, as Lucille rose to her feet and shrugged herself into a vast, banana-yellow cardigan which reached past her knees.

'This charming gentleman,' Izzy ventured weakly, because it seemed that here at last was her chance to speak. 'Er . . . who is he?'

The weather had turned colder. Lucille, pausing in the act of winding a turquoise-and-yellow striped scarf several times around her plump neck, looked surprised. 'To be sure, the fellow didn't give me his name but he said he was a friend of yours so I thought it best to tell him to come on round here anyway. I knew you wouldn't mind, and he did sound awful *nice*.'

It was hard, trying to imagine what kind of male voice would most appeal to Lucille. Izzy didn't know Terry Wogan, so it couldn't be him. But on the other hand there was always Doug . . .

'So, he's coming round for dinner,' she said, realizing that she was hungry. 'OK, fair enough. What are we having to eat?'

'And who exactly is it that you think I am?' This time Lucille's orange eyebrows arched in astonishment. 'Super-woman, maybe? Haven't I spent the entire afternoon workin' me poor fingers to the bone, cleanin' every window in the house and ploughin' me way through that damn great heap of ironing you wanted done so that you could look halfway decent in Rome . . . ?'

Izzy forestalled her. 'There's nothing to eat, then.'

'Sure an' there's plenty to eat,' scolded Lucille, already halfway through the door. 'There's food in the freezer. All it needs is a bit of attention, you lazy article. Heavens above, anyone'd think you didn't know how to cook a simple meal without makin' a pig's ear of the event! What are you, Izzy Van Asch? Completely helpless?'

'You've made a conquest,' said Izzy, rubbing her wet hair with a towel as she led the way into the sitting room. 'My housekeeper is besotted with your voice. Even more strangely, she's under the impression that you're a gentleman.'

Sam, who had been both startled and amused by the impromptu invitation issued to him over the phone by an unknown Irish woman, replied equably, 'It's not that strange. Some people really quite like me.'

'Hmm.' Izzy, who still hadn't properly forgiven him for bawling her out at The Chelsea Steps the other week, cast him a doubtful look. Stung by Lucille's scathing remarks earlier, she had wrestled irritably with a packet of chicken breasts and concocted a casserole of sorts which Doug would have enjoyed. She had a feeling, however, that Sam might laugh at it.

But Sam, who was in a good mood, made himself comfortable on Izzy's new, dark green velvet sofa and grinned up at her.

'OK, misery. Maybe I was too tough on you, so if I really have to apologise, I will. But only if you promise to cheer up.'

'You *were* tough,' Izzy reminded him, assuming an

injured expression, but at the same time inwardly encouraged by such an admission. As far as she could remember, Sam was never in the wrong. She hadn't known he was capable of even pronouncing the word 'apology'.

He shrugged. 'In that case, I'm sorry.'

'Good.'

'So, are we friends again?'

'Could be,' conceded Izzy, beginning to relent.

'In that case, can I ask a personal question?'

Damn. He was going to make fun of her hair, she just knew it. Slowly, she said, 'Mmm?'

'That smell!' exclaimed Sam, gesturing towards the kitchen. 'That *terrible* smell! What on earth is it?'

This time there was no question about it; Sam was right. The indescribably awful casserole tasted every bit as bad as it had smelled. Izzy simply couldn't imagine how some ingredients could be so burnt, while at the same time the vegetables had managed to stay rock-solid raw. Worst of all, having out of sheer desperation blamed the absent Lucille for the disaster, she realised that Sam hadn't been fooled for a moment.

'No, this is one of yours,' he admonished her. As if to prove it, the piece of carrot he'd been attempting to spear ricocheted off his plate and landed in Izzy's lap.

'Definitely one of yours.'

'I have other talents,' she replied crossly, frustrated by such dismal failure. 'Oh, stop trying to *eat* it, Sam, for God's sake. Why don't we just stick to what we know and send out for a pizza?'

He smiled. 'Why don't we open another bottle of wine

instead? I'm supposed to be drowning my sorrows, after all.'

'What sorrows?' demanded Izzy, when they had by mutual consent abandoned the dreadful meal and settled down in front of the fire in the sitting room. Sam was hardly looking distraught; in fact it was ages since she'd seen him in such good spirits.

He threw her a swift sideways glance. 'The Argentinians you assaulted. They're suing the club.'

'*What*?'

Sam burst out laughing. Izzy, realizing that she'd been had, cursed her own gullibility.

'Not fair,' she grumbled. 'I'm flying to Rome tomorrow. Blame it on pre-jet lag.'

'As an excuse, that's even worse than the casserole.'

Sipping her wine, she repeated slowly, 'What sorrows?'

'Well, Vivienne moved out two days ago.'

He still didn't look upset. Bizarrely, she found herself feeling guilty on Vivienne's behalf. She had been the one who had urged her friend to take action, after all.

'Are you upset?'

Sam's eyes glittered with amusement. 'Oh, distraught. My flat's so tidy it looks like a show home. There's room in the wardrobes to hang up my own clothes, the TV isn't constantly tuned to the soaps and I don't have to sleep in the spare bed any more.'

Even Izzy, herself a veteran of so many such crimes, couldn't help smiling. 'If she asks me, I'll have to tell her you were at least a little bit upset.'

He nodded. 'Of course you will. Poor Vivienne. The decision to leave had to be one she made for herself, for the sake of her pride. I'm just glad she finally realised it couldn't go on any longer.'

'You're cruel,' she protested, feeling sorry now for Vivienne.

'No.' Sam, unrepentant, simply grinned. 'I'm free.'

With two-thirds of a bottle of Sancerre inside her, Izzy began to relax. It was comforting, having Sam back as a friend, and nicer still being able to discuss the failure of their respective love affairs in appallingly indiscreet detail.

'I can just see myself at seventy,' she mused, twirling her hair around her fingers and surveying its colour with a lack of enthusiasm. 'I'll be one of those eccentric spinster ladies surrounded by mountains of newspapers and half-empty tins of sliced pineapple. I shall keep a parrot, train it to sing all my old songs, and bore all my visitors rigid by reminiscing about the time I was famous. Kat will be deeply ashamed of me and try to put me into one of those homes for doolally ex-entertainers . . .'

Sam leaned forward to refill her glass. 'And what about me?'

'Oh, easy. You'll be the sergeant-major type, lining up all the bottles in your drinks cabinet, writing pithy letters to *The Times* and terrifying your poor, down-trodden wife. You'll iron all your own shirts because she never manages to get the creases exactly right, and keep terribly well-trained labradors.'

He raised his eyebrows. 'Don't I get any children?'

Izzy had been poking gentle fun at him. Now, thinking about it, her expression grew serious. 'I don't know. Do you want them?'

He would make a brilliant father, yet for some reason

the idea hadn't even occurred to her. It was hard enough trying to imagine the kind of woman he would choose to marry.

'Is that what you want, Sam? A wife and family?'

He grinned, sensing her disbelief. 'Of course I do. Eventually. Why, d'you think I'm on the shelf? A lost cause? Too . . . *old?*'

Izzy hastily shifted position as he made a grab for her bare toes. 'Don't you dare tickle me! And of course you aren't too old. Men never are. It's unfair.'

Sam looked at first amazed, then intrigued. 'What's this, feeling broody?'

'Not *me*, stupid. I meant Gina. All she's ever wanted was a family and her time's practically up. Whereas you could give yourself another thirty years if you wanted. Then all you'd have to do would be to find yourself some nubile young thing in her twenties and start . . . firing away.'

'I wasn't planning on leaving it quite that long,' he protested mildly.

'Yes, but at least you have the option . . . that's what's so unfair.' She paused, then said, 'What an amazingly grown-up conversation we're having! My God, Sam – we'll be discussing pension plans next.'

Sam didn't care what they discussed; he was just glad to be here. Now that she had forgiven him, Izzy was on great form and her new-found success clearly agreed with her. In her dark blue jersey top and leggings she looked more like a 'nubile young thing in her twenties' herself than a thirty-seven-year-old woman with an almost-adult daughter. She might not be able to cook, he thought wryly, but she certainly possessed more than her share of alternative assets.

Gazing across at her now, remembering those few brief moments during the past months when things had so nearly come right between them, he was struck afresh by the irony of the situation. With Vivienne clinging stubbornly on like a burr, he hadn't allowed himself to think about it too deeply, but if he were honest with himself, the attraction he felt towards Izzy was greater than anything he had experienced for any other woman for longer than he could remember. And yet their relationship had been so ludicrously *chaste* . . .

'What?' she demanded now, long-lashed dark eyes narrowing with suspicion. 'You've gone quiet. I hate it when you go quiet. Oh God, is it food poisoning?'

'More likely the thought of trying to discuss pension plans with someone who thinks an investment is a two-hundred-pound silk shirt.' Rising to his feet, he removed the glass of wine from her hand. 'Come on, show me your new home. I haven't seen it yet and I want the full guided tour.'

# Chapter 47

As Izzy led him from one room to the next, her sense of shame increased. Being subjected to Katerina's despairing cries of, 'Oh, Mum!' every time she arrived home from a shopping trip with yet more unnecessary purchases was bad enough, but Sam's silent incredulity was even more galling.

It wasn't until she opened the door leading into the old nursery, however, that he finally spoke.

'An exercise cycle. A sunbed. A Nautilus machine. Izzy, this is bloody ridiculous.'

'We've used the sunbed,' she replied defensively. 'It's great.'

'Well, hooray for that. And the rest?'

'I need to be fit. MBT are setting up a European tour for the new year . . .'

'And you've never exercised in your life.' He gave her a pained look. 'Izzy, you're throwing your money away. You're *never* going to use this stuff.'

'I will!' The words sounded unconvincing, even to her own ears.

Sam's expression switched to one of impatience. 'Take it from me,' he said flatly, 'you won't. And you have to understand that you can't carry on like this, spending as fast as you earn. What happens when the supply dries up? What'll you do then?'

'It isn't *going* to dry up.' He meant well, so she kept her temper. ' "Never, Never" was a top-ten hit in seventeen different countries. The cheques just keep coming . . .'

'And you haven't received a tax demand yet.'

'Sam, don't be so boring! "Kiss" is doing brilliantly . . . I don't have to worry about tax bills . . .'

'You're still wasting your money on rubbish.' He spoke more gently this time, and Izzy's shoulders sagged in defeat. He wasn't, after all, telling her anything she hadn't already figured out for herself.

'I know,' she said in a low voice. 'It's stupid, of course it's stupid. I'm beginning to think I'm not cut out for this being-rich business. I'm just not very good at it.'

Touched by the admission, Sam turned to face her. 'Of course you aren't used to it,' he reminded her. 'But you don't have to rush out and spend, spend, spend. It isn't compulsory, you know.'

All at once Izzy's dark eyes filled with tears. 'Of course it is,' she wailed. 'I'm miserable! It *helps*.'

He steered her swiftly out of the depressing room. 'If it helps so much, why are you crying?'

Izzy wiped her eyes with her sleeve. She herself hardly knew the answer to that. Somehow, though, Sam's being here tonight had made her realise just how *empty* she'd been feeling for the past few weeks. Before, she'd blamed it on her problems with Katerina, but Kat had come back and the gnawing, inner emptiness had persisted.

'I don't know.' She shook her head like a child, deeply ashamed of such inexplicable weakness. 'I've got every-thing I've ever wanted . . . I have no *right* to be miserable

. . . but something still seems to be missing and I don't even know what it is.'

'Or who he is.' Sam, hazarding an unpalatable guess, said slowly, 'It's not Tash Janssen, is it?'

It was some comfort to see her attempting a watery smile.

'*Definitely* not him. Oh hell, I'm just being stupid. Don't take any notice of me.'

It was about the silliest statement she could have made. Even if he'd been carved out of granite he could scarcely have failed to take notice of her.

In an attempt to cheer her up, he gave her a crooked grin. 'You're certainly a lousy tour guide. Come on, let's go back downstairs.'

'I haven't shown you my bedroom.' Izzy was particularly proud of her glamorous, newly redecorated master bedroom with its emerald-green ceiling, crimson wallpaper and lavishly swathed crimson-and-green four-poster bed. Turning left and leading the way along the corridor, she opened the door. 'And now that you're here, you can carry my cases down for me.'

Now that he was here, Sam could think of far more interesting things to do than haul a set of matching luggage around. It wasn't something he'd planned, but Izzy's unhappiness had touched a chord in him, affecting him more deeply than any amount of outright flirtation could ever have done. There had been so many missed opportunities in the past, yet the mutual attraction underlying their chequered, sometimes volatile relationship had always been there . . .

'I haven't been able to get this one closed,' Izzy

explained, anxious to divert his attention from her embarrassing outburst. The last thing Sam needed now was yet another hopeless, whingeing female crying all over him.

Having crammed far too many clothes and at least a dozen pairs of shoes into the largest pale grey suitcase, she had struggled unsuccessfully for some time to fasten the zip. Now, plonking herself down on top of the case and mentally making herself as heavy as possible, she said, 'Come on, Sam – you're the one with the muscles. If you can just do the zip . . .'

He had to crouch down in order to secure the suitcase. Izzy, perched cross-legged on the lid like a fairy on top of a toadstool, gave him an encouraging smile.

Sam leaned back on his heels and took a deep, measured breath.

'Izzy, I think it's about time.'

'Time for what?' She gazed at him, her expression blank, her lips slightly parted.

'Time you stopped being miserable,' said Sam slowly. Her hands were resting on her knees and when he covered them with his own, she didn't move away. 'And I think it's also about time we stopped kidding ourselves. It's still there, isn't it?'

It was a statement rather than a question and Izzy knew at once what he meant. To Sam's great relief she didn't pretend not to.

'Of course it's still there,' she replied in a low voice, her pulse beginning to race. Admitting it to herself, and realizing that Sam still felt the same way as well, was like allowing a great weight to fall from her shoulders. By tacit unspoken agreement, Vivienne's arrival in London and Izzy's own subsequent ill-fated relationship with Tash had put paid to any thought of continuing what had so nearly been started.

Now, however, the obstacles had been smoothed away; there was no reason on earth why it shouldn't happen. Unless . . .

Sensing her hesitation, he said, 'What?'

Izzy pushed her hair away from her face. 'It's been there all this time,' she said hesitantly. 'So, why now? Why tonight in particular?'

At this, Sam had to smile. Then he glanced briefly at the sumptuous four-poster behind her. 'Well, call me an opportunist, but this is the first time you've ever actually invited me into your bedroom. That is, if you don't count the time at Gina's house when you found a spider in your bed and screamed the place down . . .'

It was a good answer, but Izzy had to be sure. 'Look,' she tried again, her expression serious. 'I don't want this to be happening just because I burst into tears and said I was miserable. I don't want you to feel *sorry* for me, Sam.'

'I have never, in my life, felt sorry for you,' he answered truthfully, and she breathed a sigh of relief.

'OK,' said Izzy, this time with a glimmer of amusement. 'I believe you.'

He raised his eyebrows in mock despair. 'I should bloody well hope so.'

'And now I want you to do something else for me.'

'What's that?'

'Oh, Sam.' Awash with anticipation and longing, wondering if he could hear the frantic thudding of her heart against her ribs, she slid down from the suitcase and into his arms. 'Stop wasting time and seduce me . . .'

Afterwards it seemed to Izzy as if everything had happened in slow motion, each stage of the exquisite mutual seduction becoming so miraculously elongated that time no longer held any recognizable meaning.

And when at last he had explored and caressed her naked body until she'd ached to feel him inside her, her wish was fulfilled. As a lover, Sam was more perfect than she had ever dared imagine. No words were necessary because he knew intuitively – almost before she knew it herself – what to do in order to heighten and prolong each magical moment to such a degree that she couldn't have formulated the simplest of words anyway . . . Closing her eyes and giving herself up to the sheer mindless ecstasy of it all, Izzy moved with him, her fingernails raking his shoulders, her parted lips brushing his neck. The moment was approaching and she knew Sam was holding back, waiting for her. It wasn't fair . . . she wanted it to go on for ever . . . but the sensations were spiralling out of control and nothing – not even Sam – could stop them now . . .

'Oh . . . !' cried Izzy, clutching him and almost sobbing with joy.

The next moment, Sam's mouth brushed her ear. 'I've waited so long for this,' he murmured, his body tensing as he pulled her closer still. 'Izzy . . . I love you . . .'

She awoke at six-thirty to find herself wrapped in Sam's arms. Their legs, too, were comfortably entwined. He wasn't asleep.

'I'm hungry,' she said, smiling up at him and revelling in the blissful security of his embrace.

His fingers trailed suggestively across the lower part of her stomach. 'Hmm, me too.'

'For food,' protested Izzy, gasping as he rolled her gently on to her back and began to explore the swell of her breasts with a lazy tongue. Seconds later, she gave in and whispered weakly, 'But maybe I can wait . . .'

This time the lovemaking was slow and languorous, almost dreamlike. Afterwards, Sam said, 'Do you remember what I told you last night?'

'You mean that stuff about how I shouldn't be throwing my money away?' Izzy pulled a face. 'Sam, don't tell me you're going to try and sell me a time-share.'

He gave her bare bottom a reproving pinch. 'Don't be a smart-ass. I'm being serious.'

'Sorry.'

'And I'm talking about three words in particular.'

It didn't take much effort to guess which three he was referring to. Izzy, who had heard those words uttered at such crucial moments before, tended to take them with a wagonload of salt. Ducking the issue, she gazed innocently at Sam and said, 'Three words in particular? Like "Oh God – cellulite"?'

He pinched her again, hard.

'I told you I loved you.'

'It's OK,' she assured him. 'I'm sure it isn't legally binding.'

'If you carry on like this for much longer,' he warned, 'I shall—'

'Tie me to the bedposts with silk stockings and teach me a lesson I'll never forget?'

Sam closed his eyes in mock despair. 'I think I prefer you miserable . . . Can you be serious for one moment?'

'OK.' She nodded, trying to look penitent. 'But only if you promise to make breakfast afterwards. I'm *still* hungry.'

But Sam wasn't to be put off. 'Those three words,' he said simply, gazing down at her. 'I meant them. And it isn't something I make a habit of saying, in case that's what you thought. If you must know, this is a first.'

Izzy's string of one-liners abruptly died in her throat. Her stomach did an ungainly flip-flop and her mouth went dry. Oh God, she thought, he really *was* serious. And while it was possibly the most wonderful thing he could have said, it was also the most terrifying.

Hopelessly unprepared for such a declaration – and so early in the morning too – she said weakly, 'Oh Sam, don't do this. Please.'

Leaning across, he tilted her chin with his hand so that she was forced to look at him. 'Why not?'

'Because it scares me.' It hurt even to say the words. Sam meant so much to her – far more than he could possibly know – but it only made the situation that much more frightening. Tash Janssen had said, 'I love you,' and it hadn't meant a thing. Ralph had said it dozens of times; so had Katerina's father. And what good had it done, what had it ever *achieved*? As far as Izzy was concerned, the fact that Sam could so easily say the same thing when it clearly wasn't true only proved beyond a shadow of a doubt how little such words meant, and how ridiculously gullible she had been in the past to believe them. God, men were such treacherous shits, she thought with renewed sadness. Why couldn't they just treat women honestly? Why did they deliberately have to confuse them?

'What are you talking about?' Sam demanded now, pushing his fingers through his dark blond hair with an impatient gesture. 'Nothing scares you.'

Being fed a line and being stupid enough to fall for it was what scared Izzy. This time she wasn't going to make a fool of herself.

'It doesn't matter,' she said easily. 'No big deal, Sam. I just don't want you to say those things, that's all.'

'*I* wish I hadn't bloody well said them,' he replied with feeling. This wasn't turning out at all as he had expected.

'Yes, well.' Izzy shrugged. 'It only mucks everything up, doesn't it? I mean, let's be honest; after fancying each other for months we've finally . . . done something about it. And I have to say that on my part at least, it lived up to all expectations. It was great – maybe it can even carry on being great – but there's absolutely no need to spoil it by pretending it means more than it really does.'

Sam hadn't been pretending, but he was damned if he was going to say so now, in the light of Izzy's illuminating comments. He had, it seemed, been a good lay and satisfied Izzy's curiosity to boot. But as for anything more . . . well, that would only *spoil* it.

'I'm being sensible,' she continued, bunching the duvet up around her and hugging her knees. 'Realistic. Don't get funny, Sam.'

'Getting funny wasn't exactly uppermost in my mind,' he replied, his expression sardonic.

It was Sam's turn now to avoid Izzy's gaze. Sliding closer, losing half the duvet in the process, she grinned and landed a kiss on his rigid jaw. 'But you're in danger of doing it anyway,' she said between kisses, 'and there's really no need. We aren't having an argument, after all.'

'Hmm.'

He was weakening; she could sense it. Feeling her stomach beginning to rumble, Izzy stretched a little further, manoeuvring the kisses closer to his mouth. 'So, no getting funny,' she murmured in wheedling tones. 'If, on the other hand, you were thinking of getting breakfast . . .'

Despite himself, Sam smiled. 'You're a hard bitch.'

She was almost on top of him now. 'Oh no,' she said, stifling irrepressible laughter. 'I'm a hungry bitch. Forgive me for mentioning something so personal, Sam, but you're the one who's hard.'

Sam was downstairs in the kitchen when Izzy, emerging from the shower, remembered the phone. Having unplugged it last night in order to avoid any untimely interruptions, it occurred to her now that Joel McGill probably would have been trying to get through for the last hour. As soon as she reconnected the bedside phone, it started to ring.

'No need to panic,' said Izzy, balancing the receiver between chin and collarbone as she wriggled into primrose-yellow silk knickers and kicked last night's dark blue jersey top in the general direction of the washing basket. 'I'm awake, packed and ready to go.'

But it wasn't Joel, phoning to bully her out of bed. It was Gina, sounding distinctly odd.

'I've been trying to get hold of you all night,' she said, her tone jerky. In the background, Izzy could hear the clatter of pans and an unearthly wailing noise.

'All night? Gina, where *are* you? It sounds like Whipsnade Zoo.'

There was a pause, then Gina's voice cracked. 'It's worse than a zoo. Oh, Izzy, I need you here. I'm in St Luke's Hospital and nobody will tell me what's going on . . .'

'But why are you there?' Izzy sat down abruptly on the edge of the rumpled bed. 'Gina, don't cry. Has there been some kind of accident?'

'No . . . no accident.' Gina was crying in earnest now. 'Oh God, Izzy . . . I've been trying to phone you all night! I tried to phone Sam, but he wasn't answering, either. Will you come down and find out what's happening . . . ?'

'Of course I will,' said Izzy automatically, her mind racing. 'But, why are you *there*?'

'My eyes.' Gina's reply was barely audible now. 'It's my eyes. I think I'm going . . . blind . . .'

# Chapter 48

Up until now Izzy Van Asch had been a model protégée, writing songs practically to order, singing when she was asked to sing, good-naturedly smiling and posing for hours on end during gruelling photographic sessions and interviewing like a dream. Her endless enthusiasm and down-to-earth sense of humour had won Joel McGill over completely, and although no one could call her the most punctual person in the world, she had never let either him – or herself – down.

Until now. Oh, until now. And how he wished he hadn't answered the damn phone.

'Look,' he said, struggling to remain calm and wondering if Izzy had any idea how much damage she could be doing to her career. 'Everything's been arranged. For God's sake, Izzy – you can't do this to me! You can't *not* go to Rome.'

But Izzy, it seemed, wasn't open to persuasion. She was utterly determined.

'I'm sorry, I know I'm mucking everything up,' she replied, her tone even. 'But I have no choice. Gina needs me and I can't let her down.'

Joel, close to despair, said, 'The Italians aren't going to be amused.'

'I know that.' The fourteen-day schedule of TV appearances, concerts and interviews was a hectic one. Izzy was only too well aware of the phenomenal amount of work that had gone into organizing it. She sighed, a deep and sorrowful sigh. 'And I wish I didn't have to do this. But you see, Joel, now that it's happened . . . there's no way in the world I *can* go to Rome.'

St Luke's Hospital, with its intimidating red-brick exterior and endless corridors of pea-soup-green walls and beige linoleum flooring, was about the most depressing building Izzy had ever seen. The antiseptic smell of the place was all-pervading, the lifts positively antique; even the expressions on the faces of the medical staff they passed along the way seemed uncompromisingly grim.

But if she had found her initial impression disturbing, it was nothing compared with the shock of actually entering the ward to which Gina had been allocated. Now the stench became all too recognizably human. Izzy held her breath and gazed around in dismay at the pitiful sight of thirty or so women, none of whom were a day under eighty, either slumped in chairs or lying corpselike in regimented beds. Some were silent, while others mumbled unintelligibly to themselves. One, frenziedly clawing the air above her head, emitted a series of ear-splitting squawks as they passed by. The terrible smell intensified. Another ancient female with wild hair hurled a plastic beaker on to the floor and cackled with laughter as cold tea splattered Izzy's highly polished, sage-green boots. Two young nurses, frantically busy at the far end of the ward with yet another recalcitrant patient, hadn't even noticed their arrival. The place was pitifully understaffed and there wasn't a doctor in sight.

'It's OK,' said Sam, although it clearly wasn't. Tightening his grip on Izzy's arm, concerned for a moment that she might actually pass out, he continued in reassuring tones, 'Look, there's Gina. Second from the end, on the left.'

It was a measure of Gina's deep distress, Izzy felt, that she was no longer even able to cry.

'You're here,' she whispered almost in disbelief when she turned her head and saw them. 'Oh God, you're both here . . .'

'Of course we're here,' said Izzy, in a voice that sounded as if it didn't belong to her. Appalled by Gina's listlessness as much as by her dreadful pallor, she reached for her hand and squeezed it. 'And you mustn't worry any more, because we're going to get this sorted out. But Gina, what *happened* to you?'

Gina knew only too well what had happened to her, but for a long moment she couldn't speak. Gazing helplessly up at Sam, she raised her left arm – her good arm – and curled it around his neck as he bent to kiss her.

'I tried to phone you,' she croaked, her throat constricted and dry. 'Oh Sam, I kept trying and trying, but you were never there . . .'

The portable telephone-box-on-wheels was still there, pushed against the wall. Izzy said quickly, 'I managed to get hold of him just after you rang me. I unplugged my phone last night because I wanted to get some sleep . . . oh Gina, I'm so sorry.'

Realizing that Izzy was on the verge of tears, Sam took over. Pulling up an orange plastic chair, he said firmly,

'Now, tell us everything. From the beginning. Don't miss anything out.'

He was so strong, so in-control. Now that Sam was here, thought Gina, it was almost possible to believe that everything would be all right.

'Yesterday eve-evening, I was late home from the office,' she began, licking parched lips and reaching once more for the security of his hand. 'Doug's away in Manchester for a couple of days, so there was a lot of extra work. Anyway, I got back at around eight o'clock, and fell asleep on the sofa. When I woke up a couple of hours later I thought I was dying – my head felt as if it was about to burst, I couldn't see out of my right eye and I knew I was going to be sick. So I tried to stand up – to get to the bathroom – but it was as if the whole of my right side wasn't there. I just fell on to the floor.' She paused, then added wearily, 'And was sick anyway.'

To her horror, Izzy realised that the hand she had been holding – Gina's right hand – was indeed as floppy and lifeless as a doll's. 'Then what?' she asked, her voice hushed. 'What did you do after that?'

'Dragged myself across the floor to the phone.' Gina closed her eyes briefly. 'I must have looked an idiot. And Jericho was no help, leaping around and thinking it was all some brilliant new game. Anyway, I managed to dial 999 and an ambulance brought me here. They've been poking and prodding me . . . I've got to have tests done today . . . but they won't tell me what's *wrong* with me . . .'

'That's because they haven't carried out the tests yet,' Sam admonished her gently. The smile he gave Gina was reassuring but Izzy sensed how concerned he really was.

And Gina, it seemed, wasn't falling for it either.

'Come off it, Sam,' she said wearily. 'You met my mother how many times? You know how she died.'

'How did she die?' demanded Izzy, when a doctor had finally appeared on the scene. Drawing the curtains around Gina's bed with a flourish, he had banished Izzy and Sam to the cheerless waiting room while he carried out yet another examination. Now, all thought of last night's shared intimacies banished from her mind, she sat rigidly opposite him and searched his face for clues.

Sam hesitated, then said brusquely, 'She had a brain tumour. It was all pretty traumatic. Gina looked after her at home, almost until the end.'

Izzy, stunned by his words, felt her heart begin to race. 'A brain tumour? But what does that have to do with Gina? She can't possibly have a tumour. She's too . . . young!'

'Yes, well.' He didn't bother to contradict her on that score; even Izzy had to recognise the absurdity of such a statement. 'We *don't* know what it is, yet. Until we do, the most important thing is to keep Gina's spirits up as much as possible.'

'In this hell-hole?' As she gestured helplessly in the direction of the doorway, a fresh chorus of squawks greeted their ears. 'What was it you had in mind, Sam? A quick song-and-dance routine?'

'Miss Van Asch, I appreciate the fact that conditions here aren't ideal, but when Mrs Lawrence was admitted last night, no beds were available on the neurological ward. I can assure you, however, that your friend is receiving the best possible care and attention.'

The doctor was overworked, the hospital underfunded. It wasn't his fault, thought Izzy, but that still didn't make it all right.

'I'm sorry,' she said, ignoring the fact that Sam was giving her one of his what-the-hell-do-you-think-you're-doing stares, 'but the best *possible* care isn't good enough. What Gina needs is the best care, full stop. And she certainly isn't getting it on this ward.'

'I can assure you,' said the doctor stiffly, 'that as soon as a neuro bed does become free, Mrs Lawrence will be moved. In the mean time, however, we have no alternative but to keep her here.'

He was trying to intimidate her. Izzy stood her ground. 'We *do* have an alternative,' she insisted. 'Look, Gina needs treatment, I know that. But she should be comfortable as well. She needs peace and quiet ... and good food ... and nurses who aren't permanently rushed off their feet ...'

'I asked her whether she had private medical insurance,' intercepted the doctor, glancing at his watch. 'She doesn't.'

'I know, but I want her moved to a private hospital anyway,' said Izzy flatly. 'I'll pay.'

He cast her a look of doubt. 'We don't know yet what the problem is with Mrs Lawrence. It could be extremely expensive.'

Izzy was glad. At long last she had found something worthwhile to spend her money on. 'I don't care about the expense,' she said. 'It doesn't matter how much it costs. I'll pay.'

# Chapter 49

When Gina had first learned that she was being transferred to Cullen Park Hospital in Westminster, she almost wept with gratitude. Not only was it famous for the unrivalled luxuries with which it cosseted its largely star-studded clientele, but also for its exceptional standards of medical care. The Cullen was a good hospital, equipped with all the very latest high-tech machinery. Wealthy patients from all over the world flew in to be treated there. Gina, who had only ever read about it in the newspapers before now, knew that if anyone could cure her, it would be the incomparable medical staff at the Cullen.

*If* anyone could cure her. That, of course, was the stumbling block. Because it didn't matter how brilliant the staff might be, or how space-age the technology; some illnesses were still incurable. And after two of the longest, most terrifying days of her entire life, nobody was giving her any clues either way. Nobody, it seemed, was prepared to tell her anything which might indicate whether she could expect to live or die. Everybody, on the other hand, smiled a great deal and chatted brightly about any subject under the sun. As long as it wasn't related to her illness . . .

It was, naturally enough, the subject which occupied Gina's every waking thought. Her mother had been fifty-two when her own brain tumour had first manifested itself. The sudden onset of migrainous headaches – blinding pain and vomiting – had been treated with extra-strong painkillers and hearty reassurance from the family doctor, who had talked about the menopause and told her she needed to start taking things easier at her age.

Over the course of the next few months, however, she had metamorphosed from an active, tennis-playing, smiling crossword enthusiast into a frightened, introverted woman at the mercy of bewildering mood changes and slowly deteriorating eyesight. By the time the tumour was finally discovered, it was beyond treatment. The headaches worsened, a creeping paralysis of the left side of her body made day-to-day living increasingly difficult, and the unpredictable changes of mood were replaced by a pathetic eagerness to please, and finally mild euphoria.

It had been heartbreaking for Gina, having to witness the gradual destruction of the mother she adored, struggling to care for her during that last terrible summer. She had done everything she could, bringing her home from the hospital and nursing her at Kingsley Grove, but love hadn't been enough. The malignant growth had been unstoppable, eroding her mother's memory until she was no longer able to understand that her husband had died three years earlier. Most heartbreaking of all, as far as Gina was concerned, had been having to listen to her mother crying out in endless bewilderment, 'Thomas, where *are* you? Help me . . . don't leave me here on my own . . . oh Thomas, I'm so afraid . . . please don't leave me . . .'

Deep down, Gina knew that the similarity between her own symptoms and those of her mother was too great to be merely a coincidence. The battery of tests continued in earnest, but during the breaks between them she was doing her best to prepare herself – mentally at least – for the realization that she, too, had developed a brain tumour.

And she, too, was afraid . . . so terribly, *desperately* afraid . . . of being left to die on her own.

'I've just been given a funny look by one of those nerve-wracking nurses outside,' grumbled Doug, bursting into the room and thrusting a bunch of crumpled pink carnations into Gina's lap. 'I didn't realise we were expected to dress for visiting hour, here.'

Gina, glad of the diversion, smiled up at him. 'Maybe she's just never seen anyone wearing an orange shirt with a maroon suit before.'

'Oh. Is it bad?' Doug looked so crestfallen, she had to bury her nose in the carnations in order to hide her laughter.

'Not bad, just . . . individual. Mmm, these flowers smell gorgeous.'

Wanting to kiss her but unable to summon up the courage, he sat down beside her instead. 'How are you feeling?'

Her ability to keep up a cheerful front still amazed her. Being asked the same question maybe twenty times each day, she had become adept at telling people what they wanted to hear, rather than the less palatable truth. In a way, too, she was ensuring that they would continue to ask. Weeping and wailing, Gina now realised, would only frighten people away.

'Much better,' she replied, running the fingers of her good hand through her freshly shampooed blonde hair. 'They did more tests this morning, stuck electrodes all over my head and took a recording of my brainwaves. One of the nurses washed my hair afterwards.'

'Good, good.' Doug, who had been frantic with worry since returning from Manchester, looked visibly relieved. 'I expect you'll be out of here soon. And you'll need to convalesce for a while before we get you back to work . . .'

Work, that was a joke. But she played along, glancing up at the clock on the wall and nodding as if in agreement. 'You may have to get a temp in, though. For a few weeks or so. Is the office chaotic?'

For a moment he looked flummoxed, having had neither the time nor the inclination to worry about the state of the office. Gina was all that mattered. 'I don't know. Probably. What did they say about the brain scan you had yesterday?'

She swallowed, not wanting to think about it. The doctors, gathered in a cubicle adjacent to the scanning room itself, had conversed in whispers; all she had been able to make out were disjointed mentions of ventricles, white-matter and hemispheres, whatever they might be. As far as she was concerned, their unsmiling faces and covert sidelong glances were of far greater significance than any stupid words.

The awful panic rose in her throat once more. She didn't want to die, alone and unloved . . .

'They didn't say anything.' Her gaze slipped past Doug once more, to the wall clock, which still said four-fifteen. 'Not to me, anyway.'

Her guard had slipped. Doug, glimpsing the bleak expression in her eyes, thought that if there was anything he could do to make her well again . . . anything at all . . . he would do it.

I love you, he thought, willing her to be able to read his mind. He didn't dare speak the words aloud. I love you *so much* . . .

'Is there anything you need?' he said instead, his forehead creasing with concern. 'Anything I can get you?'

Brightening slightly, Gina nodded. Pushing his flowers to one side, she said, 'Thanks, Doug. On your way out, if you could ask Nurse Elson to come and give me a hand.'

'What's the matter?' He looked alarmed. 'Are you feeling ill again?'

'No, no.' She was reaching into her bedside locker now, pulling out her make-up bag. 'I just want her to help me change into a clean nightie. Sam's coming to see me at five and I want to look nice for him. Oh, and if you could pass me that bottle of perfume on top of the chest of drawers over there . . .'

The looks Sam received from the nurses upon his arrival forty minutes later were far from funny. Katerina, who had bumped into him in the plush foyer downstairs, noticed the effect he was having and grinned.

'Don't look now,' she said, tucking the glossy copies of *Vogue* and *Harpers* under her arm and almost having to break into a trot in order to keep up, 'but I think you're about to be offered a bed bath.'

'Hmm.' Sam, unimpressed, quickened his pace.

'Hmm?' mimicked Katerina in admonishing tones.

401

Having taken a break from studying and spent a long and enjoyable weekend visiting Simon up at Cambridge, she was in high spirits. 'Whatever's the matter with you, then? Now that you've got rid of Vivienne I thought you'd be making the most of being free again. Or,' she added slyly, 'have you realised you miss her, after all?'

'Did I ever tell you how much I loathe smart-aleck teenagers?' countered Sam equably. As far as he was concerned, there was no earthly reason why Kat shouldn't know about Izzy and himself, but Izzy had come over all coy and born-again-virginal and begged him not to breathe a word of their relationship to anyone.

The lift stopped at the third floor. Katerina pulled a face as they got out. 'I'm only interested.'

'You're nosy. Maybe I like to keep my affairs private.'

'And you think I'd run off to the *News of the World*,' she said with good-humoured resignation. 'Sam, I'm the soul of discretion. I'm my mother's daughter, for heaven's sake. I've had enough practice!'

On entering Gina's room they were almost knocked sideways by the overpowering scent of Miss Dior. Katerina observed with inward amusement the way Gina cried out, 'Sam!' before realizing he wasn't alone. 'Oh and you, Kat, how nice,' she amended somewhat less effusively. 'Pull up a couple of chairs and make yourselves comfortable. I can ring for coffee if you'd like some.'

'Relax, you don't have to play party hostess,' Sam told her gently, as he gave her a brief kiss. 'We've come to see how *you* are.'

Katerina, settling back in a pink-and-green upholstered chair which exactly matched the flowery wallpaper, was further entertained by the sight of Gina blushing beneath her careful make-up. Surely there hadn't been something clandestine going on between these two? Not Sam and *Gina . . . ?*

Two days later, the consultant paid her the visit she'd been waiting for. The tests had all been carried out and now he was here to give her his verdict. With her heart pounding, Gina submitted to yet another neurological examination and braced herself for the news.

But the tortuous game, it appeared, wasn't over yet.

'You're a puzzle,' he told her finally, when he'd finished testing what felt like every reflex in her body. 'The good news, of course, is the fact that the paralysis on the right side is lessening, the headaches have stopped and your eyesight's almost back to normal.'

He was wearing an exceedingly well-cut grey suit and a pale pink Armani shirt. I'm a private patient, thought Gina; of course he's going to smile and give me the good news first.

'And the bad news?' she asked, wishing she had Sam here with her now to give her the support she so badly needed.

'I'll be perfectly frank with you, Mrs Lawrence.' The consultant sat on the edge of the bed in order to be frank. The smile was replaced by a professionally serious expression. 'The tests we've been running have shown up an abnormality, but the precise nature of that abnormality isn't clear.'

If she had been an NHS patient, Gina wondered, would he have simply come out with it and said, 'You have a brain tumour and you're going to die'? It was, after all, more or less what they had told her mother all those years ago.

'So, what happens next?' she persisted, having braced herself for the very worst.

'Well, I think that poor old brain of yours needs a while to recuperate.' He flashed dazzlingly white teeth at her and Gina winced. Such jocular remarks were all she needed. 'There's clearly some swelling in the left hemisphere' – reaching across, he lightly tapped the left side of her head for emphasis – 'and until that recedes, we can't really come to any firm conclusions. So what I suggest is that we send you home for a week or two, then get you back here for another scan. By that time, hopefully, you'll be as right as rain!'

'And what if I'm not as right as rain?' she countered with rising anger. This so-called bloody miracle-worker in his flashy designer suit and hand-made shoes was fobbing her off with ridiculous platitudes. She couldn't just sit around and *wait*, for God's sake. She needed to know. *Now*.

'Why don't we cross that hurdle when we come to it?' This time he tried to give her hand a consoling pat, but Gina snatched it away.

'Just tell me,' she said evenly, 'what *you* think is wrong with me.'

'Ah, but the tests are inconclusive. It really isn't possible to . . .'

He was shaking his head. Prevaricating. Fixing him

with a steady gaze, Gina said, 'But you can't assure me that I *don't* have a brain tumour, can you?'

# Chapter 50

Katerina, despatched by Lucille to answer the front door, was delighted to see Vivienne standing on the doorstep.

'I was beginning to think we'd never see you again,' she cried, giving her a hug and almost having her eye taken out in the process by an enormous gold earring curved like a scimitar to match Vivienne's flawless cheekbones. 'And I thought that if we *did* ever see you, we wouldn't recognise you. Now that you're a country doctor's lady, aren't you supposed to trudge around in tweed skirts and wellies?'

'Tried it once, didn't like it,' deadpanned Vivienne, glancing down at her cyclamen-pink silk jacket and short black skirt. Then she broke into a grin. 'OK, that's a lie. Thought about it once and couldn't face it. Hell, at least this way the patients have something to gossip about. I figure it brightens their day.'

'We've got a patient whose day could do with a bit of brightening.' Katerina drew her inside, kicking the door shut behind them. 'Come on, I'll break open the gin, if Lucille hasn't got there first. And I warn you, you're going to need it.'

Vivienne was both appalled by the change in Gina, and enchanted by bossy, bustling Lucille who appeared to run the entire household and whose welcome entailed swiping the bottle of Gordon's from Katerina's grasp and all but emptying its contents into two enormous glasses.

'That girl pours terrible small measures,' she declared expansively, above the clatter of ice cubes. 'Not that I'm much of a gin-person myself, ye understand, but I'm willing to join you for decency's sake. And none of this poison for *you*,' she added, swinging round to address Gina. 'It does desperate things, y'know, to the human brain.'

'Hear, hear,' said Vivienne cheerfully, taking her drink and sinking down on to the dark green sofa next to Gina. 'I was so sorry to hear you were sick. Still, it must be great to be out of hospital.'

Gina managed a wan smile. She looked, Vivienne decided, like a stiffly jointed wooden doll.

'Everyone's been very kind. Izzy insisted I stay here until I'm well enough to . . . cope on my own.' Her tone of voice indicated that this was an unlikely prospect. Behind her, Katerina raised her eyebrows in an I-told-you-so manner.

'So, what exactly *was* wrong?' persisted Vivienne, who had only heard the vaguest details from Izzy when she'd phoned and whose curiosity was now thoroughly aroused. It wasn't like Katerina to be so unsympathetic where illness was concerned.

'I have to go back for more tests before they decide whether or not it's worth trying to operate.' Gina's eyes glittered with unshed tears, but she soldiered on. 'Although if the tumour's malignant, they probably won't bother . . .'

Vivienne's eyes widened. 'You have a *tumour?*'

'Not definitely,' said Katerina, with a trace of

impatience. 'Gina, it isn't *definite*.'

'Of course not.' Gina shrugged apologetically and gave Vivienne a brave smile. 'Well, they're ninety per cent sure, but that isn't definite. Did Izzy tell you my mother died of a brain tumour?'

This was awful, unbelievable. Suddenly ashamed of herself for having asked, Vivienne shifted in her seat and said, 'Where is she? Izzy, I mean. I told her I'd be here at seven-thirty . . .'

'Ah,' said Lucille, who evidently wouldn't recognise an emotionally charged atmosphere if it were to leap up and poke her in the eye, 'but she's a crafty article, that one. She told me you were never anywhere you were supposed to be without losing an hour in the process, so she was goin' to take a nice hot bath while she was waitin' for you to turn up late.' She gave Vivienne a great beaming smile. 'It's thinkin' like that, I said to her, that brings down governments and loses wars. And I'm right, aren't I, because she's still wallowing upstairs in the tub and here *you* are, not so late after all, havin' fun and drinkin' all the gin.'

By nine o'clock Izzy and Vivienne had the sitting room to themselves, Gina having retired to bed in order to rest and Katerina having disappeared to do some revision. Lucille had gone home to her much-beleaguered husband.

'Well, I love your housekeeper, but isn't Gina acting kinda weird?' said Vivienne with characteristic bluntness.

Izzy sighed. 'I suppose so. But then I suppose she's entitled to act weird, under the circumstances. It just doesn't make things easier.'

'This place is like *Little Women*,' Vivienne mused, curling her long legs beneath her. 'Ever read that book? You've got Gina doing her impression of saintly Beth, Kat can be Amy . . . hell, your problem is that none of you has a man!'

'Not so long ago we had problems,' Izzy countered drily. 'And they were *all* caused by men. It's a no-win situation.'

Vivienne looked smug. 'I've won.'

'And we aren't totally starved of male company,' said Izzy, glancing at her watch. 'Doug's round here all the time. He won't admit it, but I'm sure he's carrying a secret torch for Gina.'

'Well, hooray for Doug.'

'And there's Sam, too.' Izzy paused, awaiting her reaction. 'He calls round every night to see Gina, usually at around nine-thirty on his way to The Steps. I expect he'll be here soon.'

But all Vivienne did was laugh. 'What are you doing, testing me? To see if I'm well and truly cured? Honey, I can read you like a book!'

No, you can't, thought Izzy with some relief. Vivienne and Sam might not be a couple any more, but she still felt guilty about what had happened between Sam and herself.

'And if I am testing you?' she said cautiously.

'Everything's different now. Like I said, I've won. Hit the good old jackpot. Oh Izzy, it's like a dream come true! Terry's the one for me and now that I've finally managed to convince him I'm not just messing him around, it's got better and better. I'm living with a man who really *wants* me . . .'

409

'You haven't explained how that came about either,' said Izzy, curious to know how she'd managed it. 'Sam told me you'd moved into an hotel. The next thing I know, you're out of it and into the love-nest.'

'I moved into *the* hotel,' Vivienne corrected her triumphantly. 'The Ritz, to be precise. When poor old Terry heard what the nightly rates are for that place he all but fainted on the spot. At first he tried to persuade me to move into someplace cheaper, but I told him it was either his place or I stayed put. And since he couldn't cope with the idea of being responsible for such *vast* sums of money disappearing by the hour, he had to give in.' She grinned and said, 'The bill for four days at the Ritz came to just over a grand, what with laundry and room service. But in the end, you see, it was a brilliant investment.'

This was the kind of logic with which Izzy happily concurred. It was also the kind that drove Sam to despair. For a moment she almost wished he could be there to hear it; the expression on his face would be miraculous.

'And you're changing the subject, sweetie,' Vivienne continued, fixing her with a shrewd look. '*You* don't have a man in your life and it isn't right. Aren't you meeting hordes of handsome hunks these days, now that you're mixing in the most glittering showbiz circles?'

'Mainly balding, overweight hunks,' said Izzy, wondering if she should tell her now. It was about as good an opportunity as she was likely to get, after all. But the words wouldn't come. She felt her nerve – quite uncharacteristically – slipping away. 'Not that they're all bald,' she amended lightly. 'Some of them have hair. Well, toupees.'

True to her word, Vivienne didn't even flinch when the doorbell rang. Izzy, answering the door, ducked away before Sam could kiss her and pressed herself like a fugitive against the wall.

'It's OK.' He looked amused. 'I don't have a gun.'

'Sshh. Vivienne's here.'

'So?' Totally unfazed, he gave Izzy a kiss anyway. She only managed to squirm frantically out of reach a fraction of a second before Vivienne appeared in the sitting-room doorway.

'Hi, Sam. Come to visit the invalid? Since our hopeless hostess hasn't offered, I was just about to make some coffee. Would you like some?'

It was all so civilised, thought Izzy wonderingly, ten minutes later. She could hardly have believed that there had ever been anything between Vivienne and Sam. Now, with no apparent awkwardness at all, they were chatting away like old friends, the conversation moving effortlessly from the latest gossip at The Chelsea Steps to Sam's about-to-be-divorced neighbours, and then on again to Vivienne's new-found happiness.

'It's so great,' she enthused, green eyes alight with adoration. 'I keep having to pinch myself to make sure it isn't all a dream. And do you know, Terry doesn't even *care* if I leave my shoes in the kitchen, or burn dinner?'

Sam looked startled. 'You actually cook *meals* for him?'

'Are you kidding?' Vivienne burst out laughing. 'We

have a sweet woman in from the village. She does all the cooking; I heat it up.'

'He'll come to his senses. When the novelty wears off.'

'No, he won't,' she replied simply, not even taking offence. 'Because he accepts me, just the way I am. And it isn't a novelty, it's love.'

Gina was sitting up in bed, waiting for him. Holding out her arms for her customary hug, she said, 'You've been downstairs for ages. I was beginning to think you'd forgotten me.'

Sam looked and smelled wonderful. He was wearing a new, dark grey suit, a pink-and-grey striped shirt and her favourite aftershave. She wondered if he had any idea how much his visits meant to her, how very much he had come to mean to her during these last, nightmarish few days. For while Izzy had been brilliant, footing the ludicrously expensive medical bills and insisting she stay in order to be properly looked after, Gina sensed that only Sam truly understood what she was going through. And he really *cared* . . .

'Of course I hadn't forgotten you,' he said, idly turning over the paperback she'd been reading. 'But Vivienne's still down there. I had to sit through the whole happy-ever-after story before I could escape. Oh, for heaven's sake, Gina!' His expression changed as he read the title of the book. 'What are you doing with this?'

'I'm being sensible,' she replied, an aching lump coming to her throat as she realised the extent of his concern. 'We have to face facts, Sam. It's no good pretending everything's fine.'

'*Arranging Your Own Funeral?*' he demanded, staring aghast at the discreet, dark blue lettering of the title and then at Gina's pinched white face. Hurling the book across the room, he said, 'This is ridiculous . . . you shouldn't even be *thinking* about it!'

Gina, who had never seen him so angry before, promptly burst into tears. 'It needs to be done. There are so many things I have to think about! Making a will . . . organizing the service . . . please, Sam, don't look at me like that. I don't want you to be c-cross with me . . .'

Sam, who was seldom at a loss for words, took her into his arms and let her sob. Eventually he said, 'I'm not cross with you. It just doesn't seem right, that's all. I don't think you should be dwelling on what might not even happen.'

His embrace was so warm, so comforting, Gina didn't want it to stop. But she was scared, and exhausted with the effort of putting on a brave face. The fear of what lay ahead was too much for anyone to bear; she couldn't go through it alone.

Gradually, however, she began to feel better. Having heard muted scrabbling sounds at the door moments earlier, she tilted her tear-stained face and saw Jericho crouched at the foot of the bed, wrestling with the paperback.

'You see?' murmured Sam, stroking her hair. 'Even the damn dog agrees with me.'

'I don't know what I'd do without you.' Gina gave him a weak smile.

'You don't have to know. I'm here, aren't I?'

'As if you don't have enough to worry about. Was it

413

awful, seeing Vivienne again and having to listen to her going on about how happy she is with her new boyfriend?'

'Are you kidding?' Relieved to see that Gina was looking more cheerful, he carefully wiped her eyes with the back of his hand and grinned at her. 'It's the best news I've had all year.'

# Chapter 51

'Well, you've certainly got a bit of colour in your cheeks today,' declared Lucille approvingly at eleven-thirty the following morning, as she wielded the vacuum cleaner with some vigour around the bedroom. Prodding Jericho with the nozzle until he let out an indignant yelp, she added cheerfully, 'Looked like a wee ghost, so you did yesterday . . . will you shift yer carcass, you dumb crazy animal . . . I'll tell you now, I said an extra prayer or two before I went to bed last night.'

'Maybe it worked,' suggested Gina, trying not to flinch as Jericho's tail came perilously close to being sucked into the Hoover.

Lucille, however, wasn't about to let the Almighty take all the credit for this particular small miracle. Switching off the machine – to the profound relief of both Gina and Jericho – she tilted her head to one side and said slyly, 'Somethin' surely worked, but since I'm not entirely convinced the good Lord was able to hear my prayers above all the noise of me old man's drunken snores, I'm thinkin' that maybe it has more to do with a certain visitor . . .'

Doug Steadman, Lucille had decided, was a lovely fellow. Deeply appreciative of her ham-and-mustard sandwiches, which comprised more ham than bread, and always willing to regale her with gossip about her favourite old Irish singers, she enjoyed his daily visits immensely. And he was kind, too; this morning he had brought her a dog-eared programme of a Val Doonican concert from the Seventies, signed by the great man himself.

If Doug wasn't so clearly besotted with Gina, Lucille could almost have had a go at him herself.

At the mention of the word 'visitor', however, Gina's thoughts had flown immediately to Sam. Since stating so emphatically last night that Vivienne meant nothing to him at all, her tentative hopes had soared and she had slept well for the first time in a week.

Now, since Izzy's perceptive housekeeper had virtually raised the subject anyway, she decided to take the plunge and say aloud the question that had been buzzing around in her mind ever since she'd woken up.

'OK,' she said, bracing herself. 'Lucille, if *you* really liked a man and knew he liked you in return, but because you were old friends nothing was actually happening . . . well, would you carry on as you were and just hope it might happen naturally? Or do you think it would be better to come out and say something?'

She could feel perspiration prickling the back of her neck. God, it was hard enough even saying this to Lucille . . .

But the housekeeper's broad smile told her all she needed to know.

'Bless you,' declared Lucille triumphantly, feeling almost as if she had engineered the entire fairy-tale herself. 'And there I was, wondering how long it was going to take you to come to your senses! Of course you must tell him. He'll be relieved and delighted to know how you feel, and that's a promise!'

'Are you sure?' said Gina, sagging with relief. 'Really? I wouldn't want him to think I was being . . . well, pushy.'

'Sure, I'm sure,' Lucille replied, her sweeping gesture towards the window encompassing the entire male population of north London. 'Don't three-quarters of them need a bit of a push and a shove to get them started at the best of times? You mark my words, a fine man is a rare enough creature to track down these days. If you're fortunate enough to find one, you have to thank your lucky stars and then hang on to him by your very fingernails.'

'Bugger, bugger and damn!' shrieked Izzy, slamming down the phone just as Gina wandered into the kitchen.

Katerina, who was standing at the stove stirring a great panful of molten chocolate fudge, raised her eyebrows.

'My mother, the celebrated song-writer. Can't you just picture Michael Parkinson introducing her on next week's show? And now ladies and gentlemen, here to give us a rendition of her latest single, "Bugger, bugger and damn", will you please welcome—'

'That was Doug,' snapped Izzy, ignoring her. 'The concert organisers in Rome have just informed him that if I don't get over there tomorrow night they're going to sue the pants off me for breach of contract.'

'Oh, I get it now.' Katerina grinned. 'Bugger, bugger and damn is a firm of solicitors.'

'I could always have you adopted, you know.'

Gina, sitting down at the kitchen table, interceded. 'Is it really so terrible?' she asked cautiously, in case Izzy rounded on her as well. 'I thought you were looking forward to going to Rome.'

Izzy was exhausted. Weeks of working punishing hours in the recording studios had taken more out of her than she'd realised. The dozens of interviews and personal appearances had been mentally draining too, since she always had to guard against saying the wrong thing and permanent perfection didn't come easily, particularly when the subject of Tash Janssen was so often on every interviewer's lips. She was tired of smiling and endlessly being diplomatic. She was tired of working, sometimes until midnight, with her brilliant but unbelievably picky producer. The only thing that hadn't been tiresome had been the prospect of a week in Rome, which was somewhere she'd always longed to visit, but that had had to be cancelled when Gina was taken ill.

And this is all the bloody thanks I get, she thought mutinously. So much for making the great sacrifice and promising to look after the invalid. Here was Gina, sitting opposite her, wearing violet eyeshadow and urging her to bloody well go anyway.

'Don't be cross,' said Gina, bewildered by her obvious irritation. 'I'm trying to help, that's all.'

'You're ill,' replied Izzy bluntly. 'I thought *I* was supposed to be the one trying to help *you*.'

Finally understanding, Gina's face cleared. 'And you have,' she said with genuine gratitude. 'More than you'll ever know. But you've made enough sacrifices already, and you can't possibly let those Italians sue you. I'll be *fine*,' she added persuasively, thinking of Sam but smiling at Izzy. 'Really. It's only going to be for a few days, after all.'

'Ah, but a lot can happen in a few days,' put in Katerina, sighing with pleasure as she tasted the first spoonful of still-warm chocolate fudge.

Izzy, somewhat mollified, said, 'Such as?'

'Mum, I know what you're like with Italians. You could go over there to do the concert and come back married.' Rolling her eyes for emphasis, she added solemnly, 'To a devastatingly attractive Roman solicitor called Buggeri . . .'

The last time she had packed her suitcase for Rome, Sam had ended up making love to her on top of it.

Izzy felt it suitably ironic, therefore, that Gina should have chosen this particular evening and this moment in which to confide her earth-shattering decision.

The difference, of course, was that this time she was having no fun at all.

'. . . so you see, I know it sounds crazy, but I really do love him,' Gina concluded, while Izzy, like an automaton, continued to pack. 'Oh God, it's such a relief to be able to tell you this! But do *you* think I'm crazy?'

Unable to speak for a moment, Izzy shook her head. How could falling in love with Sam Sheridan be crazy, when she'd done the very same thing herself? And how desperately she wished now that she hadn't insisted upon keeping their relationship a secret.

'You really should be using tissue paper,' said Gina, eyeing the haphazard jumble of silks and cottons spilling over the rim of the case. 'It stops things getting creased.'

'Mmm.'

'Everything that's happened, you see, has made me rethink my life. Particularly now that I might not have much of it left.'

'Don't say that,' said Izzy numbly, but this time Gina wasn't being self-pitying.

'I'm just trying to explain,' she went on, willing Izzy to understand. 'Whenever you've wanted something, you've gone out and got it. I've always admired you for that. And here you are, happy and successful . . . you have everything you could possibly want! So I've decided to be like you. I love Sam and he's what *I* want. I would have been too scared to tell him before, but now I know that life's too short to be scared.' She shrugged, with more bravado than she felt. 'The worst he can do, after all, is turn me down.'

Except that he can't, thought Izzy, her expression bleak and her stomach a clenched knot. Because you've got a brain tumour and Sam's practically your dying wish. So he doesn't really have a lot of choice.

# Chapter 52

Knowing that she was entirely responsible for her own misery wasn't making Izzy feel any better. Last night she had dreamt that during a fearful confrontation she'd told Gina she couldn't have Sam because he loved *her*. Gina, utterly distraught, had drowned herself in Izzy's weed-choked fish pond and Sam, in turn rounding on Izzy, had icily informed her that Gina was the only woman he'd ever really loved anyway.

It was all very disturbing and she had woken up in floods of tears, only to realise that what actually *had* happened was just as hopeless. Gina had begged for reassurance that she was doing the right thing and all she'd been able to do in return was agree. How, after all, could she deny her friend that last chance of happiness when she had already endured a year of such awful misery and despair?

It would have been so much easier, as well, not to have had to face Sam and pretend that nothing had happened, but even that small luxury had been denied her. By sheer chance, an urgent business meeting had prevented him visiting Gina the previous night and when he'd phoned to explain, she had told him of Izzy's imminent departure. Izzy, consequently, hadn't had any choice in the matter when Gina had happily informed her that Sam would pick her up at nine-thirty

421

the following morning and drive her to the airport himself.

It was an unfairly beautiful November morning too, brightly sunny and glittering with frost like something out of a Disney cartoon. Still haunted by her earlier dream, Izzy gazed silently out of the car's side-window at the dazzling blue-whiteness of Hyde Park and didn't even notice they were slowing down until Sam had brought the car to a full stop.

'What?' she said, startled, as he switched off the ignition.

'My sentiments exactly,' replied Sam, his tone dry. Leaning across her, undoing her seat belt and opening the passenger door, he added, 'Come on, we're going for a walk.'

Anticipating somewhat warmer weather in Rome, Izzy was wearing a pink-and-green striped blazer over a short pink dress. She shivered as an icy blast of air invaded the car, but all Sam did was hand her his own scuffed leather jacket and motion her to get out.

'Why don't you tell me what's wrong?' he said eventually, when she had trudged along beside him in silence for several minutes.

It was the last thing Izzy felt able to do. Instead, she gave him a brittle smile. 'I'm cold.'

'You're playing some kind of game,' he countered, not returning her smile. 'And I want to know what it is. Even more, I'd like to know why you're doing it.'

And I want to tell you, she thought miserably, more than anything else in the world. But I can't, because that would mean betraying Gina's confidence. It wouldn't be fair. Worse than that, it would be downright cruel . . .

'Look,' she said, shoving her hands deep into the pockets of the leather jacket and quickening her pace in order not to have to meet his unnervingly direct gaze, 'I'm really not playing games. I've thought a lot about . . . what happened the other night, and I know now that it was a mistake.'

'Oh, right.' Even though she couldn't see his expression, the sarcasm in Sam's voice was unmistakable. 'Of course it was. The biggest mistake ever. I thought of writing to Clare Rayner myself—'

'Don't start,' she said unhappily. 'I'm trying to explain, that's all, and you aren't making it any easier.'

A hand on her arm stopped her in her tracks. Frosted leaves crunched beneath Izzy's feet as Sam swung her round to face him.

'But I don't want to hear this bullshit. So, why should I make it easier?'

It was unfair. Everything was unfair. Even the fact that Izzy knew her nose and cheeks were red with cold yet Sam's face remained as smooth and brown as a ski instructor's was unfair. Why on earth, she thought with mounting resentment, couldn't he at least go blotchy like everyone else?

'Look,' she said, trying again. 'When it comes to mistakes, I'm an expert. I can spot them a mile off. And I'm fed up with *making* them . . . so for the first time in practically my entire life I'm trying to do the sensible thing instead.'

She stood her ground as Sam stared at her in disbelief.

'Maybe,' he said finally, 'you should define *sensible*.'

This wasn't easy. She hadn't had time to practise. And it had to sound believable . . .

'I don't want to make any more mistakes,' said Izzy, pushing her hair away from her face with a defiant gesture. 'Sam, we're an unmatched pair. Look at how Vivienne drove you up the wall with her untidiness and the way she couldn't cook a meal to save her life . . . I'm *just* like her, only worse! I know that if we even tried to make a go of it we'd end up hating each other. It simply wouldn't work.'

'I think it would.'

'Only because you're being pig-headed,' she retaliated. 'And because you've probably never *been* turned down before.'

'I've certainly never heard such feeble excuses before.' He was almost smiling now. 'Got any more, or was that the entire repertoire?'

'I'm being serious!' Izzy shouted, infuriated by his refusal to believe her. 'We have no future, so what *would* be the point of even pretending we have?'

He raised his eyebrows. 'So that really is all you're worried about? The fact that you can't cook?'

'No.' Slowly, she shook her head. 'We have no future because I'm thirty-seven years old. I have a grown-up daughter and a career that's finally taken off. You want a nice little wife, and children of your own.' She paused, giving the words time to sink in. 'And that's what you should be looking for, Sam. A wife.'

He wasn't smiling now. 'Perhaps that's what I am doing.'

'No, you aren't.' Izzy, who'd had no idea he was this serious, briefly closed her eyes. Gina was all but forgotten by this time. She was no longer making up excuses; this was the unvarnished, unpalatable truth and not even Sam could argue with it. 'I've had my family and it's too late to start again now. I can never give you what you want, Sam. That's all there is to it. I'm just too *old* . . .'

'We don't have to have children,' he said, but the words didn't sound entirely convincing. Izzy, her eyes already watering with the cold, swallowed hard in an effort to dispel the lump in her throat. It was all so terribly sad; here she was, receiving what virtually amounted to a proposal of marriage from the nicest man she had ever known, and there was absolutely no way in the world she could allow him to talk her into saying yes.

'But you'd always want them,' she said miserably. 'And sooner or later you'd resent me for not being able to give you what you wanted. It's no good, Sam; I can't make myself younger and I couldn't bear to be a stop-gap, a temporary diversion until the right woman comes along. You have your life to lead and I have mine, and the next thing I have to do is catch my flight to Rome, before frostbite well and truly sets in. So, if we could just get back to the car . . .'

The scheduled Alitalia flight from Heathrow wasn't as busy in November as it would have been in season. Izzy, thankful to find she had a double seat to herself and praying she wouldn't be recognised, shielded her eyes with sunglasses and wept quietly all the way to Rome. She'd done the right thing . . . the *sensible* thing . . . and it hurt like hell. All she could do now was remind herself that any kind of future with Sam would, in the long run, only result in more pain than even this.

\* \* \*

Despite making a terrific effort to pull herself together, Rome's magnificence and beauty were wasted on her today. Even the maniacal manœuvres executed by her excitable taxi driver as he zig-zagged and hooted his way across the city failed to dispel her gloom. Izzy, whose eyes were still swollen behind her dark glasses, gazed dismally out at the sunny streets, until the taxi eventually pulled up outside the Hotel Aldrovandi Palace where she would be staying for the next few days.

But her schedule was tight, there was work to be done and she had little time to appreciate the style and splendour of the five-star hotel. A note at reception from the concert organisers informed her that at four o'clock someone would be arriving to take her to the hall for sound checks and rehearsals. As soon as she reached her room, which overlooked the Borghese Gardens in all their glory, she stripped off her clothes and stepped into the shower.

When she emerged from the bathroom fifteen minutes later, Tash was waiting for her.

'I don't believe this,' said Izzy flatly. 'How the hell did you get into my room?'

The seductive smile was so familiar, her departure from his life might never have existed.

'Sweetheart, in Italy I'm a national hero,' he drawled. These pretty little chambermaids will do *anything* for me.'

'I knew an Italian man once,' she retaliated in withering tones, making quite sure the towel wrapped around her body was firmly secured. 'He had no taste either.'

He looked reproachful. 'Izzy. No bitterness, please!

I've come here to make the peace. I've *missed* you.'

She shivered. His words were uncannily similar to Sam's, when he had turned up on her doorstep just a week earlier. And now here was Tash, as dark and dangerous as a panther in his black sweatshirt and jeans, giving her that look of his and so confident of his own irresistibility that it didn't even seem to have occurred to him that she might say no.

'No,' said Izzy, sparing a glance at her watch. 'And if you'll excuse me, I'm in a hurry.'

But all he did was make himself comfortable in one of the plush velvet chairs. 'Of course you are, angel. I'm here to take you to the hall myself. We have a run-through rehearsal at four-fifteen, after all.'

There was something going on. Warily, Izzy said, 'We?'

'Did they forget to tell you?' He raised his dark eyebrows in mock amazement. 'My manager organised it a couple of days ago. I'm the surprise guest. Halfway through the set, you launch into "Never, Never" and after the first verse I appear on stage to tumultuous applause and screams of ecstatic delight from several thousand nubile Italian virgins. We sing, we hug, we kiss . . . we hit the front page of the papers . . . sweetheart, that's show business!'

'No,' repeated Izzy, realizing that he had orchestrated the entire thing. 'I won't do it. I don't want you there.'

'Ah, but the organisers do. And if you refuse now, you'll have two massive lawsuits to contend with.' Tash shrugged, then smiled again. 'Copies of the amended contract were sent to your agent forty-eight hours ago. With his customary inefficiency, no doubt, he forgot to

427

read them. You should get yourself a smart manager, Izzy, if you want to get ahead in this world. If you wanted to, you could even share mine.'

He was loathsome, but he was also right. Izzy, recognising a fait accompli when she heard one, knew that she had no choice but to go along with the revolting, publicity-courting charade. Out of sheer desperation, and to make him realise just how much she despised him, she said quietly, 'How's Mirabelle?'

Tash, however, didn't even flinch.

'Funny you should say that,' he replied in cheerful tones. 'When I saw her yesterday I mentioned the fact that I was flying over here to do a gig with you.' He paused, then added triumphantly, 'She said, "Izzy who?" '

# Chapter 53

Sam, unable to quite believe that a day which had begun so dreadfully could get this much worse, was unable to speak. At almost exactly this time last week the room in which he was now trapped had contained an expensive assortment of exercise machines and he had been telling Izzy in no uncertain terms to stop wasting money and get her life into some kind of order.

Today, no exercise equipment remained. Banished to a small box-room on the top floor of the house, it had been replaced by conventional bedroom furniture and an incumbent invalid. Izzy, having taken his advice and refused point-blank even to consider the possibility that they might have a future together, had buggered off to Rome instead in order to further her career.

He, meanwhile, now found himself having to face rather more than just the music.

His sensation of claustrophobia intensified as Gina clutched his hand with thin fingers, forcing him to return his attention to her.

'. . . and I realise that maybe I'm not being fair to you,' she continued rapidly, 'but I'm just not brave enough to go through this by myself. I'm not scared of dying . . . but I *am* scared of dying alone. And that's why I had to tell you how I feel about you. I love you, Sam. And I need to know how you feel about me, because I don't think I'm brave enough to get through it on my own. Good friends aren't enough ... I need someone who loves me ... to *be* with me.' She faltered, her eyes brimming with tears, her grip on his hand tightening with the effort of maintaining control. 'Otherwise it would be ... unbearable ... I don't honestly know if I could go on ...'

She was evidently so distraught she hadn't even recognised that what she was inflicting upon him was emotional blackmail. Much as Izzy had done yesterday, Sam appreciated that he was being given absolutely no choice in the matter. It was a fait accompli from which there was no escape, an offer he simply couldn't refuse. As far as Gina was concerned, she was being punished for a crime she hadn't committed and now, without even realizing it, she was punishing him in return. Trapped, he thought bleakly, wasn't the word for it.

But Gina's desperation was genuine enough. She needed him, and he couldn't let her down.

'I'm here,' he said, taking her thin, shuddering body into his arms and feeling her hot tears of relief soak through his shirt front. 'You're not alone. You've got me. You'll always have me ...'

'Oh, Sam,' wept Gina, clinging to him. 'I love you. I really do.'

'Sshh,' he murmured, rocking her like a baby and forcing himself not to think of Izzy. 'You mustn't cry. I love you too.'

Katerina, busy putting the finishing touches to an essay, looked up and grinned as Sam entered the room.

'I know I'm in love with my word processor,' she said,

leaning back in her chair and offering him a Liquorice
Allsort, 'but you really don't need to knock before coming
in. Our relationship is purely platonic.'

'Don't talk to me about relationships.' With a shudder,
Sam sent up a prayer of thanks that at least Gina didn't
expect him to perform in that respect. He could go along
with the charade just so far, but anything even remotely
sexual would be out of the question.

Intrigued, Katerina said, 'Problems with Vivienne?'

'Worse.' For a moment he was tempted to tell her
about Izzy and himself, but he knew he couldn't do that.
She would have to know, however, about the farcical
situation with Gina.

'Oh my God,' said Katerina finally, when he'd finished.
'I don't know whether to laugh or cry. However are you
going to wriggle out of this one?'

He shrugged. 'No way out.'

She gazed at him, genuinely appalled. Sorry as she felt
for Gina, she felt sorrier still for Sam. 'She's got you by
the short and curlies.'

'Not quite that.' He winced at the unfortunate
metaphor. 'But it's bad enough.'

'Maybe next week's brain scan will be OK,' suggested
Katerina, not very hopefully. 'If she isn't going to die,
you're off the hook.'

The other alternative – that Gina's death would be
mercifully swift – hung unspoken in the air between them,
too callous to even voice aloud.

'We'll just have to wait and see.' Sam glanced at his
watch. 'Hell, I'd better go. I was supposed to be at the
club an hour ago.'

Jumping to her feet, Katerina gave him a big hug. 'Poor old you, what a shitty thing to have happen. And just when you'd got yourself free of Vivienne, too.' Drawing away, starting to laugh as she realised that yellow fluff from her mohair sweater had moulted all over his dark blue jacket, she said, 'Look, even my jumper's hopelessly attracted to you! Has it ever occurred to you, Sam, that maybe you're just too irresistible for your own good?'

It was a shame, thought Sam wryly, that Izzy should be the only one who didn't share her views.

'Thanks,' he deadpanned, brushing stubborn crocus-yellow mohair from his lapels. 'That's comforting to know. At least I'm . . . irresistible.'

'Oh, except to me,' Katerina assured him earnestly. 'I'm totally exempt. I don't quite know why,' she added, breaking into a grin, 'but for some weird reason I see you as more of a father figure than a man!'

Struck by this further irony, Sam allowed himself a crooked smile. 'Thanks . . .'

The atmosphere inside the concert hall was amazing. Izzy, pausing for breath and gazing out in wonder at the bobbing, seething mass of the audience as seven thousand Italians applauded wildly and screamed for more, realised that here was the antidote she so desperately needed. It was a magical evening and the crowd loved her. It was all she'd ever worked for, all that really mattered. For while eventually . . . hopefully . . . she would be able to forget Sam, the exhilaration of singing here would remain indelibly imprinted on her memory. She was, at long last, a real success and nobody could take that away from her.

The heat, too, was stifling. Shaking damp tendrils of hair away from her face and undoing another button of the peacock-blue-and-gold shirt which clung to her perspiration-drenched body, she turned and nodded to the band behind her. Dry ice was already billowing from the back of the stage, signalling Tash's impending entrance. In response to her nod, the drummer and sax player moved into the now-famous opening bars of 'Never, Never'. The audience, recognizing the song at once, sent up a roar of approval that almost shook the hundred-year-old building to its foundations.

Izzy, acknowledging their appreciation with a wave, took a small step backwards and smiled. The clouds of dry ice were close behind her now, sliding noiselessly towards the front of the stage. Above and all around her, spots of lilac-and-blue light darted like moonbeams, illuminating her solitary, unmoving figure. The pure, clear notes of the tenor sax soared and a shiver of pleasure snaked down her spine. Taking a deep, measured breath, Izzy lifted her face to the lights, opened her mouth and began to sing.

> 'Never, never
> *Understood how*
> *The rest of the world*
> *Felt, until now.*
> *Was I ever, ever*
> *Alive before now?*
> *You showed me how*
> *It could be.*'

And then an even greater roar of amazement and delight went up from the audience as, dressed all in black like the devil himself, Tash emerged from the backlit clouds of dry ice and made his way slowly towards Izzy. The unexpectedness of his appearance was almost too much for them to take in; for the first few seconds, when only his silhouette was visible, the crowd weren't certain that it was actually Tash Janssen. But then, when the spotlights finally beamed down on him, they knew for sure and their tumultuous welcome brought the house down. Screams, whistles and frantic applause raised the noise level to new heights. Izzy, who still hadn't turned to look at him, had to concede that the surprise appearance was indeed a master-stroke of planning. Tash might be a bastard, she thought, but he was undoubtedly a clever one.

'*Never, never Understood how,*' sang Tash, behind her. Seemingly startled, she spun around to face him just as his hand slipped around her waist, and the audience erupted once more. Tash, grinning broadly, murmured, '*Mi amore,*' into the microphone, just loud enough for seven thousand pairs of ears to catch the whispered endearment. Then, expertly picking up on the missed beat, he resumed the song. '*Lucky me, lucky world, You're a woman, not a girl.*'

The husky, powerful voice had enraptured every female in the building except Izzy. But this, as he had told her earlier, was show business and she could feign rapture with the best of them.

'. . . *You taught me how To love. And now,*' she sang back, her voice soaring with emotion, '*As long as I have you, You'll al-ways, al-ways Have . . . me . . .*'

It was a triumphant finale. The audience, delirious with joy, simply refused to let them go. The applause went on for ever, reaching new heights when Tash finally signalled the band to lead them into 'Kiss'. Izzy had already sung it alone, but it would be unthinkable now not to repeat it as an encore. Besides which, the audience knew the words so well themselves that when Tash broke off from singing, '*I want you to kiss me, To know that you've missed me*,' in order to kiss Izzy, they could happily carry on without him.

The kiss, when it came, went on far longer than Izzy had anticipated, but since an undignified tussle was out of the question she had little choice other than to keep her mouth resolutely shut and tolerate it while the audience, avid romantics that they were, whistled approval and bombarded the stage with flowers.

'*I want you to kiss me, to know that you've missed me*,' whispered Tash finally, his fingers stroking the nape of her neck beneath her tumbling damp curls, his hips moving imperceptibly against her own. 'And I think you *have* missed me, sweetheart . . .'

The explosion of flashbulbs was dazzling. Izzy, gazing adoringly up at him for the benefit of a thousand cameras, smiled and said, 'If you think that, you really *are* deranged.'

Tash's glance flicked momentarily to her heavy emerald-and-sapphire Bulgari earrings. 'You wouldn't be wearing those if I didn't still mean something to you.'

Izzy fingered her left earlobe. 'I like them.'

'So you bloody well should! They cost nine and a half thousand pounds.' He grinned. 'But what the hell, you were worth it.'

Behind them, the band continued to play the refrain of 'Kiss'. All around them, the concert hall reverberated to the sound of seven thousand word-perfect Italians singing the chorus. Just then, a Cellophane-wrapped bouquet of yellow roses sailed through the air, landing almost at Izzy's feet.

'See?' said Tash, picking them up and presenting them to her. 'They think you're worth it, too.'

With her free hand Izzy swiftly unfastened first one earring, then the other. The next moment, before Tash had time to react, she'd hurled them into the audience.

'You bitch,' he said, the amusement dying in his eyes.

'Not at all,' countered Izzy sweetly. 'These are our fans, Tash. Surely *they're* the ones who are worth it . . . ?'

# Chapter 54

In order to escape Gina's claustrophobic attentions, Sam found himself inventing work and arriving at The Chelsea Steps earlier and earlier each evening.

When he let himself into the club at eight-fifteen on Tuesday night, four days after Izzy's departure to Rome, only Sarah, the blonde receptionist, was there before him. Lounging on one of the charcoal-grey curved sofas adjacent to the main bar, she was eating a Mars bar and racing to finish a fat, lurid-looking paperback before work began. She glanced up with some surprise when Sam came in.

'Well, I know why I'm here early,' she said in reproving tones. 'I hate my husband. So, what's your excuse?'

'I hate mine, too.' Sam tipped her feet off the chair opposite, picked up her glass and sniffed it. 'And I like to check up on my staff now and again. Is this straight bourbon?'

Sarah, a teetotaller and life-long Pepsi addict, giggled. Then, remembering something, she said, 'Oh!' and reached for her handbag, rummaging energetically until she unearthed a folded sheet of newspaper. 'I saved this in case you hadn't seen it. It was in this morning's *Express*.'

The Chelsea Steps, with its illustrious clientele, was frequently mentioned in various gossip columns. Taking the clipping, Sam hoped it wasn't a scathing comment upon the fact that one of the minor Royals had been observed leaving the club the other night slightly the worse for wear.

'It's OK, it's not about us,' said Sarah, reading his mind. Pointing to the photograph with a manicured damson-red fingernail, she added, 'You're a friend of Izzy Van Asch, aren't you? I thought you'd like to see it. Looks like she and Tash Janssen are back together again.'

It certainly did. Sam had enough experience to know not to believe everything one might read in the papers, but it was hard not to believe this. The picture, taken at her concert in Rome, showed Izzy with her arms around Tash and an unmistakable expression of triumph on her face. The short accompanying article reported the concert's riotous success and dwelt lasciviously on the apparent resumption of their affair. Tash Janssen, it seemed, had told the avid reporters that their temporary estrangement was now behind them, and that the lyrics of 'Never, Never' had never been more apt. The blissfully happy couple, furthermore, were staying at the Hotel Aldrovandi Palace and were rumoured to be extending their stay . . .

Sam wished he could dismiss the possibility that Izzy and Tash were back together from his mind, but Izzy's unpredictability and notorious lack of judgement where men were concerned made it impossible. And if she was determined to pursue her career, as she had so ruthlessly informed him the other morning, who better to do it with than Tash Janssen?

'I think she's incredible.' Sarah prattled cheerfully on,

craning her neck to take another look at the photograph. 'She's nearly forty years old, but she looks younger than I do. Mind you, Tash Janssen's pretty stunning himself. If they got married, they'd have the most amazing-looking children, don't you think?'

The urge to socialise having temporarily deserted him, Sam remained upstairs in his office until nearly midnight, concentrating instead on a backlog of paperwork.

The phone on his desk finally interrupted him.

'Meredith Scott's here, Sam,' announced Sarah, ringing from reception. 'She's just gone in, but she was asking for you so I told her you'd be down shortly. Was that OK?'

'It rather looks as if it has to be OK,' he replied, his tone brusque. Meredith Scott, one of the few child stars of the Fifties who had made the successful transition to adulthood and even greater stardom, simply wasn't accustomed to rejection in any form. Now based in Hollywood and – handily – married to a plastic surgeon of some repute, she was an intermittent visitor to The Chelsea Steps and a wonderfully bitchy gossip whose innocent violet eyes belied a lethal tongue.

Her presence at the club, however, was good for business and Sam had always found her to be entertaining company. 'Tell Marco to uncork the Veuve Clicquot,' he said into the phone. 'I'll be right down.'

'Darling, it's been simply ages!' cried Meredith, in time-honoured Hollywood fashion. Faultlessly de-bagged eyes sparkled with fun as she studied Sam carefully for a second before raising her face for a kiss. 'And you're looking more gorgeous then ever, I must say. Go on Sam, break my heart and tell me you're married!'

Glancing with amusement at her shapely, astonishingly uplifted breasts, he nodded in the direction of her heart and said, 'Don't panic, it's safe.'

'Well, hooray for that.' Smiling, she reached up and kissed him once more for good measure. 'If nothing else, it does my husband the world of good to know there are still one or two handsome, eligible men on the circuit. Keeps him on his toes, you know...'

'He isn't over here with you?' Sam poured the champagne and handed her a glass. Meredith Scott was always good value and his mood was beginning to improve.

She gestured dismissively in the general direction of America. 'Poor man had to stay behind to do a chin-lift on some wizened old ex-president whose wife, I *happen* to know, is about to leave him anyway. I'm here to promote my new film. I have *the* most stultifying series of chat-show appearances lined up ... I just know I shall fall asleep during one of them ... so, I thought I'd at least seize the chance to have some fun first. Oh, and to make the most of my last few days as a forty-something. It's my birthday next week, darling ... the dreaded half-century ... and my manager's planning the most tremendous party for me. You simply must come!'

Sam grinned. Meredith Scott was fifty-five if she was a day, but who would ever dare to remind her of such an unpalatable fact?

'Of course I will. But tell me about the new film. What's it like?'

The awe-inspiring bosom, only semi-encased in plunging white velvet, heaved. 'An absolute stinker! Every member of the cast hated each other, we all hated the director even more and the storyline's putrid. But when you see me being interviewed on TV, of course, I shall praise the damn thing to the skies and declare it the most wonderful experience of my life.' She paused and took a sip of her drink, then added with a trace of sadness, 'I might not get any awards for acting in this Godawful film, but I deserve an Oscar for promoting it.'

'It certainly sounds as if you need a good party to make up for it.'

But Meredith's eyes had grown misty. 'I think I'd prefer a good man. I do love my husband, Sam, but he isn't here. I don't suppose you'd consider doing the honourable thing? Escort a lonely actress back to her hotel and . . . keep her company?'

When he didn't reply, she said falteringly, 'I'm sorry, but a woman in my position has to be careful. And at least I know I can trust you to be discreet.'

She was staying at the Savoy. When Sam pulled up outside the entrance, he left the ignition running. In the darkness, Meredith managed a half-smile.

'So, this is your discreet way of turning me down?'

The car was filled with the voluptuous scent of her perfume. For a fraction of a second, Sam wondered what it would actually be like to make love to a world-famous sex symbol.

Instead, he took her hand and gave it a squeeze. The fifteen-carat diamond on her wedding finger dug into his palm.

'You're happily married,' he said, his tone gentle. 'And although I've only met your husband a couple of times, I liked him. He's a nice man.'

She nodded. 'And now you're being an honourable one. I suppose you're right, really.'

'You know I'm right.' Leaning across, he planted a swift kiss on her cheek. 'Come on, cheer up. Think of all those Oscar-winning performances you have to give in the next few days.'

With a rueful grin, Meredith said, 'I could have given one for you, tonight. Except I don't think they hand out Oscars for that kind of performance, more's the pity. Hey, now there's an idea for my party! Everyone gets an Oscar . . . Biggest Jerk, Most Repulsive Paunch, Least Believable Toupee, Smallest Willy . . .'

Relieved to see that she had regained her sense of humour, Sam said, 'Am I still invited?'

'Of course! You can be the Greatest Disappointment in Bed.' Tilting her head to one side she added wickedly, 'That's because I couldn't persuade you into one, of course, but nobody else is going to know that.'

The danger period was over. Sam, having successfully negotiated it, raised his dark eyebrows and said, 'What's wrong with Most Honourable Night-Club Manager?'

'No way! It's insults only, at this Oscar party. And that reminds me . . .'

'What?'

'I forgot to ask you earlier, but somebody mentioned

that you were friendly with Izzy Van Asch, and then I saw in the paper this morning that she and Tash Janssen are back together again.'

Sam felt as if he'd been punched in the stomach. His tone carefully neutral, he said, 'Ye . . . es.'

'It's that song of theirs, "Never, Never",' Meredith continued with enthusiasm. 'I just love it so much, I thought how brilliant it would be if they could sing it at my party. My manager's going to contact theirs, but since you already know Izzy Van Asch, I thought you could have a word with her yourself. Will you ask her to ring me, Sam?'

Was he destined to spend the rest of his life, he wondered painfully, listening to people singing Izzy's praises?

'If I see her,' he replied tonelessly, 'I'll tell her. But it isn't certain that I will. And just because we're . . . friends doesn't necessarily mean she'll say yes.'

'Just if, then,' agreed Meredith, her cheerfulness renewed. Gathering her coat around her, she searched in the darkness for the door handle. Then, with a throaty laugh, she added, 'But I have to tell you, Sam, you certainly slipped up there. She's a beautiful girl. What kind of man would ever want to be "just friends" with someone like Izzy Van Asch?'

Katerina and Lucille were gossiping in the kitchen when he arrived at the house the following morning.

'I've seen it,' said Sam wearily, as Katerina waved a copy of yesterday's paper under his nose.

'That total dickhead!' Kat was outraged. 'Honestly, I

sometimes wonder if my mother has more than three brain cells to rub together. I don't know how she can even bear to *speak* to him, let alone . . . ugh!'

Sam, who shared her sentiments entirely, helped himself to a slice of Katerina's heavily buttered toast and marmalade. 'It might not be true.'

'I've been trying to call her at that hotel, but she isn't in her room.' She shot him a dark glance across the table. 'And Tash's phone has been left off the hook. God, if she ever brings him round here, I'm leaving home again.'

Sam's efforts to change the subject were sabotaged at every turn by Lucille, who was intensely interested in the Izzy-Tash affair. 'Such shenanigans,' she said in gleeful tones, deftly appropriating the last slice of toast and demolishing it with relish. 'We'll have Trevor McDonald here on our doorstep before ye know it. Maybe I should be gettin' me perm topped up, just to be on the safe side.'

Katerina looked horrified. 'Why? Don't tell me *you* think Tash Janssen's irresistible as well!'

'Ah, he's not my type,' replied Lucille comfortably. 'The fellow's too skinny by half, if you ask me. But Trevor McDonald, now; I've always had a bit of a sneakin' fancy for that one . . .'

'Did you hear about Izzy?' asked Gina, when Sam went up to her room.

Later, as he was leaving, he encountered Jericho lying outstretched in the hall, toasting his back against the radiator.

At the sight of him, Jericho thumped his tail with half-hearted enthusiasm. 'Are you quite sure there isn't something *you'd* like to ask me?' said Sam drily, bending to stroke his sleek, golden head. 'Like have I seen the piece in the paper about Tash and Izzy?'

# Chapter 55

University life evidently agreed with Simon. When he turned up at the house on Friday evening, all smiles and wielding his battered weekend case as easily as if it were a biscuit tin, Katerina was struck afresh by the change in him. He seemed to have grown both in confidence and in stature, and when the irrepressible Lucille insisted upon feeling his biceps and pronounced herself deeply impressed, he took all the attention effortlessly in his stride. Katerina, one of whose favourite pastimes had always been teasing poor Simon until he didn't know whether he was coming or going, was rather startled to discover that she was no longer even capable of making him blush.

'That was brilliant,' he pronounced, having demolished a vast supper of home-made shepherd's pie followed by two helpings of blackberry-and-apple crumble. As befitted a future member of the university's rugby team he patted a cast-iron stomach and drained the glass of Guinness which Lucille had pressed upon him. With a broad wink in her direction, he added, 'I need to keep my strength up, after all.'

He *had* changed, Katerina decided. Not so long ago, she would have been the one passing that kind of faintly suggestive remark and Simon would have been turning scarlet with embarrassment. Now, however, fully in control and at the same time almost flirting – heaven forbid! – with Lucille, he was scarcely recognizable as the awkward fumbling schoolboy with about as much sex appeal as a teddy bear. It was completely ridiculous, but in the face of such an abrupt role-reversal, she realised that if anyone was in any danger at all of blushing, it was her . . .

Determined to nip such a humiliating prospect in the bud, she countered briskly, 'You certainly will need to keep your strength up if you're going to help me with my physics revision.'

But Simon, apparently, had other ideas. Shaking his head, he said, 'You've done enough work. We can do a final run-through tomorrow, if you like, but there's no point in overloading yourself now. I've come down here to give you a break before the exams start next week. Mental relaxation is what you need at this stage. It's a proven fact.'

In the old days, Katerina had always made the decisions and Simon uncomplainingly had gone along with them. Now that he was being masterful, however, all that had changed. And although she would never normally have allowed herself to be dragged within a mile of a cinema premièreing the latest Arnold Schwarzenegger movie, this time she gave it a chance and found to her astonishment and secret dismay that it was really rather entertaining.

The crowded pub in Holborn where a favourite amateur rock band of Simon's was playing was also more fun than she would ever have imagined, having steadfastly refused to accompany him to such unprepossessing venues before now. It was noisy, it was hot and it certainly wasn't a piano concerto by Debussy, but with a half-pint of shandy clutched to her chest, the security of Simon's muscled arm to protect her from the jostling crowd and the infectious enthusiasm of the band themselves, Katerina realised that once again, despite her initial misgivings, she was actually enjoying herself.

It was past midnight before they returned to the house. Having drawn the line at a doner kebab, Katerina switched on the kettle instead and watched Simon wolf his down.

'So, what exactly were you doing tonight?' she asked when the last shreds of salad had been efficiently disposed of. 'Testing me?'

He looked surprised. 'Testing you for what?'

'I don't know.' Deciding that she didn't want a coffee after all, she came and sat down on the sofa next to him. 'I just thought you might be trying to prove something to me.'

Simon broke into a broad grin. 'Have you been reading Sigmund Freud again?'

'No!' Her curiosity was well and truly piqued now. Where was the old Simon, whom she had been able to manipulate so easily and at will? And why was this new Simon seemingly so much more attractive?

Determined to make him blush at least once, Katerina kicked off her flat, black leather pumps and swung her legs across his lap, wriggling her bare toes and giving him a self-deprecating smile. 'I still think I should have been revising, but I've had a great time tonight. Thank you.'

Not only did Simon not blush, but he picked up one of

her feet in order to examine it more closely and said in conversational tones, 'How strange. I'd never noticed before that your middle toes are longer than the big toes. Have they always been like that?'

This was too much. Having long ago become accustomed to his adoration, Katerina couldn't cope with this new-found lack of it. Stung by the implied criticism of her toes, she wrenched the shameful objects smartly away. 'Don't you dare laugh at my feet.'

'I wasn't *laughing*,' replied Simon mildly. 'Merely making an observation.'

'Well, don't.'

The expression in her brown eyes was unmistakable. It took all his self-control not to burst out laughing. He could still scarcely believe that Jessie had been so *right*.

'If you've put this girl on a pedestal, how can you ever expect her to look up to you?' Jessie Charlton, his flatmate's girlfriend, had made it all sound so simple when, one drunken night, Simon had miserably confided in her. 'Of course she's going to treat you like dirt. That's the way it happens, Si. I'm not saying you have to come over all he-man and chauvinistic, because too much of that is a turn-off as well, but it sounds to me as if a bit of table-turning wouldn't go amiss. Try treating this girl as if *she's* the lucky one. Be macho, be enigmatic, be uninterested . . . and before you know it she'll be wondering what on earth *she's* doing wrong . . . Take it from me, Si. You'll end up practically having to fight her off.'

Good old Jessie, he thought with renewed admiration and fondness. He really owed her one for those inspired words of wisdom. All he had to hope now was that he could maintain the façade of disinterest, both mentally and physically . . .

'How about that coffee?' he suggested, still struggling to keep a straight face, and Katerina stomped into the kitchen. Returning to the sitting room two minutes later with mugs of hideously strong instant coffee, she shoved one into his hands and said, 'You've got a girlfriend, haven't you?'

'Hmm?' Simon pretended to be engrossed in his drink, which tasted even more disgusting than it looked. 'No . . . no . . . of course not.'

She shot him an accusing look. 'You must have. You've changed.'

'Well, my hair's longer.'

'Simon, don't be so flippant! What is the *matter* with you?'

He shrugged. 'I'm OK.'

'Oh yes, *you're* OK.' Realizing that she was losing her cool but by this time beyond caring, Katerina landed an ineffectual punch on his shoulder. 'You're *fine*. You're just treating me as if I was something from another planet. You used to *like* me . . .'

Females were funny creatures, thought Simon. His shoulder didn't hurt but he rubbed it anyway.

'I still like you, Kat.'

'You used to *really* like me,' she countered accusingly. 'I suppose you think that since the Andrew thing I'm some kind of fallen woman. I suppose your mother warned you to keep away from me.'

'She said no such thing.' This was chiefly because he had never mentioned 'the Andrew thing' to his family, but now wasn't the time to sound wimpish. 'And I don't think of you as a fallen woman, either,' he added in reassuring tones. 'After all, you're only eighteen.'

Out of sheer desperation Katerina leaned across and kissed him, hard. Then, because hard didn't appear to be working, she softened the kiss, sliding her arms around Simon's neck and moving slowly against him.

He did his very best to think about something else . . . dustbins . . . rugby practice . . . ice-cold showers . . . anything but what Katerina was doing to him with her hands and mouth.

And failed, miserably.

'You do still like me,' murmured Katerina, her warm lips brushing his neck, her body squirming with triumph and pleasure.

'I didn't say I didn't,' he replied reproachfully, breathing in the clean scent of her skin. 'And this isn't fair. It's a purely biological response—'

'Not so long ago, you wanted to give me a practical biology demonstration.'

Simon had never stopped wanting to, but despite the intensity of his desire, some sixth sense warned him that if he gave in now, his new-found advantage would be lost and he'd find himself back at square one. He no longer would be a challenge and Kat would lose interest all over again. So far, Jessie's advice had been spot-on. If, therefore, there was to be any future for this relationship, he absolutely had to remain aloof, macho and . . . oh, hell . . . uninterested . . .

'Actually,' he said, doing his best to shrink away from actual physical contact, 'it was quite some time ago. And you, if you remember, turned me down.'

For the life of her, Katerina couldn't think why. Neither was she able to imagine how she could have failed to notice until now how attractive Simon really was. He might not be what the girls at school would call 'drop-dead gorgeous' – their true heroes, after all, were currently Leonardo DiCaprio and Robbie Williams – but with his straight blond hair, kind face and American football player's strapping physique, Simon was a million times more interesting than the girls' puny real-life boyfriends.

'So now you're turning me down,' she said, her self-confidence in tatters, the disappointment evident in her eyes.

Simon shifted uncomfortably in his seat, willing his erection to subside and only hoping he was doing the right thing. Knowing his luck, he thought wryly, Kat would meet some other boy next week and fall madly in love . . .

Placing all his trust in Jessie Charlton, however, and furtively crossing his fingers at the same time, he said, 'You didn't want to jeopardize our friendship, if you recall. And I realised afterwards that you were right. Far better to be good friends, Kat, without the hassle of all that sex and stuff.'

To his relief, she broke into a grin. 'Sex and stuff. It isn't that terrible, you know.'

Simon didn't know. Deeply shaming though it was, he had yet to discover the delights of actually making love to a real live girl. If his flatmates ever found out, he would die . . .

'Of course it isn't terrible,' he replied easily, giving

Katerina the benefit of his man-of-a-thousand-conquests smile. Little realizing that he was echoing Izzy's argument with Sam – and lying, just as she had done, through his teeth – he added, 'But friendship's more important than sex, every time. And we don't want to spoil that, do we?'

# Chapter 56

Izzy, unaware of the furious speculation surrounding her supposed romance with Tash, was both amused and amazed when – upon arriving home on Saturday morning – she found herself on the receiving end of a decidedly severe mother-daughter lecture.

Since Katerina clearly needed to get the talk out of her system, however, she sat obediently on her bed and waited until it was over before saying, 'But darling, I *know* he's a jerk. This silly newspaper article doesn't mean anything at all. I'm really not seeing him again, scout's honour.'

'Oh,' said Katerina, deflating like a balloon. Lamely, she added, 'Well, good.'

'And I haven't married any Italian solicitors either,' continued Izzy, humouring her. 'In fact, as far as I'm concerned, men are off the agenda for the foreseeable future. I'm going to be concentrating on work, work, work.'

'Me too.'

Dying to ask how things were between Sam and Gina, but sensing that something was still bothering Kat, Izzy gestured for her daughter to sit down beside her. Idly playing with her long, sleek brown hair, she said, 'Is everything all right, sweetheart? Simon isn't . . . making a nuisance of himself, is he?'

Katerina leaned against her mother's shoulder, as she had always done when she was a child. 'No. He's taking me to see a rugby match this afternoon.'

'Oh my God, whatever for? You don't like rugby!'

Katerina smiled. Her mother was looking positively indignant. 'I suppose I might change my mind. I've never watched a real match before. It might be fun.'

Curiouser and curiouser, thought Izzy. Tentatively, she said, 'So, things are going well between the two of you?'

Her expression rueful, Katerina replied, 'If you must know, I've decided that I fancy Simon like mad and he's decided we should be just good friends.'

'The nerve of that boy!'

Katerina shrugged. 'But then why should I be any less miserable than anyone else? Mum, I swear there's a jinx on this house . . . this thing with Gina and Sam is so farcical it's embarrassing. There's Doug, *obviously* in love with Gina, mooning around the place like a lost soul.' She paused, ticking the disasters off on her fingers. 'Then there's Simon and myself, of course. You and . . . nobody at all. Lucille and anyone at all, but preferably Trevor McDonald—'

'What?'

'At this very moment,' said Katerina with heavy irony, 'Simon is downstairs in the kitchen being seriously chatted up by our housekeeper. Yesterday morning she had the milkman closeted in there with her for over an hour. And as for Doug, well . . . the poor man just isn't safe when she's around.'

'And Trevor McDonald?'

'It's only a matter of time,' Katerina replied darkly.

'Heavens.' Izzy thought hard for a moment. 'But Jericho's OK?'

Her daughter grinned. 'Oh, Jericho's happy enough.'

'That's something, I suppose.'

'But the next-door neighbours aren't too thrilled. It seems he's been getting on rather too well recently with their labrador bitch. And now she's developed a craving for Mars bars and pickled mackerel.'

Izzy knew within minutes that accepting Vivienne's supposedly impromptu dinner invitation had been a dreadful mistake.

It was sheer desperation that had driven her to say yes in the first place. Back in the recording studios to complete her album, she was able to avoid bumping into Sam during the day, but evenings at home were a nightmare. Unable to cope with the increasingly strained atmosphere, she had leapt at the chance of escape. Just an informal supper and a couple of good bottles of wine, Vivienne had assured her, and an opportunity for her finally to meet Terry Pleydell-Pearce, the most wonderful man in the entire universe.

And if he *was* the most wonderful man in the universe, she thought drily, what on earth was he doing with a sneaky, conniving, traitorous old bag like Vivienne Bresnick?

'It's a set-up,' she announced, her expression bleak. 'Vivienne, how *could* you?'

Vivienne was just glad that Malcolm Forrester had arrived at the cottage first. Judging by Izzy's reaction, she might otherwise have taken one look at the table set for four and walked straight back out.

'What's the big deal?' she countered innocently, taking care to keep her voice down so that neither Terry nor Malcolm, in the next room, could overhear. 'Like I said, it's just a cosy evening with friends ... no pressure ... Malcolm's a real nice guy.'

'Hmm.' Izzy, not taken in for a moment, said, 'Well, excuse me if I don't marry him.'

Vivienne, showing off her domestic skills, pressed the start button on the microwave. 'You could do a hell of a lot worse,' she replied lightly. 'He's divorced, charming and a real gentleman. He's nothing like Tash Janssen at all.'

This was certainly true. Putting on a brave face, Izzy admired the cottage, which was enchanting, got to know Terry, who was every bit as nice as Vivienne had promised, and exchanged pleasantries with Malcolm Forrester, who was of all things an obstetrician.

He was also *old*, probably knocking fifty, with silver wings in his dark, swept-back hair, a paisley cravat and an avuncular manner that reminded Izzy of her grandfather. Vivienne, having found real happiness with Terry, had evidently decided that Izzy should broaden her horizons and at least consider a man of similar vintage.

But the excruciatingly polite conversation, which ranged from the latest exhibition at the Tate to the genius of Dizzy Gillespie, only succeeded in making Izzy realise how desperately she missed Sam. The sense of longing, so acute it was almost a physical pain, was showing no signs at all of going away. Every time Malcolm Forrester called her 'my dear Isabel' she found herself imagining the expression on Sam's face if he could only have been there to hear it. His grey eyes, glittering with suppressed amusement, would have locked with hers as they had done so many times at The Chelsea Steps, and later they would have rocked with laughter together over a shared Chinese takeaway.

Her appetite by this time had all but disappeared. Uncharacteristically picking at the delicious meal – *boeuf Bourgignon* with fresh asparagus and tiny new potatoes – Izzy listened in silence as Terry and Malcolm swapped 'And-then-she-said' stories about their respective grandchildren. Her sense of aloneness increased when she realised that beneath the table, Terry and Vivienne were holding hands. Nor could they keep their eyes off each other for more than a few seconds; with each newly touted example of infant cuteness Terry would glance at Vivienne as if unable to quite convince himself she was still there. Then, his face lighting up once more, he would give her a brief, secret smile . . .

Finally, unable to contain herself a moment longer, Vivienne leapt to her feet and disappeared into the kitchen. Returning with a bottle of champagne, she said, 'OK folks, this was supposed to wait until after the meal but patience was never my forte. Sweetheart, can you get this thing open? I don't want to wreck my nails.'

It wasn't exactly the surprise of the century, but Izzy dutifully assumed a blank expression. While Terry wrestled somewhat inexpertly with the cork, Malcolm said in hearty tones, 'What's all this, then? Do we have something to celebrate?'

Vivienne, her amethyst silk dress shimmering in the

candle-light, let out a squeal of delight as the cork ricocheted off the ceiling and champagne cascaded over Terry's corduroys. When their glasses had eventually been filled, she clung to his arm and raised her own glass in a toast.

'Ladies and gentlemen, we'd like you to be the first to know. Terry and I are going to be married!'

Amid the flurry of congratulations, with hugs and kisses all round, Izzy found herself being forced to submit to a decidedly firm kiss from Malcolm Forrester.

'Marvellous news,' he declared, straightening his cravat and looking smug. 'How about that, Isabel? Isn't it simply the most marvellous news?'

Izzy, fighting the childlike urge to wipe her mouth with her sleeve, said, 'Absolutely splendid news, Malcolm,' and glanced across at Vivienne to see if she, at least, was sharing the joke.

But Vivienne, who had never looked more radiant, hadn't even been listening. 'And of course,' she continued joyfully, 'we'd like the two of you to be godparents . . .'

Izzy stared at her. 'You're *pregnant?*'

'Oh, not yet. But we certainly aren't going to waste any time in that direction.' Pausing, in order to give Terry another hug, she added, 'I'm nearly twenty-eight, after all.'

'But that isn't old,' Izzy protested, turning to Malcolm Forrester for corroboration and feeling hollow inside. 'Twenty-eight isn't *old!*'

But Vivienne had been reading all the books. 'The sooner it happens, the better,' she said simply. 'You weren't even twenty when Katerina was born, but in the baby-making stakes I'd already be classed as an "elderly primagravida". My fertility is decreasing, the chances of complications only increase with every passing year ... all *sorts* of things could go wrong!'

'Twenty-eight still isn't old,' repeated Izzy stubbornly.

'Good heavens, of course not.' Malcolm Forrester, swooping diplomatically to the rescue, refilled their glasses and adjusted his cravat once more. 'Why, more and more women these days wait until they're in their thirties before starting a family. Professionally, I'm all for it.' To emphasise the point, he gave Izzy the benefit of his best Harley Street smile. Then, in a jocular undertone, he went on, 'Although personally I can't say I envy them. At least you and I have been through that stage and put it well and truly behind us now. We're the lucky ones, my dear Isabel, don't you agree? At our age we simply don't need to worry about that kind of thing any more.'

# Chapter 57

Having for the past week and a half been plagued by nightmares in which the second brain scan had shown up a tumour the size of a melon, the reality was almost disappointing. Gina, sitting in the consultant's immaculate grey-and-white office on the fourth floor of the Cullen Park Hospital with Sam beside her, gazed in silence at the reality for several seconds before placing the films carefully back on the desk. Reaching for Sam's hand, inwardly amazed by her ability to remain calm, she said, 'So, what happens now?'

The consultant was no longer smiling. Gliomas – fast-growing malignant tumours formed from the central nervous system's supporting glial cells – weren't funny. And from the appearance of the scan, he had no doubt at all that this was the type of tumour with which Gina Lawrence had been afflicted.

'We operate,' he replied, his tone carefully matter of fact. Experience had taught him that this was the best way to avoid hysterical outpourings of grief. 'The plan is to remove as much of the tumour as possible before commencing radiation therapy. I've already made the necessary arrangements. Surgery is scheduled for nine o'clock tomorrow morning.'

'It *is* a glioma then,' said Gina, only the convulsive tightening of her fingers as she clutched Sam's hand

461

betraying her agony. It was a glioma which had killed her mother.

The consultant hesitated for a second, then nodded. 'I'm afraid that's what it looks like,' he admitted quietly. 'Mrs Lawrence, I wish I could have given you more hopeful news. I really am very sorry indeed.'

The operation the following day went on for three and a half hours. Doug, unable to cope with the interminable waiting, had gone for a walk in the rain. Izzy and Sam, left alone in the waiting room, occupied seats opposite each other and drank endless cups of coffee. Since idle conversation would be too cruelly inappropriate, neither said much. Izzy tried hard not to imagine the surgical procedures being employed in the theatre downstairs. She wondered what Sam was thinking. Then she tried not to think about Sam and how differently things could have turned out if only there hadn't been all those stupid obstacles between them.

'You're fidgeting,' said Sam.

Putting down her cup and jamming her hands into the front pockets of her jeans, she rose to her feet and went over to the window. Outside it was still raining; a sea of multi-coloured umbrellas bobbed in the streets below. Katerina would be finishing her final biology paper around now. Thousands of city workers were taking their lunch break, wondering whether to choose cottage-cheese salad or lasagne and chips. And Doug, umbrella-less and no doubt by this time soaked to the skin, was still out there somewhere, just walking . . .

Wishing she'd gone with him, Izzy said, 'I don't even

know why we're here. There's nothing we can do.'

'Gina wanted us to be here.'

'Yes, but I hate it.' Unable to look at him, she continued to gaze blindly out of the window. 'I feel so *useless*.'

'Don't be so bloody selfish,' Sam replied evenly. 'There are some things in life that even you can't control.'

When the surgeon erupted into the room ninety minutes later, Izzy reached for Doug's hand and found it as clammy as her own.

'Well?' said Sam, only the muscle ticking in his jaw betraying his tension.

'It wasn't a tumour.' The surgeon, his mask still dangling around his neck, beamed at them. 'Quite extra-ordinary . . . I must say, I haven't seen anything like it in all my years of working. The scan appearances were so typical I'd have bet a year's salary we had a glioma on our hands . . .'

'So, what was it?' Izzy almost shrieked, unable to bear the suspense. 'Is she going to be all right? What *was* it if it wasn't a tumour?'

'It was an angioma,' explained the surgeon in pacifying tones. 'It's a collection of abnormal blood vessels, rather like a bundle of tangled wool. As the vessel walls weaken the likelihood of haemorrhage increases, and that of course can be fatal.' Pausing for effect, he rubbed his hands together and beamed triumphantly once more. 'Happily, we got there first and were able to . . . defuse the time-bomb, as it were! Mrs Lawrence's angioma was very amenable to surgery; I simply tied off the offending vessels and effectively disconnected them from her circulatory system. The operation was a complete success in every respect, and there's no reason at all now why Mrs Lawrence shouldn't enjoy a long and healthy life.'

Izzy promptly burst into tears.

'She isn't going to die,' whispered Doug. Sweating profusely and looking quite dazed, he enveloped her in a mighty bear-hug.

'Thank you,' said Sam, shaking the surgeon's hand.

When the three of them were alone once more, he handed Izzy a clean white handkerchief. 'It's good news,' he said, sounding faintly exasperated. 'There's no need to cry.'

'The bastard,' sobbed Izzy, still clinging to Doug. 'He could have sent someone in here *hours* ago to tell us that.'

'I cut my best friend's hair once, when I was seven years old.' Izzy, her tongue between her teeth, gingerly combed Gina's blonde hair over the shaved area. 'It ended up looking just like this. Her mother belted the living daylights out of me when she saw it.'

'Let me see in the mirror,' said Gina. Turning her head this way and that, she smiled with relief. Now that the dressing was off and the stitches had been removed, her remaining hair fell naturally over the scar, concealing it so well that it hardly showed at all. 'I can't believe it . . . I thought they'd shave my whole head.'

'You look fine,' said Izzy, giving her a hug. 'You *are* fine, thank God. And it's great to have you back home.'

Gina was glad she was looking her best when Sam arrived to see her a couple of hours later.

'More flowers,' she protested, burying her nose in the pale apricot roses and inhaling their delicate scent. 'I'll soon be able to open my own branch of Interflora.'

Sam, looking distinctly edgy, pulled up a chair and sat down. Gina raised a quizzical eyebrow.

'Is something wrong?'

The fact that he had been planning this speech for days didn't make it any easier now, but the words had to be said. And at least, he'd reasoned with himself, he had a legitimate excuse for getting them out of the way sooner rather than later.

'I have to leave for New York tomorrow,' he said without prevarication. 'There are serious problems with the club over there which may take some time to sort out.'

'Sam, that's terrible.' To his profound relief, Gina seemed more concerned for him than for herself. 'What kind of problems?'

'It seems the acting manager has been embezzling the accounts on a major scale, in order to finance his drug habit.' Sam paused, then shrugged. 'Maybe it's my own fault for not keeping a closer eye on the business myself. But the IRS are involved now and it's evidently going to take a while to work out.'

'You poor thing!' she cried sympathetically. 'And with Christmas coming up, too. What rotten luck.'

'Yes, well.' That was the easy part over with. His grey eyes serious, he said, 'Gina, there's something else we have to sort out before I leave. I don't quite know how to say this . . .'

But Gina, the colour rushing to her cheeks, forestalled him. 'Please,' she begged, reaching for his hand. 'You

don't have to say it. I know what it is and you really don't
have to say anything. It was all a silly mistake on my part
... I panicked, and you were nice enough to humour me
... but all that's behind us now and I don't expect ...
expect you to...' Stumbling over the words, by this time
redder than a beetroot, she silently pleaded for his
forgiveness. She was guilty of having put him under the
most terrible pressure and, being Sam, he had shouldered
it without a word of complaint. All she could hope for
now was understanding and absolution.

'... I was just so afraid,' she concluded in a whisper.
'Of dying. Alone.'

Sam, scarcely able to believe it had all been so effortlessly sorted out, felt the great weight of responsibility
lift from his shoulders. The sense of freedom was
indescribable.

'Anyone would have been afraid,' he assured her, lifting
her thin hand and kissing it out of sheer relief. 'Considering what you've been through, I think you were amazingly
brave. Now all you have to do,' he added solemnly, 'is get
on with the really tricky part.'

Gina smiled. 'And that is?'

This time, leaning out of his chair, Sam planted a brief
kiss on her cheek. 'My dear Mrs Lawrence,' he said, his
expression deadpan, 'living, of course.'

'I don't know how Lucille's going to cope when Gina
moves back to Kingsley Grove,' said Katerina drily, ten
days later. 'If we aren't careful, she might even defect.'

Izzy, who had been engrossed in the task of dyeing her
hair good old Glossy Blackberry, wiped a trail of dark

blue dye from her cheek and spun around to gaze at her in surprise.

'What?' she demanded. 'Why on earth should she?'

From her position in the bath, Katerina watched as a shower of inky droplets hit the basin. Hoping that none were also staining the expensive ivory carpet, she soaped her arms and explained patiently, 'Where Gina goes, Doug follows. It just occurred to me that Lucille, in turn, might want to follow Doug.'

'Hell.' Izzy nodded. It made sense. Not normal sense, maybe, but certainly Lucille-type sense.

'Mum, you're dripping.'

But Izzy, lost in thought, barely noticed. 'She mustn't leave. I'll give her a pay rise.'

Katerina grinned. 'She'd prefer Doug, gift-wrapped.'

'Well, she can't have him. Poor Doug . . . all *he* wants is Gina, and she treats him like a piece of old furniture.' She shook her head. 'No, what we need if we're going to hang on to Lucille is some kind of incentive.'

'You mean another man.' Reaching for the bottle of bubble bath, Katerina poured herself a generous extra helping and turned on the hot tap with her toes. 'We don't seem to be doing terribly well at the moment, where men are concerned. No wonder Lucille's fed up. Simon's gone off me, Sam's gone off to the States . . . even the milkman's too scared to ring the doorbell any more. There's nothing else for it, Mum – you'll just have to find yourself a toyboy.'

'Either that,' said Izzy, gloomily surveying the dye-spattered carpet, 'or we start writing begging letters. To Trevor McDonald.'

# Chapter 58

Izzy barely had time these days to so much as fill in a Dateline questionnaire, let alone find herself a toyboy. Christmas was approaching, the album was finally nearing completion and the success of 'Kiss' ensured a steady stream of interviews, photo-shoots and public appearances. To her intense frustration, however, being rushed off her feet hadn't succeeded in getting her over Sam.

Absent Sam, still over in New York, occupied her mind at the most inconvenient times. Izzy tried to tell herself that it was only because she didn't have a sex life, but it didn't help. Everyone else was happy – even Doug, still pursuing Gina with dog-like devotion, seemed happy enough in his own way – and it only made her own unhappiness that much harder to bear. Christmas had always been her absolute favourite time of year, but this time she possessed no festive spirit at all. Festive, she thought dismally, was above and beyond the call of duty right now. The only thing she really wanted for Christmas was a decent night's sleep.

Major Reginald Perrett-Dwyer, ex-Grenadier Guards, veteran of the Second World War and regular contributor to the letters column of *The Times*, disapproved of most things. More than almost anything else at all, however, he disapproved of female singers with disreputable lifestyles moving into the house next door to his own and disrupting his own highly ordered existence. Despite maintaining watch from his drawing-room window, he had yet to ascertain who actually *lived* at Number Forty-five and who was merely visiting, but the non-stop comings and goings of so many people – at what seemed like all hours of the day and night – only served to increase his annoyance and send his blood pressure soaring.

'Drug-taking and orgies,' he boomed, slamming down his binoculars and glaring at his poor long-suffering wife. 'Mark my words, Millicent. That's what they're up to in there. If I had my way, I'd launch a dawn raid on that house. These types of people need teaching a lesson . . .'

'I thought they seemed quite pleasant,' protested Millicent Perrett-Dwyer, her eyebrows twitching with anxiety. Personally, she thought it rather exciting to be living next door to a pop star, and Izzy Van Asch couldn't have been nicer when she'd plucked up the courage last week to ring the doorbell and ask to borrow a jar of mustard. Her husband, however, who disapproved passionately of domestic inefficiency, didn't know about this. Just as he didn't know that each time he set out on his brisk morning constitutional his wife furtively turned the wireless from the World Service to Radio One and sang along to the music while tackling the breakfast dishes.

'Nothing but lazy, good-for-nothing vagabonds,' snorted the major, bristling once more as the Van Asch woman herself drew up outside in her flashy German car and ran, long hair flying, into the house. 'Look at that, I ask you! Can't park straight and hasn't even bothered to lock the damn thing. It's an open invitation to car thieves . . .'

'Oh, do come away from the window, dear,' begged his wife, terribly afraid that he was on the verge of making another of his infamous scenes. 'They aren't doing us any harm, after all.'

But scenes, unfortunately, were what made life worth living for Reginald Perrett-Dwyer. 'Harm?' he barked, staring at his wife as if she was quite mad. 'Is your sense of judgement really as poor as your memory, woman? How can you stand there and say they haven't done us any harm, after what that vicious brute did to Bettina!'

Here, thought Izzy, was living proof that not all dogs resembled their owners. The major, gaunt, upright and congenitally stroppy, was still in full flow and showing no sign at all of running out of breath. Bettina, by contrast, rested peacefully at his feet. Plump and sweet-natured, she seemed to tolerate her master's ranting with almost benevolent amusement. Whenever Izzy caught her eye she wagged her tail as if silently apologizing for all the fuss.

'. . . and it is *no* laughing matter!' stormed the major, intercepting Izzy's smile. 'That irresponsible hound of yours has violated an innocent young bitch, and I demand to know what you intend doing about it.'

'Look, I really am very sorry,' said Izzy in soothing tones. 'But are you absolutely sure Jericho's the father?'

The major's agitation reached new heights. 'Of course I'm sure!' he spluttered furiously. 'That animal arrived here six weeks ago. According to the vet, Bettina is five weeks pregnant. No other dog has been near her . . . has *ever* been near her . . . and I take great exception to the fact that you should even suggest otherwise.'

'It was just a—' began Izzy, but he quelled her with a look.

'Maybe such a suggestion is only to be expected from someone of your . . . type,' he concluded heavily. 'But I can assure you, Miss Van Asch, that Bettina has been brought up in a household of the very *highest* moral repute.'

It was deeply ironic, thought Izzy several hours later, that it should have been Major Reginald Perrett-Dwyer who – in effect – had broken the news to her. Until then, it hadn't so much as crossed her mind.

Now that they had been spelt out for her, however, the facts were inescapable. It was six weeks since Jericho had come to board with them.

Six weeks since she and Sam had made love.

More than six weeks since her last period . . .

'Oh, Bettina,' murmured Izzy with resignation, in the privacy of her darkened bedroom. 'Pregnant. You and me both.'

'That's no good,' Gina sighed. 'Doug, stop . . . you're doing it all wrong . . . that doesn't *go* there . . .'

Doug, his forehead creased with concentration, straightened up and took a step backwards. Something went *crack* under his left shoe.

'Oh, brilliant,' said Gina in despairing tones. 'Now you've trodden on the fairy. Well done.'

Just for a moment, he was tempted to tell her to decorate her own bloody tree. What should have been an enjoyable evening was threatening to turn into yet another major disappointment, and he was beginning to tire of them. It was all very well for Gina, lounging on the sofa and barking instructions like some parade-ground sergeant-major, but hanging baubles and draping garlands of tinsel simply wasn't his forte and he was damned if he was going to apologise for that.

'Look, why don't you get Izzy and Kat over here to do this?' he said levelly, stripping the imperfectly hung garlands from the tree and dropping them back into their box. 'Seeing as I'm clearly not up to it.'

Gina, unaware that the worm was on the verge of turning, simply shrugged. 'I suppose I'll have to,' she replied with irritation. 'At least they understand how it's meant to be done. Where are you going?'

'Home.' Doug reached for his jacket.

'But I thought you were staying for supper.' She looked up, startled. 'I've defrosted a chilli.'

But Doug had had enough. Winding his scarf around his neck, he said recklessly, 'I'm eating out tonight.'

'Who with? A client?'

'No. With Lucille Devlin.'

'You'll never guess what,' said Gina when Izzy arrived at Kingsley Grove an hour later. Sounding intrigued and at the same time faintly put out, she went on, 'Doug's gone out to dinner tonight. With Lucille.'

You'll never guess what, thought Izzy, struggling to keep a straight face, but Lucille is at this precise moment in my house, drinking gin and bawling her eyes out over a video rerun of *Ryan's Daughter*.

Then her gaze slid sideways, to the pile of half-written Christmas cards on the coffee table with Gina's address book lying open next to them.

'Why shouldn't they have dinner together?' she said lightly. 'They get on wonderfully well. Doug's an eligible bachelor.'

Gina's mouth narrowed with disapproval. 'And Lucille's a married woman.'

'I'll let you into a secret,' Izzy confided. 'It's a marriage in inverted commas only.'

'Really?'

'Really. Now come on, tell me what you want me to do with this poor naked tree of yours. And I'm going to need the step ladder. Where is it?'

'In the cupboard under the stairs,' replied Gina absently, her mind still occupied by thoughts of Doug and Lucille.

Izzy rolled up the sleeves of her yellow MBT sweatshirt in a businesslike manner and began investigating the glittering contents of the Christmas box. 'I'll make a start here,' she said, lifting out a tangled skein of lilac-and-silver fairy-lights, 'and you can take that chilli out of the oven. I'm hungry.'

The moment Gina was out of the room, Izzy dropped the string of lights and made a grab for the address book on the coffee table. Feeling like a sneak thief, riffling through the pages until she came to S, she breathed a sigh of relief when Sam's New York phone number and address leapt out at her. Hastily, she scribbled them down

on the back of an unused Christmas card and stuffed it
into the pocket of her jeans. She hadn't decided yet quite
*how* she was going to break the news to Sam, but at least
she now had the means with which to contact him. Even
if it had been necessary, she thought wryly, to do a James
Bond and practically *steal* the information from an
unsuspecting accomplice . . .

# Chapter 59

Having boarded the jumbo jet eight hours earlier buoyed up by determination and a sense of exhilaration at her own daring, Izzy's self-confidence seeped steadily away as the plane came in to land. No longer separated from Sam by the mighty stretch of the Atlantic Ocean, she had effectively sealed her fate. There could be no backing out now. She was here, in person, to see him . . . to tell him that she was pregnant . . . and to gauge his reaction first-hand.

And although it was a distinctly scary prospect, it was really the only way. Writing a letter, she had concluded after the fortieth failed attempt, was beyond her. The words simply wouldn't come. Neither, she realised, would a phone call work. Apart from the fact that she undoubtedly would lose her nerve, burble incoherently and get everything wrong, she wouldn't be able to tell what he was really thinking. She'd witnessed his ability to mime despair while speaking soothingly into the phone too many times to be able to take his words at face value.

No, doing it that way was out of the question. She definitely needed to *be* there, to say the words and gauge his true reaction for herself.

And now I am here, she reminded herself, as the plane approached the runway at JFK and began to engage reverse thrust.

'Nervous?' asked the middle-aged businessman next to

her, having observed her sudden pallor.

Izzy nodded. She had never been so scared in her life.

'You can hold my hand if you like.'

She had to smile. With a brief shake of her head, she replied, 'Thanks, but it's not that kind of nervous.'

Already cloaked with snow, New York had been promised a further blizzard before nightfall. Having retrieved her suitcase – *the* infamous suitcase – and cleared customs without difficulty, Izzy jostled for a cab outside the main terminal.

'Seventeen below zero,' the driver laconically informed her, glancing over his shoulder and looking unimpressed. 'An' it's gonna get worse. Where to, lady?'

Her teeth were chattering so much, she sounded like a typewriter on speed. Struggling to get the words out between shivers and combing frozen fingers through her damp, dishevelled hair, she said, 'C-can you rec-commend a d-decent hotel?'

'Hey lady, I can recommend the Waldorf-Astoria.' He had an accent like the pregnant one in *Cagney and Lacey* and his tone of voice betrayed his exasperation. 'I can *also* recommend the Tokyo Hilton and the Happy Traveller Motel in Milwaukee. Couldya be, like, more specific?'

Smartass, thought Izzy, glaring at the back of his horrible head. And to think that when Vivienne had told her about New York cabbies she'd refused to believe her.

'No problem,' she replied shortly, and with as much sarcasm as she dared muster. 'The Waldorf will do just f-fine.'

\* \* \*

The hotel was more than just fine; it was unbelievably opulent. Upon hearing the price of a room, Izzy very nearly wheeled round and headed back out of the lobby into the street. But the street was awash with grey slush, she desperately needed a hot bath, and there was always the hideous chance that her cab driver might still be outside, waiting to greet her reappearance with a knowing smile . . . Besides, now that she had come this far, what difference did a few hundred dollars more make? She was here on a mission, possibly the most important mission of her life, and she might as well do it in style.

A long scented bath, she concluded, was a great way of putting off something that had to be done but which you weren't looking forward to doing. Izzy stayed submerged as long as possible, gazing at her flat stomach, realizing how it had looked eighteen years ago and envisaging the repeat performance ahead of her. By next summer, taking a bath would mean submerging the rest of her body and watching the water lap against the sides of a smoothly rounded protruding belly the size of a football. Every so often the perfect symmetry would be distorted by a miniature arm or leg kicking out. At other times – rather less pleasurably – an invisible kick would be aimed at her bladder. And the inconveniently positioned bump would make painting her own toenails a virtual impossibility.

The burning question, of course, was whether or not Sam would be there with her, to witness the miraculous changes her body was about to undergo. Would they be a proper couple, like Vivienne and Terry, or had she driven him away when she'd insisted that such a future was out of the question because her career came first, and because she was just too old to start having babies all over again?

But although she would never have chosen for this to happen, she didn't resent the fact that it had. Maybe it was the hormones taking over, but the thought of being thirty-seven years old and accidentally pregnant no longer seemed as alarming in reality as it had in theory. With or without Sam she would cope, just as she had coped all those years ago when Katerina had arrived on the scene.

Biting her lip, Izzy envisaged once more the process of picking up the phone and dialling Sam's number, which she now knew off by heart. It had to be done, before she lost her nerve completely. Although maybe she'd just repaint her toenails first . . .

The phone rang seven times before it was picked up, by which time Izzy had begun to feel quite sick. All she was doing, she reminded herself, was calling Sam to let him know she was in New York to promote 'Kiss', and to suggest they might meet for a drink. It wasn't, after all, as if this was the big one, the moment when she had to take a deep breath and tell him about the baby . . .

But the voice at the other end of the line didn't belong to Sam. Furthermore, it was a female voice, sexy and slow and sounding as if its owner had just been woken up.

Praying that in her agitation she'd got the wrong number, Izzy cleared her throat and said, 'Er . . . is Sam there?'

But the fickle dialling-finger of fate wasn't that kind. The sleepy, sexy voice, sounding unperturbed, replied, 'I'm afraid he isn't, right now. I'm expecting him home in a couple of hours, though. Can I ask him to call you back?'

Oh shit, thought Izzy, feeling sicker than ever. That something like this might happen hadn't even occurred to her. Whoever she was speaking to certainly didn't sound like any kind of domestic hired-help.

'Um. OK.' It was no good, she couldn't chicken out now. Not leaving a message would be downright immature, and maybe there *was* some perfectly innocent explanation for the girl's presence in Sam's apartment.

'Right, I've found a pen,' said the voice at the other end. 'Fire away.'

'Could you tell him that Izzy Van Asch called.' Giving her full name, Izzy felt, made it sound more businesslike. 'I'm in New York, staying at the Waldorf-Astoria in Room 317. If he could phone me as soon as he gets in . . .'

'Room 317, the Waldorf,' repeated the girl. 'Right, got that. I'll pass the message on.'

'Thank you.' Taking the deep breath she hadn't been planning on using so soon, Izzy added, 'I'm sorry if I woke you up.'

'Oh, no problem,' came the good-natured reply. 'It's about time for my bath anyway. Bye.'

The next two hours crawled past. Izzy, who had never felt more alone in her life, alternately flicked through fifty odd channels of atrocious cable television and paced the luxurious hotel room coming up with reason after plausible reason why Sam might have a female staying in his apartment. The only trouble was she didn't believe any of them for more than a single moment.

Gazing out of her fifth-floor window only served to

increase the gnawing sense of loneliness. The snow was falling heavily now, white flakes hurling themselves against the glass and sliding down like tears. Below her, Park Avenue glittered with lights and life as Manhattanites bent on celebrating Christmas thronged the street on their way home from work and out to parties.

Any minute now, thought Izzy as ten o'clock came and went, the phone would ring and she would hear Sam's blissfully familiar voice. Without even needing to be prompted, he would volunteer the information that his secretary – or maybe the sister she'd never known he possessed – had passed on her message, and that he hoped she was dressed and ready to go because he'd booked a table for the two of them at Spago . . .

Except Spago, she belatedly recalled, was in Hollywood and the phone wasn't ringing anyway.

By eleven-thirty it still hadn't rung and jet lag was beginning to set in. Not having slept at all the night before, Izzy fought the urge to do so now, terrified that she might go out like a light and not hear the phone when it did finally ring.

But at the same time, the prospect of escaping into unconsciousness was an enticing one. Exhausted as she was, prolonging both the mental and physical agony wasn't doing her poor fraught body any favours. It had certainly played havoc with her fingernails . . .

'Honey, it's getting late and you still haven't returned those calls,' chided Rosalie Hirsch. The front of her dove-grey silk wrap fell open as she reached across the bed to refill Sam's wineglass. 'Tom wants to know if you can meet him for lunch tomorrow. And Izzy Van-somebody asked you to ring her at the Waldorf as soon as you got in. You really should phone, Sam. It might be important.'

'Hmm.' Sam, admiring the view of Rosalie's cleavage, trailed his hand across her equally exposed thigh. 'I doubt it.'

'You have no conscience,' she protested mildly, holding her breath as the hand moved higher.

'On the contrary.' Pushing her gently back against the pillows, smiling and unrepentant, he said, 'I feel just terrible about not returning those calls. But some things in life are simply more important. Don't you agree . . . ?'

Rosalie genuinely hadn't minded being woken up by the phone four hours earlier. This time, however, the intrusion came at a particularly crucial moment.

But whereas Sam would have let the damn thing carry on ringing, she couldn't ignore it. Grabbing the receiver, intent only upon getting rid of the caller, she gasped, 'Yes?'

'Oh. Is Sam back yet?'

The woman from the Waldorf, thought Rosalie, closing her eyes. With a breathy laugh, she said, 'Uh . . . well . . . he's pretty busy at the moment. Look, I'm sorry . . . oh! . . . but he'll speak to you later . . . OK?'

Disconnecting the call, leaving the phone off the hook this time, she returned her attention to Sam.

'Who was it?' he murmured with some amusement.

'Nobody important,' sighed Rosalie, her toes curling in ecstasy as she arched against him. 'Don't stop, honey . . . oh my God, whatever you do, don't stop now . . . !'

# Chapter 60

Doug was up to his ears in paperwork when Gina entered the office.

'Well, this is a surprise,' he said, carefully concealing his delight.

Gina, unaccountably nervous, removed her olive-green beret so that if he wanted to kiss her, he could. But it didn't happen. Instead, perching awkwardly on the chair opposite, she placed a large gift-wrapped parcel on the desk.

'I haven't seen or heard from you for over a week,' she said brightly.

Doug nodded his head in agreement. 'I know.'

'So . . . I thought I'd pop in and see you. See how you were getting on.'

'Fine,' he replied, glancing at his watch and deliberately ignoring the parcel on the desk.

Abruptly, Gina's fragile defences crumbled. She had rehearsed this meeting a dozen times over the last day or so, but Doug evidently hadn't learned his lines. He didn't even seem pleased to see her.

'Look, I'm sorry if I was rude to you the other day,' she blurted out, twisting her fingers together in her lap. 'It was wrong of me, but I just didn't expect you to walk out like that.'

Doug hadn't expected himself to walk out either, but it

appeared to have had the desired effect. Encouraged by her conciliatory tone, he replied evenly, 'There didn't seem much point in staying.'

'I know. I behaved like a spoilt bitch.' Gina looked unhappier than ever. Smoothing her dark green skirt over her knees, she inclined her head in the direction of the parcel. 'And I really am sorry. I didn't know if I'd be seeing you at all over Christmas, so I thought I'd better give you your present now.'

'That's very kind of you,' he replied gravely. 'Thanks.'

'So, what are your plans for Christmas?' Gina had been biting her tongue, willing herself to remain calm, but the words tumbled out anyway. 'Will you be staying in London, do you think, or going away?'

He shrugged. 'I haven't made up my mind yet, although I'll probably stay here. See some friends, you know the kind of thing.'

It was extraordinary, but she'd never noticed before the slight but definite resemblance between Doug and Anthony Hopkins. The eyes were the same, Gina now realised, gazing at him for what seemed like the very first time. And the shape of their mouths was virtually identical . . .

Pulling herself together and struggling to conceal her jealousy, she said, 'I expect you'll be seeing Lucille.'

'I expect so.' Relaxing in his chair, inwardly amazed by the success of his campaign, Doug felt he could afford to be magnanimous. With a brief smile he said, 'And what will you be doing?'

It's my own fault, thought Gina miserably. All he's ever been to me is kind and in return I've treated him like dirt. I deserve this.

'Oh, I'll be fine.' Her voice sounded unnaturally high. 'I'm not quite up to wild parties at the moment, of course . . .'

'What about Christmas Day?'

She didn't even want to *think* about Christmas Day. If she did, she might cry. 'Oh,' she murmured, flapping her hands in a vague gesture of dismissal. 'I'll be fine, really . . .'

Doug, who had never deliberately hurt anyone in his life, found her stoical sadness almost unbearably poignant.

'If you don't have any other plans,' he ventured, clearing his throat, 'maybe we could spend it together. There are plenty of restaurants open on Christmas Day, and we wouldn't have to go anywhere too . . . wild.'

'Really?' Colour flooded Gina's pale cheeks. 'On Christmas Day? You'd have lunch with *me*?'

'Only if you'd like to.' Doug broke into a grin. There, he'd done it. And it hadn't been so difficult after all.

'I'd *love* to,' cried Gina, her eyes glistening and her body sagging with relief. 'I can't think of anything nicer. But you don't need to book a restaurant, I can do all the food and we can spend the day at my house.'

Doug pretended to hesitate. 'Only if you promise not to ask me to decorate your tree.'

'I won't ask you to do anything,' declared Gina joyfully. 'Except be there. That's all that matters, after all.'

'So, you're back,' Lucille observed, having heard the taxi pull up outside and rushed to open the front door. Giving Izzy a shrewd up-and-down, she added, 'And you're lookin' a bit peaky. That jet lag's gone to yer eyes . . . what you need, my girl, is a bowl of hot soup and a good piece of soda bread to mop it up with.'

What Izzy needed was Sam, but she managed a feeble smile and allowed herself to be ushered into the kitchen, where a vat of Lucille's famous soup simmered on the stove.

'There ye go,' exhorted her housekeeper, plonking a brimming bowl in front of her. 'Get that down into yer stomach and you'll start feelin' better in no time at all.'

If only, thought Izzy. Her appetite had deserted her on the other side of the Atlantic, but with Lucille standing guard she had little choice other than at least to try a spoonful of the soup.

'How's Jericho?' she said, glancing in the direction of his empty basket.

Lucille rolled her eyes. 'Love's young dream! He howls outside Bettina's window until he catches a glimpse of her. It's like Romeo and Juliet all over again and it's drivin' the major demented. But I'm more interested in findin' out how *you* are,' she continued, folding her plump arms across her chest and fixing Izzy once more with that unnervingly direct gaze. 'From the desperate look of you, I'm thinkin' that things in New York didn't turn out quite as you'd planned.'

'What?' hedged Izzy, disconcerted by the note of sympathy in her voice. 'It was a business meeting, that's all. It went OK.'

But Lucille wasn't about to be fobbed off. Her eyes softened as she glanced momentarily in the direction of Izzy's stomach. 'Bless you, girl,' she said gently. 'Ye might be able to get away with foolin' some people, but this is an Irish Catholic ye're talkin' to, now. We can spot a pregnant woman at fifty paces.'

'*What?*' Izzy gasped, appalled. Inadvertently gazing down at her still-flat stomach, she cried, 'How? How can you *possibly* tell?'

'Easy,' said Lucille with a modest shrug. 'I found a crumpled-up letter to the fellow himself, when I hoovered under yer bed.'

Having sworn Lucille to secrecy, and so that Christmas at least could be spent in relative peace, Izzy waited until the day after Boxing Day before breaking the news to Kat.

But it had to be done, and although she still leapt a mile each time the phone rang or the doorbell went, there had been no word at all from Sam, not even so much as a Christmas card.

He had, it seemed, made his own decision to put their ill-fated relationship behind him and involve himself with a sensual American girl instead.

She was probably a blonde, Izzy had mournfully concluded, trying hard not to feel jealous. A beautiful, nubile blonde with great teeth, who was utterly devoted to Sam Sheridan and undoubtedly a good ten years younger than herself.

Katerina was stretched out across the sofa watching *The Wizard of Oz* and working her way methodically through a Terry's Chocolate Orange when Izzy sidled into the sitting room.

'Sweetheart,' she began, perching on the arm of the

sofa and listening to her own voice echoing in her ears. 'I've got something to tell you.'

'You're pregnant.'

So much for Lucille's ability to keep a secret, thought Izzy, torn between outrage and relief. Frantically twiddling her hair around her fingers, she said humbly, 'Yes.'

Kat jerked upright. The remaining segments of Chocolate Orange fell to the floor. 'My God, I was joking!'

'Oh.' Izzy twiddled more furiously than ever. 'I wasn't.'

'You're really and truly pregnant?' cried Katerina, her brown eyes wide with horror. 'It's not just a false alarm?'

Izzy shook her head and tried not to listen to Dorothy, on screen, giving the poor old cowardly lion a pep-talk. Right now she understood just how he felt.

'No, it's real.'

'Ugh!' Katerina yelled. 'That's disgusting! Mother, how *could* you?'

'It isn't disgusting,' countered Izzy, appalled by the ferocity of her daughter's reaction. 'I'm sorry, darling, I know this must have come as a bit of a shock to you, but that still doesn't make it disgusting.'

'You're nearly forty.' Katerina, whose face had drained of all colour, felt physically sick. 'You're *supposed* to be old enough to know better. Has it even occurred to you to stop and think how humiliating this is going to be for all of us?'

Much as she would have welcomed it, Izzy hadn't been naïve enough to expect instant understanding and a pledge of undying support. But the sheer selfishness of Kat's attitude was positively breathtaking.

'I haven't *murdered* anyone,' she retaliated, dark eyes

flashing. 'I haven't done anything to even hurt anyone, for heaven's sake! All I'm doing is having a baby . . .'

'Who will be known throughout his or her entire life,' spat Katerina with derision, 'as Tash Janssen's unwanted "love child".' She shuddered once more at the hideous thought. 'Poor little bastard, what a label. Of all the unsuitable men in the *world*—'

Izzy stared at her, open-mouthed in astonishment. 'Kat, listen . . .'

But Katerina, misinterpreting her expression and looking more appalled than ever, shouted, 'Oh no, don't tell me you're going to marry him. *Please* don't tell me that.'

Not knowing whether to laugh or cry, Izzy could only shake her head. 'Sweetheart, I'm not going to marry anyone, least of all Tash Janssen. He isn't the father.'

'He's *not*?' Now it was Katerina's turn to look dumb-struck. 'Then who the bloody hell is? Oh Mum, don't tell me you had a Roman fling after all!'

'No.'

Outrage had given way to curiosity. To Izzy's profound relief, Kat's main objection appeared to have been to the thought of Tash Janssen's imagined involvement.

'Go on then,' prompted Kat, her voice calm. 'I'm not going to play twenty questions. Just tell me who it is.'

Izzy held her breath. 'Sam.'

'What? It can't be. You haven't slept with him!'

'Isn't a mother allowed to have some secrets from her daughter?' she protested, struggling to keep a straight face.

'So, you did sleep with him? I mean, you *are* sleeping

with him?' Katerina corrected herself. Gazing accusingly at her mother she said, 'OK, just how long has this secret affair been going on?'

By the time Izzy had finished explaining the whole sorry tale, Dorothy was waking up back in her own bed in Kansas and wondering whether or not it had all been a dream.

'. . . so I caught the first flight out of New York the following morning,' she concluded with a shrug, 'and decided that was that. I was the one, after all, who told Sam to find himself another woman so I can't really blame him for going ahead and doing it. It wasn't great fun, realizing that I'd effectively shot myself in the foot, but it isn't the end of the world, either.'

'Oh, Mum.' Katerina hugged her. 'You know what you are, don't you?'

'Hopeless.'

Eyeing her with affectionate despair, Katerina said, 'If the cap fits . . .'

'Oh, the cap fitted all right.' Izzy's mouth began to twitch. 'It's just that the stupid thing had a hole in it.'

# Chapter 61

'You'll have to speak up, it's a bad line,' shouted Simon, in Cambridge. Half-covering the receiver with his hand, he said, 'Stop it, Claire.'

'Who's Claire?' demanded Katerina, bridling.

'Nobody. Sorry, what did you say just now? For a moment I could have sworn you'd said Doug and Gina were getting married.'

'They are!' Katerina started to laugh. 'Isn't it amazing? Apparently Gina's divorce was finalised last week. She realised she was madly in love with Doug, and was terrified that Lucille would snatch him away . . . so she proposed to him in the office the very next morning. Oh Simon, it's so funny and so sweet, they're going around like a couple of moonstruck teenagers!'

The trouble with Kat, thought Simon with a trace of exasperation, was that she never seemed to regard herself as a teenager. And what was so funny, after all, about being moonstruck? He'd been crazy about *her* for years.

'So, when's the wedding?' he said, above the crackle of interference on the line.

'That's what I'm ringing about. It's fixed for next weekend, and you're invited. You will be able to come, won't you?' Katerina paused, then added fretfully, 'Who *is* Claire?'

'I told you, nobody. And of course I'll come.'

'For the whole weekend?'

He grinned. 'Yeah, all right. I suppose I can manage that. I'll get to your house at around six on Friday evening. Look, I have to go now ... we're on our way out to a party. Bye, Kat.'

Replacing the receiver with an air of triumph, he pushed up the sleeves of his crumpled rugby shirt and rejoined the poker game currently in progress at the kitchen table. His two flatmates raised quizzical eyebrows as he shuffled, then rapidly dealt the cards.

'What party's this then?' said Kenny Bishop, pinching the last digestive biscuit.

'And who the bloody hell,' demanded Jeff Seale, 'is Claire?'

Izzy, amazed and delighted by the news and happily taking full credit for having introduced Gina and Doug in the first place, had insisted upon being allowed to pay for the reception.

Gina almost fainted when she realised how much it was all going to cost.

'We can't let you do that,' she protested, horrified. 'Izzy, no! All we were planning to do was take over the private dining room at Cino's restaurant in Kensington. We'd all have a wonderful meal and nobody would need to go bankrupt. Why can't we just go there?'

'Because if I don't spend my money on important things like wedding receptions,' replied Izzy firmly, 'I'll only fritter it away on silly inessentials like sunbeds and tax demands.'

'It looks gorgeous,' said Gina longingly, clutching the

glossy brochure. 'But it's awfully extravagant.'

'So am I.' Izzy grinned. 'And for heaven's sake stop arguing. It's too late now, anyway. I've booked it.'

'Gosh.' Gina squirmed with gratitude and pleasure. Her eyes bright, she added, 'And I'm phoning Sam tonight to see if he can come to the wedding. Just wait until *he* hears about this.'

For Izzy, who had wanted so desperately to be looking her best when she saw Sam again for the first time in three months, the almost inaudible pop of the button breaking free at her waist was the final insult.

Her heart was in her mouth as he made his way across the Register Office's crowded waiting room towards her.

This is unfair, she thought miserably. Sam, *of course*, was immaculately dressed in a dark suit and white shirt. Tall, handsome and still possessing that indefinable charisma which marked him out from other men – and which other women found so hard to resist – he had never looked better. New York, and the love of a younger woman, evidently suited him. Izzy, wishing that she could melt into the wall behind her, tried to take comfort from the fact that at least he hadn't brought her along with him, but somehow even that didn't help.

'Hallo, Izzy.' His brief, polite smile didn't reach his eyes. 'You're looking . . .' He hesitated. Izzy, who knew exactly how she was looking, winced.

'Wet,' she supplied flippantly, deciding that it was the only way to play it. With a nod in the direction of the window, at the torrential rain outside, she went on, 'It was sunny when we left the house, so I didn't even bring a coat, let alone an umbrella. Kat was furious with me . . . she spent thirty minutes putting my hair up this morning and by the time we arrived here I looked like a half-drowned rat, so it all had to come down again. And I managed to ladder a stocking as I was getting out of the car,' she concluded defiantly, before he had a chance to point it out to her himself. 'So all in all, I'm a complete mess.'

'I was going to say you were looking well,' observed Sam mildly. 'But if you'd rather I didn't . . .'

When people said, 'well', in Izzy's experience, they almost invariably meant fat. Horribly conscious of the fact that she had, in the past fortnight, put on almost half a stone and praying that he wouldn't spot the popped-off skirt button at her feet, she sucked in her stomach and hurriedly changed the subject.

'Did Kat tell you she'd got top grades in her exams and been offered a place at medical school?'

Sam nodded. 'You must be very proud of her.'

'And Gina . . . what about Gina?' Izzy feverishly rattled on. 'Can you *believe* she and Doug are actually getting married?'

'These things do happen,' he observed, his tone dry.

'Oh, you don't know about Jericho, either! He's—'

Sam, interrupting her in mid-flow, placed a hand briefly on the damp velvet sleeve of her jacket. 'The registrar's calling us in now. We'd better not keep him waiting. You'll have to tell me about Jericho later.'

'Right.' Flustered by his obvious lack of interest, Izzy pushed her fingers through her still-damp hair. 'Yes, of course.'

'And Izzy . . .'

'Yes?'

The thickly lashed grey eyes remained absolutely expressionless. 'There's a pearl button on the floor by your left foot. I think it must belong to you.'

The reception, held at the Laugharne Hotel in Mayfair, was a splendid affair. Gina, looking more radiant than ever since becoming Mrs Douglas Steadman two hours earlier, threw her arms around Izzy and whispered, 'This is the happiest day of my life. And none of it would have happened if it hadn't been for you.'

'It was nothing,' quipped Izzy. Away from Sam, it was at least easier to behave normally. 'I just happened to be riding my motor bike down the right street at the right time . . .'

'And that's not all,'Vivienne chimed in. 'Think about it . . . if she hadn't invited me to that party at Tash Janssen's place, I would never have met Terry.' Rolling her emerald eyes in soulful fashion, she tightened her grip on his hand. 'And I would've spent the rest of my life a miserable spinster.'

'Like me, you mean,' Izzy suggested with a wry smile.

'Oh yes, you're a fine example of a miserable spinster,' drawled Vivienne. 'On our way here we passed an advertising hoarding with your picture plastered all over it, promoting the new album. It said, "Experience Izzy Van Asch's Kiss," and someone had sprayed underneath it, "Yes please." '

'I'm still a spinster.' For a terrible moment, tears pricked her eyelids.

'Bullshit,' Vivienne declared fondly. 'You could have any man you wanted.' Then, turning to Terry and planting a noisy, fuchsia-pink kiss on his cheek, she added, 'Except, of course, this one.'

'Who's Claire?' demanded Katerina. Simon, forking up smoked salmon and deciding that it definitely had the edge on tinned, hid his smile.

'You keep asking me that,' he complained good-naturedly. 'And I keep telling you, she's nobody.'

'I don't believe you.'

'Why not?'

'Because she must be your girlfriend.'

'And if she is?' Cocking his head to one side, he studied her beautiful, mutinous profile. 'Would you be jealous?'

Katerina wasn't eating. Having demolished a bread roll with agitated fingers, she was now reduced to rolling the dough into pellets.

'Of course I'd be bloody jealous,' she muttered, her cheeks burning with shame. 'I don't even know her, and I hate her.'

Bingo, thought Simon, breaking into a grin. Putting down his fork, he took her trembling hand in his and said, 'In that case, maybe it's just as well she really doesn't exist.'

It was weak and pathetic of her, Izzy knew, but after four solid hours of being relentlessly cheerful she needed a break. Her mouth ached from smiling, her new high heels pinched like crab claws and her stupid skirt – even without its button – was still far too tight. It was hard work socializing without the aid of champagne and harder still avoiding Sam without making the distance between them seem obvious. Other people's happiness, Izzy ruefully concluded, wasn't catching at all. It was making her downright miserable.

# Chapter 62

'What are you doing in here?'

Sam's voice made her jump. Izzy, who had been curled up in the corner of a Wedgwood-blue sofa in the otherwise deserted hotel sitting-room for the last twenty minutes, felt her stomach do its familiar ungainly flip-flop.

Avoiding you of course, she thought. But since she couldn't very well say so, she replied shortly, 'Nothing. Having a rest.'

With an inward sigh, Sam realised that this wasn't going to be easy. Discussing anything of any real importance with Izzy had *never* been easy and the signals she was sending out at this moment were unpromising to say the least.

But he was damned if he was going to give up without having even tried. Not when he'd come this far . . .

'You haven't told me about Jericho,' he reminded her, nudging her feet out of the way and making himself comfortable on the sofa next to her.

Oh God, thought Izzy, close to despair, not more polite conversation.

'It isn't exactly the most riveting gossip in the world,' she said with a dismissive shrug. 'He got some poor bitch pregnant, that's all. She gave birth to three puppies last week.'

'Hmm. It sounded more riveting the way Katerina told it.'

497

Izzy glared at him. 'If you already knew, why did you bother to ask me?'

'Well, we've already discussed the weather...'

He was almost-but-not-quite smiling. Realizing that he was making fun of her, she snapped back, 'Don't patronize me.'

'Don't sulk then,' Sam replied easily. 'Izzy, look. It doesn't have to be like this. I thought we were supposed to be friends, at least.'

The more *reasonable* he was, the more she hated it. Childishly, she said, 'Real friends send Christmas cards.'

He started to laugh. 'You didn't send me one.'

'Only because you didn't send me one first.'

'Izzy, is that *really* what this is all about?' Rising to his feet, taking out his wallet, he said, 'Would you like me to go out to the shops and buy you a Christmas card now?'

'Oh, shut up!' she howled, determined not to smile. He had always been able to *do* this to her and she needed so badly to remain in control...

But Sam had crossed to the mantelpiece, upon which was stacked a sheaf of the glossy brochures extolling the delights of the Laugharne Hotel. Removing the top from his pen he sat down beside her once more, wrote 'Happy Christmas, Izzy' across the front of one of the brochures, then opened it up and scrawled on the inside page, 'With all my love, Sam.' 'There,' he said, his expression deadpan once more. 'Better?'

But it wasn't better. Izzy, awash with jealousy and realizing that she was once again in danger of bursting into tears, muttered, 'You can't put that. You mustn't put "*all* my love". What would your girlfriend think?'

'My girlfriend.' Sam paused, giving the matter some thought. Then he said, 'What girlfriend?'

Izzy flushed. She was sailing close to the wind now, but the urge to say it . . . and the masochistic need to know what Miss America was really like . . . was irresistible.

'I'd heard you'd got one,' she said, her heart hammering against her ribs, but her tone carefully casual. 'Is she nice?'

But Sam no longer appeared to be listening. Instead, having removed the impromptu greetings card from Izzy's grasp, he was scrawling an additional line below his name.

Barely able to contain her impatience, Izzy repeated, 'Sam. Is she nice?'

'Who?'

'You know damn well who!'

He sighed and handed her the card. 'I can't imagine where you've been getting this highly dubious information from, but there *is* no girlfriend. If you must know, I've been shamefully celibate for the last three months. Now, come on, open your Christmas card and read the last line.'

It said, 'PS Why don't you stop arguing and just say you'll marry me?'

The words swam on the page as Izzy's eyes filled with tears, but this time she made no effort to hold them back. Sam was telling her everything she'd wanted to hear. The trouble was, he was *lying* . . .

'I spoke to her on the phone,' she said, her voice barely above a whisper. 'I phoned you and she was there at your apartment. Sam, I realise that she never did pass on the message for you to ring me back, so you can't be blamed for that. But the second time I phoned, you were there in bed with her. The two of you were . . . together. So please don't try and pretend you've been celibate for three months because I *heard* you . . . and I can't bear the fact that you're telling me lies!'

Sam was silent for several seconds. Finally, he said, 'Which number did you ring?'

'Oh, shut up,' wailed Izzy. 'It was *your* number.'

He reeled it off. When she nodded – because for some ridiculous reason it had remained indelibly imprinted on her mind – he smiled.

'That's where I used to live,' said Sam gently. 'I sold it eight weeks ago. To a TV producer called Sam Hirsch.'

Izzy stopped crying. She stopped breathing. She couldn't remember how to breathe . . . When she was able to speak, she said, 'Are you sure?'

His dark eyebrows lifted. 'Well, I'm fairly sure. And I used the money from the sale of the apartment to pay off the debts at the club . . . But if you wanted to double-check, you could always phone the Hirsches and ask them yourself.'

Every detail of the nightmare thirty-hour trip to New York was hurtling through Izzy's mind: sixteen hours of flying, that beastly cab driver, the sheer torture of sitting in her hotel room waiting for the phone to ring, and then the ensuing anguish . . .

'Oh, Sam,' she said weakly, gazing at him in exasperation, 'why didn't you *tell* anyone you'd moved?'

'I did,' he replied with mock indignation. 'When I sent Gina a Christmas card I gave her my new number and address. All you had to do was ask her.'

'I flew all that way for nothing.'

'You mean you were *in* New York when you called me?'

Izzy closed her eyes for a moment, unable to believe this was really happening. She nodded.

'Well, this is encouraging news.' Intrigued, Sam said, 'Does this mean you actually wanted to see me?'

'Maybe.' Her tone was cautious, but the corners of her mouth were beginning to twitch. 'Oh bloody hell, Sam! Do I have to spell it out? Yes, I flew to New York because I wanted to see you and managed to make a complete idiot of myself in the process. There, I've said it. Are you happy now?'

'Maybe,' he mimicked gently, grinning and pulling her at long last into his arms. 'Although I'll be a lot happier when you've said you'll marry me.'

Izzy's lower lip was starting to tremble again. He kissed it, very briefly, then drew back and gazed into her brown eyes, his expression this time deadly serious.

'I mean it, Izzy. I've had three months to think about it, and it's the only answer. I don't want anybody else. I can't imagine *ever* wanting anyone else. I know now you were trying to be sensible when you told me I'd want children of my own, but that's simply no longer an issue. *I* know I'd rather be married to you and not have children, than marry somebody else and . . .' He shrugged, dismissing the argument. 'Well, it would be totally pointless.'

'Oh.' Suffused with love, Izzy clung to him. In a moment, when she was able to think coherently once more, she would break the news to him that Mother Nature had decreed a change of plan.

But Sam's arms, around her waist, were making a

voyage of discovery of their own.

'Your zip's undone,' he said, looking perplexed and glancing down at her short, topaz-yellow velvet skirt. 'What's the matter, are you ill?'

'We . . . ll,' Izzy began, but at that moment the door to the blue-and-white sitting room flew open.

'There you are,' declared Katerina accusingly. 'For heaven's sake, you two! I've been looking *everywhere* for you.'

It wasn't the most well timed of interruptions. Izzy, struggling to pull herself together, said, 'Why, is something the matter?'

'Of course not.' Advancing towards them, Katerina held out a sealed brown envelope. 'We wondered where you were, that's all. Doug's only just remembered that he was supposed to give this to Sam, so I offered to deliver it.'

'Looks like one of my tax demands,' joked Izzy feebly. Then, glimpsing the loopy, uneven scrawl on the front of the envelope, she said in surprise, 'That's Lucille's writing.'

Katerina winked at Sam. 'Lucky old you, then. It's probably an indecent proposition. Now that Doug's out of the picture she's fixing her sights on the next best thing.'

'Thanks,' said Sam drily, tearing open the envelope and removing a once-crumpled, now flattened-out sheet of paper. Then he frowned. 'But Lucille didn't write this.'

With a shriek, Izzy made a lunge for it. 'You mustn't read that!' she yelled, struggling to wrench the half-finished letter from his grasp. 'It's mine! I was just about to *tell* you—'

'It says Dear Sam,' he pointed out, effortlessly fending

her off and skimming the contents in seconds. Then, his expression changing, he turned his gaze back to Izzy.

'Is this true?'

Trust Lucille, she thought, to take matters blithely into her own meddling Irish hands. Carefully keeping a straight face, she said, 'Maybe.'

Oblivious to the presence of his future stepdaughter, Sam dropped the letter to the floor and pulled Izzy into his arms. This time the kiss he gave her wasn't brief.

'Young love,' said Katerina cheerfully. Unembarrassed, she perched on the edge of the coffee table and waited patiently for the grown-ups to finish. Sam, she decided, had evidently taken notice of the advertising posters exhorting him to Experience Izzy Van Asch's Kiss.

'OK,' she said eventually, fixing Sam with a determined gaze. 'This is all very well, but before it goes any further there's something I really must ask you.'

'What's that?' said Sam, his expression suitably deferential. Hidden from Katerina's view, his left hand was surreptitiously exploring the gaping zip at the back of Izzy's skirt.

'I need to know,' said Katerina slowly, 'whether or not your intentions towards my mother are honourable.'

# Sheer Mischief

To Lydia with my love

## Acknowledgements

A huge thank you to Mum, as ever, for all those hours at the word processor; Dad, the only one who understands it; Tina, babysitter extraordinaire; and Pearl, Sarah and Cino who helped too.

# Chapter 1

Running away from her boring old fiancé had seemed such a brilliant idea at the time. It was just a shame, Maxine decided, that running out of boring old petrol four hours later should be turning out to be so much less fun.

'Oh please, don't be mean,' she begged, but the middle-aged petrol-pump attendant remained unmoved.

'Look,' he repeated heavily, 'you've filled your car up with twenty pounds' worth o' petrol. Now you tell me you've only got seventy-three pence on you. You ain't got no credit cards, no cheque book, nor no identification. So I don't have no choice but to call the police.'

Maxine's credit cards, house keys and cheque book were back in London, lurking somewhere at the bottom of the Thames. Exasperated beyond belief by the man's uncharitable attitude, she wondered how and when the inhabitants of Cornwall had ever managed to acquire their reputation for friendliness. As far as she was concerned, it was a filthy lie.

'But I'll pay you back, I promise I will,' she said in wheedling tones. 'This is just silly. I don't know why you won't trust me . . .'

1

The attendant had a glass eye which glinted alarmingly in the sunlight. Fixing her with the bloodshot good one and evidently immune to the charms of hapless blondes with beguiling smiles, he exhaled heavily and reached for the phone.

'Because it's seven o'clock in the morning,' he replied, as if she were being deliberately stupid. 'Because you can't pay for your petrol. And because you're wearing a wedding dress.'

Janey Sinclair, peering out of her bedroom window overlooking Trezale's picturesque high street, was embarrassed. She'd had twenty-six years in which to get used to being shown up by her younger sister but it still happened. What was really unfair, she thought sleepily, was the fact that none of it ever seemed to faze Maxine.

'Sshh,' she hissed, praying that none of her neighbours were yet awake. 'Wait there, I'm coming down.'

'Bring your purse!' yelled Maxine, who didn't care about the neighbours. 'I need twenty pounds.'

What Maxine really needed, Janey decided, was strangling.

'OK,' she said, opening the front door and wearily surveying the scene. 'Don't tell me. You're eloping with our local policeman and you need the money for the marriage licence. Tom, are you sure you're doing the right thing here? Your wife's going to be furious when she finds out, and my sister's a lousy cook.'

Tom Lacey, Trezale's local policeman, had been married for ten months and his wife was due to give birth at any moment, yet he was blushing with pleasure like a

2

schoolboy. Janey heaved an inward sigh and wished she'd kept her mouth shut.

Maxine, however, simply grinned. 'I did offer. He turned me down.'

Janey pulled her creased, yellow and white dressing gown more tightly around her waist. That was something else about Maxine, she always managed to upstage everyone around her. And although it was still relatively early on a Sunday morning, it was also mid-July, practically the height of the holiday season. Tourists, unwilling to waste a moment of their precious time in Cornwall, were making their way along the high street, heading for the beach but pausing to watch the diversion outside the florist's shop. They couldn't quite figure out what was going on, but it looked interesting. One small boy, deeply tanned and wearing only white shorts, deck shoes and a camera slung around his neck, was even taking surreptitious photographs.

'So why *are* you wearing a wedding dress?' she demanded, then flapped her arms in a gesture of dismissal. Maxine's explanations tended to be both dramatic and long-winded. 'No, don't bother. Here's the twenty pounds. Can we go inside now or are you really under arrest?'

But Maxine, having whisked the money from her sister's grasp and popped the rolled-up notes into her cleavage, was already sliding back into the passenger seat of the panda. 'My car's being held hostage,' she said cheerfully. 'Tom just has to take me to pay the ransom first, but we'll be back in forty minutes. Tom, are you as hungry as I am?'

3

'Well . . .' Tom, who was always hungry, managed a sheepish grin.

'There, you see. We're both absolutely starving,' declared Maxine, gazing with longing at the array of switches studding the dashboard and wondering which of them controlled the siren. Then, fastening her seatbelt and flashing her sister a dazzling grin, she added, 'But you mustn't go to too much trouble, darling. Just bacon and eggs will be fine.'

Tom, to his chagrin, was called away instead to investigate the case of the stolen parasol outside the Trezale Bay Hotel.

'Toast and Marmite?' Maxine looked disappointed but bit into a slice anyway. Rearranging her voluminous white skirts and plonking herself down on one of the wrought-iron chairs on the tiny, sunlit patio, she kicked off her satin shoes and wriggled her toes pleasurably against the warm flagstones.

'Why don't you change into something less . . . formal?' Janey, who was wearing white shorts and a primrose-yellow camisole top, poured the coffee. 'Where's your suitcase, in the car?'

Maxine, having demolished the first slice of thickly buttered toast, leaned across and helped herself to a second.

'No money, no suitcase,' she said with a shrug. 'No nothing! You'll just have to lend me something of yours.'

Janey had looked forward all week to this Sunday, when nothing was precisely what she had planned on doing. A really good lie-in, she thought dryly, followed by hours of blissful, uninterrupted *nothing*. And instead, she had this.

'Go on then,' she said as Maxine stirred three heaped spoonsful of sugar into her coffee cup and shooed away an interested wasp. 'Tell me what's happened. And remember, you woke me up for this so it had better be good.'

She had to concede, ten minutes later, that it was pretty good. Three years at drama school might not have resulted in the dreamed-of glittering acting career, but Maxine certainly knew how to make the most of telling a story. In the course of describing the events of the previous night her hands, eyebrows – even her bare feet – became involved.

'. . . So there we were, expected to arrive at this fancy-dress party in less than an hour, and bloody Maurice hadn't even remembered to tell me it was on. Well, being Maurice, he phoned his mother and she was round in a flash with her old wedding dress tucked under her skinny arm. It's a Schiaparelli, can you believe? So we ended up at this chronic company party as a bride-and-sodding-groom and everyone was sniggering like mad because the thought of us ever actually tying the knot was evidently too funny for words. And I realized then that they were right – I didn't want to spend the rest of my life pretending to be a dutiful banker's wife and having to socialize with a bunch of boring stuffed shirts. So I told Maurice it was over, and then I told the stuffed shirts and their smirking wives exactly what I thought of them too. Poor Maurice; as far as he was concerned, that really was the last straw. It didn't matter that I'd humiliated him, but insulting all

5

the directors was too much. Janey, I've never seen him so mad! He dragged me backwards out of the hotel and told me I wasn't worth his mother's old slippers, let alone her precious wedding dress. I screamed back that as he was such an old woman *he* should be wearing the bloody dress! Then I kicked him because he wouldn't let go of me, so he called me a spoilt, spiteful, money-grabbing delinquent and chucked my evening bag into the Thames.' She paused, then concluded mournfully, 'It had everything in it. My favourite Estée Lauder eye-shadow palette . . . *everything*.'

All the toast had gone. Janey, reminding herself that it didn't matter, she was supposed to be on a diet anyway, cradled her lukewarm coffee in both hands and remarked, 'Bit daring, for Maurice. So then what did you do?'

'Well, luckily we'd taken my car. All my keys were in the river, of course, but I've always kept a spare in the glove compartment and the driver's door is a doddle – you can open it with a hair slide. I just jumped in, drove off and left Maurice standing in the middle of the road with his mouth going like a guppy. But I knew I couldn't break into the flat – he's got that place alarmed to the eyeballs – so I headed for the M4 instead. And because the one thing I *did* have was a full tank of petrol, I thought I'd come and visit my big sister.'

With a grin, Maxine ran her fingers through her tumbling, gold-blond hair and shook it back over her shoulders. 'I'm seeking sanctuary, darling. Just call me Quasimodo.'

'Don't call me darling,' grumbled Janey, who hated it. 'And whatever you do, don't call me *big*.'

But it was no good. Maxine wasn't going to go away. Neither – despite having driven all night from London to Cornwall – did she apparently have any intention of falling asleep.

Janey, who loved but frequently despaired of her sister, followed her upstairs and sat on the edge of the bed whilst Maxine carried out a brisk raid on the wardrobe. She wondered what Maxine had ever done to deserve a twenty-two-inch waist.

'These'll be fine.' Forcing another hole through the tan leather belt, she patted the size fourteen khaki shorts with approval and admired her reflection in the mirror. The white shirt, expertly knotted above the waist, showed off her flat brown midriff and her dark eyes sparkled. 'There, ready to face the world again. Or dear old Trezale, anyway. Where shall we go for lunch?'

'You don't have any money,' Janey reminded her with a sinking heart, but Maxine was already halfway to the bedroom door.

'I'll sort something out with the bank tomorrow,' she replied airily. 'They'll understand when I tell them what that pig of an ex-boyfriend of mine did with my cheque book. Now come along, Janey, cheer up and tell me where we can meet all the most gorgeous men these days. Is the Dune Bar still good?'

'He wasn't your boyfriend,' said Janey, wondering at the ease with which Maxine had apparently discarded him from her life. 'He was your fiancé.'

Maxine looked momentarily surprised. Then, waving her left hand in the air so that the large, square-cut emerald caught the light, she said gleefully, 'Of course he was! How clever of you to think of it. If the bank gets stuffy I can flog the ring, instead.'

'You think I'm a heartless bitch, don't you?'

They were sitting out on the crowded terrace of the Dune Bar. Janey tried not to notice the way practically every male was lusting after Maxine. Maxine, who genuinely appeared not to have noticed – it was a particular speciality of hers – sipped her lager and looked contrite.

'I *know* you're a heartless bitch,' said Janey with a faint smile. 'But at least you're honest about it. That's something, I suppose.'

'Don't try and make me feel guilty.' Maxine glanced down at her engagement ring. 'I didn't love Maurice, you know.'

'Surprise, surprise.'

'I liked him, though.' With a trace of defiance, she added, 'And I adored the fact that he had money. I think I managed to convince myself that ours would turn out to be like one of those arranged marriages, where love eventually grows. He was generous and kind, and I did so hate being broke . . .'

'But it didn't work out like that,' Janey observed, shielding her eyes with her forearm and gazing out over the sea. A pillarbox-red speedboat, skimming over the waves, was towing a water skier. Ridiculously, even after eighteen months, she still had to convince herself that it wasn't Alan before she could bring herself to look away.

'It might have worked, if Maurice hadn't been so boring.' Maxine shrugged, then grinned. 'And if I weren't so easily bored.'

Not for the first time, Janey wondered what it was like to be Maxine. Maybe her cool, calculating attitude to life wasn't such a bad thing after all. It might not be romantic, but at least it meant she spared herself the agonies of unrequited love and those endless, gut-wrenching months of despair.

I married for love, thought Janey, the cold emptiness invading her stomach as readily as it ever had. And look where it got me.

'Oh God,' cried Maxine, intuitively reading her sister's thoughts and grabbing her hand in consolation. 'I am a callous bitch! Now I've made you think about Alan.'

But Janey, managing a wry smile, shook her head. 'I think about him anyway. It's hardly something I'm likely to forget, after all.'

'I'm still an insensitive, clod-hopping prat,' insisted Maxine. Her expression contrite, she lowered her voice. 'And I haven't even asked how you're coping. Does it get better, or is it as hideous as ever?'

'Well, I'm not crying all over you.' Finishing her drink, Janey met her sister's concerned gaze and forced herself to sound cheerful. 'So that has to be an improvement, don't you think?'

'But it's still hard?'

'It *is* getting better,' she admitted. 'But the not knowing is the worst part of all. The awful limbo of not knowing what I am.' Pausing for a moment, she added bleakly, 'A widow or a deserted wife.'

# Chapter 2

They were married on the first of May, the happiest day of Janey's life.

'I'm sure there's something I'm supposed to be doing today.' Alan, emerging from beneath the navy blue duvet with his blond hair sticking up at angles, sounded puzzled. 'What is it, the dentist . . .? Ouch!'

But Janey didn't let go of his big toe. 'Much worse,' she mocked. 'Much, *much* worse.'

'Aaargh, I remember now! The Registry Office. And you should be covering your eyes, you shameless female. You aren't supposed to see the blushing groom on the morning of his wedding.'

'Too late, I've already seen you.' Whisking back the duvet, she surveyed him solemnly. 'All of you.'

Alan grinned and reached out for her, pulling her back into bed and unfastening the belt of her flimsy dressing gown. 'In that case we may as well have a quickie. One last, glorious, pre-marital quickie. How many hours before we're married, Miss Vaughan?'

Janey glanced at her watch. 'Three.'

'Hmm,' he murmured, rolling on top of her and kissing the frantically beating pulse at the base of her neck. 'In that case, we might even have time for two.'

Once they'd torn themselves away from the bedroom to complete the formalities, Janey found she adored every moment and every aspect of being married. Each morning when she woke up she almost had to pinch herself to check that it was all real. But it always was, thank God, and the sheer joy of being Mrs Sinclair showed no signs of waning.

She enjoyed looking after their tiny flat, experimenting with new recipes and socializing with his surf-crazy friends. And because she was only twenty-five years old she enjoyed above all else knowing that they had the rest of their lives to spend together. Nothing need ever change.

No body was ever found.

'But something *must* have happened to him.' Janey, grief-stricken yet dry-eyed, simply couldn't believe that it hadn't. In an effort to convince the police, she uttered the words for what seemed like the hundredth time. 'He's my husband . . . I know him . . . he wouldn't just *disappear*.'

The police, however, whilst sympathetic, were less convinced. Every year, they explained, hundreds of people in Britain with no apparent problems or reasons to disappear, did precisely that, leaving behind them distraught families, endless unanswerable questions and countless shattered lives.

Janey's life was certainly shattered. On a sunny afternoon in July, after just fourteen months of marriage, her beloved husband had vanished without trace. Nothing had been taken from the flat and there were no clues as to the reason for his disappearance.

11

During the first few frantic days she'd pinned all her hopes on an accident, not serious enough to be life-threatening, just a bang on the head resulting in temporary amnesia. At any moment, she had fantasized helplessly, the phone would ring and when she picked it up she would hear his dear, familiar voice.

But although the discovery of Alan's body was what she'd most dreaded, as the weeks dragged into months she found herself almost beginning to wish that it would happen. She felt like a murderer, even thinking such a thing, but at least it would be conclusive. The torture of not knowing would be over. And – most deeply shaming of all – she would be spared the humiliation of thinking that her husband had vanished because he could no longer tolerate his life with her.

Nobody else had ever voiced this possibility aloud, of course, but whenever she was feeling particularly vulnerable Janey was only too easily able to imagine what was uppermost in their minds. As time passed she found herself, in turn, the object of macabre curiosity, whispered gossip and pity. And it was hard to decide which of these was worst.

Maxine drifted into the shop at ten-thirty the following morning, yawning and clutching a mug of tea. 'God your sofa's uncomfortable,' she grumbled, rubbing her back.

Janey, who had been up for over five hours, lifted an armful of yellow irises into a bucket and slid them into position between the gypsophila and the white roses. The shop had been busier than usual and she still had three wreaths to make up before midday.

'Sorry,' she replied wryly. It would never occur to

Maxine to bring her a cup of tea as well.

But Maxine was still massaging her back and pulling faces. 'I'll be a cripple by the end of the week.'

'Are you really planning to stay?'

'Of course!' She looked surprised. 'I'm not going back to Maurice-the-Righteous, and there's nothing to keep me in London. Besides,' she added dreamily, 'I'd forgotten how lovely it is down here. Much nicer than smelly old London. I think a summer by the sea would do me the world of good.'

'Hmm.'

'Oh come on, Janey. Don't look at me like that! It'll be fun; we can cheer each other up.'

Having consulted the notes on her clipboard, Janey began sorting out the flowers for the wreaths. 'You'll be too busy complaining about your back to have any fun,' she said brusquely. 'And having to listen to your endless whingeing is hardly going to cheer me up.'

'You don't want me to stay?' Maxine looked hurt and Janey experienced a twinge of guilt.

'I do,' she protested as the shop door swung open and Paula, having completed the morning's deliveries, dropped the keys to the van on the counter. 'Of course I'd like you to stay. It's just that the flat's so small, and I don't have a spare bedroom.'

'I see.' Maxine shrugged 'Well, that's OK. I'll go and see Mum.'

Janey looked doubtful. Their mother would only complain that nothing cramped one's style more effectively than a stray daughter hanging around the place. And Thea Vaughan's highly individual lifestyle didn't take kindly to cramping. She wasn't exactly the slippers-and-home-made-sponge-cake type.

But Maxine knew that as well as she did, so Janey didn't bother to voice these thoughts. Instead, she said, 'And you'd need some kind of job.'

'Oh God.' Maxine was looking gloomier by the second. Working had never been one of her strong points. 'I suppose I would. But what on earth can I do?'

Paula, who was a lot more thoughtful than Maxine, returned from the kitchen with two mugs of tea.

'Paula, this is my sister Maxine,' said Janey, seizing one of the mugs with relief. 'Now, take a good look at her and tell me what kind of work she might be able to cope with.'

Maxine, perched on the stool next to the counter with her long brown legs stretched out before her, gave the young girl an encouraging smile. But nothing fazed Paula.

'Here in Trezale, you mean?' As requested, she studied Maxine for several seconds. 'Well, selling your body's out for a start. Too many giggling girlies on the beach at this time of year, giving it away for free.'

Maxine burst out laughing. 'That's too bad.'

'Seriously,' protested Janey, weaving fronds of fern into the circular mesh base of the first wreath.

'Bar work?'

'Ugh.' Maxine cringed, rejecting the idea at once. 'Too hard on the feet.'

'Hotel receptionist?' suggested Paula, unperturbed. 'The Abbey's advertising in the paper this week.'

But Maxine shook her head. 'I'd have to be polite to ghastly tourists.'

'Nannying.' Paula looked pleased with herself. 'The family my mother cleans for is losing theirs. You could be a nanny.'

Maxine looked amused. 'Oh no I couldn't.'

But Janey's interest was aroused by this item of news. 'That's an idea!' she exclaimed, temporarily abandoning the wreath. 'You'd be able to live in. That way, you'd have a job and a place to stay. Max, it'd be great!'

'Apart from one small problem,' replied Maxine flatly. 'If there's one thing I hate more than tourists, it's children. Children and babies and nappies. Yuk!' she added with a shudder of revulsion. 'Especially nappies.'

'These two are a bit old for nappies,' said Paula, ever practical. 'Josh is nine and Ella's seven. I've met them a few times. They're nice kids.'

'And they'd be at school during the day,' put in Janey, her tone encouraging.

But Maxine, sensing that she was being ganged up on, pulled a face. 'I'm just not the nannyish type. I mean, for heaven's sake, do I look like Julie Andrews?'

Losing patience, Janey returned her attention to work. 'OK, you've made your point. You probably wouldn't have got the job anyway,' she added, unable to resist the dig. 'Most people prefer trained nannies and there'd be enough of those queuing up when they realize who they'll be working for.'

Needled by the insult, Maxine's brown eyes glittered. 'Why, who is it?' she demanded, ready to find fault with any prospective employer who wouldn't choose her.

'Guy Cassidy.' Janey shook droplets of water from the stems of a handful of yellow freesias. 'He moved into

Trezale House just over a year ago. He's a—'

'Photographer!' squealed Maxine, looking as if she was about to topple off her stool. 'Guy Cassidy,' she repeated faintly. '*The* Guy Cassidy? Janey, are you having me on?'

*Bingo*, thought Janey, exchanging glances with Paula and hiding her smile.

'Of course not.' She looked affronted. 'Why ever should I? And what difference does it make anyway? You hate kids. You just said so, yourself.'

'What difference does it make?' echoed Maxine, her eyebrows arching in disbelief. 'Janey, are you quite mad? It makes all the difference in the world. That man is *gorgeous . . .*'

# Chapter 3

'God, this is hard work,' complained Guy, crumpling up yet another sheet of paper and lobbing it in the general direction of the wastepaper basket at the side of the bed. Fixing his son and daughter with a stern expression, he added, 'And it's too early in the day for this kind of thing. I don't know why you two can't write your own advert, anyway.'

Ella, squirming at his side, nudged his arm. 'Daddy, I can't spell!'

'And you hate those kind of adverts,' chided Josh, who was sprawled across the foot of the bed. Running his finger down the 'Help Wanted' columns of the slim magazine in which the finished advertisement would be placed, he found a shining example and began to read aloud in an exaggerated baby voice.

'Hello, my name is Bunty and I am two yearth old. I need thomebody to look after me whilst Mummy and Daddy are working. We live in a big houthe in Thurrey, with a thwimming pool. You muthn't thmoke . . .'

'OK, OK,' said Guy with resignation. 'So it wasn't one of my better ideas. Maybe I'll just put, "Two spoilt brats require stern battleaxe of a nanny to feed them cold porridge and beat them daily." How about that?'

Ella giggled. 'I don't like cold porridge.'

'You should say, "Widow with two children needs kind nanny",' suggested Josh, who had been giving the matter some thought.

'Widower,' Guy corrected him. 'Widows are female. Men are called widowers.'

'I know why you're a man,' Ella chimed in. Josh, at the foot of the bed, grinned.

It was too early in the day for this, too. Guy, closing his eyes for a moment and mentally bracing himself, said, 'Go on then. Why am I a man?'

'Because you haven't any bosoms on your chest,' declared his daughter with an air of importance. 'And you don't wear a bra.'

It was four-thirty when the doorbell rang. Berenice, the soon-to-be-married departing nanny, had taken Ella into St Ives for the afternoon on a shopping trip. Guy was busy in the darkroom, developing black and white prints, when Josh knocked on the door and informed him that he had a visitor.

'She said it was important,' he told Guy, his forehead creasing in a frown as he struggled to remember. 'I don't know who she is, but I'm sure I've seen her somewhere before.'

Maxine was standing before the sitting-room window, admiring the stupendous view of clifftops and sea. When she turned and smiled at Guy, and came towards him with her hand outstretched, he realized at once why his son had thought her familiar yet been unable to place her.

'Mr Cassidy?' she said demurely. 'My name is Vaughan. Maxine Vaughan. It's kind of you to see me.'

She was here in his house, thought Guy with inward amusement. He didn't really have much choice. But he was, at the same time, intrigued. Maxine Vaughan was an undeniably attractive girl in her mid-twenties. Her long, corn-blond hair was pulled back from her face in a neat plait, her make-up carefully unobtrusive. The dark green jacket and skirt were a couple of sizes too big for her and she was wearing extremely sensible shoes. It was all very convincing, very plausible. Guy was impressed by the extent of the effort she had made.

'My pleasure,' he replied easily, taking her proffered hand and registering short fingernails, a clear nail polish and – oh dear, first sign of a slip-up – a genuine Cartier wristwatch. 'How can I help you, Miss Vaughan?'

Maxine took a deep, steadying breath and hoped her palms weren't damp. She'd known, of course, that Guy Cassidy was gorgeous, but in the actual flesh he was even more devastatingly attractive than she'd imagined. With those thickly lashed, deep blue eyes, incredible cheekbones and white teeth offset by a dark tan, he was almost too perfect. But the threat of perfection was redeemed by a quirky smile, slightly crooked eyebrows and that famously tousled black hair.

He exuded sex appeal without even trying, she realized. He possessed an indefinable charisma. Not to mention a body to die for.

'I'm hoping we can help each other,' said Maxine. Then, because her knees were on the verge of giving way, she added, 'Would you mind if I sat down?'

'Please do.' Having concluded that she must be either a journalist or a model desperate for a break, Guy gently mimicked her formal style of speech. Either way, he would give her no more than ten minutes; he was all for a spot of personal enterprise but her unexpected arrival wasn't exactly well timed. He had work to do, phone calls to make and a nine-year-old son demanding to be taken for a swim before dinner.

He glanced at his watch. Maxine, sensing his veiled impatience, took another deep breath and plunged in. 'Right, Mr Cassidy, I understand you'll shortly be requiring a replacement nanny for your children. And since I myself am an experienced nanny, I'd like to offer my services.'

It was a good start, but the rest of the interview wasn't going according to plan, she realized several minutes later. And she hadn't the faintest idea why not.

On the surface, at least, Guy Cassidy was asking the appropriate questions and she was supplying faultless replies, but at the same time she had a horrible feeling he wasn't taking her seriously. Worse, that he was inwardly laughing at her.

'They're in Buenos Aires now,' she continued valiantly, as he studied the glowing references which she'd slaved for an entire hour to produce. 'Otherwise I'd still be with them, of course. The children were adorable and Angelo and Marisa treated me more as a friend than an employee.'

But her potential employer, instead of appearing suitably impressed, was glancing once more at his watch.

'I'm sure they did,' he replied. Rising to his feet, he

shot her a brief smile. 'And it was thoughtful of you to consider us, Miss . . . er . . . Vaughan. But I don't think you're quite what we're looking for.'

Maxine's guard slipped. 'Why not?' she wailed, remaining rooted to her chair. 'I've shown you my references. They're brilliant! What can possibly be wrong with me?'

Guy, enjoying himself, maintained a serious expression. 'You're too dowdy.'

'But I don't have to be dowdy,' said Maxine wildly. She knew she shouldn't have worn Janey's horrible suit. 'I'm not usually dowdy at all!'

'OK.' Gesturing for her to calm down, he continued. 'You're too prim and proper.'

'I am not prim!' Maxine almost shrieked. 'Please, you have to believe me. These aren't my own clothes . . . I'm not the least bit proper either and I *hate* these shoes!'

But Guy hadn't finished. Fixing her with his deadpan gaze, he said remorselessly, 'And you're a liar, Miss Vaughan. Which wouldn't set a particularly good example to my children. I'm afraid I can't employ someone who is dishonest.'

Maxine felt her cheeks burn. He was bluffing, he had to be. Stiffly, she replied, 'I don't know what you mean.'

'Don't you?' This time he actually smiled. 'In that case, wait here. I'll just go and find my son.'

He returned less than two minutes later with the boy in tow. Although nine-year-old Josh Cassidy had straight, white-blond hair in contrast to his father, Maxine was struck by the similarity of their extraordinary dark blue eyes.

'Hello, Josh,' she said, dredging up a brave smile and wondering why he was staring at her in that odd way.

But Guy was handing his son a large brown envelope. 'Here,' he said casually. 'I developed that film you gave me earlier. Take a look at these prints, Josh, and tell me how you think they've turned out.'

Maxine spotted the offending item a fraction of a second before Josh. Having tipped the photographs out of the envelope and spread them across the coffee table, he was still studying them intently, one at a time, when she let out a strangled cry and made a grab for it.

Guy, standing behind her, whisked the photograph from her grasp and handed it, in turn, to his son.

'Golly,' said Josh with a grin. Staring at Maxine, who was by this time redder than ever, he added, 'I thought I knew you from somewhere!'

'And the moral of this story,' she muttered sulkily, 'is never trust a member of the *paparazzi*.'

'You look different today.' Studying the glossy ten-by-eight at close quarters and looking pleased with himself, he said, 'I think I prefer you in the white dress. It's a good photograph, isn't it?'

It was a bit too good for Maxine's liking. No wonder Guy Cassidy had been able to recognize her. There she was, captured for posterity in that stupid wedding gown, laughing as she clambered out of the panda car and not even realizing that her skirts had bunched up to reveal white stocking tops and a glimpse of suspender. And the expression on Tom-the-policeman's face, she observed with resignation, didn't help. He was positively leering.

'Hang on a minute.' Josh was looking puzzled again.

'If you got married yesterday, why aren't you on a honeymoon?'

'I wasn't getting married,' said Maxine impatiently. '*Or* arrested. It was a fancy-dress party, that's all. Then I ran out of petrol on the way home and the policeman gave me a lift.' Fixing Guy with a mutinous glare, she added, 'It was nothing sinister, for heaven's sake.'

He shrugged. 'Nevertheless, I'm sure you understand why I can't consider you for the job. I'm sorry, Miss Vaughan, but I do have the moral welfare of my children to take into account.'

'At least I'm not dowdy and prim,' she muttered in retaliation.

'Oh no.' This time, as he drew a slim white envelope from his shirt pocket, he laughed. 'I'll grant you that. But I'm afraid I have work to do, so maybe I could ask my son to show you out. And Josh, I've written out the advert. If you run down with it now, you'll just catch the last post.'

'Well?' said Guy, when his son returned twenty minutes later.

'She gave me five pounds and a Cornetto.' Josh looked momentarily worried. 'Was that enough?'

Amused by his son's concern, Guy ruffled his blond hair. 'Oh, I'd say so. Five pounds and a Cornetto in exchange for a first-class stamp and an empty envelope. It sounds like a fair enough swap to me.'

# Chapter 4

The response to the advertisement when it eventually appeared the following week wasn't startling, but it was manageable. Guy preferred to do his own hunting as a result of the futile experiences he'd had three years earlier when he'd tried using an agency. Having also learned to expect applications from star-struck girls and would-be second wives, he had omitted his name from the advertisement.

But last time he had struck lucky. Berenice, profoundly unimpressed by his celebrity status, had fitted the bill to perfection. Stolid, hard-working and not the least bit glamorous, what she lacked in sparkle she'd more than made up for in dependability. Guy, whose work required him to travel abroad at short notice, was able to do so without a qualm, safe in the knowledge that his children would be competently looked after by someone who cared for them and who would never let him down.

It had come as something of a shock, therefore, when Berenice had shyly informed him that she was shortly to be married, and that since her future husband had been offered a job in Newcastle, she would be leaving Trezale.

Guy hadn't even been aware of the existence of a man in her life, but discretion had always been one of Berenice's major attributes – as he had himself on numerous occasions had cause to be thankful for. The courtship, it appeared, had been conducted on her days off. And although she was sorry to be leaving, she now had her own life to pursue. She hoped he wouldn't have too much trouble finding a replacement.

Interviewing the half dozen or so applicants, however, was both tedious and time-consuming. What Guy wanted was a clone of Berenice with maybe a sense of humour thrown in for good measure.

What he got, instead, was a succession of girls in whom it was only too easy to find fault. Josh and Ella, dutifully trotted out to meet each of them in turn, were equally critical.

'She smelled,' said Ella, wrinkling her nose in memory of Mary-from-Exeter.

'She laughed like a sheep,' Josh observed bluntly when Doreen from Doncaster had departed.

Neither of them could make head nor tail of Gudren-from-Sweden's singsong accent.

'She's all right, I suppose.' Josh, referring to another contender, sounded doubtful. 'But why did she have a bottle of vodka in her handbag?'

They finally settled on Maureen-from-Wimbledon, a pale, eager-to-please twenty-five-year-old who was keen to move in and start work as soon as possible. Carefully highlighting her good points – she didn't smell, possess an irritating laugh or an incomprehensible foreign accent – Guy prayed the children wouldn't make mincemeat of her before she had a chance to find her feet. She barely seemed capable of looking after herself, but maybe she'd just been too nervous to create a dazzling first impression.

And at least, he thought dryly, recalling the very first candidate, she hadn't fluttered inch-long eyelashes at him, surreptitiously edged up her short skirt and treated him to a flash of emerald-green knickers each time she'd crossed and re-crossed her legs.

Janey was working in the shop when Guy Cassidy and his children walked in.

'I need some flowers,' he said without preamble, removing his dark glasses and surveying the myriad buckets lined up against the wall. 'For a wedding reception next Saturday. If I place the order now, would you be able to bring them to my house on the Friday afternoon and arrange them?'

'Of course I would.' Janey was delighted. Men for whom money was no object were definitely her kind of customer. Reaching for her clipboard she said, 'Tell me what type of arrangements you have in mind and which kind of flowers you think you'd like.'

Flowers, however, evidently weren't Guy Cassidy's strong point. Looking momentarily helpless, he frowned and said, 'Well, blue ones?'

'Berenice likes daffodils,' supplied Ella, tugging his white shirt sleeve. 'Remember? We picked her some for her birthday and she said they were her favourite.'

Janey had already guessed that the flowers were for

Berenice's wedding but now that Guy's daughter had given her the excuse she needed, she raised her eyebrows and said, 'You mean Berenice Taylor? Oh, I'm doing her bridal bouquet.'

'Put it on my bill,' said Guy casually, producing his wallet and pulling out a wad of twenties. With a self-deprecating smile he added, 'She's been our nanny for the last three years. Holding the reception at our house is my present to her.'

'How lovely.' Janey returned his smile, then gave Ella an apologetic shrug. 'I'm afraid daffodils are out of season now, but maybe we could see which flowers Berenice has chosen for her bouquet and work from there. I'll have to check to be sure, but I think she decided on a yellow and white colour scheme. Yes, that's it . . . white roses and sweet peas with mimosa.'

Guy Cassidy didn't even flinch when she eventually wrote down the estimated cost of the work involved.

'As long as it looks good,' he said good-humouredly, dealing the notes on to the counter. Then, as an apparent afterthought, he glanced down at his children and added, 'Actually, whilst we're here, why don't you two pick out a bunch of something-or-other for your new nanny? She's arriving tomorrow afternoon and some nice flowers will make her feel welcome.'

Josh liked the green, earthy smell of the shop but he was bored sick with flowers.

'They haven't got dandelions or deadly nightshade,' he said, his tone dismissive.

'Or stinging nettles,' put in Ella with a smirk.

Poor new nanny, thought Janey. Without speaking, she

selected a generous bunch of baby-pink spray carnations, wrapped them in pink-and-silver paper and calmly handed them to Josh.

Appalled, he said, 'Boys don't carry flowers,' and shoved them into Ella's unsuspecting arms.

Janey, watching the expression on his face, burst out laughing.

And Guy, who had in turn been watching her, said, 'Of course. You're Maxine Vaughan's sister.'

'Oh help!' said Janey. 'Not necessarily. Not if it means you cancelling the order.'

He looked amused. 'Don't panic, I don't think I could face the prospect of going into another shop and starting all over again.'

'But how did you know?' She flushed. 'We aren't a bit alike.'

Tilting his head to one side and studying her in greater detail, he disagreed. 'Physically, there are similarities. She's skinnier . . . blonder . . . wears more make-up than you do, but the resemblance is still there. And you have the same laugh.'

This must all be part of the famous Cassidy charm, thought Janey. By cleverly reversing the usual comparisons he had actually managed to make her sound more attractive than Maxine. What a neat trick.

'And at least you've managed to find a new nanny.' Changing the subject, she nodded at the gift-wrapped carnations. With an encouraging smile at Josh and Ella, she said, 'Is she nice?'

'She's a wimp,' replied Josh flatly.

'But honest,' Guy interjected, shooting him a warning

look before returning his attention to Janey. 'Unlike your sister.'

'Look, Maxine isn't as bad as you think,' she bridled, springing instinctively to her defence. 'She really wanted to work for you. And children adore her. If you ask me, you could have done a lot worse.'

'Of course children adore her,' drawled Guy. 'She bribes them with money and ice cream.'

Josh brightened. 'I liked her. The lady in the wedding dress, you mean? She was good fun.'

'She had good references too,' Guy remarked tersely, 'but that still doesn't make her ideal nanny material. Has she found another job yet?'

Janey shook her head. Maxine's efforts in that department had been half-hearted to say the least. 'Not yet.'

'Hardly surprising,' said Guy, his blue eyes narrowing with amused derision. 'Tell her from me, the next time she writes out her own references not to use violet ink. At least, not if she's planning to trot off to the interview with a smudge of it on the inside of her wrist.'

# Chapter 5

Janey was leaning into the back of the van, stretching for the box of flowers which had slid up to the front and wedged itself behind the passenger seat, when Bruno gave her sticking-out bottom a friendly pat.

'You'll do that gorgeous body of yours an injury,' he said, nudging her out of the way and taking over. 'Come on, leave it to me.'

She flushed and smiled, and glanced quickly over her shoulder in case anyone was watching. Bruno, a notorious flirt, didn't mean anything by the playful gesture, but she still wouldn't like Nina to get the wrong idea.

Intercepting her glance as he carried the box into the empty restaurant, he winked. 'It's OK, she's still asleep.'

'*She* might be,' Janey protested. 'But you know what people are like for gossip around here.'

'Exactly. And they know what *I'm* like,' Bruno countered with an unrepentant grin. 'They'd be far more suspicious if I didn't lay a finger on you. Then they'd really know they had something to gossip about.'

He was pouring them both an espresso, as he invariably did when she arrived with the twice-weekly delivery of flowers for the restaurant.

It was ridiculous, thought Janey; since nothing had ever happened between them, there was no reason at all why she should feel guilty. But she felt it just the same, because no matter how many times she told herself that circumstances made him the most wildly unsuitable choice, her muddled emotions had taken charge and made the decision for her.

At the age of twenty-eight, she had developed a humiliating crush on Bruno Parry-Brent. And all she could do now was hope and pray that it would burn itself out before anything did happen.

In the meantime, however, it was so nice to feel human again, after all the endless months of aching deep-frozen nothingness. And Bruno was undeniably good company. A ladies' man in every sense of the word, he possessed that happy knack of being able to talk about anything under the sun. Even more miraculously he was a great listener as well, always genuinely interested in hearing other people's views. He paid attention, asked questions, never appeared bored.

It was, of course the great secret of his success with the opposite sex. Janey had watched him at work in the restaurant before now, weaving his magic in the simplest and most effective way possible. Real conversation with a real man was a powerful aphrodisiac and the women succumbed to it in droves, as Janey herself had done. But it was better this way, she felt, at least there was safety in numbers.

'New earrings,' he observed, bringing the tiny white cups of espresso to the table where she was sitting and leaning forward to examine them more closely. 'Very chic, Janey. Are those real pearls?'

'They're Maxine's.' Self-consciously, she fingered the slightly over-the-top earrings and prayed he wouldn't guess that he was the reason she was wearing them. Even Maxine had raised her eyebrows when she'd caught Janey digging around in her jewellery box. 'Earrings, lip gloss *and* mascara?' she'd remarked in arch tones. 'Darling, are you sure there isn't something you'd like to tell me?'

But diplomacy was another of Bruno's assets and, if he'd noticed such additional details himself, he was too nice to comment on them. Instead, stretching out in his seat and pushing his fingers through his long, sun-streaked hair, he said, 'I was going to ask you about Maxine. So you haven't managed to get rid of her yet?'

Janey pulled a face. 'She won't go, she won't look for work and she's so untidy: it's like living with a huge, unmanageable wolfhound.'

'But house-trained, presumably.' Bruno grinned. 'You haven't told me yet, what does she look like?'

'Maxine?' As she sipped her coffee, Guy Cassidy's words came back to her. 'Skinnier, blonder and noisier than me.' Then, because it sounded catty when she said it, she added shamefacedly, 'And much prettier.'

'Hmm. Well, we're pretty busy here at the moment. Maybe I could offer her a couple of evenings a week behind the bar.'

'She wouldn't do it,' said Janey hurriedly. 'Her feet, they'd ache . . .'

Bruno shrugged, dismissing the suggestion. 'Just a thought. But you'll have to bring her down here one evening, I'd like to meet her.'

Of course he would. And she could only too easily imagine Maxine's reaction when she, in turn, met Bruno Parry-Brent. They were two of a very particular kind.

'I will.' Janey tried not to sound unhappy, evasive. She had no intention of introducing them but Maxine had a talent for seeking out . . . well, talent, and Trezale wasn't a large town. It would surely be only a matter of time before she discovered Bruno for herself.

'Oh come on, cheer up.' He took her hand and gave it a reassuring squeeze. 'We all have our crosses to bear. Look at me, I have Nina!'

Janey tried not to laugh. He really was disgraceful.

'And where would you be without her?' she countered. Bruno and Nina made an odd couple, certainly, but after ten years together they still seemed happy enough in their own way. It wasn't something Bruno had ever discussed in detail but, as far as Janey could figure out, Nina didn't ask any questions and in return he was discreet. Indeed, although he was such a notorious flirt, she didn't even know whether he actually had affairs.

'Where would I be without Nina?' he repeated, teasing her. 'Probably in big trouble, because she'd have a contract out on me.'

Janey burst out laughing. Nina was the most placid woman she'd ever met. She doubted whether Nina could even summon the energy to read a contract, let alone organise taking one out.

'You'd be lost without her,' she told him in mock-severe tones. Rising to her feet, she smoothed her pink skirt over her hips. 'I'd better be getting back to the shop. Thanks for the coffee.'

Bruno grinned, unrepentant. 'Thanks for the pep talk. If you bring your sister down here maybe I'll be able to return the favour.'

'Hmm,' said Janey, renewing her vow to keep Maxine as far away from the restaurant as humanly possible. She could imagine what kind of favour he had in mind.

Maureen-from-Wimbledon wasn't on the four-o'clock train.

Guy, who had cut short a session in the darkroom and driven hell for leather in order to reach the station in time, couldn't believe it. If she'd missed the train at Paddington, she could have bloody well phoned and let him know, he thought furiously. And now what was he supposed to do, hang around on the platform and wait an hour for the next train to roll in?

But he hadn't waited and the would-be nanny hadn't phoned. By eight-thirty, when there was still no sign of her, he dialled the London number she had given him.

'Oh dear,' said Berenice, thankful that at least Ella, whom she had put to bed half an hour earlier, wasn't there to witness his language.

Josh, who was used to it, wondered if this meant his prayers had actually been answered. 'What is it, Dad?'

'No wonder she was in such a hurry to come and live down here,' Guy seethed, pouring himself a hefty Scotch and downing it in one go. 'I've just spoken to her mother. The lying, conniving bitch was arrested this morning and charged with credit-card-fraud! This is all I bloody need . . .'

'Does that mean she isn't going to be our nanny?' said

Josh, just to make absolutely sure.

Guy raised his eyes to heaven. 'I knew that expensive private education of yours would come in useful one day. Yes Josh, it means she isn't going to be your nanny.'

Hooray, thought Josh. Aloud he said, 'Oh. So what are we going to do?'

'Only one thing for it.' It was Wednesday night, Berenice was getting married on Saturday and he had to fly to Paris for a prestigious calendar shoot on Monday morning. 'We cancel Berenice's wedding.'

'You'll have to answer it,' said Maxine, when the doorbell rang. She was wearing bright orange toe separators and the crimson nail polish on her splayed toes was still wet. 'I look like a duck.'

'You look like a duck,' Guy Cassidy remarked when Janey showed him into the sitting room two minutes later.

Maxine, sitting on the floor with her bare legs stretched out in front of her, carried on eating her Mars bar. 'Just as well,' she replied equably. 'It means your insults roll off my back.'

Mystified by his unexpected appearance on her doorstep, Janey said, 'Would you like a cup of tea?'

'Thanks.' He smiled at her and lowered himself into an empty armchair. To Maxine, whose attention was fixed upon an old re-run of *Inspector Morse*, he said, 'Haven't you seen this one before? Lewis did it.'

Her gaze didn't waver from the television screen. With thinly veiled sarcasm she countered, 'Who's lying now?'

Janey fled to the safety of the kitchen.

'Go on then,' said Maxine eventually, when she had

finished the Mars bar and dropped the wrapper on to the coffee table. 'Tell me why you're here.'

There wasn't much point in beating around the bush. Guy said, 'The job. If you still want it, it's yours.'

'You've been stood up, then.'

He nodded.

'Gosh,' said Maxine, her expression innocent. 'You must be desperate.'

His mouth twitched as he allowed her her brief moment of triumph. 'I am.'

'And here am I, such an all-round bad influence . . .'

'You might well be,' he replied dryly, 'but your sister put in a few good words on your behalf and for some bizarre reason my son has taken a liking to you.'

'And you're desperate,' Maxine repeated for good measure, but this time he ignored the jibe.

'So are you interested, or not?'

'We-ll.' Tilting her head to one side, she appeared to consider the offer. 'We haven't discussed terms, yet.'

'We haven't discussed your funny webbed feet either,' he pointed out. 'But live and let live is my motto.'

Janey had been eavesdropping like mad from the kitchen. Unable to endure the suspense a moment longer, she seized the mugs of tea and erupted back into the sitting room.

'She's interested,' she declared, ignoring Maxine's frantic signals and thrusting one of the mugs into Guy Cassidy's hand. 'She'll take the job. When would you like her to start?'

# Chapter 6

Guy Cassidy was twenty-three years old when he met Véronique Charpentier. It was the wettest, windiest day of the year and he was making his way home after a gruelling fourteen-hour shift in the photographic studios where his brief had been to make a temperamental forty-four-year-old actress look thirty again.

Now the traffic was almost at a standstill and his car was stuck behind a bus. All he could think of was getting back to his flat and sinking into a hot bath with a cold beer. In less than two hours he was supposed to be taking Amanda, his current girlfriend, to a party in Chelsea. It wasn't a prospect that particularly appealed to him but she had insisted on going.

There was no room to overtake when the bus came to a shuddering halt and began to spill out passengers. Guy amused himself by watching them scurry like wind-blown ants across the pavement towards the relative shelter of the shop canopies lining the high street.

The last passenger to disembark, however, didn't make it. As her long, white-blond hair whipped around her face she struggled to control her charcoal-grey umbrella. At the exact moment the umbrella flipped inside out, she stumbled against the kerb and crashed to the ground. Her carrier bag of shopping spilled into the gutter. The inverted umbrella, carried by the wind, cartwheeled off into the distance and a wave of muddy water from the wheels of the now-departing bus cascaded over her crumpled body.

By the time Guy reached her, she was dragging herself into a sitting position and muttering 'Bloody Eenglish' under her breath.

'Are you hurt?' he asked, helping her carefully to her feet. There was a lot of mud, but no sign of blood.

Her expression wary, she shook her wet blond head, then cast a sorrowful glance in the direction of the spilled carrier bag lying in a puddle. 'Not me. But my croissants, I theenk, are drowned. Bloody Eenglish!'

'Come on.' Smiling at her choice of words, he led her towards his car. When she was installed in the passenger seat inspecting the holes in the knees of her sheer, dark tights, he said, 'Why bloody English?'

'Eenglish weather. Stupid Eenglish umbrella,' she explained, gesticulating at the torrential rain. 'And how many kind Eenglish people stopped to 'elp when I fell over? Tssch!'

'I stopped to help you, he remarked mildly, slipping the engine into gear as a cacophony of irritated hooting started up behind them.

The girl, her face splashed with mud and rain, sighed. 'Of course you did. And now I'm sitting in your car and I don't even know you. It would be just my luck, I theenk, to get murdered by a crazy person. Maybe you should stop and let me out.'

'I can't stand the sight of blood,' Guy assured her. 'And I'm not crazy either. Why don't you tell me where you live and let me drive you home? No strings, I promise.'

She frowned, apparently considering the offer. Finally, turning to face him and looking puzzled, she said, 'I don't understand. What ees thees no strings? You mean like in string vests?'

Her name was Véronique, she was eighteen years old and she lived in an attic which had been shabbily converted into a bedsitter but which had the advantage – in daylight at least – of overlooking Wandsworth Common.

As a reward for not murdering her on the way home, Guy was invited up the five flights of stairs for coffee. By the time his cup was empty he had fallen in love with its maker and forgotten that Amanda even existed.

'Let me take you out to dinner,' he said, wondering what he would do if Véronique turned him down. To his eternal relief, however, she smiled.

'All wet and muddy, like thees? Or may I take a bath first?'

Grinning back at her, Guy said, 'I really don't mind.'

'It is best if I take a bath, I theenk,' Véronique replied gravely. Rising to her feet, she gestured towards a pile of magazines stacked against the battered, dark blue sofa. 'I won't be long. Please, can you amuse yourself for a while? They are French magazines, but maybe you could look at the pictures.'

The tiny bathroom adjoined the living room. Guy smiled to himself as he heard her carefully locking the door which separated them. The magazines, he discovered, were well-thumbed copies of French *Vogue*, one of which contained a series of photographs he himself had taken during last spring's Paris collections. The thought of Véronique poring over pages which bore his own minuscule by-line cheered him immensely. It was, he felt, a good omen for their relationship.

But the magazines were also evidently a luxury for her. The bedsitter, though charmingly adorned with touches of her own personality, was itself unprepossessing and sparsely furnished. The sofa, strewn with hand-embroidered cushions, doubled as a bed. Strategically situated lamps drew the attention away from peeling wallpaper and the posters on the wall, he guessed, were similarly positioned in order to conceal patches of damp. Neither the cinnamon-scented candles or the bowls of pot pourri could eradicate the slight underlying mustiness which pervaded the air.

And there was no television; a box of good quality writing paper and a small transistor radio seemed to comprise her only forms of entertainment. Guy, exploring the meticulously tidy room in detail, greedy to discover everything there was to know about Véronique Charpentier, felt an almost overwhelming urge to bundle her up and whisk her away from the chilly, depressing house, to tell her that she no longer needed to live like this, that he would take care of her . . .

And when she emerged from the bathroom twenty-five minutes later, he actually had to bite his tongue in order not to say the words aloud. Mud-free, simply dressed in a thin black polo-necked sweater, pale grey wool skirt and black tights, she looked stunning. The white-blond hair, freshly brushed, hung past her shoulders. Silver-grey eyes regarded him with amusement. She was wearing pastel pink lipstick and *Je Reviens*.

'OK?' she said cheerfully.

'OK!' Guy nodded in agreement.

'Good.' Véronique smiled at him. 'I theenk we shall have a nice evening.'

'I know we will.'

She blew out the cinnamon-scented candles and picked up her bag. 'Can I make a confession to you?'

'What?' Guy's heart sank. He couldn't imagine what she was about to say. He didn't want to hear it.

But Véronique went ahead anyway. 'I theenk I begin to be glad,' she confided, lowering her voice to a whisper, 'that I fell off the bus in the rain. Maybe Eenglish weather isn't so bloody after all.'

Oliver Cassidy wasn't amused when his son informed him, three weeks later, that he was going to marry Véronique Charpentier.

'For God's sake,' he said sharply, lighting a King Edward cigar and not bothering to lower his voice. 'This is ridiculous. She's eighteen years old. She's French. You don't even know her.'

'Of course I do!' Guy retaliated. 'I love her and she loves me. And I'm not here to ask your permission to marry her, because that's going to happen anyway. I've already booked the Register Office.'

'Then you're a bloody fool!' Oliver glared at him. 'She's in love with your money, your career; why on earth can't you just live with her for a few months? That'll get her out of your system fast enough.'

'There's no need to shout,' said Guy. Véronique was in the next room.

'Why not? Why can't I shout?' His father's eyebrows knitted ferociously together. 'I want her to hear me! She should know that not everyone is as gullible as you obviously are. If you ask me, she's nothing but a clever, scheming foreigner making the most of the opportunity of a lifetime.'

'But I'm not asking you,' Guy replied, his tone icy. 'And Véronique isn't someone I want to get out of my system. She's going to be my wife, whether you like it or not.'

Oliver Cassidy turned purple. 'You're making a damn fool of yourself.'

'I'm not.' His son, sickened by his inability even to try to understand, turned away. 'You are.'

They were married at Caxton Hall and Véronique accompanied Guy on a working trip to Switzerland in lieu of a honeymoon. Upon their return, she moved her few possessions into his apartment, gave up her job in a busy north London delicatessen and said, 'So! What do we do next?'

Joshua was born ten months later, a perfect composite of his parents with Guy's dark blue eyes and Véronique's white-blond hair. With no family of her own, Véronique said sadly, 'It's such a shame. Your father hates me, I know, but he should at least have the chance to love his grandson.'

Guy, though not naturally vindictive, wasn't interested

in a reconciliation. 'He knows where we live,' he replied in dismissive tones. 'If he wanted to see Josh, he could. But he clearly doesn't want to, so forget him.'

The arrival of Ella two years later brought further happiness. Contrary to Véronique's plans that this time the child should have silver-grey eyes and dark curly hair, she was a carbon copy of Josh. Guy, his career sky-rocketing, took so many photographs of his family that they had to be stored in suitcases rather than albums. It wasn't until he received a large Manila envelope through the post, addressed to him in familiar handwriting and containing a selection of the choicest photographs, that he realized Véronique had sent them to his father. 'Don't ever do that again,' he said furiously, hurling the envelope to the ground. 'He doesn't deserve anything. I've told you before . . . just forget him!'

But Veronique could not forget. All children were supposed to have grandparents, and her enduring dream was that her own children should know and love the only living grandparent left to them. As the years passed and the rift remained as deep and unbridgeable as ever, she became quietly determined to do something about it. Both her husband and her father-in-law were clearly too proud to make the first move but for Josh and Ella's sakes she was prepared to take the risk. If Oliver Cassidy were to come face to face with his grandchildren, she reasoned, the rift would instantly be healed. It would be a *fait accompli*, following which human nature would take its course and all would be well.

Knowing that her fiercely protective husband would never allow her to make the initial move towards reconciliation, however, she planned her campaign with secretive, military precision. Oliver Cassidy was at that time living in Bristol, so she waited until Guy was away on a two-week assignment in New York before booking herself and the children into an hotel less than a mile from her father-in-law's address.

By the time of their arrival at the station, Véronique's head was pounding and she was feeling sick with apprehension, but there was no backing out now. For the sake of Josh and Ella she struggled to maintain a bright front. At their hotel, overlooking the Clifton Suspension Bridge, she treated them to ice-cream sundaes on the sweeping terrace and said gaily, 'Eat them all up, and don't spill any on your clothes. We're going to see a very nice man and he might not be so impressed with chocolate ice-cream stains.'

Josh, six years old and enjoying the adventure immensely, said, 'Who is he?'

But Véronique, whose headache was worsening by the minute, simply smiled and shook her head.

'Just a very nice man, my darling, who lives not far from here. You'll like him, I'm sure.'

Josh wasn't so sure he would. The big house to which his mother took them was owned by a man who didn't look the least bit pleased to see them. In Josh's experience, very-nice-people smiled a lot, hugged you and, perhaps, gave you sweets. This man, with fierce grey eyebrows like caterpillars, wasn't even saying hello.

'Mr Cassidy,' said Véronique quickly. It was an unpromising start and her palms were sticky with perspiration: 'I have brought Josh and Ella to see you

. . . I thought you would like to meet them . . . your family—'

Oliver Cassidy didn't like surprises. Neither did he appreciate emotional blackmail. A man who seldom admitted that he might be in the wrong, he saw no reason to revise his opinion of his only son's French wife. In her flowered dress and with her straight blond hair hanging loose around her shoulders, she still looked like a teenager, which didn't help. And as far as he was concerned, the fact that she thought she could simply turn up out of the blue and expect some kind of fairytale reunion proved beyond all doubt that she was either stupid or staggeringly naïve.

'What's the matter?' he said coldly, eyeing her white face with displeasure and ignoring the two children at her side. His gesture encompassed both the Georgian house and the sloping, sculptured lawns. 'Afraid they'll miss out on all this when I'm gone?'

'No!' Appalled by her father-in-law's cruelty, Véronique took a faltering step backwards. 'No,' she cried again, pleading with him to understand. 'They are your grandchildren, your family! This isn't about any inheritance . . .'

'Good!' snapped Oliver Cassidy as Ella, clinging to her mother's hand, began to cry. 'Because they won't be seeing any of it anyway.'

'I feel sick,' Ella sobbed. 'Mummy, I feel—'

'And now, I have an urgent appointment.' He glanced at his watch in order to give credence to the lie. Then, with a look of absolute horror, he took an abrupt step sideways.

But it was too late. Ella, who had eaten far too much chocolate ice-cream, had already thrown up all over her grandfather's highly polished, handmade shoes.

It wasn't until they were back at the hotel that Véronique realized she was ill. The headache and nausea which she had earlier put down to nervousness had worsened dramatically and she was aching all over.

By early evening a raging fever had taken its grip and she was barely able to haul herself out of bed in order to phone downstairs and ask for a doctor to be called. Summer flu, she thought, fighting tears of exhaustion and the shivers which racked her entire body like jolts of electricity. Just what she needed. A fitting end to a disastrous visit. Had she been superstitious she might almost have believed that Oliver Cassidy had cast a malevolent jinx in order to pay her back for her impudence.

The doctor, however, took an altogether more serious view of the situation.

'Mrs Cassidy, I'm afraid we're going to have to get you into hospital,' he said when he had completed his examination.

'*Mais c'est impossible!*' Véronique cried, her fluent English deserting her in her weakened state. '*Mes enfants
. . .*'

But it wasn't a suggestion, it was a statement. An ambulance was called and by midnight Véronique was being admitted to the neurological ward of one of Bristol's largest hospitals. The hotel manager himself, she was repeatedly assured, was contacting her husband in New

York and had in the meantime assumed full responsibility for her children who would remain at the hotel and be well looked after for as long as necessary.

By the time Guy arrived at the hospital twenty-seven hours later, Véronique had lapsed into a deep coma. As the doctors had suspected, tests confirmed that she was suffering from a particularly virulent strain of meningitis and although they were doing everything possible the outlook wasn't good.

'Mummy said we were going to see a nice man,' said Josh, his dark eyes brimming with tears as Guy eased the truth from him 'But he wasn't nice at all, he was horrid. He shouted at Mummy, then Ella was sick on his shoes. And when we came back to the hotel Mummy wasn't very well. Daddy, can we go home now?'

It was as Guy had suspected. He didn't contact his father. And when Véronique died three days later without regaining consciousness, he saw no reason to change his mind. Oliver Cassidy might not have caused Véronique's death but he had undoubtedly ensured that her last few waking hours should have been as miserable as possible. For that, Guy would never forgive him.

# Chapter 7

Guy watched from the kitchen window as Maxine's Jaffa-orange MG screeched to a halt at the top of the drive.

'I don't know,' he said, looking doubtful. 'I'm still not sure about this. Somebody tell me I'm not making a big mistake.'

Berenice followed his gaze. The girl climbing out of the car was wearing white shorts and a sleeveless pale grey vest with MUSCLE emblazoned across her chest. She also possessed a great deal of gold-blond hair and long brown legs.

'Just because she doesn't look like your idea of a nanny,' she replied comfortably. Then, secure in the knowledge that by this time tomorrow she would be a married woman, she added with a slight smile, 'She certainly doesn't look like me.'

There really wasn't any diplomatic answer to that; the differences between the two girls were only too evident. But Berenice had been such relaxing company, thought Guy, and it had never occurred to anyone who'd met her that there might possibly be anything going on between the pair of them.

The arrival of Maxine Vaughan, on the other hand,

was likely to engender all kinds of lurid speculation.

'I don't care what she looks like.' His expression was deliberately grim. Above them came the sound of thunderous footsteps as Josh and Ella hurled themselves down the staircase. 'I just want her to take care of my kids.' He was about to continue but his attention was caught by the scene now taking place on the drive.

'OK,' Maxine was saying, leaning against her car and surveying the two children before her. 'Just remind me. Which one of you is Ella and which is Josh?'

Josh relaxed. She wouldn't, he was almost sure, force them to eat cold porridge. He had high hopes, too, of being allowed to stay up late when his father was away. Berenice had always been a bit boring where bedtimes were concerned.

'I'm Ella,' said his sister, meeting Maxine for the first time and struggling to work out whether she was being serious. 'I'm a girl.'

'Of course you are.' Maxine grinned and gave her her handbag. 'Good, that means you can carry this for me whilst I get my cases out of the boot. Isn't your dad here?'

'He's in the kitchen,' supplied Josh. 'With Berenice.'

'Hmm. Nice of him to come out and welcome me.' With a meaningful glance in the direction of the kitchen window, she hauled the heavy cases out of the car and dumped them on the gravelled drive. She'd been so serious about the live-in aspect of the job that she'd been up to Maurice's flat in London to collect all her things. 'Well, he can carry them inside. That's what men are for.'

By the time Janey arrived at Trezale House in the van,

Maxine appeared to have made herself thoroughly at home. Her enormous bedroom, flooded with sunlight and nicely decorated in shades of pink, yellow and cream, was already a mess.

'Berenice has given me a list of dos and don'ts,' she said, rolling her eyes as she tossed an armful of underwear into an open drawer and kicked a few shoes under the dressing table. 'She seems incredibly organized.'

'Nannies have to be organized,' Janey reminded her.

'Yes, well. I pity the chap she's marrying.'

'And you're going to have to be organized,' continued Janey remorselessly. 'If these children have a routine, they'll need to stick to it.'

Maxine gazed at her in disbelief. 'We never did.'

This was true. Thea, engrossed in her work, had employed a cavalier attitude to child rearing which involved leaving them to their own devices for much of the time, whilst she, oblivious to all else, would lose herself in the wonder of creating yet another sculpture. Janey, in the months following her own marriage, had traced her love of domesticity and orderliness back to the disorganized chaos of those early years when she had longed for order and stability. It had never seemed to bother Maxine, however. More adventurous by nature, and less interested in conforming than her elder sister, she positively embraced chaos. Janey just wished she could embrace the idea of work with as much enthusiasm.

'That's different,' she said sternly. 'At least we had a mother. Josh and Ella don't. It can't be easy for them.'

'It isn't going to be easy for me.' Maxine looked glum

and handed over the list, painstakingly written in neat, easy-to-read capitals. 'According to this they get up at six-thirty. And I'm supposed to give them breakfast!'

'Oh please,' sighed Janey, exasperated. 'You wanted this job! You were desperate to come and work here. Whatever's the matter with you now?'

'I wanted to work for Guy Cassidy.' Maxine stared at her as if she was stupid. 'But he's just been going through his diary with me and from the sound of it he's going to be away more often than he's here. Whilst he's leaping on planes and jetting off all over the world, I'm going to be stuck here in the wilderness with the kids like some frumpy housewife.' She paused then added fretfully, 'This wasn't what I had in mind at all.'

Guy emerged from his study as Janey was putting the finishing touches to the flowers in the hall. Crossing her fingers and praying that it wouldn't pour with rain overnight, she had garlanded the stone pillars which flanked the front entrance to the house with yellow and white satin ribbons, and woven sprays of mimosa and gypsophila between them. Together with the tendrils of ivy already curling around the bleached white stone they would provide an effective framework for the bride and groom when they stood on the steps to have their photographs taken by none other than one of the country's best-known photographers.

'It looks good.' Standing back to survey the overall effect with a professional eye, he nodded his approval. 'You've been working hard.'

'So has the hairdresser,' Janey observed, as a car drew

up and Berenice stepped out, self-consciously shielding her head from the light breeze coming in off the sea. Her mousey brown hair, pulled back from her face and teased into unaccustomed ringlets, bounced off her shoulders as she walked towards them.

'How are you going to sleep tonight?' said Guy, and Janey glimpsed the genuine affection in his eyes as he admired the rigid style.

Berenice, turning her head this way and that, said, 'Upright,' then broke into a smile as she inspected Janey's work. 'This is gorgeous; it must have taken you hours!'

'I think we all deserve a drink.' Placing his hand on her shoulder, Guy drew her into the house. When Janey hesitated, he added, 'You too.'

Berenice said, 'Where are the children?'

'Upstairs with the new nanny.' He grinned. 'And a pack of cards. I heard her saying she was going to teach them poker.'

'Enjoying yourself?' asked Guy, coming up to Janey in the sitting room the next day. She was perched on one of the window seats overlooking the garden, watching Maxine flirt with the best man.

'It was nice of Berenice to invite me,' she replied with a smile. 'And even nicer for her, being able to have the reception here. She's terribly grateful – she was telling me earlier that otherwise they would have had to hold it in the skittle alley at the Red Lion.'

He shrugged. 'No problem. Weddings and bar-mitzvahs a speciality. And forty guests is hardly over the top.'

'You'll miss her,' said Janey, nodding in Berenice's direction.

'The kids certainly will. We were lucky to keep her as long as we did.' He hesitated, a shadow coming over his face. 'She's been with us since my wife died.'

Weddings were an integral part of Janey's job but she still found them difficult to handle at times. They invariably brought back memories of her own marriage to Alan.

'It can't be easy for you,' she said, guessing what would be uppermost in his own mind. Out in the garden, Berenice and Michael were posing with their arms around each other's ample waists whilst Josh, his expression exquisitely serious, finished up yet another roll of film. Through the open window they could hear him issuing stern commands: 'Don't laugh . . . stay still . . . just look happy . . .'

Moving her half-empty wine glass out of the way, Guy eased himself down next to Janey and stretched out his long legs.

'Not easy, but bearable,' he said, his tone deliberately even. 'I don't resent other people's happiness. And Véronique and I had seven years of it, after all. That's more than some.'

More than I had, thought Janey sadly, but of course he didn't know anything of her own past. Since she wasn't about to try and compete in the tragedy stakes, she said nothing.

Now that the subject had been raised, however, Guy seemed to want to continue the line of conversation.

'Other people's attitudes are harder to cope with,' he

said, breaking the companionable silence between them. 'In the beginning I just functioned on automatic pilot, doing what had to be done and making sure Josh and Ella suffered as little as possible. Everybody was so concerned for us, everywhere you turned there were people being helpful and sympathetic . . . I couldn't do a thing wrong in their eyes. Then, after about six months, it was as if I couldn't handle any more sympathy. I kicked against it, went back to work and started, well, it was a pretty wild phase. Subconsciously, I suppose, I was looking for a replacement for Véronique but all I did was pick up one female after another, screw around like it was going out of fashion and get extremely drunk. All I managed to do, of course, was make an awful lot of people unhappy. Including myself. And everyone who'd been so sympathetic in the early days changed their minds and decided I was a real bastard instead. Sleeping with girls and dumping them – deliberately hurting them so they'd understand how *I* felt – seemed like the only answer at the time but all it did was make me more miserable. In the end, I came to my senses and stopped doing it.' With a rueful smile and a sideways glance at Janey, he added, 'I suppose I was lucky not to catch anything terrible. At the time, God knows, I deserved to.'

Janey, who had read books on the subject of coping with grief, said hesitantly, 'I don't know, but I think it's a fairly normal kind of reaction. Probably men are more likely to go through that kind of phase than women, but once it's out of their system they . . . settle down again. What's it like now? *Do* you feel more settled?'

It was an amazingly intimate conversation to be having

with someone who was, after all, a virtual stranger. But she was genuinely interested in finding out how he had coped and was continuing to cope. She wondered too whether she would ever enter a promiscuous phase . . .

Guy didn't appear in the least put out by her questions. Reaching for a bottle of white wine, he refilled both their glasses. 'There's still the problem of other people's attitudes.' His eyes registered mild contempt. 'Not that I particularly care what they think, but it can get a bit wearing at times. After three years, it seems, I'm expected to remarry. And the pressure's always there. Nowadays, every time I'm introduced to some new female at a dinner party I know it's because she's a carefully selected suitable candidate. Sometimes I half expect to find a tattoo on her forehead saying "Potential Wife". The next thing I know, everyone's telling me how marvellous she is with children and saying how hard it must be for poor Josh and little Ella, at their ages, not having a mother.' He shuddered at the unwelcome memory. 'God, that's happened to me so many times. It's like a recurring nightmare. And it's a bigger turn-off, of course, than a bucketful of bromide.'

'What's bromide?' said Ella, and they both jumped.

Guy, recovering from the surprise of her unexpected appearance, said, 'It's a kind of cold porridge. You wouldn't like it.'Then, pulling her on to his lap, he added, 'And what you need is a cowbell around your neck. Have you been eavesdropping, angel?'

'No.' She shook her head so vigorously that her white velvet headband slipped off. 'I was listening to you. Daddy, when can *I* get married?'

55

He assumed a suitably serious expression. 'Why? When would you like to get married?'

'Tomorrow.' Ella giggled and smoothed her lilac cotton dress over her knobbly knees. 'I'm going to marry Luke.'

Luke was eight years old and Berenice's nephew.

'I see.' Guy looked thoughtful. 'Well, tomorrow sounds OK to me. But maybe I should have a word with him first.'

Ella frowned, anxious that he shouldn't hear about the glass of lemonade she had accidentally spilled into a handbag left open and unattended in the kitchen. Biting her lower lip and looking dubious, she said, 'Why?'

'Marriage is a serious business,' Guy told her. 'I'd definitely need to speak to Luke, man to man. Apart from anything else,' he added severely, 'I have to ask him about his future prospects.'

'You seemed to be getting on rather well with my boss,' said Maxine, polishing off a slice of seafood quiche and sounding faintly put out. 'What were you doing, giving him the rundown on my sordid past?'

'Not at all.' It was early evening now and they were sitting outside on a wooden bench enjoying the light breeze. For most of the day the temperature had been up in the eighties. Janey, examining her arms for signs of sunburn and hoping she wouldn't wake up tomorrow with strap marks, said, 'I was the one who stuck up for you, remember? I'm hardly likely to scare him to death by telling him what you're really like. He might drag me into court and sue me for misrepresentation.'

'So what *were* you talking about?'

Despite having wolfed down at least half a dozen sausage rolls and a slice of wedding cake as well as the quiche, Maxine's lipstick was still immaculately in place. Shielding her eyes from the sinking sun, she was surreptitiously watching Guy Cassidy as he stood at the far end of the terrace talking to Berenice's new mother-in-law.

'He was telling me how fed up he gets, being chased by women hell-bent on becoming the next Mrs Cassidy.' Jancy's tone of voice was casual but she felt it necessary to point out this fact, both to save her sister from making a fool of herself and to ensure that Guy wouldn't dispense with Maxine's services. Now that she had her flat to herself once more she wanted to keep it that way.

But Maxine only laughed. 'They can't have been very good at it then. The whole point of chasing a man – and catching him – is to make sure he doesn't realize it's happening. It's a delicate process, Janey! Practically an art form in itself.'

'Well, it sounds as if he's had plenty of practice at being on the receiving end.' Janey, having at least made her point, changed the subject. 'And you seemed to be getting on rather nicely with the best man anyway,' she observed. 'What was his name, Colin? He looked keen.'

'He was.' Maxine, licking her forefinger and dabbing at the crumbs of pastry on her plate, sounded gloomy. 'And I may as well change my name to Cinderella. Guy wants me to stay here for the rest of the weekend so the kids have a chance to get used to me before he leaves for Paris on Monday morning. Then I'll be here on my own with them until he gets back on Friday. I'm allowed next weekend off, apparently, but by that time Colin will have left on a cricket tour.' She shrugged. 'We did try, but we couldn't seem to get ourselves synchronized. At this rate my social life looks set to have all the sparkle of a squashed snail.'

'Welcome to the real world,' said Janey shortly. Her own social life had been practically non-existent for the past eighteen months.

Maxine cast her an impatient glance. 'Yes, but it's all right for you,' she replied with characteristic lack of tact. 'You're used to it.'

# Chapter 8

The heatwave continued. On Sunday morning Janey packed a canvas holdall and headed down to the beach. It would be packed solid but she could amuse herself by guessing, according to the various shades of pallor, redness and tan, how long the holidaymakers had been in Trezale. And eavesdropping on their conversations – bickering couples were a particular favourite – was always entertaining.

The beach *was* crowded but the tide was on its way out, which helped. A lot of sandcastles were being constructed along the stretch of damp sand, leaving more room for the serious sunbathers on the dry sand. Janey chose a promising spot where she could stretch out, make a start on the latest Danielle Steel novel and simultaneously overhear the lively argument already in progress between a pair of big, sunburnt Liverpudlians who couldn't decide whether to go for cod and chips later or splash out on a proper Sunday lunch at that posh place in Amory Street. She wondered idly whether to tell them that the posh place, Bruno's, was closed on Sundays, but it seemed a shame to interrupt them. Uncapping her bottle of Ambre Solaire she smoothed the lotion

59

haphazardly over the bits of her most likely to burn and promptly fell asleep instead.

She awoke with a start some time later. Ice-cold liquid was being dripped into her navel.

Grinning, Bruno held the Coke can aloft.

'It should be Bollinger of course,' he said, admiring her exposed body in the brief, fuchsia-pink bikini, 'but sometimes one just has to improvise. Can I sit down?'

'I don't know.' Shielding her eyes from the sun, Janey deadpanned, 'Can you?'

'OK. May I be permitted to share a corner of your towel?' He lowered himself down beside her anyway and offered her the Coke. 'You're looking rather gorgeous, I must say. I hardly recognized you at first, without your clothes on.'

Behind them, the Liverpudlian couple tittered. Janey tried hard not to flinch as Bruno ran a hand lightly across her stomach. It was a disturbingly pleasant sensation; she just wished her diet had been a bit more of a success.

But he wasn't stopping. 'Don't,' she protested, pushing his hand away. 'I'm too fat.'

'Rubbish!' replied Bruno firmly. The female predilection for dieting was a source of constant irritation to him, particularly when they tried to do it in his restaurant. 'Everyone else is too thin.'

Out of sheer desperation, she said, 'Where's Nina?'

'Gone to visit her parents.' He gave her a soulful look. 'She comes back on Tuesday morning. I'm all alone for two whole days.'

'You poor thing.' Janey smiled at the expression on his face. 'Whatever will you do with yourself?'

He knew what he'd like to do, but he also realized that he would have to tread very carefully indeed. Janey Sinclair was one of those rare females who seemed genuinely unaware of her own attractions. Since getting to know her, he had been struck by the aura of sadness surrounding her, and impressed by her refusal to seek sympathy from those who knew what she had gone through.

She was certainly no holiday bimbo. If she had been, he would have seduced and discarded her long ago. As it was, however, the sense of intrigue and interest had been maintained. She was, in a way, forbidden fruit. Time and again Bruno had told himself that in view of his own track record he should simply leave it at that and not get involved, but the attraction was definitely there and he was expert enough to know that it was mutual. Behind the awkward, diffident exterior he sensed Janey's own interest. It was heady stuff, all this self-denial and surface badinage. It had been years since he had experienced the pain and pleasure of such a slow-burning, tentative friendship. But at the same time Sunday and Monday stretched emptily ahead and he was certainly no saint . . .

'I'm too hot,' he said, finishing off the Coke and eyeing her glistening, Ambre-Solaired body. 'And if you stay here you're going to burn. Come on, let's go and get some lunch.'

It was a tempting offer. Hungrier than she'd realized and delighted at the prospect of company, Janey raised herself up on her elbows and said, 'Where?'

'My place.'

'Oh.' Nina wasn't there. She wasn't sure she should. 'But—'

'Oh dear,' he mocked, sensing her doubt. 'Now I've got you worried and you're desperately trying to think of a diplomatic way to say no.'

Janey, floundering, felt her cheeks redden. 'Well . . .'

'For heaven's sake,' said Bruno, sounding faintly exasperated. 'Live a little. All I'm talking about is a spot of lunch. I'm not inviting you to have wild sex with me.'

Embarrassed, she replied, 'I didn't think you were.'

'Oh yes, you did.' He grinned and helped her to her feet. 'But there's no need to panic; you'll be quite safe. Come on, let's go.'

Like Janey, Bruno and Nina lived above the shop, but whereas her own flat was tiny, their apartment was both spacious and stylish.

Janey, who had never visited it before, was impressed. Immaculate white rugs on the tiled floors offset the lavender and green décor. Modern, semi-abstract paintings were ranged around the walls and well-tended plants spilled out of white porcelain pots. The main ceiling was palest lavender, exactly matching the two three-seater leather sofas, and the cat occupying the one closer to the windows was white with luminous green eyes.

'You're surprised,' said Bruno, handing her an ice-stacked Pimm's.

'A bit,' she admitted. The almost clinical perfection of the apartment was so at odds with languorous, faintly hippyish Nina.

But once again he seemed able to read her mind. 'This

is me. Nina isn't bothered about interior design; she just goes along with my ideas.' As far as Janey could make out, Nina went uncomplainingly along with most things. Following him into the well-equipped kitchen, she leaned against the wall and watched Bruno prepare lunch. There was something almost irresistible about a man who could cook and talk at the same time. Before she had a chance to put down her empty glass, he had refilled it and added an extra dash of gin for good measure.

The unaccustomed strength of the drink went straight to her head. By the time they sat down to eat, her knees were like cotton wool and she was feeling deliciously uninhibited.

'Why aren't you two married?' she asked, intrigued.

'I don't make promises I can't keep.'

'So you aren't faithful to Nina.' Gosh, she couldn't believe she'd actually said that. To make up for it, Janey tried to look disapproving, although the effect was slightly spoiled when she attempted to fork up a frond of radicchio and it slipped, landing on the pale green tablecloth instead.

This time his smile broadened. 'Actually, I was thinking of the for richer, for poorer bit.'

'Oh.' She wondered if he was joking. It was difficult to tell, with Bruno.

But this time, it seemed, he was serious. 'Nina's the wealthy one,' he explained guilelessly, the sweep of his arm encompassing both the apartment and the restaurant below. Then he shrugged. 'She bought this place, I run it, and the arrangement suits us both. But if she didn't have any money, well . . .'

'That's terrible,' Janey protested, but Bruno wasn't in the least put out.

'No it isn't. It's honest.' Finishing his omelette and pushing his plate to one side, he lit a cigarette. 'There are trade-offs in every relationship. Ours simply happen to involve money. And Nina does realize this,' he added, pausing to execute a perfect smoke ring. 'She understands. If she decided she didn't like it she could always kick me out.'

The Brie omelette and tomato salad were delicious but Janey had lost her appetite. It was all very well for Bruno. He made it sound so simple and natural, but as far as she was concerned his theories were too unnervingly close for comfort. She wasn't wealthy by any means, but after meeting Alan she had worked hard and long enough to acquire the lease on her own small shop and the flat which went with it. He, on the other hand, had been falling behind with the rent on his own shared apartment and taking on casual work only when it became absolutely necessary in order to eat. Surfing and water skiing, his two great passions in life, weren't exactly profitable. During the moments of dark despair following his disappearance, Janey had wondered uneasily whether she had ever been more than a convenient stop-gap, supplying bed and board to a man whose love she'd only imagined.

But she was here now, with Bruno, and she damn well wasn't going to cry. He and Nina had an understanding: they were more of a business partnership than a real couple, and they weren't even married. Taking another gulp of Pimm's, she felt her own resolve weakening. She'd been alone for eighteen months, mourning the loss of her husband and wondering if life would ever be truly enjoyable again. Maybe it was time she had a little fun. Maybe she should take the plunge and find out.

'So your life is perfect,' she said, her smile deliberately provocative. 'You have everything you want.'

'Pretty much.' He nodded in agreement, those devastating bedroom eyes roaming lazily over her body. Janey shivered with sudden longing; it had been so long since she'd felt *wanted*.

Bruno certainly wanted her, but he had no intention of doing anything about it. Not yet, anyway. Tempting though the thought was, he knew that Janey had her preconceived ideas about him and that if he lived up to them this afternoon she would undoubtedly have her regrets by tomorrow. And he didn't want their relationship prematurely curtailed by a guilt attack. Where Janey Sinclair was concerned, he had decided, a single afternoon of pleasure simply wouldn't be enough.

Janey, walking home several hours later, didn't know whether to be relieved or disappointed. Her virtue was still intact, which was good in one way, but at the same time her ego had taken a bit of a knock. For Bruno, true to his word, had behaved like a perfect gentleman. Lunch had been followed by coffee on the sunny balcony, easy conversation and absolutely no untoward moves whatsoever. When she had succumbed to the effects of the Pimm's and closed her eyes, he had brought cushions for her head and left her to doze whilst he dealt with the washing up. When she awoke, it was to the muted strains of Vivaldi emanating from the stereo and the sight of

Bruno, sitting opposite her, quietly reading the *Sunday Times*. Glancing up, he'd grinned and said, 'Oh good, you can help me with the crossword. I'm stuck on eight across.'

# Chapter 9

Over at Trezale House Maxine found herself on the receiving end of a similar lack of interest, but in Guy Cassidy's case it was entirely genuine. Spending his working life surrounded by some of the most beautiful women in the world, she decided sourly, had evidently had some kind of immunizing effect. Instead of the admiration to which she was accustomed, she was only too well aware that when he looked at Maxine Vaughan all he saw was the new nanny. And when he had observed the haphazard way in which she tackled the ironing, he'd been even less impressed.

'I can't do it if you're standing there watching me,' she'd said defensively, seizing Ella's fiendishly difficult pink cotton dungarees and realizing that she should have checked the pockets before chucking them into the machine earlier. Shreds of blue paper tissue clung to the bib like burrs.

'Don't worry,' he'd replied, backing out of the kitchen in horror. 'I can't bear to watch.'

And now here she was, stuck in the rotten kitchen with the beastly ironing, feeling more like bloody Cinderella than ever. Outside, Guy was fooling around with Josh and Ella, threatening them with the garden sprinkler. Ella, shrieking with laughter and making a desperate bid for freedom, tripped and landed in the flowerbed. As she scrambled to her feet once more, Maxine sucked in her breath; the clean white tee-shirt and jeans were clean no more. And no prizes for guessing who would have to deal with them.

Josh, skidding into the kitchen, grabbed a carton of orange juice from the fridge and emptied the contents into a mug, rubbing ineffectually with his muddy toes at the drops spilled on the floor.

'Why don't you come out and play?' he asked kindly when he had gulped down the orange juice in one go. 'We're having fun.'

'Fun?' Maxine echoed, glancing out of the window at Guy. Her voice heavy with irony, she said, 'Oh dear, I'd better not then. Your father wouldn't approve of that.'

Josh looked troubled. 'Don't you like it here?'

Softening, she turned and smiled at him. It was hardly his fault, after all, that coming to work for Guy Cassidy wasn't turning out as she had expected.

'Of course I do. I'm just not that keen on ironing.'

'You aren't going to leave then?'

Maxine, reminding herself that she didn't really have anywhere else to go, shook her head. 'No.'

'Good,' he said not bothering to hide his relief. 'I know Dad's a bit strict sometimes, but we like you.' Brightening, he added, 'And he's going out tonight, so we'll be able to have fun without him. We can play poker again. For real money, if you like . . .'

In the event, the evening was more entertaining than she had anticipated. Guy, preparing to go out, was in a good mood. To Maxine's utter amazement, he had even asked her if she'd like him to bring back an Indian takeaway.

'Where's he gone?' she said, when the cream Mercedes had disappeared down the drive. Josh was sitting cross-legged on the floor, practising his shuffling technique. Ella, curled up next to her on the sofa wearing red spotted pyjamas and furtively sucking her thumb, was engrossed in a video re-run of Friday night's *Coronation Street*.

'Dad?' Josh shrugged. 'Seeing one of his girlfriends, probably.'

'*One* of his girlfriends?' Maxine's spirits plummeted. Despite having got off to a not-terribly-promising start, she still entertained fantasies of her own in that department. The ridiculously handsome widower and the pretty nanny, living and working together and eventually falling in love had a certain ring to it. But this was the first she'd heard of any girlfriends. When Guy had remained un-partnered during yesterday's wedding reception, she'd assumed the field was clear.

Josh, however, was more interested in mastering the art of the shuffle. 'He's got lots,' he said vaguely. 'I expect it's Imogen tonight, because she phoned up this morning.'

Pushy, thought Maxine. Aloud, she said, 'Is she nice?'

*Coronation Street* had finished. Ella, who was humming along with the theme tune, took her thumb out of her mouth and said, 'I like Imogen. She's pretty.'

Hmm. Maxine decided she couldn't be that fantastic. Guy had said he'd definitely be home by eleven.

'She's *quite* pretty,' Josh corrected his sister. 'But Tara's better.'

'Tara can sit on her hair,' agreed Ella happily, confirming Maxine's suspicion that the girl in question was Tara James, currently one of the most sought-after models in Europe. Hell, she thought gloomily. Talk about competition.

Josh was now painstakingly dealing out the cards. Looking up and glimpsing the expression on Maxine's face, he said in matter of fact tones, 'They're OK I suppose. But none of them is as good as Mummy. She was prettier than anyone.'

'Really?' Maxine was intrigued. 'I'd love to see some photos of her.'

'We've got loads,' said Josh cheerfully. 'I'll bring them downstairs later and show them to you.'

She looked hopeful. 'We could do it now.'

'We have to play poker first,' he replied firmly. 'And I need to buy some new batteries for my Gameboy tomorrow, so we can't stop until I've won at least two pounds.'

It took some deft manipulation on Maxine's part, but she managed; a respectable forty minutes later, Josh was two pounds and twenty pence up and he hadn't noticed the sleight of hand which had been necessary in order to achieve it.

'Well done,' said Maxine, clearing away the cards with some relief. 'Go on then, run upstairs and find those albums. I love looking at other people's photographs.'

Particularly when they belonged to Guy Cassidy. And there were hundreds of them, depicting his life over the past decade. Josh steered her through the albums, pointing with pride to the many pictures of Véronique.

'That's Mummy with Ella, just after she was born. This is me with Mummy in Regent's Park when I was four. And this one's Mum and Dad at a party in St Tropez. He's laughing because Sylvester Stallone just asked her for a dance and she said no.'

Véronique Cassidy had certainly been beautiful. Maxine pored over the close-ups which revealed stunning blond good looks in all their glory. Even more dauntingly, she had been a natural beauty, never over-embellishing herself, simply allowing the exquisite basics to speak for themselves.

But what shone through most of all was happiness. Maxine knew instinctively which of the photographs of his wife had been taken by Guy. And those featuring the two of them together were almost unbearably poignant. Their obvious love for each other shone out; it was almost a tangible thing.

Quite uncharacteristically, she felt tears pricking at the back of her eyelids. Something approaching envy curled in her stomach; not for Véronique, but for their shared happiness. Looking at them with their arms around each other, Maxine was reminded that she herself had never been in love, not really. Her own experiences were of a string of tumultuous and usually short-lived relationships where lust had figured high on the agenda. Instinctively drawn to men whose volatile personalities mirrored her own, it was almost as if she was ensuring that the affairs wouldn't last. For all their similarities, she and her partners never seemed to have much in common in so far as ordinary, day-to-day living was concerned. Within weeks of the initial dazzling attraction, boredom would set in and she would find herself looking for a way out. Invariably, the way out involved another man.

Yet she was, it seemed, doomed to failure. In a deliberate attempt to break the sad and sorry pattern she had got herself involved with Maurice Stanwyck and that, thought Maxine ruefully, had turned out to be the biggest mistake of all. Poor, pedantic Maurice, hellbent on conforming to his mother's ideas of success, simply hadn't been able to cope with a wayward fiancée. And she in turn had tried to conform, she really had, but all she'd managed to do in the end was to hurt and humiliate him.

Returning to London last week to pick up her belongings, she had attempted to apologize. The meeting, however, had been an awkward one. Maurice, his stiff upper lip super-glued into place, had initially betrayed no emotion at all. Then, after twenty minutes of following her around whilst she packed her cases, his guard had dropped. Maxine had been forced to endure the far more harrowing ordeal of listening to him as he begged her to change her mind. At one point he had been on the verge of tears. All she'd been able to do was to remind him how miserable she would undoubtedly have made him if she'd stayed, and what a disaster she would have been as a corporate wife.

Poor Maurice, she thought now, gazing numbly down at the photographs of Guy and Véronique in her lap. She hoped he'd put the experience behind him and find himself another more suitable girlfriend soon.

Josh, meanwhile, was still sorting through the piles of

photos which hadn't made it into the albums. Thrusting a selection into Maxine's hands, he said in matter-of-fact tones, 'This is us after Mummy died. That's me when I was seven, on my new bike. That's Ella's birthday party when she was five. And these are some of Dad's girlfriends.'

It was as if Guy had deliberately chosen women who in no way resembled his wife. Véronique, with her straight blond hair and Madonna-like beauty, couldn't have been more different from these gypsy-eyed, dark-haired females who pouted and smiled for the camera and who were evidently trying too hard to impress.

The difference in Guy, she observed, was equally apparent. Just as earlier she had been able to tell at a glance which photographs of Véronique had been taken by him, so now she could have guessed which of those featuring him had been taken after her death. It was almost indefinable, but there nevertheless; a hardening of the expression in the eyes . . . the loss of carefree pleasure . . . concealed sorrow reflected in the wryness of his smile.

Feeling uncomfortably as if she was intruding upon his private grief, Maxine bundled the photographs together and handed them back to Josh. Ella, still sucking her thumb, had fallen asleep at her side.

'They're lovely.' Maxine smiled as Josh replaced them with care in the cardboard box. 'You're lucky to have so many pictures of your mum.'

'Yes.' The boy looked thoughtful for a moment. 'I wouldn't have forgotten what she looked like but Ella might have. She was only young when it happened.'

She wondered how he felt about the string of subsequent girlfriends but sensed that she had done enough prying for one night. Outside, it was growing dark. It was past both children's bedtime. Tugging tentatively at Ella's thumb, Maxine found it plugged into the rosebud mouth as firmly as a sink plunger.

'Come on, I'm still on parole. Your father will shoot me if he finds out how late I've let you stay up. You take the photographs back upstairs and I'll carry Ella.'

*They Think It's All Over* was about to start on TV. Josh said jealously, 'What will you do when we've gone to bed?'

Maxine gathered Ella into her arms. She was only small but she weighed an absolute ton. 'What else?' she countered, with a long-suffering sigh. 'The rest of the rotten ironing.'

True to his word, Guy was back by eleven with the Indian takeaway. Maxine, having watched *They Think It's All Over*, switched the television off and the iron on the moment she heard his car pull up the drive and promptly assumed the kind of saintly-but-weary expression which indicated that whilst he'd been out enjoying himself with one of his floozies, she had been hard at work for hours.

Her mouth watered as he unwrapped the brown carrier bag and lifted the cardboard lids from their foil containers. Prawn korma, scented and golden, was piled over pilau rice. Massaging her back for good measure, she switched the iron off.

'What time did they get off to bed?' said Guy, turning his attention to the lamb dhansak and naan bread.

'Nine o'clock.'

He grinned. 'That means ten.'

'Well . . .' It was on the tip of her tongue to ask him

what time he'd gone to bed, but she didn't want to risk spoiling his good mood. 'Ella fell asleep on the sofa and Josh thinks he's the Cincinnati Kid. At this rate I can see my entire salary disappearing into his piggy bank.' She pulled a face. 'I wish now I'd never taught him how to play poker.'

'If it makes you feel any better,' said Guy, deadpan, 'you didn't. I did. Last Christmas.'

For the first time, Maxine realized, they were actually sitting down and discussing the children rather than engaging in a battle of verbal wits. The sparring subsided, she began asking suitably intelligent questions about Josh's education and the atmosphere, helped along by a bottle of Sancerre, grew positively relaxed.

Before she knew it, she was asking Guy the question she hadn't felt able to ask Josh.

He frowned. 'Why? What's he been saying?'

'Nothing really.' She crushed a poppadum and licked her fingers. 'Just that you have lots of girlfriends, but none of them is as pretty as his mother was.'

'I see.' The dark blue eyes registered amusement. 'Well, he's probably right about that. Although I don't know about the actual number. "Lots" sounds pretty alarming.'

'Aren't there?' Maxine cast him an innocent look. 'Lots, I mean.'

'One or two.' He shrugged. 'I've tried to keep it low key, for the kids' sakes. On the other hand, I'm only human. And they've never seemed to mind the occasional . . . visitor.'

'Children are adaptable,' agreed Maxine, reassured by his reply. 'And it isn't as if you went through a traumatic

75

divorce. At least they know you were happily married.'

'I hadn't thought of it like that.' Guy looked pensive. 'Maybe it does help.'

Pleased with herself for having said the right thing, she nodded. 'I'm sure it does.'

'I could show you photographs of Véronique, if you're interested.'

Maxine wondered if this was some kind of test. She didn't want him to think of her as morbidly curious.

'There's no hurry,' she replied easily, getting to her feet and taking his empty plate from him. 'Maybe Josh and Ella will show them to me whilst you're away.'

And then it was all spoiled. By the time she returned from the kitchen Guy was standing by the sofa with his back to her. When he turned around, she saw the crumpled photograph in his hand and the look of disdain on his face.

'Why did you lie?' he said coldly. 'I wouldn't have minded if you'd told me you'd already seen them. But why the bloody hell did you have to lie?'

The photograph of Véronique must have slipped down the side of the sofa when she had lifted the sleeping Ella and taken her upstairs. Since then, she had been sitting on it.

'I'm sorry . . .' began Maxine. To her horror, she saw that it was not only crumpled, but torn.

'Don't be sorry,' Guy replied, his tone curt. 'Just be careful, that's all. These pictures might not mean much to you, but they do to us. They're all we have left.'

# Chapter 10

Never at her best at the ludicrously early hour of seven in the morning, Maxine propped herself up on her elbows at the breakfast table and wondered how on earth Janey managed to get up at five in order to visit the flower market. It simply wasn't natural.

And as for having to cope at the same time with two starving children and their picky, irritable father, she thought as she battled to stay awake, it was downright unfair.

'There's a pink elephant in my Sugar Puffs,' squealed Ella, waving the plastic toy in Maxine's face and sprinkling her with milk.

'Eat it. It's good for you.'

'Don't forget we've got to go and buy my batteries today,' Josh reminded her, speaking through a mouthful of toast and blackberry jam and jingling the money in his shorts' pocket for added emphasis. 'Maxine, open your eyes. I said we've got to buy new batteries for my—'

'Gameboy,' she supplied wearily. 'I heard you. And don't talk with your mouth full – you look like a cement mixer in overdrive.'

'You shouldn't have your elbows on the table,' Josh

retaliated, unperturbed. 'Berenice says it's rude. Doesn't she, Dad?' He turned to his father for confirmation. 'Berenice says elbows on the table are rude.'

Having to get up at six-thirty evidently didn't bother Guy Cassidy. Fresh from the shower and wearing a white linen shirt and faded Levi's, he was looking unfairly good for the time of day. Although it was all right for him, thought Maxine mutinously; he was zipping off to Paris. Whilst she spent the week looking after his monsters, he would be surrounded by beautiful semi-naked models only too eager to show him their version of a really good time.

He was standing by the dresser painstakingly checking the cameras he would be taking with him and piling rolls of film into the small case which would accompany him on to the plane. Ignoring Josh, he turned that unnervingly direct dark blue gaze upon Maxine.

'Now, are you sure you're going to be able to cope whilst I'm away?'

She wished she'd had time to brush her hair before stumbling downstairs. 'Don't worry, I'll manage,' she replied evenly, thinking that he'd be stuffed if she said no. 'And you'll have Paula's mother coming in to keep an eagle eye on me in case I'm tempted to do anything drastic, like tape their mouths up and lock them in the cellar.'

'We haven't got a cellar.' Ella, dive-bombing the elephant into her cereal bowl, looked triumphant.

'In that case, it'll just have to be the attic.' Maxine confiscated the elephant. For the first time that morning, a glimmer of a smile crossed Guy's face.

'There you go then,' he warned. 'You'd better behave yourselves. A week in an attic wouldn't be much fun, would it?'

Ella, who was devoted to *Coronation Street*, said, 'I wouldn't mind if I could have a television up there.'

'Oh, you could have a TV set,' Maxine exclaimed, cheering up and buttering herself a slice of toast. 'But no plug.'

The next week, despite Maxine's misgivings, was a greater success than either she or Guy had anticipated. After one or two inevitable power struggles as the children tested the limits of her patience and she in turn exerted her own particular brand of authority, they settled into a routine of sorts and began to enjoy each other's company. Josh and Ella could be noisy, argumentative, boisterous and infuriating but Maxine, retaliating in kind, found she didn't hate them after all. In some ways, she realized with amusement, they reminded her quite a lot of herself.

'Yuk, I don't like cauliflower,' declared Ella, her tone fractious.

To the child's astonishment Maxine replied, 'Neither do I,' and promptly lobbed the offending vegetable out through the kitchen window. 'Let's have frozen peas instead.'

'We like Big Macs,' said Josh hopefully the following evening.

Maxine, who had been burrowing through the contents of the freezer in search of fish fingers, because she knew how to cook them, closed the door with relief.

'OK,' she said to Josh's amazement and delight.

Berenice had always been a stickler for proper, home-cooked meals. 'But don't tell your father.'

Guy phoned every evening. Maxine, hovering unseen in the doorway, eavesdropped shamelessly whilst his children sung her praises. Nannying wasn't so bad once you got the hang of it, she decided, priding herself on her success. And letting the children stay up until midnight had been a stroke of genius; no more horrendous six-thirty starts. She couldn't imagine why more households hadn't cottoned on to such a perfect scheme.

'Everything all right?' Guy would enquire, when she was summoned to the phone for interrogation.

'Perfect!' Determined to impress the hell out of him to pay him back for ever having doubted her, she boasted, 'They've been absolute angels.'

Josh and Ella, sitting on the stairs, collapsed in giggles.

'Hmm,' said Guy, not believing her for a second. 'In that case you've got the wrong children. Return them to the spaceship and make sure the real ones are home by the time I get back.'

'You didn't tell Dad you'd reversed his car into the gatepost,' Josh reminded her when she had replaced the receiver.

Maxine's smile was angelic. 'Don't you remember, darling? That stupid man in the Reliant Robin drove into the back of the car whilst we were parked on the seafront.'

'No he didn't. You reversed into the gatepost.'

'Fine.' She picked up the phone once more. 'I'll call and tell your father now. Oh, and maybe you'd like to explain to him how you managed to smash the kitchen window with your sister's Sindy doll . . .'

Josh's shoulders sagged and he waved his hands in a gesture of defeat. He might have known he didn't stand a chance against an expert like Maxine. 'OK, OK. Put the phone down. You win.'

But whilst being with the children was fun, it had its restrictions. Maxine found herself yearning for adult company. By Thursday she realized she was even looking forward to Guy's phone call from Paris, and felt absurdly put out when he spoke to Josh and Ella, then hung up.

'He was in a hurry,' Josh explained. 'He said some people were waiting for him and he had to go out.'

'How nice for him,' said Maxine sourly. It was five o'clock and the evening stretched ahead interminably. All she had to look forward to was beating Josh and Ella at Monopoly and maybe the added thrill of washing her hair.

Janey, who enjoyed washing her hair, was in the bath when the phone shrilled at six o'clock. Inwardly cursing but unable to leave it to ring – there was always that infinitesimal chance that it might be Alan, after all – she climbed out of the bath and made her way, naked and dripping bubbles, into the sitting room.

'Big favour,' Maxine beseeched, on the other end of the line. 'Big, big favour. How would you like to save your poor demented sister's life?'

'Not very much.' If Maxine was planning a moonlight flit from Trezale House, Janey didn't want her flitting back to the flat. With a trace of suspicion she said, 'I thought Guy was away this week.'

'Exactly,' declared Maxine, then giggled. 'What a strange thing to say. I wasn't asking you to play hired assassin.'

That was a relief, Janey supposed. Shifting from one foot to the other, she watched the bath bubbles melt into the carpet. 'So what do you want?'

'I'm suffering from cabin fever,' cried Maxine with suitable drama. 'If I don't get out of here for a couple of hours I won't be responsible for my actions. And Colin's just phoned, inviting me to have a drink with him.'

'I'm in the bath,' complained Janey.

'No you aren't, you're in the sitting room. Sweetie, it's not too much to ask, is it?' Maxine switched into wheedling mode. 'Josh and Ella would absolutely love to see you again. And you know how brilliant you are at Monopoly . . .'

It really was a gorgeous house. Janey, kicking off her shoes and stretching out across the long sofa, gazed around appreciatively at the beamed ceiling, matte burgundy walls and glossy, rug-strewn parquet floor. Maxine and her incurable mania for clutter had reduced her own small flat to chaos but Trezale House was evidently large enough to handle it. The style of the sitting room was elegant but at the same time relaxed. The paintings hanging on the walls vied for space with a selection of framed photographs, expertly lit. Thanks to Jessica Newman, Paula's mother, the antique furniture was lovingly polished, the indoor plants immaculately tended. Janey was pleased to see that her own flower arrangements were still looking as fresh as they had the previous Saturday.

But it was midnight, the children were in bed and she was starving. 'Help yourself to anything,' Maxine had declared, the expansive sweep of her arm encompassing the contents of the entire kitchen. That had been at seven-thirty when Janey hadn't been hungry. Now, checking her watch and marvelling at her own gullibility – Maxine had promised faithfully to be back by eleven at the very latest – she padded barefoot into the kitchen and opened the fridge. Josh, who was the most appalling cheat, had beaten her at Monopoly and a girl deserved some compensation, after all.

Abandoning her diet, she'd just finished piling a dinner plate with French bread, pâté and a hefty slice of Dolcelatte when a car snaked up the drive, its headlights dazzling her as she peered out through the kitchen window.

Maxine was back at last. Too hungry to stop now, Janey gave her a wave and picked up the already opened bottle of red wine which had been left balancing precariously on the edge of the windowsill. She wouldn't have bothered if she'd been on her own, but now that Maxine was here they might as well finish it up between them.

By the time the front door opened, Janey was comfortably ensconced once more on the sofa. Through a mouthful of pâté she called out, 'And about time too! Come in here this minute and tell me what you've been doing to that poor defenceless cricketer. I hope you haven't been tampering with his middle wicket . . .'

'Absolutely not,' said a cool male voice behind her, and Janey turned pale.

'Oh God, I'm s . . . sorry,' she stammered, hideously

embarrassed at having been caught out. The attempted witticism had been feeble enough anyway, but at least Maxine would have laughed.

Guy Cassidy, however, wasn't looking the least bit amused. Janey's complexion, unable to make up its mind, promptly reddened. The dinner plate clattered against the coffee table as she shoved it hurriedly away from her, like a shoplifter caught in the act. It was ridiculous, she told herself; she had a perfect right to be here. She just wished Guy wouldn't look at her like that.

'Well,' he said finally, glancing at the two brimming glasses of wine on the table and at the almost empty bottle beside them. 'You appear to have made yourself at home. Aren't you going to offer me a drink?'

Bastard, thought Janey. To add insult to injury, her hand shook like a leaf as she silently passed him the nearest glass.

'And I suppose I don't need to ask where Maxine is. Screwing some unfortunate cricketer, from the sound of it.' Collapsing into one of the chairs opposite her, he consulted his watch. 'It's past midnight. Is this a regular occurrence?'

'What?'

'You, doing the babysitting. Has it been going on all week?'

'Of course not!' Janey retaliated. Outraged by the unfairness of the suggestion, she took a great slug of wine. There was really no need for him to take his irritation out on her. 'I thought you weren't supposed to be flying back until tomorrow, anyway,' she said in accusing tones, wishing she didn't feel at such a disadvantage. He must have been travelling for hours, but in his olive-green cashmere sweater and white jeans he still looked as fresh as if he'd just got up, whereas she was only too conscious of the fact that she was wearing an ancient grey tee-shirt and leggings, and no make-up at all.

'Maybe I wanted to check up on what happens when I'm away,' he countered evenly, those unnerving dark eyes boring into her as she emptied her glass. 'I hope you enjoyed that.'

By this time thoroughly fed up, Janey responded with a belligerent stare. 'It was OK.'

He nodded 'So it should be. That was a bottle of seventy-eight Châteauneuf du Pape. It cost two hundred and forty pounds.'

# Chapter 11

Swarming tourists were all right in their place but unless they were prepared to put their money where their mouths were, Thea Vaughan was a lot happier when she had her beloved studio to herself.

All day long she'd smiled and silently suffered the endless stream of visitors who'd trooped in and out of the gallery. Most had temporarily tired of the beach and were simply seeking a diversion out of the sun. Some, treating Thea as if she didn't exist, openly criticized her sculptures. Others, feigning interest, admired her work and engaged her in pointless, time-wasting conversation. Occasionally they fell in love with a particular piece and only balked when they saw the price tag.

So far this week she hadn't sold a single sculpture. With the rent overdue, it was especially demoralizing. All those wasted smiles and dashed hopes. She was tempted to tell the next influx of ignorant, sunburnt visitors to get stuffed, just for the hell of it.

'I'm sorry, did you say something?'

The visitor, a lone male in his early sixties, turned enquiringly in Thea's direction as she emerged from the back of the gallery where she had been making a fresh pot of coffee.

'Not a word,' Thea lied smoothly, having glanced down at his shoes. No holiday flip-flops these, but polished brown leather brogues of the very highest quality worn with traditional lighter brown trousers, a brown and cream checked shirt and a Harris tweed jacket. In these temperatures the man had to be on the verge of heat-stroke. One simply didn't tell the owner of such an outfit to get stuffed.

It was one of her better decisions.

The prospective customer was standing in a pool of sunlight beside the open window, thoughtfully stroking his moustache as he studied one of the sculptures of which Thea was particularly proud. The almost life-sized figure of a ballerina, sitting on the floor to tie the ribbons on her shoes, was priced at £3,000. Earlier in the day a skinny Welshman had elbowed his wife in the ribs and said loudly, 'There now, Gwyneth, maybe I could put you in your slippers, dip you into a tank of concrete and flog you in some fancy gallery.' The wife had cackled with laughter and Thea had gritted her teeth, longing to punch them both down the stairs. To add insult to injury the sniggering couple had left Starburst wrappers strewn across the bleached wooden floorboards. Oh, the joys of cretinous bloody tourists . . .

But this man, even if he was a tourist, which she doubted, was in a different league altogether. Anxious not to put him off, Thea decided to wait for him to initiate any conversation. Resuming her seat before the half-finished figure upon which she was currently working, she rinsed her fingers in the bowl of water next to it and continued moulding the clay over the wire base of the torso.

Within the space of a minute she became aware of the fact that the man was now watching her. Calmly ignoring him, she concentrated instead upon the job in hand. The naked female required breasts and she had to decide on an appropriate size for them. It was also tricky ensuring they didn't end up looking like improbable silicone implants. The figure was of a middle-aged woman; they had to have the correct amount of droop.

Oliver Cassidy, in turn, was studying the interesting outline of Thea Vaughan's breasts beneath her ivory cheesecloth blouse. She was wearing several heavy silver necklaces and no bra, and as far as he was concerned her figure was admirable.

He was drawn, too, to the strong facial features of the woman who seemed so absorbed in her work. With those heavy-lidded dark brown eyes and that long Roman nose, she looked almost like a bird of prey. The swirl of white hair, caught up in a loose bun, contrasted strongly with her deep tan, but although he estimated she must be in her late forties, the lines on her face were few.

Observing her clever, capable hands as they moulded the damp clay, he said, 'Did you do all these?'

Thea glanced up and responded with a brief smile. 'Yes.'

'You're very good.'

'Thank you.'

Intrigued by her apparent lack of interest in engaging him in conversation, Oliver Cassidy thrust his hands into his trouser pockets and surveyed the ballerina once more.

'I particularly like this one.'

'So do I,' said Thea easily. Leaning back and resting

her wrists on her thighs, careful not to get clay on the full, navy blue cotton skirt, she added, 'It's for sale at three thousand pounds.'

She liked the fact that he didn't even flinch. She liked it even better when he frowned and said, 'What's the matter, are you trying to put me off? Don't you want to sell it?'

'I'm an artist, not a saleswoman.' Narrowing her eyes and tilting her head to one side in order to survey the figure currently in progress, she said, 'And since three thousand pounds is a great deal of money, I doubt very much whether anything I say would have much impact either way. I couldn't persuade you to buy something you didn't want, so why on earth should I even try?'

Accustomed to the cut-throat machinations of the property business which had made him his fortune and rendered him impervious to the hardest of hard sells, Oliver Cassidy almost laughed aloud. Instead, however, and much to his own surprise, he heard himself saying, 'But I do want it. So persuade me.'

Thea, enjoying herself immensely, replied, 'No.'

'Why not?'

'Because you might not be able to afford it. I couldn't live with my conscience if I thought I'd inveigled you into buying something you couldn't afford.'

In fifty-one supremely selfish years she had never yet been troubled by her conscience, but he didn't need to know this. Her eyes alight with amusement, she shook her head.

'Do I look,' demanded Oliver Cassidy in pompous tones, 'as if I can't afford it?'

This time she gave him a slow, regretful smile. 'I wouldn't know. As I said, I'm not a saleswoman.'

He replied heavily, 'I can tell.'

The ensuing silence lasted several seconds. Thea, determined not to be the one to break it, carried on working.

'I'll buy it,' said Oliver Cassidy finally. 'On one condition.'

She raised her eyebrows. 'Mmm?'

'That you have dinner with me tonight.'

Openly teasing him now, she said, 'Are you sure you can afford both?'

For the first time, Oliver Cassidy smiled. 'I think I can just about manage it.'

'Oh well then, in that case it's an offer I can't refuse. I'd be delighted to have dinner with you, Mr—'

'Cassidy. Oliver Cassidy. Please, call me Oliver.'

For buying the ballerina I'd call you anything you damn well like, thought Thea, struggling to conceal her inner triumph. Rising to her feet, she wiped her hands on her skirt. What did a few clay stains matter, after all, when you'd just made a mega sale? The contract was sealed with a firm handshake.

'Thank you! It's a deal, then. Oliver.'

# Chapter 12

'He's a pig,' said Janey, who still hadn't forgiven Guy for his snide comments of the previous night. Overcome with a sudden need for companionship she had arrived at Thea's house at eight only to find her mother getting ready to go out.

Thea, wearing her favourite crimson silk shirt over a peasant-style white skirt, was doing her make-up in the mirror above the fireplace. With an ease borne of long practice, she swept black liner around her eyes, enlarging and elongating them just as she had done for the past thirty years.

'You mean that photographer chap?' she said vaguely, having been only half listening to her elder daughter's grumbling. 'I thought he was supposed to be rather gorgeous.'

'That's beside the point.' Janey, immune to Guy Cassidy's physical attractions, threw her a moody glance. 'And that stupid bottle of wine was just about the last straw. It was Maxine's fault, of course, but he automatically assumed I'd opened it.'

Thea completed her make-up with a dash of crimson lipstick and treated herself to an extra squirt of Mitsouko for luck. Chucking the bottle into her bag, she said briskly, 'Well, he isn't your problem. And I'm sure Maxine can deal with him. She's always been good with difficult men.'

Luckily, Janey hadn't expected motherly support and reassurances; they simply weren't Thea Vaughan's style. Now, listening to her airy dismissal of the problem which as far as her mother was concerned wasn't even a problem, she managed a rueful smile.

'Speaking of difficult men, who are you seeing tonight?' Is all this really in aid of Philip?'

Thea froze with her bag halfway to her shoulder. Her eyebrows lifted in resignation. 'Oh, sod it.'

Philip Slattery wasn't difficult at all. One of Thea's long-standing and most devoted admirers, he was as gentle as a puppy. Janey liked him enormously, whereas her mother took him almost entirely for granted, seeing him when it suited her and ditching him unmercifully whenever somebody more interesting came along. As, presumably, somebody now had.

'You mean, Oh sod it, you *were* supposed to be seeing Philip but you'd forgotten all about him,' she said in admonishing tones. Then, because Thea was showing no sign of reaching for the phone, she added, 'Mum, you'll have to let him know. You can't just stand him up.'

Thea pulled a face. 'He's going to be awfully cross with me. He's holding a dinner party at his house. Now I suppose he'll accuse me of lousing up the numbers.'

'Mum!' Janey protested, dismayed by this act of thoughtlessness. 'How could you possibly forget a dinner party? Why don't you just cancel your other date?'

'Out of the question,' declared Thea, picking up the

phone and frowning as she tried to recall Philip's number. Her own, it went without saying, was practically engraved on his heart. 'I sold the ballerina this afternoon.'

'So?'

'He invited me to have dinner with him, on the strength of it. Darling, he's seriously wealthy, not to mention attractive! This could be so *important;* I'd have to be a complete idiot to turn him down.'

Poor, faithful Philip and cruel, mercenary Thea. Janey listened in silence to her mother's side of the phone call as she blithely excused herself from the dinner party which he had undoubtedly spent the past fortnight planning to the nth degree.

'Who is he, then?' she said when Thea had replaced the receiver.

Her mother, whose memory was notorious fickle, checked her reflection in the mirror and smoothed an eyebrow into place. 'Oliver. Kennedy, I think.' With a vague gesture, she dismissed the problem in favour of more important details. 'He wears extremely expensive shoes, darling. *And* drives a Rolls Royce.'

'You mean he's a chauffeur.'

Thea gave her daughter a pitying look. 'Janey, don't be such a miserable spoilsport. He's rich, he's interested, and I like him. I mean this is the kind of man I could even be persuaded to *marry.*'

It was the kind of lifestyle she could easily get used to, the kind she had always felt she deserved. Hopeless with money herself, however, Thea had got off to a poor start when, at the age of nineteen, she had met and fallen even more hopelessly in love with Patrick Vaughan. Big, blond and a dyed-in-the wool Bohemian, he was the mercurial star of his year at art college, adored by more women than even he knew what to do with and a dedicated pleasure-seeker. Within six weeks of meeting him, Thea had moved into his incredibly untidy attic apartment in Chelsea, embracing with enthusiasm the chaotic lifestyle of her lover and encouraging him in his work.

But Patrick only embraced her in return when no other more interesting women were around. Incurably promiscuous, his wanderings caused Thea such grief that, looking back over those years, she wondered how she'd ever managed to stand it. At the time, however, she had loved him so desperately that leaving had been out of the question. When Patrick, laughing, had told her that fidelity was bourgeois, she'd believed him. When he'd told her that none of the others meant anything anyway, she'd believed him. And when – quite seriously – he'd told her that he was going to be the greatest British artist of the twentieth century she'd believed that too. She was lucky to have him, and nobody had ever said that living with a genius would be easy.

It wasn't. The never-ending supply of eager women continued to troop through their lives and turning a tolerant blind eye became increasingly difficult. Furthermore, Patrick Vaughan only painted when he felt like it, which wasn't often enough to appease either the buyers or the bookmakers.

Gambling, always a passion with him, fulfilled yet another craving for excitement. And although it was fun when he won, the losses far outweighed the gains. As his

addiction spiralled, Thea began to realize that maybe love
wasn't enough after all. The all-consuming intensity with
which Patrick gambled might divert his attention from
the numerous affairs but it scared her. Patrick, still
laughing, told her that worrying about money was even
more bourgeois than fidelity but this time she had her
doubts. Neither the promised luxurious lifestyle nor his
glittering career were showing any signs of materializing
and the novelty of being poor and perpetually cheated
on was beginning to wear off.

Unable to find a market for her own work she had
reluctantly taken a job in a Putney craft shop, but Patrick
was spending everything she earned. Bailiffs were
knocking on the door. She deserved more than this. It
was, she decided, time to leave.

Fate, however, had other ideas. Discovering that she
was pregnant threw Thea into a flat spin. She was only
twenty-two, hopelessly unmaternal and deeply aware of
her own inability to cope alone. All of a sudden Patrick-
and-all-his-faults was better than no Patrick at all.

To everyone's astonishment Patrick himself was
delighted by the news of the impending arrival. Never
having given much thought to the matter before, he was
bowled over by the prospect of becoming a father and
didn't – as all his friends had secretly imagined – do one
of his famous runners. He had created a son who would
inherit his artistic genius, good looks and charisma, he
told everyone who would listen. This was his link with
immortality. What could be more important than a child?
At Patrick's insistence, and to his friends' further
amazement – they had assumed he would think it far too

bourgeois – he and Thea were married at once. The wedding was funded by a timely win on the Derby. Fascinated and inspired by his new wife's condition, he resumed painting with a vengeance, insisting that she sit for him whilst he captured her voluptuous nakedness in oils. The paintings, among the best he'd ever done, sold easily through a West London gallery. Gradually the creditors were paid off. And if Patrick was still seeing other women, for once in his life he exercised discretion. For Thea, the months before the birth were some of the happiest she had ever known.

Janey, when she arrived, was a monumental disappointment to both of them. Squashed and ugly, not only did she bear no resemblance whatsoever to either parent, she was entirely the wrong sex.

With all his visions of Madonna and child shattered and the reality of fatherhood failing abysmally to live up to fond expectations, Patrick promptly reverted to type. The painting ground to an abrupt halt, the gambling and womanizing escalated to new and dizzy heights, and in order to escape both the noisy wails of his daughter and the silent tears of his wife, he spent less and less time at home.

Maxine, born twenty-two months later as a result of a last-ditch attempt at reconciliation, failed to do the trick. Another daughter, another shattering disappointment. Knowing that it was hopeless to go on trying and by this time so miserable that it was hardly even a wrench, Thea packed her things, gathered up the two girls and left.

Not wanting to stay in London, she moved to Cornwall in order to start a new and happier life. From now on, she vowed, she would learn by her mistakes and Patrick's example. Being a doormat was no fun; selfishness ruled. Never again would she let herself be emotionally intimidated by a man. She was going to make damn sure she kept her self-respect and enjoyed the rest of her life.

For twenty-five years she had kept her promise to herself. Bringing up two young daughters single-handed wasn't easy, but she'd managed. And whilst it would have been easy to let herself go, she deliberately didn't allow this to happen.

Janey and Maxine learned to fend for themselves from an early age, which Thea felt was all to the good and the only sensible way to ensure that they would grow up with a sense of independence. She wanted them to realize that the only person one could truly rely on was oneself.

She had been divorced, now, for over twenty years and never been tempted to remarry. Patrick had disappeared to America, leaving her with nothing but his surname, and although alimony would have been nice, it wasn't something she'd ever expected from him. Managing on her own and struggling to balance her meagre finances had become a matter of pride.

And, on the surface, she was content with her modest lifestyle. Now that her children were grown up, the struggle had eased. Her home was small but comfortable. The studio where she created and sold her sculptures was rented. She made just enough money, as a rule, to enjoy herself, and when business was slow there was always Philip, happy to help out in whichever way he could. Not a wealthy man himself, he was nevertheless heartbreakingly willing to dig into his own pockets when the need arose. He really was a very nice man, as devoted to Thea as she had once been to Patrick. Sadly for him, she was unable to prevent herself treating him as badly as Patrick had once treated her.

But Oliver Cassidy was in a different league altogether. After years of struggling and making do, Thea was ready to be spoiled by a man who wasn't afraid to wave his wallet. And although she'd only just met him, she knew instinctively that here was a man who wasn't afraid of anything at all.

It had been a dazzling evening. Arriving in the Rolls less than five minutes after Janey had left, Oliver had picked her up and taken her to the five-star Grand Rock Hotel where he was staying. The hotel restaurant, one of the best in Cornwall, was as impressive as she had hoped. And her dinner companion, Thea decided as she sipped her cognac, had definitely exceeded all expectations.

'How long are you staying down here?' she asked, having already learned that he lived in Bristol.

Oliver Cassidy shrugged, adjusting snowy shirt cuffs. 'A week, maybe two. I've been looking at properties in the area, thinking of moving down here.'

Better and better, thought Thea happily, admiring his discreet gold cufflinks and breathing in the scent of Penhaligon cologne. 'Well, I'm pretty familiar with the area. Perhaps I could help you there.' Pausing, she broke into a smile. 'Helping other people to spend their money is a great hobby of mine.'

As far as Oliver Cassidy was concerned, her bluntness made a refreshing change. Over the years he had become something of an expert on the subject of gold-digging females and what he'd discovered was that, to a woman, they would tear out their own professionally manicured fingernails rather than admit that his money held any interest for them or that it could make any difference to their attraction towards him. It was all so tiresome, so bloody predictable.

Thea Vaughan, on the other hand, was making no secret whatsoever of her interest in both him and his money, and he found her honesty quite disarming. He wanted to get to know this charming, teasing woman; she interested him more than anyone else had done for years. He also, quite urgently, wanted to take her up to his suite and make love to her. Ever the perfect English gentleman, however, he felt he should allow her to finish her cognac first.

It wasn't difficult to read his mind. Thea was looking forward to the hours ahead just as much as he was. Beneath the immaculate, dark blue suit and white shirt she could only too easily imagine the contours of his body. Oliver Kennedy – no, Cassidy – had the erect stance of a guardsman and he'd kept himself in remarkably good shape. His chest was broad, his stomach flat and he sported an impressive tan. Going to bed with him, she thought as her fingers idly caressed the stem of her brandy glass, would be fun.

But there was no hurry. No hurry at all.

'Go on then,' she said with a provocative smile. 'I've told you all about my miserable marriage. Now it's your turn.'

'Which particular miserable marriage did you have in mind?' Oliver, after puffing meditatively on his cigar, leaned back in his chair and signalled for the waiter to replenish their drinks. If she could wait, so could he. 'There are three to choose from.'

'All of them,' said Thea cheerfully. 'In chronological order. And I want to hear the gory details . . .'

Since picking wives had never been one of his strong points, there were plenty of those, too. Over the next half hour he regaled her with hair-raising tales of his three scheming, volatile wives. If Thea suspected that he was bending the facts in order to present himself in a blameless light, she didn't voice such thoughts aloud. And it was riveting stuff anyway, better than any soap opera. According to Oliver – trusting, innocent Oliver – he had been bamboozled in turn into matrimony by Liza, Milly and Fay. All three, it appeared, had been blonde, beautiful and absolute hell to live with. They made Macbeth's witches look cute.

None of the marriages had lasted longer than three years. Each wife had departed in a flurry of recriminations and alimony. Following the third divorce, Oliver had vowed that he would stick to mistresses. They might be expensive but they were a damn sight less expensive than greedy, vengeful wives.

'And there were no children?' said Thea, totally engrossed and not in the least put out by the declaration. She couldn't imagine anything more thrilling than being an expensive mistress. This kind of scenario was right up her street.

Oliver looked momentarily uncomfortable. 'I have a son by my first wife,' he replied, after taking another puff of his cigar. 'But we had . . . er . . . a disagreement some years ago. I'm afraid we haven't been on speaking terms since then.'

With a directness which so often made her elder daughter cringe, Thea rested her chin on her clasped hands and said, 'Really? What happened?'

'I tried to stop him making the same mistake I had.' Oliver Cassidy didn't make a habit of admitting that he could have been wrong. He still wasn't entirely convinced that in the matter of Véronique he might have been, but her untimely death had come as a great shock to him nevertheless. 'I'd been through three disastrous marriages and realized too late that my wives were only interested in my money. My son was living in London, doing very well for himself in his own career. Then, when he was twenty-three, he met a young French girl. She was eighteen years old and penniless. He was besotted with her. Within a few weeks of meeting her, he brought her down to Bristol and informed me that they were planning to get married.' He paused, remembering the ensuing argument as plainly as if it had happened yesterday. 'Well. To cut a long story short, I told him he was a bloody fool, and he went ahead and married her anyway. They had two children, and a few years later she died. I attempted to contact my son afterwards, but I'm afraid he wasn't able to forgive me for disapproving of the marriage in the first place.'

'But that's terrible!' cried Thea, suffused with indignation on his behalf. 'You only had his best interests at heart. You were trying to help him!'

'I know, I know. But my son had ideas of his own. You know how stubborn children can be.'

'So you've never ever seen your grandchildren?'Thea persisted, her dark eyes sympathetic.

Oliver shook his head. There was no need to mention that fateful afternoon when Véronique had brought them to his house. The encounter wasn't something of which he was particularly proud.

'Never.'

'It's a tragedy,' she declared expansively. 'And those poor children . . .'

Smiling, he leaned closer. 'Between ourselves, that's one of the reasons I'm thinking of buying a house down here. They moved to Trezale a year ago. I'm not getting any younger.' He spread his hands and added sorrowfully, 'I'd like the chance to get to know them.'

Her emotions heightened by Chablis and champagne, Thea was on the verge of tears. She took his hand in hers. 'You know, you really are a very nice man.'

Oliver Cassidy's plush suite was decorated in peacock blues and greens, and subtly lit.

Unashamed of her body, Thea removed her clothes with neither coyness nor ceremony, then crossed the bedroom to stand naked before him.

'Who's seducing who?' he said, appreciating her lack of artifice.

Thea, loosening his tie, looked amused. 'Does it really matter? We're adults. I think we both know why we're here . . .'

He removed his jacket and watched her capable fingers unfastening the buttons of his white shirt. She was still smiling, evidently enjoying herself. And she was right, of course; any further games were unnecessary.

Aroused by her straightforward attitude, as well as by the proximity of her unclothed body, Oliver realized that it was years since he had wanted a woman this badly. He put his arms around her, drawing her against him. He was sixty-one years old and his life wasn't over yet.

'Yes,' he said, inhaling her warm scent and pressing a kiss to her temple, where white hair met tanned, enticingly perfumed skin. 'And I think you are a very nice woman.'

'You're so right.' Closing her eyes, Thea slid her hands inside his unbuttoned shirt. 'I am.'

# Chapter 13

'If you don't eat your Weetabix,' said Maxine, hating the sound of her own voice and frantically casting about for an appropriate threat, 'I'll—'

'What?' Josh challenged her, his eyes narrowing. In the two days since his father had been back from France, Maxine had definitely changed for the worse. No longer any fun, she had taken to bossing them around, ruthlessly rationing their television time and insisting they do boring school work even though it was still the middle of the summer holidays. If she hadn't demanded to see his exercise books he would never even have found the squashed Mars bar in the side pocket of his satchel, so the fact that he wasn't hungry was all her fault anyway. 'If I don't eat my Weetabix,' he repeated mutinously, 'you'll what?'

Hell, thought Maxine, who couldn't have cared less whether or not he ate his stupid breakfast. All she was trying to do was prove to Guy Cassidy that she could do the job he so obviously didn't think her capable of, and all she was doing was making everyone miserable, including herself.

And Guy, damn him, wasn't even paying attention. Buried behind his paper, apparently engrossed in the racing pages, he was drinking strong black coffee and ignoring his young son's act of rebellion. Maxine, who had been so determined to impress him, wondered why she even bothered.

'I shall begin by shaving your head,' she replied sweetly, because Josh was inordinately proud of his spiky blond hair. She had also observed the first furtive flickerings of interest in ten-year-old Tanya Trevelyan, whose parents ran the local post office. 'And then I shall paint red spots all over your face with indelible felt pen. Then I'll tell Tanya that you're madly in love with her!'

Ella screamed with laughter. Josh, turning purple, shot Maxine a look of fury.

'You wouldn't!'

'Oh yes, I would.'

Grabbing Guy's arm, he wailed, 'Dad, tell her she can't do that! She can't tell Tanya I love her . . .'

But Guy, who appeared to have other matters on his mind, wasn't interested. 'Of course she won't.' His tone brusque, he glanced at his watch and stood up. 'Damn, I'm going to be late. I'll be back this evening at around nine.'

'Make her promise not to say anything to Tanya,' Josh begged, still mortified by the prospect of hideous humiliation.

'Make him promise to eat his Weetabix,' said Maxine, imitating his nine-year-old whine.

Guy merely looked exasperated. 'For heaven's sake!'

'Thanks for your support,' muttered Maxine, seizing the bowl of beige mush and clattering it into the sink. 'You're a great help.'

Ella, who detested having her hair washed, tugged at her sleeve. Her eyes shining, she said hopefully, 'Maxine? If I'm naughty, will you shave *my* head?'

Since attempting to instil discipline and show Guy what a treasure she was had been such a dismal failure, Maxine left the children to their own devices for the rest of the morning. If non-stop TV cartoons were all they wanted to watch, why should she care?

Having washed up the breakfast things and gazed morosely out at the rain sweeping in from the sea, she sat down at eleven o'clock with a big gin and tonic and the portable phone. To cheer herself up and get her own back on Guy for being so stroppy, she was going to phone all her London friends for a good gossip. The fact that it was peak time and would cost him an absolute fortune only made the prospect more enjoyable.

'You make him sound like an ogre,' exclaimed Cindy, from the opulent comfort of her four-poster bed in Chelsea. Recently married to a rich-but-ugly industrialist, some twenty-five years older than herself, whose vast stomach, thankfully, was a serious impediment to their sex life, she couldn't imagine what Maxine had to moan about. 'I met Guy Cassidy at a party last year and he was absolutely charming. All the women were drooling like dogs! Maxi, you have to admit he's sensationally attractive...'

'Looks aren't everything,' Maxine drawled, jiggling the ice cubes in her glass and tucking her bare feet beneath her on the sofa. Then, relenting slightly, she added casually, 'Well, he's not bad I suppose.'

'Don't give me that,' crowed Cindy, who knew her

too well. 'What are you trying to tell me, that you've had your hormones surgically removed? You must fancy him rotten!'

Maxine grinned. Cindy, in London, was a safe enough confidante.

'OK,' she admitted, taking a slug of gin. 'So maybe I do, a bit. But I'd fancy him a lot more if only he'd show a smidgeon of interest in return. You have no idea how demoralizing it is, slapping on the old make-up and making myself generally irresistible when he takes about as much interest in me as he does in the bloody milkman.'

'Sometimes make-up isn't enough,' replied Cindy, ever practical. 'Sometimes you just have to rip off your pinny and get naked.'

'You mean I should seduce him?' At such an awesome prospect, even Maxine blanched.

'Works every time,' Cindy said happily. Maxine doubted whether Cindy would even recognise a pinafore if it leapt up and strangled her. She'd certainly never worn one in her life.

'It wouldn't work with Guy.' Gloomily contemplating her almost empty glass, she imagined the scenario. She had a horrid feeling he would laugh his handsome head off. Before firing her, naturally.

'Why?' countered Cindy. 'Have you got fat?'

'I've got Guy Cassidy as a boss,' Maxine sighed. 'So far, he's seen through everything I've tried, and all he does is sneer. He's too smart to fall for an old trick like that.'

'You're losing your nerve, girl. Living out in the sticks is doing something to your brain. Isn't he worth taking a chance on?'

'It's all right for you.' As Maxine spoke, the doorbell rang. 'All you did was meet him at a party. You want to try living with him.'

'Darling, I'd be there like a shot!' Cindy, her interest aroused, sounded excited. 'Now *there's* an idea. You could invite me down for a weekend. If you're too chicken, I'll have a crack at him myself!'

'I'll have to go.' Maxine, uncurling herself, realized that her left leg had been seized by pins and needles and was now completely numb. 'There's someone at the door.'

'Oh pleeease,' Cindy urged. 'I'm your friend, aren't I? Go on, invite me!'

'No,' said Maxine bluntly. 'You're married.'

'Don't be so boring,' protested Cindy. 'At least I'm not chicken!'

Cindy didn't understand, thought Maxine as she made her way awkwardly to the front door, clinging to furniture as she went. She wasn't chicken either, she just wasn't prepared to make a complete prat of herself and lose both home and job into the bargain. And she would have her wicked way with Guy Cassidy eventually, she was quite determined on that score. It was simply a matter of timing and technique. And pouncing on him buck-naked, Maxine decided with a small, wry smile, didn't exactly rate highly in terms of finesse.

She needn't have bothered to stop en route and grab a handful of fivers from the tin in the kitchen, because it wasn't the milkman after all.

'Yes?' said Maxine, staring at the woman on the doorstep and mentally noting the style and quality of the clothes she wore. She'd bet her last Jaffa cake it wasn't the Avon lady either.

'Is Guy here?' The visitor eyed Maxine in turn, instantly homing in on the blackcurrant jam stain which, courtesy of Ella, adorned her yellow tee-shirt.

The rain was still bucketing down, driven in from the sea by a ferocious wind and hammering against the windows like gravel. Anyone else, caught out in such a storm, would have looked like a scarecrow.

But this woman, wrapped in a long, lean leather coat the colour of toffee apples, worn over a cream and toffee-apple striped silk shirt and cream trousers, seemed impervious to the weather. Screamingly elegant from her short, sleek black hair to her beige Ferragamo shoes, she simply wasn't the kind of female whose mascara ever ran. Maxine couldn't bear people like that. Most ominous of all, however, was the fact that in her elegant hand she carried an elegant suitcase. Naturally, it matched the outfit.

Feeling very down-at-heel by comparison, Maxine replied with a trace of belligerence. 'He's away on a shoot in Wiltshire. We aren't expecting him back until late this evening. He may even decide to stay there overnight.'

The woman, however, simply shrugged and smiled. Even her teeth were elegant. 'So much for surprises.'

Deeply engrossed in her telephone conversation with Cindy, Maxine hadn't heard an approaching car. Now she realized there wasn't one.

'I came by taxi,' said the woman, intercepting her glance in the direction of the drive.

'Don't worry.' Maxine stepped aside and gestured her

to step inside. 'I'll phone for another one. I'm sorry you've had a wasted journey, but if you'd like to leave a message for Guy I'll make sure he gets it. As I said, he probably won't be back tonight . . .'

'It's quite all right,' said the woman easily, making her way past Maxine into the hall and dismissing her offer with a nonchalant wave of her wrist. Indicating the suitcase in her other hand, she added, 'This isn't a fleeting visit. I'm down here for a week at least.'

Bugger, thought Maxine. It hadn't worked. 'Really? How nice,' she said aloud.

Her name was Serena Charlton and in confined spaces the reek of her scent was positively overpowering. One of Guy's ruthlessly slender model 'friends', she was showing every sign of making herself at home.

'We're extremely good friends, she told Maxine as she slithered out of the leather coat and handed it to her. 'I expect Guy's told you all about me.'

Not so much as a syllable, thought Maxine, taking comfort from the fact. It was going to be interesting seeing Guy's reaction when he returned and found an uninvited guest comfortably installed in his home. What fun if he booted her out . . .

'Then again,' said Serena, observing her deliberately blank expression, 'he always did like to keep his private life to himself. And gossiping with the household staff isn't quite the done thing, after all.'

'Of course not.' No m'lady, sorry m'lady, Maxine silently mocked, only just resisting the urge to tug her forelock and bob a fetching little curtsey. She was expected, it seemed, to hang the coat up. To amuse herself, she dumped it instead over the back of the nearest chair.

But Serena appeared genuinely unaware of the fact that her words might have given offence. Making herself comfortable on the sofa, she smiled across at Maxine and said, 'A cup of tea would be nice. White with two Hermesetas, please.'

Having heaped at least a hundred calories' worth of brown sugar into the cup, Maxine felt a little better. When she carried it through to Serena in the sitting room she said, 'Josh and Ella are playing upstairs. Shall I tell them you're here?'

Serena was undoubtedly beautiful but she hadn't featured in Josh's list of favourite females, which was another bonus. Maxine soon found out why.

'The children are here?' Serena's face fell. Her tone of voice registered distinct lack of enthusiasm. 'Why aren't they at school?'

'Summer holidays.' Maxine had to work hard to suppress a grin. Serena Charlton, presumably, was childless.

'Oh. No, don't worry about getting them down here. No need to disturb them. You carry on with your work, um . . . Maxine. I'll just sit here and enjoy my tea in peace.'

And get fat into the bargain, thought Maxine smugly, remembering the amount of sugar she'd put in. Dying to get the low-down on Serena, she raced upstairs to interrogate Josh. The lack of enthusiasm, it transpired, was entirely mutual.

'She's staying for a whole *week*?'

Reaching for the remote control, Maxine reduced the volume on the television.

'She thinks she is. Why, don't you like her?'

'Her face is quite pretty,' said Ella helpfully. 'And she's got really short hair.'

'She's OK I suppose.' Josh was making an effort to be fair. 'She brought us some sweets once. But she'd rather be with Dad than us. We've only met her a few times and she always thinks we should go outside and play.' He pulled a face. 'Even when it's raining.'

Their earlier row forgotten, Maxine retorted indignantly. 'And what does your father have to say about that?'

Sometimes Josh seemed wiser than his years. His gaze drifting back towards the television screen, where Tom was beating hell out of Jerry, he replied absently, 'Most of Dad's girlfriends make too much of a fuss over us because they think it'll make him like them more, and then maybe he'll marry them. I think Dad likes Serena because she doesn't do that. He says at least she's honest.'

Nifty reasoning, though Maxine appreciatively. On both sides.

'If I go and get the scissors,' said Ella, 'will you cut my hair off now?'

# Chapter 14

Thanks to the appalling weather, business in the shop was slow. Few people, it seemed, were interested in buying flowers when it was pouring with rain. Janey and Paula, guiltily eating cream cakes from the bakery next door, passed the time by doing the crossword in the local paper and taking it in turn to make endless mugs of tea.

'What's a nice chap like me doing in an advertisement like this?' Paula read aloud as Janey emerged from the back of the shop with yet more tea.

'How many letters?' Janey asked, easing herself back onto her stool and peering across at the paper. 'Could it be Jeremy Beadle?'

'God forbid!' Paula grinned and pointed to the next page. 'I'm on to the Personal column. Don't you ever read it?'

'No.' Pulling a face, Janey followed Paula's index finger and read the rest of the advert. ' "I am a good-looking male, thirty-four, with a whacky sense of humour." Hmm, probably means he's into serious spanking. "Fun-loving partner required, five feet three or under." Ah, so he's an extremely short spanker. "Age, looks and marital status unimportant." That means he's totally desperate.'

'OK,' said Paula, conceding the point. 'He doesn't sound great, I'll admit.'

'Great? He sounds like a nerd.'

'But they aren't all like that. How about this one? "Divorced male, forty, own home and car, new to the area. Likes dining out, theatre, tennis, long walks . . ." What's wrong with him?'

Janey said unforgivingly, 'BO I expect.'

'Don't be mean! Why are you so suspicious?'

'I don't know.' She shrugged. 'If he's so terrific, why does he need to advertise in the Lonely Hearts?'

'He's new to the area and he doesn't want to cruise the bars picking up girls,' said Paula, springing to his defence. 'Because the type of girl he likes doesn't hang around bars waiting to be picked up. There's nothing weird or sinister about advertising in the Personals,' she added firmly. 'Sometimes it's just the most sensible thing to do.'

Janey had never thought of it like that. Neither would she ever have imagined that Paula would argue the case so strongly. Her curiosity aroused, she said, 'Have you done this kind of thing yourself?'

'No, but a friend of mine tried it once. And it worked for her.'

'What happened?'

The younger girl broke into a grin. 'She met a tall blond airline pilot. Within six weeks, they were married. And they're amazingly happy.' Paula, who could give Maxine a run for her money where bluntness was concerned, added, 'You should try it.'

Startled, Janey laughed aloud. '*Me?*'

'It's been two years now since Alan . . . disappeared.' Paula fixed her with a steady gaze. 'I know it's been hard for you, but you really should be starting to think about the rest of your life. You're only twenty-eight, Janey. You need to start going out, meeting new people . . . having fun . . .'

'And you seriously think this is the answer?' Deeply sceptical, Janey said, 'That by answering a few crazy adverts in the local paper I'll change my life?'

'I don't know.' Paula, having made her point, crossed her fingers beneath the counter and prayed that Janey would never find out she'd made up the fairytale romance between her friend and the pilot. Reaching for the paper and returning her attention to the crossword, she added casually, 'But if you don't try it, you'll never know. Now, have a look at fourteen across. Do you think it could be pfennig?'

Paula had a way of saying things which stuck in the mind. As she tackled a pile of ironing that evening, Janey found herself recalling their earlier conversation and beginning to wonder if she had a point after all. Having overcome her initial misgivings, she now conceded that for some people, circumstances beyond their control made it hard for them to socialize in the traditional manner. When she'd pressed Paula for further details about her friend, for example, she'd explained that as an airline pilot, Alistair had been so busy flying all over the world, he simply hadn't had time to meet any girls in his own country. Not interested in the air hostesses with whom he worked, he had placed an advert instead, in *Time Out*, and received sixty-seven replies. The first date hadn't worked out and Geraldine, Paula's friend, had been the second. True love had blossomed almost instantaneously and the remaining sixty-five females hadn't had a look-in.

Janey hadn't believed this story for a moment. Even if Paula hadn't own-goaled herself, calling the pilot Alistair one minute and Alexander the next, she would have seen through the enormous fib, but that didn't mean it couldn't happen. Janey herself had read magazine articles detailing such meetings and subsequent marriages. Paula had undoubtedly been right when she'd declared that sometimes it was simply the most sensible thing to do.

Abandoning the ironing before she wrecked something she was particularly fond of, Janey switched on the kettle. Her stomach was rumbling and she could have murdered a bowl of spaghetti but the cream cakes that afternoon had probably used up her calorie quota for the next three weeks.

Gloomily surveying the contents of the fridge, she set about making herself a boring salad sandwich instead.

'Widower, 62, seeks the company of a lively lady 45–60, for friendship and old-time dancing. Resilient toes an absolute must.'

He sounded lovely. Janey was only sorry she wasn't old enough for him. Wondering if maybe she couldn't get away with lying about her age, she read on.

'Lonely vegan (Sagittarius) wishes to meet soulmate,' pleaded the next ad. 'Non-smoking, teetotal young lady required. Capricorn preferred.'

Aaargh, thought Janey. Oh well, it took all sorts. And who knew, maybe there was a soulmate out there somewhere, reading this advert and experiencing a leap of joyous recognition.

'Gentleman required for plumpish but well-preserved divorcee, 55. Fond of walking, gardening, cooking and dancing.'

That was nice, she could pair up with the foxtrotting widower.

'Discreet businessman seeks ditto lady, 30-50, for mutually pleasurable meetings, afternoons only.'

A typographical error, surely, thought Janey with a grin. Didn't he mean 'matings'?

'Tall, presentable, divorced male, 35, would like to meet normal female.'

She paused and re-read the words, attracted by their simplicity and intrigued to know more. Had his wife been spectacularly abnormal? How tall was tall? And did 'presentable' mean a bank-managerish grey suit with accompanying dandruff, or clean jeans and a tee-shirt that had actually been ironed?

Twenty minutes later, after having absently flipped through the rest of the paper and finished her sandwich, Janey found herself back once more at the Personal column. With a guilty start, she realized she was studying the advertisement placed by Mr Presentable. Even more alarming she was actually giving it serious consideration.

'You should try it,' Paula had said in her uncompromising way. 'You need to meet new people. If you don't try it, you'll never know what you might be missing.'

If the Sagittarian vegan was anything to go by, Janey suspected she did. But maybe . . . just maybe Paula had a point. Mr Presentable didn't sound weird and there was always the chance that he might turn out to be genuinely nice. There was, after all, an undeniable gap in her life, and a cautious toe in the water – nothing too alarming, perhaps a brief meeting in a wine bar for a lunchtime drink – would satisfy her own curiosity and at the same time show Paula that she had at least been willing to make some kind of effort on the man-front.

Or more aptly, the unmanned front.

Although there was Bruno, of course, whom Paula didn't know about. Janey wasn't sure whether he really counted. In addition, knowing how she would have felt if Alan had cheated on her, she hated the thought of getting involved and upsetting Nina. Bruno had assured her that theirs was an open relationship but she was, after all, only hearing his side of the story.

If she was being honest, her attraction towards Bruno was yet another good reason why she should consider replying to the advert. Any real involvement with someone like him could only eventually end in tears. What she really needed to do, Janey decided, was to diversify.

'I don't believe it!' cried Maxine, who had only phoned up in order to relieve her own boredom and have a good moan about Serena. Riveted by the news of Janey's decision, she quite forgot her own irritations. 'Darling, what an absolute scream! I know, we could both answer a few ads and compare notes afterwards. Marks out of ten for looks, brains and bonkability!'

'It isn't a joke.' With great firmness, Janey interrupted her. Her sister, of course, was about the last person in the world in whom she should have confided. Maxine simply couldn't comprehend the idea that meeting new men wasn't always easy. She could scarcely take five paces without tripping over likely contenders in nightclubs, on the street, at supermarket checkouts, even on one occasion in Asprey's. The man in question had been in the company of his girlfriend at the time, choosing from a selection of wildly expensive engagement rings. Maxine, broke as usual and shamelessly trying on jewellery for the hell of it, had fallen into conversation with the two of them and came away with the bridegroom-to-be's phone number in her jacket pocket. When you were Maxine, Janey remembered, men were there for the taking. They practically queued up to be taken, in fact. Usually for everything they had.

'What do you mean, it isn't a joke?' Maxine demanded. 'Of course it's a joke. You can't seriously be serious!'

Janey had known she was making a big mistake. Patiently, she said, 'Why not? If I was looking for a new car, I'd see what was being advertised in the paper. If I wanted to move house I'd find out what the estate agents had on their books. Why should looking for a new man be any different?'

I sound like Paula, she thought with amusement. Maybe we should forget selling flowers and set up a dating agency instead.

'I don't believe it,' repeated Maxine, as close to being struck dumb as it was possible for Maxine to get. 'You *are* serious!'

Having made up her mind, Janey had no intention of allowing herself to be bulldozed out of it now. Before

Maxine had a chance to get her teeth into a really below-the-belt argument on the subject, she said, 'OK, OK. You're right, it was a bad idea.'

'About the worst you've had since you decided I should come and work at the Hotel Cassidy,' declared Maxine, remembering why she had decided to phone her sister in the first place. 'As if I wasn't enough of a skivvy already, some ghastly tarty girlfriend of Guy's rolled up earlier today with wagonloads of cases and announced that she was here for the week. All she's done is sit on her fat bum watching television and demanding endless cups of tea.'

'Funny, that's what you do when you visit me.' Janey grinned to herself. 'Has she really got a fat bum?'

'She soon will have, by the time I've finished with her.' Maxine spoke in self-satisfied tones.

'And she's tarty? I wouldn't have thought that was Guy's style at all.'

This time she was almost able to hear Maxine's shoulders slump in defeat.

'OK, so maybe she isn't tarty. If she were, I might not hate her so much.'

'Ah, so she's a threat,' Janey teased. 'You had your designs on Guy and now she's put your nose out of joint.'

Gloomily, Maxine said, 'She even has a designer nose.'

It was cheering to discover that even Maxine could feel inadequate when the odds were stacked against her. Janey, who knew only too well how it felt, said, 'Is she really stunning?'

'Hmm.' Maxine sounded resigned. 'Come up and see us sometime, then you might understand what I'm up against.'

'Isn't your sparkling personality enough?'

'Don't be stupid, of course it isn't. Men like Guy aren't interested in personalities.' Maxine paused, then added, 'I mean it, Janey. Come over tomorrow morning, then you can see for yourself.'

'I can't just turn up,' protested Janey. 'That really would look stupid.'

'Florists deliver flowers, don't they?' Maxine spoke with exaggerated patience. 'So, if you're going to be boring about it I'll place an order. How about a nice bouquet of deadly nightshade?'

'Oh dear.' Janey grinned. 'Are you sure you wouldn't prefer a wreath?'

It was eleven-thirty by the time Guy returned home, and to Maxine's disappointment he didn't boot Serena unceremoniously out into the night.

Staying put in her armchair, she eavesdropped like mad on the reunion out in the hall. If she twisted round and craned her neck all the way over to the left she could have watched them through the crack in the door, but that would have been too tacky. Besides, Guy would probably catch her at it.

He sounded surprised, though not unhappy, to find Serena waiting for him at the front door. Maxine heard her say, 'Darling, Thailand was cancelled so I found myself with a free week. I've been here since about midday.'

Maxine was only too easily able to envisage the accompanying embrace; Serena was the lithe, wrap-around type. The kiss that went with it, thankfully, wasn't audible.

'You should have phoned,' said Guy, eventually.

'It doesn't matter now. I'm just glad you decided not to stay away overnight after all.'

Maxine winced. Guy didn't miss a trick.

'Has Maxine been looking after you?' she heard him say. There was a faint edge to his voice. She winced again, this time in anticipation.

'Mmm,' Serena replied vaguely. 'Well, in her own way I suppose. She served up the most extraordinary supper, a kind of fish pie made with instant mashed potato.'

She made 'instant' sound like maggot-infested. Maxine heard Guy say, 'The children like it.'

'And it was positively teeming with garlic.'

All the better to repel you with, my dear, thought Maxine happily. With six whole cloves of the stuff to contend with, she doubted whether Guy had much enjoyed his welcome-home kiss.

'Yes, well. Maxine's culinary techniques are . . . interesting,' he replied dryly. 'Where is she now, in bed?'

'In the sitting room.' Serena didn't bother to lower her voice. 'Darling, is it wise to allow the nanny the run of the entire house? She's been there all evening, hogging the most comfortable chair and the remote control. And she's been helping herself to your gin.'

Maxine turned and smiled at Guy as he entered the room. Since there wasn't much point in pretending not to have overheard, she said brightly, 'Only one gin. Oh, and a splash of tonic and two ice cubes. You can deduct them from my wages.'

'Don't be silly. Are the children all right?'

'Bound, gagged and manacled to their beds.' She

beamed. 'Don't worry, they can't escape.'

'Good.' He gave her a brief smile. Serena, as she had anticipated, clung lovingly to his arm. 'Well, we're off to bed now. Don't forget to turn everything off before you go up.'

With any luck, thought Maxine, I did that when I mashed six cloves of garlic into the fish pie.

# Chapter 15

Janey saw what Maxine meant when she turned up at Trezale House the following morning. The storms had cleared, Cornwall was bathed in glorious sunshine once more and Serena Charlton was sunning herself topless in the garden. Observing the sheer flawlessness of her long, lean body and deeply envious of such perfect breasts – the pert kind, which wouldn't dream of sliding down to nestle in each armpit as her own unruly pair invariably did – Janey was glad she didn't share her sister's need to compete. When the opposition was this stunning, it was a daunting prospect to say the least.

'For me?' said Guy, coming into the kitchen behind her and spotting the cellophane-wrapped bouquet of lemon-yellow roses in her arms. 'How kind. Nobody's given me flowers for years.'

He seemed to be in a good mood. Janey, moving out of the way as he reached into the fridge for a bottle of milk, tried not to stare at his naked torso. All he wore was a pair of Levi's and delicious aftershave. Yet another faultless body, she thought enviously. Such dazzling perfection was almost too much to bear.

'Maxine ordered them. She's gone to track down a vase.'

'Who?' Rubbing his wet hair with a green towel slung around his neck, he said cryptically, 'Ah, you mean our in-house saboteur.'

Janey's heart sank. 'What's she done now?'

But Guy merely grinned. 'I'm sure she'll tell you. When she does, perhaps you would let her know that it didn't work.' When Janey continued to look blank, he added enigmatically, 'Tell her that for lunch yesterday I had chicken Kiev.'

'Found one,' said Maxine, coming into the kitchen with a slender, very elongated smoked-glass vase. 'It looks like Serena, don't you think? Except that the vase has a higher IQ. Oh . . . sorry!' Spotting Guy and not looking the least bit apologetic, she stood the vase on the table. 'I thought you were still in the shower.'

Guy raised his eyebrows in good-humoured disbelief. Turning to Janey, he said, 'Do me a favour, will you? Take her out somewhere tonight.'

'Can't afford it,' said Maxine promptly. 'I've got to get the clunking noise in my car sorted out before the wheels fall off. I thought I'd stay in and save my pennies.'

Serena, taking a break from sunbathing, appeared in the kitchen doorway. The gauzy white blouse she had thrown on over her bikini was virtually transparent. Up close, Janey thought with a twinge of envy, she looked even more stunning than she had at a distance.

'I'd like a cup of tea,' she announced with a brief, pointed glance in Maxine's direction. 'And this time, maybe I could have Hermesetas in it instead of sugar.'

'Of course you could,' Maxine replied smoothly, filling the lookalike vase at the sink and busying herself with

125

the task of flower arranging. 'The kettle is that round metal object next to the toaster. The teabags are in the cupboard.'

Exchanging yet another glance with Janey, Guy said, 'I've changed my mind. Take her away with you now.'

Maxine, thrilled at the prospect of almost a whole day off, protested, 'But I can't afford to go anywhere . . .'

'Here.' With a look of resignation he reached for his wallet. Peeling off eighty pounds, he handed the notes to Janey. 'Have fun. On one condition.'

Janey, who didn't trust conditions, looked wary. 'What's that?'

'You have to promise not to send her back before midnight.'

'It's a deal.' Maxine, cheered by her success, promptly abandoned the flowers in the sink.

Serena, frowning as Janey pocketed the money, said, 'I've never heard anything so ridiculous in my life.'

'Don't worry about it,' riposted Maxine, her smile angelic. 'I'm worth every penny. Just ask Guy . . .'

'Down here on holiday then, girls? Come on, don't be shy, we'll buy you a drink. Come and sit down with us.'

At Maxine's insistence, because 'you said you wanted to meet some men', they had set out at seven in the evening on a seafront bar crawl. And there was no doubt about it, thought Janey with a suppressed shudder: they were certainly meeting some men.

'Don't let them do it,' she whispered frantically in Maxine's ear, at the same time tugging her in the direction of the door. But Maxine, for someone so lacking in bulk, was surprisingly untuggable. She was also flashing the kind of smile that meant they were staying put.

Within seconds, two glasses of house white had materialized and the short one with the beer belly stretching a salmon-pink Lacoste shirt to its limits was leading Janey to the table. Maxine, brown eyes gleaming as she settled herself into one of the vacant chairs, was already nose to nose with his far better-looking friend.

'I'm Phil and he's Ricky,' said the little fat one, before diving enthusiastically into his pint and downing it in seconds. Having wiped the moustache of froth from his upper lip, he returned his attention to Janey. 'So how long are you down here for? Where d'you come from? What kind of work d'you do and what's your name?'

Janey stared at him. Fat Phil roared with laughter. 'Hey, it's a joke! Time is money, babe, and why waste time getting to know each other when we could be having fun? That's what I say!'

'I couldn't agree with you more.' Janey, suppressing a shudder, handed him her untouched glass of wine. 'And I hope you have lots and lots of fun, I really do. But I'm afraid I have to go now. The babysitter's expecting me back at nine and she'll kill me if I'm late—'

'What *is* the matter with you?' Maxine cried indignantly, catching up with her thirty seconds later. 'You wanted men, I got you men. Janey, you didn't even give him a chance!'

'Are you sure he was a man?' Janey countered, stung by her sister's insensitivity. 'He looked seven months pregnant to me. *And* he had breasts.'

'But he had a kind face.'

127

Maxine's ability to point out redeeming features in the most hopeless of cases never failed to amaze Janey. Provided, of course, that they were somebody else's hopeless cases and not her own.

'Maybe.' It was no good, she wasn't going to feel guilty. 'But I can't pretend to be interested in people. It just isn't me. Besides, he was a pillock.'

'You don't have to fall in love with him.' Maxine was trying hard to understand but it was an uphill struggle. 'You aren't supposed to take men like that seriously. They're just good to practise on, until the real ones turn up.'

This time Janey laughed because nobody would ever change Maxine. She had her own strategy in life and it would never even occur to her to question it. And why should she want to, anyway? As far as Maxine was concerned, it worked.

'OK, I'm sorry. What shall we do now?'

Maxine, straight-faced, said, 'I know. Back to your place, into our woolly dressing gowns and slippers. We'll watch that nice cookery programme on the telly and take it in turns to make the cocoa. If you're really good, I'll teach you how to crochet a tea cosy that looks like a thatched cottage.'

'Or?'

'Blow the money on a stupendous meal,' Maxine replied promptly. 'I'm starving.'

Janey threw her a look of disbelief. Whilst she'd been working in the shop all afternoon, Maxine had been out on the patio, sunbathing and stuffing herself with food. An entire tub of Häagen Dazs rum and raisin had vanished from the freezer and when she'd gone out to

128

clear up at six o'clock, empty crisp packets and Coke cans had littered the wrought-iron table.

But since it didn't even occur to Maxine that she shouldn't be hungry now, she misinterpreted the expression on Janey's face.

'Oh, all right! I absolutely promise not to talk to any strange men for the rest of the night.'

Janey doubted whether she was physically capable of such a feat, but it was a noble offer. Beginning to relax, she said, 'OK. How about La Campagnola?'

'Boring,' declared Maxine. 'The cricketer took me there last week and it was practically empty. No, I asked Guy about restaurants. He said the best one was in Amory Street. I think it's called Bruno's.'

'Janey, my gorgeous girl!' shouted Bruno when he saw her coming through the door, and Maxine's eyebrows shot up in amazement.

Janey, praying she hadn't turned red, explained hurriedly, 'He says that to all the girls.'

'Hasn't said it to me,' murmured Maxine as Bruno made his way across the restaurant to greet them. 'Hmm, and very nice too. Is he gay?'

'Is the Pope Jewish?' countered Bruno, who possessed 20-20 hearing. Embracing Janey and at the same time studying Maxine over her shoulder he murmured, 'Darling, what have you been telling this poor girl?'

'She isn't a poor girl, she's my sister.' As if Bruno hadn't already guessed, Janey thought morosely. Hadn't she, after all, been complaining to him about Maxine for the past fortnight?

'Maxine Vaughan,' said Maxine, gazing with interest at possibly the only man on the planet capable of making Janey blush. He wasn't what you'd call startlingly good-looking but the eyes were the greenest she'd ever seen and the grin was irrepressible. He was, she decided, one of those men with an indefinable aura of attractiveness about them . . . a wonderfully wicked, *tantalizing* aura of attractiveness.

Janey, in turn watching Maxine survey Bruno, prayed she hadn't made a hideous mistake in agreeing to come here. On the one hand, Bruno's attentions were always guaranteed to boost her morale, and whenever Maxine was around, God knows, it needed boosting.

On the other hand, however, just introducing Bruno and Maxine was playing with fire. A bloody great bonfire, thought Janey ruefully, for already the inevitable sparks of interest were there. She could almost predict what would follow. Maxine and Bruno, both brimming with confidence and rapier-like repartee, were a perfectly matched pair. Whilst she, in dismal contrast, could practically feel herself melting into the wallpaper.

As she had known he would, Bruno ushered them to the most favoured table in the restaurant, next to the window.

'Come on, forty minutes over coffee is long enough,' he informed the diners already seated there. Whisking away cups and liqueur glasses and signalling to one of the waitresses to bring fresh linen and cutlery, he added briskly, 'Time's up, off you go, don't forget to leave an enormous tip.'

'Charming,' muttered the younger of the two men.

Bruno, winking at Janey and Maxine, slipped an arm around their waists and gave them both an appreciative squeeze.

'Charming isn't the word, sir. These ladies are stupendous . . . magnificent . . . the jewels in my own personal crown. And just think, if you hadn't spent practically a week's wages earlier on that ludicrously expensive bottle of wine, you might even have been able to afford to take them home with you for the night.'

'Hmmph,' snorted the older man, eyeing Maxine's bare legs with disdain as he rose to his feet.

'And hmmph to you too,' said Bruno cheerfully, guiding them towards the door. 'Goodbye, gentlemen. Have a wonderful evening. See you again very soon.'

'Gosh,' said Maxine, watching with admiration as Bruno waved them off the premises. 'Is he always like this?'

Janey, who was studying the menu, nodded. 'All the time.'

'But doesn't he lose an awful lot of customers?'

Janey shrugged. 'Bruno says it keeps them on their toes. And the ones he doesn't kick out are so grateful they leave bigger tips.'

Maxine was clearly impressed. When Bruno returned to their table with a bottle of Pouilly Fumé and pulled up another chair, Janey was surprised she didn't offer to sit on his lap.

'I love this place,' Maxine declared, her expansive gesture encompassing the green and white decor, the latticed ceiling and the spectacular view from the window. 'Thank goodness we didn't go to La Campagnola! And why on earth hasn't my big sister brought me here before?' Having given Janey a look of mock reproach, she returned her attention to Bruno. 'She's a sly one, I must say. She told me she didn't know any interesting men in Trezale.' With an arch smile, she added, 'And to think that you were here all the time.'

Janey, who would have torn out her own tonsils rather than come out with such a line, stared at her in disbelief. Was she being serious? Did other women really say things like that and get away with it? Had Maxine no shame?

The answer, it seemed, was no. If anything, her sister was looking more entranced than ever. The thin straps of her indigo camisole were slipping off her shoulders now and she was making no attempt to pull them up again. Her dark eyes, illuminated by candlelight, were bright with unconcealed interest.

'But how do you know each other?' she was asking Bruno, her chin cupped in one hand and the camisole top gaping to reveal more chest than ever.

In reply, he touched the arrangement of lilac and white freesias in the centre of the table. 'She brings me flowers.'

Maxine grinned. 'How romantic.'

'Come on, pay attention,' said Janey firmly, thrusting the menu into her free hand. 'You're the one who was so hungry. I'm having the seafood risotto and the lamb.'

By the time their food arrived, Maxine was in her element. Having discovered as much about Bruno Parry-Brent in the space of thirty minutes as Janey had learned in a year, she was now regaling him with her own life history. By the time they had moved on to the coffees, she was launching into a bitchy attack on Guy Cassidy.

'He's the one paying for this meal tonight,' Janey pointed out in Guy's defence.

Maxine looked scornful. 'Only because he wanted me out of the way.' Turning back to Bruno, she went on, 'You wouldn't believe this girlfriend of his. I didn't think anyone could treat me worse than Guy, but at least he's been known to say the odd please and thank you. Serena Charlton's a living nightmare; I can't believe what terrible taste in women some men have.'

Janey couldn't resist it. 'Maxine's only saying this because Guy isn't interested in her,' she explained. 'She had visions of moving into Trezale House and dazzling him, and it hasn't happened. It's been a great disappointment to her.'

'Oh, crushing,' Maxine agreed with a trace of mockery.

'But her ego, of course, won't allow her to admit it.' Janey smiled. Two could play at bitchery. Besides, Maxine had been showing off for long enough. She deserved it.

'He comes in here quite often,' said Bruno, aware of the undercurrents and of Janey's irritation with her sister. It didn't take a genius, he deduced, to figure out the reason for it. 'Brings some spectacular women with him, too.'

'His harem.' Maxine gave a dismissive shrug and spooned brown sugar into her coffee.

'So are you going to stick it out?' Bruno grinned. 'Or leave?'

Maxine hesitated. Rattling on about Guy's pigheadedness was one thing, but she had no intention of jacking in her job.

'He's a pain,' she said with a brave smile, 'but the kids

are OK. It wouldn't be fair to leave them.'

Janey pulled a face. 'My sister, the patron saint of children.' Turning to address Bruno once more, she said evenly, 'Take it from me, nothing interests Maxine more than a man who isn't interested in her. As long as Guy puts up with her, she'll stay. She doesn't give up on anyone without a fight.'

'So how long have you had this raging crush on Bruno?' said Maxine, on the way home.

Janey concentrated on driving. The lane leading up to Trezale House was narrow and unlit. 'Don't be silly,' she replied, her manner offhand. 'He's a friend, that's all.'

'And I'm your sister,' declared Maxine, not fooled for a moment by her apparent lack of interest. 'Come on, Janey! First you don't even mention him, then you have a go at me, deliberately putting me down in front of him. Why else would you do it?'

'You were showing off.'

Maxine shot her a triumphant grin. 'I'm always showing off. What's so interesting is the fact that this time you minded like hell. Darling, it's nothing to be ashamed of . . . there's no reason on earth why you shouldn't fancy him! He's an attractive man. I thought he was lovely.'

'I know you thought he was lovely,' said Janey in cutting tones. In her less-than-serene state, she crunched the van's gears. 'The entire restaurant knows you thought he was lovely. I just don't understand why you have to be so obvious.'

'Because that's the way I am.' Maxine shrugged. 'But

we're getting away from the point. The reason I asked
you about your own little crush was because I wanted to
know how serious it was. If you're madly in love with
him, I'll do the decent thing and steer clear. After all,'
she added infuriatingly, 'I wouldn't want to waltz in and
snatch away the first man you've been interested in since
Alan.'

Janey gritted her teeth, sensing that they were on the
verge of their first real quarrel for years. Even more
annoying was the fact that, deep down, she knew she
was the one at fault. She was also in serious danger of
cutting off her nose to spite her face.

As they approached Trezale House, she took a deep
steadying breath. 'OK, I do like him. He *is* the first man
I've been interested in since Alan, and the reason I didn't
tell you about Bruno was because I didn't want you to
say anything embarrassing when you met him.' She drew
the van to a halt, switched off the engine and gazed out
into the darkness ahead. 'There, so now you know.'

'Well, hallelujah!' Maxine retorted. 'I don't know why
you couldn't have said all that in the first place. Darling,
it's no big deal. Sometimes you're just too proud by half!'

Unlike Maxine, thought Janey, who had no pride at
all. She still wasn't entirely happy, either. The last thing
she needed was to be patronized by a younger sister who
thought the entire situation too amusing for words.

'You needn't worry,' Maxine assured her now. 'From
this moment on, he's all yours. I shall treat Bruno like a
brother. We shall be friends.' She grinned. 'And I shan't
even *try* to imagine what he looks like naked.'

Janey was tired. She sensed, too, that Maxine was still

poking gentle fun at her. 'It's past midnight,' she announced pointedly. 'You're allowed back into the house now. And I have to be up at five.'

But Maxine was still prattling on about Bruno. 'He is fun, though. I still can't believe he practically booted those customers out into the street just so we could sit at the best table. You have to admit, darling, that takes style!'

'Oh, please,' sighed Janey. 'Don't tell me you fell for that old routine. Nick and Tony run the antique shop next door to the restaurant. Bruno does that to them every night.'

# Chapter 16

In for a penny, in for a pound. Having given the matter a great deal of thought, Janey replied to the advertisement in the paper, posted it at once so she couldn't change her mind, then began drafting out an ad of her own. The chances of Mr Presentable turning out to be Mr Ideal might be slim, but if she received a dozen replies she would at least have a selection to choose from. And if eleven of them were duds it wouldn't even matter, because number twelve could be perfect and *one* perfect male was all she needed.

It really was extraordinarily difficult, though, describing oneself in just a few brief sentences. If she exaggerated the facts she risked ridicule when she eventually came to face it out. The prospect of being greeted with a look of horror and a derisory 'I thought you said you were attractive', was positively bone-chilling. The bald facts, however, – 'plumpish, blondish deserted wife' – might be so off-putting that no man would even be tempted to reply.

It took longer than filling out a tax return and was about as harrowing. Every time a customer came into the shop she jumped a mile and shoved her writing pad under the counter. When Paula returned from making the morning deliveries, Janey was so engrossed she hardly heard her words.

'I've had a brilliant idea.'

The pad was hidden but the pen was still in Janey's hand. Twiddling it frantically between her fingers and pretending she'd been writing down an order, she managed, 'What?'

'If you placed one of those ads yourself, you could arrange to meet each man somewhere busy and ask them to wear a white carnation in their buttonhole.'

'So?'

Paula, looking pleased with herself, pulled herself on to the spare stool and swung her legs. 'So, all we have to do is sit here and wait for men to come in asking for a single white carnation. You'll be able to have a good look at them first, incognito. And if they're too hideous for words you wouldn't have to bother turning up.'

'Cruel!' protested Janey, starting to laugh.

'Sensible. Not to mention good for business.' Paula threw her a sidelong glance. 'Do you think you might advertise, then?'

Paula was trustworthy, but some items of gossip were just too good to pass up. Her mother worked at Trezale House and Janey was determined that Maxine shouldn't find out about this. Now, more than ever, she needed to keep the last vestiges of her self-confidence intact.

'Maybe when I'm fifty,' she replied with tolerant amusement. 'But for now, I think I'll give it a miss.'

Maxine, unable to understand why she couldn't simply

scrawl the names on with pink Magic Marker, was struggling ill-temperedly to sew name tapes into Josh's school shirts. Guy hadn't helped, earlier, when he had remarked, 'Not that anyone else is likely to mistake Josh's shirts for their own, the way you iron them.'

He had said it jokingly, but Maxine had detected the dig. And although she'd been sewing for the last two and a half hours the pile of new school clothes still waiting to be attacked seemed more mountainous than ever.

'Dad's taking photographs of Serena,' Josh reported from his position in the window seat overlooking the back garden. He frowned. 'She doesn't have very big bosoms for a grown-up.'

Maxine suppressed the memory of what she'd imagined working for Guy would be like. In her innocence she'd envisaged organizing games of hide-and-seek for the children, accompanying them to the pantomime and in her free time socializing happily with Guy. In her more elaborate fantasies, she was the one being endlessly photographed. And because Guy was so famous and respected, interest in his stunning new model would spread like wildfire . . . the life of a super model beckoned . . . she would become wealthy, a celebrity, loved by everyone . . . especially Guy Cassidy.

'But then your bosoms are only little, as well,' said Josh, who had been studying her with a critical eye. 'Your sister has much bigger ones than you.'

'A word of advice.' Maxine clenched her teeth as she bit off a length of thread. 'You'll find life a lot easier if you don't go through it telling people what small bosoms they have.'

'Bosoms' was currently his favourite word. Josh smirked.

'And don't you think you should be getting changed into something more suitable?'

Guy and Serena were supposed to be taking both Josh and Ella into St Ives for lunch and it was one o'clock already. Maxine, who had set her heart on an afternoon of serious sunbathing, was beginning to wonder if they'd forgotten.

Josh shrugged. 'Oh, we aren't going now. Dad's taking Serena to meet some of her friends instead. They've got a yacht moored at Falmouth.'

Maxine's heart sank. Bang went her peaceful afternoon. She wondered whether Serena had done it on purpose.

'So we're staying here with you,' said Josh cheerfully. Then, in conversational tones he added, 'Why do you keep pricking your fingers, Maxine? I hope all that blood's going to wash out.'

Maxine was battling with the washing machine, which was making alarming noises like a jailer rattling his keys, when the doorbell rang. Glancing out through the kitchen window she saw a silver-grey Rolls Royce parked majestically in the drive. What fun, she thought, if the visitor was yet another of Guy's ritzy model girlfriends, complete with sneer and a bootful of suitcases. He could install her in the other spare bedroom and visit them on alternate nights like some Arab sheik.

But just as the identity of the last unexpected caller had turned out not to be the milkman but Serena, so this one appeared not to be a pouting, leggy model at all.

Wrong again, thought Maxine, realizing that she was grinning inanely at the visitor on the doorstep. What a good job she hadn't set her heart on a career as a fortune teller.

'Good afternoon,' said the man, and although she was certain they hadn't met before, he looked vaguely familiar. Hastily rearranging the grin into a more suitable smile, Maxine shook his outstretched hand and wondered if he might know something about erratic washing machines.

'You must be Maxine, the new nanny,' he continued warmly. 'I'm Oliver Cassidy.'

Realization dawned. 'I spoke to you on the phone earlier,' she said, recognizing the deep, well-bred voice. 'How nice to meet you, but I'm afraid Guy isn't back yet. We aren't expecting him home until this evening.'

'I know.' Oliver Cassidy looked a lot like his son but Maxine felt he possessed a great deal more charm. Now he shrugged and smiled. 'But it seemed a shame to pass up the opportunity to see my grandchildren. It's been quite a while, you see, and I'm only down here for the afternoon.'

Delighted to see him and mightily impressed with his car – which even had personalized plates – Maxine said at once, 'Come in! Of course you couldn't miss seeing the children. They're playing in the summer-house at the moment; shall I go and call them or would you prefer to take them by surprise?'

'Oh, surprise, I think.' Guy's father winked at her. He really was tons nicer than Guy, she decided. She'd never really gone for older men before, but he was almost enough to make her think again.

'Can I get you a drink?' she said brightly, but Oliver Cassidy shook his head.

'That's kind of you, my dear, but I'd better not. I'm driving.'

'It's a beautiful car,' said Maxine.

'My great pride and joy.' He nodded, acknowledging her admiration. 'I thought Josh and Ella might enjoy a ride in it before I leave. If you have no objections, that is.'

'Of course not!' Maxine's reply was almost vehement, her approval of Guy's father was increasing in leaps and bounds. And now she would be able to sunbathe in peace after all.

'Take them out for as long as you like,' she told him happily. 'I'm sure they'd love a trip in your car. What a shame, though, that you'll miss seeing Guy.'

'I cannot . . . simply *can not* believe you could be so stupid!'

He was more furious than Maxine had ever imagined possible. 'Fury' wasn't enough to describe his emotions. 'Rage' wasn't good enough either. Guy simply looked as if he wanted to kill her.

This is it, she thought numbly. Now I really am out of a job and on to the streets.

Almost more galling, however, was the fact that Serena appeared to be on her side.

'Look,' said Maxine, struggling to defend herself and willing herself not to lose her temper. 'I've already said I'm sorry, but how on earth was I supposed to know I was doing the wrong thing? He just turned up on the doorstep like any normal grandfather and said he'd come to see Josh and Ella. From the way he acted, I assumed he was a regular visitor. And he seemed perfectly nice—'

'Yes, darling,' put in Serena, her tone soothing.

Her defence of Maxine's actions was wholly astonishing as far as Maxine was concerned, and coming from any other quarter it would have afforded her some small comfort to know that she wasn't as negligent as Guy was making out.

'It isn't Maxine's fault that you and your father aren't on speaking terms,' Serena went on. 'If you didn't want him to see the children you should have told her.'

His eyes glittered. 'He's seen them once before. Only once, when he wasn't given any alternative. So it was hardly likely that he'd turn up.'

Serena shrugged as if to say, *Well, there you are then*, but Guy hadn't finished.

'Besides, that's hardly the point.' Turning back to Maxine, he said icily, 'He could have been anybody. Josh and Ella could have been kidnapped, held to ransom . . . murdered.'

'He wasn't a kidnapper,' shouted Maxine. 'He was your father.'

'You mean he told you he was my father.'

Stung by his derisory tone, she snapped back. 'He looked like you. Only better.'

'Oh, for God's sake!'

Maxine had had enough. It wasn't as if Josh and Ella had been at all harmed, anyway. True to his word, Oliver Cassidy had taken them out in the Rolls, given them afternoon tea at one of the better beach-front hotels and delivered them back safely at five o'clock, as promised. He had even left them each clutching a crisp fifty-pound note because, as he'd explained to Maxine, it was hard to know what to buy children these days now that train sets and dolls were passé. It wasn't until after he'd left that she'd made the alarming discovery that Josh and Ella didn't actually know their grandfather. Although being on the receiving end of fifty-pound notes certainly went some way towards persuading them that they should.

'Go on then,' she said abruptly, rising to her feet and glaring back at Guy. 'You're dying to do it, so sack me. Find yourself a new nanny who'll safety-pin the children to her ankles and shoot any strangers on sight. In the meantime, I'm sure Serena would just adore to stay on for a few more weeks and look after them herself.'

Too late she remembered that Serena had been sticking up for her, although it hardly mattered now. If she was out on her ear she'd never see either of them again anyway.

As far as Serena was concerned, however, the bitter jibe was too true to be offensive. 'I've got work lined up,' she said hurriedly. 'My agent would kill me if I tried to cancel anything now.'

Guy crossed to the drinks tray and poured himself a stiff Scotch. Part of him still wanted to kill Maxine but he was making an effort to calm down. Since even Serena had defended Maxine's actions, he realized now that the hatred he bore his father had led him to overreact. Maxine undoubtedly had her faults, but the fact remained that Josh and Ella adored her. And although he still didn't have the faintest idea why his father had turned up out of the blue, they had enjoyed themselves. Josh had only been six and Ella four when Véronique had taken them to meet him and even if they dimly recalled the events of that day they clearly hadn't connected them with this afternoon's surprise visitor. Both children had thoroughly enjoyed themselves and Josh, who was smitten with expensive cars – not to mention crisp new bank notes – was already asking when they might see him again.

As far as Guy was concerned, 'when hell freezes over' was the phrase that sprang most readily to mind, but it was a reply he'd kept to himself. And he supposed that, given the circumstances, Maxine couldn't really have been expected to refuse entry to an *apparently* charming relative visiting his much-loved grandchildren.

Draining his Scotch, he turned back to find Maxine, the picture of belligerence, still glaring at him. With her blond hair ruffled, she looked like an indignant parakeet.

'Oh cheer up,' he said with a trace of exasperation. 'I'm not going to sack you. Just take a bit more care in future, OK? They might not be the best behaved kids in the world but they're all I've got, so I'd quite like to hang on to them if I could.'

# Chapter 17

It was all happening amazingly quickly. Janey, who had envisaged a wait of at least a fortnight before hearing anything back from Mr Presentable, had been caught so off-guard by his phone call that before she could gather her wits she heard herself agreeing to meet him that evening. Profoundly grateful that Paula wasn't in the shop at the time, she added hurriedly, 'Why don't you wear a carnation? Then I'll be able to recognize you.'

'Why don't you just look out for a tall, dark-haired man in a navy blue blazer and grey flannels?' he countered, sounding faintly amused. 'I'm not really the carnation-wearing type.'

'Oh.' Crestfallen, and on behalf of florists everywhere, Janey said, 'Why not?'

'Every time I put one in my buttonhole,' he replied, 'I find myself getting married.'

His name was Alexander Norcross and he had two ex-wives, a dark blue Porsche and a small cottage on the outskirts of Trelissick. Janey also suspected that his refusal to wear a carnation was due to the fact that it would have meant buying one.

'No, we decided against children,' he explained, over lukewarm coffee in a quiet bar away from the seafront which Janey had suggested because nobody she knew ever went there. 'They cost an absolute fortune. My wives tried to make me change my mind, of course, but I wasn't having any of it. There's no way I could have afforded to keep the Porsche on the road and bring up kids as well.' Leaning across the table he added confidentially, 'So I got out each time they started hankering, before they had a chance to pull the old "Oops, how did that happen?" routine. It isn't as if they really wanted children, after all. They just saw their friends doing it and didn't want to miss out. It didn't even occur to them to consider the expense.'

It was truly astounding, thought Janey, that someone so mean with money should be so generous with his aftershave. Great wafts of Old Spice were whooshing up her nose. It even seemed to have invaded her cup of coffee, which hadn't tasted great in the first place. She wondered how soon she could decently leave.

But meeting Alexander was an education, at least. He wasn't bad looking, he had a nice voice and he was tall. The packaging, she decided, was as much as anyone could possibly hope for. The only let-down was the fact that it belonged to a complacent, penny-pinching bore.

But there was also the irresistible challenge of discovering just how awful he could be. Summoning up a Maxine-ish smile and working hard not to inhale too much Old Spice, she said, 'So has advertising been a success? I expect you've met lots of girls.'

'Ah, but it's quality that counts.' Alexander gave her a

147

knowing look. 'Not quantity. I've found the initial telephone conversations to be revealing, Jane. All some of these females are interested in is a free meal, which is when I make my excuses. That's why I was so interested in meeting you,' he added happily. 'As soon as I read your letter, I felt we had something in common. And when you suggested we meet for a quick drink, I knew I was right.'

'Thank you,' murmured Janey, by this time struggling to keep a straight face. 'After all, why should people need to eat in order to get to know one another?'

'Exactly my point!' Alexander looked positively triumphant. Finishing his cold coffee, he pushed the cup and saucer an inch or two in her direction. 'And when you consider the ridiculous prices restaurants charge for an omelette . . . well, I call it money down the drain. I'd rather stay at home and know I wasn't being ripped off. How about you Jane?' he added, gazing at her with renewed interest and approval. 'Do you cook?'

Thanking her lucky stars she hadn't pinned all her hopes on Alexander Norcross, Janey was longing to tell someone the story of the brief encounter which – bizarrely – had gone some way towards restoring her own self-confidence.

'It was so ghastly it ended up being funny,' she said to Bruno the following morning, grinning as she recalled the way Alexander had complained to the bar manager about the price of a cup of coffee. 'He was so awful, but he really thought he was Britain's answer to Mel Gibson. If you could have seen the look on his face when I said I wouldn't be seeing him again—'

'Was he handsome?'

'Oh yes, but such a jerk! When I got back to the flat I was dying to phone Maxine to give her all the gory details, but I'd already decided not to tell her anything about answering the ad. I shouldn't be telling you, either.' Janey tried to look repentant, and failed. 'You're just as likely to make fun of me as she is. But it *was* funny, and I had to tell someone.'

'It certainly seems to have cheered you up,' remarked Bruno, inwardly appalled that she should have been driven to reply to a newspaper advert in the first place. 'But Janey, aren't you taking a bit of a risk? You don't need to do that kind of thing. A gorgeous girl like you could take her pick of men.'

Colouring at the compliment, even if it was only Bruno saying what he would no doubt say to anyone under the age of ninety, she resorted to flippancy. 'Yes, well. The neighbours were starting to complain about the queues outside my front door so I thought I'd try going about it another way.'

'Hmm.' Bruno, who wasn't stupid, surveyed her through narrowed eyes. 'Or does it have something to do with that noisy, pushy sister of yours?'

Janey could have hugged him. She'd been so sure he would be entranced by Maxine. Her self-confidence rose by yet another notch. 'Not at all,' she lied, relaxing visibly but still not quite daring to admit that she'd placed an advertisement of her own. 'I just thought I'd give it a go. It didn't work out. End of story.'

'I should bloody well hope so.' Bruno glanced at his watch and saw that he'd have to get a move on if they were to open for lunch. Janey *was* gorgeous, he thought. She deserved a hell of a lot better than a guy with a Porsche and a padlocked wallet. 'Look, I could get away early tonight.' As he spoke, he began unpacking the box of flowers she had brought to the restaurant, pink carnations and sweet-smelling lilac today to match the new tablecloths. 'If you aren't doing anything, why don't we go out for something to eat?'

'Oh!' Janey looked astonished. After a moment's hesitation, she said, 'But this is your restaurant. Shouldn't we eat here?'

'That would make it business.' Bruno gave her one of his most irresistible smiles. 'What I had in mind was pleasure.'

'But you're—'

'I'm not married,' he reminded her. 'And I don't argue with bar managers about the price of coffee, either.'

'But—'

'No more excuses,' said Bruno, his tone firm. 'I'll pick you up at ten.'

'Oh, but—' said Janey, torn between delight and the hideous prospect of having to get up at five o'clock tomorrow morning.

'Stop it,' said Bruno, very firmly indeed. 'It'll be fun.' Then he winked. 'Besides, better the devil you know . . .'

The drawback to being picked up at ten o'clock in the evening was that it left one with far too much time to get ready. Instead of flinging on the first decent thing that came to hand, Janey found herself racked with indecision. None of the more casual skirts and tee-shirts she wore for work would do; Bruno had seen them all a hundred times. The black sequinned dress was wonderfully slimming but it would be way over the top, and the only other really decent outfit she owned, a violet crêpe-de-Chine affair with no back and swirly skirts, made her look like something out of *Come Dancing*.

Clothes littered the bed as she tried on and discarded one outfit after another. A white, dripping-with-lace blouse resembled nothing so much as an overdone wedding cake. The black trousers were too tight, her favourite red silk shirt had a hole in the sleeve and Maxine had spilt make-up down the front of her cream lambswool sweater.

Finally settling for a sea-green shirt and white jeans, Janey did her make-up and fiddled with her hair. After putting it up, experimenting with combs and taking it down again because the combs wouldn't stay in anyway, it was still only eight-thirty. When the phone rang fifteen minutes later she almost hoped it would be Bruno calling to tell her he couldn't get away after all. Her stomach could only stand so many jitters. She had been looking forward to the evening far more than was good for her. Bruno might not be married to Nina but he still wasn't properly single, either.

'Janey? Now listen to me. Get out of that old dressing gown and do yourself up this instant!'

Maxine was shouting into the phone to make herself heard above a background of loud music and roars of male approval.

'Where are you calling from?' said Janey. 'It sounds like a strip-joint.'

'What?We're down at the Terrace Bar of the Manderley Hotel. My lovely cricketer's come back to Cornwall and he's brought the rest of the team with him, so I'm hopelessly outnumbered. They're calling for reinforcements, Janey, and as soon as I mentioned a fancy-free sister they insisted I get you down here.' She giggled. 'In fact they carried me to the phone.'

Janey, listening to the ear-splitting whistles of eleven over-excited cricketers, said, 'I can't, I'm going out.'

'Who with?'

'A friend.'

'Who?' demanded Maxine.

'Nobody you know.'

'That means nobody at all! Darling, don't be so *boring*. You wanted to meet new men and here I am, granting your wish with a dazzling selection . . . they're dying to meet you and now you're chickening out. Oh, look what you've done to them. They're starting to cry.'

From the chorus of boo-hoos now drowning out Maxine's protests, it certainly sounded as if they had a collective mental age of around seven. Janey could only wonder at the amount of beer they must have consumed.

'I really can't,' she repeated patiently. 'I'm meeting a friend for a quick drink and then I must get an early night. I have to be—'

'—up at five o'clock in the morning to go to the flower market,' chanted Maxine, who had heard it all before. 'Janey, how many times do I have to tell you, there are more important things in life than getting enough sleep? These boys are *raring* to go. You're missing out on the opportunity of a lifetime here!'

'Then I'll just have to miss out,' she said firmly, so that Maxine wouldn't be tempted to persist. 'And I'm sure you can handle them all beautifully without my help. I'll ring you tomorrow to see how your hangover is, but I really do have to go now. Bye.'

'If I'd known we were coming here I would never have worn jeans,' whispered Janey for the third time as they were finishing their meal. The black sequinned dress wouldn't have been OTT after all, she decided, glancing around at the other diners. And she wouldn't have needed to fumble under the tablecloth surreptitiously in order to loosen her belt three more notches. 'Heavens, I haven't eaten so much in years. This food is perfect!'

'But not too perfect,' said Bruno, who liked to keep an eye on the opposition. Looking pleased with himself, he said, 'The mange-touts were a fraction overdone and the Bordelaise could have used a touch more black pepper. This Burgundy's good though,' he admitted, twirling the stem of his glass and sniffing the wine appreciatively. 'Very nice indeed. I may have to order some of this for the restaurant. Nick and Tony would go into raptures over it.'

Janey, mindful of the last time Bruno had plied her with wine, was rationing herself severely. Determined that tonight she was going to stay in control – and awake – she shook her head as he held the bottle towards her.

'Maxine was most impressed with the way you kicked them out the other night.'

'Ah, well. I expect it made her feel important.' Bruno looked amused. 'I imagine it's the kind of thing she enjoys.'

'It's what she lives for,' said Janey dryly. Then, glimpsing the expression on his face, she added, 'I know I'm being bitchy and disloyal, but I don't care. Sometimes Maxine goes too far.'

'No need to apologize.' Calmly, Bruno leaned forward and examined the slender gold chain around her neck. 'I've only met her once but it was enough to put me in the picture. I don't think I'd walk too far out of my way for one of her dazzling smiles.'

It was reward enough to know that just one man was impervious to Maxine's charms. That the man in question should be Bruno was positively blissful. Like a puppy yearning to have its ears tickled, Janey moved fractionally closer so that the fingers investigating her necklace could brush against her skin. When they did so, she experienced once again the delicious tingle of anticipation only Bruno's touch could evoke.

'I thought you'd adore her,' she confessed, trying to sound matter-of-fact.

'Then you don't know me as well as you think you do.'

'I suppose not.'

The green eyes glittered. 'So in future, maybe you should leave it up to me to decide whom I adore.'

It was only Bruno, she reminded herself breathlessly, coming out with his usual banter. She wasn't expected to take it seriously. He didn't mean it.

It seemed, however, that he hadn't lost the knack of reading minds, either. Trailing his fingertips along her collarbone he said, 'Come on Janey, have a little faith.'

She gulped. 'In what?'

'Me. You never know, I might just be serious.'

It was what half of her longed to hear. Yet it was nerve-racking too. Relieved to spot the waiter approaching with their bill, she said, 'You're never serious.'

'Never say never.' Bruno remained unperturbed. 'Who gave you that necklace anyway?'

'My husband.'

'Still miss him?'

Janey opened her mouth to say yes, because that was the standard reply, the one she'd been trotting out for the past eighteen months. But was it still true?

'Sometimes,' she amended. 'It isn't as unbearable now as it used to be. Whenever anyone said time heals all wounds, I wanted to punch them.'

Bruno grinned. 'Good.'

'Why, do you think I should have punched them?'

'No.' He shook his head. 'It's good that you only miss him sometimes. You're getting back to normal.'

Right now, Janey wasn't feeling the least bit normal. She was hopelessly attracted to Bruno and she was sure it wasn't wise. And since it was by this time almost midnight she wasn't likely to be feeling too normal when she woke up tomorrow morning either.

'Here, let me pay half,' she said, reaching for her handbag as he placed a credit card over the folded bill. She couldn't bear to think how much such a spectacular dinner must be costing him.

'Because you don't think you deserve to be taken out for a decent meal?' Raising his eyebrows, Bruno gave her a knowing look. 'Put that purse away, for God's sake. My name isn't Alexander Norcross.'

'Oh help,' murmured Janey minutes later as they were leaving. Almost wrenching Bruno's arm out of its socket, she dragged him behind one of the magnificent marble pillars flanking the main entrance to the hotel. 'That's my mother over there.'

'Pity.' Bruno grinned. 'For a moment I thought my luck was in.'

'Sshh.'

'Why the panic anyway?'

'You don't know my mother.' Janey pulled face. 'She'd interrogate you.'

'She's over-protective?'

'No, just incurably nosey. Before you knew it, she'd be asking when we were going to get married.' Edging a cautious inch away from the pillar, she peered across at the man with her mother. 'I don't believe it, they're holding hands! This must be the new chap she was so excited about the other week, the one with the Rolls.' Really, she thought with a trace of despair; if her mother had taken to frequenting five-star hotels the least she could do was wear a bra. That glossy white shirt was practically transparent.

'He must be sixty at least,' said Bruno, watching as they picked up their room key and headed for the lift. Grinning, he added, 'Isn't it reassuring to know that old people can still enjoy sex? When I was younger I was always terrified it might stop at thirty.'

'I'm sure I've seen him somewhere before,' whispered Janey, who could only see his profile. 'I can't place him, but he definitely looks familiar.'

'He's certainly familiar with your mother.' Bruno's grin

widened as the lift doors slid shut. 'He's got his hand inside her shirt. Janey, did you notice that your mother isn't wearing a bra?'

# Chapter 18

Back at Janey's flat, Bruno pointed out the splash of red wine on the knee of her white jeans.

'You should soak them in cold water. Go and take them off,' he said matter-of-factly. 'I'll make the coffee.'

Janey, standing in the bedroom and gazing at her reflection in the wardrobe mirror, wondered what on earth she was supposed to do now. Slip into something more comfortable? Lever herself into another pair of jeans and pray the zip would stay up? Envelop herself in her oldest towelling dressing gown and furry slippers, surely the most effective contraceptive known to woman?

By the time she emerged from the bedroom Bruno had made the coffee, switched off the overhead light in the living room in favour of a single table lamp, and mastered the stereo. Ella Fitzgerald was crooning in the background and the cushions had been rearranged on the sofa.

Feeling absurdly self-conscious, Janey sat down at the other end.

'That's better.' He nodded approvingly at her pale pink shorts. 'You should show off your legs more often.'

Janey immediately wished she'd settled for the dressing gown and slippers after all. When all you were wearing were a pair of shorts, trying to hide your legs was a physical impossibility.

'They're fat.'

'They're the best legs in Trezale,' Bruno replied evenly. 'What you mean is, they aren't a pair of matchsticks like your sister's.' He gave her a sidelong, knowing look. 'Janey, we're going to have to do something to get you over this ridiculous complex. You're a gorgeous girl and you don't have to compare yourself unfavourably with anyone, least of all Maxine.'

It was nice that he should say so, but the belief was so deeply ingrained that she couldn't take him seriously. Scatty, extrovert Maxine, forever embroiling herself in drama and emerging unscathed, was the beautiful slender sister to whom all men were drawn like magnets. Janey, hard-working and about as scatty as Margaret Thatcher, was the one best known for the fact that her husband had disappeared without trace. What a riveting claim to fame.

'Won't Nina be wondering where you are?' Compliments embarrassed her anyway. And it was almost one o'clock.

'No,' said Bruno simply. Then his face softened. 'OK, no more pep talk. Why don't you just move over here instead?'

When Janey stayed put, he smiled and edged his way slowly towards her instead. 'Well, if the—'

'—mountain won't come to Mohammed?' guessed Janey, when he hesitated. 'That's what you were going to say, wasn't it? But you thought I'd be offended if you called me a mountain.'

'Don't be so silly.' Bruno slid his arms around her waist. As he pulled her towards him, his mouth brushed her ear. 'Take it from an expert, sweetheart. You're not fat. If anyone should be envious of their sister, it's Maxine.'

It had been so very long since she had last been made love to. It sometimes seemed more like eighteen years than eighteen months and Janey had wondered if she would remember how it was done.

But magically . . . miraculously . . . she was remembering now, and the reality was even more blissful than the memories. Bruno, the self-acknowledged expert, was proving to her that he wasn't all mouth and no trousers, and she had no complaints at all. She no longer even cared that it was ridiculously late, and that she had to be up early. Just for once, the flowers could wait. She was having the time of her life and she had no intention of asking him to hurry such delicious proceedings along . . .

The hammering at the front door downstairs sounded like thunder, making them both jump.

'What the . . . !' exclaimed Bruno, rolling away from her and cracking his ankle against the leg of the coffee table. 'Ouch. *Bloody* hell!'

Janey froze as the hammering started up again. As she scrambled to her feet a loud, authoritative voice from the street below shouted: 'Open up! Police. This is an emergency.'

'Oh my God, what is it?' She stared fearfully at Bruno. Her knees were trembling and all she was wearing was her jewellery.

'Police. Open up!' repeated the voice outside.

Running to her bedroom, Janey grabbed her dressing gown and threw it on, fumbling to tie the belt as she made her way downstairs. An emergency could only be a bomb scare or a major gas leak, she thought frantically, her mind whirling as she considered the possibilities. Unless something terrible had happened to Maxine.

As soon as she unlocked the door it crashed open.

'Surprise!' yelled Maxine gleefully. Clinging to the arm of one of her companions, who was six and a half feet tall and built like Arnold Schwarzenegger, she ricocheted off the open door and clutched Janey's shoulder with her free hand.

Before Janey could react, four more men piled through, squeezing themselves into the narrow hallway and chorusing: "Ello, 'ello, 'ello, what 'ave we 'ere then?'

'This wallpaper, Constable,' barked one of them. 'Arrest it immediately.'

'What about the dressing gown, Detective Inspector?' demanded another.

'Arrest the wallpaper first, Constable. Charge it with being pink.'

'Aye, aye, sir. And the dressing gown, sir? What shall I charge that with?'

'Easy peasy,' yelled Maxine, by this time almost helpless with laughter. 'Grievous bodily harm!'

Each of the cricketers was over six feet tall. Janey had never felt so small in her life.

'OK, very funny,' she said evenly. 'Now get out.'

'Can't get out, only just got in,' protested the man she had seen at Berenice's wedding, the one who was with Maxine. Behind him, his even taller friend was solemnly

161

addressing the wall: '. . . but I have to warn you that anything you do say will be taken down and used in evidence.'

'*Out*,' repeated Janey, her voice firm.

'In-out-in-out, shake it all about,' chanted the other two. To her absolute horror they were pushing past her, hokey-cokeying towards the stairs.

'She said you'd make us a cup of coffee,' explained Maxine's cricketer with what he no doubt thought was a beguiling grin. 'Oh come on, Janey, don't be cross. We won't stay long. We aren't really arresting your wallpaper.'

Frantic with worry that any minute now they were going to come face to face with Bruno – there wasn't even room for him to hide in her wardrobe – she wrenched the front door open again and glared at Maxine as ferociously as she knew how.

'No! You're all drunk and you aren't getting any coffee. Now *leave*.'

Maxine, unperturbed by the lack of welcome, simply giggled. 'Gosh, Janey, has anyone ever told you you're beautiful when you're angry? And we're not drunk, just . . . merry. I've told you a million times, don't exaggerate.'

This was awful. Janey considered bursting into tears to show them she meant it.

But Maxine was on a mission and she wasn't about to allow an unco-operative elder sister to put her off. 'One quick coffee,' she insisted, attempting to prise Janey away from the door. 'Well, one each would be even better. You see, darling, we felt sorry for you . . . no man, no social life . . . so we thought we'd come and cheer you up. Now isn't that a kind gesture?' She broke off, observing Janey's stony expression, and pouted. 'Oh cheer up, Janey. You could at least be a teeny bit grateful.'

Janey would have preferred to be a teeny bit violent. The next moment she swung round in panic. The hokey-cokeyers, after several wobbly false starts, had actually made it up the staircase. As she watched them lurch towards the door at the top of the stairs, one of them bawled: 'Open, sesame!'

And to her horror, it did.

'I say, what a brilliant trick,' said Maxine. Then, as Bruno appeared in the doorway, she did a classic double-take. 'Oh I *definitely* say! No wonder you didn't want to let us in. Two's company, seven's a crowd. Or an orgy . . .'

Bruno's pink-and-grey striped shirt and grey trousers were only slightly crumpled, and he had combed his hair. Having had time to compose himself, he was also looking amazingly relaxed.

'I've made the coffee,' he said, meeting Janey's petrified gaze. 'But there's no milk left, so it'll have to be black.' Pausing to survey the state of the astonished, bleary-eyed cricketers, he added pointedly, 'Under the circumstances, maybe it's just as well.'

'So now we're getting down to the nitty gritty,' crowed Maxine when Bruno had made his excuses and left. The cricketers, having piled into the tiny kitchen, were trying to remember whether or not they took sugar. Maxine, sitting cross-legged on the floor, was avid for details. 'The secret life of Janey Sinclair! Not only is she having a rip-roaring affair with a practically married man, but she has the confidence to do it in a ten-year-old towelling dressing gown.'

'I am not having an affair with Bruno.' Janey struggled to remain calm. If she lost her temper, Maxine would know for sure she'd struck gold. She had to be plausible. 'If I was,' she added, improvising rapidly, 'I wouldn't *be* wearing this dressing gown, would I?'

'Hmm. I wouldn't put it past you,' retorted Maxine, still looking deeply suspicious. 'In that case, why are you wearing it?'

'We went out for a meal. I spilled red wine on my jeans.' This, at least, was the truth. Gesturing towards the bathroom she said, 'They're soaking in the basin, if you'd like to check for yourself. Or maybe you'd prefer to send them off to Forensic.'

'So you went out to dinner and came back here afterwards for a nightcap? You sat here chatting and didn't notice the time? I'm sorry darling, but I don't believe you.'

Inwardly close to despair, Janey said. 'Well you're just going to have to. Because if I was having an affair with Bruno I'd tell you. But I'm not, so there's nothing *to* tell. Got it?'

'Don't be-lieve you,' repeated Maxine in a singsong voice.

'Oh for God's sake, it's the truth! Why can't you see that?'

Maxine unravelled herself and leaned slowly forwards. 'Because I'm the untidy sister,' she said joyfully, 'and you're the efficient, organized one.'

'What?'

Reaching under the sofa, Maxine pulled out the primrose bra which Janey had been wearing earlier and which Bruno had missed when he'd bundled up the rest of her clothes and slung them on the bed. 'Exhibit number one, m'lud,' she said, her expression triumphant. 'And no need for further cross-examination. Leaving items of lacy underwear beneath the settee? Janey, it just isn't you.'

# Chapter 19

Elsie Ellis, who lived above the bakery next door and who thrived on gossip, wasted no time the following morning. Bustling into Janey's shop with a self-important air and exuding as she always did the aroma of chocolate doughnuts, she was scarcely able to contain her impatience as Janey served the customer who'd beaten her in there by thirty seconds.

The customer was Serena Charlton, looking very chic in a midnight-blue off-the-shoulder tee-shirt, slender white skirt and navy-and-gold shoes. 'It's my mother's birthday tomorrow,' she explained, flipping a credit card on to the counter. 'It's so hard to know what to get them, isn't it? And I've left it rather late. As a matter of fact, it was Maxine who suggested I came to you.'

At the mention of Maxine's name, Elsie's chins began to wobble. Janey, steadfastly ignoring her and thinking that putting a bit of business her way was the least Maxine could do to make up for last night, took out her order pad and uncapped a biro.

'Something around the fifty-pound mark,' Serena continued vaguely, gazing around the shop in search of inspiration. 'Oh I don't know. Flowers aren't really my thing. Any kind, as long as they're white.'

*Fifty pounds, white*, wrote Janey. Lifting her head she said, 'And the message?'

Serena cast around for further inspiration. Finally, it came. 'Happy Birthday, Love Serena.'

My word, thought Janey. You ought to write a book.

When Serena had finished reciting her mother's address she added, 'Oh yes, I nearly forgot. Maxine wanted me to ask you how you're feeling this morning. She mentioned something about a late night.'

Elsie's chins exploded into life once more. This time she couldn't control herself. 'Funny you should mention Maxine,' she said, dying to know exactly what had happened and equally curious to discover the identity of the glamorous, dark-haired girl. 'I could hardly believe it when that incredible racket started up at two o'clock this morning. All that hammering on your front door and thumping around . . . nearly fell out of bed with the shock of it, I did!'

'Really?' Serena looked faintly amused. 'And what was it?'

Janey, saying nothing, gazed at Elsie.

'Well, I peeped out of my window.' Elsie's chest now swelled with self-importance as she turned to address Serena. 'It was dark, mind you, and I didn't have my glasses on, but I could see enough. It was young Maxine herself, with a whole bunch of plain-clothes policemen, and they said it was an emergency. Looked to me like she'd been arrested.'

Janey, who didn't see why she should have to explain anything, simply gave Elsie an unhelpful smile.

'So that's why I felt I should pop round and find out if you were both all right,' said Elsie, disappointed by the lack of response. 'It's only natural, after all, to worry when something like that happens. I just hope Maxine isn't in any *serious* trouble.' she concluded with relish.

'There's no need for you to worry about anything,' Janey assured her, running Serena's credit card through the machine and giving her the slip to sign. 'It's all been sorted out now, and Maxine is fine. It was nice of you, though, to be so concerned.'

Serena watched Elsie leave the shop. 'Well,' she said, calmly sliding the credit card back inside an expensive purse, 'you can say one thing about Maxine.'

Janey could think of several but they weren't wonderfully polite. Instead she said, 'What's that?'

Senena smiled. 'She certainly lives life to the full.'

When the cricketers had departed to play cricket somewhere in the north of England, Maxine had been briefly despondent. Only briefly, though. The very next day, whilst walking along the beach with Josh and Ella, she had encountered Tom.

'Bleeeuchh!' yelled Tom, coming awake with a jolt. Josh, who had been running, had stumbled against an abandoned shoe and inadvertently sent up a fountain of sand. Tom, spitting it out of his mouth, glared at Josh.

'Gosh, sorry,' said Josh. 'I didn't mean to do it.'

'It was my fault.' Maxine, removing her sunglasses, grinned down at the body on the sand. It was quite the nicest body she'd seen in . . . ooh, twenty-four hours. 'If I hadn't been chasing him, he wouldn't have tripped.'

She was wearing a pastel pink bikini and her long, blond hair was tied back with a pink scarf. Tom's mood improved almost at once.

'It doesn't matter.' Ruefully wiping his cheek, he said, 'It's a long time since anyone kicked sand in my face.'

'I should think it was.' Maxine admired his biceps. 'Do you weight-train?'

'Three times a week.' Tom was intensely proud of his physique. 'Have to,' he added, because he was also an incurable show-off. 'When you're out in the lifeboat it might mean the difference between life and death.'

'The lifeboat?' gasped Maxine, playing it to the hilt and deciding that Josh had earned himself an ice cream at the very least. The dazzling smile came into play. 'Goodness, you must be incredibly brave . . .'

But going out to dinner with a man who carried a beeper had its drawbacks. Maxine, who had worked long and hard on Guy in order to wangle another night off, and who had promised to babysit for the next three evenings to make up for it, was dismayed when she realized what was happening: one minute they were in Bruno's restaurant, about to dive into great bowls of mussels swimming in garlic butter sauce, and the next minute Tom was responding to his beeper as if he'd been stuck with an electric cattle prod.

'You're leaving now?' Maxine stared at him as he leapt up from the table. He could at least stay to finish his first course, surely.

Everyone in the restaurant had by this time turned to stare at the source of the beeping. Tom loved it when that happened. He felt just like Superman.

'Vessel in distress,' he said, just loudly enough for them all to hear. Snatching up his car keys he added, 'Every second counts. Sorry, love. I'll be in touch.'

That's what you think, Maxine thought moodily. Whilst she appreciated the urgency of the situation, she still wasn't happy about it. She'd never been stood up in the middle of dinner before. Even more disturbing, it looked as if she was going to be stuck with the bill.

'Bugger,' she said aloud, pouring herself another glass of wine and now wishing she hadn't chosen such an expensive bottle.

'Oh dear.' Bruno materialized at the table as the door swung shut behind Tom. 'Lovers' tiff?'

Maxine, poking at the mussels with her fork, gave him a wry smile. 'Saving lives, apparently, means more to him than my scintillating company and your stupendous food.'

'Some people have no sense of priority.'

'If he only knew what a struggle I had, getting the night off,' she went on with a trace of irritation. 'I wouldn't have bothered if I'd thought this might happen. What a waste!'

'Some people are so selfish,' Bruno mocked. Interestingly, he observed, she was no longer bothering to flirt with him as she had done on her previous visit. Since discovering him in Janey's flat, presumably, she had decided he was off-limits.

'You'd better go and tell the chef to stop cooking the steaks,' said Maxine. 'I can't afford to pay for them as well.' Gloomily she added, 'I don't even have enough cash on me for a taxi home.'

But Bruno was hungry and the Scotch fillets this week were superb. 'Please,' he said, in the same wry tone. 'You'll have me in tears next. I'll eat with you, if you like. If you're good,' he added with a brief smile, 'I'll even give you a lift home.'

If the mussels had been great the steaks *au poivre* were even better. Maxine, demolishing hers with enthusiasm, soon cheered up. 'Tell me all about it then,' she demanded, when the party at the table closest to theirs had left. 'How long have you been sleeping with Janey? And why on earth was she so desperate to keep this ravishing little item of gossip from me?'

'I think you've just answered that one yourself.' Bruno raised an eyebrow as he picked up his glass. 'Janey's hardly the type to enjoy being an item of gossip.'

'Oh you know what I mean,' said Maxine crossly. 'But she could at least have told me. I'm her sister! It isn't as if I'd go rushing out, broadcasting the news to all and sundry. I can be discreet, you know. When I have to be.'

Having heard all the lurid tales of Maxine's past conquests, Bruno didn't doubt it. But he was more interested right now in discovering whether she really knew why Janey had been so determined to keep their relationship a secret.

'In that case,' he said mildly, 'there must have been other reasons.'

Maxine, however, just looked puzzled. 'What other reasons?' she demanded. 'Your girlfriend? Her absent husband? She could still have told *me*.'

'Don't be dense,' sighed Bruno. '*You're* the reason she didn't want to tell you.'

'What?'

'You make her insecure. She thinks you're more attractive than she is,' he said bluntly. 'On her own, she's fine. When she's with you, she loses all faith in herself.'

Maxine looked appalled. 'You mean she doesn't trust me?'

She genuinely hadn't known. Bruno smiled slightly. 'I don't know, maybe I'm the one she doesn't trust. I don't have the greatest reputation in the world . . .'

'And that's why she didn't want us to meet in the first place,' said Maxine, her tone thoughtful. 'She thought you might prefer me.'

'Of course she did.' With a trace of exasperation, Bruno said, 'I can't believe it's never occurred to you. How can you not notice something like that?'

'Easy.' She drained her glass and inspected the bottle. 'I'm selfish and thoughtless, aren't I?'

'So what are you going to do now?'

'That's easy, too.' She smiled. 'See if I can't persuade you to open another bottle of wine.'

As he drove her back to Trezale House, Maxine said, 'You still haven't told me how long it's been going on.'

'You mean how long I've been sleeping with your sister?' There was a note of irony in his voice. 'Why don't you ask Janey?'

Maxine shrugged. 'She isn't speaking to me at the moment.'

'And I'm not telling you,' said Bruno. With a sideways glance in her direction, he added, 'There, doesn't that prove how discreet I can be?'

'It certainly proves how bloody infuriating you can be.' Peering into the darkness ahead, she said, 'Next turning on the left, just past that big tree. I know you didn't believe me earlier, but I can keep the odd secret . . . no, I said next left.'

Bruno, who knew the country lanes well, ignored her. A couple of hundred yards further along the road he turned the car into a gateway.

'This isn't next left,' said Maxine, as he switched off the ignition.

'We haven't finished talking yet. There's something I'm curious about.'

'What's that?'

The sky was inky black and sprinkled with stars, but the moon was almost full. The darkness wasn't total; she could see Bruno's white shirt and green eyes. She could also see that he was smiling.

'I've told you what Janey was afraid of,' he said in conversational tones. 'But you haven't asked me whether or not she was right.'

'Oh.' Maxine thought for a moment, aware of what he might be leading up to. 'OK then. Was she?'

'Janey's an attractive girl.' Bruno shrugged. 'Who needs her self-confidence building up.'

'And?'

'I think you already know how attractive you are.'

Maxine half-smiled. 'But when you first saw me, did you like me more than you like Janey?'

'I like you both, very much,' he said slowly. 'But you and I are more alike. We understand each other. And as I said before, I'm very discreet.'

Maxine didn't bother to look surprised. Bruno Parry-Brent was every bit as unscrupulous as she had suspected. They might be alike in many ways, she thought, but even she wasn't that two-faced. 'I see,' she murmured, pushing back her hair with her fingers. 'You mean, what Janey doesn't know about won't hurt her?'

'Exactly. You said you could keep a secret when you had to.' His smile broadened, his teeth gleaming white in the darkness. It had evidently not even crossed his mind that she might turn him down. 'It could be fun. A lot of fun. You and I.'

Charisma was a powerful aphrodisiac, and Bruno had more than his fair share of it. He really was amazingly attractive, thought Maxine. But then he had to be. Only men at the very top of the league in the attractiveness stakes could expect to get away with this kind of thing. And most of the time, presumably, they did.

Wishing, now, that she hadn't worn four-inch heels – although at least she was only a quarter of a mile from home – she ran her hand lightly over the soft leather upholstery.

'Do these seats go right back?'

Bruno grinned. 'All the way.'

'Hmm,' said Maxine. 'Somehow I thought they would.'

'Where are you going?' he protested as she opened the passenger door and climbed out of the car.

Yuk, thought Maxine as her heels sank into three inches of mud. So this was her reward for making a noble stand. No wonder she'd never bothered in the past.

'Home,' she said, her tone brisk. 'I realize this may come as a bit of a shock to you, but you aren't totally irresistible. And if you really want to know, I think you're a complete shit.'

'Maxine—'

'Poor Janey,' she continued, slamming the door shut and addressing him through the open window. 'What chance does she have, falling for a two-faced bastard like you?'

'OK,' said Bruno, making calm-down gestures with his hands. 'I get the message.'

'And here's another message,' Maxine snapped. 'I may not be perfect, but did you seriously think I'd play a dirty trick like that on my own sister?'

Bruno sighed good-naturedly, 'Spare me the moral lecture. It was just a suggestion, after all. Some girls would take it as a compliment.'

'My God, you're amoral!'

'And you're some kind of saint?' Bruno was grinning once more. 'Come on now, there's no need to make this much of a fuss. All you had to do was say no.'

'I don't care about me,' Maxine said icily. 'I care about Janey. You're going to hurt her.'

'I'm rehabilitating her,' he protested. 'Where's the harm in that? I haven't made any false promises.'

'You're just incredible.' She shot him a look of disdain. 'When I tell Janey what you've said to me tonight . . .'

'Now that really would hurt her,' said Bruno reasonably.

Maxine, who had already worked that out for herself, glared at him. She knew she couldn't tell Janey but she still didn't see why Bruno should escape scot-free.

'Come on, sweetheart,' he said again, patting the seat

beside him. 'No hard feelings. Now you've got that little outburst out of your system, I'll drive you home.'

Maxine, however, hoisted the strap of her evening bag over her shoulder and shook her head. 'I'd rather walk.'

'Why?'

Because I've just dropped an opened bottle of traffic-light-red nail polish on to the passenger seat, thought Maxine, still gazing at him through the wound-down window. And I don't want to get it all over my nice white skirt. Explain that one away to your girlfriend tomorrow morning, sweetheart.

'I'd just rather walk,' she said, straightening up and stepping away from the car. 'Don't worry, I'll be safe.'

'I'm sure you will,' murmured Bruno, realizing that he had well and truly blown it and switching on the ignition once more. Well and truly, he mused as he reversed out of the muddy gateway. And what on earth was that peculiar smell . . . ?

# Chapter 20

Oliver enjoyed watching Thea at work in her studio. Never having considered himself a suitable candidate for retirement, taking it easy for the first time in forty years had come as a pleasant surprise. Now, with the sun streaming through the windows and nothing to do but relax, he found it extraordinarily soothing simply to sit and admire her skill.

And Thea was such good company, too. She didn't indulge in idle gossip. If she had something worth saying, she said it. If she didn't, she kept quiet. As far as Oliver was concerned, the companionable silences, together with her down-to-earth attitudes and innate sensuality, made her about as perfect as any woman could be. Now that he had found her, he had absolutely no intention of letting her go.

'I wish you'd marry me,' he said, but all Thea did was smile and reach into the bucket beside her to rinse her hands.

'I thought you might have learned your lesson by now.'

Each of his three ex-wives had squealed with delight when he had proposed, the pound signs glowing practically neon in their eyes as they accepted. Thea, however, calmly continued to fashion a jawline from clay, studying it intently as a cloud passed over the sun, altering the shadows on the semi-constructed face.

Moving over to where she sat, Oliver stood behind her and rested his hands on her shoulders. 'They were the wrong women. You're the right one. Thea, you know how I feel about you.'

She knew, she knew. And if she had been young and foolish she would have married him in a flash, as recklessly as she'd once married Patrick. But independence was sweet, and learning both to achieve and enjoy it had taken half a lifetime. Thea was superstitious enough to believe that if she married Oliver their relationship would be spoiled. Furthermore, like snakes and ladders, she would then be forced to start all over again . . .

'I do know how you feel about me,' she said, tilting her head and smiling up at him. 'And I love you, darling. But we're allowed to feel this way. We don't need a vicar to give us permission.'

'I want us to be together,' he protested. 'Properly together.'

'And you think a silly scrap of paper would do the trick?' She leaned back, sounding amused. 'I'm not going to say yes, Oliver. I'll be your mistress but I won't be your wife. Just think, people might call me Mrs Kennedy the fourth. I'd end up feeling like the consolation prize in a raffle.'

She was always doing that, getting his name wrong. 'Cassidy,' he corrected her with mock severity.

'Of course.' Thea grinned, then looked puzzled. 'Why is that name so familiar?'

178

'It belongs to the man who wants to marry you. If you weren't so bloody obstinate, it could be your name!' Faintly exasperated, he added, 'Then you'd have to remember it.'

But her expression had cleared. 'Of course. Guy Cassidy, the photographer. That's the chap my younger daughter works for. You've probably heard of him, darling . . . I believe he's rather famous.'

'Ah.' Oliver, who had been waiting for some time for her to make the connection, realized he may as well get it over with. Clasping Thea's hand in his, he took a deep breath. 'As a matter of fact, I have heard of him . . .'

'One question,' said Thea, when he had finished. 'Was I part of this plan? Did you know I was Maxine's mother when you came into the studio that day?'

'No.' Oliver shook his head. 'You definitely weren't part of the plan. Just a glorious, unexpected bonus.'

Thea smiled, satisfied he was speaking the truth. 'That's all right then, and I suppose you'd rather I didn't mention any of this to Maxine?'

'It might be best.' He kissed her teasingly on the forehead. 'Not until the wedding, at least.'

'How have the children been?' asked Guy, sitting down at the kitchen table and watching Maxine wash up. Serena had left for a fashion shoot in Barcelona and he'd spent the day in London after seeing her off at Heathrow.

'Wonderful.' Maxine, immeasurably cheered by Serena's departure, grinned at him. 'I took them to the supermarket this morning. When we got back here I found a packet of Jellytots in Ella's pocket. I felt like Fagin.'

Guy frowned. 'I hope you told her off.'

'Told her off? I stood in front of her and ate every last one. And I've told her that next week she has to go back, apologize to the manager and hand over two weeks' pocket money. If she's lucky he won't send her to prison.'

'She won't do that again in a hurry, then.' He looked amused.

'She won't speak to me again in a hurry either,' said Maxine. 'According to Ella, it was my fault for not allowing her to buy any Jellytots in the first place.'

Guy rose to his feet and picked up a tea towel. When he started drying the plates she'd washed, Maxine knew at once something was up.

'But they do speak to you,' he said, his tone casual. 'Tell me, what do they think of Serena?'

*Uh-oh*. It hadn't escaped Maxine's notice that Serena had arrived with four suitcases and only left with two. She might have known she shouldn't get her hopes up. 'Why? Are you thinking of marrying her?'

'I'm just interested in hearing anything you may have picked up,' said Guy.

Serena had stuck up for her, Maxine remembered, when he had bawled her out over the Oliver Cassidy incident. She'd also given her a Monopoly board-sized box of expensive make-up, an unwanted gift which she said she'd never use. In her own vague way, Maxine supposed, she wasn't really that bad. Not scintillating, but bearable.

'They think she's OK,' she replied, washing a teaspoon with care. 'They don't dislike her, anyway. She doesn't really talk to them that much.'

Guy raised an eyebrow. 'Is that it?'

Maxine handed him the teaspoon. 'As far as Josh is concerned, most of your girlfriends go so far over the top they're practically in orbit. At least Serena doesn't do that. She doesn't gush over them.'

'Hmm.' He paused, then said, 'And how about you?'

She gave him an innocent look. 'I don't gush either.'

'What's your opinion of Serena?'

He wasn't being very fair. If she said anything remotely bitchy it could only go against her. With a trace of resentment, Maxine said, 'Why are you asking me? My opinion hardly counts. You're old enough to make up your own mind about whether or not you like her.' Furthermore, she thought grumpily, she couldn't for the life of her understand why he should be so apparently taken with Serena and so uninterested in herself.

'I know.' There was a glimmer of a smile on his face. 'I have. But it is going to affect you. Serena's sold her flat in London and she's going to be moving in with us when she gets back from Barcelona.'

Oh hell, thought Maxine. If Guy and Serena were going to play happy families, did that mean she was out of a job? Aloud, she said, 'Permanently?'

He shrugged. 'We'll see how it goes. She was looking at other flats, but completion on her own went through more quickly than expected, so it seemed an appropriate time to . . . well, try it.'

Maxine turned, gave him a look and said nothing.

'I know, it's hardly the romantic gesture of the decade,' hedged Guy, 'but it's tricky, with the children . . . I just don't want to make any mistakes.'

'And what do Josh and Ella think of all this?' she countered. 'They haven't said anything about it to me.'

'I'm speaking to them this evening.' He smiled. 'I asked you first.'

'What for, my permission?'

'Your opinion.'

Maxine dried her hands on a tea towel. 'Don't their opinions matter?'

'Of course they do,' Guy retorted. 'If they really couldn't handle it, Serena wouldn't move in. And this isn't a cue,' he added severely, 'for you to put the boot in behind my back.'

She kept a straight face. 'Would I?'

'Of course you would.' He raised an eyebrow. 'That's why I'm saying don't even think of it. This is important to me.'

Me too, thought Maxine. Leaning against the sink and folding her arms she said mildly, 'If Serena's moving in, does that mean you won't need me any more?'

'Good God, of course not!' Guy looked astonished. 'Is that what you thought? No, Serena has her career . . . she travels abroad more often than I do. You'd still be needed to look after the children.' He paused, then added, 'If anything, I was more concerned that you might decide to leave.'

It was the nicest thing he'd ever said to her, Maxine decided. Heavens, it was practically a full-scale compliment. 'Does that mean you really *want* me to stay?' she said, milking the situation for all it was worth.

But Guy wasn't that easily fooled. 'The children do,'

he replied neatly. 'But then they don't know about the incident the other night outside your sister's flat.'

'Oh, but I hadn't really been arrested—'

'I know.' He looked amused. 'I'm just saying there isn't much point in fishing for compliments. There's such a thing as pushing your luck too far.'

'If you want to marry someone, why don't you marry Maxine?' said Ella, as if that solved the problem. 'Then Serena wouldn't need to move in.'

Guy tried to imagine what was going on in her seven-year-old mind. Ella's memories of her mother were becoming sketchy. She had been cared for by nannies – first Berenice, now Maxine – for over three years.

'I'm not marrying Serena,' he replied carefully. 'We just thought it might be nice if she came to live here.'

Ella frowned. 'But she's your girlfriend. Does that mean she'd be sort of like a mummy?'

Guy didn't know the answer to that. In darker moments during the past year or two when other people had made pointed comments and guilt had mingled with the weight of parental responsibility, he had wondered whether he should simply find himself a wife, a suitable stepmother for the children, and stop waiting for *it* to happen. It, he thought, was taking its time. Love didn't grow on trees. There had been more than enough willing candidates, God knows, but the ones who would have made ideal stepmothers had never captured his interest and those with whom he had become briefly involved had on the whole been wildly unsuited for the task.

And it was a hell of a task for any woman; he knew

183

that. But of all of them, at least Serena had had the guts to be honest with him from the start. Young children weren't something she was familiar with. She was sure Josh and Ella were perfectly nice but if he didn't mind she'd prefer to take her time getting to know them. Besides, she had added, who knew how their own relationship would work out? There didn't seem much point in getting too emotionally involved with the kids if all they ended up doing was splitting up. That would only cause them more unnecessary pain.

It might be a pessimistic attitude, but it was practical. Guy was willing to give it a go. Just because he had fallen in love with Véronique within minutes of meeting her didn't mean it always had to happen that way. Maybe this time with Serena, it would simply unfold at a gradual pace.

Ella, wearing pale pink pyjamas and Mickey Mouse slippers, was curled up beside him on the sofa. Reaching for the doll she had been playing with earlier she began replaiting its blond nylon hair.

'No, Serena's just . . . Serena,' said Guy cautiously, in reply to her question. 'She's a friend.'

'So we aren't going to be a whole family?' Ella gazed up at him, eyes serious.

He gestured towards Josh, sitting on the floor in front of them. 'The three of us are a family, sweetheart. You know that.'

'Serena's just Dad's girlfriend.' It was Josh's turn to explain the situation to his young sister. 'She isn't part of our family because she isn't related to us. The only way she can get related is if Dad married her, but even then she'd only be a distant relation.' Glancing at Guy for confirmation, he added cheerfully, 'Like that man who gave us the money the other week, our grandfather. He's a distant relation too. It means they can buy you presents but they aren't allowed to tell you off.'

Guy hesitated, then nodded. This particular matter had yet to be sorted out. All he'd got so far each time he'd attempted to call his father was the answering machine.

Ella, however, brightened. 'He was nice! When are we going to see him again?'

'I don't know, sweetheart. We'll have to see. Now, are you happy about Serena moving in? Is there anything else you'd like to ask me?'

She shrugged. 'I don't mind. As long as she isn't allowed to tell us off.'

'That's what Maxine does,' said Josh earnestly. 'It's her job.'

Ella finished fiddling with the doll's springy hair. 'And teaching me how to do plaits,' she said with pride. 'Daddy, will Serena sleep in the same bed as you when she starts living here?'

Guy nodded once more. For the sake of appearances, Serena had been occupying the guest room for the past week. From now on, however, the subterfuge was going to have to come to an end. 'Yes sweetheart, she will.'

'Poor Serena,' said Ella with a sigh. 'She's really going to hate it when you snore.'

# Chapter 21

The trouble with liking the sound of someone from the letter they had written in reply to an advert, Janey decided, was that it didn't tell you everything about them. Certain vital details only emerged later, when it was too late to say you'd changed your mind after all and that although you hadn't even got to know them yet you just knew it wasn't going to work out.

If James Blair had only mentioned in passing that he had a laugh like a donkey on helium, for example, she would have crossed him off her list faster than you could say snort. As it was, he only hit her with the awful reality of it after introducing himself in person, in the foyer of the theatre where they had arranged to meet prior to seeing a play in which his sister had a starring role.

He wasn't afraid to use it either. To her dismay, Janey realized that the play was billed as a comedy. All James had done so far was buy her a gin and tonic prior to curtain-up, and he'd laughed five times already. Everyone was turning to stare. One poor woman, standing unsuspectingly with her back to him, was so startled by the incredible noise that she'd spilled her drink down her blouse. It was a loud laugh that erupted abruptly,

186

exploded out of all control and didn't know when to stop. If James Blair had wanted to forewarn her about it in his letter, he could have described it as: Bleugh-huuu . . . eek . . . bleugghh-huuu . . . eek eek eek . . . blaaaahhhuuu-huuu . . . eek. Now she was stuck with it for the next ninety minutes at the very least. She didn't know which was worse, the sound of the laugh or the curiosity and barely concealed amusement of every other theatre-goer within earshot.

I'm a shallow, spineless person, Janey reprimanded herself, and James is probably a very kind man. Just because he doesn't laugh like other people, there is absolutely no reason at all to wish I was anywhere in the world but here.

But it was no good. James was still laughing, people were still staring and the play, now due to start in less than three minutes, was described in her programme as 'rip-roaring, rib-tickling, fun, fun, fun!'

'Marvellous play,' declared James, taking her arm in order to steer her back towards the bar when it was over. 'I can't remember when I last enjoyed myself so much. Didn't you think it was marvellous, Janey?'

'It's awfully late.' Damp patches of perspiration had formed under Janey's arms; she could feel them as she glanced at her watch. 'I really think I should be making a move.'

'Oh, but I told my sister we'd meet her for a drink after the show. You can stay for another ten minutes, surely?'

He looked so crestfallen she hadn't the heart to refuse. He wasn't her type, but he was undeniably decent.

'OK,' she heard herself saying out of sheer guilt, 'just a quick drink. Then I'm afraid I really will have to leave.'

'Jolly good!' James beamed, his boyish face alight with such enthusiasm that she felt guilty all over again. If she hadn't been feeling so ashamed of herself she would never have allowed him to slide his arm in a proprietorial manner around her waist. 'What'll you have then, a quick gin? Or a slow one? Sloe gin . . . geddit? Bleugh-huuu . . . eek . . . bleugghh-huuu . . . eek eek . . .'

Janey could have died on the spot when she saw Guy Cassidy ahead of her at the bar. All evening she'd been consoling herself with the thought that at least she hadn't bumped into anyone she recognized. It might be shallow and spineless of her, but it was a comfort nevertheless. Or it had been, up until now.

'Hello, Janey.' Breaking off his conversation with a balding middle-aged man, he turned and smiled at her. Perspiration prickled once more beneath her arms and down her spine as for a fraction of a second his gaze flickered to James, still caught up in the throes of his own unfunny joke.

Feeling sicker than ever, because he was also bound to relay every detail to Maxine, Janey made an effort to return his smile. 'Guy, what a surprise!'

'I know,' he replied with mock solemnity. 'I don't make a habit of visiting the theatre but I'd heard such great things about this production . . .'

'What he means,' explained his balding companion, 'is that he was dragged here against his will because we've been friends for years and I happen to be the play's director. I told him he had to suffer first if he wanted dinner afterwards.'

Guy grinned. 'I felt like a girl out on a blind date.'

Janey felt herself go scarlet. James, who had been listening to the exchange with interest, guffawed. 'Like a girl out on a blind date? Oh I say, that's jolly funny, bleugh-huuu . . . eek eek eek . . .'

'Why don't you like me?' said Serena suddenly.

Guy was upstairs saying goodnight to Josh and Ella. Maxine, who was busy stuffing clothes into the washing machine, hadn't even realized she was no longer alone in the kitchen. She looked up, surprised.

'Who says I don't like you?'

'I'm not stupid,' said Serena calmly. Pulling out a chair, she sat down and examined her perfect fingernails. Maxine, who thought that anyone capable of spending one and a half hours buffing and manicuring their nails had to be stupid, didn't reply.

'Is it envy?'

'I don't dislike you,' Maxine protested, because the situation was bordering on the embarrassing. She half smiled. 'And no, I'm not envious. I've always liked being five feet six and blond.'

'I'm used to being envied for my looks.' As if to prove it, Serena ran a hand through her sleek dark hair then fixed her unswerving gaze on Maxine, who was still kneeling on the floor with a box of Persil in one hand and an armful of Ella's socks in the other. 'But that isn't what I meant.' Slowly she added, 'I'm talking about Guy.'

'Guy!'

'He's an attractive man.' Serena smiled slightly. 'Please, Maxine. Don't tell me you hadn't noticed.'

'And you think I'm jealous because you're living with him,' cried Maxine, outraged. This was too much. Of course Guy was attractive, but the fact that she had been secretly lusting after him for weeks didn't even enter into it. If Serena hadn't been so distant and stand-offish from day one, things might have been different. If, Maxine thought crossly, she'd made even the slightest attempt to fit in, it might have helped – regardless of her own small crush on Guy. But Serena, it appeared, had eyes only for Guy and no interest at all in either his children or herself. Maxine knew only too well that she wasn't the most likely nanny in the world but she'd grown extremely fond of Josh and Ella, who were friendly, cheerful and endlessly entertaining. Serena's persistent and total disregard for them, she now felt, was downright weird.

'Yes, I think you're jealous.' Serena picked up and investigated a half-full cup of tepid coffee.

If she asked me to make a fresh pot, thought Maxine, she'll get it over her head.

'Well you couldn't be more wrong!' she snapped back. 'OK, he might not look like Quasimodo, but as far as I'm concerned Guy Cassidy is irritable, moody and not a great deal of fun to work with. I came here because I wanted to stay in Trezale and I needed a job.' Shovelling the last of the laundry into the washing machine – which ran a lot more smoothly now that her spare set of car keys had been removed from the outer drum – she added crossly, 'And if I was really interested in chasing after your boyfriend, you'd know about it.'

Serena merely raised an immaculate eyebrow. 'No need to lose your temper,' she observed, her tone mild. 'Maxine, I don't *want* us to be enemies. What I'm trying to say is that if you are interested in Guy, I can understand that. Personally, I'd be amazed if you weren't.'

'Well I'm not,' lied Maxine. Serena sounded like a benevolent schoolmistress; the urge to act like a five-year-old and stick out her tongue was almost overwhelming.

'All right.' Serena, looking more tolerant then ever, said soothingly, 'We'll leave it at that then, shall we? I truly didn't mean to upset you, Maxine; all I was going to say was that if you were hoping some kind of relationship might develop, well . . . I'm afraid it isn't really on the cards.'

This was getting crazier by the minute. Maxine, shaking with suppressed rage, spoke through clenched teeth. '*What*?'

'I discussed the matter with Guy,' explained Serena, unperturbed. 'He told me that you absolutely weren't his type.'

# Chapter 22

The cliff path leading down to the cove was stony and narrow but worth the effort. The beaches at the heart of Trezale would, at eight o'clock in the evening, still be overrun by holidaymakers, whereas Shell Cove, on the outskirts of the town, was virtually empty. Few people could be bothered to stray the mile or so from the shops and bars; fewer still could face the prospect, at high tide, of clambering back up the steeply sloping track to the road at the top of the cliff.

Which was really just as well, thought Janey, since it enabled Maxine to rant and rave as loudly as she liked without fear of alarming the tourists.

'. . . so Serena said, "We'll say no more about it,"' Maxine spat furiously, continuing the monologue which had started 300 feet up, 'and walked out of the kitchen. I had plenty more to bloody say about it, I can tell you!'

'But you couldn't tell her so you're telling me instead.'

They had reached the bottom; rocks and crumbling gravel gave way to fine dry sand. Janey removed her shoes and wiggled her toes in its delicious warmth.

'Damn right I'm telling you,' said Maxine, pushing her hair away from her face with an indignant gesture.

'It's the only way to make sure I don't explode. The bloody nerve of that woman!'

'She was right, though.' Janey, who hadn't completely forgiven her sister yet for barging into the flat the other week, couldn't resist pointing it out. 'You *are* after Guy.'

'Not any more.' Maxine's dark eyes glittered with disdain. Then, catching Janey's sidelong glance, she added forcefully, 'And it isn't because Serena says he isn't interested, either. I wouldn't have anything to do with a man who had anything to do with her. I can't for the life of me imagine what he even sees in her, anyway.'

'We've been through this before,' Janey pointed out. 'Perfect face, perfect body . . .'

'Oh that!' Maxine threw her a look of derision. 'Physically, she's perfection on a sodding stick. But mentally she's nothing, no personality whatsoever. Half the time it's like trying to hold a conversation with a bowl of fruit.'

'You mean she isn't temperamental.' Janey grinned. 'Like you.'

'I mean I've never seen her laugh,' snapped Maxine, aiming a kick at a heap of seaweed. 'Josh was telling her jokes yesterday and I swear she didn't even get them. And then she has the nerve to discuss me with Guy, for God's sake!'

Janey was struggling to hide her amusement. 'At least that means they have conversations.'

'But you should have heard the way she said it,' howled Maxine. Kicking a bundle of seaweed along the shoreline was no longer enough; picking up the largest pebble within reach she hurled it into the sea. 'She was so bloody superior and all the time I was having to bite my tongue because she thinks that now she's moved in with Guy she's home and dry. Except that I know,' she added darkly, 'what he's really been getting up to whilst she's away.'

'Oh?' This was more like it, Janey, whose attention had begun to wander, looked interested.

'Exactly,' Maxine declared with an air of triumph. 'Those other women of his haven't given up on him yet. They still phone up, and he didn't come home on Tuesday night until gone three. That would wipe the smirk off Serena's face, if she only knew.'

Tuesday, thought Janey. That was when she had bumped into him at the theatre. Innocently she asked, 'Why, who was he with?'

'Which particular female, you mean?' countered Maxine, her voice awash with sarcasm. 'Well, it was one of them, and that's all that matters. When I asked Guy he told me it was none of my business and not to be so damn nosey, so I knew he'd been up to no good.'

If Guy had walked out of the sea at that moment, Janey would have thrown her arms around him and covered him with kisses. Tempted though she'd been to beg him not to mention their chance meeting to Maxine, she hadn't had the nerve to do so. But Guy hadn't said a word about it anyway. Her shameful secret was safe.

'Maybe there's an innocent explanation,' she suggested cheerfully, but that wasn't what Maxine wanted to hear.

'What's the matter with you?' Seizing another pebble and tossing it into the waves, she almost decapitated a passing seagull. 'Taking his side all of a sudden? Give me a break, Janey – he has more women than he knows what to do with and he was hardly going to spend the night playing Monopoly. The man's about as innocent as Warren Beatty, and the least he could do is have the decency to let me in on the agenda. After all, I'm glad he's seeing somebody else. Anyone's better than that smug bitch Serena.'

'Perhaps he thinks you might run off and tell her,' said Janey.

'If I thought it would get rid of her, and if it didn't mean risking my job,' Maxine replied crossly, 'I bloody would!'

As children they had always taken the same route around the cove. Now, reaching the rock pools, they made their way across the slippery boulders to their favourite pool, the one that always contained the most interesting wildlife and which provided two comfortable seats worn into the rock by centuries of tides.

Maxine, having finally run out of invective, dabbled her bare feet in the sun-warmed water, and watched two miniature crabs skitter out of the way in alarm. 'You haven't been very sympathetic,' she grumbled, casting a sidelong glance at Janey's fuchsia toenails. 'What's the matter, are you still mad because we invaded your flat and spoiled your fun with Bruno?'

It was the first time the subject had been mentioned. Janey had been waiting for it to come up. She had also decided that there was no longer any point in holding back. 'Don't worry,' she replied cheerfully, 'we've made up for it since then.'

'Oh. So you're still seeing him.'

195

Maxine sounded disappointed. This had to be a first for her, thought Janey with a flicker of triumph. Two attractive men, neither of them the least bit interested in ever-popular, oh-so-irresistible Maxine Vaughan. Not what she was used to at all.

'I am,' she said with pride.

'Hmm.'

Now it was Janey's turn to be annoyed. 'Such enthusiasm,' she snapped. 'You were the one who nagged me to find myself a man, and now I have. Couldn't you at least pretend to be pleased?'

Maxine sighed. Although diplomacy had never been one of her strong points, she recognized that she would have to tread with care. 'But he's somebody else's man,' she said, her tone even. 'Janey, is this wise? What about the girl he's living with?'

Janey's mouth narrowed. This was rich; couldn't-care-less Maxine was giving her a moral lecture. Talk about double standards.

'Look, Nina knows what he's like and she accepts it. If she doesn't mind, why should I?'

'Oh, so you've asked her.' Maxine threw her a challenging stare.

'Of course I haven't asked her.' Beginning to feel cornered, Janey retaliated crossly, 'And I can't believe I'm hearing this holier-than-thou rubbish from someone who once had an affair with a man because she'd "forgotten" he was married!'

'That was me,' said Maxine, forcing herself to keep calm. 'I'm different. But darling, sneaking around with a married man simply isn't your style. You're too *nice* . . .'

196

'Bruno isn't married.'

This was Janey's mantra, the phrase with which she endlessly comforted herself in order to justify her actions. Of course the situation wasn't ideal, of course she wasn't proud of herself, but at least Bruno was not married.

'She's his common-law wife,' Maxine continued remorselessly. 'They've been together for years.' Then she softened. 'Oh Janey, that isn't why I'm against it. I just don't want you to end up getting hurt, and I'm so afraid you will. Bruno isn't your type of man. He's—'

'You mean he's your type,' Janey countered bitterly. 'And you don't want me to have fun. Well I've spent the last twenty months not having any fun and I'm not going to go back to that again. I like Bruno and he likes me. A lot.'

For the first times their rôles had been reversed. Maxine, struggling to keep her older sister on the straight and narrow, and to prevent her from being hurt, realized that she wasn't making a roaring success of the operation. It wasn't as simple, she thought ruefully, as Janey had always made it look. But if she told her exactly what Bruno had suggested the other night she would only splatter Janey's fragile self-confidence and probably lose her friendship into the bargain. Hell, it was hard being a good guy.

'I'm sure he likes you,' she said cautiously. 'But I still don't think he's the right man for you, sweetheart.'

'Stop it!' Janey had had enough. With a look of disdain she rose to her feet. 'I know it's come as a shock to the system but you're just going to have to face up to it. Bruno prefers me. And you're jealous.'

★  ★  ★

Life at the moment, Maxine decided, wasn't being very fair. Returning to Trezale House, she ran into Guy at the foot of the stairs.

'I've been trying to work,' he said, gesturing with a handful of contact prints in the direction of the darkroom, 'and the bloody phone keeps ringing. Someone called Bruno has rung three times asking to speak to you. He wants you to phone him back as soon as possible.'

Serena's car was parked on the driveway outside. Glancing at it through the hall window, Maxine said, 'Can't Serena answer the telephone?'

'She's in the bath.'

Josh and Maxine had taken to laying bets on the duration of Serena's famous baths. The longest so far had been an hour and forty minutes. Maxine hoped Josh was upstairs, timing this one. Keeping a straight face, she said, 'Oh, right.'

'She also tells me that you lost your temper with her this afternoon.'

Maxine's dark eyes flashed. 'And did she happen to mention why?'

Guy nodded. For a moment she thought she detected a glimmer of a smile.

'OK, maybe she went a bit far but there was still no need for you to fly off the handle like that. We all have to make allowances if we're going to get on together.'

'Nobody else does,' Maxine retorted sulkily. 'I don't see why I should have to be the one who makes all the allowances around here.'

'You aren't the only one,' he countered, his tone brisk.

'I've answered the phone three times this evening, haven't I? And I'm passing on the message, even though I don't approve of what you're up to.'

'What I'm up to?' She looked astonished. 'Tell me, what am I up to?'

'Oh come on,' Guy drawled. 'It isn't too difficult to figure out. Bruno, I presume, is Bruno Parry-Brent. I might not know him that well, but I've heard enough to know what he's like. And now he's panting down the phone after you. Or as near as dammit.'

'It's none of your business why he's ringing up,' Maxine countered furiously.

'Of course it isn't. I just thought you might have had a bit more sense than to get involved with a married man. He's hardly ringing up to check table reservations, is he?'

'He isn't married,' hissed Maxine. This was ridiculous, now she sounded like Janey. 'And I'm not involved with him! I don't even like the man.'

'Oh please.' At this, Guy rolled his eyes. 'If they're male, you like them. If they're female, Bruno likes them. Let's face it Maxine, the two of you are a perfectly matched pair.'

'Come out with me tomorrow night,' said Bruno.

'No, I don't want to go out with you tomorrow night.' Maxine, who had deliberately waited until Guy was in the room before returning Bruno's call, spoke the words slowly and clearly. For good measure she added, 'Or any other night. Bruno, I've told you before; I'm just not interested.'

'I know.' He sounded amused. 'But I am. And the

harder you play to get, the more interested I become.'

Maxine shot a triumphant glance at Guy, who was reading the paper and eating the children's Jaffa cakes. 'The answer's still no.'

Guy, apparently engrossed in his horoscope, didn't react.

At the other end of the line Bruno laughed. 'Hasn't anyone ever told you that the saintly act doesn't suit you? Come on now, you owe me one night out at least. Have you any idea how much it cost me to get the nail varnish cleaned off that car seat?'

'Serves you right,' said Maxine briskly. 'And no, I don't owe you anything. If you're so determined to go out tomorrow night I suggest you take Nina.'

Guy ate another Jaffa cake.

'She's gone to stay with her sister in Kent.'

Maxine almost blurted out: 'Take Janey, then, instead,' though why she should bother to protect her gullible sister's reputation from Guy she didn't know. Instead, she said smoothly, 'Well, I'm sure you'll be able to find someone else to keep you company.'

'I'm sure I will,' Bruno replied good-naturedly. 'It's just that you were my first choice.'

'What a shame you aren't mine,' Maxine retorted. 'Goodbye.'

When she hung up, Guy lifted his head from the paper. Returning his gaze with pride, Maxine said, 'There.'

'Totally believable,' he remarked dryly, shaking the last Jaffa cake out of the box. 'The best piece of acting I've seen in years. Who were you talking to, the speaking clock?'

# Chapter 23

Sunday mornings were funny creatures, Thea decided. Waking up alone on a Sunday morning, as far as she was concerned, was downright depressing. In the first months after the break-up of her marriage, she had spent each week dreading those few hideous hours above all others. Solitary Sunday mornings, like solitary Christmases, were the absolute pits.

And then there were the other kind . . .

'What are you thinking?' asked Oliver, leaning across and brushing a croissant flake from her cleavage.

Thea smiled at him. 'That there really isn't anything more wonderful than lying in bed on a Sunday with fresh croissants, lots of newspapers and a superb lover.'

'Does that mean I trail in third?' he protested. 'Behind food and *The Times*?'

'No.' As she kissed his cheek, the newspapers crackled between them. 'They're nice but they aren't crucial. Having you here is what makes it so wonderful.' Her smile widening, she pushed back her long white hair. 'And of course there is the even more wonderful added bonus . . .'

Oliver smirked. 'That I'm a superb lover.'

'Actually,' said Thea, 'it's that you're so good at crosswords.' She chuckled in delight. It was the most gorgeous day but she didn't even want to venture outside. Oliver was here with her and that was all that mattered.

Oliver, however, was still hungry. 'If we'd stayed at the hotel we could have called room service,' he grumbled.

Remembering to buy the croissants and a jar of black cherry jam had stretched Thea to the domestic limits. Never having been the type to keep a fridge bursting with cold roast chicken, smoked ham, good wine and strawberries, she knew with certainty that the only items currently in occupation were three opened jars of mayonnaise in various stages of senility, a Body Shop eye mask for hangovers, and a mango. But what the hell, she decided comfortably. I'm an artist. I'm allowed to be a slob.

'I don't have any more food, we shall have to starve,' she told Oliver, lifting her face to his for another kiss. 'There, you see? A prime example of why I must never marry you. I'm hopeless in the kitchen. Within weeks you'd be a shadow of your handsome former self and screaming for a divorce.'

'I would not!' He looked astonished. 'We'd have a housekeeper.'

'To cater for our every whim?' Thea mocked. 'How exotic!'

'I'm being serious. And meanwhile . . .' Picking up the phone beside the bed, he punched out the number of his hotel.

'How marvellous,' Thea sighed, when he had spoken to the restaurant manager and arranged for two three-course lunches to be sent over by taxi within the hour. 'The power of the favoured customers.'

'The power of money.' Oliver dismissed it with a shrug. 'It's not such a big deal.'

'It's a big deal when it means you get to eat rack of lamb with fennel instead of dial-a-pizza,' Thea said happily. She might not cook but she still adored exquisite food.

'If you're that easily impressed,' Oliver retorted, 'I don't know why you won't marry me. Then you could eat whatever you liked, go wherever you liked . . .'

As Thea sat up, the sheet dropped away, revealing her nakedness. Trailing the back of her hand across Oliver's cheek, she felt the bristly soft texture of his moustache against her skin. 'Don't be cross with me,' she chided, her tone gentle. 'If I said yes, people would wonder if I'd married you for your money. I would wonder if I'd married you for your money! But this way it doesn't matter, because I love you anyway. I'm already where I want to be and I'm doing exactly what I want to do. As far as I'm concerned, this is as perfect as it gets.'

Oliver was in the shower when the doorbell rang. Thea, only vaguely decent in an embroidered black silk robe which showed off her splendid bosom, and with her long white hair still hanging loose down her back, was padding barefoot around the kitchen in search of matching cutlery.

As she headed for the front door, her stomach rumbled. Lobster mousse, rack of lamb, fresh fruit salad and two bottles of Chardonnay were going to go down very well indeed. But three figures were silhouetted through the patterned glass and none of them appeared to be carrying trays of sumptuous food.

One outline was instantly recognizable, the other two were short. Thea groaned. It was too late to shrink back and pretend not to be at home. Whilst she hesitated, she heard a young girl enquire in high-pitched tones, 'So if she's your mother, does that mean she's really old?'

'Ancient,' Maxine replied. 'Over forty.'

Thea took a deep breath and opened the door. 'But young at heart,' she declared, praying that Oliver wouldn't choose this moment to break into song upstairs. 'Darling, how lovely to see you, but you really should have phoned. I'm in a tearing hurry, about to go out . . .

'Just five minutes then.' Since it hadn't for a moment occurred to Maxine that she might not be welcome, she was already halfway through the door, ushering her two small charges into the hallway ahead of her. 'Mum, this is Ella, and this is Josh, and am I glad you're home. We've walked all the way from Trezale House and I forgot to bring any money with me. If you could lend me a fiver for cold drinks . . .'

'I'll go and find my purse,' said Thea, backing away. 'Wait here.'

'. . . and if Ella could just run upstairs and use the bathroom,' Maxine went on, scarcely pausing for breath. 'She's had her legs crossed for the last twenty minutes. It's been painful to watch.'

Damn, thought Thea, glancing down at the small blond girl whose knees were pressed tightly together. 'Right, um . . . give me a couple of minutes first.'

'Is that the shower?' Maxine, listening to the distant

sound of running water, gave her mother an enquiring look. 'Who's upstairs?'

'No one.' Thea gathered her black robe around her and moved towards the staircase. 'I was just about to jump in. I'll go and turn it off.'

'Out,' she hissed moments later, grabbing Oliver's soapy arm and dragging him out of the shower. 'My daughter and your grandchildren are downstairs, waiting to use the loo. You'll have to hide in the bedroom.'

'Bloody hell!' Shampoo cascaded down his face and chest, half blinding him. Stubbing his toe against the edge of the door he cursed once more beneath his breath as Thea pushed him naked on to the landing. 'I knew we should have stayed at the hotel. How long are they here for?'

'As long as it takes to pee.' Thea, stifling laughter, steered him towards the bedroom. 'Don't worry I'll get rid of them. Stay in here. And whatever you do, don't sneeze.'

By the time she returned downstairs, Maxine and the children had moved into the front room. Maxine, glancing out of the window, said, 'If you ordered a taxi to pick you up, it's already here. Shall I go out and tell the driver he'll have to wait?'

'I'll do it.' Thea hurried towards the door but the taxi driver was already out of the car, reaching into the back seat and sliding out a vast wicker hamper.

'Can I go to the bathroom now?' cried Ella, frantic with need.

'First left at the top of the stairs,' Maxine replied absently, her gaze still fixed on the driver as he struggled up the path with the hamper. 'Mum, what's going on? Have you adopted a puppy?'

'I've invited someone to dinner.' Thea looked shamefaced. 'He doesn't know I can't cook and I wanted to make a good impression so I ordered the food from a restaurant.'

'Good heavens,' said Maxine, because Thea had never worried about making a good impression before. 'I hope he's worth it.'

'Don't worry.' Thea smiled to herself, because Oliver was worth millions. 'He is.'


'Do you know, Maxine, your mother wasn't telling the truth?' Josh remarked as they made their way back along the beach.

Maxine licked a blob of chocolate ice-cream from her wrist. 'No?'

'She hadn't had a shower when we got there,' he continued seriously, 'and her hair was dry. But when I went up after Ella, there were wet footprints all along the landing and blobs of shampoo on the bathroom carpet.'

'Gosh.' Maxine looked shocked. 'You mean—?'

Josh, who was deeply interested in becoming a detective when he grew up, nodded. 'Somebody else was upstairs.'

'I knew that,' Ella piped up, anxious not to be outdone. 'I went into the wrong room by mistake and there was someone hiding under the duvet in a big bed.'

Josh was a particular fan of Inspector Poirot. His expression serious, he said, 'Were they dead?'

'Well, I could hear breathing.'

'That's a relief then,' said Maxine cheerfully. 'At least he was alive.'

Josh stared at her. 'Why did you say he? How do you know it was a man?'

She grinned. He wasn't the only one to be intrigued. For the first time in her life Thea was being secretive and there had to be a particularly good reason why.

'I don't know,' she told Josh. 'Lucky guess.'

# Chapter 24

Janey, hampered by the tray of flowers in her arms, was about to push open the door of the restaurant with her bottom when it was done for her. She tried not to look too taken aback when she saw that it was Nina.

'Oh . . . hi,' she said quickly, terrified that her voice sounded artificial. Nodding down at the tray, brimming with delphiniums, pinks and snowy gypsophila, she added stupidly, 'Just delivering the flowers.'

'Bruno told me to expect you,' Nina replied. 'One of the waitresses dropped twenty-eight dinner plates last night so he's gone out to get replacements.'

She was wearing a long, droopy dress of pale blue cheesecloth, several silver necklaces and flat, hippyish sandals laced around the ankles with leather thongs. No matter how many times Janey had tried, she simply couldn't envisage Bruno and Nina in bed together. She couldn't even imagine them sharing the same laundry basket.

'Heavens!' Putting the tray down, she wondered how quickly she could arrange the flowers and get away. 'He must have been furious. He'll be looking for a replacement waitress.'

'It wasn't her fault.' Nina, lighting a cigarette and sitting down to watch Janey at work, appeared unconcerned. 'She was taking the stack of plates down from a high shelf in the kitchen and Bruno pinched her bum. She screamed and dropped the lot. Under the circumstances, there wasn't a great deal he could say.'

Here, thought Janey, was the opportunity she'd been waiting for. This was her chance to assuage her own conscience, to gain first-hand proof of the understanding shared by Nina and Bruno, to prove without a shadow of a doubt that what she was doing wasn't wrong.

'Doesn't it bother you?' she said, her tone ultra-casual, her fingers trembling only slightly as she pushed cones of bottle-green oasis into each of the vases. 'Bruno, I mean, flirting with other women?'

Nina, looking amused, blew a perfect smoke ring.

'By that I presume he's been flirting with you.'

'No . . .' Flustered, Janey felt the colour rising in her cheeks. 'Well, maybe a bit, but not me in particular.'

'Of course not,' Nina replied mildly. 'Just you and every other woman he sets eyes on. That's Bruno's way, I'm used to it by now . . . and it is only flirting, after all. Harmless enough stuff.'

Janey felt her stomach begin to churn. What she and Bruno had been doing went way beyond a harmless flirtation. Was Nina bluffing, playing the part of the tolerant partner, or had Bruno been lying to them both? Not having the nerve to ask outright, however, she resorted to lies of her own.

'My husband was the same,' she said, improvising rapidly, 'but I found it harder to cope with than you do. I kept wondering if, well, if that was all it was.'

'You thought he might be having an affair?' Nina looked interested. 'And was he?'

Despising herself, Janey shook her head. 'I don't know. If he was, he disappeared before I could find out.'

'Of course.' Remembering, Nina nodded. The next moment she added unexpectedly, 'But you only felt that way because you were jealous.'

Janey looked up at her. 'Aren't you?'

'I have no reason to be jealous.' Leaning forward, Nina stubbed out her cigarette. Clasping her hands together in her lap, she said simply, 'I love Bruno. I trust him. And I know he would never be unfaithful to me.'

This was no bluff. Her calm belief in him was staggering. Feeling sicker by the minute, Janey said, 'What would you do if he was?' Hastily she added, 'In the future, I mean.'

Nina gave the hypothetical question some thought. 'I'd be devastated,' she said at last, and smiled. 'Goodness, it's not something I've ever really considered. Bruno's my whole life. It would mean he'd betrayed me and my love for him.' She paused, then said, 'I could never forgive him for that.'

Janey wanted to cry, because Bruno had betrayed them both and because her own newfound happiness had been nothing but a sham. She too had trusted him, had believed him when he told her he loved her. For the first time in almost two years she had felt like a human being, experiencing emotions she'd thought she might never feel again.

And it had all been an illusion because Bruno didn't have an understanding with Nina and had lied to them both in order to satisfy his own selfish craving for adulation and sex. Janey wondered how many other gullible woman had fallen into the same trap. Most of all she hoped Nina would never find out.

But ignorance was bliss and whilst her own world crumbled around her, Nina's train of thought was moving on to more relevant matters. Happily lighting up another cigarette and flicking back her long straight hair, she settled herself more comfortably in her seat. 'Come on, Janey, cheer up. No use dwelling on the past. You're coming to Bruno's party on Friday night, aren't you?'

Dumbly, Janey nodded. Her name was already on the guest list. She wouldn't go, of course, but a last-minute excuse was easier than coming up with something plausible just now.

'It's going to be great fun,' said Nina with more enthusiasm than Janey had known she possessed. Then she sighed and added plaintively, 'The trouble is, I haven't a clue what to get him for his birthday. I'm hopeless at choosing presents. What do you think, Janey? Any ideas?'

A monogrammed chastity belt, thought Janey. And a muzzle. Aloud, she said, 'I don't really know. How about aftershave?'

'Oh!' Nina started to laugh. 'I think Bruno's worth a bit more than that, don't you? He is my life partner, after all. I was thinking more along the lines of a new car.'

During the next two days, Janey didn't have a chance either to see or speak to Bruno. By Friday night she was in a turmoil about whether or not to go to the party. The thought of turning up, being sociable towards Bruno and

Nina, and allowing him to think that nothing had changed seemed hideously hypocritical.

But on the other hand, and for purely selfish reasons, she was tempted to go anyway. Bruno's famous birthday parties were a social landmark in Trezale, enormous fun and always riotously successful. His friends, glitzy and glamorous and all at least as extrovert as Bruno himself, descended from all corners of the country for the event which invariably carried on into Saturday. Last year the gossip columns had been full of the stories about the playboy racing driver, water-skiing naked at dawn across Trezale Bay and eloping the next day with the only just divorced young wife of a particularly pompous Tory MP. The marriage had lasted seven months and six days, which was seven months longer than anyone who knew either of them had predicted. Earlier in the week Bruno had shown Janey the fax sent by the same racing driver accepting his invitation to this year's party: 'Me and my skis say yes, yes, please,' he had scrawled across the top of the page. Below it, he had written out fifty times: 'And this time I must not elope.'

Oh sod it, thought Janey, throwing down the evening paper and switching off the television. She'd been looking forward to this party for weeks. The prospect of sitting alone in her flat mourning the loss of a bastard with whom she should never have got involved in the first place and consoling herself with a hefty bar of Cadbury's fruit and nut was too depressing for words. She was going to do herself up, take herself along to the party, flirt with strangers and have an all-round bloody good time. Telling Bruno to get stuffed could wait until next week.

And who knew whom she might meet, Janey decided, daydreaming as she turned on the bath taps and tipped in at least half a pint of peach bubble-bath. As long as she maintained a positive attitude the possibilities were endless. And if the worst came to the very worst, there was always the water-skiing racing driver . . .

By eight-thirty she was almost ready and for once, to her immense relief, everything seemed to be going right. The black sequinned dress she so seldom had the opportunity to wear looked as good as it always did, enhancing the curves she wanted enhanced and discreetly skimming over those she preferred to keep to herself. Wickedly expensive but worth every penny, it imbued Janey with self-confidence and glittered like coal when she moved.

Her hair, too, had decided to behave this evening; the bronze combs holding it up at the sides were staying firmly in place and even the loose blond tendrils at the nape of her neck were falling naturally into place instead of sticking out at silly angles as they so often did when she tried to look chic.

Bronze eyeshadow, black mascara, a bit of eyebrow pencil and two coats of pinky-bronze lipstick later, Janey was done. Stepping back and surveying her reflection in the mirror, she decided that if she said so herself, she looked pretty damn good.

She was going to the party and she was ready for anything.

Except maybe water-skiing at dawn, she thought ruefully. At least, not in this dress . . .

# Chapter 25

The restaurant had been transformed. Tonight, minus its twenty-five tables, with wild music pulsating from loudspeakers and the lighting subdued, it looked more like a nightclub. And although it wasn't yet ten o'clock the place was already heaving with glamorous bodies intent on having a fabulous time.

Bruno, wearing a new, raspberry-pink silk shirt, monopolized what was now the dance floor. With a bottle of Remy Martin in one hand and a fetchingly dishevelled brunette in the other, he was performing the lambada and simultaneously carrying on a shouted conversation with a tall blond actor, star of a long-running series of coffee commercials. Watching him as he laughed, joked and didn't miss so much as a single move of the complicated dance, Janey realized that this was Bruno's speciality; here, as if she needed it, was yet another example of his ability to have it all. He wanted to dance and he enjoyed talking to his friends, so why waste time doing first one thing, then the other? And when he liked two women, why miss out, she thought bitterly. Why not have both?

Gazing around, she realized she couldn't see Nina

anywhere. All the women were amazingly done-up, there wasn't a shred of sprigged Laura Ashley cotton in sight.

The next moment, in mid-gyration, Bruno saw her. Whispering something in the giggling brunette's ear, he pressed the bottle of cognac against her cleavage and turned her in the direction of the actor. As he made his way over to Janey she felt the familiar tug of longing in the pit of her stomach. The man was a liar and a cheat but sexual attraction didn't automatically evaporate into thin air. Willing herself to overcome it, she returned his welcoming grin with a brief smile and urged herself to remain in control. She supposed she ought to feel honoured that he had abandoned the brunette in order to come and see her instead.

'Janey, you look incredible! Mmm, and you smell of peaches . . .'

As she submitted awkwardly to his embrace, Bruno murmured, 'Sweetheart, relax. It's my birthday; I'm expected to kiss my guests.'

'Here's your card.' Taking a step backwards, she pulled it from her bag. Then, eyeing the table stacked with elaborately wrapped gifts she added, 'I didn't buy you a present.'

'Don't worry, you can give it to me later.' Bruno winked. 'Upstairs.'

He simply didn't care, thought Janey. He wasn't even bothering to lower his voice. Taking another step back, she flinched as her high heel landed on someone else's foot. Behind her, more and more guests were arriving, piling in through the double doors like customers on the first day of Harrods' sale. The stifling, perfumed heat combined with the green and gold decor gave the place a jungle atmosphere. Over to her left a tall woman screeched with laughter like a parrot. The place was noisy and chaotic but Bruno, she thought crossly, shouldn't assume he couldn't be overheard.

'. . . absolutely gorgeous,' he continued, sliding an appreciative forefinger along her exposed collarbone. 'Janey, you should do yourself up like this more often. I can hardly wait to unwrap you. Happy birthday to me, happy birthday to—'

He was, Janey realized, well on the way to getting drunk. She hadn't seen him like this before. Removing his hand from her shoulder before it could weasel its way anywhere embarrassing, she said abruptly, 'Where's Nina?'

'Nina?' Bruno laughed. 'Do I know a Nina? Come on sweetheart, make my day. Tell me you're wearing stockings underneath that delicious dress.'

'Don't be stupid.' Trying to sound brisk, Janey slapped away the errant hand now threatening to slide down her thigh. 'Where is she?'

'I say, you sound just like my old headmistress.' Bruno gazed at her in admiration. 'Now there's an idea.'

'Where is Nina?' repeated Janey, loudly enough for those around her to hear. People were beginning to stare. 'I need to speak to her.'

'Her grandmother's been taken ill.' He grinned once more, totally unrepentant. 'She was rushed into hospital this morning. Nina's gone up to Berkshire to see her. She won't be back until tomorrow night at the earliest.'

So that was why he wasn't bothering to be discreet,

thought Janey. Feeling sorry for Nina she said, 'Is it anything serious?'

'Chronic affluence.' Bruno helped himself to a glass of pink champagne from the table behind her and raised it in mock salute. 'Dear old Granny Bentley. Seriously wealthy and ninety-three to boot. Well past her sell-by date, wouldn't you say?'

At first Janey didn't say anything at all. At that moment her task became easier. To Bruno it had simply been a flip one-liner, but as far as she was concerned it was downright cruel. And wonderfully, miraculously off-putting.

'My grandmother is ninety-four,' she lied, her tone icy. 'Maybe you think she's past her sell-by date, too.'

André Covel, who owned the hugely successful surf shop where Alan had spent most of Janey's hard-earned money, and who had been a particular friend of his, refilled Janey's glass with white wine. Glancing across at Bruno, who was now back on the dance floor with the stunning Italian wife of a well-known rock singer, he raised his sun-bleached eyebrows and said, 'You seem to know Bruno rather well. Anything going on that I should be told about?'

Definitely not, thought Janey with a suppressed shudder. She liked André but he was the most appalling gossip. And he knew *everyone* . . .

'No.' She made it sound as if the idea was an amusing one, because anything the least bit emphatic would only bring out the Sherlock Holmes in him. 'Not my type, thanks.'

'Bruno?' Jan, André's girl friend, had been only half listening. With a giggle she said, 'Everyone's *his* type, though, lecherous old sod! D'you know, last Christmas he tried to seduce me in the kitchen of this very restaurant? It was right at the end of the evening but there were still three tables of customers out here. Bruno invited me through to the back to see his Sabatier knives and told the washer-up to take a ten-minute coffee break. I told Bruno to take a running bloody jump,' she declared with pride. 'I mean to say, ten minutes!'

Bruno's reputation was evidently common knowledge. Janey, who had never known of it until now, realized that she simply hadn't been mixing in the right circles. Gossip, it appeared, had its uses after all.

But anger and humiliation churned inside her. She just wished she could have had this conversation six weeks ago, before falling blindly into Bruno's arms and kidding herself that it was love.

'That's nothing,' André was saying, oblivious to the effect his revelations were having. As he offered Janey a cigarette, he lowered his voice to a conspiratorial whisper. 'Remember Natasha, the blonde with the tattoo on her bum who came to work for me last year? Bruno had an affair with her mother. Fifty years old and the manageress of that building society in Pink Street. She was totally besotted with him, apparently. Natasha said she only just managed to persuade her not to have a face lift.'

'Fifty!' squealed Jan, who was twenty-four. 'Practically old enough to be his mother. Yuk, totally gross.'

Janey had heard more than enough for one night. The white wine wasn't going down too well; her stomach felt like a nest of snakes. Moving away in search of food, hoping it might help, she found Nick and Tony, the antique dealers from next door, who were admiring the splendid buffet. Tony, wearing a magenta cravat and a new, extremely glossy toupee in a startling shade of chestnut, was piling his plate with scampi tails and endive salad. Nick, who had been greedily envying the whole fresh salmon, slipped his arm around Janey's waist and gave her a welcoming peck on the cheek. He smelled of Penhaligon's cologne and garlic, and Janey smiled because at least it was safe to assume that neither of them had ever slept with Bruno. They were devoted entirely to each other.

'Here you are, my darling. Teeny Cornish potatoes coated in breadcrumbs, deep-fried and rolled in garlic butter.' Nick popped one into her mouth, selected another for himself and rolled his eyes in appreciation. 'Sheer heaven. Better than sex.'

'Lovely,' agreed Janey, when she had swallowed. With a grin she added, 'So Bruno hasn't thrown you out yet.'

'Too busy philandering,' Nick remarked, with a nod in Bruno's direction. Following his gaze, Janey saw that Bruno and a blonde appeared to be playing pass-the-orange without the orange.

'Bless him,' said Tony with an indulgent smile. 'He works hard; he's just letting off steam. If you can't philander on your birthday, when can you?'

According to André, Bruno had been doing it day in, day out throughout most of his adult life. He practically made a career out of it. Reminded once more of her own gullibility, she said, 'He's getting too old to be a philanderer. Before long he's not going to find it so easy to impress the girls.'

'Ah, but he has charm,' Tony observed through a mouthful of salmon. 'Charisma. Mark my words, that boy will always get by.'

Nick and Tony adored Bruno. Janey couldn't decide which was the most painful, being regaled with André's scurrilous gossip or having to endure this paeon of praise. Belatedly, she wished Maxine could have been here with her tonight. Maxine, who didn't yet know the sordid truth, had sensed instinctively what Bruno was really like and had tried to warn her away from him.

I was wrong and she was right, thought Janey wryly, sipping her drink. *Ouch.*

It would have been nice to have company, too. Doing herself up and telling herself that the party would be fun was all very well, but now she was actually here Janey was beginning to feel conspicuously single. Most of the guests were from out of town and she didn't know as many people as she had imagined she would. Sometimes even being driven to distraction by Maxine's over-the-top chat-up lines was preferable to standing alone and wondering who to talk to next.

# Chapter 26

The next moment, just to prove she looked as solitary as she felt, a male voice behind her said, 'Speak of the devil's sister. Hello, Janey, all on your own tonight?'

Turning, she saw that it was Guy Cassidy, looking ridiculously handsome in a black dinner jacket and white shirt. Next to him stood a tall, titian-haired woman wearing a strapless topaz silk evening dress. Janey smiled as Guy, making no mention of Serena, introduced her as 'Charlotte, a friend of mine'. From what Maxine had told her, he had almost as many female friends as Bruno.

'I was just telling Charlotte about Maxine's latest adventure,' Guy went on, his tone dry. 'She got on to Josh's skate-board, shot down the lane at the end of our drive and landed up in the back of a milk float. The milkman almost had a heart attack.'

Janey winced. 'Was she hurt?'

'No, but she spent the rest of the afternoon washing strawberry yoghurt out of her hair. And the milkman, in a state of shock, ran over the skate-board.'

'Poor Josh.'

'Poor Maxine! Very poor Maxine, in fact. As soon as her hair was dry, Josh dragged her down to the shops and made her buy him a new one.' With a grin, he added, 'It cost thirty-eight pounds. When I found out what he'd done I didn't have the heart to tell her he'd bought the old one in Oxfam for a fiver.'

This time Janey laughed. Grateful that Guy hadn't asked her where laughing-boy James was tonight and eager to keep him away from the subject, she said, 'When she was seven, Maxine rode her bike into a fish pond and ended up covered in frogspawn. You'd think she would have learned her lesson by now.'

Guy stepped to one side as a man wearing a crash helmet, white silk boxer shorts, a tropical suntan and a pair of water skis made his way past. 'This party would suit Maxine down to the ground,' he observed. 'She could have brought Josh's new skate-board along and challenged that chap to a race.'

'She'd certainly enjoy herself.' Janey wondered where Serena was. 'Is Maxine at home with the children?'

'I thought it would be safer,' Guy replied enigmatically. 'Bruno invited her, of course, but I told her it was her turn to babysit and for once she didn't kick up a fuss.'

Surprised and faintly put out because she hadn't realized Maxine had been invited to the party by Bruno, Janey said, 'Oh.'

Charlotte, who was gazing with fascination at the water-skiing racing driver, drawled, 'Do you know, those boxer shorts are completely see-through.'

'Enthralling.' Guy returned his attention to Janey. 'We hadn't planned to come here ourselves; Charlotte pressganged me into partnering her at a charity dinner at some castle in Bodmin but it was so Godawful we escaped at half-time.'

'Between the main course and the sweet.' Charlotte, gazing fondly up at Guy, slid her hand into his.

'I didn't particularly want to come here, either,' said Guy. 'Bruno Parry-Brent isn't one of my favourite people but he knows how to throw a party. And at least the food's edible.'

Janey raised her eyebrows. 'Does this mean you're gate-crashing?'

'Oh, I was invited too.' He looked amused. 'Probably because I'm a good customer and Bruno felt I deserved to be thanked.'

Charlotte, who evidently felt that Guy was spending too much time talking to a rival female, gave his arm a possessive tug. 'Come on, darling, we're missing all the fun.'

'Hooray,' said Guy. On the dance floor the water-skier had now been joined by a fat man in a bikini with a surfboard under his arm. 'Why don't you go and dance with them?'

'I've got a much better idea.' Charlotte wasn't about to give in. Her green eyes glittered. 'Why don't you come and dance with me?'

'Oh look, there's Suzannah.' Embarrassed and terribly afraid that Guy was only staying because she was on her own and he felt sorry for her, Janey waved at a girl she barely knew. With a brief smile she said, 'Do excuse me, I must go and say hello.'

At least Suzannah didn't mention Bruno. 'My boyfriend's buggered off to Ibiza,' she pouted. 'Men, honestly. He didn't even have the nerve to tell me to my face! All I got was a message left on my answering machine saying he'd be back in three weeks. How about you, Janey? Are you seeing anyone at the moment?'

Out of the corner of her eye Janey glimpsed Bruno, murmuring into the ear of yet another blonde. The next moment he was kissing her neck.

'No,' she replied firmly. 'Nobody at all.'

Suzannah, who was also blonde, and whose parents owned the largest yacht in Cornwall, didn't work. Getting her hair highlighted and zipping around in her open-top jeep evidently occupied all her time.

'Ah, but it's all right for you,' she told Janey. 'You're running your own business. At least you've got something to take your mind off not having a man.'

'Of course.' Janey managed to hide her smile. 'It's a great help.'

'You're really lucky,' sighed Suzannah. 'I sometimes wonder if I should think about getting a little job.'

How about Governor of the Bank of England, thought Janey. But at least she was talking to someone, even if it was only Suzannah. At this moment she couldn't afford to be choosy. Feigning interest, she said, 'What kind of work are you interested in?'

'God, I don't know.' Suzannah flicked back her hair with a tanned arm and half a dozen solid gold bangles jangled in unison. 'Something easy, I suppose. Like your job.'

Janey tried to envisage Suzannah getting up at five every morning, working flat out for twelve hours a day and settling down at night to do the books. Determined to keep a straight face even if it killed her, she said, 'I didn't realize you were interested in floristry.'

'Oh, I love flowers.' To prove her point, Suzannah gestured vaguely in the direction of a frantically gyrating girl whose purple taffeta dress was patterned with enormous yellow daisies. 'They're so . . . um . . . pretty, aren't they?' Then, brightening, she added, 'In fact my boyfriend bought me a big bouquet of flowers for my birthday. *And* he got them from your shop.'

'Really?' Every cloud, thought Janey. Men, incapable of coming up with anything more imaginative for the women in their lives, were what kept her in business. 'What were they?'

'Red ones,' said Suzannah, pleased with herself for having remembered. 'Roses, I think. With bits of funny white stuff mixed in.'

'Cocaine?'

'What?'

'Sorry.' Biting her lip, Janey said, 'It's called gypsophila.'

'Oh, right.'

'Did the roses last a long time?' Janey couldn't help it. She always wanted people to get the very best out of their flowers. 'If the heads start to droop after the first week you can re-cut the stems and plunge them into boiling water for a few seconds. It works wonders.'

'Really?' Suzannah looked blank. 'I forgot to put them in water when he gave them to me. When I woke up the next day they were all dead.'

The dedicated revellers were moving up a gear. People were stripping off to reveal swim suits beneath their party clothes, ready for a moonlight dip at high tide. A state-of-the-art camcorder ended up in a bowl of punch and one of the male guests, suspected of working on behalf of one of the more down-market tabloids, was handcuffed to a tree in the restaurant garden, his hairy ankles tied together by the reel of exposed film from his camera.

For Janey, introduced by Nick and Tony to an hotelier who *was* interested in flowers, the evening was turning out to be not so bad after all. He needed regular arrangements for his foyer and sitting rooms and a deal was struck over two hefty measures of cognac, both of which were drunk by the hotelier.

'Sign here,' said Janey, having written out details of the agreement on one of Bruno's linen napkins. 'You may not remember this tomorrow. I want something I can jog your memory with.'

'You sound like my wife,' he grumbled goodnaturedly. 'I still don't remember asking her to marry me. She just woke me up the next day and told me I had.'

'Don't worry.' Janey grinned as he scrawled a haphazard signature across the bottom of the napkin. 'This isn't going to tie you down nearly as much as a wife.'

Bruno caught up with her as she was on her way to the loo.

'I saw you,' he murmured, catching her around the waist and pulling her towards him. 'You've been talking to Eddie Beresford for the last twenty minutes.'

'I'm amazed you even noticed.' Bruno reeked of Shalimar. Janey tried to pull away, but he was stronger

226

than she was. Now he was drawing her back towards the dance floor.

'I notice everything.' With a derisory glance in Eddie Beresford's direction, he drawled, 'He could hardly take his eyes off your cleavage.'

'Don't worry,' said Janey in pointed tones. 'I'm sure he's faithful to his wife.'

But Bruno didn't make the connection. 'He's so ugly I shouldn't think he could find anyone to be unfaithful with. Anyway, it's my turn now.' His green eyes glittered as he studied Janey's rigid face. 'And don't think I've forgotten about my birthday present either. How about a couple of dances to put us in the mood, then you head on up the stairs and make yourself . . . comfortable? I'll have a quick drink with Guy Cassidy and the redhead, and follow you up five minutes later. If anyone spots you on the way, just tell them you feel faint.'

He'd got her as far as the dance floor but Janey wasn't moving. Causing a major scene was the last thing she wanted.

'I see,' she said carefully. 'But what should I do if the bed's already occupied?'

Bruno laughed. 'Sweetheart, the keys to the flat are right here in my pocket. I'm hardly going to rent out my own bedroom to whoever fancies a quickie!'

'It's *your* quickies I'm talking about.' It was no good, she hated Bruno about as much as she despised herself for having been so weak-willed in the first place and she couldn't contain herself a moment longer. With icy disdain she said, 'I can't seem to spot the blonde you were dancing with earlier. Are you sure she isn't still up there, hunting for her knickers and hoping for a repeat performance?'

'Oh dear.' He gave her a mock-sorrowful look. 'Are we jealous?'

Janey, who'd said it but hadn't meant it, realized with a sickening jolt that she'd been right.

'I'm not jealous.' The urge to punch him was almost overwhelming. 'I just can't believe it's taken me this long to find out what you're really like. I can't believe I've been so stupid. Believe it or not, I actually trusted you . . .'

Bruno, who liked Janey a lot and who found her innocence particularly appealing, decided that he could bluff his way out of this one. True, she was upset, but only because she didn't realize the sacrifices he'd made since their relationship had begun.

'Sweetheart, there's no need for this.' Still smiling, he tried to draw her towards him. It was like dragging a child into the dentist's chair. 'You can trust me. OK, so maybe I've played the field a bit in the past, but if you only knew how many women I *haven't* slept with since we've been together . . . I'm a reformed character, truly I am!'

'Liar,' hissed Janey. 'I spoke to Nina. You don't have any kind of understanding.'

Bruno, determined to chivvy her out of her mood, gave her a disarming look. 'OK, call it an unspoken agreement. Whichever, she's hardly likely to admit it to you.'

'And what about all the others?' Janey countered bitterly. 'My God, I don't know when you find time to sleep! Let go of me . . . !'

This was more than a mood, he realized. Janey meant business. Oh well, it had been good fun while it lasted.

'So what are you saying?' He released his grip on her arms so abruptly that she almost staggered backwards. 'That you don't want to meet me upstairs in ten minutes after all?'

'You arrogant bastard.' Without her even realizing it, Janey's eyes had filled with tears. 'I never want to meet you again anywhere. I never want to see you again!'

Bruno's relationships ended when he wanted them to end. He had never been dumped in his life. And if Janey thought she could get away with doing it in public, with making a fool of him at his very own party, she could suffer the consequences in return.

At that moment, by chance, the dance music which had been blaring through the speakers came to a halt. The tape had finished.

'Oh dear,' Bruno drawled into the ensuing silence. 'And there I was, doing my good Samaritan bit and thinking you'd be grateful for the attention. I'm beginning to realize now why your husband might have wanted to disappear. Is that what you yelled at him, Janey? Did you tell him you never wanted to see him again?' He paused for a second, then added with a cruel smile, 'If you ask me, the poor sod probably couldn't believe his luck.'

# Chapter 27

It was a nightmare. A nightmare with an audience. With tears streaming down her face, Janey turned and searched frantically for the way out. All she could see was a blur of faces. Mascara stung her eyes and she didn't know where the hell she'd left her handbag. Her face burned with shame as she pushed her way through the crowd of riveted partygoers in what she prayed was the direction of the door.

The next moment a pair of strong arms were guiding her. Behind her a voice murmured reassuringly, 'It's OK, I've got your bag. Just keep walking.'

Janey stumbled on the steps outside the restaurant and the arms tightened their grip on her shoulders, keeping her upright. When they reached the pavement she turned to face her rescuer.

'I'm all right. Thanks . . . I'll be f-fine now . . .'

Her voice wavered and began to break as a fresh wave of humiliation swept over her. Fumbling blindly for her bag, she tried to hide her blotched face, cruelly exposed by the bright spotlighting outside the restaurant. She must look a complete wreck; this was almost more awful than having to endure Bruno's sneering jibes.

'Don't be so bloody stupid,' said Guy, handing over

her bag but keeping a firm hold on her arm. 'You aren't all right at all and you're certainly in no state to drive home. Come on, give me your car keys.'

He might have come to her rescue but he wasn't being wildly sympathetic. Still sobbing, Janey said, 'I'm not drunk.'

He sighed. 'I know you aren't drunk, but you can't see where you're going, either. Why don't you just give me the keys and let me drive?'

'Because the van isn't here.' She sniffed loudly. 'I walked.'

For some reason he seemed to find her reply amusing. Turning her around and leading her briskly across the road towards his own car, he said with a brief smile, 'Fair enough.'

'You can't take me home.'

'Why not?'

Janey wiped her wet face with the back of her sleeve. Sequins, like miniature knives, grazed her cheeks. 'What about . . . thingy? Charlotte?'

'Oh, thingy will understand.' This time he grinned. 'Besides, you only live half a mile away. All I'm doing is giving you a lift home; we aren't eloping to Gretna Green.'

It was dark inside the car, which was a relief, but Janey still flinched each time another vehicle passed them, beaming sadistic headlights over her face. She couldn't seem to stop crying, either; the harder she tried not to think about Bruno and the degrading scene back in the restaurant, the more insistently the tears slid down her face. She hoped Guy Cassidy couldn't see them plopping into her lap.

The journey took all of two minutes. Janey was free of

her seat belt and reaching for the door handle before the car had even drawn to a halt outside the shop.

'It's customary to invite the man in for a coffee, you know,' he observed, when she had mumbled her thanks and scrambled out on to the pavement.

Janey, who had been about to slam the passenger door shut, forgot to avert her swollen eyes. 'Look, you've been very kind but I'd really rather be on my own. Don't you think I'm embarrassed enough as it is?'

But Guy had switched off the ignition and was already stepping out of the car. 'I think it wouldn't be fair to leave you on your own bawling your eyes out.' His tone of voice was more gentle now, and reassuringly matter of fact. 'Come on, we can't stand here arguing in the street. People will think you're Maxine.'

'She said you were a bully,' Janey grumbled, realizing that he wasn't going to go away. 'And what about Charlotte, anyway? You took her along to the party. She won't be very pleased with you if you don't go back.'

'She'll survive.' Guy dismissed the protest with a careless gesture. Taking the keys from her trembling hand, he opened the front door and guided Janey into the hallway ahead of him. 'Besides, rescuing damsels in distress is as good a reason as any for escaping. I grew out of those kind of parties years ago, and I've already told you I don't much care for Bruno Parry-Brent.' With a brief sidelong glance at Janey, he added, 'That's something we appear to have in common, at least.'

So much for looking great, thought Janey, gloomily surveying her reflection in the bathroom mirror. Having scrubbed her face, soaping away every last vestige of make-up, it no longer looked like a ploughed field but it was certainly in a sorry state. The whites of her eyes were pink and her cheeks, normally pink, were white. Her eyelids remained hopelessly swollen too, despite her best efforts with a cold flannel. And somewhere along the line she had managed to lose one of the combs holding her hair back at the sides. All in all, she looked like a lop-eared rabbit.

But since she wasn't about to run off to Gretna Green, as Guy had so caustically reminded her earlier, what did it matter? Pulling a face at herself in the mirror, chucking the other bronze comb on to the windowsill and running her fingers through her no longer perfect hair, Janey unlocked the bathroom door. Guy was in the kitchen making coffee. If he was so hellbent on hearing her side of the unflattering story behind Bruno's contemptuous outbursts tonight, she would give it to him. She had no reason to want to impress him; he was only another rotten man anyway.

'You're looking better.' Guy, having made the coffee and brought it through to the sitting room, handed her the pink mug with elephants round the side. Stretching out in the chair by the window, he added, 'Not wonderful, but better.'

'Thanks.' He certainly had a way with words, thought Janey. Flattery like that could turn a more susceptible girl's head.

'So what was it all about?'

She shrugged. There was no reason on earth why Guy Cassidy should be interested in hearing this, yet he was certainly giving a good impression of an agony aunt. One of those brisk, no-nonsense ones, Janey decided, who wouldn't hesitate to tell you what a prat you'd been.

'Well, Marje,' she began with a rueful smile, 'I suppose you could say I got myself involved with the wrong kind of man. I fell for the old chat-up lines, and even managed to convince myself that we weren't doing anything wrong.'

'Don't tell me. He said his wife didn't understand him.'

'Quite the reverse. He said Nina understood him only too well, and that she didn't mind.'

'Of course.' Guy's dark eyebrows twitched with suppressed amusement. 'And you believed him.'

'I don't make a habit of getting involved with attached men,' Janey protested. 'I know what you must be thinking, but I'm really not like that. I suppose I believed him because I wanted to. And he was plausible,' she added defensively. 'I'm not trying to excuse myself, I'm just explaining how it happened. It simply didn't occur to me that he might not be telling the truth.'

'Until tonight, presumably, when you learned otherwise.'

'I found out a couple of days ago,' Janey admitted. 'I asked Nina.'

'Good God.'

'I didn't tell her!' she said crossly. 'I'm not that much of a bitch.'

'OK. So what happened after you'd made your momentous discovery?'

'You were there.' To her shame, she felt fresh tears on her cheeks. 'You heard the rest. I told Bruno what I thought of him and he retaliated.' Fumbling for a tissue, she took a deep breath. 'He . . . he hit back where it hurt. I wasn't expecting him to say what he did.'

'About your husband?' Once again, Guy's tone was reassuringly matter of fact. 'I didn't even know you'd been married. How long ago were you divorced?'

'I'm not divorced,' said Janey, her voice beginning to break. 'My husband . . . disappeared. We hadn't had a fight or anything like that. He just went out one day and n-never came b-b-back. Nobody knows what happened to him . . . We don't even know if he's alive or d-d-dead.'

It should have been embarrassing, breaking down in tears all over again in front of a man she barely knew. But Guy took it all in his stride, allowing her to get all the pent-up despair out of her system, making more coffee and showing no sign at all of wanting to slope off.

'Stop apologizing,' he said calmly when Janey, lobbing yet another sodden tissue into the waste paper basket, mumbled 'Oh hell, I'm sorry' for the fifth time. 'You haven't exactly just had the best two years in the world. You're entitled to cry.'

'I don't usually talk about it,' she admitted in a small voice.

'You should. It helps to talk.'

'Did you?' Janey hesitated, wondering if he would be offended. 'Talk, I mean. After your wife died.'

'Probably bored a few close friends rigid,' said Guy. 'But they were kind enough not to let it show.'

'And now here I am, boring you.'

'Not at all.' He grinned across at her. 'If I was hearing it for the twentieth time and knew the words off by heart, then I'd be bored. But I'm being serious, Janey. It doesn't

235

help, bottling it all up. You really need to get it out of your system.'

'I know, I know.' The tears had dried up now, making it easier to speak. 'But it's so . . . unfinished. If I knew what had happened, it would help. If Alan had wanted to leave me, why didn't he just say so? Sometimes I think . . . oh hell, it doesn't matter—' Mindful of Guy's own past experience, she bit her tongue before the shameful words could spill out. But he was already nodding in agreement, having understood exactly what she was about to say.

'Sometimes you think it would be easier if he were dead.'

Plucking at the sequins on her dress, Janey nodded.

'Of course it would be easier,' he continued gently, 'but you can't put your life on hold while you wait to find out one way or the other. You could carry on like that indefinitely and still not get an answer.'

Beginning to feel like one of those novelty dogs in the backs of cars, Janey nodded again. Guy's voice was wonderfully soothing and now that her nose was no longer blocked from crying she was able to taste the hefty measure of brandy he'd added to her coffee.

Guy, however, was really getting into his stride. 'I'm going to be brutal,' he said, fixing her with his unnervingly direct gaze. 'If Alan is dead, he's dead. If he's alive, it means he did a particularly cowardly runner. Either way, the marriage is over.'

He wasn't telling her anything she didn't already know, but Janey still winced. Having clung so fiercely in those first few weeks to the total-amnesia theory, she had never been able to discard it from her subconscious.

'Yes,' she replied obediently. 'I know that.'

'So what you have to do is put it behind you anyway and rebuild your life.'

Janey managed a brief smile. 'That's what I was trying to do. With Bruno.'

'Heaven help us.' With a rueful shake of his head, Guy said, 'Now that's what I call choosing the wrong man for the job. Tell me, who would you go to if you needed brain surgery? A lumberjack?'

'Don't. I think I must need brain surgery.' This time she laughed. All of a sudden, the Bruno fiasco didn't seem quite so terrible. Guy had certainly been right when he'd said it helped to have someone to talk to.

'OK, so now you forget him,' he declared briskly. 'He's an unscrupulous little shit and he'll get his comeuppance sooner or later. With any luck,' he added suddenly, 'it'll be with Maxine. Punishment enough for any man, I'd have thought. Even a bastard like Parry-Brent.'

By the time Guy rose to leave it was gone three o'clock. Janey, opening the front door for him, found herself suddenly and unaccountably overcome by shyness.

'Well, thank you.' Clutching the door handle for support, she shifted from one stockinged foot to the other. 'For um . . . bringing me home. And for staying to talk.'

'No problem,' said Guy easily. 'I've enjoyed myself.'

Without her high heels, she was dwarfed by him. And since he'd seen her lose both her dignity and her makeup, Janey realized, there wasn't a great deal of point in being shy. She owed him so much for having come to her rescue, the very least she could do was reach up on tiptoe and give him a quick kiss on the cheek.

But her courage failed her, and she remained firmly rooted to the carpet. Some people, like Maxine, did that kind of thing all the time but she herself just wasn't the quick-kiss-on-the-cheek type. Besides, thought Janey, how awful if Guy thought she was making some kind of amateurish pass at him . . .

'I'm glad you decided to sneak away from the charity dinner, anyway,' she said hurriedly, before he could read her mind.

'Not half as glad as I am.' He grinned. 'It was pretty dire.'

'And I hope Charlotte isn't too furious with you for abandoning her at the party.'

'Well at least you've managed to stop apologizing,' said Guy, sounding amused. 'All you have to do now is stop feeling guilty on my behalf. If I'm not worried about Charlotte, I don't see why you should be.'

'Oh, but isn't she—'

'Absolutely not. She's a friend, but that's as far as it goes. And shame on you,' he added in mocking tones, 'for even thinking otherwise. What has your fiendish sister been saying about me?'

'Nothing at all,' lied Janey. 'I'm sorry. It was just me, getting it wrong as usual. I suppose it was because Charlotte seemed so . . . well, so keen.'

'She did?' Guy looked genuinely surprised. Then he shrugged. 'I'm not encouraging her, anyway. As I told you once before, I gave up behaving like Bruno Parry-Brent a couple of years ago. It isn't worth the hassle.' He paused, then added severely, 'And whilst we're on the subject of faithfulness, who was that chap I saw you with at the theatre the other week? I don't suppose you mentioned him to Bruno.'

*Aaargh*, thought Janey, blushing in the darkness. Just when she thought she'd got away with it. 'Oh, him. He wasn't worth mentioning,' she said, her tone off-hand. 'I hadn't even met him before that night. A so-called friend set me up on a blind date.' She shuddered. 'I could have killed her; I'd never been so embarrassed in my life.'

'Until tonight,' Guy reminded her. 'And I'm afraid you're really going to have to learn not to feel guilty on your own behalf.'

Janey's blush deepened. 'What do you mean?'

'After you'd left, I was introduced to your blind date's sister,' he replied evenly. 'She told me he'd met you through a Lonely Hearts column in the local paper.'

'Oh God,' sighed Janey, mortified.

'I don't know why you're so embarrassed,' Guy continued briskly. 'He might have a loud laugh but he can't be as much of a bastard as Parry-Brent. You need to make up your mind about what you really want.'

Now he'd managed to make her feel deeply ashamed of herself. Was there no end to this man's talents?

'Sleep, I think.' Janey glanced at her watch. It was three-fifteen.

'I'm going. Just one more thing.'

Eyeing him warily, she said, 'What?'

'Something you said earlier.' Guy broke into a broad grin. 'It's been bothering me. Do you really think I look like Marje Proops?'

# Chapter 28

'Oh please,' Maxine begged, thrusting the letter into Guy's hands. In her excitement she'd almost torn it in two. 'Look, the audition's tomorrow! I'll just die if I can't go up for it . . . and think how thrilled Josh and Ella would be if I was chosen! They'd be able to see me on television . . .'

'Sitting on the loo,' said Guy acerbically, having scanned the contents of the letter. 'Maxine, this is an audition for a toilet-roll commercial. It's hardly *Macbeth*.'

'You mustn't say that word; it's always referred to as the Scottish play,' she replied in lofty tones. Then, because she didn't want to irritate him, she waved her arms in a gesture of apology. 'But you can call it anything you like.'

'I still call this a toilet-roll commercial.' Guy remained unimpressed. 'And I can't imagine why you should even want to do it. What's happened, have they run out of puppies?'

Maxine was practically hopping up and down with frustration. It was all right for him, she seethed; he was already successful and famous.

'It's a brilliant opportunity,' she explained, struggling to control her impatience and giving him a beseeching

240

look. 'It means I'd be seen by millions, and that includes other directors. A break like this gets you known. And the pay is fabulous too. All those repeat fees!'

'It's still only an audition.' Guy frowned. 'I don't know what makes you think you stand a chance anyway.'

'I do,' said Maxine happily. 'The casting director's a friend of mine. Oh please say I can go! It isn't too much to ask, is it? If I catch the eight o'clock train tomorrow morning I can be home again by six.'

'And I'm flying out to Amsterdam tonight. What are you planning to do with Josh and Ella, cart them up to London with you?'

He was being deliberately unhelpful, Maxine decided, because he didn't want her to win the part, get famous and leave him with the task of finding a new nanny. How selfish could a man be?

'Serena's here,' she reminded him. 'She isn't doing anything tomorrow. Why can't she look after the kids?'

'I'm not a kid,' declared Josh, wandering into the kitchen and looking cross. 'I'm nine years old and a half. Maxine, we're still hungry. Could you make some more peanut-butter-and-jam sandwiches?'

'You aren't a kid,' Maxine retaliated briskly. 'You're nine years old and a half, and I'm busy arguing with your father. Make your own horrible sandwiches.'

'What are you arguing about?'

'I want to audition for a TV commercial.' Maxine looked sorrowful. 'And your father won't let me take the time off to do it.'

'How long does it take?'

She sighed. 'Only a few hours.'

Josh's eyes lit up with excitement. Turning to Guy he said, 'Oh Dad, say yes! If Maxine's on television I can tell all my friends at school. They'll be dead jealous . . . *please* say she can go to the audition!'

Maxine crossed her fingers behind her back, assumed a saintly expression and silently vowed never to tease Josh about Tanya Trevelyan again.

Guy, looking suspicious, addressed Josh. 'Is this a set-up? Did she tell you to come in here and say that?'

'No.' Bewildered, Josh said, 'What's a set-up?'

'OK.' Returning his attention to Maxine he said wearily, 'But only if Serena agrees. And you'll have to ask her yourself.'

Maxine could have kissed him. Instead, more prudently, she said, 'Thank you thank you thank you,' flashed him a dazzling smile, and made a dash for the kitchen door before he could change his mind. 'I'll go and speak to her right away . . .'

Josh caught up with her at the top of the stairs.

'My angel,' cried Maxine, picking him up and showering kisses on his blond head.

'Yeeuk!' said Josh. 'Put me down. Kissing's for cissies.'

'You were *brilliant*.'

'I know I was.' He wiped his hair, then grinned. 'You aren't the only one around here who can act, you know. Come on Maxine, hand over the ten pounds.'

It wasn't that Serena actively disliked children, she had simply never found much use for them. An adored only child of parents who had themselves been only children, she had wanted for nothing and enjoyed their undivided attention to the full. Extended networks of brothers and sisters and cousins, as far as the young Serena could make out, only meant having to share your toys and wear hand-me-downs. And if there were four children in one family, she deduced, each child could only receive a quarter of the love. She couldn't understand for the life of her why any parents should ever want more than one.

Those had been Serena's thoughts throughout her own childhood. People change, however, and by the time she reached her early twenties she had revised her opinions. The prospect of having to endure pregnancy in order to produce a baby had become more and more off-putting. Not only would it mean putting her career on hold for almost a year, but there was no sure-fire guarantee that you wouldn't turn into a blimp and lose your figure for good. Besides, there was no rule that said you had to bear offspring anyway. She could go one better than having one child, she concluded happily. She needn't have any at all.

And, as time passed, Serena looked around at her friends and saw that she had made absolutely the right decision. Children were expensive, time-consuming and inconvenient. As for their table manners . . . well, they could be positively grotesque.

But then along had come Guy, a coveted catch by any standards, and Serena, who up until now had made a point of steering well clear of men-with-children, realized that he was simply too good an opportunity to pass up. Josh and Ella were something of a drawback but at least there was no neurotic ex-wife lurking in the background. And Guy employed a full-time nanny, which Serena decided was another bonus. She wouldn't actually be expected to look after them herself.

'Serena, Josh has got his toast jammed in the toaster and there's all smoke coming out of it.'

Serena, who had been reading *Harpers & Queen* with her fingertips carefully splayed, suppressed a sigh of irritation. As children went, Ella and Josh weren't bad – and their table manners, at least, were faultless – but they certainly knew how to pick their moments.

'Tell him to switch the toaster off,' she said. 'I can't do anything now. My nails are wet.'

Ella gazed enviously at Serena's glistening nails, the exact colour of pink bubble-gum.

'Could you paint my nails for me?'

'Your father wouldn't like that.'

'Daddy isn't here. He's in Holland.'

'I think you're too young for nail polish.' Serena's attention was drifting back to Galliano's autumn collection. Darling John, one of her favourite designers, had such an eye for colour and line. Those velvet jackets were divine . . .

'When your fingers are dry, will you do my hair in plaits then? With ribbons threaded through them?'

Serena raised her gaze from the glossy pages. Ella was shifting from foot to foot in front of her, looking hopeful.

'What?'

'With pink and white ribbons threaded all through them, like when Maxine does it for me.'

Serena had observed this ritual on numerous occasions during the past weeks. Even Maxine, with her practised, nimble fingers, couldn't complete the complicated procedure in less than twenty minutes.

'Sweetheart, your hair looks fine as it is,' she said in soothing tones. 'It's much prettier hanging loose. Now why don't you run back into the kitchen, and tell Josh to switch off the toaster? Your father isn't going to be very pleased if he sets the kitchen on fire.'

The result of such lack of interest was that by mid-afternoon Ella was deeply bored. Josh, addicted to computer games and taking full advantage of Maxine and Guy's absence, was closeted in his bedroom with his beloved Gameboy, going glassy-eyed over Pokémon. Normally limited to thirty-minute sessions, he was in heaven. Guy always confiscated the batteries when half an hour was up. Maxine, even more infuriatingly, swiped the whole thing and started playing the game herself.

'Go away,' he told Ella, who was perched on the end of his bed kicking her heels.

'Can't I have a turn?'

'No. I've got fourteen thousand points.'

Ella stuck out her bottom lip. 'But Jo-osh—'

'And stop kicking the bed, you're making me blink.'

Ella kicked the bed harder. Josh, putting the game on pause, leaned across and shoved her on to the floor.

'Look, you make me blink and I haven't got *time* to blink. Just go away and leave me alone.'

'I hate you,' whined Ella, but Josh wasn't going to be drawn into a fight. Fourteen thousand points was his highest score ever and he had no intention of stopping now.

'Good,' he murmured as Ella flounced towards the

bedroom door. 'I hate you too.'

If she couldn't have her hair in plaits and she couldn't play with Josh, Ella decided, she should at least be allowed to buy sweets instead. It was only fair.

Serena, who had finished with *Harpers & Queen*, was now engrossed in the *Tatler*. Several of her more glamorous friends were featured in this month's edition and it was always fun seeing who'd been doing what. Even better, the fact that they were often caught unawares by the camera meant there was always the chance of spotting an unflattering expression, an exposed bra strap, even a lethal hint of a double chin . . .

'Can we go down to the shop and buy some sweets?'

Glancing up from the pages of Bystander, Serena saw that Ella was back. This time she was clutching a yellow purse shaped like a banana.

'Of course you can, darling.'

'I've got eighty pence.'

'How lovely.' Serena gave her a benevolent smile.

When she showed no sign of moving from the sofa, however, Ella tried again.

'Can we go now, please?'

As realization dawned, Serena's smile faded. 'Isn't Josh going with you?'

'He won't. He's playing his stupid Gameboy game. It isn't far away, though.' Ella gave her a pleading look. 'And it's stopped raining now so we won't get wet.'

Trudging half a mile down a muddy lane overhung with dripping chestnut trees wasn't Serena's idea of fun, although it was gratifying to think that Ella wanted her company. 'Thank you, darling,' she replied, her tone soothing, 'but I'm not really in the mood for a walk right now. Maybe tomorrow.'

Ella was by this time thoroughly confused. Serena appeared to be saying no to the walk, but she hadn't said no to the sweets. Desperate for Rolos and Maltesers, she said in hesitant tones, 'Does that mean I can go down to the shop?'

'Of course you can,' Serena replied absently, her attention captured by a familiar face amongst the guests at a recent society wedding. Good heavens, she hadn't seen Trudy Blenkarne for years and now here she was, complete with nose job, collagen-inflated lips and an ugly Texan husband to boot . . .

It absolutely wasn't fair, thought Josh, shaking the Gameboy and willing the batteries to surge back to life. Just when there was nobody to stop him playing, they'd had to run out. And it was all Maxine's fault, he decided crossly. She was the one who'd kept confiscating the game and playing it instead of doing the ironing. Now she'd used them up.

Feeling vaguely remorseful for having driven Ella away earlier, he went in search of her. His sister's bedroom was empty, however, and when he got downstairs he found Serena alone in the sitting room, drinking orange juice and watching television.

'Oh,' said Josh, surprised. 'I thought Ella was down here with you.'

A girl was abseiling down the side of a tall building. Serena, evidently enthralled, waited until she'd reached the ground before turning to smile at Josh.

'I'd probably be sick if I had to do that, wouldn't you? No . . . I haven't seen Ella for a while. Perhaps she's upstairs.'

He frowned. 'I've already looked in her room.'

'Oh well.' Serena shrugged, sipped her orange juice and glanced up at the grandfather clock. 'She's around somewhere. Go and find her, Josh, and ask her what she'd like for tea. It's either fish cakes or poached eggs on toast.'

When Josh returned to the sitting room ten minutes later, Serena still hadn't moved.

'She isn't anywhere,' he said, his voice taut with worry. 'I've looked all over the house and in the garden and she isn't anywhere at all.'

Serena sighed. 'Well when did you last see her? What time did she get back from the shop?'

'What shop?'

'The newsagent's,' said Serena patiently. 'She went to buy sweets.'

Twitching with agitation, Josh stared at her. 'On her own?'

She stared back. 'Of course on her own. She said you wouldn't go with her because you were playing with that silly Gameboy machine.'

'But Ella isn't allowed to go to the shop without someone with her.' Abruptly, Josh's eyes filled with tears. 'Because of strange men. She's only seven years old.'

# Chapter 29

Having waved Paula off, Janey closed the shop at five o'clock and settled down to the fiddly business of constructing a fourteen-foot flower garland, commissioned by a local dignitary to festoon the buffet table at his wife's sixtieth birthday celebrations. Linen bows, stiffened with flour-and-water paste and sprayed silver, were to be interspersed along the swagged length of the garland and the flowers – summer jasmine, champagne roses and stephanotis – needed to be wired painstakingly into place. It was a time-consuming but rewarding task and the end result, Janey hoped, would be spectacular. The party, too, sounded very much a keeping-up-with-the-Joneses affair and could bring plenty more business her way, so long as the dignitary's wife didn't try and pass off the flower garland as a little something she'd knocked up in her own spare time.

She was up to her elbows in damp sphagnum moss, packing it securely around the wire which formed the basis of the garland, when the phone rang.

'Janey, is that you?'

It was a young voice and at first she didn't recognize it. 'Yes, it's me. Who's that?'

'Josh. Josh Cassidy. Maxine gave me your number in case anything was ever wrong, and she's not due back home until tonight . . .'

He sounded very scared. Janey, her heart racing, wiped her wet hands on her sweater and said, 'It's OK, Josh. I'm here. What's the matter?'

'Dad's away.' His voice was high and strained, as if he was struggling to hold back tears. 'Serena's been looking after us today but Ella went down to the shop an hour and a half ago on her own and she hasn't come back. I said we should phone 999 but Serena thinks I'm making a fuss about nothing. She says I mustn't call them and that Ella will be back soon, but she isn't even supposed to go out on her own and I'm worried about her. Janey, what do you think I should do?'

Janey's blood ran cold. Was Serena out of her mind? 'Darling, don't worry,' she said urgently, as memories of Alan's disappearance flooded back. 'I'm sure Ella will be just fine, but to be on the safe side I'll phone the police myself.'

'What about Serena? She'll be cross with me.'

His voice began to break. Janey, trying to sound as reassuring as possible, said, 'Don't you worry about Serena. As soon as I've phoned the police I'll come on over. You've done absolutely the right thing, Josh. Just hang on for a few minutes and I'll be there with you. And you needn't say anything to Serena if you don't want to. I'll speak to her myself.'

Abandoning the flower garland on the shop floor, Janey drove the van faster than it had ever been driven before in order to reach Trezale House before the police did. Thankfully, Tom Lacey had been on duty when she'd phoned and explained the situation, and he was on his way.

Serena opened the front door. From the expression on her face Josh had evidently spoken to her after all.

'Have you really called the police?' she said, frowning at the sight of Janey in her unflattering work clothes. 'I must say you're making an extraordinary fuss about this. Ella's probably bumped into a friend.'

'And maybe she's bumped into a maniac with a penchant for attacking little girls,' Janey retorted, only managing to keep her voice down because she'd spotted Josh hovering white-faced in the hallway behind her. 'For God's sake, Serena. How long were you planning to wait before you did anything . . . a few *days*?'

'But this is Cornwall.' For the first time Serena began to look worried. 'If we were in London . . . well, OK, there are weirdos about . . . but it's different down here.'

'That is the most pathetic excuse I've ever heard in my life,' Janey replied icily, pushing past her and reaching for Josh. Flinging his arms around her waist, he buried his blond head in the folds of her sweater in order to hide his wet face.

'You can't let the police try and blame me for this,' Serena protested. 'No one told me Ella wasn't supposed to go out alone. It isn't my fault if something's happened to her.'

Josh's whole body was trembling. Having led him gently into the sitting room, Janey pulled him on to her

251

lap whilst Serena remained outside. 'Nothing's happened to Ella,' she murmured, cradling him in her arms as he choked back tears. 'I expect she's just wandered off and forgotten the time.'

'But I t-told her to leave me alone,' Josh sobbed. 'She said she hated me because I was playing with my Gameboy and I said I hated her back. What if she's run away for ever?'

It was a fear with which Janey was only too painfully familiar. In the distance she heard the sound of a fast-approaching car. At the same moment the rain started up again, giant droplets splattering noisily against the windows.

'Ella knows you don't hate her,' she said in soothing tones. 'You might have said it, but you didn't mean it any more than she did. Come on now, sweetheart, use this handkerchief and blow your nose. Tom's here. What you have to do now is try and think where Ella may have gone, so we know where to start looking. What about schoolfriends living nearby . . . ?'

Tom Lacey, himself the proud new father of six-week-old twin boys, questioned Josh with kindly understanding and attention to detail. When he'd finished, he put away his notebook and stood up.

'Right then, all you have to do it wait here. I'll check out the addresses of those names you've given me, and call in at the shop on my way. If young Ella turns up back here in the meantime, you can phone the station and they'll contact me on the car radio.'

The thought of staying at the house and doing nothing, however, was too much for Josh.

'Can't we come with you?' he pleaded, but Tom shook his head.

'Best not,' he said gently.

'But I want to help look for her!'

Sensing his need to do something, Janey squeezed his hand.

'If she's gone to a friend's house, Tom will find her.'

'And if she's run away, he won't,' said Josh. 'Will you come out with me, Janey? I want to look for her too.'

The rain was torrential by the time the two of them set out on foot to investigate the wooded areas bordering the narrow lane which led away from the house. The woodland, dark and forbidding, separated the lane from the clifftop a quarter of a mile away. Janey, who had borrowed one of Maxine's hopelessly impractical jackets, was soaked to the skin within minutes.

'If we move too far away from the road we won't be able to hear Tom sounding his siren,' she warned. This was to be the signal that Ella had been found.

But Josh, already clambering over fallen branches and pushing his way through the woody undergrowth, didn't stop. Turning, he glanced up at her from beneath his drooping yellow sou'wester. 'If she was close to the road she would have come home.'

Janey wiped the rain from her face. The trees grew more densely here and there were no clear paths, yet Josh was moving purposefully on ahead. She almost said, *Do you come here often?* but caught herself in time. Instead, catching up with him, she turned him back round to face her once more. 'Josh, do you know where you're going?'

For a second, the dark blue eyes flickered away. Josh

253

drew a breath. 'Well, we've been through here a few times. It's a short cut to the top of the cliffs, but Dad told us we weren't allowed to come through the wood, so . . .'

He shrugged, his voice trailing away.

'. . . So you know this area like the back of your hand,' Janey supplied, giving him a brief smile and refusing even to think about the clifftop ahead. 'Don't panic, I'm not going to tell you off; come on, Josh, lead the way.'

They found Ella fifteen minutes later, lying in a small crumpled heap against a fallen tree. Cold and extremely wet, her face was streaked with mud and tears.

So relieved she found it hard to breathe, Janey said unevenly, 'Here you are then. We wondered where you'd got to.'

But for Josh, who had been fearing the worst and blaming himself, relief took another form. Unable to control himself, he shouted, 'How dare you run away! I didn't mean what I said . . . How could you be so *stupid*!'

When Janey tried to help her to her feet however, Ella let out a piercing shriek. 'I didn't run away, I tripped over a blackberry branch and hurt my ankle . . . ouch, it hurts!'

Carefully investigating the ankle, Janey saw that it was badly swollen but probably not broken. 'It's OK, sweetheart. Put your arms around my neck and let me lift you up.'

'Stupid,' repeated Josh, choking back fresh tears. 'Serena's mad as hell, and we called the police in case you'd been murdered.'

Ella, clinging to Janey, shouted, 'Well I wasn't murdered and I hate Serena anyway. I went to the shop and bought some sweets and on the way back I saw a rabbit going along our secret path so I followed it, to give it some chocolate. But then I fell over and the rabbit ran off and it started raining. If you hadn't told me to go away,' she added, her voice rising to a piteous wail, 'we could both have gone to the shop and I wouldn't have been all on my own when I fell over.'

*The Waltons* it wasn't.

'OK, OK,' Janey said soothingly, struggling to get a secure grip on Ella and mentally bracing herself for the trek back through the woods. 'Stop arguing, you two. Josh, you'll have to go before me and hold the branches out of my way. And Ella's very cold; why don't you take off your oilskin and drape it round her shoulders?'

'Because I'll get wet.'

'He's a pig,' sniffed Ella. 'It's all Josh's fault anyway. I still hate him.'

'And you're a litter-bug,' Josh retaliated, pointing an accusing finger at the Rolo wrapper and shreds of gold foil on the ground. 'I'm going to tell the policeman you left that there. You'll probably have to go to prison.'

The time had come to be firm. Janey, whose arms were aching already, said, 'All right, that's enough. Josh, pick up that sweet wrapper and stop arguing this minute.'

'I'm c-cold,' whimpered Ella, whose blond, raindrenched hair was plastered to her head.

'And take off that oilskin. Your sister needs it more than you do.'

'I thought you were nicer than Maxine.' Obeying at the speed of mud, Josh gave her a sulky look. 'But you aren't.'

255

\* \* \*

Maxine returned to the house at eight-thirty, by which time Tom Lacey had left, the local doctor had also been and gone and the only physical reminder of the afternoon's events was a neat white pressure bandage encasing Ella's left ankle, of which she was fast becoming inordinately proud.

'What's going on? Why's Janey's van parked outside?'

Looking puzzled, Maxine dropped her coat over the back of an armchair. Serena, hogging the sofa as usual, was apparently engrossed in a frantic game show on the television. An ancient skinny man, having evidently just won himself a vacuum cleaner and a weekend at a health farm, was leaping up and down in ecstasy.

'Nothing's going on.' Serena finally turned to meet her gaze. 'Ella sprained her ankle, that's all. Your sister has been making an incredible amount of fuss over a simple accident.'

Maxine stared back. 'Janey doesn't make incredible amounts of fuss unless there's a damn good reason for it. What kind of simple accident are we talking about?'

But Serena merely shrugged. 'You may as well ask her, she's so much better at lurid detail than I am. She's upstairs, putting the children to bed. Probably giving them nightmares, too, with that neurotic imagination of hers . . .'

# Chapter 30

Janey was working in the shop three days later when Guy Cassidy came in. Having been kept bang up to date with the goings-on at Trezale House by Maxine gleefully relaying each new instalment over the phone, Janey could almost have timed his entrance to the second.

'He's leaving now,' Maxine had shrieked, minutes earlier. 'Put in a good word for me, Janey, and tell him I deserve a pay rise.'

In order not to give the game away, however, she looked dutifully surprised to see him.

'I've come to thank you,' Guy said simply. Then, breaking into a grin, he added, 'But I have a bit of a problem. If it had been anyone else, I would have brought them flowers . . .'

If there was one major drawback to this job, thought Janey, it was that nobody ever brought you flowers.

'The story of my life,' she replied with a good-humoured shrug. 'But you don't need to thank me, anyway. You helped me when I had a problem; all I did was return the favour.'

'Rather more than that,' said Guy. 'And I'm still grateful. I was going to bring you chocolates but Maxine insisted they'd wreck your slimming campaign.' Studying her figure for a moment he frowned and added, 'Are you really on a diet?'

'Oh dear.' Janey looked amused. 'Does that mean it isn't working?'

'It means you don't need to lose weight.'

Acutely aware of his speculative gaze still upon her, Janey flushed with embarrassment. It was all very well for Guy Cassidy to say she didn't need to diet, but she couldn't help noticing that men like him only ever chose girlfriends as thin as sticks, the kind who could step out of a size-fourteen skirt without even undoing the zip.

'How is Ella?' she said, changing the subject.

'Recovering nicely.' Guy smiled. 'And passionately attached to the bandage. She doesn't really need it any more but whenever we suggest taking it off, the limp gets worse.'

'And Josh?'

This time he pulled a face. 'You mean my modest son? He's cast himself in the role of rescuing hero. By the time he goes back to school next week he'll probably have awarded himself an OBE at the very least.'

Janey laughed. 'So everything's all right then, at home. Business as usual.'

'Well, I wouldn't quite say that.' He gave her an ambiguous look. 'And it's nice of you to ask, but I'm sure you know all the latest developments. Every time I've picked up the phone during the last few days,' he added pointedly, 'it's wafted Maxine's perfume back at me. And the receiver's always warm.'

Caught out, she said, 'Ah.'

'So I'll just say the situation has been dealt with.'

At that moment a customer entered the shop behind him. Guy, leaning against the counter, lowered his voice. 'And since flowers and chocolates are out of the window, how about a couple of theatre tickets instead?'

'You really don't have to,' protested Janey.

'I want to. And the tickets are for Saturday night. Do you have someone you'd like to take with you?'

Flustered by the unexpectedness of the question, she said, 'Um . . . well. Maybe Maxine?'

'What a shame, she has to stay at home and babysit,' Guy replied briskly. 'Never mind, perhaps I'll do instead.'

Behind him, the woman customer waved a bunch of dripping gladioli. Distracted, wondering whether he had just said what she thought he'd said, Janey stammered, 'Y-you mean . . .?'

'Well you can hardly invite Bruno, can you?' Guy grinned. 'So that's settled. I'll pick you up on Saturday. What time do you close the shop?'

'Um . . . f-five o'clock.'

'Good. It doesn't take you too long to get ready, does it? I'll pick you up at six.'

From her upstairs window, Janey watched as Guy expertly reversed the Mercedes into a parking space just outside the shop. As she had suspected, he was bang on time. Her stomach squirmed, the jitters refusing to subside. It was silly to be nervous, since it wasn't even a proper date, but still the adrenaline coursed through her bloodstream, working overtime practically of its own accord.

It would be far easier, she thought, if only Guy Cassidy

weren't so physically attractive. Such exceptional good looks were downright intimidating. Talking to him the other night in the privacy of her own home had been one thing, but this evening they were going to be seen out together in public, looking for all the world like a *real* couple. She was only too well aware of how she measured up against such willowy exotic beauties as Serena Charlton. In the back of her mind lurked the nightmare scenario that other people, observing them together, might be sniggering behind her back at such an unlikely pairing.

But it wasn't a real date, and at least she knew that even if they didn't. As Maxine had carelessly remarked, upon learning of the outing, 'I expect he just feels sorry for you because you never have any fun.'

My sister, thought Janey, such a comfort to have around. At least with Maxine to remind her of her failings, she wasn't likely to get ideas above her station. And, as she had done with James, she was trusting to fate that they wouldn't bump into anyone they knew at the theatre. Then, she had been the embarrassed one. This time, she thought ruefully, the tables of justice had been well and truly turned. If anyone was going to be embarrassed tonight, it was Guy.

When she opened the front door, however, he looked both surprised and pleased to see her.

'You're ready! Amazing.'

He was used to being kept waiting, of course, by glamorous women incapable of leaving the house until their three-hour beauty routines were complete. Janey, who had showered, changed and done her face in less than thirty minutes because she hadn't been able to close the shop before five-thirty, felt intimidated already.

But it wasn't a proper date, she reminded herself for the tenth time in as many minutes, so it really didn't matter. All she had to do was relax, stop feeling nervous and enjoy the evening for its own sake.

'Well, I hate to say it,' she said, as Guy opened the passenger door for her, 'but aren't we going to be horribly early? What time does the play start?'

'Ah.' He smiled. 'I have a favour to ask.'

Oh, that disarming smile. Like magic, Janey's butterflies disappeared. The prospect of seeing Guy again might have been nerve-racking but she'd forgotten how good he was at putting her at her ease. Now, miraculously, her anxieties melted away.

'A favour?' She gave him a deadpan look. 'Don't tell me. You want me to pay for the tickets.'

'Much worse than that.' Guy grinned. 'Some friends of mine are having a party and I promised I'd drop in on them. We'd just stay for an hour or so, then go on to the theatre for eight.' He paused and gave her a swift sidelong glance. 'Would that be OK with you, or is it a complete pain?'

It wasn't what she'd expected, that was for sure. Pulling a face, Janey said, 'Parties aren't exactly my favourite thing at the moment. Look, why don't I wait here? You could go on to the party on your own, see your friends and meet me at the theatre later.'

'Don't be such a wimp.' Guy was already putting the car briskly into gear. 'It isn't that kind of party, anyway.

Mimi and Jack are extremely nice people. You'll love them.'

He hadn't been asking her whether she'd like to go with him, Janey realized. He'd been telling her.

'Won't they mind, when you turn up with me in tow?' she protested.

'Mind?' He laughed. 'They'll be thrilled to bits. They're expecting me to bring Serena.'

# Chapter 31

Mimi and Jack Margason lived in a splendid old rectory on the outskirts of Truro. Mimi, welcoming them at the door, gave Guy an immense hug and did a delighted double-take when she saw Janey.

'My darling man! Come along now, make my day and tell me you've dumped dreary Deirdre for good.'

Guy, turning to grin at Janey, said, 'Told you they didn't like her.'

'Serena? Ghastly girl,' Mimi declared, planting a big kiss on his cheek. 'As skinny as a string bean and about as interesting to talk to. Or is that an insult to string beans?'

Having steeled herself for the worst – because with a name like Mimi the very least one could expect was glamour, glitz, drop-dead chic and probably a French accent to boot – this Mimi came as a marvellous surprise to Janey. It wasn't hard to understand, either, why Mimi considered Serena dreary and thin. At a conservative estimate, she had to weigh all of fifteen stone herself. Her long, extremely yellow hair was piled up and loosely secured with blue velvet bows, two biros and a chopstick. A billowing pink-and-silver blouse was worn over a long violet skirt. Mimi's round, laughing face was dominated by a wide mouth, many chins and a great deal of haphazardly applied violet eyeshadow. Her age wasn't easy to gauge but she was probably in her late fifties. She was also wearing the largest, most elaborate silver earrings Janey had ever seen in her life.

'This is Janey,' said Guy, performing the introductions. 'And she's just a friend so spare her the in-depth cross-examination because it won't get you anywhere. Janey, this is Mimi Margason, my very own Beryl Cooke character come to life. She's also the nosiest woman in England, so hang on to your secrets . . .'

'Oh, don't be so boring.' With a chuckle, Mimi ushered them into the house. 'But since you're the first guests to arrive, it's lovely to see you anyway. Now come through to the kitchen – oops, mind those wellies – and let Jack get you a drink. If he offers you the elderflower champagne,' she murmured furtively, 'for Pete's sake smack your lips and look appreciative. It might taste like old pea pods but it's his pride and joy.'

The kitchen was vast, rose-scented and hugely untidy. Mimi had evidently raided the garden that day; upon the twelve-foot-long windowsill stood three enormous, unmatched vases. The poor roses themselves, jammed in willy-nilly irrespective of size and colour, looked like far too many strangers squashed uncomfortably together in a lift.

'I know!' said Mimi cheerfully, having intercepted Janey's glance in their direction. 'I can't organize flowers to save my life. Poor Jack spends all his spare time in the garden, pruning and chivvying them along, and then I have to do that to them. Ruined, in ten minutes flat.'

'They aren't ruined.' Moving closer, Janey admired the blooms which had evidently been tended with devotion. 'They're beautiful. All they need is a bit of . . . sorting out.'

'I suppose I'm just not the sorting-out type.' With an unrepentant shrug, Mimi indicated the rest of the chaotic kitchen where, at the far end, the two men were already deep in conversation. She elaborated, 'We love this house, but let's face it – we're never going to be featured in *House & Garden*. Now come along, let's find you that drink and then we can get down to some serious gossip. I can give you all the dirt on dreadful Deirdre.'

'Actually,' said Janey, 'I did meet her a few times. I already know how dreadful she is.'

Mimi's eyes gleamed. 'In that case, you can tell me how you got yourself involved with gorgeous Guy.'

'Oh dear, this is going to come as such a disappointment to you.' Janey gave her an apologetic smile. 'But I'm afraid we really aren't involved.'

Mimi, however, was not easily swayed. 'You mean it's early days yet and you don't want to say too much about it,' she stage-whispered with the smug air of one who knows better.

'I mean there's nothing to say too much about.' Janey, beginning to realize that the more she protested, the more convinced Mimi would become that something delightfully illicit was going on, decided that this was a problem only Guy could sort out. Glancing once more at the poor, half-suffocated roses on the windowsill, she said suddenly, 'Look, why don't you find me a nice sharp knife—?'

'Help!' Mimi burst out laughing. 'Who are you thinking of using it on – me for asking too many questions? Or Guy, just to prove you aren't madly in love with him?'

Janey grinned. 'Your flowers. Let me do something to them before the rest of your guests arrive. And if you could lay your hands on some old newspapers and a couple more vases . . .'

'Amazing.' Having rummaged in a drawer, Mimi handed her a well-used Sabatier boning knife. Eagerly, she grabbed the bowls of roses and lined them up in front of Janey. 'The lengths some people will go to in order to get out of sampling my husband's beloved elderflower champagne. I say,' she added admiringly as Janey set to work with the knife, 'you really know what you're doing, don't you!'

With deft fingers, Janey separated a dozen or so deep, creamy yellow Casanovas from a tangle of coppery pink Albertines, trimmed their stems and stripped them of their waterlogged lower leaves. 'Plenty of practice,' she said, with a brief smile. 'I'm a florist.'

'How marvellous,' Mimi cried. 'At last, a girlfriend of Guy's who can actually do something besides flick her hair about and pose for a stupid camera.'

'Except I'm not a girlfriend of Guy's,' Janey patiently reminded her.

'Of course you aren't, darling.' Mimi, her silver earrings tinkling like sleighbells, shook her head and gurgled with laughter. 'But just think of the advantages if the two of you *should* decide to get married! Guy could take the photographs, you'd organize the flowers . . . how much more DIY can a bride and groom get?'

'Goodness.' Janey kept a straight face. 'I hadn't thought of it like that. We could get my brother the bishop to perform the ceremony, my sister Maxine could play "Here comes the bride" on her mouth organ and Josh and Ella could stab all the sausages on to little sticks . . .'

Jack Margason, having evidently decided that in the immediate-impact stakes he couldn't even begin to compete with his wife, wore a pale grey shirt and oatmeal trousers which exactly matched his pale grey hair and oatmeal skin. Tall and thin, with liquid, light brown eyes, an apologetic smile and a very long, perfectly straight nose, he reminded Janey of an Afghan hound.

And she wasn't going to get away with it after all, she realized. He had brought her a drink.

'You deserve one,' he told her, 'for doing justice to my poor, beloved roses. I can't tell you how grateful I am.'

Janey, putting the finishing touches to the final arrangement of blush-pink Fritz Nobis and creamy Pascali, tweaked a couple of glossy leaves into position in order to hide the chipped rim of the terracotta bowl in which they stood. Stepping back, she smiled and accepted the glass he offered her. It was the infamous elderflower champagne, and it definitely had character. Manfully she swallowed it.

'Go on then,' said Guy, having given her a ghost of a wink. 'What's the old bag been saying about me?'

'Don't flatter yourself.' The taste of old pea pods clung to Janey's teeth. 'She's been far too busy. Organizing the honeymoon.'

'The brazen hussy; she's already married.'

'Not her honeymoon.' Janey had been so entertained

by Mimi's endless suppositions and fantasies that it hadn't even occurred to her to be embarrassed. 'Ours.'

'Really?' Guy's eyebrows shot up. 'Where are we going? Somewhere nice, I hope?'

Evidently finding nothing strange in the idea that less than a week after Serena's departure Guy should have found himself a new future wife, Jack glanced with regret at the half-empty glass in his hand.

'What a shame, I only have three bottles of elderflower left. But if you think you might be interested, Guy, I could let you have three cases of last year's damson and crab-apple. That would certainly make the wedding party go with a swing.'

By seven-thirty the house was overflowing with guests, an eclectic mixture of smart, arty and downright Bohemian types complete with children and dogs for added informality. Janey, proudly introduced by Mimi as 'a whizz with flowers', almost had to forcibly restrain her from adding, 'She's Guy's new girlfriend but I'm not allowed to tell you because it's all terribly hush-hush.'

What struck Janey about the assortment of guests was their friendliness. Mimi and Jack clearly had no time for the kind of people who might turn up their noses at terrible wine or gaze askance at a messy home.

Two or three of them she even knew slightly, through the shop, whilst others, on hearing about it, bombarded her with questions. There was always someone desperate to learn how a wilting yukka could be sprung back to life, exactly how to go about preserving beech leaves with glycerine, when and how to trim a bonsai . . .

She was in the middle of demonstrating the method of putting together a *pot-et-fleur* arrangement to the glamorous wife of a pig farmer when Guy reappeared at her side.

'I'm thinking of setting up evening classes,' Janey told him with a grin.

'It looks to me as if you've already started.' He showed her his watch. 'Eight o'clock. Definitely evening.'

'Eight o'clock already?' The play started at eight thirty; he had come to tell her it was time to leave. Janey, feeling like a six-year-old at a birthday party, looked crestfallen.

'We shouldn't be late,' said Guy. 'Apart from anything else, I can't stand being glared at when I'm trying to squeeze past all the people already in their seats.'

'This play,' she said in neutral tones. 'Is it . . . good?'

'Oh, terrific. Riveting. Unmissable.'

'And these tickets. Expensive?'

'Cost an absolute fortune.'

'Do we have to go?'

Guy shook his head. 'We don't *have* to.'

Feeling guilty, she said, 'Do you want to?'

He smiled. 'Of course I don't. I hate the bloody theatre.'

The party was proving to be a great success. An enormous game of charades was interrupted at nine o'clock by the arrival of a caterer's van bringing Chinese food for sixty. At ten o'clock, everyone was ushered out into the garden for the firework display.

'I haven't had a chance to ask you yet how you've been getting on.' Guy led Janey towards a wooden bench from which they could view the proceedings in comfort. When she shivered in the chilly September night air he removed his green sweater and draped it across her shoulders.

Janey breathed in the scent of aftershave emanating from the soft folds of wool. It was a curiously intimate sensation, wearing an item of clothing still warm from someone else's body. Glad of the darkness she said, 'You mean meeting your friends tonight?'

'I mean sorting yourself out and getting Parry-Brent out of your system.'

'Don't worry, he's well and truly out.' She gave him a rueful smile. 'A little public humiliation works like a charm.'

'It didn't exactly make him look good, either,' Guy reminded her. 'A scene like that won't improve his street-cred.'

'I suppose not.' Janey thought about it for a moment. 'Well, good.'

'And you haven't seen him since?'

'Not at all. He's doing his own flowers from now on . . . or sweet-talking some other gullible female into doing them for him.' She fidgeted with the sleeves of the sweater, twisting them around her cold hands. 'But that's enough about my failed relationship. How about you? Does it feel strange, not having Serena around any more?'

'Ah.' Guy sounded amused. 'You mean it's time to talk about *my* failed relationship.'

Janey laughed. 'Well, it seems only fair. And it's so encouraging, knowing I'm not the only one who makes mistakes.'

Maxine had told her, of course, about Guy's return from Holland and the subsequent departure – amid a flurry of Louis Vuitton suitcases – of Serena and all her worldly goods. There had been no question of either forgiveness or reconciliation; such overwhelming lack of concern for the safety of his children was unforgivable.

'What can I say?' He shrugged, to indicate his own misjudgement. 'I've spent the last three years getting myself involved with unsuitable women and Serena turned out to be the icing on the cake. She was beautiful and she didn't try to suck up to Josh and Ella. Somehow I'd got it into my head that it was how my wife would have behaved if I'd already had children in tow when I first met her. Véronique would never have used them in order to get to me. She'd have taken her time getting to know them and allowed them to make up their own minds about her in return. When I met Serena she said much the same thing and it struck a chord. I was impressed by her honesty.' Pausing for a second, Guy added ruefully, 'I even managed to persuade myself that at last I'd found someone whom Véronique would approve of.'

The first fireworks were being set off, exploding against the night sky in a dazzle of colour and light, each rocket climbing higher than the last. The children squealed with delight. After watching them for a few moments, Guy spoke again. 'A couple of years ago I took the kids to a bonfire-night party,' he said in a low voice, 'and Ella asked me if her mother could see the fireworks from Heaven. The thing is, nobody ever teaches you the answers to questions like that.'

Janey was no longer cold but she shivered anyway.

Brushing a leaf from her black trousers she tucked her feet up on the bench and hugged her knees.

'Now you've really made me feel ashamed of myself. The only person I have to look after is me. If I make a pig's ear of things, at least I'm the only one who has to suffer the consequences. I can't imagine how much more difficult it must be for you, always having the children to consider as well.'

'Hmm,' said Guy. 'The trouble is, it doesn't stop you making the mistakes. You just feel a hell of a lot guiltier afterwards, and hope to God your kids don't say "I told you so".'

In an attempt to cheer him up, Janey said, 'Oh well, you're bound to meet the right girl sooner or later. Who knows, by this time next year you could be married and living happily ever after with someone who adores children . . .'

'You're beginning to sound like Mimi.' With mock-severity he demanded, 'Have you been reading her books?'

'Mimi writes books?' Janey was instantly diverted by this piece of news. 'What kind?'

'The kind where you end up married and living happily ever after with someone who adores children,' said Guy dryly. 'She sat me down and forced me to read an entire chapter, once. Real fingers-down-the-throat stuff it was too. I told her they ought to be sold with detachable sick bags.'

'That's because you're a man,' she explained in comforting tones. 'Women love that kind of thing because the men in the books are so much nicer than any in real life. We call it escapism.'

'The trouble with Mimi is she's written so many she's started believing them,' he protested. 'You wouldn't believe the problems I had with her when she heard about Maxine coming to work for me. She was practically uncontrollable. Pretty-nanny-meets-widowed-father, it seems, is one of her all-time favourite plots.'

It was one of Maxine's, too, thought Janey with secret amusement. But the opportunity to tease him was too good to pass up. 'These things do happen,' she said mildly. 'Who knows how your feelings might change?'

'Oh *please*.' He heaved a great sigh of despair. 'Not you as well. Maxine? Never. Not in a million years!'

'That's what they always say in the books,' Janey replied cheerfully. 'All the way through. Right up until the very last chapter . . .'

# Chapter 32

Maxine's high hopes for the lucrative toilet-roll commercial – founded on the basis of having once slept with the casting director – had been cruelly scuppered by his decision to give the job to the actress with whom he was currently sleeping instead. The disappointment of losing out was made all the harder to bear by the almost universal lack of sympathy.

'What a waste,' said Guy, straight-faced. 'All that talent down the pan.'

'If you'd got it,' Josh innocently enquired, 'would it have been a leading rôle?'

Ella, who didn't get the so-called jokes, said loyally, 'Well I'm glad you aren't doing it. I told my teacher Mrs Mitchell that you were going to sit on the toilet on television with your knickers down and she said it sounded horrible.'

'I was not going to sit on the toilet with my knickers down,' said Maxine through gritted teeth. No wonder Mrs Mitchell had given her such a sour look when she'd picked Ella up from school yesterday.

'Josh said you were.'

'Josh is a little toad about to get his Gameboy confiscated.'

'That's not fair!' protested Josh. 'Dad was the one who told me the joke.'

'Ah, you mean the hysterically funny leading rôle joke.' Maxine glared across the breakfast table at Guy. 'I suppose it took you hours to think that one up.'

He looked modest. 'Not at all. As a matter of fact, it came to me in a flush.'

Josh fell about laughing. Even Ella cottoned on to that one.

Maxine realized she was hopelessly outnumbered. 'You'll be sorry when I'm famous,' she snapped. 'In fact you're going to be sorry a lot sooner than that.'

There was a familiar glint in her eye. Recognizing it, Josh said weakly, 'Oh no, she's going to cook dinner. Not the fish pie, Maxine. Please, anything but that.'

'Oh yes.' She smiled, because revenge was so wonderfully sweet. 'Definitely the fish pie.'

Disappointment gave way to delight, however, when the director phoned Maxine a week later. Katrina, the actress whom he'd intended to favour, had somehow managed to fall out of his bed and break her arm in three places. Shooting started tomorrow. Could Maxine possibly get away at such short notice and step into the breach . . .?

Guy was busy in the darkroom. Since she wasn't prepared to risk life and limb opening the door – limbs being a precious commodity just now – Maxine yelled the news from outside.

'Oh, what next,' she heard him sigh. Hardly the encouraging response she might have hoped for. A minute passed before the door opened and Guy, frowning as his eyes adjusted to the light, emerged irritably.

'No,' he said, before she could even open her mouth to begin. 'This is too much, Maxine. Especially after what happened last time. You're either working for me or you're not, but you can't expect me to allow this kind of thing to carry on. I need someone who's reliable.'

What a pig, thought Maxine, outraged by his selfish, uncompromising attitude. The fact that Serena was a hopeless incompetent was hardly *her* fault. Guy had seemed to be so much more good-humoured during the past couple of weeks. And now here he was, reverting to type all over again.

'But this could be my big break,' she pleaded, silently willing him to pick up on the pun. If he smiled, she was halfway there.

Guy, however, saw through that little manoeuvre in a trice. He had no intention of smiling, either. 'Don't be obvious,' he said shortly. 'The answer's still no.'

'But it's fate . . . a chance in a million . . . and the kids are back at school now,' gabbled Maxine, bordering on desperation. In four days she would be earning almost as much as Guy paid her in an entire year. 'Oh please, let me find you a really and truly one-hundred-per-cent reliable nanny . . .'

'Maxine, forget it. You aren't going.'

'But—'

'No.' He spoke with a horrible air of finality.

Both Josh and Ella attended the local village school, which made it easy for Janey to pick them up at three-thirty and return them to Trezale House. Paula, thrilled to have been entrusted with the responsibility of visiting the flower market and running the shop single-handedly during Janey's absence, was almost more excited than Maxine at the prospect of watching her on television when the commercial was finally aired. Janey, less easily impressed, was nevertheless prepared to take care of the children for a few days whilst her sister was away. It was no hardship unless you counted having to sleep in Maxine's pigsty of a bedroom, and she was glad to be able to do a favour for Guy.

When she pulled up outside the school, Josh and Ella seemed equally pleased to see her.

'You're looking after us until Friday,' Ella declared, and promptly handed her a rolled-up sheet of paper. 'Here, Janey. I painted a picture of you in class. It's good, isn't it? What you have to do is say "How lovely" and pin it up on the kitchen wall when we get home.'

Janey studied the portrait. Ella had given her yellow hair, an unflattering purple face and fingers like tentacles. Next to her on a two-legged table stood a vast crimson cake complete with a staggering number of candles.

'Whose birthday is it?'

'Nobody's,' said Ella. 'But Maxine said you were good at cakes and they're my favourite, so I thought you might like to make some.'

'Tell Janey what else you thought,' prompted Josh slyly.

Ella beamed. 'I said Maxine was thin and she doesn't like cooking, but you aren't thin so that means you must like doing it a lot.'

Guy, who had spent the day working in Somerset

photographing an ancient countess and her fabulous jewels for a county magazine, arrived home at seven-thirty. The unfamiliar aroma of gingerbread hit him the moment he opened the front door. The sight of Janey, sitting at the kitchen table with Josh, Ella and practically an entire army of gingerbread men lined up on cooling racks was unfamiliar, too.

Nobody else, however, appeared to have noticed anything out of the ordinary.

'Hello, Daddy,' Ella greeted him airily, over her shoulder. 'We're just waiting for them to get cold enough to eat. I did the tummy buttons myself, with real currants.'

'I'm going to eat the arms and legs first,' Josh told him with ghoulish pride. 'Then the heads, until there's only bodies left.'

Janey, unaware of the smudge of flour on her forehead, smiled and said, 'Hi. Don't worry, I made them a proper tea at six. It's only chicken casserole and mashed potatoes, but there's some left if you're starving . . .'

It hadn't been the best of days as far as Guy was concerned. The countess, who was over eighty, had examined the preliminary Polaroids and haughtily demanded to know why someone reputed to be so clever with a camera couldn't even manage to take a moderately flattering snap.

The raddled old bag, it transpired, had delusions of passing for fifty, which not even all the soft focusing in the world could hope to achieve. It had been a long and tiresome session, throughout which Guy had endured being addressed as 'That boy'.

And now, this.

It didn't take a genius to work it out, but he said it anyway. 'Where's Maxine?'

Janey, evidently the innocent party, looked surprised.

'What? She caught the ten o'clock train this morning. Did you think she wasn't leaving until tonight?'

'Bloody hell,' said Guy. The girl was uncontrollable. Was there anything she wouldn't do in order to get her own way? '*Bloody* Maxine.'

'Oooh!' Ella squealed with delight. When she'd said bloody the other day it had caused all kinds of a fuss. Just wait until the next time her father tried to tell her off for saying it.

'What?' repeated Janey, bewildered by Guy's response. 'I'm sorry. I don't understand. Is there a problem?'

'Go on then,' he said heavily. 'Tell me how she managed to talk you into it.'

It didn't take long for realization to dawn. Maxine had done it again. 'You didn't know she was going,' Janey sighed.

'Damn right I didn't know,' said Guy icily. 'But then she was hardly likely to tell me, was she? My God, I told her she couldn't just waltz off . . .'

*Damn*, registered Ella, beside herself with glee. Surely that was another bad word? She wondered whether it was worse than 'sodit', which was what Maxine had said when she'd burnt the scrambled eggs the other night.

For once, however, Janey was on Maxine's side. Had she stopped to think about it, she supposed she wouldn't have agreed to take over if she'd known the full story, but she also knew how much the job offer meant to Maxine.

Besides, she was here now, and it wasn't as if she was a crazed axe-murderer.

'Look,' she said reasonably, 'there really isn't a problem. I'm enjoying myself, Paula's going to be looking after the shop . . .'

'Maxine asked me if she could go and I said no,' Guy repeated defiantly. 'And I don't know how you can even begin to defend her. She can't seriously expect to do this kind of thing and get away with it.'

Josh and Ella watched, enthralled, as Janey squared up to their father.

'If you didn't have any intention of allowing her to take the job, you should never have let her go up for the audition. That's unfair.'

'If she'd given me enough warning, I wouldn't have objected.' Guy found it hard to believe that Janey was defending Maxine. 'But I employ her to look after my children. She cannot expect to skip off at a moment's notice, leaving them in the care of God-knows-who . . .'

'She only found out yesterday that she'd got the job,' Janey countered hotly. 'And I'm not God-knows-who. I'm her sister. I'm sorry if that isn't good enough for you, but—'

'Don't be ridiculous.' Realizing that the situation was getting out of hand, he made an effort to calm down. Removing his leather jacket, he tipped Ella off her chair, sat down in her place and pulled her on to his knee.

'And don't look at me like that,' he told Janey. 'You know I'm not criticizing you. This is all Maxine's fault, as usual. That girl is enough to drive any man to distraction.'

And she'd even been flattered when she'd thought Guy had wanted her to look after the children. Janey, still indignant on Maxine's behalf, didn't return his smile. When he reached past Ella and helped himself to a gingerbread man, she hoped it would burn his mouth.

It did. Guy pretended it hadn't.

'These are brilliant,' he said, in an attempt to mollify her. 'Oh come on, Janey. Cheer up. Have a gingerbread man.'

'Is the tummy button nice, Daddy?' asked Ella.

The currant tummy-button was molten. Swallowing valiantly, Guy gave her a squeeze. 'Sweetheart, it's the best bit.'

'Look, you're back now,' said Janey in level tones. 'You don't need me here. Why don't I just go home and leave you to it?'

Belatedly, Guy realized just how affronted she really was. The expression in his dark blue eyes softened. 'OK, I'm sorry. I know you think I'm an ungrateful bas— person, but I'm not really. And of course you can't leave; we want you to stay. How could I not want someone to stay when they can make gingerbread men like these?'

'She did mashed potato with real potatoes, too,' offered Josh.

'And washed my hair,' Ella put in helpfully, 'without getting shampoo in my eyes.'

Janey was threatening to smile. Guy, glancing around the kitchen and counting on his fingers, continued the list.

'*And* she's made a chicken casserole. *And* she's ironed my denim shirt. *And* she's managed to tear Josh away from his Gameboy without even having to handcuff him to the kitchen chair . . .'

Josh, ever-hopeful, said, 'And she's promised I can stay up to watch *Bride of Dracula*.'

'No I haven't!' Janey started to laugh.

'That settles it,' declared Guy. 'I can't possibly watch *Bride of Dracula* on my own. It'll remind me of Maxine and give me hideous nightmares. You're going to have to stay.'

Ella, reaching across him, picked up one of the gingerbread men. To her dismay the all-important currant rolled on to the floor.

'Oh, sodit,' she squealed indignantly. 'What a little bugger. His bloody tummy button's come off.'

# Chapter 33

Discretion was all part and parcel of a florist's job, Janey had discovered. When a man who had been married for twenty years began placing a regular order for white freesias to be delivered to an address several miles away from his own home, you kept your mouth shut and delivered them. When your very own middle-aged bank manager suddenly spruced himself up, discovered after-shave and took to popping in for single long-stemmed red roses, you kept a straight face at all costs. And on Valentine's day, when any number of men might request two – or even three – identical cellophane-wrapped bouquets of mixed spring flowers, you didn't bat so much as an eyelid.

Which was how she was managing not to bat an eyelid now. But there could be no doubt about it; the man standing before her was definitely the same man she had seen with her mother all those weeks ago. And the gold American Express card she was holding definitely bore the name 'Oliver J. Cassidy'.

Which was why, of course, he had looked so familiar to her when she'd spotted him at the Grand Rock Hotel.

'I'd like to write the message on the card myself, if I

may,' said Oliver Cassidy with a brief smile.

Janey, who had only popped into the shop for a couple of hours whilst Josh and Ella were at school, watched him uncap a black and gold Mont Blanc fountain pen. She felt like a voyeur.

'There.' The task completed, he passed the card back to her and smiled once more. The brief message: *You have all my love. Counting the days*, was written in a courtly, elegant hand. 'Will they be sent this afternoon?'

'Don't worry, they'll reach her before two o'clock,' Janey assured smoothly. 'I shall be delivering them myself.'

'Darling, what a lovely surprise!' Thea, opening the front door, kissed Janey on both cheeks. Her eyes lit up at the sight of the enormous cellophane-wrapped bouquet. 'And what heavenly lilies . . . how kind of you to think of your poor old mother.'

'They aren't from me,' said Janey dryly. 'They're from an admirer. I'm just the delivery girl.'

Thea, evidently in a buoyant mood, said, 'Oh well, in that case I won't invite you in for a drink.'

'Yes you will.' Handing over the bouquet, Janey headed in the direction of the kitchen and switched on the kettle. By the time she'd spooned instant coffee into two mugs, Thea had opened the envelope, read the message written on the card and slipped it into the pocket of her blue-and-white striped shirt. It was an extremely well-made man's shirt, Janey noted. No prizes for guessing the identity of the original owner.

She waited until the coffee was made before saying anything.

'So who is he, Mum?'

'Good heavens,' countered Thea, a shade too brightly. 'You're the one who sold him the flowers, sweetheart. Surely you know who he is. Or did he run off without paying and you're desperate to track him down?'

'I know who he is. I wanted to know if you did.'

Thea laughed. 'Well of course I do, darling! His name is Oliver and he's madly in love with me.'

'I meant do you know *exactly* who he is?' Janey paused and sipped her coffee. 'But it's pretty obvious now that you do. For goodness sake, Mum, whatever do you think you're doing? What's going on?'

'I don't know why you're making such a fuss,' said Thea crossly. 'There's absolutely nothing to get dramatic about. OK, so his name is Oliver Cassidy and he just happens to be the father of the photographer Maxine's working for. Is that so terrible? Am I committing some hideous crime?'

'You tell me.' Janey, inwardly amazed at her ability to remain calm, sat back and crossed her legs. 'Were you the one who came up with the idea of abducting his grandchildren?'

'Of course I wasn't. And there's no need to make it sound like some kind of kidnapping,' Thea countered. 'He wanted to see them; he knew Guy would kick up all kinds of a fuss if he asked his permission, so he waited until he was away. Those children had a splendid afternoon, Oliver did what he came to Cornwall to do and nobody came to any harm.'

'So you do know all about it,' said Janey accusingly.

'Maxine nearly lost her job as a result of that little escapade. And did dear Oliver tell you how he came to be estranged from his son? Did he explain exactly why Guy would have kicked up such a fuss?'

'It was all a misunderstanding.' Thea dismissed it with an airy gesture. 'Oliver realizes now that he made a mistake, but it's only gone on as long as it has because Guy overreacted. All families have disagreements, unfortunately. Oliver was unlucky enough to have his turned into some ridiculous, long-running feud. Darling, he was heartbroken about it! Seeing those dear little children, even if it was only for a few hours, did him all the good in the world.'

'It wouldn't have, if Guy had found out about it. He would have called the police.'

If there was one thing Thea couldn't bear, it was being criticized by her own children. 'And you're on his side of course,' she countered irritably. 'Despite knowing nothing about what really happened. Just because he no doubt has a pretty face.'

Janey, determined not to rise to the bait, gritted her teeth. 'But it's OK for you to defend his father, just because he's mad about you and stinking rich? Mum, what he did was *wrong*!'

'Oh Janey, don't get your knickers in a twist.' Thea banged her coffee mug down on the table. 'What happened wasn't tragic. The real tragedy is Guy Cassidy's pig-headed refusal to let bygones be bygones, because the children are the ones who suffer. All Oliver was trying to do was make it up to them.'

'Really?' Janey remained unimpressed. 'And what's he

planning to do for an encore? Whisk them out of the country for a few months?'

This was ridiculous. Thea's expression softened. 'Oliver would never do anything like that. He's a wonderful man, darling.'

Janey, who had thought Bruno was wonderful, replied unforgivingly, 'I'm sure he is. As long as he's getting his own way.'

There was a long silence. Finally, Thea said, 'All right, so what happens now? What are *you* going to do for an encore?'

Janey, having already considered the options, shrugged. 'You mean am I going to tell Guy? I don't know, Mum. The thing is, can you be sure his father isn't, in some obscure way, just using you? I'm serious,' she went on, when Thea started to smile. 'It's all highly coincidental, after all. You're Maxine's mother, and Maxine looks after Josh and Ella. How do you know he hasn't hatched some sinister plan?'

'Dear me.' Her mother shook her head and gave her an indulgent look. 'And I thought Maxine was the drama queen of the family. Janey, take it from someone old enough to know. There's nothing even remotely sinister about Oliver Cassidy, and there are no ulterior motives on his part. He loves me, and I love him. I'm sorry if that doesn't meet with the approval of Maxine's employer but as far as I'm concerned, my private life is none of his business anyway. And if you feel you have to tell him, then do it, though personally I can't see the point. From what I hear, hugs and smiles and forgiveness-all-round is pretty much off the cards, so all you'd be doing would be stirring it up again for no useful reason. Still,' she concluded with a take-it-or-leave-it gesture, 'Those are just my thoughts. As I said, it's entirely up to you.'

Janey was now more undecided than ever. What her mother had said made sense. Keeping quiet, on the other hand, meant assuming responsibility for the secret. And it also meant not telling Maxine, who would be sure to tell Guy herself. If anything should ever go wrong, she thought with unease, she would be at least partly to blame.

But Oliver Cassidy had seemed charming, and imprinted in her mind was the expression on his face as he'd written the brief message to accompany Thea's flowers.

'How do you know he loves you?' she asked, gazing into her mother's dark eyes.

'I've had nearly thirty years to learn from my mistakes in that field,' Thea replied simply. 'This time it's the real thing. Trust me, darling. When it happens like this, you *do* know . . .'

In that case, thought Janey as memories of Alan and Bruno flooded back, why don't I?

Torrential rain the next day meant an early wrap for the fashion shoot Guy had been working on in the Cotswolds. Home by four-thirty, he found Janey on the phone in the kitchen, the receiver tucked under her chin whilst she mashed parsnips with one hand and stirred a pan of gravy with the other. Her blond hair was loosely pinned up and the violet sweatshirt she wore over white jeans was slipping off one shoulder. Her cheeks, pink from the heat of the oven, turned pinker still when she realized he was back.

'Oh, I didn't hear you come in. Dinner won't be ready for another hour yet . . . but there's tons of hot water if you'd like a bath.'

Maxine, on the other end of the phone, groaned. 'Uh oh, enter the dragon. Don't tell him it's me.'

'Who are you talking to?' said Guy, his tone deceptively mild.

'Nobody.' Janey's innocent expression was foiled by the tell-tale deepening flush. 'A friend.'

'Did anyone ever tell you you're a hopeless liar?' With a brief smile he crossed the kitchen, took the phone from her and said, 'Hello, Maxine.'

'Oh God.' In London, Maxine sighed. 'Are you still mad at me?'

'What do you think?'

'You're still mad,' she said penitently. 'And I know that what I did was wrong, but you just didn't understand how important this job is to me. I'm sorry Guy, but I really was desperate . . .'

'Hmmm.' Glancing across at Janey, who was frenziedly tackling the parsnips and trying to look as if she wasn't listening, he drawled, 'Lucky for you you've got an understanding sister. I hope you appreciate the favour she's done you.'

'I do, I do.' Maxine's tone was fervent. Much to her relief, the expected bawling-out hadn't happened. Not yet, anyway. Deciding to chance it, she added, 'And aren't *you* glad she's there, too? She's so much better at cooking than I am.'

'She could hardly be any worse.'

'And Josh and Ella think she's terrific!'

'Carry on like this and you'll end up talking yourself out of a job. Or was that what you had in mind?' he enquired evenly. 'If you've landed the lead in some dazzling West End production, Maxine, I'd rather you told me now.'

'Oh, but I haven't! And I really don't want to leave, Guy. I like working for you.'

'But?' he prompted, when it became apparent that Maxine hadn't the courage to say the word herself.

She crossed her fingers, hard. 'But we aren't going to finish shooting until Saturday, so I won't be able to get back before Sunday morning.' The words came out in an apologetic rush. 'I've already asked Janey and she doesn't mind a bit, but is that OK with you?'

If he was ever going to blow his top, it would happen now. As the silence lengthened, Maxine realized she was holding her breath.

'Why,' drawled Guy finally, 'do I feel like a schoolboy who's just found out the summer holidays are carrying on for an extra week?'

'Was he furious?' asked Cindy, who was wallowing in the jacuzzi. It was nice having Maxine as a temporary house-guest whilst her husband was abroad; it was almost like being single again, sharing a flat and gossiping until three in the morning over bottles of wine, about men.

'He wasn't furious at all.' Maxine, perching on the edge of the bath, looked distinctly put out. 'He was delighted.'

'Isn't that what you wanted?'

'There's a difference between agreeing to let me stay

and being delighted,' said Maxine moodily. 'It would be nice to feel a little bit missed. From the sound of it, they're having a whale of a time down there without me.'

'Who knows?' said Cindy, holding out her glass for a top-up. 'Maybe something's going on between them. They could be having a rip-roaring affair.'

'Janey and Guy?' Maxine laughed. 'Now I know you've had too much to drink.'

'I don't see why it's so funny. You told me he'd taken her to a party the other week,' Cindy reminded her. 'And he's pretty irresistible, after all. Are you seriously telling me your sister would turn down the opportunity of a fling with Guy Cassidy?'

'I'm telling you that I spent a good couple of months trying to persuade him to have a fling with me,' said Maxine, tossing back her long blond hair and admiring her reflection in the full-length mirror. 'And it didn't bloody work. Boasting aside, darling, if he can ignore an offer like that, he's hardly likely to be interested in Janey.'

# Chapter 34

The phone rang again whilst Guy was taking a shower. Janey, picking it up, recognized titian-haired Charlotte's voice at once. She could almost smell the perfume, too, oozing down the line at her from St Ives.

'He's upstairs in the shower,' she told Charlotte, who had asked to speak to Guy in deeply husky tones. 'Can I take a message?'

'That isn't Maxine.' Huskiness gave way to suspicion. 'Who am I speaking to?'

For a moment, Janey was tempted. Then, deciding that that would be cruel, she said, 'Maxine's taken a few days off. I'm just here looking after the children whilst she's away.'

Charlotte, however, sounded unconvinced. 'And you are . . .?'

'Janey. Maxine's sister.' She wondered whether an apology might be expected, for having been the cause of Charlotte's abandonment at Bruno's party. But she hadn't dragged Guy away; if anything, he had dragged her.

'Oh. Right.' Thankfully, Charlotte didn't mention it either. She sounded unflatteringly relieved, though, to hear that she wasn't facing Serena-standard competition. 'Well in that case, maybe you could ask Guy to call me back.'

'Will do.' Josh had crept barefoot into the kitchen behind her. Janey watched his reflected image in the window as he surreptitiously reached for the biscuit tin. 'No more Jaffa cakes.'

Startled, Charlotte said, 'I beg your pardon?'

'Sorry, I was speaking to somebody else.'

'How did you know I was there?' Josh protested. 'I didn't make any noise.'

'I heard the Jaffa cakes screaming for help.'

'Good Lord.' Charlotte sounded amused. 'Look, whilst you're there, would you happen to know whether or not Guy has anything on tonight?'

'Nothing at all at the moment,' said Janey. 'He's in the shower.'

'I mean any plans.'

'I don't think so. He told me I could go out for the evening if I wanted, so he must be staying in.'

'Oh. And where are you going, somewhere nice?'

The CIA had nothing on Charlotte. Smiling to herself, Janey replied, 'I don't have any plans either. I'll probably just stay here.'

'That sounds nice.' Charlotte sounded immeasurably cheered by the news. 'OK then, if you could just ask Guy to ring me back as soon as he's out of the shower. You won't forget now, will you?'

'Oh hell.' Guy looked bored. 'That means she's going to invite me round for dinner.'

'Stop eating, then,' scolded Janey, because he'd already helped himself to three sausages and she hadn't even dished up yet.

'But I don't want to go. No, I can't face it.' He shook his head. 'She'll float around in some kind of negligée and try to get me drunk so I won't be able to drive home. When she phones back, say I've gone out.'

'Then I'll get the blame for not passing on the message,' she protested. God, men were callous beasts. 'No, you've got to ring her.'

Guy shrugged. 'OK, I'll tell her I've already made other arrangements.'

Janey looked shamefaced. 'I said you hadn't.'

'Then I'll tell her I have to stay in and look after the kids because you're going out.'

'Oops,' said Janey. 'She's already asked me that. I told her I wasn't.'

He mimed mock despair. 'So how long have you been taking this truth drug?'

'I can't help it,' Janey protested with a grin. 'I'm just a naturally honest person.'

'One of you must have been adopted then. You can't be Maxine's sister.'

'And you can't keep changing the subject like this.' In order to spur him into action, she whisked his plate out of reach. 'She's sitting at home, waiting for you to call her back. Do it.'

'Now who's being bossy?' he grumbled, pinching yet another sausage from Ella's plate as he headed for the kitchen phone. 'You're far nicer to my children than you are to me.'

Janey gave him a guileless smile. 'You pay me to be nice to your children.'

'She'd be nicer,' Josh told his father, 'if she didn't make us help with the washing up.'

Just listening to Guy's side of the phone call was uncomfortable enough. Janey, squirming on the other woman's behalf, decided that if she were Charlotte she would have died of embarrassment. But still it went on, Guy tactfully saying no and Charlotte – clearly not embarrassed at all – shooting one excuse after another down in flames.

'Look, maybe another time,' he said eventually, several toe-curling minutes later. 'But not tonight, Charlotte. Really. I have to be in London first thing tomorrow morning and it's been a tough few days. Yes, I know that's what I said last week, but that doesn't mean it isn't still true.'

More muffled protests ensued. Guy glanced across at Janey for help. She, unable to look at him, picked up the pepper mill and over-seasoned her baked tomatoes.

'OK.' He lowered his voice to a conspiratorial whisper. 'If you must know, I *have* to stay here tonight. It's Janey; she's absolutely petrified of being left alone in this house. Yes, I know it sounds ridiculous but she has this thing about burglars breaking in with shotguns. We're so isolated here, you see; I only have to mention going out for the evening and she starts gibbering with fear. Charlotte, I'm sorry but you have to understand, I can't possibly abandon her . . .'

'Thanks a lot,' said Janey, when he returned to the table. 'Why are all men such shameless liars?'

'The first four excuses were true.' He gave her a what-can-you-do shrug. 'And she didn't believe any of them. Sometimes you have to resort to a little elaboration.'

It was certainly instructive, seeing the situation from a male point of view. Curious, she said, 'But if you aren't, you know . . . well, interested in her, why don't you just say so?'

Josh and Ella, evidently accustomed to such goings-on, were unfazed by the conversation.

'He tried doing that last week,' Josh explained kindly. 'But all she did was cry. Then she phoned Dad back, right in the middle of *Coronation Street*, and cried some more.'

'So he took the telephone off the hook,' said Ella. 'But that didn't work either. She got into her car and came here, *still* crying. It was really mean of her,' she added, her expression indignant. 'It was only eight o'clock and it wasn't even our fault, but we had to go up to bed.'

'You see?' protested Guy. 'I get the blame for everything. I can't do anything right.'

Janey, still acutely aware of the fact that she had made almost as much of an idiot of herself with Bruno, couldn't help feeling sorry for Charlotte who was probably weeping buckets right now.

'You must have led her on.' She tried to look disapproving. 'If you really don't want to see her again, it would be far kinder to say so and put her out of her misery.'

He looked surprised. 'Rather than let her down gently?'

'There's nothing worse than not knowing where you stand.' Janey spoke with feeling. She lowered her voice, although Josh and Ella had by this time lost interest. 'You should tell her, you know. It'll be easier all round if you do. Even Charlotte will appreciate it in the long run.'

'Oh hell.' He gave a sigh of resignation. 'I hate these emotional showdowns. This is going to be no fun at all.'

At least he wasn't the one being dumped. Janey wondered if he'd ever been on the receiving end of a verbal 'Dear John'. Somehow, she seriously doubted it.

'You'll go and see her then? Tonight?'

With reluctance, he nodded. Then grinned. 'Only if you're sure you can cope with being left alone in the house for an hour or so?'

'Oh, I think I can stand it,' said Janey bravely. 'If any burglars turn up, I'll just send them into Maxine's bedroom. That should be enough to put them off looting and pillaging for life.'

By the time he got back it was almost nine-thirty. Janey had put Josh and Ella to bed and was finishing the washing up.

'Leave that,' said Guy, opening a bottle of wine and taking two glasses out of the cupboard. 'Come and help me drink this. I need it.'

'Was it awful?'

He ran his fingers through his dark hair and pulled a face. 'Pretty much. Shit, I feel like such a bastard. She said she wished she'd never met me.'

'She didn't mean it,' said Janey consolingly. 'She just feels let down. Charlotte liked you more than you liked her, that's all. And when it ends, it hurts.'

'That's what she said,' mused Guy. 'The trouble is,

she blames me. But you have to get to know someone before you can decide whether or not you're suited. By the time you realize the relationship doesn't have a future, it's too late. They like you, so they end up getting hurt.' He paused, then added, 'Hardly an earth-shattering revelation, I know. It's just that I've never really discussed it with anyone before.'

'Whereas we women discuss it all the time,' said Janey with a grin. 'I told you, you should have stuck at those books of Mimi's. They'd have taught you everything you needed to know.'

'I thought you were supposed to be having an early night,' she protested three hours later.

This was an altogether different Janey from the one he had taken away from Bruno's party, Guy reflected. Now, relaxed and perfectly at ease, interested in hearing what he had to say yet at the same time totally unpushy, she had managed to make him forget the time completely. And he, too, was relaxed; it was such a relief to be able to talk to someone who wasn't even attempting to flirt with him or advance her own cause.

But despite Janey's apparent conviction that she was less attractive than her younger sister, he didn't agree. Tonight, wearing virtually no make-up, with her honey-blond hair loosely held up with combs and her violet sweatshirt still slipping off one shoulder, he found her uncontrived beauty infinitely more attractive. Her summer tan showed no signs of fading, her complexion was flawless and those conker-brown eyes, alight with humour, didn't need shadows and eyeliners to make them spectacular; just as the soft, perfectly shaped mouth had nothing to gain by being plastered with lipstick.

He found himself comparing their manner with the children too, for although Josh and Ella adored Maxine and her slapdash, highly individual ways, her wit was on occasions too acute for comfort, leaving them unsure whether or not she had actually meant it. Maxine could be unpredictable, which in turn made Ella edgy and Josh mildly resentful. Young children appreciated continuity and the security of knowing just where they stood. Berenice, of course, had been stability personified, whilst Maxine was all fun and back-chat, but if he could choose the ideal nanny, Guy realized, it would be someone like Janey, who tempered control with gentle humour. She was also easy on the eye – unlike poor Berenice, he thought with a stab of guilt – extremely good company and not the least bit interested in shooting off at short notice to star in toilet-roll commercials.

'Any more news about your father?' she said suddenly.

Guy, who had been pouring out the last of the Beaujolais, gave her a stern look.

'And there I was, just thinking what a nice person you were.'

'I'm still a nice person,' said Janey innocently. 'I wondered whether there'd been any developments, that's all.'

'None. Every time I rang his home number the answering machine was switched on. In the end I stopped trying.'

'What would you have said, though? If you had spoken to him?'

'I'd have told him to keep away from my home and my children.' Guy's expression was stony, unforgiving. 'I'd have told him that if he ever tries a stunt like that again I'll call the police.'

'But if he apologized,' she persisted, tucking her bare feet beneath her and leaning forwards to reach for the refilled glass, 'and begged you to forgive him, do you think you could?'

'Oh yes.' His eyes darkened. 'Highly likely.'

'I mean it,' said Janey. 'Come on, think it through. He might really regret what happened and now all he wants to do is get to know his grandchildren and make up for lost time.' Her expression was oddly intense.

Guy, however, had made his own mind up long ago. 'You've been watching too much *Little House on the Prairie*,' he told her, before she could open her mouth and say more. 'No, Janey. I never want to see my father again and I don't want the children to have anything to do with him either, so don't even try and talk me round. This is one happy family reunion that definitely isn't going to happen.'

Oh well, thought Janey. Sorry, Oliver. At least you can't say I didn't try.

# Chapter 35

Every year in the second week of October the travelling fair came to Trezale, setting up its comfortably familiar pattern of stalls, side-shows, candy-floss stands and mechanical rides along the high street with the dodgems, ghost train and big wheel taking pride of place at the top end.

Everyone went to the fair; it was a landmark event on the social calendar. Josh and Ella, in a frenzy of excitement at the prospect of spending all their money and spinning themselves sick on the waltzers, were practically counting the minutes until Friday night.

Janey was stunned, however, by Guy's reaction when he called her from his car phone on the M5 on his way back from a fashion shoot in Bath.

'Josh says you've promised they can stay out until midnight,' she told him. 'I need a voice of authority here. What time do they have to be home?'

'What do you mean, they?' Guy demanded. '*We* go home whenever we like.'

'You mean you're coming with us?'

'Why else would I complete a six-hour shoot in three and a half hours?' He sounded amused. 'And skip dinner with Kate Moss. Of course I'm coming with you.'

'Gosh,' said Janey. 'Somehow I hadn't imagined you as a fairground lover.'

'No? What kind of lover had you imagined me as?'

'I meant—'

'I know what you meant.' Guy laughed. 'And it's OK, you can stop blushing now. Look, I'll be home by six, so just tell the kids to hang on. Don't you dare leave without me.'

Josh and Ella had, over the years, grown used to it. Since it was practically the entire reason Maxine had taken the job in the first place, she would have enjoyed every minute. Janey, however, cringed. It was a frosty evening, her nose was probably pink with cold and her hair had been whisked to a frenzy on the Octopus. It was all right for Guy; he was the one taking roll after roll of film with the new camera, but she wasn't used to finding herself on the receiving end of a lens. As far as she was concerned, it was a distinctly nerve-racking experience.

And he was using up film at a rate of knots.

'Haven't you finished yet?' It sounded ungracious, but she wished he would stop. Being asked to test out the latest Olympus was all very well, but this was downright off-putting. She didn't know where to look.

'No need to panic,' said Guy. 'It isn't as if I'm asking you to pose and smile. Just ignore me.'

Janey scowled. 'How can I ignore you when I know my nose is red?'

'Don't be so vain,' he chided briskly. 'I'm trying out a new camera, not using you for the cover of *Vogue*. So relax . . .'

'Quick, Daddy!' Ella, who wasn't the least bit camera-shy, screamed with delight. 'Take one of me with candy floss all over my face.'

Janey was eating a toffee apple when a male voice behind her said, 'Well, hello. Having fun?'

Swinging round, she saw that it was Alexander Norcross, Mr Presentable himself, looking very smart in a charcoal-grey Crombie and with a plump, shivering brunette in tow.

'Oh hi.' She probably had bits of toffee stuck to her teeth but she smiled anyway. 'Yes, we're having a great time.'

Ella tugged at her arm. 'Janey, can you lend me fifty pence for the hoop-la?'

'Rip-off, these places.' Alexander glanced down at Ella, who had just proved his point. 'How these people have the nerve to charge fifty pence for the opportunity to win something that costs ten, I don't know. If you ask me, there should be a law against it.'

Smart but mean, recalled Janey, pressing a pound coin into Ella's gloved hand. With exaggerated politeness she said, 'Oh dear, does that mean you aren't enjoying yourself?'

'I'm not saying that,' protested Alexander. 'Fairgrounds can be entertaining, so long as you don't waste your cash. We've been here for almost two hours now,' he added with evident pride, 'and it hasn't even been necessary to open my wallet. Now that's what I call real value for money.'

The brunette didn't just have a red nose, she was almost blue with cold all over.

'You mean he hasn't bought you a cup of coffee?' Janey

looked shocked. 'Alexander, this poor girl is going to end up with frostbite. What she needs is a hot espresso and a couple of stiff brandies to warm her up.'

The girl, looking almost pathetically grateful, said, 'That would be nice. Alex, could we do that?'

'Are you cold?' He sounded surprised. 'Well, maybe it is time we made a move. I know. We'll get back to my house and have a nice cup of tea.'

Janey had the urge to scream: 'Make him take you to an expensive restaurant! Better still, tell him to take an almighty running jump into the sea . . .'

But she didn't, and the next moment Josh and Guy arrived back from the shooting gallery. Guy, realizing that she was talking to someone she knew, hung back and maintained a discreet distance. Josh, who was far more interested in money than discretion, charged up to Janey and yelled frantically, 'Quick, I've run out of change!'

'Two kids,' Alexander remarked, when Josh had pocketed another pound coin and shot off to join Ella. 'Well, well. So you found yourself a family man. Bad luck, Jane.'

Janey risked a glance over his shoulder. Ten feet away and eavesdropping shamelessly, Guy grinned.

'Bad luck?'

'Oh well, maybe you get on well with them.' Alexander shuddered with disapproval. 'Some girls don't mind that kind of set-up, after all. But you do want to be careful, Jane. Single mothers are bad enough, but single fathers are an even dodgier prospect. Is he interested in you, or is he just desperate to find someone to look after the house and kiddies?'

'Gosh.' Not daring to meet Guy's gaze, Janey bit her lip and looked worried. 'I hadn't thought of it like that. You mean all he's really after is some kind of substitute nanny?'

'That's exactly what I mean,' Alexander declared with a knowledgeable nod. 'You see, nannies don't come cheap and they aren't always one hundred per cent reliable. As far as the man's concerned, it's simpler and more economical in the long run to find himself a new wife.'

Guy, approaching them, gave Janey a ghost of a wink. She didn't even flinch when he slipped his arm around her waist and gave her a fleeting kiss on the cheek.

'Darling, I thought I'd lost you. We really should be getting home, you know. It's way past Ella's bedtime.'

Janey gave him a cold stare. 'Oh dear, is it? Well in that case we'd better run.'

'What's the matter?' Guy raised his eyebrows. 'Is there a problem?'

'I don't know,' she replied evenly. 'But I think I'm about to find out. Let me ask you a question, Guy. Did you invite me to move in with you because you loved me or because you needed someone to take care of your children?'

His smile faded. After some consideration he said, 'Well, sweetheart. If you think back, I didn't actually invite you to move in with me at all. As far as I recall, I arrived back from Amsterdam one night and there you were, unpacking your suitcases and generally making yourself at home. Not that I'm complaining of course, but—'

'But you do *love* me?' A note of hysteria crept into Janey's voice. 'If we're going to get married next week I need to know if you really love me.'

Alexander and the brunette stood in fascinated silence. Janey prayed Josh and Ella wouldn't pick this moment to come back.

'Sweetheart, of course I do.' Guy gave her a placatory hug. 'We all do. In fact the kids are so smitten, I've decided to sack the nanny. From now on you can look after them all by yourself. Now isn't that just the most wonderful surprise?'

'That's it,' she said flatly. 'The wedding's off.'

The brunette, who had been staring at Guy, snapped her fingers. 'I know who you are. You're Guy Cassidy, the photographer.' Her eyes widened. 'You're famous.'

'Doesn't stop him being a cheapskate double-crossing toad,' Janey snapped.

'Guy Cassidy?' said Alexander, deeply impressed. '*The* Guy Cassidy? Of course you are! Hey, it's really nice to meet you.'

'I don't believe I'm hearing this.' Janey glared at Alexander. 'You've just told me not to marry him and now you're fawning all over him like some kind of groupie!'

Guy frowned. 'He told you not to marry me? Why ever would he say a thing like that? Janey, you're making it up.'

'Look, I'm sorry.' Alexander shook his head. 'I didn't know it was you.'

'Too late,' declared Janey, prising Guy's hand from her arm. 'I wouldn't marry him now if he was Mel Gibson.'

# Chapter 36

'And I thought Maxine was the actress.' He caught up with her by the win-a-goldfish stall, where Ella and Josh were engrossed in the task of flipping rubber frogs on to lily pads. 'Carry on like that and you'll end up starring in toilet-roll commercials.'

Janey grinned. The expression on Alexander's face had been superb. It was a shame Guy couldn't have captured it on film.

'You started it.'

'Couldn't resist it. My God, when I heard what he was saying to you; no wonder you're wary of men.' He shook his head in disbelief. 'I must say, you certainly know some extraordinary people.'

At least he didn't know how she'd met Alexander, Janey thought with some relief. He'd already caught her out once, and that was enough.

'My *bloody* frogs keep falling in the water!' complained Ella, unaware of Guy behind her.

He tapped her on the shoulder.

'Oh, sorry Daddy.' She gave him an angelic, gap-toothed smile.

'Good.' Guy winked at Janey. 'Because we don't

want any bloody goldfish anyway.'

'My feet ache,' said Janey as they made their way back to the car two hours later.

Josh and Ella, clutching helium balloons, armfuls of Day-Glo furry toys and an inflatable giant squid, were running on ahead, the squid's pink plastic tentacles wrapping themselves around Ella's legs as she struggled to keep up with Josh.

'My wallet aches.' Guy gave her a rueful look. 'I'm financially destitute. And all because my daughter fell in love with a squid.'

'And you didn't enjoy trying to win it?' Janey mocked. 'Come on, you loved every minute on that rifle range.'

'I would have loved it even more if the sights hadn't been ninety degrees out. Fifteen quid for a squid,' he groaned. 'And what's the betting that by tomorrow morning it'll have a puncture.'

'Stop complaining. You've had a wonderful time.'

'OK, so maybe I have.' He grinned. The next moment, he grabbed her arm and pulled her towards him, so abruptly that Janey almost lost her footing.

'Wha—'

'Sorry, dog shit on the pavement,' said Guy romantically. 'You almost stepped in it.'

'My hero,' Janey murmured, because although she had regained her balance he hadn't released his hold on her. If she moved away she would feel silly – it was hardly the romantic gesture of the decade, after all – but at the same time she couldn't help wondering what Josh and Ella would make of it if they should choose this moment to turn round. Why, she thought with some embarrassment, was he doing this? Why wasn't he saying anything? And why didn't he just let go?

Guy was deep in thought. He wasn't normally slow off the mark but something had just occurred to him, something quite unexpected, and it needed some serious thinking about.

The big stumbling block, he now realized, had been the fact that Janey's unfortunate past had rendered her so totally off-limits from the start. With a history like hers, the last thing she needed was the kind of involvement which could only bring more pain. And when you were a man with a history like his, thought Guy grimly, it was easier simply to steer clear. As he'd told her himself only days earlier, his relationships had a habit of coming to grief. He didn't do it deliberately but it happened anyway. He always seemed to be the one at fault. And it was always the other person who got hurt.

But although he hadn't even allowed the possibility to cross his mind before, Guy now acknowledged the fact that he had been deluding himself. Throughout the past week he'd been telling himself what a great nanny Janey was. In truth, he realized, it was the simple fact of her being there that had been great.

One of the major points in her favour, however, was also one of the major drawbacks, and it was something else with which he was woefully unfamiliar. Janey didn't flirt, and he didn't know if that was because she simply wasn't a flirtatious person, or if it meant she didn't find him worth flirting with. Consequently, he had no idea whether or not she was even faintly attracted to him. Their relationship up until now had been entirely platonic. Over the months – and not without the occasional hiccup along the way – a friendship had been forged. Aside from that, he just didn't know how Janey felt about him.

And all of a sudden it mattered terribly. The idea that she might not return his feelings was galling to say the least. It wasn't the kind of problem he'd ever had to deal with before; he wanted Janey to like him, but how on earth was he going to find out if she did?

Belatedly, Guy realised he was still holding on to her arm. Now he felt plain stupid. Should he carry on and see if she objected, or oh-so-casually let go? It was the kind of dilemma more normally faced by teenagers.

It was his own daughter who came to the rescue. Ella, struggling to disentangle her legs from the tentacles of the squid, slipped off the kerb and landed, with a piercing shriek, flat on her face in the gutter.

She was shaken but not hurt. As he lifted her to her feet and brushed a couple of dry leaves from her white-blond hair, Guy was reminded of his first meeting with Véronique, in another gutter all those years ago. She hadn't flirted with him either, he recalled; she had simply been herself, take it or leave it, and allowed him to make all the running. Falling in love with her had happened so fast, and had been so easy, he would never have believed at the time that waiting for it to happen again could take so long. But finding someone else to fall in love with, he reflected ruefully, hadn't been easy at all.

'You're all right,' said Janey, wiping a lone tear from Ella's cheek with her knuckle. 'No damage, sweetheart. The squid broke your fall.'

'He's hissing.' Ella stopped crying in order to listen. 'I

can hear him making a funny noise.'

'That's because he's a hero,' Janey replied gravely. 'He saved you from being hurt, and punctured a tentacle in the process. Don't worry, we'll stick a plaster on it when we get home.'

By the time they reached the car, Guy had come to a decision. He didn't want to risk rocking the boat whilst Janey was looking after the children. But Maxine would be back on Sunday, and it would be perfectly in order for him to take Janey out to dinner on Sunday night by way of thanking her for having stepped into the breach. This meant he had two days in which to plan what he was going to say . . .

The traffic was nose to tail along the high street where the fair had set up, so he took a left into the road which would take them past Janey's shop and up out of the town. He would take her somewhere really special on Sunday, he decided; maybe the new restaurant in Zennor that everyone was talking about. Would vintage champagne impress or alarm her? Should he take the car or would a cab be better? Or how about flying to Paris, would she think he was being flash? Was that too over-the-top for—?

'Stop!' shrieked Janey. 'Oh my God, stop the car!'

So wrapped up in his own thoughts that for a fraction of a second it seemed as if she had read his mind, Guy slammed on the brakes and screeched to a halt at the side of the road. Janey, white-faced, was staring back at the darkened shop. Guy followed her gaze; something was evidently wrong but he didn't know what. The windows were still intact, the door hadn't been smashed down, the building wasn't going up in flames . . .

'What is it?'

He put out his hand but she was already struggling out of her seatbelt, still staring and apparently unable to speak. As she fumbled for the door handle he saw how violently her hands were shaking.

'Janey, what's the matter?' He spoke more sharply than he had intended. In the back seat, Josh and Ella were craning their necks in order to see what was going on.

'Is it a burglar?' Josh sounded excited. He had glimpsed a figure sitting in the shadows of the recessed entrance to the shop, but burglars, he felt, didn't usually stop for a rest.

'It isn't a burglar.' Janey's voice sounded odd, as if she hadn't used it for a long time. The handle of the passenger door having defeated her, she said numbly, 'Can you open this for me please?'

'Who is it?' Guy had already figured it out for himself but he asked the question anyway.

'My husband. Alan. It's . . . my husband.'

She was evidently in a state of deep shock. Guy hesitated, wondering what he should do. At this moment he doubted whether Janey could even stand upright, let alone cross the road unaided.

He was also seized, quite abruptly, with the almost overwhelming urge to cross the road himself and batter Alan Sinclair to a pulp. Because he wasn't dead, he'd never been dead, and he had no right to put Janey through two years of hell and still have the nerve to be alive.

'Why don't you wait here?' He spoke in soothing tones,

as if she were a child. 'Just stay in the car and let me speak to him.'

But Janey turned to stare at him as if he had gone irredeemably mad. '*What*?'

Josh and Ella, in the back seat, listened in dumbstruck silence.

'I said, let me just—'

'I heard you,' she replied through gritted teeth. 'And I can't believe you have the bloody nerve to even think of such a thing. If you saw your wife, Guy, what would you do? Sit in the car and let *me* go and have a word with her?'

As a counter-attack it was horribly below the belt, but Janey didn't even stop to consider what she was saying.

'Véronique is dead,' Guy murmured. 'Your husband is alive.'

'Of course he's alive,' shrieked Janey, almost beside herself with rage. 'That's why I'd quite like to see him, you stupid bastard, except that I can't bloody see him because you won't switch off the stupid child-lock on this stupid bloody door!'

He flicked the switch.

'There. Janey, all I'm saying is be careful. Ask yourself why he left and why he's decided to come back.'

But it was too late. She was already out of the car.

'Oh Dad!' wailed Ella, as he put the car into gear. 'This is exciting! Can't we stay and watch?'

'No.' Guy's jaw was set, the expression in his eyes unreadable. 'We can't.'

# Chapter 37

'My God, I don't believe it,' sighed Maxine. 'What is this, some kind of sick joke? Did they move April Fool's day?'

Bruno put his hand out to steady her glass, which was tilting alarmingly.

'Careful,' he said, at the same time admiring her cleavage. 'Didn't you read the government health warning on the bottle? Red wine on a white dress can seriously damage your night.'

The dress, which had cost a scary amount of money, was an Azzedine Alaia. Moreover, it belonged to Cindy, who had threatened her with certain death if anything untoward happened to it. Mindful of the warning, Maxine placed the glass on a table out of harm's way.

'My night's already been damaged,' she said rudely. 'What the hell are you doing here?'

Bruno grinned. 'Just one of those fateful coincidences, I suppose. Jamie Laing's an old friend of mine. When he called last week and invited me to the party I didn't even think I'd be able to get up here, but my new assistant manager was keen to work this weekend, so . . .' He shrugged and gestured around the room. 'It seemed like a nice idea. Now why don't I ask how you came to be invited to this party? Or maybe it isn't a coincidence at all. Maybe you're following me.'

'Oh, absolutely,' declared Maxine, the words dripping sarcasm. But the urge to show off was simply irresistible. Glimpsing a semi-familiar face in the crowd, she waved over Bruno's shoulder, realizing too late that the face belonged to an actor whom she had only seen on television. At least Bruno hadn't witnessed the actor's blank stare. 'Sorry, so many old friends,' she said airily. 'Me? Oh, Jamie's a darling, isn't he? I've been up here all week, shooting a commercial with him. It's all gone wonderfully well, he's predicting great things for me if I decide to give the acting business another go.'

'So you'd leave Trezale?' Bruno, equally unable to resist putting her down, looked sympathetic. 'Oh dear, you mean persuading Guy Cassidy that you were the woman of his dreams didn't work out? Must have been a bit of a kick in the teeth for you.'

'A kick in the teeth for *me*?' Maxine gave him a condescending smile. 'Bruno, men like you are the reason women like me wear stiletto heels. Is being obnoxious a hobby of yours, or are you just particularly miffed because I turned down your own touching little offer of a quickie in the back seat of your car?'

She was wonderful, he thought, filled with silent admiration. He adored almost everything about Maxine Vaughan, from those fabulous bare shoulders right down to that pair of ridiculously high heels. But if the body was terrific, the mind was even more entrancing. She could trade insults like no female he had ever met before, she was sharp and funny, a talented liar, and out for everything she could possibly get. They were alike in every way. Best of all, he thought with a barely suppressed smile, she was as mad about him as he was about her.

'I wasn't miffed,' he replied easily, leaning against the wall and running his fingers carelessly through his hair. The emerald-green wallpaper matched his eyes and offset his deep purple jacket to perfection. 'You were being loyal to your sister; an admirable quality in any girl, but especially you.'

He thought he looked so great, thought Maxine, with all that streaky blond hair and that toffee-brown tan. He was only resting against the wall because the colour of it went so well with his jacket. And he had some nerve, too; you had to be unbelievably un-gay in order to get away with wearing a jacket like that over an ochre tee-shirt and pale yellow trousers. She was only surprised it wasn't smothered in bloody sequins . . .

'I told Janey she should never have got involved with you,' she declared, ignoring the last jibe. 'I knew exactly what would happen and I was right. Tell me, does it give you some kind of thrill, finding some vulnerable female and tearing her to pieces like that?'

'I didn't actually set out to hurt her,' Bruno protested with a good-humoured shake of his head. 'Believe it or not Janey couldn't accept the way I am, that was all.'

'You mean she couldn't accept the fact that you're such a bastard?' There was derision in Maxine's eyes. 'Or that you deliberately humiliated her in front of two hundred people at your stinking rotten party?'

'Maybe I went a bit far.' Despite the admission, Bruno

was still smiling. 'But she started it. All I did was retaliate and she didn't even fight back. Let's face it, Janey's too nice.' He shrugged. 'We really weren't suited at all.'

'You can say that again.'

'Ah well, these things happen. I suppose she hates me now.'

Cindy, who had appeared behind Bruno, was wriggling her eyebrows in a gesture of deepest appreciation. Maxine, pretending she hadn't noticed, snapped, 'You can definitely say that again.'

'Good.' He glanced over his shoulder, winked at Cindy, then returned his attention to Maxine. 'So loyalty is no longer an issue. You can stop pretending, sweetheart. We just take it from here.'

As he said the words he moved closer, lowering his voice accordingly. For something to do, Maxine reached for her drink and took a great slug of red wine. The glass remained in her hand, between them, on a level with Bruno's trousers.

'Armani versus Alaia,' he observed in conversational tones. 'We're talking serious money.'

'You think you're so irresistible,' Maxine drawled. 'Don't you?'

'Not at all.' Bruno removed the glass from her hand, drained it and put it out of reach. 'I'm just honest. Maxine, I admire you enormously for your loyalty towards your sister, but it's different now. You can relax. We're both three hundred miles from home. Janey hates me. As far as I'm concerned, you are the most delectable female I've ever known and as far as you're concerned, you fancy me rotten. So why don't we stop playing games and simply admit how we feel about each other? OK,' he conceded, 'so it's a massive coincidence, but since we're both here in London at the same party, why waste time? Why don't we just take advantage of the situation and enjoy it?'

Coincidence had had precious little to do with it, other than the fact that Jamie Laing really was a friend of Bruno's. Upon hearing from his new waitress that according to her son – who attended the same school as Josh Cassidy – Josh's nanny was doing a TV commercial with someone called Jamie, all it had taken was a phone call. He had practically invited himself along to the end-of-ad party at Jamie's elegant, three-storey Chelsea home. His appearance there tonight might have caught Maxine off-guard but he had been rehearsing these lines for days.

Maxine fixed him with an unswerving gaze. Beneath a great deal of gold eyeshadow and at least three coats of mascara, her dark eyes were serious.

'You really think,' she said, very slowly, 'I fancy you rotten?'

'I don't think.' Bruno gave her a modest smile. 'It's a fact.'

'Shit!' howled Maxine. 'That is just so unfair. How could you possible *know*?'

The fact that she was wearing those ludicrous high heels didn't bother Bruno in the least; he didn't care that at this moment she was a couple of inches taller than him. Leaning across, he kissed her very lightly on the mouth.

'I'm an expert,' he said, then broke into a grin. 'But even if I hadn't been, I would still have known. It was obvious from the start, angel. You might be able to act but even you aren't that good.'

This was unbelievable. Talk about one-upmanship, thought Maxine, torn between admiration for such a talent and annoyance because if there was one thing she couldn't stand, it was being seen through. And she had thought she'd done so well, too. Damn, damn, damn!

'You don't even know me.' She looked cross. 'Not properly, anyway.'

'Don't sulk,' Bruno chided. 'And of course I know you, as well as I know myself. I told you before, we're alike. I've never met anyone as much like me before in my life. That was why it was so easy. Looking at you is like looking into a mirror.'

'Except I wear more make-up.' Hopelessly unprepared for such a turn of events, Maxine resorted to flippancy. It gave her time to think.

But she had reckoned without his ability to read minds.

'You're also more nervous,' Bruno replied, sliding his arm around her waist. 'And there's no need to be. Stop trying to analyse it, sweetheart. It's happened, whether you like it or not. Some things are just out of our control. All we have to do now is enjoy it.'

He was breathtakingly self-confident. Maxine decided with some regret that he was also right.

'Has it even occurred to you that I might say no?' she asked, because it went against the grain to be too much of a pushover.

Bruno grinned. 'What would be the point? We both know you're going to say yes.'

Everything seemed to be happening in ultra-slow motion.

Just crossing the street was like climbing Everest. Janey, dimly aware of Guy's Mercedes accelerating away behind her, felt the muscles in her legs contract with each step. She listened to the sound of her own uneven breathing and she saw the figure in the shop doorway turn in her direction, tilting his head in that achingly familiar way.

Still numb with shock, she tried to formulate some kind of plan. It was so strange, she had no idea what she was going to say. All she could think of was the fact that her hands were cold. Alan had always hated being touched by cold hands. If she touched him, would he wince and draw away? Should she just keep her hands jammed in her pockets? God, was this really happening?

'Janey.'

It had taken forever but somehow she had made it across the street. Her heart was pounding in her ears and she still couldn't speak but to Janey's immense relief she didn't need to because Alan was saying it all for her, pulling her into his arms and hugging her so tightly she could hardly breathe. Over and over again, as he covered her face with kisses, he murmured 'Janey, oh Janey, I've missed you so much . . . you don't know how long I've dreamt of this day.'

'You're alive,' she murmured finally, touching his face as if to prove it beyond all doubt. His cheek was warm and her hands were cold but he didn't flinch away. She had almost forgotten how good-looking he was. The sun-bleached hair was shorter; the face, confusingly, looked both older and younger and a new, pale scar bisected his left eyebrow. But the eyes, light blue and fringed with long lashes, were as clear as they had always been. They, at least, were unchanged. The eyes, and that hypnotically reassuring voice . . .

'Oh my poor darling,' Alan whispered tenderly, taking her icy fingers and pressing them to his lips. 'Don't say that; I can't bear to imagine what I must have put you through. All I can say is that at the time I thought I was making the right decision for both of us. The trouble was,' he went on, breaking into a sad smile, 'no matter what I did or how hard I tried, and God knows I tried, I could never stop loving you.'

# Chapter 38

Stupidly, she had almost forgotten that the flat had been Alan's home too. It seemed odd, watching him walk into the kitchen and know without having to ask where things were.

'It should be champagne, of course,' he said cheerfully, uncapping the half-empty bottle of cooking brandy that was all Janey had in the way of something to drink, 'but you look as if you could do with warming up, so . . . cheers.'

He had filled her balloon glass almost to the brim. With a trembling hand Janey raised it to her lips and gulped down several eye-watering mouthfuls, willing it to have some kind of effect on her numbed brain. She had fantasized over this scene a thousand times, her fevered imagination running riot as she covered every possible eventuality. It had never even crossed her mind that she might be so lost for words she would barely be able to say anything at all.

There were still too many questions to be answered. Alan had disappeared from her life and she didn't know why. Now he was back and she was still none the wiser. The brandy, however, was beginning to make its presence known; she could feel that much, at least.

'Sit down,' she said haltingly, when Alan had switched on the gas fire and paused to admire the new painting above the mantelpiece. 'You'd better explain everything. Right from the start. I need to know why you did it.'

She had chosen the armchair for herself. Alan sat on the sofa opposite, nursing his drink and looking contrite.

'I want you to know, Janey, that I'm desperately ashamed of myself. I took the coward's way out, I realize that now, but it really didn't seem like that at the time. I was under pressure, confused, I couldn't figure out any other way of going about it without causing you even more pain.'

As far as Janey was concerned, even more pain was a physical impossibility. She had hit the threshold and stayed there, trapped like a bluebottle stuck to flypaper.

'Go on,' she said briefly, her eyes clouded with the unbearable memories of those first months. 'What are you trying to tell me, that you'd met someone else?'

'No!' He looked appalled. 'Janey, absolutely not. Oh God, is that what you thought?'

Impatience began to stir inside her. 'I didn't know what to think,' she replied evenly. 'I tried everything, but there were never any answers. And you weren't there to ask.'

Alan had known this wasn't going to be easy. He shook his head and tried again. 'I know, and it was all my fault. What's the expression? Be careful what you wish for, because you may get it.'

Janey stared at him.

'Don't look at me like that, sweetheart, please. The truth is, I loved you too much. You were what I wished for, and I got you.' He hesitated for a second, then went on, 'And it scared the hell out of me. It became a kind of obsession, you see; I managed to convince myself that sooner or later you would fall out of love with me. It's a terrible feeling, Janey, to think you aren't good enough for your own wife. It was all right for you; you knew how much you meant to me, but all I felt was more and more insecure. Every single morning I'd wake up and ask myself whether this would be the day you'd decide you'd had enough of being married. To someone,' he concluded brokenly, 'who didn't deserve you.'

He'd stopped speaking. It was Janey's turn. Her glass was empty and she'd almost forgotten how to breathe.

'But that's crazy,' she managed to say, her voice barely above a whisper. Of all the possible reasons she had come up with, this was one she had never for a moment even considered. 'We were married, we were happy together.'

'Yes, it was crazy.' Alan nodded, his expression regretful. 'I know that now, but at the time I think I was a little bit crazy myself. It was a kind of self-torture, and I couldn't break the cycle. The more I thought about it, the more real it became. And the fact that you seemed happy no longer counted for anything, because I'd convinced myself that you were only putting on some elaborate act for my benefit. You read about it all the time in the papers; it happens every day, for God's sake. Perfect couples with apparently perfect marriages, except they aren't perfect at all. Suddenly, out of the blue, the wife or husband says they can't stand it any more; they hire a hit-man or simply up and leave with their secret lover. Janey, it got so bad I had to get away. I didn't want to go, but it seemed like the only option left to me. You have to try and understand, sweetheart. I was desperate.'

Wordlessly, she held out her glass and watched Alan refill it. He still wore Pepe jeans, still moved with that same casual, confident grace. He had always exuded such an air of confidence; how could she possibly have known that beneath the surface lurked a maelstrom of insecurity and self-doubt?

The brandy was no longer lacerating her throat. This time it slipped down like warm honey. 'You should have asked me,' she said, tears prickling the back of her eyes. 'If you'd told me how you felt, I could have—'

'I didn't want to hear it,' Alan interjected, his own eyes filled with pain. 'Don't you see, Janey? If you'd reassured me, I would only have convinced myself you were lying. And that would have been almost as unbearable as hearing you say you didn't love me.'

'Oh God.' With a trembling hand, Janey covered her face. What he was telling her made an awful kind of sense. Such paranoid beliefs, once they took a hold, made reassurance impossible. 'You should have gone to see a doctor.'

'I did. After I'd, um, left.' Alan gave her a crooked half-smile. 'And a world of good that did me, too. He said that, in his experience, any man who harboured suspicions about his wife most probably had every right to do so. Then he told me that his own wife had walked out on him three weeks earlier and it wasn't until she'd gone that he found out she'd been having an affair with their dentist for the past five years.'

'I wasn't having an affair,' said Janey, her voice

beginning to break. 'I would never have done anything like that. Never.'

'Yes, well.' He dismissed the protest with a shrug. 'You can understand it didn't help.'

Janey could understand that such a bloody useless doctor should be struck off the medical register. She shuddered at the thought of the damage he might have inflicted on countless innocent people.

'Are you still cold?' Alan patted the empty cushion on the settee. 'Why don't you come over here, sweetheart? Sit by me.'

But Janey needed to hear everything first. There were nearly two whole years separating them, two blank years in which anything might have happened. She couldn't relax until she knew it all. She also needed more brandy . . .

'Where did you go?' she pleaded, suddenly desperate to get it over with. 'Where have you been living? What have you been doing?'

His smile was bleak. 'Existing. Trying to stop loving you. Telling myself a million times that I'd been a complete fool who'd made the worst mistake of his life, but that it was too late to go back.' He stopped for a second, gazing into space and swallowing hard. 'I'm sorry, Janey. Here I go again, moaning on about my own stupid feelings when what you want to hear are the facts. OK, well they aren't exactly riveting but here goes. I hitch-hiked to Edinburgh, did a bit of bar work, got myself a filthy little bed-sitter and spent most of my spare time shaking cockroaches out of the duvet. After a few months, when I couldn't stand the place a moment longer, I travelled down to

Manchester. That was just as awful, but the customers had different accents and at least the pub employed bouncers to break up the fights, instead of expecting me to tackle them myself.'

Janey shuddered. 'That scar on your forehead . . .?'

'A bloody great Scotsman with fourteen pints of lager inside him and a broken bottle in each fist.' He touched the scar as if to remind himself. 'I was lucky. One of the other barmen almost died.'

Janey bit her lower lip. Alan could have died. She had thought he was dead . . .

'Go on. How long were you in Manchester?'

He thought for a moment. 'Three, four months? Then I moved down to London. Another lousy bed-sit, another family of cockroaches to get to know. I did some casual work here and there when I could get it, but it was pretty much of a hand-to-mouth existence. Not to mention lonely.'

'But you must have met people, made new friends?'

'I didn't want to,' he replied simply. 'I didn't think I deserved any. Unless I was working, there were times when I didn't even speak to a soul for days on end. London's like that; you can almost begin to believe you no longer exist.'

'Girlfriends?' said Janey, needing to know. It had been almost two years, after all.

But Alan smiled and shook his head. 'Hadn't I suffered enough? Janey, my feelings for you were what got me into this mess in the first place. I was hardly going to risk it again, was I? Besides,' he added sadly, 'I was still in love with you. I didn't want anyone else. And even if I had, it would have been too much of a betrayal.'

'And now you're back.' Janey still felt as if she were in suspended animation. It was a curious feeling, like one of those near-death experiences people reported, when they hovered on the ceiling and gazed down at their own lifeless bodies. She had no idea of the time, no conception of what she might say or do next. It was as if all this were happening to somebody else.

Alan nodded. Again, the hesitant half-smile. 'I'm back.'

'Why?'

He took a deep breath. 'Please let me get it all out in one go. Wait until I've finished before you say anything. I haven't been able to stop loving you, Janey. I tried, but it didn't work. I've no idea how you feel about me, now. I don't know, maybe you've put the past behind you, met someone else and forgotten you even knew me . . . but I had to find out. I need to know if you do still care for me. And if you can ever forgive me. I have to know whether there's a chance for us to carry on as we were before. As husband and wife.'

He looked so unsure of himself, so scared of what she might say. Only sheer desperation had given him the strength to admit his own weakness and declare his feelings for her with such heart-wrenching honesty. And he had always been the stronger partner in the past, thought Janey, so seemingly secure and laid-back with his devil-may-care attitudes and freewheeling lifestyle.

But he hadn't been secure at all, she realized; he had needed her, more than she had ever imagined. He hadn't abandoned her for another woman, either. Nor had he ever stopped loving her. And now he needed understanding, love and forgiveness in return.

It's like a dream come true, Janey realized hazily. Tears were beginning to roll down her cheeks and she thought how stupid, to cry now. This is the happiest night of my life.

'Of course we can carry on,' she said, rising unsteadily to her feet. The tears fell faster as Alan came towards her, his expression one of joy mingled with relief.

'You don't know how much this means to me,' he murmured, his mouth grazing her wet cheek. 'I wouldn't have been able to bear it if you'd said no. The scariest part was not knowing whether you'd met someone else.'

Janey, breathing in the wonderful familiarity of him, closed her eyes. 'There's no one else,' she whispered, stroking his hair and revelling in the sensation of his warm hands against her back. 'There's never been anybody else. Only you.'

# Chapter 39

'Oh good!' said Maxine, when Cindy finally picked up the phone. 'You're there.'

'It's four o'clock in the morning,' Cindy replied in arch tones. 'Of course I'm here. The question is, where are you? More to the point, who is that man lying stark naked in the bed next to you?'

Maxine grinned. 'That's two questions.'

'And that's no answer,' said Cindy briskly. 'Besides, I haven't finished yet. You were seen tiptoeing away from the party at midnight, sweetie, and that was four long hours ago. The thing is, what on earth could you possibly have been doing since then that's kept you so busy you couldn't call your oldest and dearest friend to let her know about it?'

'Gosh.' Maxine sounded deeply impressed. 'You mean you were worried about me?'

'Worried? Of course I wasn't worried. I was jealous!' Abandoning all self-control, Cindy screeched down the phone. 'So stop buggering about and tell me who he is before I explode!'

'OK, OK,' sighed Maxine. 'His name's Jim Berenger and he's an actor. We're here at his flat in Belsize Park and I just rang to let you know that I'll be back tomorrow morning. Well, this morning,' she amended, glancing up at the clock. 'If you're good, I'll give you all the girly gossip then.'

Cindy was still screaming, 'Oh my God, is he spectacular in bed?' when Bruno leaned across and seized the phone.

'Hi,' he said, lying back against the pillows and daring Maxine to stop him. 'Actually, my name is Bruno Parry-Brent; I'm a restaurateur and we're in my hotel room at the Royal Lancaster. And yes, since you ask, I am most definitely spectacular in b—'

'Stop it!' hissed Maxine. Struggling to her knees, she wrenched the receiver back from him and slammed it down, cutting Cindy off in mid-shriek. 'How could you do that?'

'Relax darling.' Effortlessly, Bruno fended her off. 'We have nothing to hide. We're going legit.'

'I don't want to go legit,' Maxine howled. 'This is a one-off, an aberration, a never-to-be-repeated—'

'It's been a two-off already,' Bruno reminded her, his green eyes glittering with amusement as he surveyed her in all her naked glory. 'Play your cards right and we can make it three.'

'Bastard.' She threw a pillow at his head.

'And it isn't an aberration, either. I thought it was rather nice.'

'This is stupid, cried Maxine, wrapping a sheet around herself and debating whether to risk tipping the contents of the ice bucket over him. Somehow, she didn't quite dare. The prospect of retaliation was too awful. 'Cindy's the biggest gossip in the world, she's got a mouth like a megaphone . . . and you think it's funny!'

'Not at all. I'm quite serious.'

'So am I bloody serious.' Maxine looked fierce. 'I have a sister who will probably never speak to me again if she ever hears about this. Even more to the point,' she added heavily, 'you have Nina.'

Bruno said nothing for a while. No longer smiling, he studied Maxine's face for several seconds, his own expression oddly intense. Then, reaching out, he traced the line of her cheek with a warm forefinger.

'I told you I was serious,' he said eventually. 'This is it, Max. We were always meant to be together. I love you.' He paused, then added, 'I'm going to leave Nina.'

'Go on,' persisted Bruno, pinning Maxine down on the bed and expertly avoiding her flailing limbs. 'Say it. You won't get any breakfast until you do.'

The tray was outside the door, tantalizingly out of reach. Maxine, who was starving, made another hopeless bid for freedom before falling back, exhausted, against the pillows. She ached too much to put up a decent fight and it was all Bruno's fault. He was the most insatiable man she had ever known.

'Say what?'

'Tell me that you love me.' He enunciated the words slowly and clearly, as if addressing a dim child.

Maxine's brown eyes narrowed. 'Why?'

'Because I've said I love you, and it's only fair. And if you don't,' he added with an air of triumph, 'well, no breakfast. I shall just have to seduce you all over again.'

Desperate to eat, Maxine said in a small voice, 'I love you.'

'Louder.'

'I love you.'

'Come on, don't be shy,' Bruno persisted. 'Much louder than that.'

She sighed. Then, at the top of her voice, screamed, 'I LOVE YOU!'

'Tell us something we don't know,' came the shouted reply from the room adjoining theirs. 'You've been proving it all bloody night. Bloody honeymooners!'

Maxine burst out laughing.

'Honeymooners,' Bruno mused. 'Now there's an idea.'

'I think you have to be married to come into that category.' Still grinning, Maxine ruffled her hair and glanced at her reflection in the mirror. Not bad, considering the excesses of the past nine hours. Thank goodness for smudge-proof mascara.

But Bruno was giving her an odd look. For the first time he no longer seemed entirely sure of himself. 'That's what I mean.'

'Oh,' she mocked. 'So now you think we should get married?'

'That's exactly what I mean.'

Maxine's eyebrows shot up. The next moment she started to laugh once more, so uncontrollably that the bed shook.

'Don't do that,' Bruno retaliated crossly. Jesus, would she ever take anything he said at face value? 'I'm serious.'

It was a while before she could manage to speak again. 'Oh please! Bruno, you just aren't the marrying kind.'

He looked offended. 'Nobody is, until they meet the person they want to marry. Think about it, Max, you and me, together.'

'How can I think about it?' she gurgled. 'It's the most ridiculous idea I ever heard. Look at our track records; we were born to cheat! Can you imagine the chaos it would cause if we ever tried to stay faithful to each other?'

He watched her fling back the bedclothes, and make her way to the door. Naked, she briefly checked that the coast was clear before reaching for the breakfast tray.

'But that's just it,' Bruno protested, meaning every word and willing her to take him seriously. 'We're the same, so we understand each other. God, you're such a pig,' he added, as Maxine tore into a croissant. Within seconds it was gone and she was starting on the toast, slathering it with butter and honey and sprinkling brown sugar on top before stuffing it greedily into her mouth.

'There, you see?' she countered between mouthfuls. 'You're going off me already.'

He watched her set to work on the second slice; she looked like a bricklayer on speed, and the butter was going on thicker than cement. It didn't stop him loving her, but it was a miracle she wasn't the size of a Sherman tank.

'I'm a restaurateur,' he reminded her. 'I like to see people enjoying their food, not shovelling it down like porridge.'

'I am enjoying it.' With immense satisfaction, Maxine licked her fingers one by one. Then, with a determined smile she added, 'And there's another good reason why you can't leave Nina. You love that restaurant. Imagine how she'd react if you told her about us – she'd have you out of there like a shot.' She fired an imaginary pistol into the air for emphasis. 'Boom. And then what would you be? An ex-restaurateur.'

Bruno shrugged. It wasn't a welcome forecast, but it was fairly accurate, given the circumstances. The restaurant belonged to Nina; giving her up would mean giving up his livelihood. Until now, such an action had been unthinkable.

It was a measure of his feelings towards Maxine that it no longer even seemed to matter. 'Sacrifices have to be made,' he said lightly. 'I can always get another job. The lifestyle may take a bit of a dive, but . . . well, I happen to think you're worth it.'

'Don't.' Maxine felt suddenly afraid. This was so unlike Bruno, so totally out of character for him. 'In five minutes you could be telling me it's all a joke.'

But when Bruno reached for her, the expression in his eyes was deadly serious. 'No joke. I've waited nearly twenty years for this. I don't even know if I like it, yet. I love you more than you love me, and that makes me the vulnerable one. This has never happened to me before.'

More moved than she dared admit, Maxine said briskly, 'Evidently not. Rule number one is never tell people you love them more than they love you. It's asking to get kicked in the teeth.'

'I know.' Bruno kissed her collarbone. 'But it's the only way I can think of to convince you I'm not bullshitting.'

A shudder of sheer longing snaked its way down her spine. 'OK,' she said simply. 'I believe you. But it still isn't going to be easy.'

'And I'm going to be poor. Well,' he amended with a forced smile, 'relatively poor, anyway. Is that a major problem for you?'

To her absolute horror, Maxine realized she was in danger of bursting into tears. Staring hard at the tops of the trees outlined against a pale grey sky, which was all she could see from their third-floor window overlooking Hyde Park, she willed the lump in her throat to subside. Nobody made her cry and got away with it. Least of all, she thought crossly, a bloody man.

But Bruno, misinterpreting her silence, was growing impatient. 'Is it?' he persisted. 'Are you only interested in men with money? Is that what you're trying to tell me?'

Maxine hit him with a pillow.

'You bastard,' she howled. 'What do you think I am, some kind of bimbo gold-digger? How dare you!'

'Ouch.' Bruno dodged out of reach as she lunged at him again. Overcome with relief, he broke into a grin. 'Look, I wasn't accusing, I was asking. And it's a perfectly reasonable question, anyway. Lots of people are attracted to money. What about that ex-fiancé of yours?' he added in ultra-reasonable tones. 'Janey told me about him. He was loaded, and you can't tell me you didn't enjoy it.'

Just for a second, Maxine experienced a pang of longing for those lost luxuries. Of course she had loved living in a splendid house, swanning around in smart cars, flashing a diamond ring the size of a beech nut at anyone who came within a two-mile radius, never having to worry about the next gas bill . . . But it hadn't been enough. And, having left that life behind her, she had never even for a moment regretted doing so.

'Oh yes, it was nice,' she said. 'But I gave it all up, didn't I? *And* I gave the engagement ring back to him, in case you were wondering. It cost nine thousand pounds but I still did it.'

'Pity,' murmured Bruno. 'That's one noble gesture you might live to regret.'

'Yes, well.' Maxine couldn't help agreeing with him there, but a girl had to have some scruples. Brown eyes flashing, she said proudly, 'At least it proves I'm not a fortune hunter.'

Unable to resist making the dig, he countered, 'What about Guy Cassidy? Would you have lusted after him if he'd been penniless and unknown?'

'Guy doesn't count,' Maxine declared flatly. 'I wanted to work for him because he could have boosted my career. Not that it did the slightest bit of good,' she grumbled. 'Do you know, in all the time I've been there he hasn't taken so much as a single photograph of me? I'm sure that's out of spite.'

'Don't worry.' Bruno gave her a hug. 'I've got a Kodak Instamatic. I'll take thousands of photos of you.'

'You aren't influential and famous.'

'I'm not rich either.'

She smiled. 'I don't care. Really.'

'So what's the verdict?' Bruno realized that he was holding his breath. There are only a few moments in a lifetime when real decisions have to be made. This was one of those moments. 'Do we give it a whirl?'

Maxine, both exhilarated and afraid, said in a low voice, 'It isn't going to be easy, you know. Being poor is the least of our worries. We're going to upset quite a few people. You have Nina to deal with. I have Janey.'

'What are you,' Bruno demanded, 'a bloody politician? Answer the question, Max. Does that mean yes or no?'

'You idiot.' Fondly she caressed his tanned arm. 'How can you even ask? You saw through me right from the start. You knew I loved you almost before I knew it myself.'

'You're going to have to say it,' he persisted evenly. 'Yes, Maxine? Or—'

'Darling!' she exclaimed, loving him even more for his insecurity and hurling herself into his arms. 'Don't panic! I *am* the original girl who can't say no.'

# Chapter 40

'This is terrible,' said Janey, looking at her watch and seeing that it was almost ten o'clock. 'There are so many things we should be doing. We really ought to get up.'

'What could be more important than this?' Alan, who didn't want to move, kissed the top of her head. 'Making love, catching up on lost time, getting to know one another all over again . . .'

'Phoning the police,' she continued dryly.

'What?'

Janey smiled. 'You're on the missing persons' register. One of us is going to have to let them know you're no longer missing.'

'Oh God.' Alan shuddered. 'You can do that. What do you suppose they'll do . . . come round and rap my knuckles for running away without leaving a note?'

'I haven't the faintest idea, but we still have to phone them.' Janey, wriggling out of reach, slid out of bed and grabbed her dressing gown. 'And Paula's downstairs, running the shop on her own. She doesn't even know I'm up here. If she starts hearing footsteps, she'll think we're burglars.'

'Why?' Alan's eyes narrowed. 'Where does she think

you spend your nights? Come to that,' he added with growing suspicion, 'who were you with last night? That was a pretty smart car you leapt out of. Are you sure there isn't something you aren't telling me?'

Janey hadn't given Guy Cassidy so much as a thought until now. Belatedly she realized that she must have caused him considerable inconvenience. He had been due to fly up to Manchester at seven for a photo session with the much sought-after, deeply temperamental supermodel, Valentina di Angelo. She prayed that in letting him down at such short notice he wouldn't have had to cancel the entire shoot.

'There's nothing to tell,' she said in reassuring tones, still mindful of the unfounded suspicions which had prompted Alan's disappearance in the first place. 'Maxine moved back down here a few months ago and took a nannying job up at Trezale House, but for the past week she's been in London making a TV advert. I offered to look after the children whilst she was away, so I've been staying at the house and Paula's taken over in the shop. Everyone's been doing everyone else's job,' she added cheerfully. 'It's been fun.'

'You always liked children.' Alan's expression grew bleak. 'That was something else that scared me. I knew you wanted a family of your own, but I was afraid you'd love them more than you loved me.'

Janey stared at him, appalled. 'It doesn't work like that.'

'Sometimes it does.' A note of urgency crept into his voice. 'Look, sweetheart. I've come back and we're going to make it work this time, but I still wouldn't be happy if you suddenly announced you were pregnant. So, no little accidents. No "Surprise, surprise, darling, I can't think how it happened, but . . ." announcements. Because that's something I just couldn't handle. OK?'

'No little accidents,' Janey repeated numbly, stunned by the bombshell and by the suddenness with which it had been dropped. She would never have dreamed of intentionally becoming pregnant without Alan's knowledge and approval, but neither would she ever have guessed the strength of his own feelings on the subject. He was evidently deadly serious.

Having got that bit of information off his chest, however, he cheered up and changed the subject.

'So Maxine's been working as a nanny, you say? Heaven help *those* poor kids! What mother in her right mind would employ someone like Maxine, anyway?'

Janey picked up her hairbrush and sat in front of the mirror. 'It isn't a mother, it's a father. A widower.'

'Oh well.' Alan stretched and yawned. 'That explains it. Old or young?'

'Thirtyish.' Janey set about restoring some semblance of normality to her hair. 'Coming up to thirty-five, I think.'

'Really,' he drawled, watching her reflection in the mirror. 'And is he good-looking?'

Janey carried on brushing. 'I suppose so. If you like that sort of thing,' she added, her tone deliberately off-hand.

'And do you like that sort of thing?'

'Stop it.' As she swivelled round to face him, the dressing gown fell open to reveal her bare legs. Her knuckles were white as she gripped the brush. 'Don't try and read something into a perfectly innocent situation. I

341

was doing Maxine a favour, that's all. I'm not interested in Guy and he certainly isn't interested in me.'

'Why not? Is he gay?'

'Of course he isn't gay.' Janey replied wearily. 'He has women coming out of his ears. And he isn't interested in anyone unless they're drop-dead gorgeous, OK? You'd have to have at least half a dozen covers of *Vogue* under your belt before Guy Cassidy would even notice you. Even Maxine didn't qualify, which really pissed her off.'

'Guy Cassidy the photographer? Is that who you're talking about?' Alan sat up and took notice. Evidently impressed, he said, 'And he's the one whose kids you've been looking after?'

Janey nodded. He was also the one she'd been hideously rude to last night. She would have to phone and apologize.

'Oh well, that's all right then.' Alan grinned with relief. 'And there I was, thinking I had a rival on my hands. I see what you mean now about the gorgeous girls. He can have just about anyone he wants.'

And although it was undoubtedly true, Janey couldn't help feeling a bit miffed. Having allayed Alan's suspicions, she now had to bite her tongue in order not to blurt out: 'Yes, but he held my hand last night, and he kissed me . . .'

But that would be childish and it had only been a jokey kiss anyway, not a real one. Instead, feeling very second-best, she said lightly, 'Of course he can have anyone he wants. So he's hardly likely to be interested in me, is he?'

'Exactly.' Nodding in vigorous agreement, Alan then leaned over and gave her bare knee a consoling pat. 'Sorry, sweetheart, it isn't very flattering, but you know what I mean. He's had some of the best in the world, lucky sod. I even heard he had a bit of a thing going with that dark-haired model, Serena Charlton. Christ,' he added, rolling his eyes in deep appreciation, 'if that isn't drop-dead gorgeous, I don't know what is.'

Maxine, guiltily in love and desperately confused, wasn't looking forward to the next twenty-four hours.

'I don't know what you're getting so worked up about,' said Bruno, as their train drew into Trezale station. He had insisted they travel back together, and Maxine had grown more and more jittery by the mile. 'It isn't like you. Here, d'you want to finish this?'

She took the lukewarm gin and tonic from him, swallowed and pulled a face. 'The whole thing isn't like me. Look, I may have been involved with married men before, but they were just flings. Nobody's ever done anything as drastic as leaving their wife on my behalf. And even if they'd wanted to, I wouldn't have let them.'

The breathe-if-you-dare Alaia dress had gone back into Cindy's walk-in wardrobe. Now, wearing her own jeans and a striped shirt knotted at the waist, she looked younger and infinitely more vulnerable.

'Relax. Let me take care of Nina.' Bruno grinned. 'And how many times do I have to tell you, anyway? She isn't my wife.'

Maxine gazed gloomily out of the window as the train creaked to a halt. 'That doesn't make me feel any less guilty. It's still going to be horrible.'

'Ah, but I'm worth it.'

She thought of Janey, whose fragile self-confidence was about to be shattered, and of Guy's disdainful reaction to the news. Even people she only vaguely knew were going to disapprove, on principle. But she really did love Bruno, and he loved her. Besides, she no longer appeared to have any choice in the matter.

'You'd better be worth it,' she murmured, rising to her feet and mentally preparing herself for the fray. 'For everyone's sake, you'd better be.'

It was nine o'clock when she let herself into the house. Guy, of all people, was cooking in the kitchen. Highly diverted by the spectacle, Maxine watched him pile burnt oven chips and enormous fillet steaks on to three plates. Ella, cringing at the sight of blood, was wailing, 'Ugh, I hate fillet steak. Why can't we have proper food instead?'

'I like fillet steak!' announced Maxine, from the doorway. 'Is there enough for me? And where's Janey?'

Ella, sensing salvation, ran over and gave her a hug. 'Hooray, you're back. If you cook me some beefburgers you can have my steak. Janey went home after the fair last night. She called Daddy a bastard and jumped out of the car because she wanted to see her husband. Actually, I'd rather have fish fingers than beefburgers but not burnt like the chips. Daddy's a terrible cook. I'm really hungry,' she added boastfully, 'because I've been up in a helicopter to Manchester.'

Where convoluted storytelling was concerned, thought Maxine, Ella could give Ronnie Corbett a run for his money. Thoroughly confused, she turned to Guy. 'I think I need a translator. So what really happened last night?

You and Janey had an argument and she stormed off in a huff?'

Guy threw the frying pan into the sink, which was already overflowing with washing-up. 'Her husband came back.'

'What!' Maxine gazed at him in disbelief. 'You mean Alan? Are you sure?'

'I already said that,' Ella complained. Having rifled the freezer, she now shoved three icy fish fingers into Maxine's unsuspecting hands. 'Why didn't you listen to me? Shall I tell you all about the helicopter while you cook my tea?'

'He's back,' continued Guy evenly. 'I don't know any more than that. We were driving past the shop and he was waiting outside.'

Still stunned, Maxine said, 'So what did you argue about?'

'I told her to be careful, to find out why he'd turned up after all this time.' He shrugged. 'Maybe I wasn't very subtle. It didn't go down well.'

'I still can't believe it.' Maxine sank into the nearest chair. 'My God, that man has a nerve! Poor Janey.'

'Quite. I was going to phone her this evening, but I'm not exactly flavour of the month.' Guy picked up an overdone chip, gazed at it for a second and put it down again. 'Maybe you should do the honours. Make sure everything's all right.'

'How can it be all right?' Maxine, who had never had much time for Alan Sinclair, looked gloomy. 'He's back, isn't he? It's bad news all round, if you ask me.'

But she found herself faced with a moral dilemma. As

the news gradually sank in, it became more and more obvious that since Alan had returned, telling Janey about herself and Bruno was going to be an awful lot easier if Janey was happy. Telling Janey that in her opinion Alan was a no-good, selfish sonofabitch who deserved a boot up the bum, on the other hand, wasn't going to make her very happy at all.

'Haven't you phoned her yet?' Guy, coming into the kitchen at ten-thirty, found her half-heartedly tackling the mountain of washing-up.

'I tried,' fibbed Maxine, who had been putting it off as long as she could. 'No answer. She must be out.'

'Out of her mind.' Guy picked up a Day-Glo pink fluffy rabbit – one of Ella's trophies from last night's trip to the fair – and placed it on the dresser next to a cross-eyed furry pig. 'My God, hasn't he done enough damage already?'

'All this concern,' she said in lightly mocking tones, 'when you don't even know him.'

'I've heard enough. And you aren't exactly his greatest fan yourself.' He gave her a sharp look. 'You were the one who told me what a bastard he was in the first place.'

'I know, but I've been thinking.' Maxine concentrated on the washing-up, scrubbing furiously at Josh's cornflake-encrusted breakfast bowl. 'You know how stubborn Janey can be. If you ask me, the more critical we are of Alan, the more likely she is to dig her heels in and take his side. I really think the best thing we can do is pretend to be pleased he's back. That way, she can

346

make up her own mind, in her own time, without sacrificing her pride.'

Guy nodded in grudging agreement. 'Maybe you're right.'

'Of course I'm right.' That had gone well. Maxine, pleased with herself, said, 'I always am.'

'And it makes things so much easier for you,' he continued smoothly. 'What a happy coincidence.'

Damn. She raised her eyebrows. 'A happy coincidence? Sorry, I'm not with you.'

'I know you aren't,' said Guy. 'You're with Bruno Parry-Brent.'

'Oh.' Maxine gave up. So he had recognized Bruno's car when he'd dropped her off earlier, after all.

*No more deceit*, Bruno had told her. *No need for denials. We're going public.* Well, here goes. She raised her chin in defiance. 'Yes, I'm with Bruno. I wasn't before, when you thought I was. But I am now.'

'Dear God.'

'Is that a problem?'

Guy looked amused. 'I expect so, but at least it isn't mine. One thing I will say, about you and Janey.'

'What?' Maxine bristled, aware of the fact that it wasn't going to be flattering.

He grinned. 'You really do have the most extraordinary taste in men.'

# Chapter 41

In the event, Janey rang the house first.

'Oh, hi. It's me,' she said hesitantly when Guy picked up the phone. 'Look, I know it's late but I wanted to apologise for last night. I said some horrible things and I'm really sorry.'

'No problem.' Guy couldn't help smiling to himself because Janey's idea of horrible things was on a par with Maxine's scathing off-the-cuff one-liners. 'Believe me, I've been called worse.'

'And I let you down,' she continued, clearly racked with guilt. 'I know how important the Manchester trip was, and I feel terrible about it. Were you able to find a babysitter?'

'No.'

'Oh God, I'm sorry.'

'But it didn't matter. The kids came up with me. So if you ever want to be bored rigid for thirty minutes by a seven-year-old describing what it's like to fly in a helicopter,' he added wryly, 'just ask Ella.'

'Really?' Immeasurably relieved, Janey started to laugh. 'I didn't ruin the whole day, then.'

'Well, the pilot may take a while to recover, but all in

all it was a great success.' Guy paused, then said casually, 'And am I allowed to ask how you are? Is everything . . . sorted out?'

'Everything is completely sorted out.' Her voice grew guarded, as if in anticipation of more *Are you sure you know what you're doing?* remarks. With some awkwardness, she went on, 'Look, it's a bit complicated and I can't really explain over the phone, but I understand now why he did what he did. Now he's back and we're giving it another go. Starting afresh. And I know what you're probably thinking, but it's my life, he's my husband, and no, he didn't run off with another woman . . .'

'Sshh,' said Guy, as her voice rose. 'Calm down. You don't have to justify yourself to me. I'm not going to criticise your decision, Janey. I'm hardly in a position to, considering the lousy mistakes I've made over the past few years. Besides,' he added, choosing his words with care, 'it was what you wanted, wasn't it? And now you've got it; a second chance of happiness. For heaven's sake, it's what anyone would want.'

'I know.' Relief was tinged with caution, as if she still couldn't quite believe he wasn't going to put the boot in. 'And I am happy. Look, I have to go now, Alan's coming downstairs. Could you ask Maxine to phone me tomorrow as soon as she gets back from London?'

At that moment Maxine came into the sitting room carrying two cups of tea and a packet of Jaffa cakes.

'Well actually—' said Guy, but Janey wasn't listening.

'And give my love to Josh and Ella,' she continued hurriedly. 'Tell them I'll see them soon. I really must go . . . bye.'

Jill Mansell

'She wants you to phone her tomorrow,' Guy told Maxine, when he had replaced the receiver. 'She thinks you're still in London. She was in a hurry to hang up.'

'And?' Maxine demanded, avid for details. 'What did she say?'

'Not a lot. Just that she understands why he left, and that they're making another go of it.' He shook his head in disbelief. 'Oh yes, and she's happy.'

Considering the almost total lack of interest he'd shown in her own love life, thought Maxine, he was displaying an astonishing amount of concern for Janey's. It really seemed to have got to him. But that, she supposed, was because he knew she was capable of looking after herself. Janey, far less experienced where men were concerned, was a sitting target for unscrupulous males like Alan Sinclair. Why, she had even been hopelessly out of her depth with Bruno, and he was a pussy cat . . .

'I wonder what his excuse was,' she mused, offering Guy a Jaffa cake. 'It must have been spectacular. My God, when you think of the hard time some married men have if they just nip into the pub for a quick drink after work. They get home two hours late and their wives give them merry hell. Yet Alan gets home two *years* late and Janey's thrilled to bits.'

It was certainly ironic. Guy, who had also been giving the matter some thought, said, 'She almost expects to be treated badly. I suppose you get used to it, if all the men you've ever known are bastards.'

'You've said it.' Maxine grinned. 'And then to top it

all, she had to spend a week living here with you. Talk about the final straw.'

'I haven't treated her badly.' He looked offended. 'I was perfectly nice.'

'You!' Maxine choked on a mouthful of Jaffa cake. 'You're never nice!'

'I am when I want to be. It all depends on the company I keep.'

'You're never nice to me.'

'Exactly.' Guy was staring into his cup. 'And is it any wonder? This is the most disgusting tea I've ever drunk in my life.'

Maxine tried hers. 'Oh bum,' she said crossly. 'The sugar isn't sugar. It's salt.'

'I never thought I'd hear myself say this.' He shook his head in mock despair. 'But I'm actually beginning to feel sorry for Bruno Parry-Brent. Does the poor sod have any idea what he's taking on?'

For Bruno, it was a first. Total honesty, not something which had ever featured particularly heavily on his personal agenda before, was what was called for now.

But if it was harder than he'd imagined, it was also necessary. Maxine had turned his entire world upside down. He wanted to spend the rest of his life with her. For as long as he could remember, he had been a committed philanderer. Infidelity had come as naturally to him as breathing. But that was in the past. His mad, bad days were behind him. The only person he wanted from now on was Maxine.

It was two o'clock in the morning and Nina was sitting at the kitchen table drinking camomile tea. Her long white fingers, wrapped around the cup, appeared almost luminous in the muted glow of the shaded wall lamps. Her face, bare of make-up, seemed paler still, but her voice remained calm.

'So it was Janey Sinclair's sister all the time.' She nodded thoughtfully. 'How interesting. Janey talked to me about you, you know. I thought she was the one you were involved with.'

'Not my type,' said Bruno, because total honesty was all very well but some things were undoubtedly better left unsaid. He wasn't concerned about his own reputation, but at least he could protect Janey's.

'And Maxine is?'

'Yes.'

'You're absolutely sure?'

He nodded. 'Absolutely.'

'Oh well.' Nina shrugged and recrossed her legs. 'It was bound to happen sooner or later. If I'm honest, I didn't expect us to last this long.'

She was taking it well, thought Bruno with gratitude. But then nothing ever fazed Nina. It was what he'd always liked about her. 'I didn't expect it to happen like this,' he admitted with a rueful smile. 'And to me, of all people.'

'Where will you live?'

'I'm going to see Don Hickman tomorrow. Now the summer season's over he should be able to find me a cheap holiday cottage. I suppose I'll have to start looking out for another job, too.' He paused, then added, 'Unless you want me to carry on here . . .?'

'No.' Nina shook her head. 'Better not. I think we need a clean break.'

'Right.' Bruno gave her a concerned look. 'Are you sure you'll be OK?'

She smiled. 'Of course I will. We had a good partnership, and now it's over. It's hardly the end of the world.'

Leaning across the table, he kissed her pale forehead. 'Thank you. For making it easy.'

'My pleasure.' Nina returned the kiss, stroking his streaky-blond hair for a moment before rising to her feet and placing her empty teacup in the sink. 'But it isn't going to be quite so easy for you, financially. Does Maxine have plenty of money?'

'No.'

'Oh dear,' she said with affectionate amusement. 'In that case, it really must be love.'


Bruno, fast asleep in the spare room, lay spread-eagled across the bed with one foot dangling over the side. With tears streaming silently down her cheeks, Nina stood in the doorway and watched the man she had loved for the past ten years dream of the girl he loved.

Sadly, that girl wasn't herself. But she had done absolutely the right thing, Nina reassured herself. Breaking down and begging him to stay – maybe even attempting to bribe him with yet more money – would only have earned his contempt. Instead she had been cool, calm and understanding, and it was much the best way because now they could part as friends. More importantly, it kept the door open. Bruno would know he could always return.

You're leaving me now because you're besotted with someone called Maxine Vaughan, thought Nina, who is undoubtedly beautiful and who makes you laugh. She's probably brilliant in bed, too. But she can't possibly love you as much as I do, and that's why I'm letting you go. Because it doesn't matter how long it takes. I'm prepared to wait for you to come back.

# Chapter 42

'Oh Janey, I'm so happy for you!' Maxine enveloped her sister in a bear hug and swung her round in the narrow hallway, trampling all over the Sunday papers which had only just been pushed through the letterbox. 'Look, I've brought champagne to celebrate. Where's Alan, still in bed? Tell him to get up this minute and come and give his long-lost sister-in-law an enormous kiss!'

Janey, abandoning the mangled newspapers, followed her up the stairs. 'You've missed him. He's gone to the surfing club. He'll be back at around midday.'

Inwardly relieved, Maxine squeezed Janey's hand. 'Oh well, never mind. There'll be plenty of time for that later. Maybe it's nicer this way; we can have a proper talk without interruptions, and drink all the champagne ourselves. Come along, grab a jacket and a couple of glasses; it's time to hit the beach.'

It was cold but sunny, and the tide was on its way out. Down at the water's edge, Janey held up the glasses while Maxine eased the cork from the bottle, aiming it into the glittering turquoise sea.

'To you and Alan,' she said with a grin when their

glasses had been filled as they walked along. 'May you live happily ever after. Cheers!'

'Cheers,' Janey responded with a dutiful smile. She was pleased Maxine was pleased, but it had also come as something of a surprise. Having anticipated suspicion, criticism and a million questions laced with Maxine's own particular brand of sarcasm, she was still very much on her guard. Champagne on the beach and wholehearted approval weren't what she'd been expecting at all.

'This is from Guy, by the way.' Maxine waved the bottle. 'He sends his best wishes. Oh, and something else.' Rummaging in the inner pocket of her ancient leather flying jacket, she produced a crumpled cheque. Your wages for last week.'

Janey was almost embarrassed to take the cheque. It seemed odd, accepting payment for something which hadn't even seemed like work. But since refusing the money would appear even odder, she stuffed it into the back pocket of her jeans. 'Thanks, I enjoyed it.'

'So did they.' Maxine rolled her eyes in mock reproach. 'Although I'm beginning to seriously regret sending you there. Josh and Ella actually expect me to bake cakes now! And I mean real cakes,' she added darkly, 'with flour and stuff. Not even the kind you make from a packet.'

Both intrigued and amused, Janey waited to see how long Maxine could hold out. She was clearly making a heroic effort not to get down to the nitty-gritty and ask all the questions she would normally have blurted out within milliseconds. Janey, guessing that Guy must have had a stern word with her on the subject, made a silent bet with herself that Maxine would crumble somewhere between the smugglers' cave and the rock pools.

The smugglers' cave was still two hundred yards ahead of them, however, when Maxine, in the middle of prattling on about the hideous little brat with whom she'd co-starred in the toilet-roll commercial, suddenly stopped dead and ripped off her sunglasses.

'OK, that's enough,' she declared, fixing her dark eyes on Janey and daring her to move. 'You've had your fun but this is downright cruel. It's all very well for Guy bloody Cassidy to warn me against giving you the third degree but I am your sister, after all. So stop pretending to be interested in my glittering career and tell me everything, before I explode!'

Janey glanced at her watch. Nine whole minutes; whoever would have thought Maxine would be capable of restraining herself for that length of time?

'Everything you need to know?' she said innocently. 'Right. Well, first of all you sieve the flour into a bowl. Don't forget to add a pinch of salt. Then you—'

'Stop it!' Maxine shrieked, picking up a dripping, slippery mass of seaweed and advancing towards her. 'Tell me about Alan. Tell me why he left . . . why he came back . . . what he's been doing . . . what *you're* going to do.'

The trouble was, by the time Janey had finished telling her, Maxine was no longer so sure she wanted to know.

What she found almost impossible to understand was the fact that Janey actually seemed to believe the incredible line her bastard of a husband had been stringing her. As far as Maxine was concerned, she'd never heard such a heap of total and utter bullshit in her entire life.

'. . . So that's it,' Janey concluded, reaching for the Bollinger and tipping the last of it into their empty glasses. With a sidelong glance in Maxine's direction, she said with a trace of defiance, 'Go on then, your turn. You must have an opinion.'

Mere words couldn't even begin to convey her opinion of Alan Sinclair, thought Maxine, almost beside herself with silent rage. But she also realized she'd been right about Janey, who clearly wouldn't tolerate even the mildest of criticisms. One wrong word and she would leap to Alan's defence. Any suggestion that he might have been less than honest and it would be champagne corks at thirty paces.

But she was an actress, thank goodness, and she could out-act even her unspeakable brother-in-law any day of the week. For the sake of her pride, Janey was going to have to make the discovery of just how unspeakable he really was, in her own time.

For the past week, Maxine's dramatic talent had been stretched to the limit, pronouncing – in entirely convincing tones – 'When you have Babysoft in your bathroom, you know you have the best.' Now, perched on a cold rock at the far end of Trezale beach, she stretched it that little bit further and said simply, 'Oh Janey, what on earth were you expecting me to say? You're happy, and that's good enough for me. I'm *glad* he's back.'

They were making their way back along the shoreline when Janey unwittingly asked the question Maxine had been gearing herself up for.

'So what else happened in London? You must have gone to a few parties; did you meet any nice men?'

Janey was carrying the glasses. Maxine, who had stuffed the empty Bollinger bottle inside her jacket, was skimming pebbles across the water. She watched the last pebble collide with a wave and disappear from view. A gust of wind blew her hair into her eyes and she used the extra seconds it gave her to compose herself.

'I went to *a* party,' she said finally, 'and met *a* nice man.'

'And now it's my turn to be kept in suspense?' Janey protested. 'Come along now, don't be shy! Give me the gory details.'

'I've known him for a while.' Maxine took a deep breath and wished she could have persuaded Guy to part with two bottles of champagne. A little extra Dutch courage would have come in useful. 'But until the party I didn't even know I liked him. You know him too; quite well, in fact. And I don't think you're going to like it much when I tell you who it is.'

Janey thought hard for a moment. With a perplexed shrug she said, 'Well, you've got me. But if it's an actor . . .' Her eyes widened in mock amazement and she clapped her free hand to her chest. 'You don't mean . . . Mel—'

'Look, he loves me and I love him,' said Maxine rapidly. 'It's serious stuff. I know you hate him, but you have to believe me . . . for the first time in my life I really do feel—'

'Mel Gibson?' shrieked Janey, and several seagulls beat a panicky retreat.

'Bruno.' Maxine's shoulders stiffened in an unconscious gesture of defiance. There, she'd said it. Now all she had to do was pray Janey didn't burst into tears.

But Janey was starting to laugh. 'Is this a joke? Max, that's not fair. Come on now, I told you everything!'

'And now I'm telling you. It really isn't a joke.' The words spilled out fast, jerkily. Maxine took another steadying breath. 'He turned up at the party on Friday night and practically kidnapped me. Except I wanted to be kidnapped,' she amended, a shiver running down her spine even as she recalled the sheer romance of it all. 'He wants to marry me. He's leaving Nina. Oh Janey, it was as much of a shock to me as it is for you, but it just happened! I can't even begin to describe how I feel . . .'

'Well,' said Janey as the gulls continued to wheel frantically overhead. 'I'm stunned.'

'I'm sorry.'

'You're sorry I'm stunned, or sorry it's Bruno?'

'You know what I mean.' Maxine bit her lower lip. 'I've been dreading telling you. Do you absolutely hate me?'

'I don't hate you. I can't believe you're being so incredibly stupid,' sighed Janey, 'but of course I don't hate you. Max, the last time I came for a walk along this beach, *somebody* gave me the most almighty lecture. I can't remember it word for word, but it had something to do with keeping well away from Bruno Parry-Brent because he was an unprincipled, sex-crazed, triple-timing shit-gigolo-bastard who would bring me nothing but everlasting grief.' Pausing, she tilted her head to one side. 'Now does that ring any bells with you, or do you have a twin sister I don't know about?'

'Oh hell,' said Maxine uncomfortably. She braced

360

herself once more. 'Look, I know I said all those things but that's the whole point; he would only have made you miserable. You're a nice person and you expect everyone else to be nice, too. You're trusting, unselfish, honest; as far as people like Bruno are concerned, it's practically an open invitation to behave badly. They can't resist it. And I know,' she added with passion in her voice, 'because I'm like Bruno too. I don't trust men, I'm a selfish bitch and I lie like the clappers. Don't you see, Janey? Bruno and I were made for each other! We're a perfectly matched pair.'

Janey frowned. 'I thought you loathed him.'

'I did.' Maxine gave her an apologetic look. 'Well, I thought I did. But what I really loathed was the fact that I knew he'd end up hurting you. You see, it was like watching a re-run of me and Maurice. You know what I'm like, Janey. I simply can't handle nice, dependable men. The better they treat me, the worse I behave. If a man's going to keep me on my toes, keep me interested, he needs to be a bastard, someone I can fight with. I don't mean getting beaten up,' she added hastily, as Janey's eyebrows rose. 'I'm not into black eyes and teeth flying in all directions. I just need someone I don't trust enough to take for granted.'

Maxine was rattling on at a furious pace, putting across every argument she could think of. Strangely, thought Janey, it rang true. It might be weird, but it made sense.

'I know it's masochistic,' Maxine went on. 'I'm a hopeless case. But if it's easy, there's no buzz. And I need that buzz . . .'

Uncomfortably aware that she was once again echoing Maxine's own words to her, Janey said, 'There's still Nina.

You say Bruno's going to leave her. What makes you think he will?'

'I don't have to think.' The gulls were still wheeling noisily overhead. Maxine suppressed an urge to hurl the champagne bottle at them. Meeting Janey's concerned gaze, she recalled Bruno's phone call earlier this morning. 'I know,' she said simply. 'He already has.'

They had finished retracing their steps. Janey's white beach shoes were awash with sand. By the time they'd made their way back up the high street, it was almost midday.

'Alan will be home any minute now,' she said, fishing in her pocket for the front-door key. 'If you'd like to stay for lunch, you're very welcome. Or is Guy expecting you back?'

'Special dispensation,' Maxine replied with an unnecessary glance at her watch. She had already arranged to meet Bruno at the Dune Bar at twelve-thirty. Somehow a cosy foursome didn't seem appropriate. 'Guy's given me the afternoon off; he's taking the kids over to Mimi Margason's house for lunch. She's the woman whose party you went to, isn't she? I've never met her, but she sounds wild.'

'She is.' Janey wondered if she would ever see Mimi again. She had the uncomfortable feeling that bridges were being burnt. Unless they came into the shop, she might never even see Guy and the children again, either. 'She's outrageous. And very, very nice.'

'Ah well, in that case I probably wouldn't like her,' Maxine replied. 'As I said, nice people make me nervous. Apart from you,' she added cheerfully. 'Sisters don't count.'

'So will you stay for lunch?'

'I can't.' By this time they had reached the shop. Taking a step forward, Maxine kissed Janey's cold cheek. 'I'm seeing Bruno. It's a bit of an awkward situation, isn't it?'

'It's certainly unusual.' Janey smiled. 'I dare say we'll get used to it.'

'We're both happy,' said Maxine, wishing she didn't feel so guilty. 'We've both got the men we really and truly want. There's only one thing left to do now, to round it off.'

'What's that?'

Maxine grinned. 'Find some poor long-suffering female for Guy.'

# Chapter 43

Bruno evidently didn't believe in wasting time. Maxine, only a few minutes late, arrived at the Dune Bar to find him deep in conversation with an extremely pretty brunette, pouring her a glass of Chardonnay with one hand and jangling two sets of keys in the other.

'And about time too,' he complained when Maxine joined them. 'I don't think you know Pearl, do you? I've just been telling her how madly in love with you I am, and how you've changed my life for ever. Think what an idiot I'd have looked if you hadn't turned up.'

'He's definitely a changed man,' Pearl declared, eyeing Maxine with undisguised curiosity. 'I only came over to invite him to a party tomorrow night and he hasn't stopped talking about you for the last twenty minutes. He won't even come to the party.'

Bruno, eyes glittering with amusement, slid his arm around Maxine's waist. 'I'd only get chatted up by women with designs on my body,' he complained. 'There's only one woman in my life from now on. Who needs parties, when we have each other?'

'Boring old fart,' said Maxine, helping herself to wine. 'I like parties. If I was invited to one, I'd go.'

'You can both come.' Pearl scribbled the address on the back of a beer mat. Grinning at Maxine, who evidently met with her approval, she said, 'It'll be fun.'

Bruno had picked up the beer mat. Maxine promptly whisked it from his grasp.

'I'll definitely be there, but Bruno might not,' she said smoothly. 'He doesn't need parties any more, you see. He'd only get chatted up by women with designs on his body.'

'Thanks,' said Bruno, when Pearl had left.

'What's the problem?' Maxine demanded. 'Afraid you won't be able to resist a bit of temptation?'

'Look, we both know you aren't going to any party tomorrow night. Guy's away and you're looking after the kids. I only said no because I didn't think you'd want me to go on my own,' he said with a trace of exasperation. 'I thought you wouldn't trust me.'

'So what are we supposed to do?' Maxine countered. 'Trot along to the nearest hospital and ask to be surgically joined at the hip? Sweetheart, we're just going to have to *learn* to trust each other. I'm not going to try and stop you doing anything you want to do and you're certainly not going to stop me. You can chat up Michelle Pfeiffer if you like. All you have to remember is that if I ever find out you've been unfaithful to me, it's over.' With her index finger, she drew a swift, clean line across his throat. 'Finito. Kaput. Down the pan.'

Bruno kissed her. 'I love you.'

'Hmm.' People were staring, but Maxine didn't care. 'Just as well. We're going to be gossiped about from here to Land's End.'

He picked up one of the sets of keys and dangled them in front of her. 'In that case, let's really give them something to gossip about. Here, take them. Don showed me round a few properties this morning. I'm now the proud tenant of Mole Cottage.'

'You don't waste much time,' said Maxine admiringly. 'Is it nice?'

'Nice?' Bruno launched into brochure-speak. 'Mole Cottage is an *eminently* desirable seventeenth-century residence complete with *stunning* sea view, *two* charming bedrooms, *spacious* shower and delightful beamed ceilings throughout. The living room's actually smaller than the shower cubicle, the wallpaper is unspeakable and the garden's buried beneath six feet of weeds,' he added with a rueful shrug, 'but if we can ignore the décor we'll survive. At least it was dirt cheap.'

Maxine took the keys. 'I suppose these are the modern-day equivalent of a diamond ring.'

'You've done the diamond-ring bit before. You can't keep getting engaged; it's tacky.' Bruno grinned. 'Besides, I'm *nouveau pauvre*. As from today, a key-ring's about as much as I can afford.'

It was Maxine's turn to kiss him. 'I don't care. When are you going to move in?'

'As soon as you finish your drink. My suitcases are in the car.'

She experienced another spasm of guilt. 'How was Nina?'

'Fine.' Bruno drained his glass. 'Absolutely fine. She even helped me pack.'

Frowning slightly, Maxine twisted the stem of her glass

between her fingers. 'Wasn't she even a little bit upset?'

'No.' He had privately come to the conclusion that Nina felt he was in the grip of a wild passion which would be out of his system by Christmas. It wouldn't, of course, but it had certainly made leaving a whole lot easier. 'She takes things in her stride. There's only one major drawback to my leaving, as far as Nina's concerned.'

'Oh yes?'

'Bruno's Restaurant.' He pulled a face. 'She spoke to the new chef this morning and he says if he's going to take full charge, it should be named after him.'

Maxine, who had only briefly glimpsed the thin, carroty-haired individual with the bobbing Adam's apple and alarmingly pointed ears, said, 'I can't remember what he's called.'

Bruno broke into a grin. 'Wayne.'

'I'm late, I'm sorry.' Alan, bursting through the door at ten past one, gave Janey an enormous, conciliatory hug. 'I lost all track of time. All the old crowd were there; you can't imagine how much catching up we had to do.'

And you can't imagine how terribly afraid I've been, thought Janey, willing herself to stay calm. Punctuality had never been one of Alan's strong points, but that didn't mean she hadn't suffered agonies of uncertainty as each minute had ticked by. She wondered if she would ever truly be able to relax and overcome the fear that each time he left the house she might never see him again.

But that was something she was just going to have to come to terms with, she told herself firmly. Shrieking like a fishwife wouldn't solve anything, and whingeing on about how worried she'd been would only burden him with guilt.

'Don't worry, I expected you to be late.' With a casual gesture, she wiped her damp palms on her jeans. 'They're your friends; you must have had lots to talk about.'

'It was still thoughtless of me.' He stroked her blond, just-washed hair. 'But you really don't have to worry, sweetheart. I'm not going to disappear into thin air again. This time I'm here for good.'

She smiled. 'Good.'

'And to make up for being late home, I'm cooking lunch.' He began to roll up the sleeves of his denim shirt in businesslike fashion. 'You can put your feet up and relax. I'll do everything myself.'

Janey started to laugh, because the smell of lamb roasting in the oven permeated the entire flat. 'It's all done,' she said, recalling how often in the past they had gone through this routine.

True to form, Alan looked appalled. 'All of it? Roast potatoes, onion sauce, all the vegetables?'

She nodded, brown eyes sparkling. 'Afraid so.'

'Oh well, in that case . . .' Alan took her hand and pulled her gently in the direction of the bedroom '. . . maybe we should both put our feet up.'

Janey raised a quizzical eyebrow. 'And relax?'

'Hmm.' Sliding his arm around her waist beneath the fleecy lilac sweatshirt she wore, he edged towards the zip on her jeans. 'Maybe we'll leave the relaxing until later . . .'

'Oh shit.' With a groan, Janey ducked away from the window. 'I don't believe it. Oh *hell*!'

'Who is it?' Alan demanded irritably, as she wriggled across the bed and made a grab for her yellow-and-white towelling robe. Whoever it was, they certainly had a lethal sense of timing.

'Quick, get some clothes on,' hissed Janey. 'It's my mother.'

Thea Vaughan was proud of the way she had brought up her children, teaching them to be independent from an early age, allowing them to make their own decisions and never saying 'I told you so' when those decisions turned out to be mistakes. But enough was enough. This time, Janey had gone too far. And no mother, she felt, could be expected to sit back and watch her daughter make a mistake quite as monumental as the one Janey was making now.

'Mum.' Flushed and dishevelled, Janey opened the front door. 'What a surprise! You usually phone.'

'What a coincidence,' mimicked Thea briskly. 'So do you. When you have something to tell me, that is,' she added in meaningful tones. 'Some small item of news you think I might be interested in hearing.'

Janey had known it wouldn't be easy. Thea was clearly on the warpath, outraged at having been left out and determined to make a monumental drama out of the event. It was precisely why she hadn't made more than a token effort to contact her mother in the first place.

'I did try to phone you,' she insisted. 'Yesterday. There was no reply.'

'Stuff and nonsense,' retorted Thea, her crimson cape billowing out as she stomped up the stairs. 'I was out of the house for less than fifteen minutes. No doubt you were too busy to try again,' she continued scathingly. 'Which is why I have to hear the news from that nosey baggage Elsie Ellis, who from the sound of it has spent the last couple of days with her ears pinned against your adjoining wall. I dare say she's also been broadcasting the news of your husband's return to everyone who has set foot inside that bakery of hers. Personally, I'm amazed she hasn't stood on the steps of the bloody town hall with a megaphone.'

'Look, I'm sorry.' Janey's heart was pounding uncomfortably against her ribs. This was even worse than the time Maxine and the cricketers had turned up out of the blue, catching her with Bruno. 'But I don't understand why you're so angry that Alan's back. Aren't you at least happy for me?'

'My God, you are naïve.' It came out as a snort of derision. 'And I thought I was stupid, marrying your father! At least I had the guts to get out of the marriage before he ruined my entire life.'

'It isn't the same thing.' Outraged by the accusation, Janey's voice rose. 'That was completely different! You told us yourself he had non-stop affairs. Alan didn't do that. My father made you miserable for years; you can't possibly compare your marriage with mine. It's all very well for you to come storming round here with your mind already made up, but you don't even know why he left.'

She cringed as Thea reached the top of the stairs and flung open the door to the flat. If Alan had decided to hide in the bedroom, her mother's scorn would know no bounds.

But he was there, pouring Chablis into glasses and –

thank heavens – standing his ground.

'Don't be angry with Thea,' he said calmly, evidently having overheard the furious exchange on the stairs. 'She has your best interests at heart. I've turned off the oven, by the way. Why don't we sit down and discuss this whole thing in a rational manner?'

It was what Alan was best at. Janey, drinking far too much wine far too quickly, said nothing and allowed him to get on with it.

Thea, however, remained stonily unimpressed. 'Such a touching tale,' she remarked, her expression sardonic, the light of battle in her brown eyes. 'Forgive me if I don't break down in tears, but I'm less of a soft touch than my daughter.'

Alan shrugged. 'I'm sorry, I know how you must feel. But it happens to be the truth.'

'Balls,' said Thea.

Janey winced. 'Mum!'

'Oh grow up!' her mother snapped. 'I've never heard such codswallop in all my life. If he'd had the guts to say he ran off with another woman I could almost forgive him, but this . . . this complete and utter claptrap is just despicable. Janey, he's making a fool of you and I'm not going to let it carry on.'

'I can't help what you think,' said Alan, reaching for Janey's hand and squeezing it. With a sorrowful shake of his head, he met Thea's withering gaze. 'And there's no way in the world I can ever prove it, but there was no other woman. That's the absolute truth, and Janey believes me. Maybe in time you'll come to believe it too. I certainly hope you will, for Janey's sake if not for mine, but—'

'But nothing!' declared Thea with venom. 'Do I look as if I have a mental age of six? You're a liar and a cheat, and you all but wrecked my daughter's life. If you think I'm going to stand by and let you do it again, my lad, you most certainly have another think coming.'

'Right, that's enough,' Janey shouted. Red-faced, she leapt to her feet, narrowly avoiding the coffee table, and wrenched open the living-room door. 'You're treating *me* like a six-year-old, and it isn't even any of your damn business. Alan's my husband and you're just jealous because he came back and yours didn't. What's the matter, don't you want me to be happy?'

'For God's sake,' sighed Thea, frustrated by her daughter's hopelessly misguided loyalty. 'Of course I want you to be happy. That's why I came here, to try and make you see sense.'

'Well let me tell you what would make me happy,' yelled Janey, trembling all over and clutching the door handle for support. 'You leaving. Because I won't be bullied and I won't stand here and listen to another word of this garbage. You're interfering with my life and I don't need it. I don't need you, either,' she concluded with intentional cruelty. 'So why don't you do us all a favour and just get out of here, now?'

# Chapter 44

After a late lunch, Mimi walked with Guy around the garden. Ahead of them, Josh and Ella were spinning around like tops in a race to see who could make themselves dizziest and fall over in the most spectacular fashion. Within seconds, her arms flailing and her legs buckling drunkenly beneath her, Ella staggered sideways into a flowerbed.

'Masochistic little sods,' said Mimi fondly as Ella let out a scream of delight and Josh, not to be outdone, careered head first into a mass of overgrown rhododendrons. 'They'll keep going until they feel sick, then run to you for sympathy.'

'If anyone needs sympathy, it's me.' Pausing for a moment, Guy took a photograph of Ella as she emerged from the flowerbed. 'Nothing seems to be going according to plan at the moment. God knows what's going to happen next,' he added, adjusting the shutter speed and taking aim once more, 'but I'm pretty sure I'm not going to like it.'

Poor Guy. Mimi, who had heard all about Alan Sinclair's return over lunch, tucked a companionable arm through his. 'Ah, but that's the thing about masochism,' she said with the air of one who knows. 'We might grow up, but that doesn't mean we automatically grow out of it. Look at me,' she exclaimed, gesturing towards her hips. 'I wasted ten years of my life trying to diet! All that miserable calorie-counting and jumping on scales, and what did it achieve? I'd lose a stone, gain a stone, and bore everybody rigid into the bargain . . . My God, was there ever anything more pointless? I was *miserable*, darling . . . a slave to fashion. Giving up dieting and saying to hell with size twelve was the best decision of my entire life!'

Since Mimi was currently wearing a pink mohair cardigan trimmed with sequins, a mauve organza blouse and a blue-and-white gingham skirt, it was hard to imagine her ever having been a slave to fashion.

Thoroughly mystified, Guy responded with a cautious nod. 'I see.'

'And it's the same with Janey,' she continued triumphantly. 'She might think she's hooked on this wretched husband of hers but all he is, really, is a habit she hasn't broken. You have to be patient, darling. Given time, she'll come to her senses and realize she can do without him after all. Mind you, I bet you wish now you'd made your move a bit earlier,' she added with a smug, I-told-you-so smile. 'She would have had to think twice then, wouldn't she, before rushing off without so much as a backward glance? In that respect, I'm afraid you have only yourself to blame.'

'Really.' Guy struggled to keep a straight face. 'Well, this is all very interesting, but I'm afraid you're on completely the wrong track. Janey's a friend, nothing more. She's a very nice girl, but that's as far as it goes. She just isn't my type. When I said I didn't know what was going to happen next,' he explained, 'I was referring to Maxine. If this new affair of hers turns out to be more than a nine-day wonder, it's going to mean trouble for me. Before long, she'll be wanting to move in with Bruno Parry-Brent and I'll have to start looking for a new nanny.'

'Of course you will,' said Mimi blithely. 'And who would be absolutely perfect for the job? Janey.'

'You're shameless.' This time he was unable to hide his smile. 'Do you know that? Quite apart from the fact that she has a shop to run, I've already told you, Janey isn't my type.'

Mimi, not believing him for a second, pulled the mohair cardigan more tightly around her vast bosom as a sudden gust of wind whistled down her cleavage.

'You're only a man,' she said, her tone comforting. 'What would you know? You thought Serena was your type.'

'I have to get back,' said Maxine regretfully, stirring the surface of the water with her big toe and transferring an artful dollop of foam on to Bruno's shoulder. 'We can't spend the rest of our lives lying in the bath. Besides, I'm starting to prune.'

He reached for her hand and kissed her wrinkled fingertips, one by one. 'I don't want you to go. Why don't you give in your notice and come and live here with me?'

'What, leave my job?'

'I left Nina,' Bruno reminded her. 'And my job. I'm not going to enjoy sitting around waiting for you to dash over here whenever you can manage to get a couple of hours off.'

She grinned. 'You've done it to enough women yourself, haven't you? Now you can find out how it feels to be the one on the receiving end.'

'I want us to be together,' he said crossly. 'All the time.'

He was sounding more and more like a fretful mistress. Leaning forward, Maxine gave him a kiss. 'So do I, but then we'd both be unemployed. Besides, Guy's been good to me – in his own way – and I can't leave him in the lurch. Why don't we just see how things go for a while before doing anything drastic?'

'Well thanks,' murmured Bruno, who felt he had already acted pretty drastically. But Maxine, in a hurry to get back to Trezale House, was climbing out of the bath and reaching for the larger of the two towels.

'Don't glare at me like that,' she said cheerfully. 'You know what I mean. Look, I'll have a word with Guy and see if we can't come to some kind of arrangement. If he's at home, maybe he'll let me spend my nights here. And the kids are at school during the day . . .'

'Such concern all of a sudden, for Guy Cassidy,' Bruno complained, watching as she eased herself into her jeans and bent to pick up her crumpled white shirt. 'He's hardly likely to go out of his way to make things easier for us. He doesn't even like me.'

'Don't worry.' Maxine winked. 'I have ways of getting round Guy. Don't you trust me?'

'No.' He wasn't used to feeling jealous and he didn't much like it. 'That's why I want you to come and live here.'

'I don't trust you, either,' countered Maxine sweetly, doing up the last couple of buttons and knotting the shirt tails around her waist. 'So forget it. Because I'm not moving anywhere until you manage to persuade me that I can.'

Guy was leafing through a mound of contact sheets and eating a Marmite sandwich when Maxine rolled into the sitting room at seven.

'You look as if you've just crawled out of bed,' he observed, taking in her tousled hair, bright eyes and distinctly rumpled white shirt.

'It's what you do when you're in love.' She gave him an unrepentant smile.

Josh and Ella were sprawled in front of the fire, their blond heads bent over a game of Monopoly. Glancing up, Josh said hopefully, 'If you've been asleep all afternoon, I expect you'd like to play Monopoly now. I've nearly finished beating Ella.'

Guy pushed the contact sheets to one side. 'How was Janey?'

'Happy.' Maxine rolled her eyes. 'What can I say? He fed her some terrible line and she fell for it. I just went along with the whole thing and pretended to be pleased for her.' Collapsing on to the floor next to Ella, who was biting her lip at the prospect of having to mortgage the Old Kent Road, she added, 'But it was definitely the right thing to do. At the moment, she won't hear a word against him.'

'Hmm,' said Guy. 'So I gathered. Your mother phoned earlier, wanting to speak to you.'

Maxine pulled a face. If Thea had somehow heard about Bruno leaving Nina from outside sources, it was entirely possible that she was in for a lecture. Her mother was sensitive about such matters. 'Oh.' She looked wary. 'Did she say what about?'

'In Technicolor detail.' Guy glanced across at the children to make sure they weren't listening. 'And it isn't good news. She went round to Janey's place this afternoon and told Alan exactly what she thought of him. It didn't go down well at all,' he explained. 'She and Janey had a screaming row and Janey ended up booting her out of the flat.'

'Hell.' Maxine heaved a gusty sigh. 'Poor Mum. I suppose I should have warned her. Now we've got a family feud on our hands. Was she upset?'

'Upset, no. Angry, yes.' He half smiled, recalling the colourful language Thea Vaughan had employed during the course of their forty-minute conversation. 'But with herself as much as anything. She realizes now that she made a mistake.'

'Daddy, can you lend me two thousand pounds?' asked Ella in desperation. 'To stop me going bankrupt.'

'She also warned me that I had all this to come,' Guy went on, shaking his head wearily. 'Apparently, raising daughters is the pits. One calamity after another.'

'That means no,' declared Josh, merciless in victory. 'Good, you're bankrupt. You've lost and I've won. Come on, Maxine, you're next. I'm the racing car and you can be the old boot.'

'Good old Mum,' said Maxine. 'She always was about as subtle as Bernard Manning.'

'She certainly has character.' Guy grinned. 'She sounded fun though. I'd like to meet her.'

'Now there's a thought! Janey and I were only saying this morning that what you need is a woman in your life.' Maxine's dark eyes glittered with mischief. 'Maybe I should introduce you to my mother.'

# Chapter 45

Janey was in the shop putting the finishing touches to a congratulations-on-your-retirement bouquet when Guy came in.

'They're nice.' He nodded at the autumnal flowers.

'For Miss Stirrup, with love from Class 2C.' Having trimmed and curled the bronze and gold ribbons holding the bouquet together, Janey reached for the staple gun and clipped the accompanying card to the cellophane wrapper. 'She's a complete dragon; she was my English teacher, always sticking the whole class in detention when the weather was good and all we wanted to do was go tearing off down to the beach. I was tempted to write out "Have a Happy Retirement" a hundred times,' she added with a grin. 'And spell "retirement" wrongly, just to annoy her.'

She was looking well and happy, Guy realized. The habitual working uniform of jeans and tee-shirt had been replaced by a pastel pink wool dress which flattered both her figure and colouring. She was wearing make-up too, not a great deal but enough to make a difference. The overall effect was one of renewed confidence and cheerfulness. So far, he decided, everything appeared to be going well.

But he still couldn't bring himself to raise the subject of the long-lost husband's miraculous return. Instead, sticking to safer ground, he placed a large Manila envelope on the counter.

'I'm just on my way up to London. I thought I'd drop this in before I left. Go on, open it. It's for you.'

'Really?' Janey gave him a playful look. 'What is it, more wages?'

Guy smiled. 'Afraid not.'

'Oh!' As the photograph slid out of the envelope, she caught her breath. 'Oh, my God . . . this is amazing. I can't believe it's really me.'

As soon as he had developed Friday night's films, taken purely in order to test out the latest Olympus, Guy had known he had something special. The particular miracle of photography, he always felt, was the fact that although technical expertise played a part, it was never everything. The best camera in the world, coupled with perfect lighting and the most compliant subjects, could produce adequate but ultimately disappointing results, whereas occasionally – and for no apparent reason – an off-the-cuff, unplanned snap of a shutter succeeded in capturing a mood, an expression, a moment in time to perfection.

He had felt at once, even as he pegged up the still-dripping print in the darkroom, that this was one such success. It didn't happen often but it had happened last Friday, and the result was almost magical. Unaware of the camera, Janey had hoisted Ella into her arms in order to give her a clear view of Josh on the dodgems. Their faces, close together, were alight with shared laughter. Ella's small fingers, curled around Janey's neck, conveyed love and trust. The only slightly out-of-focus background managed to capture both the excitement and noise of the fairground. Ella's childish elation and Janey's pride and delight in Josh's prowess at the wheel of his dodgem car were reflected with such astonishing clarity, it almost brought a lump to the throat. Unposed, unrehearsed and using only natural available light, it was the kind of one-in-a-million shot all photographers seek to achieve. Guy, having achieved it, had known at once where its future lay.

'I don't know much about this kind of thing,' said Janey, who was still studying the print intently. She hesitated, then glanced up at him. 'But it is good, isn't it? I mean seriously good.'

'I think so.'

'It has . . . impact.' The fact that she was featured in the picture was irrelevant. Shaking her head, she struggled to express herself more clearly. 'You can . . . *feel* it. I don't think anyone could look at this photograph and not respond. And how strange, we look like—'

'Like what?' Guy prompted half-teasingly, but she shook her head once more and didn't reply. Against the darker background, which had created a kind of halo effect, both Ella's hair and her own appeared white-blond and the camera angle had managed to capture a similarity in their bone structure; but the fact that they looked like mother and daughter was sheer chance, a mere trick of the lens and far too embarrassing to voice aloud.

Instead, she said simply, 'I love it. Thank you.'

'And now I have a favour to ask.' Guy, who knew exactly what had been going through her mind, was amused by her reluctance to comment on the apparent resemblance between Ella and herself. 'I was approached by a children's charity a couple of weeks ago. They're mounting a national appeal and they've asked for my help.'

'Raising money?' He had given her the photograph. Janey, happy to return the favour, was eager to help. 'What can I do, keep a collecting tin here on the counter? I did a stint once, rattling a tin on a street corner for the RSPCA.' With a grin, she added, 'I did brilliantly, too. It wasn't until three hours later I realized most of my shirt buttons were undone. All those men stuffing pound coins into my tin had been getting an eyeful of my boobs and there I was saying thank you and thinking what lovely caring people they were.'

'All these months I've known you,' Guy drawled. 'And I never figured you for a topless model.'

'It was almost worse than topless.' Janey cringed at the memory. 'I was wearing a really awful old bra held together with a safety pin. Talk about mortifying.'

'Well you can rattle a tin if you want to, but that wasn't what I had in mind.' Leaning against the counter, Guy tapped the photograph with a forefinger. 'You see, they asked me to come up with the advertising poster for the campaign. With your permission I'd like to use this.'

She stared at him. 'You're joking.'

'Why would I joke? It's perfect. As you said yourself, you can't look at this picture and not feel something. With any luck,' he added with a wink, 'the public will look at it and feel compelled to donate pots of money.'

At that moment the door to the shop opened behind

him. Guy could almost have guessed without turning around that the waft of Paco Rabanne aftershave and accompanying footsteps belonged to Alan Sinclair. Janey had gone two shades pinker and her hand reached automatically to her hair.

But he turned anyway, taking his first look at the man who had caused her such untold grief. He saw what he had expected, too; blond, boyish good looks, an air of laid-back charm, the kind of features typical of a man who knew he stood a greater than average chance of taking risks and getting away with them. The urge to launch right in and tell Alan Sinclair exactly what he thought of him was compelling, but it was a luxury he was unable to allow himself. Thea had tried, and failed spectacularly. For once in her life, he reflected, Maxine had been right.

'Darling . . . I wasn't expecting you back so soon.' Janey sounded both pleased and flustered. 'Guy, this is Alan, my husband. Alan, meet Guy Cassidy . . . um, Maxine's boss.'

Guy was not a vain man. He nevertheless knew from experience that other men, upon meeting him for the first time, instinctively mistrusted him with their own wives or girlfriends. Even if the women didn't appear overtly interested – although, he had to admit, they frequently did – the men grew jealous. It was going to be interesting, he decided, to see how Janey's husband would react.

Alan, however, appeared disappointingly unfazed. There were no gritted teeth behind the cheerful smile as he shook Guy's hand.

'Of course,' he said easily. 'It's really nice to meet you, Janey's told me all about you and your family. I'm also a great admirer of your work.'

'Thank you.' The boy had charm, thought Guy. And since he must be almost thirty he wasn't even a boy; it was simply the impression he gave of being not altogether grown up.

'Look, darling. Guy dropped by to show me this picture.' Touching the back of Alan's wrist in order to regain his attention, Janey pushed the photograph into his hand. 'He wants to use it for a poster advertising a charity fund-raising campaign. What do you think, isn't it marvellous?'

Alan studied the print for several seconds, clearly impressed. Finally, flicking back his blond hair, he nodded. 'It is. Maxine must be over the moon. Fame at last.'

Guy bit his lip. That was always the trouble with deserting your wife, he thought with derision. When you eventually came back you didn't always recognize her.

'You idiot,' giggled Janey. 'This isn't Maxine. It's me.'

'Oh, right.' Unperturbed by his mistake, Alan took another look and nodded. Turning to address Guy he said casually, 'Very flattering. That's why you're so in demand as a photographer, of course. It's all clever stuff.'

Guy barely trusted himself to speak. No wonder Janey was so lacking in self-confidence, he thought bitterly. Between the pair of them, Alan and Bruno had sapped her of every last ounce of the stuff.

'Flattery doesn't come into it.' He had observed Janey's crestfallen expression. His dark blue eyes glittered as he removed the photograph from Alan Sinclair's grasp. 'The picture was there, waiting to be taken. All I did was capture it on film.'

'Of course,' Apparently realizing his mistake, Alan shrugged and smiled once more. 'I'm sorry, I wasn't implying otherwise. And I think it'll make a great campaign poster.'

'I still can't believe it,' sighed Janey. 'This is so exciting.'

'Not to mention well timed.' Slipping his arm around her waist, Alan gave her a brief, congratulatory hug. 'Maybe now we'll be able to take that holiday after all.' He turned to look at Guy. 'How much will she be getting for this?'

Guy stared at him. Janey, whose colour had only just reverted to normal, went bright pink all over again.

'Alan, it's for a charity campaign! The idea is to raise money. I wouldn't be paid!'

'Oh.' The disappointment was evident in his voice. This time, when he glanced down at the print, it was without interest. 'Shame.'

'I have to go.' Guy looked at his watch. Janey was embarrassed, which was maybe no bad thing, although if anyone should be ashamed it was her husband. 'Look, I'm presenting the idea to the organizers this afternoon. When they make their final decision I'll be in touch.'

'Oh dear,' said Alan, when Guy had left the shop. 'Did I put my foot in it?'

'Both feet.' Janey busied herself with a bucket of moss. She had two wreaths to complete before lunch. 'I can't believe you said that. God knows what Guy must have thought.'

'It was a simple enough mistake.' He looked injured. 'These models get paid thousands for a couple of hours' work, don't they? I was only looking after your interests. Why should you be ripped off, just because you're a friend?'

'Well nobody's being ripped off.' Shuddering at the memory of the look on Guy's face, she began packing the damp moss around the wire base of the first wreath. 'It's for a children's charity. Nobody's getting paid.'

Alan had almost entirely lost interest by now. 'In that case I can't imagine why you're so excited about it. God, I'm starving. Is there anything to eat upstairs?'

'Not unless you've bought some food.' Irritated by his manner, Janey's reply bordered on sarcasm. 'Since I've been working since five o'clock this morning, I'm afraid I haven't had time to visit the supermarket.'

He was immediately contrite. 'I didn't mean it like that. Sorry, sweetheart.'

'Well.' In her agitation, she narrowly missed slicing her finger on a protruding wire. 'Just don't expect gourmet meals, OK? I'm not Superwoman.'

'You are to me.' Alan gave her his most beguiling smile. Leaning across the counter and pulling her towards him, he kissed her soft, down-turned mouth. 'Don't be cross, Janey. You know how much I love you.'

She was still tense. He really had upset her. When she didn't reply, he smoothed a wayward strand of blond hair from her cheek and said, 'Come on, sweetheart. What is it? Is there something going on that I should know about?'

Janey hesitated. 'Like what?'

'Like the possibility that there could be more to this

so-called friendship between you and Guy Cassidy than meets the eye?'

Oh God, she thought wearily. Not again.

'Well?' he persisted.

'No.' She shook her head for added emphasis. 'Of course there isn't.'

'Hmm,' said Alan, not sounding entirely convinced. His eyes narrowed as he studied her evident discomfort. 'There'd better not be.'

The discord had unnerved Janey. It was their first semi-argument and the knot of tension in the pit of her stomach had stayed with her all afternoon. Easy-going by nature, she wished now she hadn't snapped at Alan, but at the same time she didn't feel she'd acted too unreasonably. As long as he wasn't working, she didn't see why she should put in a sixty-hour week in the shop and knock herself out cooking three-course dinners in her precious free time.

It was with some trepidation that she climbed the stairs to the flat at six-thirty. She was hungry and her feet ached. She definitely didn't feel up to an evening of verbal sparring and unease.

As she began to turn the door handle, however, she heard Alan's voice shouting from inside: 'Stop! Don't come in!'

For a fraction of a second, Janey felt her heart lurch. It was ridiculous, but the memory of a recent TV drama came flooding back to her. The wife, arriving home early from work, had been commanded to wait outside the front door in just such a manner whilst the husband's mistress, fetchingly wrapped in a bed sheet, had made her escape through the kitchen door at the back of the house. It had struck a chord at the time, because she had experienced the same situation when Maxine and the cricketers had been hammering on the door and she had been caught with Bruno. The difference, of course, was that in this flat there was no back door from which one could safely escape, only windows and an ankle-snapping fifteen-foot drop.

The next moment, Alan opened the door himself. He grinned. 'OK, you can come in now. All ready.'

She hadn't seriously doubted him, of course, but the sight that greeted her still managed to bring a lump to Janey's throat. There were no semi-naked females in the dimly lit living room. Instead, the small dining table had been set for two. Flickering candles cast an auburn glow over the tablecloth, and he had unearthed the crystal glasses she so seldom used. An unopened bottle of champagne stood in an ice-packed Pyrex bowl.

'Surprise,' murmured Alan, in her ear. 'I hope you're hungry.'

Unbelievably touched by the gesture, Janey could only nod. The fact that it was so unexpected made it all the more special. This, she reminded herself, was why she loved him.

'I'm sorry about this morning.' Taking her hand, he led her towards the table. 'My stupid jealousy. But I'm going to make everything up to you, sweetheart. Here, sit down. Didn't I say we should celebrate my return with champagne?'

It was actually '*méthode champenoise*', Janey observed,

glancing at the label. But that was just as nice as the proper kind . . .

Watching him ease the cork from the bottle, she held her breath as she always did in anticipation of the moment of release. When it finally happened, however, it was sadly lacking in oomph. The cork, instead of ricocheting off the ceiling, toppled limply to the floor. The accompanying silence was deafening.

Alan looked disappointed. 'Story of my life,' he said with a regretful grimace. 'I suppose it was bound to happen. I always seem to get everything wrong.'

'Don't be silly.' Janey's eyes filled with tears as she leap to her feet and hugged him. 'You do everything *right*. You've cooked a stupendous dinner, haven't you? Why don't I dash down to the off-licence and pick up another bottle whilst you're serving up?'

'Actually,' he said, 'it might be a better idea if you give me the money and I get the bottle. You can take a look at the food. I've done my best, but you aren't the only one who isn't Superwoman,' he added defensively. 'It may not be stupendous.'

Janey smiled. 'Why, what's the problem?'

'Well, I don't know.' Alan shook his head and looked perplexed. 'I've never cooked a stupid chicken before. Is it really supposed to have a plastic bag full of squishy bits up its bum?'

# Chapter 46

Valentina di Angelo was only temperamental when she wanted to be. Her fame had been founded upon the highly public rows between herself and her first husband, a hard-drinking but undoubtedly talented actor. Following their even more public divorce, Valentina had come to the reasonable conclusion that while displays of temperament were newsworthy, sweet, quiet, nice girls who liked sewing, reading and watching *EastEnders* were not.

She was always careful, though, to ensure that the temperamental outbursts didn't affect her work. As far as the *paparazzi* were concerned, Valentina di Angelo never turned up anywhere less than three hours late, but her modelling career was something else altogether. Always cheerful, always punctual, she worked like a trooper and never complained about anything. No supermodel, after all, was ever that indispensable. Hurling insults at chat-show hosts, journalists and horrible hangers-on, and generally acting the drama queen, was a strictly after-hours occupation.

It worked, too, like a dream. She was famous for being a beautiful, acid-tongued bitch, and only the people she cared about knew any different.

And although she'd only just met Guy Cassidy, she had already placed him on the list of people she cared about. They had worked well together, she felt, but it was the tantalizing distance he'd kept which intrigued her more than anything else. Even during the shoot itself – during which she'd been wearing not very much at all – he hadn't seemed to notice the lush perfection of her body in the way most top photographers did. The end results had been faultless of course, but as far as Valentina was concerned there was a certain amount of unfinished business to be taken care of. With two short-lived marriages and seven broken engagements behind her, she also felt she had plenty of experience. She'd met her share of Mr Wrongs and got them out of her system. Now, at twenty-five, she was ready for Mr Right. And Guy Cassidy, with his talent, toe-curling good looks and enigmatic personality, was without a doubt right up her street. Better still, he had unceremoniously dumped her arch rival Serena Charlton. It therefore stood to reason, she thought happily, that the man had impeccable taste.

If Guy was surprised to receive her phone call, he didn't show it. He was, however, curious to know how she had managed to track him down to a small hotel in Leicester Square.

'Ah, you're talking to a girl with two and a half GCSEs,' said Valentina. She wasn't entirely brainless. Not like Serena, she thought with a smirk of pride.

'I'm still intrigued.'

'I knew you were a friend of Mac Mackenzie,' she explained. 'So I rang him. He gave me your home phone number. Then I phoned your home and spoke to someone called Maxine. She told me you were staying at the Randolph and gave me the number for that. I called the Randolph, asked to speak to you . . . and here I am!' She giggled. 'There, does that put you out of your misery?'

Guy, sounding amused, said, 'Oh, absolutely. Thanks.'

'Which is nice, because I didn't even expect you to be here in London,' Valentina continued, her tone artless. 'But since you are, how would you feel about having dinner with me?'

He hesitated for a second. 'You mean tonight?'

'No, New Year's Eve, 2005.' This time she laughed. 'Of course, tonight. What's the problem, are you already booked? Tell them you've had a better offer . . .'

Guy had run across more than his fair share of up-front women in his time, but even he was taken aback. Valentina, he thought, was forward with a capital 'F'.

'I know, I know,' she said good-naturedly, reading his mind. 'I'm a pushy cow. Go on, you can say no if you want to. My ego will be crushed but I dare say I'll get over it. In a few years or so.'

It had been a long day. Guy hadn't been planning anything more arduous than a hot bath and maybe a quick drink in the bar downstairs before grabbing the opportunity of an early night and eight hours of uninterrupted sleep.

But Maxine's joking remark the other day, that what he needed was a woman in his life, had stayed in his mind. Faintly put out at the time to think that she and Janey had been discussing his imperfect love life, it had nevertheless struck a semi-painful chord. Maybe he should be making more of an effort. All he had to do, after all, was say yes.

'OK,' he said, before she started to wonder if he had hung up. 'Dinner sounds good. Where would you like to go?'

Bed, thought Valentina with a triumphant smile. But even she wasn't that blatant.

'The Ivy,' she replied. 'Nine o'clock sharp. I'll meet you outside.'

'I'd better give them a ring first.' Reaching across the bed, Guy picked up the phone directory. 'They may be fully booked.'

'Don't worry.' Valentina laughed, because she was practically their resident tourist attraction. 'They always find room, for me.'

Heads turned when Valentina di Angelo entered the restaurant. Heralded all over the world as the new Audrey Hepburn, she took the expression 'gamine' to its limits. Despite having been born and raised in Tooting, her southern Italian parentage clearly showed; skilfully cropped black hair framed an immaculate, olive-skinned face, conker-brown eyes three times bigger than Bambi's and possibly the most sensual red mouth on the planet. Around her long, impossibly slender neck she wore a narrow satin choker, a Valentina trademark copied by teenagers everywhere. And if anyone had ever thought it was impossible to look fabulous in a pink leather jacket, lime green Lycra cycling shorts and red trainers, Valentina proved otherwise.

She looked positively angelic, thought Guy, despite the bizarre, Mimi-esque outfit. Everyone else in the room was covertly watching her. He only hoped she didn't take it into her head to object and start creating her usual mayhem.

But Valentina was in high spirits. She was hungry, too. Over a dinner of watercress soup, lamb cutlets and sinfully rich chocolate pudding she set out to prove to Guy Cassidy just how much of a perfect partner she could be. The sense of distance she had noted last week was still there, but it was definitely lessening. Another bottle of Chablis, she felt, could well be all that was needed to do the trick.

'So how old are your kids?' she asked, resting her chin in her cupped palm and fixing him with her liquid brown eyes. When a man looked this good in a plain white linen shirt and dark blue chinos the prospect of checking out the body underneath was positively enthralling. 'It's a boy and a girl, isn't it? Have you got any photos I can see?'

'Josh is nine. Ella's nearly eight. And photographs of other people's children are boring.' Guy, who had a couple in his wallet, kept them there.

'Don't be so defensive,' Valentina scolded, almost disappearing under the table as she reached for her bag. After rummaging energetically, she pulled out a battered leather wallet of her own. 'Come along now, don't be shy. I'll show you mine if you show me yours.'

He smiled. 'You don't have any children.'

'Ah, but I do have an extremely fertile family. Two brothers, three sisters, five nephews and eleven nieces. So grit your teeth,' said Valentina happily, 'and prepare to be bored out of your skull.'

'Tell me if it's none of my business,' she said twenty

minutes later, 'but wasn't it weird being with Serena, knowing how much she hated kids?'

The fact that there was no love lost between Serena and Valentina was no secret. Guy, however, had no intention of providing additional fuel for gossips. There had been enough speculation already about the ending of his affair with Serena.

'She doesn't hate kids,' he replied easily. 'She just doesn't swoon over the idea of them.'

Idly, Valentina swirled her spoon through the double cream and chocolate sauce on her plate. 'How can anyone not love children?' Then, observing the expression on Guy's face – the distance was returning – she shook her head and grinned. 'I suppose you get this kind of thing all the time. Eager women dying to get their claws into you, banging on about how much they adore kids because they think it'll make you like them more.'

'Pretty close.' He found her perception and honesty appealing. 'Do you always say what you think?'

'Oh, always!' This time her eyes glittered with amusement. She had a tiny smudge of chocolate on her lower lip. Instinctively he reached across the wiped the smudge away with his thumb. Smiling, Valentina kissed it. 'There, I did warn you. Say what I think, do what I want. That's my motto.'

According to Maxine and Janey, he needed a woman in his life. They hadn't had much time for Serena; maybe Valentina would meet with their approval. Guy was entertained by the idea of parading her before them like a prospective champion at Crufts. At least she was about as far removed from Serena as it was possible to be.

'And what do you want?' he said, entering into the spirit of the game. Beneath the table Valentina had slipped off her trainers. One bare foot was now lazily caressing his thigh.

'More chocolate pudding,' she answered and the famous smile widened. 'Then you.'

The *paparazzi* were waiting outside on the pavement. The moment Valentina emerged from the restaurant with her pink leather jacket draped casually over her shoulders Italian-style, flashbulbs began exploding like fireworks.

'No pictures. I said no fucking pictures!' she yelled, glaring at them with disdain. 'We're having a private evening out, for God's sake. What are you, a bunch of animals?'

They loved her, of course. She made them a fortune. Seldom did a week go by without Valentina di Angelo featuring centre stage in the celebrity montages of the Sunday supplements. An encounter with Valentina was guaranteed to line their pockets and brighten their day. The public, it went without saying, lapped it all up like cream.

'Come on, Val, give us a smile,' one of them shouted. 'You know you can do it!'

'And you know what you can do,' she retorted, tossing her inch-long black hair.

'How about a quote then?' another ginger-bearded freelancer said hopefully. 'Are you and Guy Cassidy an item?'

'Are your legs breakable?'

397

'Hey, Guy! What's the idea? Did you take her out for a bet or something?'

Guy simply grinned and said nothing. He was content to leave the insults to the experts.

'Hey, Val. show us what you're hiding under that cheap jacket!' goaded one old hand who knew her well. 'Is it true you've had your tits fixed?'

This was the moment Valentina had been waiting for. This was the man who had started the rumour a fortnight ago, and she was ready for him.

'Why don't you come and take a closer look?' she said sweetly, and the other men grinned. Guy, who knew what was about to happen, took a discreet step to one side.

'Yeeuch, you bitch!' howled the photographer as the bowl of ice cream she had been concealing beneath the folds of the pink leather jacket cascaded down his face and chest. It was particularly splendid ice cream, honey and walnut, but well worth wasting on such a good cause and wonderfully photogenic against a black polo-neck sweater. Serve him right, Valentina thought happily, for being too stupid to tell the difference between plastic surgery and a tissue-packed Wonderbra.

Another volley of flashbulbs exploded, another feature in the tabloids was instantly guaranteed. Having made her mark, Valentina handed the empty bowl to one of the other members of the pack and reached for Guy's arm.

'Come on,' she murmured under her breath, as they moved towards their waiting cab. 'That's the business taken care of. Now for the pleasure . . .'

# Chapter 47

'No?' Valentina shrieked, scarcely able to believe what she was hearing. In her agitation, she almost catapulted off the bed. 'No? What the hell do you mean, *no*?'

The realization that he was making a huge mistake had crept up on him even as they made their way up to his hotel room. Having initially fended her off with a drink from the mini-bar, Guy had spent the last fifteen minutes searching for an acceptable way out of the situation he'd so stupidly got himself into. And it was a supremely ironic situation, he couldn't help thinking, because ninety-nine per cent of men would no doubt drool like dogs at the prospect of a night of passion with Valentina di Angelo.

It wasn't even as if she had done anything wrong. Beauty apart, she was funny and honest, great company and altogether about as engaging a person as anyone – *paparazzi* excluded – could wish to meet. But he just couldn't go through with it. For some unfathomable reason, he knew he would be making a terrible mistake.

'I'm sorry.' Guy shook his head, forcing himself to look at her. There was resignation in his dark blue eyes. 'I really am. It's been a great evening, but . . .'

'But what?' wailed Valentina, overcome with a sudden

rush of fear. 'What have I done wrong? What's the problem, for God's sake?' Casting around for a reason . . . *any* reason . . . she said helplessly, 'Am I too fat?'

'Don't be ridiculous.' It was every model's greatest fear. What was worse, he thought with an inward sigh and a glance at her stick-thin legs, was that she really meant it. 'You aren't fat and you haven't done anything wrong. It's me.'

Relief mingled with suspicion. Valentina's fingers continued to clench and unclench against the bedspread. 'What, then? If you're going to try and tell me you're impotent,' she warned, 'I may have a bit of trouble believing you.'

Guy had to smile. If he had been impotent, it would have been so much simpler. She would have felt sorry for him and he would have been off the hook. But 'won't play' was harder for Valentina to bear than 'can't play', and now thanks to him she was feeling sorry for herself.

'No,' he said gently. 'Look, you're a gorgeous girl and I'm probably going to kick myself in the morning, but right now I just know it would be . . . well, the wrong thing to do.'

Valentina didn't. As far as she was concerned it was the most absolutely right thing to do in the entire world. Her brown eyes clouded; what the hell was the big deal anyway, she thought with renewed frustration. It wasn't as if she was asking him to hitch-hike barefoot across bloody Antarctica. It was only sex, after all.

'More like you get a kick out of leading girls on,' she retaliated, still smarting from the humiliation of being rejected for no good reason at all by the most attractive man she'd clapped eyes on in years. And after such a promising start, too.

'It's not that, either.'

'Bastard,' murmured Valentina under her breath.

She wasn't taking it at all well. Guy pushed his fingers through his hair in a gesture of mild despair. 'Look, that's just what I'm trying not to be. If we spent the night together, I'd be a *real* bastard. You see, there's . . . somebody else,' he admitted with reluctance. 'I'm already involved with someone, and it wouldn't be fair to either of you if I . . .'

His voice trailed away. He took a slug of brandy, swallowed and shrugged.

'Oh.' Valentina's fingers began to unclench. A man with a conscience was something of a novelty in her experience. It was just a shame, she thought sorrowfully, he was so intent on being faithful to someone else rather than her. 'Who is it, anyone I know?'

Guy shook his head. As far as he was aware it wasn't anyone at all, but it appeared to be doing the trick, which was all that really mattered. He still didn't understand why the idea of sleeping with Valentina should suddenly have become such an undesirable proposition. It just had. Maybe, he thought with a mixture of resignation and alarm, there really was such a thing as the male menopause and it had arrived a decade ahead of schedule. Damn, what filthy rotten luck. Of all the nights to be hit with it . . .

'Well, she's a lucky girl.' Acknowledging defeat with as much good grace as she could muster, Valentina smiled and reached for her jacket. 'Whoever she is. No, don't worry, I can find my own way out. I'll ask the night porter to get me a cab.'

'I'm sorry,' said Guy, meaning it. Opening the door for her, he planted a brief kiss on her cheek. 'I was tempted, you know. This monogamy thing is pretty new to me.'

'Invite me to the wedding,' Valentina quipped. 'I'll tell her what a hero she's married. After all, I can personally vouch for your fidelity.'

He grinned. 'Thanks.'

But she was still wildly curious. Guy wasn't giving much away. Unable to resist it, she paused in the doorway.

'Is she beautiful?'

'Yes.'

'Is it . . .' – a stab in the dark, now – 'the girl I spoke to on the phone? What's her name, Maxine?'

Guy started to laugh. 'No,' he said, patting her shoulder. 'Nice try, sweetheart. But it definitely isn't Maxine.'

Thea, lying in bed with Oliver's arm around her, was looking pensive.

'What is it?' Pulling the duvet up to her shoulders, for the central heating in Thea's house was about as predictable as Thea herself, he gave her bare shoulder a squeeze. 'Worried about Janey?'

She was, of course, but that wasn't what was uppermost in her mind right now. Indirectly, she thought, the problem was Oliver himself. The trouble with being in love was the fact that it was so time-consuming. Whilst this might not be a problem for

Oliver, who could easily afford to have his time consumed, it was an undoubted drawback when you were a not altogether successful sculptress with work to do and bills to pay. The sale of the Ballerina had temporarily stalled the boring letters from the bank droning on about her overdraft, but the increasing displeasure of Tom Sparks, the owner of the studio, was somewhat more ominous. She was falling behind with the rent in a big way, and he wasn't amused. Sadly, not working meant not selling. And whilst at first it hadn't seemed to matter – how, after all, could financial security even begin to compare with all-consuming happiness? – the prospect of losing her beloved studio was fast becoming a real possibility.

All she had to do, of course, was mention this inconvenient dilemma to Oliver. Without so much as a second thought he would sign the necessary cheque like the proverbial good fairy and make everything right again. As far as he was concerned, there was no dilemma: Thea needed money and he had plenty of it. He would be happy to help out. No big deal.

But there lay the crunch. For it was a big deal. It hadn't been easy, but one way or another she had been self-supporting for the last twenty-five years, and whilst the idea of becoming a kept woman had always appealed, she now realized that some fantasies were better left unfulfilled. Maybe it was a salutary lesson, a kind of punishment for ever having wished it in the first place. Or maybe, she thought dryly, it was just sheer bloody bad luck. Because Oliver Cassidy, erupting into her life, had changed her. Here he was, the proud and generous owner of all that gorgeous money . . . and she loved him too much to take it.

It was no good, Thea decided, she was simply going to have to *make* time to work. If necessary – ugh, what a hideous prospect – she would even get up a couple of hours earlier each morning and sculpt whilst Oliver slept.

'Yes,' she lied, dragging her mind back to that other dilemma: Janey. Propping herself up on one elbow, she sighed. 'I ballsed it up completely. I should have tackled Alan on his own, of course. She was bound to take his side.'

Oliver kissed her warm shoulder. It was ironic, he felt, that they should both have been through virtually the same ordeal. In his own case, however, Véronique's untimely death had effectively prevented him from ever being able to be proved right.

'Of course she was,' he said consolingly. 'I know how hard it is; we do our best for our children, God knows, but sometimes they have to make their own mistakes. Give her time, darling, and maybe she'll come to her senses.'

'I bloody hope so.' Thea's tone was fretful; she still nurtured a fearsome longing to corner Alan Sinclair and slap him senseless. 'But how much longer is she going to need and how much more damage can he do in the meantime? Janey's so stubborn it almost frightens me,' she added, her tone bleak. 'I wouldn't put it past her to get herself pregnant, just to spite us all.'

# Chapter 48

Janey was looking wonderful, thought Bruno, watching from a distant corner as she entered the party on Alan Sinclair's arm. In a billowing white silk shirt tucked into white jeans, and with her blond hair left loose to fall past her shoulders, she exuded an air of careless glamour he had never seen in her before. The self-esteem which had been at rock-bottom for the past two years had clearly been revitalized by her husband's return, he decided, impressed by the almost magical transformation. It was as if she had been brought back to life, like a desperately wilted flower plunged into a bucket of water in the nick of time.

Hastily, Bruno pulled himself together. What was the matter with him anyway? Nauseating similes weren't his bag at all. Talk about un-macho . . .

Janey looked good because she was happy and in love, he decided, firmly banishing all thought of wilting flowers from his mind. It was as simple as that. Whether she would deign to speak to him when she realized he was here, however, was another matter altogether.

In the event, Janey didn't have a lot of choice. Having resolutely decided to ignore Bruno her plans were scuppered within minutes by Pearl, who dragged him into the kitchen. Janey, leaning against the fridge, was still waiting for Alan to uncork a bottle of Australian white. Gazing at a heavily doodled-on Chippendales calendar above the cooker, she assumed a fixed, I'm-not-listening expression. But the kitchen wasn't that big and nobody had ever called Pearl subtle.

'. . . I still don't believe you, darling!' she cried, clinging to Bruno's arm and waggling an admonitory finger at him. 'It's all very well saying you've fallen madly in love with this Maxine character, but does this mean you're actually planning to stay faithful to her, forsaking all others and all that gloomy stuff? You realize of course the whole town's laying bets on how long you'll manage to stick it out,' she added gleefully. 'So far nobody's dared risk their money on anything more than a month.'

Behind her, Alan glanced across at Janey. Eyebrows raised, he mouthed, 'Maxine?'

Nodding, she forced herself to smile as Bruno turned to face her. If she didn't, Alan would wonder why.

'Oh, I'm a reformed character.' Bruno grinned. 'It can happen, you know, even to me. Although if the odds are that good, maybe I should think about placing a bet myself.'

'So you're Bruno.' Stepping forward, Alan shook his hand. 'Hi, I'm Alan Sinclair, Maxine's brother-in-law. I've been hearing quite a bit about you.'

'That's a coincidence,' said Bruno easily. 'I've heard about you too.'

Pearl, who had been drinking double tequila slammers to celebrate the success of her party, was in high spirits.

Bruno was the greatest fun; she loved him to death. And although she hadn't actually been introduced to Alan Sinclair before, he had been one of the crowd at the surf club when she'd popped in and issued an open invitation to tonight's bash. The fact that he was deeply attractive hadn't escaped her notice at the time, either. It was just a shame, Pearl thought, that he should have chosen to turn up with a sleek blond girlfriend in tow.

'Everyone's heard about Bruno,' she told Alan with a giggle. 'Maybe I shouldn't be saying this if you're related to Maxine, but it's my party so what the hell! This man is wicked. Gorgeous,' she admitted, clinging to Bruno's arm and giving it an affectionate squeeze, 'but seriously wicked . . . possibly the wickedest man in all Cornwall.'

Janey cringed. She still couldn't believe she'd never heard so much as a single word of gossip about Bruno before getting involved with him herself. As far as everyone else was concerned, she thought bitterly, his conquests were practically the stuff of legend. And Pearl, whom she'd never met before in her life, was moving perilously close to the knuckle . . .

'You are looking at a seducer *extraordinaire*,' she continued, blithely unaware of Janey's unease. 'He's been doing it for years, you know. None of us can figure out how he manages to keep on getting away with it.'

'Thank you,' said Bruno with mock gravity. Janey, standing behind Alan, was looking positively stricken. Feeling sorry for her, he attempted to steer the conversation on to safer ground. 'But that was in the bad old days. From now on I'm a changed man, I promise you. How's your father, by the way? Has he managed to sell that yacht of his yet?'

But Pearl hadn't finished. Yachts were boring. The idea that Bruno Parry-Brent had turned over a new leaf, on the other hand, was simply too entertaining for words.

'In the bad old days!' she shrieked, gurgling with laughter and only narrowly missing the sleeve of Alan's faded denim shirt as tequila sloshed haphazardly out of her tilted glass. 'How long ago was your birthday, you old fraud? I might have missed the party but Suzannah told me all about it. She said you had the most terrific showdown with some poor girl you'd been seeing on the quiet until she found out what you were really like. Who did Suzie say she was, now?' She hiccuped, tried to think, and shook her head. 'No, I give up. Come on Bruno, remind me! I can't remember her name, but apparently she runs the flower shop in the high street . . .'

'Oh for goodness sake, will you stop going on about it.' Janey, stepping out of her clothes, left them in a heap on the bedroom floor. As she made her way through to the bathroom she added crossly, 'It was embarrassing for me too, you know.'

'I should think it was.' Alan's eyes were narrow with anger. 'You must be the laughing stock of Trezale . . . and you expect me to forgive you, just like that? Jesus, you aren't making it easy for me! You told me there hadn't been anyone else and I was stupid enough to believe you. Now I find out you've not only been screwing another man' – he spat the words out in disgust – 'but you had to make a complete fool of yourself and choose the town fucking stud.'

Not trusting herself to speak, Janey slammed the bathroom door and cleaned her teeth so hard her gums bled. Finally, taking a deep breath, she returned to the bedroom.

'Look,' she said, eyes ablaze with defiance, 'I wish it hadn't happened, but it did. And I'm not going to apologize. I said there hadn't been anyone else because that was what you wanted to hear, but what the hell did you seriously expect me to do . . . lock myself into a chastity belt and become a born-again virgin for the rest of my life? Be realistic,' she snapped, no longer caring what he thought. 'You were the one who left, for God's sake. And if sleeping with Bruno makes me the laughing stock of Trezale, so what? I'm used to it. People have been talking about me behind my back for the last two years, ever since my husband vanished off the face of the bloody earth. So if it's an apology you're waiting for,' she went on, 'you can forget it, because I've only slept with one man in two whole years . . . and that's not bad. If I'd known I was going to get this kind of grief,' Janey concluded bitterly, 'I would have slept with fifty.'

The ensuing silence seemed to go on for ever. Alan, sitting up in bed, stared at her. Finally he said, 'You've changed.'

It was late and Janey was tired but she didn't want to climb into the bed beside him. Leaning against the wall, she replied, 'I had to. When you're on your own you have to learn to look after yourself.'

Alan shook his head. 'And it's all my fault. I'm sorry,

sweetheart, I can't help it. It was the shock of finding out like that; I felt so damn jealous. Janey, come here. Please?'

He was holding his arms out to her. To her shame it was physical exhaustion rather than the prospect of reconciliation that propelled her towards the bed. Wearily, she submitted to his embrace.

'It's bound to take a while,' Alan murmured into her hair, 'getting used to being together again.'

'Mmm.'

'What are you doing?' He frowned as she adjusted the pillows and rolled on to her side, facing away from him.

Janey closed her eyes. 'Going to sleep.'

# Chapter 49

'Oh no, not you.' Sighing, Maxine wished now that she'd ignored the doorbell. 'I nearly got the sack last time you played this trick.'

Oliver Cassidy smiled. 'I'm sorry.'

'I should bloody well hope so,' she countered with indignation. 'Guy was furious with me. I was lucky to escape in one piece. And you were pretty lucky yourself,' she added. 'He was all for calling out the police. You could have been charged with kidnapping.'

She looked like her mother, Oliver realized. And although she was giving a good impression of a woman deeply outraged, he guessed it was more for effect than anything else.

'I could,' he admitted, his eyes crinkling at the corners as his smile broadened, 'but it wouldn't have been exactly fair, would it? Kidnappers have a tendency to demand ransoms. I gave Josh and Ella money.'

'You almost gave me a heart attack,' grumbled Maxine, shivering as a gust of wind rattled round the porch. Her bare feet on the stone step were icy. 'You shouldn't have lied to me, it was a rotten thing to do.'

'Growing old and never being allowed to see your

grandchildren is pretty rotten too.' Oliver, well wrapped up against the cold, in a beige cashmere overcoat, also shivered. 'Sometimes, desperate measures are called for. Maxine, I really am sorry you had to bear the brunt of my son's anger, but . . . goodness, this wind is bitter, isn't it?'

Maxine, standing her ground, forced herself not to smile. 'I expect it's nice and warm though, inside your car.'

'Go on,' said Oliver. 'Live a little. If you invite me in for a quick cup of coffee we can both relax. Guy's away, Josh and Ella are still at school; nobody need ever know I've been here.'

'What are you, the king of the door-to-door salesmen?' Maxine started to laugh. 'OK, you can come in. Just don't try and sell me any floor mops.'

'. . . So you see, Guy never forgave me for speaking my mind,' Oliver concluded fifteen minutes later. 'I felt he was too young to be married, that he was making a huge mistake, but he was too stubborn to take my advice. When Josh and Ella are grown up and he finds himself faced with the same problems, maybe he'll understand I had only his best interests at heart.' He shrugged and pushed his empty cup to one side. 'But by then it'll be too late, of course. I'll be dead.'

Maxine was well able to understand how he felt. Hadn't Thea reacted in exactly the same way upon hearing that Janey's decidedly unprodigal husband had breezed back into Trezale? And hadn't Janey reacted just as Guy had done, refusing to accept for even a single moment that her mother's opinion of him might be right?

'You might not be dead,' she ventured, struggling to say something reassuring. 'Look, I do sympathize but you must realize I'm in an impossible position here. I can't help you. And if you think I can persuade Guy to see reason, well . . . I'd have about as much chance of getting him to believe in Father Christmas.'

'I want to see my grandchildren again,' said Oliver Cassidy.

'No.'

He was no longer smiling. The expression in his eyes, she realized, was one of ineffable sadness.

'Maxine, listen to me.' Speaking without emotion, he leaned back in his chair and rested his clasped hands on the kitchen table. 'By the time Josh and Ella are grown up, I will certainly be dead. If my doctor is to be believed, I'll be dead by Christmas. I don't believe him of course – he's a notorious scaremonger – but I have to accept that there may be something in what he says. Maybe next year people can cross me off their Christmas card list but not this year.' He paused, then shrugged. 'Anyway, let's not get maudlin. I'm only telling you this because I need you to understand why I'm so anxious to see my grandchildren again.' Fixing his steady gaze upon her, he added, 'And why I need you to help me.'

'Oh hell.' Maxine shook her head in despair. 'Now I do wish you were a door-to-door salesman. Then I'd be able to say no.'

Josh and Ella were safely tucked up in bed by the time Bruno arrived at Trezale House. Since Maxine's idea of a romantic dinner *à deux* was spaghetti hoops on toast, he had brought the ingredients for a decent meal with him. Whilst he busied himself in the kitchen, slicing onions and mushrooms for the stroganoff, she sat happily drinking lager and relaying to him the events of the afternoon.

'Yeeuk! What are you doing?' she screeched as Bruno, having listened in silence for a good ten minutes, abandoned washing the leeks in order to cup wet, cold hands over her ears.

'The rest of your brain,' he explained carefully. 'I thought maybe we should save it. These medical experts can do wonders nowadays . . . if you're lucky they might be able to slide some of it back in.'

'Ha ha, very funny.' Unabashed, Maxine wriggled out of reach. 'OK, so when Guy finds out he'll have me hung, drawn and quartered, but wouldn't anyone else in my position have done the same?'

'You still don't get it, do you?' Standing back, gazing down at her with a mixture of amusement and disbelief, Bruno drawled, 'You really are full of surprises, my angel. How can anyone so smart be so incredibly dumb? How could you – of all people – fall for a line like that?'

'Like what?' The tiniest of frown lines bisected her eyebrows. Confusion registered in her dark brown eyes. 'What are you talking about?'

'And you told me Janey was the gullible one.' He couldn't resist it. The fact that razor-sharp Maxine had a hitherto unsuspected weak spot was totally, blissfully endearing. She was, he thought with a triumphant grin, never going to live this down.

'Oh come on,' she protested, as realization finally dawned. 'Bruno, no! That's sick.'

'*Maxine, yes!*' Mimicking her outraged tone, he stepped smartly back to avoid a kick on the shin. 'Look, I might not have met the man but you've already told me what he's like. What did Guy say – his father was a ruthless businessman who'd stop at nothing to get what he wanted? If he wants to see his grandchildren and you're telling him he can't, then he's going to have to come up with something spectacular to make you change your mind. What could be simpler than the old imminent-death routine? It might not be terribly original, but it usually does the trick. And it worked, didn't it?' he concluded with a cheerful I-told-you-so grin. 'My poor darling, you'd better dig out that bulletproof vest and superglue yourself into it. There's no telling how Guy Cassidy's going to react when he finds out what you've done this time.'

'Oh shit!' wailed Maxine, appalled. What she'd done this time had undoubtedly cost her her job. Travelling with Oliver Cassidy in the unimaginable luxury of his silver-grey Rolls, she had longed to ask more questions about the illness which was soon to rob him of his life. But she hadn't, for fear of appearing nosey and because it simply wasn't the kind of thing you discussed with a virtual stranger. Instead they had talked abut Josh and Ella; her soon-to-be-screened toilet-roll commercial; the wild beauty of the Cornish coastline; the stupid, sodding totally uninteresting weather . . .

Josh and Ella had been thrilled, of course, to see their grandfather waiting at the school gates. Maxine, quite choked by the poignancy of the situation, had almost been forced to blink back tears. How could anyone with even half a heart, she thought, possibly deny a dying man the chance of a last meeting with his only grandchildren?

They had returned to Trezale House to spend four blissfully happy hours together. Oliver Cassidy had even professed to adore the fish fingers and alphabetti spaghetti she'd served up, although he hadn't been able to eat a great deal of it. At the time, she had assumed his lack of appetite must be connected with the illness.

And at eight o'clock in the evening he had left. With heartbreaking innocence Ella had cried, 'Will we see you again soon, Grandpa?' and Maxine, a lump in her throat the size of an egg, had turned away. Josh, handling yet another fifty-pound note with due reverence, had said, 'When I buy my computer, Grandpa, I'll teach you to play Pokémon. If you practise long enough you might even get as good as me.'

'Maxine, how can I ever thank you?' Oliver Cassidy had smiled and rested his hand on her shoulder as she walked with him to the front door. Tilting his grey head, planting a brief, infinitely gentle kiss on her cheek, he added quietly, 'You're a very special girl and I'm truly grateful. You'll never know how much this afternoon has meant to me.'

And the fact that Guy was bound to find out what had happened – because with the best will in the world Ella was too young to keep a secret for anything exceeding fifteen seconds – didn't bother Maxine in the least. She knew she'd done the right thing, and furthermore she was going to tell him about his father's fatal illness. Surely, she thought as she stood on the step and watched Oliver Cassidy disappear down the drive in his Rolls, surely even Guy would be jolted into remorse when he learned the truth.

'Oh shit,' said Maxine again, as the irony of the situation struck her. For the last eight hours she had thought over and over again how desperately unfair it was that such a charming man should have to die. Now, riddled with self-doubt and the growing fear that maybe, after all, she had been conned in the most underhand manner possible, she found herself almost hoping he would. At least then, she thought fretfully, she'd be proved right.

On the way to school a week later, Maxine – hardly daring to raise the subject for fear of breaking some miraculous spell – turned to Josh and Ella and said in ultra-casual tones, 'You didn't tell Guy about your grandfather's visit, did you?'

It was a statement rather than a question. Maxine knew they couldn't have told him. She was still alive.

Behind her, Ella promptly erupted into fits of giggles. Josh, in the passenger seat, looked immensely proud. 'No.'

'Why not?'

He shook his head. 'It's a secret.'

'Oh come on, you can tell me,' said Maxine.

Emma mimed zipping her mouth shut. 'We can't tell anybody. It's an even bigger secret than the one about you smashing Daddy's car into the gatepost.'

'Look, I'm glad it's a big secret,' Maxine explained patiently. 'But I should be in on it. I was there, wasn't I?'

Josh considered this argument for a moment. After exchanging glances with Ella, he said, earnestly, 'OK, but you mustn't tell anyone else. Swear you won't, Maxine.'

'Bum,' said Maxine, and Ella giggled again. It was her favourite word.

'Grandpa said it had to be a secret,' Josh explained, 'because if we ever told anyone else, you'd get the sack and we'd never see you again for the rest of our lives.'

'Oh.' Overcome with emotion, Maxine's eyes abruptly filled with tears. Thankfully, they had by this time reached the school so she didn't risk killing them all.

'Well, it's nice to be appreciated,' she said gruffly, curbing the urge to fling her arms around them and smother them in noisy kisses. If she did that in front of their schoolfriends, Josh would certainly die of shame. She cleared her throat instead and attempted to turn the situation into a joke. 'So that must mean you like me a little bit, then?'

'I do,' Ella declared lovingly. 'And Josh was glad too.'

Maxine smiled. 'Was he, sweetheart?'

'Ella,' Josh murmured, his expression furtive.

But the sheer relief of having finally been allowed to break the silence proved too much for Ella. Having extricated herself from her safety belt she climbed forward between the front seats and adopted a noisy stage-whisper. 'Because Grandpa gave us extra money for not saying anything,' she confided, blue eyes shining. 'Lots of money you didn't even know about, but if we told the secret to anyone . . . except you, now . . . we'd have to give it all back.'

'Oh.' So much for thinking she'd been the one they couldn't bear to lose, thought Maxine. Mercenary little sods.

'Josh is going to buy a computer.' Ella's nose wrinkled in evident disgust. 'Ugh, computers are stupid. I don't want one!'

'That's because you're a girl,' he sneered. 'You want a stupid horse.'

Ella pushed him, then turned to Maxine, her smile angelic. 'A real, live horse,' she said happily. 'Called Bum.'

# Chapter 50

Janey, lying in the bath, told herself she was being stupid. She was a mature adult, after all, not a child for whom a birthday was a real landmark. The importance of birthdays worked according to a sliding scale; as you grew older, their significance decreased. Heavens, it was almost fashionable to forget your own birthday . . .

It was downright depressing, on the other hand, if everyone else forgot it too.

But she had dug herself into a hole from which, it now seemed, there was no face-saving escape, because her birthday was tomorrow and to mention it casually in passing at this late stage would be too humiliating for words. The trouble was, Janey thought with a pang of regret, she hadn't bothered earlier because she'd stupidly assumed everyone else would remember.

She was still in the bath when the telephone rang. Seconds later, Alan opened the bathroom door.

'Phone, sweetheart. It's Maxine.'

Superstition told Janey that if she climbed out of the water and went to answer it, Maxine wouldn't have remembered her birthday. If she stayed where she was, on the other hand, it might suddenly click.

'Ask her what she wants.' Slowly and deliberately she began to soap her shoulders. 'Take a message, or say I'll call back.'

He reappeared after a couple of minutes. 'She asked if you could babysit tomorrow evening. Guy had already said she could take a couple of days off and she and Bruno have arranged to go up to London,' he recited. 'But now Guy has to be somewhere tomorrow night, so he wonders if you wouldn't mind doing the honours. He says he'll definitely be home by midnight.'

So much for superstition. Wearily, Janey nodded. 'OK. I'll call her back in a minute.'

'No need.' He sounded pleased with himself. 'I've already told her you'll do it. She says can you be there by seven-thirty.'

Janey stared at him. 'Well, thanks.'

'What?' Alan looked surprised. 'I knew you'd say yes. All I did was say it for you. Why, have you made other plans?'

'No.' She closed her eyes. 'No other plans.'

'There you are then,' he chided, tickling the soles of her feet. 'Stroppy.'

Janey forced herself to smile. It was only a birthday after all. Not such a big deal.

'How about you? Are you doing anything tomorrow night?'

'Ah well, I was planning a quiet romantic evening at home with my gorgeous wife.' He rolled his eyes in soulful fashion. 'Just the two of us . . .'

'You could always come and help me babysit.'

'. . . but since you won't be here,' Alan concluded

421

cheerfully, 'I may as well meet the lads for a drink at the surf club.'

Janey, curled up on the sofa with a can of lager and a packet of Maltesers, was so engrossed in the book she was reading she didn't even hear the car pull up outside. When Guy opened the sitting-room door she jumped a mile, scattering Maltesers in all directions.

'Sorry.' He grinned and bent to help her pick them up. 'So which is scariest, me or the book?'

'You said you'd be back at midnight.' Still breathless, Janey glanced up at the clock. 'It's only half past nine. Oh no,' she said accusingly, 'you haven't walked out on her again. Tell me you didn't dump her at the hotel . . .'

When Charlotte had phoned Guy the night before and begged him to partner her at the firm's annual dinner, he had made strenuous efforts to get out of it. But Charlotte had been truly desperate. Everyone else was taking someone, she explained, evidently frantic, and she'd been let down at the last minute by her own partner who'd thoughtlessly contracted salmonella poisoning. 'Oh please Guy, I can't possibly go on my own,' she had wailed down the phone at him. 'It's not as if I'm asking you to sleep with me; I know it's over between us, but just this one last favour? Pleeease?'

He hadn't had the heart to refuse. But fate – for the first time in what seemed like years – appeared to be on his side. Within minutes of arriving at the hotel, Charlotte had disappeared to the loo. Finally emerging half an hour later, pale and obviously unwell, she clung to Guy's arm and groaned pitifully, 'Oh God, I think I'm going to have to go home. Tonight of all nights, as well. Bloody chicken biryani. *Sodding* salmonella.'

Guy, hiding his relief, had said goodbye to all the people he hadn't even had time to be introduced to, helped Charlotte out to the car and driven her home. Mortified at the prospect of throwing up in front of him, she had vehemently refused his offer to stay for a while and make sure she was all right. Food poisoning was a singularly unglamorous illness and all she wanted was to be left alone.

'Oh poor Charlotte!' Janey tried hard not to laugh at the expression on Guy's face. 'She doesn't have much luck, does she?'

'Every cloud,' he replied with an unrepentant grin. 'I didn't even have to give her a goodnight kiss.'

Janey looked at her watch; it was still only twenty to ten. Now that Guy was here, she supposed she could go home too. But Alan wouldn't be there, and the prospect of sitting alone in the flat on her birthday was infinitely depressing.

Sensing her hesitation, Guy said, 'Do you have to get back straight away?'

'Well, no.'

'Good. I'll open a bottle.'

When he had finished pouring the wine, he picked up the paperback Janey had been so wrapped up in. 'Hmm, so I was right. No wonder you nearly jumped out of your skin, reading horror stories like this.'

She laughed. 'I found it buried under a pile of comics in your downstairs loo. You should give it a try; it's actually very well written. I was really enjoying it.'

'As if Mimi didn't have enough fans.' With a shudder he dropped the book into her open handbag. 'Take it home with you. She always sends me a copy of her latest best-seller, though God knows why. The covers alone are enough to give me a headache.'

'You're such a chauvinist,' said Janey cheerfully. 'I like them.'

'You shouldn't need them.' Guy's expression was severe. 'Alan's back; you've got your own happy ending now.'

Janey fiddled with a loose thread on the sleeve of her pastel pink cotton sweater. 'Mmm.'

Guy decided to chance it. Very casually he said, 'Although I suppose it can't be easy. Two years is a long time. Getting used to living together again must take a while.'

She hadn't breathed so much as a word to anyone about the difficulties they'd been having. She'd barely been able to admit them to herself, Janey realized. But there were only so many excuses you could make on someone else's behalf. Alan was charming, funny and affectionate. But the flipside was beginning to get to her. Despite having been back for over a month now, he had made no real effort to find work. The amounts of money he borrowed from her in order to 'tide him over' were only small, but with no way of repaying them they soon mounted up. Janey, watching her own bank balance dwindle, was at the same time having to spend twice as much as usual on groceries, whilst Alan appeared to spend his money buying drinks for all his old friends down at the surf club.

'No, it isn't easy.' Janey attempted to sound matter of fact about it. There was no way in the world she would admit the true extent of her problems to Guy, but she was tired of pretending everything was perfect.

'I expect it's me,' she went on, taking fast, jerky sips of wine. 'When you've lived alone for a while you become selfish. It's always the silly things, isn't it? Like suddenly having to make sure there's food in the house; remembering not to use all the hot water; the toilet seat always being up when you want it down.'

'Tell me about it,' Guy raised an eyebrow. 'I share my home with Maxine. She might not leave the toilet seat up, but she drives me insane. You can't move in that bathroom for cans of industrial-strength hair spray. At the last count there were eleven different bottles of shampoo up there, and she leaves great blobs of hair mousse all over the carpet.' He shook his head in despair. 'It's like walking through a field of puffball mushrooms.'

'Why do you suppose I sent her up here to work for you?' Janey laughed. 'I've been through that mushroom field. I was desperate.'

She was starting to relax. Even more casually, Guy said, 'But at least Maxine and I aren't married.'

Janey looked uncomfortable. 'No.'

'Look.' Taking a deep breath, he decided to risk it. 'I'm on your side, Janey. Maybe this is none of my business but I can't help feeling there's more to it than hot water and toilet seats. Alan was away for two years. You've both changed. There are bound to be problems. Just because he's come back, you aren't automatically obliged to be happy.' He paused for a second, his eyes serious. 'These things don't always work out. There's no shame in that. Nobody would blame you.'

Janey bit her lip. What he said made so much sense, but she still couldn't bring herself to admit quite how torn she felt. Alan loved and needed her, after all. How on earth would it affect him if she were suddenly to announce that she had changed her mind?

Feeling horribly disloyal just thinking about it, she willed herself to remain calm. She wasn't going to pour her heart out to Guy; he'd suffered quite enough of that after the Bruno fiasco. He might be on her side, she thought, but she still had some pride. She didn't want him to think she was a completely hopeless case.

'We're fine,' Janey assured him, as convincingly as she knew how. She smiled. 'Really. I was just having a bit of a moan, that's all.'

Shit, thought Guy, not believing her for a second. He'd blown it. And he had thought he'd been doing so well.

'Shit!' Maxine yelled practically simultaneously, in London.

Bruno gave the maître d' an apologetic grin and hoped he wouldn't change his mind about giving them the last table in the restaurant.

'She's from Iceland,' he confided. 'Doesn't speak a word of English. I think she's saying "hello".'

But Maxine, staring at the reservation diary lying open on the desk before them, was too appalled to enter into the spirit of the game.

'It's the fifteenth,' she groaned. 'Oh hell, I can't believe it's really the fifteenth!'

Of November, thought Bruno, following her gaze. Big deal. Unless she'd suddenly realized her period was late, in which case it would definitely be a big deal . . .

'Quick, I need a phone!' Maxine launched herself across the mahogany desk. 'Can I use this one?'

But the maître d', who had quick reflexes, had already clamped his hand firmly over the phone. The last time someone had tried that trick, they'd called their mother in South America. 'This one is reserved for table bookings, madam. We have a pay phone for customers at the far end of the bar.'

'What is it?' Bruno demanded, as Maxine rifled his pockets for change. To his alarm, there were tears glistening in her eyes.

'That bastard,' she seethed. 'I asked him what she was doing tonight and he told me she didn't have any plans. 'I suppose *he's* gone out . . .'

'Who?'

'Bloody Alan bloody Sinclair.' The words dripped with contempt. 'Who else?'

Bruno raised his eyebrows. 'Why, what's he done now?'

'Oh, nothing much,' snapped Maxine. 'At least, not by his standards. It's only Janey's birthday, after all.'

# Chapter 51

Right, that's it, thought Guy.

Janey, watching him replace the receiver, was unnerved by his grim expression.

'Bad news?'

He nodded. 'Very bad news.'

'Oh no.' Her heart lurched. 'What is it?'

'It's November the fifteenth,' Guy replied slowly. 'Your birthday. Don't tell me you'd forgotten too.'


'The nerve of that man,' cried Maxine, flushed with annoyance. 'He wouldn't even let me speak to her!'

Bruno frowned. 'Alan? Why not?'

She looked at him as if he was being deliberately obtuse. 'Not Alan, stupid. Guy. She's babysitting up at the house. I thought he'd be out, but he's back.'

By this time thoroughly confused and too hungry to care much anyway, Bruno had begun studying the menu. But Maxine was still muttering to herself, twirling her hair round her fingers in a frenzy of indignation. He sighed. 'OK, so why wouldn't Guy let you speak to her?'

'I don't know, do I?' She glared at him across the table. 'He told me to leave everything to him; he'd deal with it.

428

What the bloody hell is that supposed to mean?'

'I'd have thought it was pretty obvious.' Bruno grinned. 'He's going to make sure Janey's birthday goes with a bang.'

'I know it's my birthday.' Janey felt unaccountably nervous. 'Who was that on the phone? Is that the very bad news, or is there something else?'

'It was Maxine, ringing from a call box.' Guy bent to refill their glasses. 'She's mortified at having forgotten, but she sends her love and says she'll bring you back a mega-stupendous present. Her words,' he said dryly. 'I wouldn't get your hopes up if I were you. She bought Josh a mega-stupendous present the other week; it turned out to be a bouncing rubber brain. When you throw it against the wall,' he added with a look of resignation, 'it screams *Ouch*.'

'I could probably do with one of those.' Janey smiled. 'So that's really the bad news, Maxine forgetting my birthday?'

But the humour had vanished from his eyes once more. Really, she thought, he was incredibly hard to keep up with.

'No,' said Guy. 'The bad news is Alan forgetting your birthday.'

Janey, opening her mouth to protest, had no chance.

'Don't even say it,' Guy warned. 'For God's sake, Janey! Why do you always have to defend him? The way he's treated you is sickening enough, but not even being able to remember your birthday – this year of all years – is downright despicable!'

'Lots of husbands forget their wives' birthdays.' She couldn't help it; now he was being unfair. 'Thousands do, all the time. It's practically a condition of marriage.' Janey realized she was shaking.

Guy's dark eyes, glittering with derision, bored into her. 'Don't be such a coward,' he drawled unpleasantly. 'Stop covering up for him. Why can't you just admit the fact that he's a selfish bastard and he's making you miserable? Why don't you give yourself a rest, Janey, say what you really think and stop being so fucking *nice*?'

This was too much. Something snapped inside her. Guy, launching into a totally unprovoked attack, was somehow managing to make her feel she was the one at fault.

'How dare you!' The words came tumbling out of her mouth but it was as if someone else was saying them for her. 'How dare you try and heap the blame on me? If you want to know what I really think, it's that you're just as much of a bastard as my husband!' She was trembling violently but the voice doing the talking didn't falter. 'OK, if you want the dirt I'll give it to you. It isn't working out because he's a selfish, idle sponger who expects me to do everything for him because that's how it used to be, and he doesn't see why it should be any different now. He's using me . . . taking advantage of me. I know he's doing it. I hate him doing it, but I don't have any choice!'

Janey paused, gulping for breath, panting as if she'd just run a marathon. But he had goaded her into this exorcism and now it was all spilling out. Her chest hurt, her throat ached and her fingernails were biting into her palms like fish hooks. But she had almost finished and she was going to force him to understand the kind of hell she'd been through if it killed her.

'I don't have any choice.' She repeated the words in a low voice. 'Because Alan needs me. I'm afraid of what he might do if I tell him it's over. I don't think he could handle it. He's dropped hints, and they scare me witless. I really believe he would harm himself: how can I possibly afford to take that risk? How could I ever live with myself if I called his bluff and he did commit suicide?' She shook her head and shuddered helplessly at the mere mention of the word. 'It would be on my conscience for the rest of my life. It would be my fault. I'd be the one who had killed him.'

'Oh Janey,' Guy gave her a ghost of a smile. 'I'm sorry I shouted at you. Do you understand now why I had to do it?'

He had been goading her deliberately, of course; forcing her to lose her temper with him and spill it all out. With a weary nod, she said, 'I understand, but it isn't as if there's anything you can do to help. You knowing about my problems isn't going to make them go away.'

'Well,' persisted Guy, 'do you at least feel better?'

'I don't know.' It was a lie. She did feel better, Janey realized, but how long was that likely to last? She would probably wake up tomorrow morning and kick herself. Ungraciously, she said, 'I suppose you do, now you've weaseled that little confession out of me. At least your curiosity's been satisfied.'

'Don't be bitchy.'

'*Don't be bitchy*?' Echoing the words, she mimed frustration. 'Five minutes ago you told me to stop being so fucking nice. You really do know how to shower a girl with compliments, Guy.'

He grinned, because there weren't many people on the planet less adept at handling a compliment than Janey. When he'd once tried admiring her new trousers she had replied, 'At least they hide my legs.' When on another occasion he had said her hair looked nice, she'd promptly told him it needed cutting. If he displayed appreciation of her chicken casserole she invariably shook her head and said either, 'Too much tarragon,' or 'Not enough salt.'

If he thought for one minute it would help, Guy told himself, he would shower her with compliments. He would tell her she was beautiful, that she had stunning legs, wondrous eyes, a deeply kissable mouth . . .

He could also tell her that the prospect of spending the night with Valentina di Angelo had left him utterly cold, whereas the thought of spending the night with Janey Sinclair was infinitely desirable.

Guy smiled, because at least he could stop worrying about the male menopause. He also, finally, understood why he hadn't wanted to sleep with Valentina. It was *because* he wanted Janey.

But it was hardly the time to make his feelings known. If anything was guaranteed to send her screaming out of the house, he decided, it was a declaration of lust from some bastard who had just bullied her into revealing the innermost secrets of her hopeless marriage to another bastard. Oh yes, that would really restore her faith in men.

'What are you thinking?' Janey demanded in accusing tones, because Guy was miles away and there was a hint of a smile around his mouth. If he was laughing at her, she would slap him.

'Nothing. Sorry.' Hastily, he composed himself. 'Look, I understand how you must feel about Alan, but this rubbish about killing himself is emotional blackmail. Janey, nobody has the right to do that to you. It's ludicrous. If he wants to jump off a cliff, that's his decision. You wouldn't have made him do it, and you wouldn't be responsible.'

'But—'

Guy's expression was severe. 'No, this time you're just going to have to sit there and let me have my say. What he's doing is sick. It's also selfish. And people who will stoop to such depths in order to get whatever they want are way too selfish to top themselves, believe me. He's threatening to do it because it's the only way he knows of making sure you don't dump him. If he really loved you as much as he says, he wouldn't dream of putting you through this kind of hell. Janey, if I thought for one moment you'd take me up on it I'd bet my house, my car – my *kids*, for God's sake – that he's bluffing. If you tell him to take a running jump, believe me, the last place he's going to visit is a handy clifftop.'

'It's so easy for you to say that.' Just listening to him made Janey's stomach squirm. 'You don't even know him. It's different when it's your own husband. I can't gamble with his life.'

More's the pity, thought Guy. But she clearly wasn't going to change her mind. At least he had forced her to admit the problem; it might not be much but it was a start.

'No. OK.' He had to agree she had a point. Maxine, faced with a similar threat, would doubtless hand the poor chap a Stanley knife and run him a nice hot bath.

But Janey was Janey, and that wasn't her style. She considered other people's feelings, had probably never deliberately hurt anyone in her entire life, and was prepared to sacrifice her own happiness in order to avoid upsetting Alan bloody Sinclair.

That was the trouble with nice girls, he thought ruefully. They had a conscience. Sometimes it was bloody infuriating.

'Now what?' Janey glared at him, because he was doing it again. She never knew what he was thinking and it unnerved her.

He grinned. 'We've finished the bottle. Shall I open another one?'

'What, so that you can lecture me for another hour?' She was only half joking. When Guy set his mind to it, he could be horribly persistent. Especially when he was determined to prove that he was right.

'We could change the subject.'

Janey looked at her watch; it was gone eleven-thirty. 'I can't drink any more and still drive home,' she said with a note of regret. 'And it's later than I thought. I'd better be making a move.'

'You don't have to drive. You could always spend the night here. In Maxine's room,' he said, before she had a chance to become flustered. 'It wouldn't do Alan any harm to wonder where you'd got to,' he added slyly. 'Serve him right for forgetting your birthday.'

But Janey was unfolding her legs, searching around

for her shoes and stuffing Mimi's book into her bag. 'And tomorrow morning I'd go to work with a raging hangover.' She pulled a face. 'Thanks for the offer, but I have to be at the market by six.'

She had ignored the dig, resolutely refusing to rise to the bait.

'Let me just go and check on the kids,' said Guy, good-naturedly accepting defeat. 'Then I'll see you out.'

Janey was waiting in the hall when he returned downstairs. She wound a red cashmere scarf around her neck. 'Are they all right?'

'Well away.' Guy nodded and grinned. 'How about you, after all that interrogation? Are you OK?'

'I'll live.' With a smile, she flipped the tasselled ends of the scarf over her shoulders. 'At least you didn't pull my fingernails out.'

'I do have something else to say,' he warned. 'Before you go.'

Janey braced herself. She might have guessed he would. 'Oh. What is it?'

'Happy birthday.' The red scarf was covering the lower half of her face. Before she realized what was happening Guy was gently pushing it down, out of the way. There was her mouth, wonderfully soft and inviting. When you wished someone a happy birthday, he reasoned, it was perfectly in order to give them a kiss to go with it.

But he didn't want to alarm her. Instead, exercising almost superhuman control, he cast one last regretful glance at those slightly parted lips and aimed, instead, an inch to the left.

'Except it hasn't been too happy,' he murmured.

Ridiculously, his heart was pounding like a schoolboy's. 'I'm sorry about that.'

Janey, startled by her own reaction to what was, after all, only a polite gesture, was deeply ashamed of herself. Just for a fraction of a second she had thought Guy was going to kiss her properly. What was even more awful was the fact that she had wanted him to.

'It isn't over yet.' Flustered, she resorted to feeble humour. 'I've still got Maxine's present to look forward to, haven't I? If Josh's brain says "Ouch", she'll probably find one for me that yells "Dimwit".'

Guy, who was still wearing his dinner jacket, reached into the inner pocket and withdrew a small, green leather box.

'Well, I can't compete with a bouncing brain.' As he took Janey's hand and placed the box in her palm, his eyes silently dared her to object. 'But at least this won't hurl insults at you.'

Inside lay a slender rose-gold bangle engraved around the outer edge with delicately entwined leaves and flowers. It was old, simple and breathtakingly beautiful. Janey, who had never been more embarrassed in her entire life, said, 'Oh for heaven's sake, you don't want to give me something like this.'

'Don't be silly. Call it making amends for giving you such a hard time tonight.' Since she evidently had no intention of taking the bracelet out of the box, Guy did it himself and pushed it over her trembling hand.

'But where . . . who . . . ?'

'I spotted it in an antique shop in St Austell a few months ago,' he lied. 'I was going to give it to Serena, then I decided it wasn't her style. You may as well have it,' he added casually. 'It's no use to me.'

Janey flushed with pleasure. It was still embarrassing to be on the receiving end of such generosity but Guy clearly wouldn't take it back. The engraved flowers were forget-me-nots, she realized, studying the bangle in more detail and loving the way it gleamed rather than glittered in the light, showing its age and quality.

'Definitely not Serena's style.' She gave him a mischievous smile. 'I'm glad you didn't give it to her. I love it, Guy. Thank you.'

This time she reached up and kissed him, her warm lips brushing his cheek a decorous inch from his mouth just as he had done earlier. The same tingle of longing zipped through her. Janey, fantasizing wildly, wondered what Guy would do if she moved towards him . . . moved her mouth to his.

The image flashed into her brain. ready-made, as if in answer. Pushy, eager Charlotte, throwing herself at Guy. Guy, good-humoured but resigned, wondering how the hell to fend her off without hurting her feelings. And Janey herself, hearing all about it, wondering how Charlotte could bear to make such an idiot of herself when he was so plainly uninterested.

No upturned bucket of ice-cold water could have shocked her to her senses more abruptly. So much for wild fantasies, Janey decided, and prayed that Guy hadn't been able to read her mind.

'Thanks again for the bracelet.' She took a hasty step backwards, pulling the scarf up over her chin once more and making a clumsy grab for the front door. 'Gosh, it's freezing outside! Look at all those stars . . . there's even ice on your bird table . . . poor old birds . . .'

One stupid kiss on the cheek, Guy realized, shaking his head in disbelief, and she'd managed to give him a severe erection. Never mind the poor birds, he thought, watching Janey as she jumped into the van, anxious to get home to her undeserving pig of a husband. To *hell* with the wildlife. What about me?

# Chapter 52

'Janey, it's me. Can you come over here right away?'

At the sound of her mother's voice, Janey felt the muscles of her jaw automatically tighten. Confiding her marital problems to Guy had been one thing, but she still considered Thea's outburst in front of Alan to have been totally out of order. Even if she had been right, it was an unforgivable action.

They hadn't spoken to each other since. And now here was Thea on the other end of the phone, expecting her to drop everything and rush over to see her. To add insult to injury, it was pouring with rain.

*Squish*, went the mister spray in Janey's hand as she aimed it at a three-foot yucca plant. 'I'm busy,' she said, stretching past the yucca and giving the azaleas a shower. *Squish, squish*. 'What do you want?'

'I need to see you.' Thea sounded quite unlike her usual self. 'Please, Janey.'

Suspecting some kind of ulterior motive, Janey kept her own response guarded. 'Why?'

'Because Oliver is dead,' said Thea quietly, and replaced the receiver.

\* \* \*

He had died the previous evening, without warning, in her bed. Thea, having slipped out of the house at eight o'clock, had gone to the studio and worked for three hours on a new sculpture. Returning finally with arms aching from the strenuous business of moulding the clay over the chicken-wire framework of the figure, and a glowing sense of achievement because it had all gone so well, she had climbed the stairs to her bedroom and found him. His reading glasses were beside him, resting on her empty pillow. The book he had been reading lay neatly closed on the floor next to the bed. It appeared, said the doctor who had come to the house, that Oliver had dozed off and suffered the stroke in his sleep. He wouldn't have known a thing about it. All in all, the doctor explained in an attempt to comfort Thea, it was a marvellous way to go.

Thea, wrapped up in a cashmere sweater that still bore the scent of Oliver's cologne, was huddled in the corner of the tatty, cushion-strewn sofa drinking a vast vodka-martini. There were still traces of dried clay in her hair and beneath her fingernails; her eyes, darker than ever with grief, were red-rimmed from crying.

Having left Paula in charge of the shop, and feeling horribly helpless, Janey helped herself to a vodka to keep her mother company. Their differences forgotten, because her own unhappiness paled into insignificance compared with Thea's, Janey sat down and put her arms around her.

'Bloody Oliver.' Thea sniffed, continuing to gaze at the letter in her lap. 'I keep thinking I could kill him for doing this to me. How could he keep this kind of thing to himself and not even warn me? Typical of the bloody man . . .'

She had found it in his wallet, neatly slotted in behind the credit cards. The plain white envelope bore her name. The contents of the letter inside had come as almost more of a shock than his death.

'Are you sure you want me to read it?' Janey frowned as her mother handed it to her. 'Isn't it private?'

'Selfish bastard,' Thea murmured, fishing up her sleeve for a crumpled handkerchief as the tears began to drop once more down her long nose. 'Of course I want you to read it. How can any man be so selfish?'

Janey recognized the careful, elegant writing she'd noted on Oliver's visit to her shop as she now read his farewell.

*My darling Thea,*

*Well, if you're reading this you've either been snooping shamelessly or I'm dead. But since I have faith in you, I shall assume the latter.*

*Now I suppose you're as mad as hell with me for doing it this way because, yes, I knew it was going to happen in the not-too-distant future. My doctor warned me I was a walking time-bomb. And no, there was nothing that could be done either medically or surgically to prevent it happening. This time even money couldn't help.*

*But think about it, sweetheart. Would you really have been happier, knowing the truth? I'm afraid I developed an all-consuming fear that you might try and persuade me to take things easy, maybe even not allowing me to make love to you as often as I liked for fear of over-exerting myself. What a deeply depressing prospect that would have been. Now perhaps you can begin to understand why I didn't tell you!*

*Right, now for something you do already know. I love you, Thea. We may not have had a vast amount of time together but these last months have been the very happiest of my life. When I came to Cornwall, it was to see my grandchildren. How could I ever have guessed I would meet and fall so totally in love with a beautiful, bossy, wonderful woman who loved me in return? And for myself rather than for my money.*

*If, on the other hand, you're reading this letter because you stole my wallet and were riffling through my credit cards, I trust you're now ashamed of yourself.*

*That was a joke, sweetheart. No need to rip this letter to shreds. If I can keep my sense of humour, so can you.*

*I don't know what else to say. I'm sorry if I've upset you, but even though my motives were selfish I still feel my decision was the right one to make. If you contact my solicitor (details in the black address book) he will organize the reading of my will. Maybe this will go some way towards making amends.*

*My darling, I love you so very much.*

*Oliver.*

'Well,' said Janey, clearing her throat as she folded the pages of the letter and handed them back to her mother. 'I think he was right.'

'Of course he was right.' With an irritable gesture, Thea wiped her wet face on her sleeve. 'But that doesn't mean

I have to forgive him. Did he think I wouldn't want anything to do with him if I'd known he was about to keel over and die?'

'He's explained why he didn't want you to know,' Janey reminded her. 'He wanted to enjoy himself without being nagged. He didn't want you endlessly worrying about him. He didn't want you to be miserable.'

'Well I am,' Thea shouted. 'Bloody miserable! After all these years I finally meet the man I've waited for all my life, and he has to go and do this to me. It isn't fair!'

Nothing she could say, Janey realized, was going to help her mother. All she could do was be there.

'At least you met him,' she said, giving Thea another hug. 'If you hadn't, think what you would have missed. Surely a few months with Oliver was better than nothing at all?'

'In a couple of years, maybe I'll think that.' Thea passed Janey her empty glass. 'All I know right now is that it hurts like hell. Get me another drink, darling. A big one. On second thoughts, just give me yours. You have to drive.'

'It's OK, Mum. I don't have to go anywhere.'

'Yes, you do,' said Thea. 'Someone has to tell Guy Cassidy his father is dead. He might not care,' she added bitterly, 'but he still has to know.'

Guy couldn't believe what he was hearing. And from Janey, of all people. So much, he decided, for mutual trust.

Maxine had gone to the supermarket and the children were at school. Janey, sitting bolt upright on a kitchen chair with her wet hair plastered to her head, had refused his offer of coffee and had come straight to the point. She was also, very obviously, on Thea's side.

'So what you're telling me,' said Guy evenly, 'is that your mother has been having an affair with my father. They've practically been living together. And you knew all about it.'

He was clearly angry. And Thea had been right, thought Janey. The fact that Oliver was dead wasn't what was bothering him. The anger was directed solely at her.

'I found out about it, yes.' Struggling to curb her impatience, she pushed a damp strand of hair away from her eye. 'But is that really important? OK, so you had a quarrel with him years ago but that's over now. Guy, your father died last night. Josh and Ella will be upset even if you aren't.'

'You knew where he was all the time.' It was as if he hadn't heard her. 'And you didn't tell me.'

Janey's dark eyes flashed. The contrast between Thea's terrible grief and this total lack of concern couldn't have been more marked. 'I thought about telling you,' she said coldly. 'And I decided against it. I'm glad now that I did.'

'Did what?' Maxine, buckling under the weight of six carrier bags, and even more sodden and bedraggled than Janey, appeared in the doorway. 'Am I interrupting something personal here?' Her eyebrows creased in suspicion. 'Are you talking about me?'

Guy, assuming that Maxine was in on it too, didn't say anything.

'Oliver Cassidy died last night,' Janey told her.

'Oh my God, you're not serious!' For a moment, Maxine looked as if she didn't know whether to laugh or cry. One of the carrier bags dropped to the floor with an ominous crash.

'No, it's a joke,' snapped Guy.

'So he wasn't lying,' Maxine wailed. 'I knew he wouldn't lie to me! Bloody Bruno . . . !'

'What?' Guy demanded, sensing that he hadn't heard anything yet. He glared at Maxine. 'Come on, out with it! What else has been going on that I don't know about?'

'Jesus,' he sighed, when she had finished telling him.

'Oh calm down.' Maxine, having rummaged energetically through every carrier, finally located the chocolate digestives. 'He's dead now, so what does it matter? I'm just glad I let him see the kids,' she added with renewed defiance. 'Go on, have a biscuit.'

It was like a jigsaw puzzle, thought Guy. Everyone had been holding different pieces. Maxine's story was clearly news to Janey.

But the oddness of Janey's presence in the house had apparently only just struck Maxine. Turning to her sister and speaking through a mouthful of biscuit, she said, 'I don't understand. Why *are* you here?'

'Janey came to tell me about my father.' Guy couldn't resist it. It was, he decided, his turn to spring a surprise.

Maxine frowned. 'But how did she know?'

'Your mother sent her over here.' His eyes glittered with malicious pleasure. 'My father, you see, was in her bed when he died.'

The funeral took place three days later. With typical thoroughness and attention to detail, Oliver Cassidy had made all the arrangements himself. Even he, however, hadn't been able to organize the weather, which had gone from bad to atrocious. Trezale churchyard, cruelly exposed to the elements, was awash with freezing rain. The small funeral party had to struggle to stay standing against the force of the bitter, north-westerly gales as Oliver's coffin was lowered slowly into the ground.

Back at Thea's house afterwards, the sitting room was warm but the atmosphere remained distinctly chilly. Guy, barely speaking to anyone, looked bored. Douglas Burke, Oliver's solicitor, had travelled down from Bristol to preside over the reading of the will as instructed by his late client and was anxious to get it over with so that he might return home to his extremely pregnant wife. Thea was desperately trying to contain her grief. Only the presence of Ella and Josh, who had insisted on attending the funeral, brightened the proceedings at all.

'At least the food's cheerful,' Maxine murmured in Janey's ear. Oliver had organized that too, making a private arrangement with the head chef from the Grand Rock where he had retained a room until the end though seldom visiting it. The hors d'oeuvres, arranged on silver platters, were ludicrously over the top; each stuffed cherry tomato had been precision carved, each quail's egg painstakingly studded with caviar. The sculptured smoked-salmon mousse, a work of art in itself, could have graced a plinth in the Tate Gallery. The champagne was Taittinger.

'There's only us,' Janey fretted. 'It doesn't seem right, but the solicitor insisted it was what Oliver wanted.'

She had phoned him herself, on her mother's behalf. Her suggestion that an announcement should be placed in the *Telegraph* had been firmly rebuffed. Not until after the funeral, Oliver had apparently instructed. He didn't want his gaggle of ex-wives descending on Trezale and upsetting Thea.

'Look at Guy,' whispered Maxine, giving him a mischievous wink just to annoy him. 'Moody sod.'

'I don't think he's ever going to speak to me again.' Janey tried to sound as if she couldn't care less. 'He said I'd betrayed him.'

'I suppose we all did.' Maxine grinned. 'I still think it's funny. It was like a mass conspiracy, except none of us realized we were all separately involved.'

'Poor Oliver. Poor Mum,' sighed Janey, toying idly with an asparagus canapé she didn't have the heart to eat.

'At least you're back on speaking terms,' Maxine consoled her. 'That's one family feud nipped in the bud. Speaking of which,' she added, 'how are things going with you and Alan?'

Speaking of conspiracies, thought Janey dryly . . .

Aloud she said, 'Oh, fine.'

The will reading lasted less than fifteen minutes. Simply and concisely, Oliver had divided his amassed fortune into three equal parts, making Thea, Josh and Ella instant millionaires. Thea, by this time beyond tears, called Oliver a bastard and said she didn't want his stinking, lousy, rotten money. Josh and Ella, entranced both by her thrilling choice of words and by the prospect of such unimaginable riches, were less than overjoyed to learn that their own inheritances were to be held in trust until they were twenty-one.

'Bugger,' pouted Ella, because if Thea could swear, so could she. 'Twenty-one's *ancient*. I'll be too old to ride a horse by then.'

'Don't worry.' Maxine, fastening her into her emerald-green coat, winked at Janey. 'You'll be able to treat yourself to a solid gold Zimmer frame.'

'Dad didn't get any money.' Josh looked thoughtful. 'Does that mean we're richer than he is now?'

Guy, darkly handsome and decidedly impatient, was already waiting at the front door to take them home. Janey, pretending she hadn't noticed him there, bent down and gave Josh a hug. 'Probably. Just think, you may have to start giving him pocket money in future.'

'But only if he makes his bed and washes the car.' Josh beamed at her, highly diverted by the prospect. Then, sounding startled, he said, 'Oh!'

His gaze had dropped. He was no longer looking at her face.

Janey, smiling, said, 'What?'

'Um . . . nothing.' Josh's long-lashed blue eyes clouded with confusion as natural good manners vied with surprise. Tentatively, he reached out and touched the sleeve of her ivory silk shirt. 'You're wearing Mummy's bracelet, that's all.'

'Janey!' wailed Ella, barging past and almost knocking him down. 'Maxine won't tell me. What's a Zimmer frame?'

# Chapter 53

It was ten o'clock in the evening by the time Janey let herself into the flat. Alan, for once not out at the surf club, had fallen asleep in front of the television with the gas fire blazing and both living-room windows wide open. Three empty lager cans and the remains of an Indian takeaway littered the coffee table upon which his feet were propped.

In the dim light, his enviable cheekbones seemed more pronounced and the corners of his mouth appeared to curve upwards as if in secret amusement. His blond hair gleamed and his eyelashes, not blond but dark, cast twin shadows upon his cheeks. Watching him sleep, Janey wondered how anyone could look so beautiful – almost angelic – and still snore like a pig.

He woke with a start when she switched off the television.

'Oh. You're back.' Rubbing his eyes, he pushed himself into a sitting position. As Janey bent to pick up the empty cans, he added, 'Leave that, I'll do it in a minute. So how did it go this afternoon?'

'Like a funeral.' Since Alan's idea of 'in a minute' was more like next weekend, she continued piling the empty curry and rice containers on to his dirty plate. In the kitchen the sink was crammed with more unwashed plates and coffee mugs, and the sugar bowl had been tipped over, spilling its contents on to the floor. Sugar crunched beneath her feet as she chucked the lager cans one by one into the bin.

'Don't worry, I'll clear it up,' Alan called from the living room. 'How's Thea, OK now?'

'Oh, absolutely fine.' Janey wondered if he had any idea what a stupid question that was. 'She's almost forgotten what he even looked like.'

Alan appeared in the doorway, looking shamefaced. 'Hey, no need to snap. You know what I meant.'

'She'll get through it,' said Janey briefly.

'Come on, sit down and relax. You look exhausted.' He took her hand and the bracelet – Véronique's bracelet, thought Janey – brushed against his wrist. When Alan had remarked upon it last week she'd simply told him that it had been a birthday present and he had assumed she'd had it for years.

'So what's the news?' he asked, when Janey had shrugged off her coat. 'You said the solicitor was coming down to read the will; that's unusual nowadays isn't it? Did Thea get anything?'

She looked at him. 'Any what?'

'Sweetheart, you aren't even listening to me!' Smiling and shaking his head in gentle reproach, Alan opened another can of lager. 'I asked you if he left Thea anything in the will. After all, from what you told me he seemed pretty smitten. The least he could do was show his appreciation with a nice little legacy.'

'He did,' said Janey tonelessly.

'Well, how much?'

'About one and a half.'

'Thousand?' Alan looked faintly disappointed. 'That's not much. I thought he was supposed to be loaded.'

'One and a half million,' said Janey.

After the endless, churning turmoil of the past weeks, finally making the decision was easy. Having listened to Alan for over an hour now, Janey knew it couldn't go on any longer. Whilst he had been crowing over her mother's inheritance and excitedly planning how they should spend the money Thea was bound to hand out to Maxine and herself, she had reached the point of no return. His shameless assumptions both appalled and sickened her. His greed revolted her. The realization that she was about to do what she had told Guy Cassidy she could never risk doing, left her feeling . . . well, Janey wasn't quite sure how she felt; presumably that would come later. Right now, all she had to do was say the words.

'. . . and we could do with a decent car,' he went on, waving dismissively in the direction of the window overlooking the high street. 'The van's OK for carting flowers around but it's hardly what you'd call stylish. How about a soft-top for next summer, sweetheart? Something with a bit of go in it?'

'Look.' Janey, unable to contain herself any longer, said evenly, 'Oliver Cassidy left that money to my mother. Not to me, and not to you. I don't know how you can even think you have any right to a share in it.'

'Janey, all I'm saying is that Thea is bound to want

you to share her good fortune!' Alan looked hurt. 'You need a holiday, you need a decent car; I'm just trying to advise you.' He paused, then broke into a grin. 'And of course you'll want to take somebody to Barbados with you, to rub all that Ambre Solaire on to those gorgeous shoulders of yours . . .'

Her heart began to race. 'Alan, I don't want my mother to give me any money and I'm not planning any holidays. But if someone came up to me in the street tomorrow and handed me two free tickets to Barbados, I wouldn't take you anyway. I'd take Maxine.'

'You're upset.' He nodded understandingly. 'This funeral's taken it out of you. Come on, you should be in bed.'

'I'm not upset.' Janey was starting to shake. 'I just don't want this to go on any longer. It isn't working, Alan. You said we needed time to get used to each other again. Well, I've had enough time to know that it isn't going to happen.'

He stared at her. As stunned, she realized, as if he had found her walking stark naked down the high street.

'Sweetheart,' he protested finally, 'what are you talking about?'

'Us.' The time had come to be brutal. She mustn't allow him to wheedle his way around her. 'This marriage. I don't want to carry on. I don't want to be married to you any more. You told me I'd changed, and I have. I'm sorry, Alan, but that's it. You're going to have to find somewhere else to stay.'

And somebody else to support you, she thought wearily. Guy had been right; Alan was a user and a taker. She just hoped he had been right about the other matter, too . . .

'I can't believe I'm hearing this.' Alan was very still, his eyes narrowed, his voice scarily low.

I can't believe I'm saying it, Janey thought, biting her lip and wishing he wouldn't stare at her like that. But she had to stick to her guns.

'I mean it.'

'Good God, woman! I came back here because I couldn't live without you! You welcomed me back with open arms . . . how can you change your mind just like that? What have I done that's so terrible?'

'Nothing.' Janey fought to stay calm. 'You haven't done anything terrible. I don't love you any more, that's all.'

But he was shaking his head. 'No. no. It doesn't work like that. I want the real reason.'

'OK, fine.' She held up her hand and began counting the real reasons off on her fingers. 'You haven't bothered to look for a job. You expect me to pay for everything. You endlessly take me for granted. You want my mother to give me money so you can spend it. And,' she concluded heavily, 'you forgot my birthday.'

He blinked. 'Any more?'

'Yes,' snapped Janey, for the hell of it. 'You snore.'

'I see.' Alan's smile was bleak. 'Oh yes, I definitely see. Your mother's the one behind all this, isn't she? That old bitch put you up to it. What did she do, threaten to cut you off without a penny if you didn't dump me?'

'Don't be ridiculous.' Enraged by his nastiness, yet at the same time almost welcoming it because it was so much easier to deal with than threats of suicide, Janey rounded on him. Her brown eyes blazed. 'You're the one who was so intent on getting your hands on that money! And no,

Mum hasn't so much as mentioned your name, so don't even think she has anything to do with this. My mother has more important things on her mind than you, just at the minute.' She paused, then added icily, 'This is *my* decision. All my own work. And since I've already made up my mind, there's no point in even trying to argue. As far as I'm concerned, the sooner you leave, the better.'

Alan's shoulders slumped. The anger in his eyes faded, to be replaced by resignation. 'So that's it,' he murmured with infinite sadness. 'It's all over.'

Janey, scarcely daring to breathe, nodded.

'Oh well, it was always on the cards, I suppose. Stupid of me.' He shook his head. 'I geared myself up to this before coming back, and now I have to get used to the idea all over again. Somehow it's even harder, this time . . .'

Guy had been right, Janey reminded herself, gritting her teeth. It was emotional blackmail, pure and simple. Alan wouldn't really do anything drastic.

'. . . like thinking you're going to the electric chair, being reprieved, then being told that it was just a joke, you're going to get it after all.'

'I'm not sending you to the electric chair,' she said quietly.

'Aren't you?' He reached for her hand. 'Janey, I love you. Where would I go, what kind of future do I have without you? What would be the point of *anything*?'

'Stop it.' Sick with fear that he might actually mean what he was saying, Janey prayed she was doing the right thing. 'You mustn't say that.'

'Why not? I'm thinking it. Jesus,' Alan sighed,

squeezing her hand so hard she felt her fingers go numb. 'I've thought of nothing else for the past two years. All I wanted was to be with you, Janey. God knows, I'm not perfect . . . I've tried to get a job, but there just haven't been any around. And I'm sorry about that. And I know I don't always do the washing up, but it's hardly a reason to end a marriage! Maybe I don't deserve you,' he murmured brokenly, 'but I do love you. Let me prove it, sweetheart. Give me one last chance and I'll turn over a new leaf, I swear I will. I'll make you happy.'

'No,' said Janey. 'I told you, I've already made up my mind. I don't care what you do from now on. I'm not responsible for you any more. The answer's still no.'

'You callous bitch.' Abruptly, he dropped her hand and pushed it away, his jaw set and a vein thudding in his cheek. 'OK. If that's what you want, I'll go. But I hope you realize what you're doing. You could end up regretting this, Janey. In a very big way indeed.'

Maxine, stretched out across Janey's settee with her hands behind her head, wiggled her toes in time to the jingle advertising a new chocolate bar. Nobody was allowed to watch BBC any more. Every time the commercials came on, her attention began to wander in anticipation. When the Babysoft commercial was shown, she stopped whatever she was doing in order to gaze, entranced, at herself on the television screen.

'Damn, the film's starting again! Maybe it'll be on in the next break. Now what was I saying . . . ?'

'You were telling me to relax,' said Janey helpfully, 'and to stop worrying about Alan.'

'Exactly. Look, kicking him out was the best thing you ever did. This should be the happiest time of your life, darling! You came to your senses, gave him the old heave-ho and now you can start afresh. He's out of your system,' she added forcefully. 'You're free at last! I can't understand why you should even care what happens to him. When did that bastard ever show any consideration for you, after all?'

Janey hadn't expected her sister to understand. When she had tried to relay her fears, Maxine had howled with laughter and said, 'You should be so lucky.'

The trouble was, wanting to put the whole miserable affair behind her was easier said than done. How could she even begin to relax when every time the phone rang she leapt a mile, petrified it might be the police . . . the hospital . . . Alan himself, with a stomachful of pills?

It had been a week now since he'd left. He was staying with Jan and André Covel, sleeping on the living-room floor of their tiny flat. Conditions, it appeared, were less than ideal; Jan wasn't happy about the set-up, he had grimly informed Janey when he had returned to pick up the last of his few possessions. Still, it was better than a sleeping bag on the beach. And it probably wouldn't be for very long . . .

'You're well rid of him,' Maxine declared, stretching out for the remote control and flipping over to Channel 4 in search of more commercials. 'And think how nice it is to have the place to yourself again. Got any more chocolate Hobnobs, Janey, or was that the last packet?'

Janey couldn't help smiling. Maxine, draped across the sofa like Cleopatra, waving an empty biscuit wrapper and hogging the remote control, could almost be Alan. And since Bruno had started work at the Grand Rock ten days earlier – his shifts clashing cruelly with Maxine's own precious time off – she had been turning up more and more often at the flat.

'Oh yes, it's great, having the place to myself,' Janey said mildly. 'And yes, we're out of Hobnobs. What time does Bruno finish tonight?'

Maxine, busy emptying crumbs into the palm of her hand, looked gloomy. 'When the last punter leaves. You wouldn't believe how long some people can just sit there, nursing a lousy cup of coffee. I'm sure they do it out of spite.'

'But you two are still OK?' She couldn't imagine how Maxine's chaotic ways must be affecting Bruno.

'More than OK.' Maxine, having licked up the last of the crumbs, stretched luxuriously. 'We're talking blissful. It's like being on a permanent honeymoon without the bother of being married . . . except he keeps wanting us to *get* married. Now will you look at that – one pink sock and one orange one. Why on earth didn't I notice that before?'

'Are you going to marry him?' asked Janey curiously.

'I don't know. We'll see.' Maxine shrugged and flicked back her blond hair. 'It's going well, but I don't see the point of rushing into anything drastic. It doesn't do him any harm to keep him in suspense. Besides, who knows what might happen now my career's taking off? The last thing I need is to be tied down . . .'

And Alan called me a callous bitch, thought Janey, marvelling at her sister's *laissez faire* attitude.

'So when he asks you to marry him and you refuse,' she said, deeply intrigued 'what does Bruno *do*?'

'What can he do?' Maxine countered with a casual shrug. 'Apart from hope for better luck next time. Don't get me wrong, I love him to death, but he's hardly in a position to argue. My career comes first and he knows that.' She hesitated, looking thoughtful. 'Does that sound selfish?'

Janey, filled with admiration, said, 'Yes.'

'Oh well.' Maxine broke into an unrepentant grin. 'Never mind. A bit of suffering never hurt anyone, especially Bruno.'

# Chapter 54

The build-up to Christmas was starting. Business in the shop was brisk and orders were already flooding in. Janey, thanking her lucky stars for ever-reliable Paula, was snowed under with requests for Christmas wreaths, table decorations and *pot-et-fleur* arrangements. Mistletoe was going down a bomb with teenagers whom she otherwise never saw from one year to the next.

Paula was out making the morning's deliveries and Janey, armed with leather gloves and secateurs, was battling her way through a mountain of holly when the shop door opened and a tall, dark-haired girl came in carrying a baby. The girl, elegantly attired in an expensive caramel leather jacket, black trousers and low-heeled black and tan boots, sported a great deal of make-up and reeked of perfume. The baby, presumably a boy, was bundled up in a navy snowsuit and a blue-and-white striped bobble hat. Wisps of ash-blond hair were plastered to his forehead and he had the most adorable blue eyes Janey had ever seen.

The girl, who looked to be in her mid-twenties, seemed nervous. It was with some relief that Janey abandoned the holly and peeled off her gloves.

'Hi.' She waved at the little boy and smiled at his mother. 'Can I help you?'

'Um . . . well, I hope so.' Long, heavily mascaraed eyelashes batted with agitation. Stalling for time, she glanced around at the hanging baskets strung from the ceiling. The baby, sensing inattention and seizing the moment, made a grab for a nearby trailing ivy frond. The terracotta pot from which it grew was dragged with an ominous grating sound from its shelf. The next moment, before anyone had a chance to move, it had crashed into a bucket of freesias, scattering leaves and compost over the tiled floor. Startled, the baby promptly let out an ear-splitting wail.

'Oh no,' cried his mother. 'Oh hell! I'm so sorry . . .'

'It doesn't matter.' Gently, Janey disentangled the long tendril of ivy from the baby's chubby clenched fist. By some miracle the terracotta pot hadn't broken. There was a mess, but not an expensive mess.

'I'll pay for the damage.' Shifting the baby from one hip to the other, the girl rummaged frantically in her shoulder bag for her purse. 'I really am sorry. Are the freesias a write-off too?'

She was shaking, Janey noticed. Bending down, swiftly retrieving the pot from its resting place amongst the poor battered freesias, she shook her head and smiled.

'It's OK, they were on their last legs anyway. I was going to bin them tonight. And look, the pot's fine.' She held it up for inspection. 'No problems, honestly. You don't have to pay for anything.'

The baby had by this time stopped yelling. After regarding Janey for some seconds with solemn intensity, he broke into a sudden beaming grin.

'Oh God,' said the girl, still distressed. 'You're being so nice about this. It doesn't make it any easier for me.'

'It was an accident,' Janey protested. 'What were you expecting me to do, dial 999?'

'I don't mean the pot.' She hesitated, flicking back her glossy dark hair. 'It's taken me weeks to pluck up the courage to come here . . . and I'm afraid you aren't going to like the reason why.'

Janey frowned. 'I don't understand.'

'You are Mrs Sinclair, aren't you?' said the girl nervously, and Janey nodded again.

'Well my name's Anna Fox.' She waited, then shook her head. 'I suppose that doesn't ring any bells?'

The baby, apparently entranced by the gold buttons on Janey's sweater, squealed with delight and made a futile grab for them.

'Sorry?' said Janey, puzzled.

'Oh dear, this is even more difficult than I thought.' Two spots of bright colour appeared on the girl's cheeks. 'Look, it was Alan I really came to see. Your . . . um . . . husband. Maybe it would be easier if he explained.' She blinked rapidly. 'Is he around at the moment?'

In less than a split second it all became clear. Stunned, Janey clutched the counter for support. The baby, chuckling with delight, revealed two pearly teeth and vast amounts of pink gum. How curious, she thought irrelevantly, that such a grin could be so irresistible. Any adult with only two teeth in his head would never get away with it.

Anna Fox bit her lip, her dark eyes bright with a

mixture of pride and regret. 'I really *am* sorry,' she sighed. 'I did say it wasn't going to be easy. You must think I'm a complete bitch.'

The door swung open. Paula, like the cavalry, had arrived in the nick of time.

'Dear old Mrs McKenzie-Smith burst into tears when I arrived with her bouquet,' she announced cheerfully. 'It's her golden wedding anniversary and this is the first time her husband's ever given her flowers. Hello, gorgeous,' she went on, wiggling stubby fingers at the wide-eyed baby. 'Oh I say, what a lovely smile! What's your name then?'

'Good, you're back,' said Janey hurriedly. 'Paula, can you take over here? We're going upstairs for a while . . .'

'His name's Justin,' said Anna, fumbling with the zip as she struggled to get him out of his snowsuit. With a defensive glance in Janey's direction she added, 'He's ten months old.'

Janey, who had switched the kettle on, was now leaning in the kitchen doorway whilst she waited for it to boil.

'Does he say anything yet?'

Anna pulled a face. 'Only "Da".'

'Da!' Justin exclaimed in delighted recognition. 'Da da da. *Da!*'

'Ma,' prompted Anna, embarrassed, and he beamed. 'Mmm . . . Da!'

'This is crazy,' said Janey, giving up on the kettle and sitting down. 'Here you are feeling sorry for me, and I'm feeling sorry for you. Look, Alan doesn't live here. We aren't . . . together, anymore. I can't say I'm not stunned by all this, but you haven't upset me. In a weird kind of way, it's the best news I've had in years.'

'Really?' Anna's eyes promptly filled with tears as astonishment mingled with overwhelming relief. 'Oh my goodness, I'm so glad . . . oh dear, now my mascara's going to run.'

Janey passed her a box of tissues. The baby, half in and half out of his snowsuit, was wriggling like an eel.

'Here, let me take him,' she offered, as Anna struggled to blow her nose and hold him on her lap at the same time. 'You don't have enough hands.'

'You really and truly don't mind?' said Anna, sniffing loudly.

Janey smiled. 'Of course not. I like babies.'

'I mean about me and Alan.' She bit her lip. 'I still feel dreadful, springing this on you.'

'I can't tell you how glad I am that you did,' Janey assured her, from the heart. 'Listen, I kicked him out. He didn't want to leave . . .' She hesitated, then shrugged and said simply, 'Well, now I know, I don't have to feel guilty any more. You can't imagine what a relief that is.'


'We only went along as a kind of joke,' Anna explained, clutching her cup of coffee and looking defiant. 'It wasn't as if I was desperate or anything, but my friend Elaine had been answering ads in the Personal columns without much luck, and I said why didn't she try a singles bar instead. Well, she found this new one advertised in *Time Out* and dragged me along to keep her company. I didn't even want to go, but she's such a nag. That's probably why her boyfriends never last longer than a week,' she added with a smile. Janey, who privately felt Personal columns and singles bars had a lot to answer for, gave her an encouraging nod.

'Well, the moment we got to this place in Kensington she spotted Alan and liked the look of him. He came over, started chatting . . . and that was how it all started. Elaine was furious with me of course, but what could I do? He was so handsome and charming that when he asked for my phone number at the end of the night I gave it to him. He wasn't the least bit interested in Elaine.' She looked at Janey. 'Now, of course, I wish he had been.'

'And that was when?' Janey silently marvelled at the story Alan had concocted about Glasgow and Manchester.

'The February before last. Nearly two years ago.'

Janey nodded. He hadn't wasted much time, then. So much for the Scottish cockroaches and seedy bedsitters. 'OK, go on.'

'Well, he just kind of moved in with me.' Anna looked helpless. 'I suppose I was pretty gullible but somehow I didn't even twig that he might be taking advantage of me. When you're madly in love, you don't think of things like that. My house, you see, was left to me by an aunt, so money wasn't a problem. I had a good job in advertising, and it was just so lovely having someone to come home to at the end of the day. To begin with, he used to do odd bits around the house: chucking clothes into the washing machine, cooking the occasional meal. And I thought that was so great! After a few months, of course, it started petering out.' Anna paused, then took a deep breath. 'Elaine had been making sarcastic remarks all along, but I'd dismissed them as jealousy. Just as I was beginning to think maybe she had a point after all, I found out I was pregnant.'

'Great timing,' said Janey sardonically.

'Yes, well. Blame it on the hormones, but the idea of coping with a baby on my own scared me witless. I managed to persuade myself that Alan wasn't so bad after all. I wanted him to marry me,' she said with a self-deprecating shrug. 'That was when I found out he wasn't actually divorced.'

'So he talked about me?'

'Not really. He just told me you were separated.'

Janey, amazed how easy it was to remain calm, murmured, 'What a shame be couldn't have told me.'

'You didn't *know?*' Anna's dark eyebrows shot up. 'I mean . . . he was your husband! What did you think, that he was working abroad or something?'

'I didn't know what to think,' Janey replied. 'He just disappeared. I thought he was dead.'

Shaking her head in disbelief, Anna reached into her bag and took out a packet of cigarettes. 'Oh well, why should that surprise me?' She gestured wearily with the box of matches. 'He did the same to me, after all.'

'Finish the story,' said Janey. 'He couldn't marry you because he wasn't divorced. So what happened after that?'

'Nothing much.' Anna gazed at the smoke spiralling towards the ceiling. 'We didn't get married. I gave up work and had the baby. Alan started going out more and more often because he said he couldn't stand the bloody noise of bloody crying, and eight weeks ago he upped and left. We'd had an awful row the night before,' she explained. 'The next morning, I took Justin to the clinic for one of his routine check-ups. By the time we got back two hours later, Alan had moved out.'

'No note?'

Anna, smiling briefly, shook her head. 'No note. But he'd threatened to leave and his clothes had gone. So I knew he wasn't dead.'

'But you did know where to find him?' Janey was deeply intrigued. Hadn't it even occurred to Alan that, for whatever reason, Anna might want to get in touch with him? Did he seriously expect to get away with it a second time when there was a baby to consider?

'Ah, but he didn't know I knew.' Folding her half-smoked cigarette into the ashtray, Anna pushed back her hair and glanced across at Justin to make sure he'd fallen asleep. 'All Alan ever told me about you was that you had a flower shop, and that you lived above it. When I asked where, he just said somewhere in Cornwall. One night though, he came home really drunk. We had a massive argument and Alan said if I wasn't careful he'd go home to Trezale. The next morning,' she added, 'he had a thumping hangover and couldn't even remember the row. I don't know why I did it but I wrote "Trezale" down in the back of my diary.'

'So you came all the way down here from London, just on the off-chance?'

'Gosh no. I did a bit of Miss Marpleing first.' Anna smiled. 'I called Directory Enquiries, got the numbers of all the Sinclairs and started ringing them, asking if they were the florist. The third person I spoke to told me the name of your shop, which meant I could phone Enquiries again and get your number . . . which in turn matched up with the next one on my list. All I had to do then was call you and ask to speak to Alan. Actually, I spoke to your assistant. But she just said Alan had gone out for the afternoon, so then I knew he was living back here, with you. That was a few weeks ago, of course,' she concluded. 'Before you booted him out.'

'Clever,' said Janey. 'He's still living in Trezale, by the way. I can give you the address.' She paused, still curious. 'So why have you come down here? Do you want him back?'

The baby stirred in his sleep, stretching his arms and briefly clenching his tiny fists.

'God no,' said Anna, running a gentle finger over his cheek. 'I just didn't want him to think he could get away with it.' Her eyes bright with defiance, she added, 'I wanted *you* to know what a bastard he was, too. For your own protection, not just to be mean. I suppose I needed to make him realize he couldn't go around treating women like dirt.'

'Well, thanks.' Janey smiled. 'I'm glad you did. I only wish you could have turned up a few weeks earlier.'

'You were really feeling guilty?'

She nodded. 'He's a convincing liar, as well as a bastard. He *made* me feel guilty. Oh . . . the relief of knowing I can stop!'

Anna said mischievously, 'Do you want to come with me when I go to see him? Would that be fun?'

'I've got an even better idea.' Janey broke into a grin. Reaching across the table, she picked up the phone. 'Why put ourselves out? Why don't I give him a ring and ask him to come over here?'

It was like exorcizing a ghost, only more fun. Janey, who hadn't enjoyed herself so much for years, made the phone call and issued the invitation in a voice overflowing with sultry promise. Alan, instantly assuming that she had come to her senses and realized she couldn't live without him, was delighted and only too happy to forgive her.

Within twenty minutes of putting the phone down he arrived, jaunty, freshly showered and bright-eyed with anticipation, on her doorstep. Janey and Anna, peeping out from behind the curtains, marvelled at the indestructible nerve of the man and struggled not to laugh out loud.

'Come on up,' Janey called huskily down the stairs when Alan had rung the bell. 'Door's open.'

The next moment, having rushed upstairs two at a time, he appeared in the living-room doorway. The expression on his face when he saw who else was waiting for him was out of this world. Indescribable, thought Janey. Better than sex . . .

'Surprise, darling,' said Anna brightly. Lifting her face, she sniffed the air. 'Oh how sweet,' she added, turning to Janey. 'He's wearing my favourite aftershave. Isn't that a thoughtful touch?'

Alan looked like a cornered animal, Janey decided, the flickering narrowed eyes reflecting his fury at having been caught out. Having come here expecting recon-ciliation, he had been made to look foolish instead. In a small way, they had succeeded in turning the tables. This time, he was the one facing humiliating rejection.

'What the hell are you doing here?' he hissed at Anna, but the trembling, nerve-racked girl who had entered the shop an hour earlier, inspired by Janey's lead, had undergone an almost magical transformation.

Now, casually confident, she gave him a sweet smile. 'It was urgent, darling. Remember that competition I entered you for? Well, they phoned. You've been short-listed for the finals.'

This was so far removed from the reply he'd been expecting, Alan couldn't take it in. 'What?' He stared at her, confused. 'What competition?'

'Don't you remember, sweetheart?' Anna protested good-naturedly. 'Father of the Year.'

Caught yet again, made to look even more foolish, he snarled, 'Oh, clever. Ha bloody ha. How did you find me, anyway?'

'Easy,' Janey murmured in an undertone. 'Just follow the trail of aftershave.'

Alan rounded on her. 'And you can shut up, spiteful bloody bitch. Was this your idea? I suppose you think it's funny.'

Janey's gaze fell briefly on the still-sleeping Justin. If she had her way, Alan would be indelibly tattooed – in the appropriate place – with a government health warning so that in future at least other women could be spared. Any minute now, no doubt, he would storm out of the flat.

Oh well, she thought, at least they could make the most of the opportunity while they still had it.

'*Funny?*' With a quizzical glance in Anna's direction,

she shook her head. 'Oh no, Alan; you're way too sad to be funny. In fact I'd probably call you pathetic. How about you Anna, any other suggestions spring immediately to mind?'

'Gosh!' declared Anna, her dark eyes alight with enthusiasm. 'I can think of *loads* . . .'

'Goodness, I enjoyed that,' Anna said happily when Alan had left, almost taking the door off its hinges as he went. 'How do you feel?'

Janey heaved a sigh of pleasure. 'Free.'

'Me too. Here we are, young, free and single. Not to mention starving . . .'

The baby, who had slept peacefully through the whole showdown, began to stretch and stir.

'Come on,' said Janey, feeling the need to celebrate. 'My treat. Let's go somewhere wonderful for lunch.'

# Chapter 55

The first week of January was always the quietest of the year. Nobody wanted to buy flowers, nobody was getting married . . . or even dying. Janey, alone in the empty shop, was perched on a stool twiddling her hair around her fingers and reading an old magazine when the door bell went and Guy walked in.

It was awful; her heart almost leapt into her throat at the unexpected sight of him. Having taken Josh and Ella to Klosters for a fortnight's skiing over Christmas and the New Year, he was incredibly tanned. The contrast between grey Trezale and Guy Cassidy – brown and breathtakingly handsome in a white shirt and faded, close-fitting Levi's – couldn't have been more marked. His eyes seemed bluer than she remembered, the teeth whiter, those faultless cheekbones more pronounced. Damn, be even smelled wonderful . . .

Hastily shovelling the magazine under the counter, Janey prayed she didn't look as overawed by his glamour as she felt. Not having seen Guy since the day of his father's funeral, when she had made the excruciating discovery about the bracelet, she had no idea what to expect now.

His smile was brief. 'Hi. Good Christmas?'

'Fabulous,' said Janey. She hadn't meant to sound sarcastic but that was how it came out. With Guy and family away in Switzerland, Maxine and Bruno had closeted themselves in Mole Cottage and – according to Maxine – had spent the week screwing themselves into a blissful stupor. With only a grieving mother for company, it hadn't been the jolliest of times for Janey. As far as she was concerned it had been a festive season to forget.

Guy, however, detected the raw edge to her voice.

'Well,' he said, softening slightly, 'maybe this will cheer you up. Childsafe are launching their campaign next week. They're holding a charity ball at the Grosvenor House Hotel. The organizers chose to go with the shot I submitted so if you can stand the thought of being surrounded by a million posters of yourself, you'd better start thinking what to wear.'

He handed Janey a thick, silver-embossed invitation. Gazing at it, the words 'For two people' leapt out at her.

'Um . . . I don't have anyone to take with me.' Hating having to say it, she mumbled the words in an apologetic undertone.

Guy smiled. 'Actually this is my invite. It seemed only fair to ask you to be my partner.'

'Oh.' Her stomach took a spiralling dive.

'It's next Friday,' he pointed out. 'You'll have to get Paula to take over here. I thought we'd fly up around lunchtime, spend the night at the hotel and come back on Saturday morning.'

'I see,' said Janey cautiously, 'How much are the rooms?'

Guy's eyes glittered with amusement. 'Don't panic, that's already been taken care of. All you have to do is chuck an evening dress into a suitcase.'

She hesitated. 'Right.'

'You do have an evening dress?' He looked concerned. The thought had evidently only just struck him.

Janey, feeling more and more like a decidedly second-rate Cinderella, experienced a surge of resentment. Maybe, she thought crossly, he'd like to take care of that too.

'Of course I do,' she lied smoothly, lifting her chin in defiance. 'No need to panic. I won't turn up in anything Crimplene.'

Whilst it was perfectly acceptable for Maxine to drool over Mel Gibson, developing a crush on someone you knew was somehow infinitely more embarrassing. Janey, unhappily contemplating her own schoolgirlish infatuation with Guy, couldn't believe how juvenile she was being. She didn't even know why it should suddenly have happened, anyway. For months she'd been fine, then . . . wham! . . . one full-blown crush, sprung up from nowhere, threatening to make her look even more of an idiot than she already felt.

It must be because of Alan, she told herself; some bizarre kind of reaction to being properly single again. Whatever, it was deeply and horribly humiliating.

'Who's that?' said Paula, peering over her shoulder. Janey, who hadn't realized she'd come up behind her, jumped a mile.

'Just some old magazine.' Hastily, she tried to turn

the page. 'I found it under the counter.'

'It's Guy!' Paula, ever helpful, pointed him out. 'Oh look, he's with Valentina di Angelo . . . isn't she stunning? You must be so excited about Friday,' she added dreamily. 'Imagine, going to a ball with Guy Cassidy. Everyone will think you're a couple. By this time next week, *you* could be splashed across the pages of some gossip column . . . what are you wearing, by the way? Have you decided yet? Not lime-green cycling shorts, I hope, like vampy Valentina!'

Janey, who had imagined nothing but going to a ball with Guy Cassidy for the last six days, and who knew only too well that he had felt morally obliged to invite her, closed the magazine and chucked it into the bin.

'I'm not wearing anything,' she murmured wearily. It really was the only answer. Turning, she caught Paula's goggle-eyed expression and forced a smile. 'Because I'm not going.'

Guy, who had been up half the night working in the darkroom, was still in bed when Janey phoned at eleven o'clock on Thursday morning.

'Hi, it's me,' she said quickly. 'Um, I'm in a bit of a rush, so I'll just say it. I'm sorry, but I won't be able to make it tomorrow after all. Paula's gone down with terrible flu so she won't be able to look after the shop, and there's no one else who can do it so I'm going to have to stay here. I really am sorry,' she gabbled, not sounding it, 'but I thought I'd better let you know as soon as possible. I'm sure you've got dozens of other girls to choose from . . .'

Guy, barely awake, propped himself up in bed.

'I chose you.' He sounded distinctly put out. 'I thought you'd enjoy it. Look, we could fly back on Friday night if it would help. Surely there's somebody capable of holding the fort for a couple of hours in the afternoon? What about your mother?'

'No, nobody.' Janey was firm. 'So it was kind of you to ask me, but I'm afraid that's it. I know you'll still have fun there, anyway. Just ring up someone else . . . oh God, more customers coming in . . . I really must go . . .'

Damn, thought Guy, when she had hurriedly hung up. Bloody Paula. Bloody flu. *Bloody hell.*

Paula, who had been lugging bottle gardens the size of coffee tables in from the back of the shop, stopped to lean against the counter and catch her breath. Bright-eyed and pink-cheeked, she said, 'I haven't got flu.'

'One little white lie.' Janey, just glad to have done the deed, excused herself with a shrug.

'What happens when he asks my mum if I'm better yet? She'll think he's gone off his rocker.'

'Your mother only works for Guy on Mondays and Wednesdays,' Janey replied evenly. 'By then it won't matter any more.'

'Hmm.' Paula looked unconvinced. 'Well *I* don't know why you won't go to the do anyway. It sounds brilliant. If anyone's off their rocker around here,' she added darkly, 'it's you.'

'Oh darling, you'll never believe it . . . the best news in the world!' Maxine, erupting through the front door of the cottage, flung herself into Bruno's arms. 'My agent just rang to tell me I've landed a part in *Romsey Road*! You're hugging the next Bet Lynch . . . the future queen of the soaps . . . the biggest new name in television since Miss Piggy!'

'Thank God.' Bruno, who loathed every minute of his job at the unbelievably stuffy Grand Rock, heaved a sigh of relief. 'You can take me away from all this. They film it in Manchester don't they? When do we leave?'

'Well . . .' Maxine hesitated. '*I* start next week, but don't hand your notice in yet. It's only a walk-on . . . or rather, a mince-on part,' she amended with a grin. 'I play a white-stilettoed trollop with a severe case of dangly-earring who tries to proposition the local vicar. He turns me down and I flounce off in a huff. But at least I'm in it!' Her brown eyes danced as she gave Bruno another almighty hug. 'And once they see how brilliant I am they're bound to want me to stay.'

'Next week?' He frowned. 'How does Guy Cassidy feel about this?'

'Oh, he's fed up with the weather. He decided this morning to take the kids to St Lucia. Some friends of his have a massive house there. I said I wanted to go too, so he was as thrilled as I was when the call came through this afternoon.' She grinned. 'Now he doesn't have to pay for my plane ticket.'

Bruno digested this in silence. If he had been offered the choice between a week in St Lucia without Maxine and a week at home with her, he would have stayed. The idea of passing up a free holiday, however, evidently hadn't so much as crossed her mind.

And although the thought of Maxine spending a week

on a tropical Island with Guy Cassidy was bad enough, the idea of her socializing with a television crew in Manchester was somehow even more menacing. He might love her, but he still didn't trust her an inch. Particularly, thought Bruno, when she was so hellbent on furthering her career.

He frowned. 'How long will you be gone?'

'Only a week.'

'A whole week? For one lousy walk-on?'

Maxine nuzzled his neck and smiled to herself. 'Hmm, I know. But I straddle two episodes. That's the kind of trollop I am.'

Bruno said nothing. That was just what he was afraid of.

'You've got a ladder in your stocking.'

Maxine, shaking back her hair and almost knocking herself senseless with her extravagantly gaudy earrings, said, 'Oh, bum.' From her seat in the studio canteen she grinned up at Zack Morrison, star of *Romsey Road* and heart-throb to millions. 'I'm supposed to have two.'

He nodded. He had a great nod. The way that lock of dark hair flopped over his left eyebrow, Maxine decided, was positively mesmerizing.

'I spotted you earlier, down on the set,' he said casually. 'You're good.'

'I know.' Maxine, too excited to eat, abandoned her Danish pastry. The part he played was that of the womanizing dodgy dealer, irresistibly wicked and altogether dangerous to know. In truth he wasn't actually that good-looking, just a damn sight better than the rest of the males in the cast. It was his character, Robbie Elliott, that really set the female pulses racing, as each woman secretly wondered whether she could be the one to tame him.

'I've seen you in the Babysoft ad, too,' he told her, and Maxine shrugged.

'Stepping stones,' she replied, crossing her legs and idly swinging one scuffed white stiletto from her toes. 'Why don't you sit down, before your salad falls off its plate?'

Zack Morrison, currently between wives, was captivated by Maxine's honesty. The rest of her wasn't bad either, he admitted to himself. He tended to go for brunettes, so blonde made a nice change. The smile was stunning. And even the terrible outfit she was wearing couldn't disguise the fact that beneath it, aching to get out, was a stupendous figure.

It was the honesty, however, which appealed above all. Women, throwing themselves at him, invariably told him how unhappy they were with the men they were currently either involved with or married to. It was their way of letting him know how available they were.

But although he was pretty certain Maxine Vaughan was throwing herself at him, practically all she'd talked about throughout lunch was her idyllic relationship with somebody called Bruno Parry-Brent.

This Bruno character, according to Maxine, was outrageously attractive, a superb chef, seriously wealthy and the best company in the world. Zack, accustomed to being made to feel he was the one with all these attributes –

apart from the cooking, of course – was almost jealous. She was practically implying that he didn't match up, he thought, feeling absurdly put out. He was Robbie Elliott, for Christ's sake, more than a match for any man.

And the more extravagantly she sang the unknown Bruno's praises, the more intrigued be became. Maxine Vaughan both mystified and intrigued him. Unable to resist such a challenge, Zack heard himself say, 'Ah, but he isn't one of us, is he? He isn't in the business. It's not as if he could pull any strings to help you in your career.'

'Of course he couldn't.' Maxine shrugged and spooned sugar into her cold coffee. 'But that doesn't matter. If I'm good enough, I'll make it on my own merit. Plenty of people do, don't they?' She brightened and added proudly, 'After all, I've got this far!'

'One toilet-roll ad and a walk-on.' Zack Morrison dismissed her dazzling achievements-to-date with a languid gesture. 'It's who you know in this game, darling. OK, this Bruno chap might be able to whip up a terrific omelette but that isn't going to put your name in lights.'

Maxine looked him. 'That's hardly his fault.'

'Whereas with the right man behind you,' Zack drawled. 'Well . . .'

'Oh come on,' she remonstrated, giving him a good-humoured smile. 'It isn't that straightforward.'

'Look, let me give you an example.' He leaned across the table towards her and lowered his voice. 'Just a for-instance. I'm what makes *Romsey Road* one of the top-rated shows on TV. I have clout. If I went to the script-writers tomorrow and suggested they expand your character . . . really bring her into the storyline . . . they'd listen to me.' He nodded, amused by the expression of disbelief in her eyes. 'Seriously. If I wanted to do it, I could. Now wouldn't you agree that's simpler than slogging round endless auditions in search of the next measly job?'

'Of course it is,' said Maxine quietly. The brightness in her eyes had faded and she was shifting almost imperceptibly away from him. She looked, thought Zack, disappointed.

'And I *could* do it,' he boasted.

'I'm sure you could.' Maxine bit her lower lip. 'Look I'm sorry, but I'm beginning to think I've been a bit naïve here. What are you saying, that if I do you a . . . favour, you'll do one for me in return? Is this the old casting-couch routine?'

Zack Morrison grinned, bewitched all over again both by her troubled expression and forthright manner. 'Why, would you go to bed with me if I asked you to? In exchange for a part in *Romsey Road?*'

'No.' Maxine shook her head. 'I wouldn't. I really am sorry, Mr Morrison, but I'm just not that sort of girl.'

She was terrific, thought Zack, filled with admiration. What a cracker! What an irresistible challenge.

'In that case I won't ask.' Giving Maxine the benefit of the famous Robbie Elliott smile, he glanced down at his watch. 'And I don't know about you, but I have to be back on set in ninety seconds. How are you fixed for this evening? Are you free for dinner?'

Maxine looked wary. 'I don't know whether I should.'

'No strings,' he assured her, still smiling.

'Well, OK.' With a trace of defiance, she added, 'But I

480

have to phone Bruno at eight-thirty.'

'Give me the address of where you're staying later.' Zack rose swiftly to his feet. 'I'll pick you up at nine. Wear something smart,' he added, deciding that Maxine Vaughan deserved the full works, no expense spared. 'We'll really hit the town.'

When he had gone, Maxine sipped her coffee. It was scummy, stone cold and unbelievably disgusting but that didn't matter. Her lips curled up at the corners as she allowed herself a small, triumphant smile.

Next year the Oscars, she thought happily. God, I'm good!

# Chapter 56

St Lucia had been spectacular, but it would have been more spectacular if Guy could have got Janey out of his mind.

He still didn't know why she had refused to go with him to the charity ball at the Grosvenor, either. All he knew, he thought dryly, was that as he had been driving through Trezale on his way to the airport that Friday lunchtime, he had overtaken Paula, giving a very poor impression of a flu-ridden invalid, pedalling furiously uphill on her bike.

But Janey had evidently had her reasons for standing him up, he concluded, and whilst half of him had longed to go round to the shop and shake them out of her, the other half had told him it wasn't the greatest idea in the world. She'd had a hell of a year, after all. The best thing he could do was back off for a while and give her time to sort herself out. It was infuriating, but undoubtedly necessary.

It had also been the reason why – out of sheer desperation – he had carted Josh and Ella off for a time-wasting week in St Lucia. Janey, Guy concluded, had cost him a goddamn fortune. She would have an absolute fit if she only knew.

But now he was back. And he had a few bridges to mend. Ready, steady . . .

Waiting silently in the doorway, Guy watched her at work. She had her back to him, and her shoes were off. Smiling to himself, he observed the holes in the elbows of her baggy, charcoal-grey sweater. The long white flowing skirt, made of light cotton, was more suited to July than February and her bare brown legs were mottled with cold. The temperature was positively arctic but so engrossed was she that it evidently hadn't occurred to her to turn on the heating. Neither did she seem to have noticed that her long white hair, having escaped from its combs on one side of her head, was trailing over her left shoulder in a tangled, clay-streaked and lop-sided mane.

'Oh,' said Thea, finally sensing his presence and swivelling round to look at him. When she saw who it was she said 'Oh,' again, this time an octave lower.

'It's OK,' Guy told her. 'I haven't come here to shout at you.'

'I should bloody well hope not.' Her eyebrows lifted. 'And I certainly wouldn't recommend it, young man. Because I'd shout right back.'

Guy believed her. 'As a matter of fact I came here to apologize,' he said. 'I was pretty uptight at the funeral, but that's no excuse for bad manners. I should at least have offered my condolences . . .'

'I didn't realize you hadn't.' Thea's expression softened slightly. 'I'm afraid the entire day passed in a bit of a blur. Goodness only knows what that poor young solicitor must have thought of me . . . according to Janey I was swearing like a sailor.'

That had been almost three months ago. Guy nodded. 'So how are things now? How are you feeling?'

She shrugged, wiping her hands on her skirt. 'Well, not full of the joys of spring ... but I'm back at work, which has helped. It's stupid; now that I no longer need to do it to earn a living, I find I'm spending more time here than ever before.' Hesitating for a second, she added, 'I suppose it takes my mind off other things. I actually believe these latest sculptures are the best I've ever done. It's just a shame Oliver isn't here to see them and tell me how brilliant I am.'

'At least the studio's your own, now.' Maxine had told him about that. Guy smiled. 'My father would definitely approve. He always loathed the idea of paying rent and never getting the chance to own anything at the end of it.'

Thea gazed at him. 'Does it bother you, the fact that he left me so much money?'

'Absolutely not.' Guy shook his head very firmly indeed. 'You deserved it. If anything, it bothers me that he left my children so much money,' he countered. 'They're in danger of becoming insufferable. Hardly a day goes by without one or other of them drawing up a new list of things-to-buy-when-I'm-twenty-one.'

'And did they enjoy their holiday?' Thea smiled. 'You're very brown. Janey told me you'd taken them somewhere hot but I can't remember where.'

'St Lucia.' Ridiculously, the mere mention of her name lifted his spirits. 'Janey was talking to you about ... us?'

'I think she was missing your children,' she replied with unconscious cruelty. 'She's extremely fond of them, you know.'

'They're very fond of her.' Guy pretended to study the half-finished figure she was currently working on. 'How is Janey, by the way? It's been a while since we've seen her.'

Thea, itching to get back to work, smoothed her thumb fondly across the ridge of the figure's cheekbone. Not quite yet, but soon, she would attempt a bust of Oliver.

'Well, what can you expect?' She spoke the words absently, her thoughts elsewhere. 'Considering her abysmal taste in men. Oh, she's getting over it now; the decree nisi comes through next week, thank God, but I can't help wondering what's going to happen next. She's a lovely girl, even if I do say so myself, but her confidence has taken a bit of a battering. What she needs is a decent man who isn't going to muck her about.' Screwing up her vision, she leaned forward to check the symmetry of the figure's eyelids. 'Although personally I dread meeting the next one she brings home. If her track record's anything to go by, I'll loathe him on sight.'

Guy didn't bother to hide his amusement. 'Are there many men you do like?'

Thea's gaze flickered in his direction. 'I liked Oliver,' she said with pride. 'As far as I was concerned, he was about as perfect as a man could get.'

'Well, that's one.'

'And I suppose you aren't bad,' she conceded with a brief smile. 'A bit too good-looking for my taste, maybe. But I dare say you'll improve with age.'

Janey howled with laughter. Tears streamed down her face and her sides ached but she was quite unable to stop. Maxine, unable to find the tissues, chucked across a piece of kitchen roll instead and waited patiently for the hysteria to subside.

'You never laugh that much when I tell you one of my jokes,' she complained eventually. 'And it's not even supposed to be funny. Poor Bruno; I'm *dreading* telling him.'

'Poor Bruno?' gasped Janey, wiping her eyes and gasping for breath. *'Poor Bruno!* I *love* it . . . !'

'And he loves me.' Maxine looked glum. 'He's not going to be thrilled, I can tell you.'

Janey struggled to compose herself. If she breathed really slowly and kept her mind a total blank, she told herself firmly, she could do it. No more laughing; this was serious stuff. Bruno was about to be dumped and she wanted to hear every last glorious detail. If she didn't get a grip, Maxine might decide not to tell her and that would be just too cruel.

'So what did he do wrong?' she asked, pressing her lips together and looking suitably concerned.

'Nothing.' Maxine sounded gloomier than ever. 'That's why it's going to be so difficult.'

'OK. In that case, why are you dumping him?'

'Oh Janey,' wailed Maxine suddenly, 'he got nice! You know what I'm like with men; I can't handle it when they're nice. Look at Maurice; it was running away from him that brought me back here in the first place. He was so nice I thought I was going to die of boredom.' She paused, shaking her head in despair. 'And that was what was so brilliant about Bruno. He had such a reputation . . . he was so wicked! I really thought I'd found someone I'd never get tired of.'

'You mean you thought you'd met your match?'

'Well, I had, then.' Maxine looked resigned. 'But somehow it all changed. I began to feel as if I'd got myself a housewife. Bruno wanted to prove I could trust him. He stopped being wicked. And I don't know . . . I suppose I stopped being interested.'

Janey struggled to keep a straight face. Oh dear, falling in love for possibly the first time in his life had turned Bruno into a bore.

'I bet he leaves Trezale,' she mused. The shame of it would undoubtedly be too great for a man of his reputation to bear. 'He won't be able to handle the prospect of bumping into you.' Grinning, because it was what Alan had done, she added, 'Maybe he'll skulk off down the coast to St Ives.'

'Ah.' Maxine blinked. 'Well he wouldn't actually need to move away. You see, I am.'

'What?'

'I am. Moving away. To Manchester,' said Maxine rapidly. 'They've given me a six-month contract to appear in *Romsey Road:* the white-stilettoed trollop is going to have a steamy affair with the vicar. And if they decide to get her pregnant I'll be sticking a cushion up my jumper and signing up for another year on top of that. Oh Janey, it's happening at last,' she sighed, her eyes glistening with tears of joy. 'I'm going to be Mandy Blenkinsop.'

'You're changing your name to *Blenkinsop?*'

'That's her name, stupid! The trollop's.' Maxine grinned. 'She didn't have one before, you see, because it was only a walk-on. But from next month she becomes a real character.' Dreamily she added, 'And I'll be a bona fide member of the cast. I'll probably have my own fan club.'

Bruno was forgotten. It was as if he had never even existed. Stunned, Janey said, 'What about Guy?'

Maxine shifted uneasily in her chair. 'Well, he knew it was on the cards. It isn't as if it's going to come as a huge surprise, is it? And when you think how many times he's almost sacked me, he'll probably be glad to see me go.'

'But you haven't quite plucked up the courage to tell him yet?' Janey spoke in faintly admonishing tones. 'Max, you must. Look at the trouble he had last time, finding a replacement for Berenice. He doesn't want any old nanny looking after his children. If it comes to that,' she amended, 'Josh and Ella won't want any old nanny either. They're going to miss you terribly.'

'Shame they didn't show a bit more appreciation, then, while they still had me.' Resorting to flippancy in order to cover up the guilt, Maxine said, 'Those little brats are forever telling me how much more fun they had when you were looking after them. Seriously, Janey, if you ever felt like selling the shop and switching careers . . . You could even have a crack at Guy while you're there, see if you don't have better luck with him than I did!'

It was like Pavlov's dogs. Maxine was only joking, but even the most frivolous of insinuations was enough to bring the colour surging into Janey's cheeks. Silently cursing her inability to keep it at bay and desperate to change the subject, she resolutely ignored the jibe and instead launched a bold counter-attack.

'Come on, Max. I'm your sister, remember? Do you seriously expect me to believe that's all there is to it?'

Maxine blinked. 'To what?'

'This whole *Romsey Road* business.' It hadn't been an innocent blink. Janey, pleased with herself for having guessed, moved in for the kill. 'Because I can't help thinking what an extraordinary coincidence it is, you getting the part and at the same time losing interest in Bruno. Call it a shot in the dark,' she suggested lightly, 'but would there happen to be any seriously wicked men in Manchester?'

This time even Maxine had the grace to look embarrassed. 'Well,' she murmured vaguely, 'now you come to mention it, maybe one or two . . .'

# Chapter 57

The fact that the weather had finally taken a dramatic turn for the better did nothing at all to lift Bruno's spirits. Outside Mole Cottage – which Maxine had insisted on calling Toad-in-the-Hole Cottage following the discovery of a mouldy cooked sausage under the bed – the sun shone with enthusiasm for the first time in months. Tiny clouds drifted across a clear blue sky, the sea – turquoise fading to aqua – glittered in the distance and daffodils had sprung up en masse, their yellow heads nodding in the warm breeze. Even the hopelessly overgrown front garden was sprouting an assortment of yellow blooms; but since he had no interest in flowers Bruno didn't have a clue what they were.

He didn't care, either. He didn't care much about anything at all right now, except the fact that forty-eight hours earlier Maxine had left him.

Standing at the living-room window, he gazed blindly out to sea as tears pricked the back of his eyes. She hadn't even let him down gently, dammit. Instead, with typically selfish haste, she had just come out with it – no, there was nobody else and he hadn't done anything wrong, it simply wasn't working. After that she'd slung the few clothes and bits of make-up she had left at the cottage into a pink raffia bag, and said gaily, 'Sorry, darling, but these things happen. Wish me luck. Bye!'

The lying bitch, he thought, pressing his lips together and turning the postcard over and over in his hands. She hadn't even bothered to cover her tracks properly. That was what you got for loving and trusting someone, Bruno concluded bitterly. They took fucking advantage of you and didn't even stop to think of the pain they were inflicting . . .

He had found the postcard stuffed into the breast pocket of his denim shirt. Maxine, who had borrowed it the previous weekend, had spilt chocolate milkshake down the sleeve and chucked it into his laundry basket. That way, of course, he could wash and iron it himself before she borrowed it again.

And it was such a naff card, Bruno thought, blinking hard and staring down at the scene depicting *Romsey Road* in all its grubby glory. Turning it over, he read for the fifteenth time the brief message scrawled on the other side: 'Don't I *always* deliver the goods? Ring me! Zack.'

Even Bruno, who didn't watch television, recognized the name. Zack Morrison might not be the most talented actor on the planet, he thought sourly, but he was renowned for his ability to deliver the fucking goods . . .

Bruno dressed with care, deliberately choosing the pink-and-grey striped shirt she had bought for him and teaming it with immaculately pressed charcoal-grey trousers. It was warm enough outside not to bother with a jacket.

Studying himself in front of the bedroom mirror Bruno nodded, satisfied with what he saw. He could still turn it on when he wanted to, he thought with renewed pride. How many women, after all, had told him he had the sexiest green eyes in the world? How many had called his smile irresistible? How many had begged him to take them away from their husbands?

*Paco Rabanne,* Bruno decided, reaching for the bottle standing on the chest of drawers. No, *Eau Sauvage.* She had bought that for him too. If that was what she liked best, it was what he would wear.

Nina was sitting up at the bar drinking tomato juice and chatting to one of the lunchtime regulars when Bruno walked into the restaurant. The good weather had brought with it an influx of customers and they all seemed to be enjoying themselves. What Wayne Simmonds lacked in personal magnetism, Bruno decided, he evidently made up for with his skill in the kitchen. At least the business hadn't suffered whilst he'd been away.

'Goodness,' said Nina shyly, her eyes lighting up when she spotted him. 'Look who's here! Bruno, how lovely to see you after all this time. And you're looking so well; working at the Grand Rock obviously suits you.'

Smiling, Bruno bent and kissed her pale cheek. Nina hadn't changed at all; that was what he'd always liked about her. Even the floppy, floral, Laura Ashley dress was utterly predictable. She'd been wearing it for the past six years.

'You're looking pretty good yourself.' Standing back, studying her shining, unmade-up face and breathing in the comfortingly familiar scent of patchouli oil, he took her hand and gave it a gentle squeeze. 'Are you busy or can we go upstairs and have a proper chat? It feels odd being down here and not having the right to insult the customers.'

The sitting room, flooded with sunlight, was less tidy than before but otherwise just as he remembered it.

Nina, intercepting his glance, smiled and said, 'You were the one who put things away around here. I'm still as hopeless as I ever was.'

'You aren't hopeless.' His tone was affectionate. 'Just . . . relaxed. Oh Nina, it really is good to see you. Tell me how you've been keeping. Tell me how you've really been.'

The dozen or so silver bracelets tinkled as she pushed her hair behind her ears. 'Well, fine. Busy at Christmas, of course, and New Year's Eve was as chaotic as ever. January was steady. We've changed the menu around and the customers seem to approve.'

'I meant how have *you* been.' Leading Nina to the sofa, he sat down next to her without letting go of her hand. 'I don't suppose it's been that easy for either of us . . .'

'Oh, you know.' She shrugged and examined a fraying hole in her skirt. 'As you said at the time, these things happen. Life goes on.'

'Nina.' Bruno's voice softened. 'I said some very stupid things at the time. And I've lived to regret them. You—'

'How's Maxine?' she said suddenly, her eyes bright with interest. 'I saw her in that toilet-roll commercial on television. I thought she was very good.'

Bruno sighed. 'Maybe she was. But Maxine isn't you,

sweetheart. She doesn't even begin to compare with you. I realize that now. I don't want Maxine any more,' he said simply. 'I want you to forgive me for behaving like a fool. I want *you*.'

For a moment Nina looked as if she were about to burst into tears. Gazing at him, hesitantly touching the sleeve of his shirt, she whispered, 'This is the one I bought you last summer.'

He nodded and gave her an encouraging smile.

'Oh Bruno, I wanted you back so badly it hurt,' Nina said softly. 'I dreamed of this happening; it was practically the only thing that kept me alive . . .'

'And now I am back.' Bruno stroked the inside of her thin wrist.

'If only you'd changed your mind sooner.' Nina spoke with genuine distress. The last thing she wanted was to hurt him. 'Oh dear, I don't quite know how to tell you this . . . but I've met someone else. I'm happy with him. We're going to be married in April; nothing flashy, just a small wedding, not even a proper honeymoon.'

'Married?' echoed Bruno, his eyes widening with horror. He stared at her, aghast. 'Who the hell to?'

She flinched. 'Um . . . Wayne.'

'You are joking!' he shouted, unable to believe what he was hearing. 'Don't be so ridiculous, Nina! You can't do that!'

Nina stuck to her guns. She loved Wayne and he loved her. She knew that.

'But we are doing it,' she said nervously. 'It's all arranged. April the twentieth.'

This was like a truly terrible dream. Bruno, not even

494

realizing that his fingernails were digging into her wrist, howled, 'For Christ's sake, cancel it! He's only marrying you for your money.'

'No he isn't.' Nina pulled free and rubbed her arm. Poor Bruno, he may as well hear all the news in one go. Straightening her shoulders, her face glowing with pride, she said, 'He's marrying me because I'm pregnant.'

# Chapter 58

It wasn't much, thought Guy ruefully, but it was all he had. Maxine's throwaway remark last night, when she had teased Josh about his new eight-year-old girlfriend – 'Goodness me, you've gone almost as pink as Janey does whenever I mention your father!' – wasn't a great deal to go on, but it was the most promising sign so far that she might actually feel more for him than she'd been admitting.

It had been enough to persuade him that the moment had arrived to do something, to find out for himself. Not knowing was beginning to get to him, Guy decided. The time had come to act. And if Maxine had been wrong, he thought, he could always strangle her with his bare hands . . .

Two dozen pink roses. Janey winced as one of the thorns ripped into the tender skin between finger and thumb. He'd had to order not one, but *two* dozen long-stemmed pink roses.

Jealousy, pure and simple, surged within her as she tried to imagine whom Guy was so eager to impress. And how tempting it was to choose less-than-perfect blooms, the ones whose petals were beginning to loosen so that within a day or two they would drop off

But pride compelled her to select the finest, just-flowering buds instead, flawless shell-pink tinged with apricot. If whoever-it-was took the trouble to look after them, they would last a good fortnight. Bitchily, Janey wondered if Guy's interest in whoever-it-was would exceed the life of the exquisite roses.

It was sheer pride too, that sent her up to the flat to brush her hair and change into a clean olive-green shirt and white jeans before setting off with the delivery. If the girl – presumably yet another svelte model – was going to be there when she arrived at Trezale House, Janey didn't want to feel any more inferior by comparison than she already did. Knowing that you had a crush on someone was bad enough. Having to face his infinitely more glamorous size-eight girlfriends was downright intimidating.

Stop it, thought Janey wearily, rubbing off the lipstick she had just applied and staring at the little pot of bronze eyeshadow which had somehow found its way into her hand. Now she was being really stupid, she told herself, flinging the eyeshadow back into the drawer of her dressing table and gazing at her reflection in the mirror. As if a bit of make-up was going to help.

Guy opened the front door as she was lifting the flowers out of the van. It would have suited Janey to hand them over to him then and there but all he did was step aside, enabling her to carry the bouquet into the house.

There didn't appear to be anyone else at home, certainly no stunning, semi-naked brunette draped across the kitchen table. In an effort to sound normal, Janey said casually, 'No Maxine?'

'No Maxine, no kids.' He shrugged and smiled. 'She's taken them to some birthday party in Truro. They won't be back for hours.'

'And there I was, thinking the roses were for her.' Janey placed them on the table, suddenly remembering that she hadn't seen Guy since the day he had come to the shop with the invitation to the charity ball. Praying he wouldn't mention it, realizing to her despair that her cheeks were hot, she turned her attention to the ribbons on the bouquet, fiddling with the curly bits and tweaking them into shape.

'Actually' – Guy's voice came from behind her – 'they're for you. And why did you make up that story about Paula having flu, by the way? Was the prospect of spending an entire evening in my company really that awful, or is there another explanation? And don't expect me to count to ten whilst you think of one,' he continued, his tone even, 'because you've had eight weeks already.'

This time Janey blushed with a vengeance. She couldn't help it. She didn't know what to say either.

'Look,' she said finally, and with at least semi-truthfulness, 'I just thought you'd enjoy yourself more if you took somebody else.'

'Janey, if I had thought I would have enjoyed myself more with somebody else, I would have asked them to be my partner in the first place.' His tone registered both amusement and impatience. 'And you aren't admiring your flowers. You're supposed to say "How lovely, you shouldn't have".'

'Well, you know what I mean.' Aware that she was gabbling, she took a step back. 'There were those photos in the paper of you and Valentina, and that's the kind of partner people expect you to turn up with. They'd wonder what on earth you were doing—'

'They might even think I was coming to my senses at last.' Guy, a million times more nervous than he was letting on, said quietly, 'Janey, did you hear what I said just now?'

'Of course I heard you.' Flustered, hopelessly confused, Janey shook her head. 'I just don't know why you're saying it. You phoned me up and ordered these flowers. You can't give them *back* to me . . .'

'Why on earth not?' He raised his eyebrows. 'I've paid for them. I gave you my Access card number over the phone.'

'But this is stupid.'

'No it isn't, it's sensible.' Guy started to smile. 'It got you here, didn't it?'

She bit her lip. 'I still don't understand.'

'You could try saying thank you,' he suggested, his eyes glittering with amusement. 'It's how people generally express their appreciation when they've been given two dozen ruinously expensive pink roses.'

Janey gave up. 'In that case, thank you. They're beautiful. How-very-kind-you-really-shouldn't-have. And they weren't that expensive,' she added with a faint answering smile. 'I thought they were very reasonable.'

It was now or never, Guy decided. He took a deep breath.

'Another way of expressing your appreciation when

you've been given two dozen very reasonably priced pink roses,' he said slowly, 'is with a kiss.'

Janey stared at him. Was this some kind of hideous practical joke? Was Maxine hiding behind the Welsh dresser, camcorder at the ready? Was Jeremy Beadle lurking inside the fridge?

Finally, she said, 'You want me to kiss the *roses*?'

But the expression on Guy's face was quite serious. No longer smiling, there was almost an air of apprehension about him. Janey, suddenly light-headed, felt her heart begin to race. Her stomach did a loop and disappeared.

'It's up to you,' said Guy, 'but I'd prefer it if you kissed me.'

As if in a dream, inwardly amazed that her legs were still capable of carrying her, she stepped forward and with infinite caution brushed her lips against his tanned cheek.

'OK?' she said stupidly, when it was done.

But Guy, half smiling down at her, shook his head. 'Terrible,' he murmured. 'Very poor attempt. I'm sure you can do better than that.'

He put his arms around her. Janey, no longer in any condition to protest, closed her eyes as his mouth found hers. Caution abandoned, this time the receiver, she gave herself up to him. This time the kiss seemed to go on for ever.

'Big improvement,' said Guy at last, speaking the words into her hair and not releasing his hold on her.

Janey, glad to be held – she needed all the support she could get – took a deep, steadying breath.

He smiled. 'All right?'

'I'm not sure.' Raising her brown eyes to his face, she said shakily, 'Is this a joke? Because if it is, I think I shall have to kill you.'

'You could always set Maxine on to me. That would be a fate far worse than death.' Guy, overjoyed by the success of his plan, broke into a broad grin. 'Except it isn't a joke, so you don't need to. My God, Janey, do you have any idea what you've put me through, these past months?'

Bewildered, still unable to take in the fact that this was happening to her, she said, 'I'm sorry.'

'So you bloody well should be.' He kissed her again, breathing in the faint scent of her perfume. 'You don't give away *any* clues; I didn't know whether you found me even remotely attractive; you *wrecked* my sex life . . .'

'What are you talking about?' Janey demanded, trembling all over and clutching the front of his shirt. Able to feel the warmth of his skin through the cotton, she suppressed an incredible urge to start undoing buttons.

'You were involved with that terrible husband of yours so I couldn't have you,' Guy complained. 'And I didn't want anyone else. It's been sheer torture.' He rolled his eyes in mock reproach. 'You aren't exactly forgettable just now either; everywhere I go, I'm haunted by that damn charity poster. I was seriously beginning to regret using that photograph, I can tell you. How was I to know they were going to plaster your face across just about every hoarding in the country?' With an extravagant sigh, he concluded, 'All in all, you're one difficult lady to fall in love with, Janey Sinclair, and I think you should apologize for all the trouble you've caused.'

'Do you really mean it?' She shivered. He had just said he was in love with her. Somewhere out there in the real world, Paula was expecting her back to close the shop, and here she was, standing in the middle of Guy Cassidy's kitchen listening to this.

'Of course I bloody well mean it,' Guy declared indignantly.

'It's just that I still keep expecting Jeremy Beadle to leap out of the fridge,' Janey murmured, glancing over her shoulder to make sure. 'What time did you say Maxine was bringing Josh and Ella back?'

'Not for ages.' He grinned. 'This was a carefully planned campaign, sweetheart. You don't seriously think I'd risk being interrupted by that rabble, do you?'

'Hmm.' Janey, her fingers still unsteady, touched his mouth. 'Just as well I didn't ask Paula to deliver the flowers.'

Guy kissed her again. 'I seem to be making all the running here.' His tone was gently admonishing. 'You haven't even told me yet how you feel about all this. Is it OK with you or do you have strong feelings about getting seriously involved with a bad-tempered photographer, two noisy juvenile delinquents and an out-of-control nanny?'

Janey's thoughts flew back to the night of the fair, when Alexander Norcross had warned her of the dangers of one-parent families.

'I don't know,' she said lightly. 'Are you only doing this because it's easier than finding a replacement for Maxine?'

Guy laughed. 'Brilliant idea. I haven't threatened to sack her for weeks. Do you really think she'd go, if we asked nicely?'

Janey breathed a guilty sigh of relief. So Maxine hadn't told him yet. She hadn't seriously suspected he would do such a thing but it was nice to know for sure.

Then she smiled, because 'nice' was such a hopelessly inadequate word to describe how it felt, knowing that Guy really did love her for herself. Not all men had ulterior motives, Janey reminded herself. Alan was a bad experience she could put behind her now. No two men in the world, after all, could be more different than Alan and Guy.

'No, I'm not looking for a cheap childminder,' he told Janey, stroking her hair away from her face and gazing into her eyes. He was looking for a wife, but there was no need to alarm her with that just now. There was no need to hurry; they had all the time in the world to get to know each other properly . . .

'Good,' said Janey, 'because I'm not cheap.'

'Unlike your very reasonably priced roses.'

'Nobody's ever given me flowers before.' She gazed lovingly at them, her eyes bright with tears of happiness. 'Oh dear, I've got a terrible confession to make.'

Guy looked at her. 'Go on.'

'I thought you were buying them for some horrible new woman in your life. I almost chose the not-so-good ones that I knew wouldn't last.'

'You'd have been sorry.' He grinned. 'So you were jealous? That's encouraging.'

'Of course I was jealous.' Janey looked ashamed. 'All

right, I'll admit something else. I couldn't face going to London with you because I was too afraid of making a fool of myself. I thought you'd be able to tell how I felt.'

If only she'd realized, thought Guy, how badly he had wanted to know how she felt.

But that was all in the past. Smiling, he stroked her cheek. The flawless skin, as soft to the touch as warm silk, was positively addictive.

'Never mind,' he murmured. 'I know now. And you feel just about perfect to me.'